Dear Arabesque Reader,

Thank you for choosing to celebrate ten years of award-winning romance with Arabesque. In recognition of our literary landmark, BET Books has launched a special collector's series honoring the authors who pioneered African-American romance. With a unique 3-full-books-in-1 format, each anthology features the most beloved works of the Arabesque imprint.

Sensuous, intriguing and intense, this special tenth anniversary series includes four must-read titles. This collector's series launched with *First Touch*, which includes three of Arabesque's first published novels written by Sandra Kitt, Francis Ray, and Eboni Snoe; followed by *Hideaway Saga*, three novels from award-winning author Rochelle Alers; and the third in the series, *Falcon Saga*, by Francis Ray. The collector's series concludes with the book you are holding by one of Arabesque's most popular authors, Brenda Jackson's *Madaris Saga*. We invite you to read all of these exceptional works by our renowned authors.

In addition to recognizing these authors, we would also like to honor the succession of editors—Monica Harris, Karen Thomas, Chandra Taylor and the current editor, Evette Porter—who have guided the artistic direction of Arabesque during our successful history.

We hope you enjoy these romances and please give us your feedback at our website at *www.bet.com/books*.

Sincerely,

Linda Gill
VP & Publisher
BET Books

D1115613

Other books by Brenda Jackson

Eternally Yours

Fire and Desire

One Special Moment

Secret Love

Surrender

Tonight and Forever

True Love

Whispered Promises

Published by BET/Arabesque Books

BRENDA JACKSON

MADARIS SAGA

ARABESQUE

BET BOOKS

BET Publications, LLC
www.bet.com
www.arabesquebooks.com

ARABESQUE BOOKS are published by

BET Publications, LLC
c/o BET BOOKS
One BET Plaza
1900 W Place NE
Washington, DC 20018-1211

All Kensington Titles, Imprints, and Distributed Lines are available at special quantity discounts for bulk purchases for sales promotions, premiums, fund-raising, and educational or institutional use. Special book excerpts or customized printings can also be created to fit specific needs. For details, write or phone the office of the Kensington special sales manager: Kensington Publishing Corp., 850 Third Avenue, New York, NY 10022, attn: Special Sales Department, Phone: 1-800-221-2647.

ISBN 1-58314-491-9

First Printing: November 2004
10 9 8 7 6 5 4 3 2 1

Printed in the United States of America

CONTENTS

TONIGHT AND FOREVER

1

WHISPERED PROMISES

155

ETERNALLY YOURS

327

TONIGHT AND FOREVER

Acknowledgments

I would like to give a heartfelt thank you to the following people:

To the man who has been my husband, best friend, love of my life, and the wind beneath my wings for twenty-three years, Gerald Jackson, Sr.

To my two sons, Gerald, Jr. and Brandon, who are proud of their mom the writer.

To a group of special friends who were kind enough to let me borrow their time—Denise Coleman, Pat Sams, Agnes Dixon, Betty Hodge, Juanita Heard, Sandra Nottenkamper, Lynn Sims, Marsher Boyd, Delores Young, Sunnie Dodd, Cynthia Grissett, Pat Render, and Emma Upshaw.

To the members of the First Coast Romance Writers for their constant encouragement; to Debbie, Anita, and Marge for their constant readings and invaluable feedback of the book in progress.

To Vivian Stephens for her timely words of encouragement.

To Syneda Walker, a very special friend.

To all my family, friends, and coworkers for their undying support.

To my eighth grade classmates at Northwestern Junior High School, Jacksonville, Florida, who enjoyed my stories even back then.

Last but definitely not least, I thank God for being the giver of all good and perfect gifts and from whom all blessings flow.

Laughter cannot mask a heavy heart. When the laughter ends, the grief remains.

Proverbs 14:13
Taken from The Living Bible

CHAPTER 1

"She's absolutely breathtaking."

The words emerged as a mere whisper from Justin Madaris's lips before he realized he'd spoken his thoughts aloud. Preferring at the moment to be apart from the growing crowd, he stood tall, a solitary figure, barely distinguishable in the shadows, as his mesmerized gaze followed the woman circulating among the other party guests. A seductive gracefulness marked her every movement. Glossy dark brown hair, stylishly cut, cascaded over her shoulders, accentuating her perfect features and complementing her nutmeg skin. She was, simply put, a strikingly beautiful woman.

Justin absently loosened the knot in his tie as a thrumming heat pulsed deep within him. The woman had a stimulating effect on his vital signs.

Who is she? he wondered, lifting a glass to his lips. The sparkling taste of the vintage wine was blotted from his mind as he continued to engage in a visual exploration of her body. The backless black dress was stunning. The delicate fabric clung subtly, defining her shapely figure. He couldn't help noticing that the side slit of the outfit revealed one long beautiful leg. He'd bet her legs fit perfectly around a man's waist while they made love.

Instinctively he took a step forward, intent on finding out who she was. His face dimpled into a smile. The woman had thoroughly aroused his curiosity and totally captured his interest.

* * *

There's nothing like seeing old friends again, Lorren Jacobs thought, making her way through the room filled with numerous people from her past. Like her, most of them had spent their childhoods here at what used to be a foster home run by Paul and Nora Phillips. To them, this large house located in the small town of Ennis, Texas—a skip and a hop from Dallas—was home.

Tonight they'd returned and had gone all out to host the party honoring Mama Nora's sixty-fifth birthday. Nora and her husband Paul, who'd died six years ago, had been instrumental in shaping their lives, providing them with food and shelter, love, friendship, and guidance.

A smile touched Lorren's lips as she glanced around the room. She knew that no expense had been spared. The food committee had special caterers flown in from New York. The decorating committee had depleted every florist shop for miles. The entertainment committee had hired a popular disc jockey to alternate with a well-known jazz band from New Orleans. A small army of people had turned out to celebrate the birthday of a woman who was a pillar of the community, a supporter of noble causes, and a dear friend.

Lorren stopped to hold a brief conversation with Mr. Monroe, the principal of her old high school, when she suddenly had the strangest feeling she was being watched. Scanning the room, she could find no reason for the peculiar sensation.

When her conversation with Mr. Monroe ended, she made her way to the buffet table, passing out quick smiles of recognition and several words of greeting to those she met. The massive spread of food looked delectable. But before she could pick up a plate, someone called her name.

Turning in the direction of the familiar voice, she came face-to-face with her closest friend, Syneda Walters, who had also grown up in the Phillipses' household. Long luxurious golden bronze curls tumbled over Syneda's shoulders, softly framing an attractive light brown face. Syneda's eyes, sea green in color, were perfect for the long curling sweep of lashes veiling them.

"So far, so good. The caterers outdid themselves. Everything's perfect," Syneda said excitedly.

Lorren smiled. "That's the reason we made you head of the food committee, Syneda. You could be counted on to make everything first-class. We didn't give you the nickname 'Classy Sassy' all those years ago for nothing."

Both women laughed. Their sound mingled with the joviality of the other guests in the room. "Let's go in here," Syneda said, pulling Lorren through a pair of double doors at the far end of the room. "It's escape time," she teased. They stepped into a large, book-lined study and closed the door behind them.

"I meant to tell you earlier how sharp your hair looks. That style looks super on you," Syneda said. "I never understood why you began wearing your hair short."

Lorren managed a half smile. "Scott preferred it that way." Saying her ex-husband's name evoked memories of a hellish marriage and the very real relief of her divorce.

"Hey, as far as this sister is concerned, there's a number of things Scott Howard preferred," Syneda responded tersely, not trying to hide the contempt she felt for the man. "One of which was being a fool and not appreciating what he had."

You better shut her up, Lorren's inner voice warned, *or homegirl will begin sounding off on Scott's cruddy attributes from now till kingdom come. Even though you agree with all of them, he's the last person you want to think about tonight,* she thought, studying the woman standing before her.

The two of them were bonded by a strong friendship. Syneda had been maid of honor at Lorren's wedding, then two years later had helped her through a shattering divorce. Although they were close, they were completely opposite in personality and temperament. Lorren had majored in English literature in college while Syneda had ventured into law and now worked for one of the most prestigious law firms in New York.

Lorren also knew her best friend had achieved the life she'd always wanted. Syneda had been adamant about not getting seriously involved with anyone until she'd blossomed in her career.

Lorren's own life hadn't turned out quite the way she had planned. Unlike Syneda, she had always hoped to be happily married by her twenty-sixth birthday, with at least one child—possibly another on the way—have a beautiful beach house on the Pacific coast where she'd be typing out her second or third award-winning book. With her birthday a few months away, all her dreams seemed unattainable.

"So much for a breather," Loren said, pulling Syneda toward the door. She didn't want to dwell on her lost dreams any longer. "Let's go back."

"Okay," Syneda agreed, sensing Lorren's melancholic mood. "The night's still a baby, and if we're lucky, we'll run into a couple of fine, unattached brothers here."

"Maybe," Lorren answered uninterestedly. "I've noticed you're not lacking attention tonight."

Syneda raised an arched brow at what could have been taken as a dig. "You wouldn't either if you'd loosen up, girlfriend, and stop being so uptight around men. Don't think I haven't been checking you out. And if I've picked up on it, so will Mama Nora, *if* she hasn't already. The last thing we need is for her to start worrying about any of us. She's done enough of that over the years."

Lorren released a smothered sigh. She'd hoped her self-imposed barriers of protection hadn't been obvious. "You're right." As they left the study she asked, "Are you still flying out first thing in the morning?"

"Yeah. I need to finalize an important case, but I'll be back Monday night. Then I'll be here for at least a week."

Lorren smiled. "Great. I can't wait to have lunch at Sophie's Diner."

Syneda grinned. "Neither can I. I hear their onion burger hasn't changed. You still get more onions than burger."

Laughter erupted between the two women again.

"The woman in the black dress, do you know her?" Justin asked the tall, distinguished-looking older man who happened to be the brother of the honoree.

Senator Roman Malone's gaze followed Justin's, and a thoughtful smile curved his mouth. "That's Lorren Jacobs. She lived here with Nora and Paul, then moved away when she graduated from high school about seven years ago."

"Married?"

"Not anymore."

"Widowed? Divorced?"

"She's divorced."

"Where's she living now?"

"Was in California, but Nora mentioned earlier tonight Lorren's moved back to Ennis." The senator grinned. "Son, you ask more questions than the *National Enquirer,* and I've given all the information I intend to." His smile faded. "But I'll give you fair warning, Justin. Nora also mentioned that Lorren's divorce left her with deep scars."

Justin glanced across the room at the woman dressed in black. His gaze took in everything about her. He suddenly remembered things he'd noticed earlier that hadn't made sense.

Now they did.

She seemed to avoid one-on-one conversation. She seemed more comfortable in a group. And so far, she'd turned down every man who'd asked her to dance.

The senator peered up at him. "I can tell by the gleam in your eyes, you aren't taking me seriously."

Justin's face split into a wide grin. "As an old college pal of Dad's, you should know a Madaris can't resist a challenge."

The senator laughed. "Do you want an introduction?"

"No, not yet. I want to enjoy the view some more," Justin replied before walking away.

Lorren, absorbed in the conversation swirling around her between Syneda and Senator Malone, who'd come to join them, again experienced an eerie feeling of being watched. Another quick scan of the room revealed nothing, but the feeling persisted. A few minutes later she took still another glance around the room.

Then she saw him.

He stood alone, casually leaning against the wall. His stance was formidable, and his gaze scanned her assessingly. The look he was giving her came from a man who knew what he liked and had no qualms about showing it.

Lorren's pulse skittered when his gaze moved appreciatively from her face and downward, over the curves of her figure and legs before returning to her face again. She quickly turned her back to him but, unable to resist a glance, discovered his gaze still glued to her, and, to make matters worse, he was heading her way. Watching him advance with long, purposeful strides, she couldn't tear her gaze from his.

Dressed in an expensive suit tailored to fit his lithe, hard body like a glove, his aura of rugged masculinity suggested he'd be just as relaxed in a pair of well-worn jeans and a chambray shirt. He appeared to be well over six feet tall, and the muscles rippling beneath the suit jacket told her his athletic build came as a result of vigorous physical activity.

His face was arrestingly carved in sharp angles and fine lines. Close-cropped, curly black hair, and a neatly trimmed mustache accentuated his sensual upper lip and emphasized the mystery in eyes the color of chocolate chips. The healthy glow of his chestnut skin tempted her to touch it to see if it really felt like warm satin.

Lorren blinked. She suspected she was finally losing her sanity. Two years of pain and humiliation had somehow slipped her mind, and she'd become utterly fascinated by a total stranger. She had to hand it to the man for giving special meaning to the description tall, dark, and handsome.

"Good evening."

"Dr. Madaris. Come join us," Senator Malone said. "Do you know everyone?" he asked, indicating the others.

"No, I don't, Senator," Justin answered smoothly, scanning the group. He quickly returned his gaze to Lorren and focused on her features. Up close she was even more beautiful. She possessed eyes the color of rich caramel, a straight nose, a nicely rounded chin, and a beautifully shaped mouth.

"Well, then," the senator replied. "Syneda Walters, Lorren Jacobs, meet Dr. Justin Madaris."

Lorren's heart hammered against her ribs from the contact of Justin's hand in a brief handshake. Long fingers gently squeezed hers before releasing them. He elicited the most powerful and intense physical reaction she'd ever experienced. It totally unnerved her. His eyes glowed with intense male interest under thick black lashes. A shiver of warning passed through her.

"Lorren, would you like to dance?" Justin asked.

His voice, deep and sensual, stirred something elemental in her blood. Refusal hovered on her lips, but when she caught Syneda's gaze, the message clearly said, *Girl, don't be a fool. Go for it!*

Against her better judgment, she said, "Yes."

The DJ had put on a slow number by Luther Vandross when Justin took Lorren's arm and led her toward the dance floor. She could feel the gentle imprint of his fingers on her skin and shivered.

"You're trembling. Are you cold?" he asked. His voice, low, strong, yet seductive, caressed the words he'd spoken. His gaze left hers and dropped to her arms as if checking for goose bumps. He returned his attention to her.

"No," she replied coolly, not liking the effect he had on her. She was unprepared for the sheer power of his masculinity. He had a magnetic, compelling charm that undoubtedly paved his way into a lot of women's hearts, not to mention their beds, she thought. When he pulled her into his arms, she tipped her head to study him.

"You hesitated before accepting my invitation to dance. Somebody tell you I've got two left feet?"

Caught off guard by his teasing, Lorren fumbled for an answer.

"No. But you didn't expect me to rush into your arms, did you?" she replied, forcing a demure smile.

"I wouldn't have complained if you had," he replied, his slow smile taunting her.

Lorren raised her eyes to meet his. Big mistake. Looking into his eyes made her breasts tingle against the fabric of her dress.

"Nice perfume," he said. "What is it?"

"Beautiful," she replied in a controlled voice.

"How appropriate," Justin said silkily. His gaze settled on her full, inviting lips, glazed with a delicious shade of red that reminded him of strawberries. They were his favorite fruit.

Their eyes met. And that sharp awareness that had cut through Justin's body like an electric shock when they'd been introduced was there again. Although he was holding her close, it wasn't close enough. The small space separating their bodies teased his senses. He felt a definite attraction to this woman. She was one of the few women he'd met who could ignite rampant emotions within him. Her beautiful eyes reflected strong will and intelligence. Looking deeper, he saw hints of loneliness and pain in them that seemed to be an innate part of her.

Justin's compliment made Lorren's heart pound out an erratic rhythm. "Thanks." She'd noticed his gaze had shifted to her mouth. Her throat went dry. Suddenly feeling a little light-headed, she blamed it on the wine she'd had earlier, but knew better. *The last thing you need is another man messing with your mind. Mama Nora didn't raise a fool. You have enough sense to see this guy is walking, breathing trouble. You can bet your Gucci he's the type who goes after what he wants and won't stop until he gets it.* Her pulse quickened at the thought.

His closeness was drugging her senses, lulling her into a euphoria. But she had no intention of experiencing a sexual high off him. She decided that holding a polite conversation would be the best way to keep from responding to his magnetic charm. "So you're a doctor?"

"Yes, I am."

"Where?"

"Here in Ennis. I took over Dr. Powers's practice when he retired ten months ago."

"Oh, I didn't know." Dr. Powers had been a very well liked and respected general physician in Ennis for as long as Lorren could remember. "I'm surprised the people accepted you as his replacement."

Justin's laugh sounded low and sexy. "Why?"

"You certainly don't look like a doctor."

"Oh? How's a doctor supposed to look?"

Lorren stared up at him as a flush stole into her cheeks. *Not like he should grace the covers of a magazine,* she thought.

"What I mean is, a lot of people in this town are set in their ways. They think competency comes with age, and compared to Doc Powers, you're rather young," she replied, proud of her quick thinking. There was no way she would tell him what she actually thought.

A sensuous smile came to life on his lips. "I don't consider thirty-five as being young. And I had no trouble being accepted in this town, once they saw my qualifications."

"You must be pretty good at what you do."

Justin grinned, his teeth strikingly white against his rich dark skin. "Yeah. I think so, and I haven't received any complaints so far," he murmured huskily.

Lorren drew a tremulous breath. They'd been talking about his profession, hadn't they? He had not even hinted at anything otherwise, but for some reason she felt he was saying more. "Where're you from?"

"Originally, I'm from Houston." He chuckled. "So I better not hear anything raunchy about the Oilers. I still have a hard time accepting that this is Dallas Cowboys country. What a waste of spirit."

For the first time Lorren gave him a dazzling smile, one Justin felt was genuine. He doubted she had any idea just how beautiful she looked with that smile. The transformation was stunning. If he'd thought her attractive before, she was now devastatingly so. Her hair tumbled around her shoulders, framing her face and highlighting her features.

"I'll try remembering that during football season when the Cowboys kick the Oilers' butts, big time, Dr. Madaris."

Justin laughed. "Whoa! The lady gets kind of rowdy in defense of her favorite team. But I can handle that. No one was a bigger Cowboys fan than my wife. Whenever they lost to the Oilers, she took it personally, and somehow I paid dearly."

Lorren blinked twice. She didn't recall seeing a ring on his finger. "You're married?"

"Not anymore," he replied somberly. "My wife died ten years ago."

The deep emotion in his voice got Lorren's full attention. "I'm sorry."

"Me, too. Denise was a very special woman. She taught me a lot during the time we were together. She especially taught me never to take anyone or anything for granted. Life's too short. She was a very courageous woman. Even at the end, she had more guts than a lot of people I know."

"She died ten years ago? She had to be rather young," Lorren said.

Justin nodded. "Yes. She was twenty-four when she died of an inoperable brain tumor," he replied. "We were married only five years, but they were the greatest years of my life. We were both young, and I was struggling through med school, but we had something a lot of young couples don't have when they get married."

A lump formed in Lorren's throat. She moistened her lips. "What?"

"We had a firm belief in commitment and in the value of marriage. We took the minister's words to heart . . . to love and to honor, in sickness and in health, forsaking all others, till death do us part."

Lorren's eyes became misty. He'd lost a lot more than she had, and apparently still believed in love. She couldn't help but think of Scott.

It was love at first sight, or so she'd thought at the time. During the months they'd dated, he'd been her knight in shining armor. But his sterling coating began tarnishing not long after their marriage. To be more precise, their problems began on their wedding night. Terrible regrets assailed her, and she looked into Justin's eyes.

Some unexplainable need pushed her to ask the next question. "Do you think you'll ever marry again, Justin?"

"Yes. Under the right circumstances, marriage is a pleasant and worthwhile institution. I believe in both love and marriage. It was meant for a man and woman to live together in holy matrimony."

Lorren frowned. "If you really believe that, then why haven't you remarried?"

He smiled. "So far, a woman hasn't come along who I can't imagine living my life without. Until she does, I'm going to remain single. I happen to believe in fate. If there's a woman out there, and we're destined to be together, I won't have to look for her. Fate will bring her to me."

Lorren gave his words some thought. She considered herself an intelligent woman who believed in reality. As far as she was concerned, his belief in fate was romantic and idealistic hogwash. Nothing in life was left to fate.

"I hate to sound cynical, but I don't share your fairy-tale ideals on love and marriage. I stopped believing in both long ago. My ex-husband made absolutely sure of that."

Justin's throat tightened with the compelling look of pain in her eyes. For some reason that he couldn't explain, he wanted to pull her closer, surround her with his strength, and somehow remove the hurt shadowing her eyes.

"Whoever he was, Lorren, you're better off without him. Any man who makes a woman lose faith in love and marriage isn't fit to be called a husband, and doesn't deserve her devotion. And I hope he pays dearly for making you feel that way."

Lorren looked up at him. His eyes had darkened, his voice, although hard, had lowered slightly. The quiet solidity in his words touched her. His arms surrounded her, drawing her a little closer to his body. Her hands rested on his powerful shoulders, and she could feel his strength.

Reluctantly, he released her when the music came to an end. She felt an odd sense of loss.

"Thanks for the dance, Lorren." Justin led her from the dance floor to the bar set up on the other side of the room. "I understand you've moved back to Ennis."

Lorren couldn't help but smile at the thought of how fast news could travel in a small town. "Yes, that's right." The pressure of his hand on her back was light, but she could feel his long, masculine fingers. They seemed to burn hot, branding her sensitized skin.

"Will you join me for dinner tomorrow night?"

Lorren stared up at him. Getting through a dance with Justin had been tough enough. An entire evening in his presence was not in her game plan. Not now, not ever. "No, I'm sorry."

A probing query came into his eyes. "How about the following night?"

She smiled inwardly, doubting many women turned him down for anything. "I don't go out with strangers."

He chuckled. "We're no longer strangers, are we? However, if you want character references, I believe I can drum up a few."

"I'm sure you can, but I'll be busy."

"What about—"

"I'll be busy for quite some time, Justin," she cut in.

"How about a rain check?"

"Sorry, I don't give them. If you'll excuse me, I need to talk with Syneda about something." She walked off, feeling the heat of Justin's intense gaze on her back.

"Back so soon? I thought the two of you made a striking couple."

Lorren gave Syneda a piqued glare. "Girl, *pleaz*. Don't even think it."

A smile touched Syneda's lips. "Evidently Justin does, sister-girl. He's on his way back over here."

Lorren's heart skipped a beat. "He's probably going to ask you to dance this time."

Syneda gave her a pointed look. "I *don't* think so. It's obvious the brother is interested in you. He's *your* Dr. Madaris."

"He's not *my* anything. The man belongs to any woman who wants him."

Syneda laughed. "From the looks the two of you got while dancing, I would say there's quite a few."

When Justin was a few feet from them, Lorren whispered, "I'm going upstairs to the ladies' room. He's all yours. I'm sure you can handle him." She gave Syneda a huge smile before turning to walk off.

Lorren strode across the room and up the stairs. Upon reaching the top landing, she glanced around, remembering the newspapers, magazines, and schoolbooks that used to lie scattered around when she'd lived here. Now everything was neat and tidy. Even with the noise of the guests from below, she was acutely aware of the house's stillness compared to how it had been years ago when ten foster children had scampered through it.

The oversize house that had once been her home since the age of eight was now a rooming house. Mama Nora's boarders were college students who thought the forty-five-minute drive into Dallas was nothing compared to Mama Nora's down-home cooking, friendship, and grandmotherly disposition.

Leaning against the wall for a moment, Lorren suppressed a sigh. Syneda thought Justin was interested in her. Even if he was, once he discovered the truth about her, he'd realize pursuing her was a waste of time. Scott had made her painfully aware she was a woman incapable of fulfilling a man's needs and desires in the bedroom. Her sexual inadequacies, he'd claimed, were the reason he had sought out other women. He'd once described her as a prettily wrapped package he'd anxiously waited for, but once he'd unwrapped it, he'd been disappointed.

Lorren struggled to fight back tears that burned her eyes. She would never place herself in a position to have to deal with that type of disappointment and rejection from any man again. And if that meant shielding herself from the male world, and choosing a life of celibacy, then so be it. Somehow, she would continue to battle the pangs of loneliness that would often hit her.

Her thoughts shifted to Justin Madaris. He wasn't the only one who had been committed to wedding vows. In the beginning, so had she. She had stayed married to Scott for those two years, deeply believing in the minister's words that . . . What God has joined together . . .

But by the time their marriage had ended, she was only thankful to God for giving her the sense to accept she'd made a big mistake in her choice of a mate, and the courage to leave Scott when she had. No one, not even Syneda, knew completely what had finally driven her away from Scott. Even thinking about it made her feel ashamed.

Shaking off the despairing memories, she returned downstairs and headed toward the table that held the huge punch bowl.

"Baby, are you enjoying yourself?"

Lorren turned toward the voice. The aged face of the older woman couldn't shroud evidence of past years of radiant beauty. Her hair, completely gray, was pulled back and up in a twisted bun.

Lorren smile. "Yes, Mama Nora. I am."

"You all did me well tonight. I feel so blessed."

"We're the ones who are blessed for being recipients of Papa Paul's and your unselfish love. Not only did you open your home to us, but you opened your hearts as well."

"Paul and I couldn't have kids of our own. That saddened us. We'd always wanted a big family. In the end, we got just what we wanted."

Lorren chuckled. "Bet you got more than you bargained for."

Nora Phillips reached out and embraced Lorren. "We never thought so. And I'm glad you came back home, baby."

"Me, too."

"Good evening, Ms. Nora. Lorren."

The deep familiar masculine voice made Lorren turn around.

"Dr. Madaris, I'm glad to see that you and Lorren have met already." Nora's sparkling eyes darted between the couple.

A disarming grin covered Justin's face. "Yes, ma'am, we met earlier tonight."

"Good. Did Lorren tell you she's a writer?"

Justin gave Lorren a smile that sent her pulse racing. "No, ma'am, she didn't mention it. What type of books do you write, Lorren?"

"Children's stories," Lorren replied, eyeing Mama Nora and Justin. It was obvious Mama Nora liked him.

"Children's stories? That's interesting," Justin said.

His comment drew Lorren's gaze to his mesmerizing eyes. As her heart skipped a beat, she became aware of a heat curling deep within her.

The disc jockey began playing an old dance song by the Pointer Sisters. The older people had cleared the dance floor, and a younger group had taken over. Syneda was among them and motioned to Lorren.

"Go on, Lorren," Mama Nora said, laughing. "Of all my children, you and Syneda were the two who really liked to boogie-woogie."

Lorren laughed. She remembered how she and Syneda had constantly practiced their dance routines, waiting anxiously for the day they would receive a call to audition for "Soul Train." Of course, that had been wishful thinking on their part. "I think I will." She left to join her friends on the dance floor.

Justin's breath caught in his throat when Lorren began swaying her hips to the music. Her shoulders dipped and rolled while keeping time with the beat. Thoroughly enjoying herself, she laughed loudly and exuberantly with the others. Her legs were moving, and her feet were effortlessly flying through the intricate steps. It amazed him that she didn't appear to be working up any kind of sweat as her body gyrated to the exhilarating beat.

He was entranced. She didn't have to sweat; he was doing enough for both just watching her. He wiped perspiration from his forehead.

"That child's got rhythm, doesn't she?" Mama Nora smiled warmly at him.

Justin didn't have to ask Ms. Nora whom she was talking about. He wondered if his interest in Lorren was apparent to the older woman. "Yes, ma'am. She, uh, moves very well." His mind swam with images of Lorren's rhythmic movements in his bed. He could only imagine what she would feel like moving beneath him.

The dance ended and everyone clapped and cheered.

The song the DJ played next was a slow number by Janet Jackson. Justin felt a sudden need to feel Lorren in his arms, following his lead. "Excuse me, Ms. Nora."

Lorren, breathless from dancing, glanced in Justin's direction and saw him coming toward her. The little bit of breath she had left was lost. Even the air held still for his approach. He appeared to be clad in an aura of tightly reined sexuality she didn't know could exist in a man.

Until now.

Dear heaven, I have to get away from him. I can't allow myself to become attracted to him.

She quickly turned to Syneda. "Do me a favor and call me a cab."

"What? You're leaving? Now?"

"Yeah."

Syneda saw Justin approaching. "The brother has really gotten next to you, hasn't he?"

Lorren didn't pretend not to know to whom Syneda was referring. "Yeah, and I can't . . . I just can't deal with it now."

"It's been a year since your divorce, Lorren. When will you be able to deal with Justin Madaris, or any man for that matter?"

"I don't know, Syneda. I really don't know." She turned and hurried out the door.

Justin stopped his approach and watched Lorren walk out the door. That was the second time tonight she'd deliberately avoided him, and he was contemplating going after her.

He was incredulous. The desire to chase after a woman—any woman—had never come over him before. But then, he'd never before encountered a woman with the ability to send fire coursing through his veins, or one who made him feel so stimulated.

Not even Denise had done that.

His hand closed over the coin medallion nestled on his chest. He could feel it through the soft material of his shirt. Denise had given the gold chain from which hung a gold coin to him on their wedding night, and he'd worn it constantly, seeing no reason to take it off—even after her death. It was a visible, tangible sign of the strong love the two of them had shared, and the commitment they'd made. He had loved her with every breath in his body.

Over the years, he'd met and dated a number of attractive women, women who'd tempted his passions but hadn't been able to tangle his emotions. His thoughts shifted back to Lorren. Tonight she had done exactly that.

He frowned. The last thing he needed after years of striving for inner peace, of pushing away painful memories, was to become involved with a bitter woman consumed in disappointment and heartache over a broken marriage. A cynical, frustrated woman who could become a threat to the harmonious niche he'd created for himself since Denise's death.

It was obvious Lorren had locked her feelings away from any man who dared to get close. The moment he'd suggested they go out, the expression on her face had been anxious, almost stricken. He resented her ability to reawaken his protective instincts. After she'd told him of her views on love and marriage, he had wanted to find her ex-husband and do the man in. He must have been some kind of a jerk.

Justin sighed deeply. Some inexplicable need made dismissing her from his mind totally impossible. Lorren Jacobs was a puzzle, one he wanted to solve. In order to do that, he'd have to see her again. And he intended to do just that.

Lorren felt exhausted during the cab ride.

Her concentration turned to the darkened countryside beyond the car window. The cab's headlights occasionally shone on the huge signs along the interstate denoting the Bluebonnet Trails.

Four well-marked trails covering approximately forty miles of good, all-weather roads had been laid out years ago by the Ennis Garden Club. The vast fields of bluebonnets had been slowly disappearing as a result of the growth of the cattle industry. The trails were intended to preserve bluebonnets for future generations to enjoy. No section of the state had broader acres or wider expanses of bluebonnets than the countryside surrounding Ennis. She smiled, remembering her bicycle rides on the trails each spring.

"Here you are, lady." The rough voice of the cab driver interrupted her thoughts.

"Thanks." She paid her fare and was glad she'd left quite a few outside lights burning. Only five houses surrounded Elliot Lake on the outskirts of town, between Dallas and Ennis. Mama Nora owned the lake house Lorren would be occupying. The other owners were out-of-towners who usually came to the lake only during the heat of the summer months.

According to Mama Nora, the son of the owners of the house next to hers was currently occupying it. Lorren hadn't seen any sign of anyone when she'd arrived earlier in the day.

Before she could step out of the vehicle, bright headlights shone through the back window of the cab. A car had pulled off the main road and onto the single lane leading toward the lake houses.

"Expecting someone, miss?" the cab driver asked when he noticed her hesitation in getting out of his cab.

Lorren welcomed the concern in his voice. "No, but since this is the only road to the lake, it's probably my neighbor coming home. But still, I'd appreciate it if you didn't leave just yet."

"No problem. I have a granddaughter about your age. I worry about her comings and goings all the time. We're living in dangerous times. Places aren't safe like they used to be. Why would you want to be out this far by yourself anyway? There's nothing around here but woods. The closest store is the Davises' gas station five miles back."

Lorren sighed. Mama Nora had asked her the same thing. "I want privacy."

"Well, you sure got it out here."

The sound of a car's engine came closer, and, moments later, a candy apple red Corvette pulled up beside the cab.

"Oh, that's the doctor, miss. You're safe. Good-night."

A funny feeling settled in the pit of Lorren's stomach. "The doctor?"

"Yeah. He's been in town almost a year now and . . ."

The man's last words were lost on Lorren as she quickly exited from the cab. Her anger had reached its boiling point. The nerve of Justin Madaris following her home. Well, it was time to throw down on the brother, who at that moment was getting out of the sports car.

Lorren watched as the cab pulled off, leaving her and Justin alone. She turned to face him, totally ticked off. "Is there a reason you followed me, Dr. Madaris?"

"I didn't follow you, Lorren."

She glared up at him. "What are you talking about? If you didn't follow me, then why're you here?"

A smile tilted Justin's lips. "I live in the lake house through the trees. I'm your neighbor."

CHAPTER 2

Justin's statement rendered Lorren speechless. *He was her neighbor? He lived a stone's throw from her house?*

"My neighbor!" she exclaimed as a cloud of anxiety swept over her, and her power of speech returned. "Is this supposed to be a joke?"

Justin gave her a huge smile. "No, ma'am. I thought you knew."

Lorren frowned. "There's no way you could have thought that. And just how long have you known?"

Justin shrugged. "I've known for a week or so that someone would be occupying Ms. Nora's lake house. I only found out tonight it was you."

She lifted a dark brow. "Exactly when tonight?"

"Moments after you left the party. I think Ms. Nora was under the impression we both knew already."

Lorren tried remembering her conversation with Mama Nora when she'd asked to stay at the lake house. Mama Nora had said the oldest son of the owners was occupying the lake house next to hers, and he had moved to Ennis almost a year ago. Mama Nora *had* mentioned the man was a doctor in town. Hell's bells! How could she have forgotten that?

"Lorren, are you all right?"

Tilting her head back, she looked up at him. "Yes, I'm fine," she replied. "I'm just surprised."

"So was I when Ms. Nora told me. She's worried about you being out here alone. I told her I'd keep an eye out for you."

Lorren's chin raised to a stubborn slant. "You may be my neighbor, but you aren't my keeper. Do try remembering that. Good-night, Dr. Madaris."

"If you'd give me the key, I'll open the door for you."

"I can do it myself."

Justin leaned back against the wood column fronting the lake house. "Just trying to be neighborly."

Lorren didn't know if it was the key not cooperating or the fact she couldn't get her fingers to relax, but the door lock wouldn't budge. When seconds ticked into minutes, she realized the futility of the situation. However, she was determined not to ask Justin for help even if she had to stay out there till morning.

"Here, let me try." Not giving her a chance to step aside, Justin's arms slid around her to the door, where the key was partially inserted inside the lock.

Lorren could feel the hardness of Justin's chest pressed against her back. His closeness overwhelmed her, and the clean manly scent of him caused her flesh to tingle. The feel of his heated breath on her neck made a pulsing knot form in her stomach.

For crying out loud. I've never experienced anything like this before in my life! What in the name of heaven is happening to me?

"There you go. You may want to get that lock changed. It's kind of old."

Lorren swallowed deeply when Justin stepped back to give her the space she needed to turn around. She did so slowly. Feeling his gaze on her face, she refused to lift her head to meet it. At least not until she felt a little less shaky, and until the tremors quivering inside of her wouldn't affect her voice.

Justin stared at Lorren, trying to cope with the feelings engulfing him from her closeness. He became enmeshed in memories of them dancing together, of him holding her in his arms, his hands wrapped around her waist, and their bodies moving slowly to the music. He also remembered her dancing with her friends on the dance floor. And how the black silk material of her dress clung to her body with every movement.

His voice was thick and unsteady when he spoke. "Do you want me to check inside to make sure everything's okay before you go in?"

"That won't be necessary."

"All right." Justin's gaze held hers, then dropped to her mouth, a mouth freshly moistened by the nervous sweep of her tongue. His muscles clenched. Heat raced through him as he tried to retain a hold on his sanity. His gaze returned to her eyes. That same electrical shock of awareness he'd experienced twice at the party hit him full force.

Lorren watched him, unsure of his next move as he stood silhouetted under the porch lights. He took a step that brought him closer to her. Automatically, she took a step back. "It's late, Justin. I'm going inside."

"Don't forget, I'm next door if you need anything. No matter how late it is."

Eyes hooded, Lorren pursed her lips and nodded before taking another step backward into the house. "Good-night, Justin."

"Good-night." He turned and walked away as she closed the door.

Lorren leaned against the door and closed her eyes. Emotional turmoil churned through her. This was not supposed to be happening. She'd been in town less than twenty-four hours, and already she had met a man who could turn her life topsy-turvy and become a threat to the placid existence she'd planned for herself in Ennis.

And if that didn't beat all, he was her neighbor. Her closest and *only* neighbor . . . for miles. She drew in a long breath, feeling tears trickle down her cheeks. She hadn't cried since that day in the judge's chamber almost a year ago. It had been the day her marriage to Scott had ended.

The tears hadn't been for the finality of her marriage; she'd been overjoyed about that. They had been for the cruel words Scott had leveled at her in the presence of the judge and their attorneys. He'd informed her he was glad to be rid of her since she had never been able to perform the natural womanly function of a wife during their marriage.

She would never forget the quick look that had passed between the other three men before the judge warned Scott against any further outburst. It had been the most humiliating day of her life. Scott had succeeded in degrading her until the very end.

Lorren slowly opened her eyes. She was too tired, both mentally and physically, to relive memories of her past or to begin pondering her future. At the moment, all she wanted was to forget about everything and go to bed.

Wiping the tears from her eyes, she straightened and went into the bedroom.

Intrusive bright sunlight flooded the bedroom, awakening Lorren. Shifting her head on the pillow, she gazed up at the ceiling. Unfortunately for her, sleep hadn't come easily. Long after going to bed last night, she'd tossed and turned. The room had been naturally cooled by the breeze blowing off the lake through the window, but her body had been hot and restless. She had been acutely aware of every inch of her naked skin left bare by the skimpy gown she'd worn to bed.

How was one man capable of making her feel things in the space of a few hours when Scott hadn't made her feel anything during the two years they'd been married? In the beginning she'd been attracted to Scott, or so she'd thought. But this attraction she felt toward Justin Madaris was completely different. And it scared her to death.

Sighing, she threw back the bedcovers and reached for her bathrobe.

Putting it on, she belted it firmly around her waist and headed for the bathroom.

A little while later, she stepped into the shower. Hot water rushed through her lathered hair, soaking her brown skin. Closing her eyes, she relished the feel of it streaming over her. Turning her face into the spray, she let the shampoo's foam slide down her back, thighs, and legs. She felt a warm glow inside her body as she remembered the feel of Justin's hard, muscular chest pressed against the curve of her back and the roundness of her bottom when he'd opened the door for her last night.

Adjusting the showerhead to release a lighter spray, Lorren threw her head back, arching her neck against the flow of water, liking the feel of it wetting her lips.

Then the unimaginable happened.

Her mind conjured up a mental image of Justin in the shower with her, placing light kisses on her lips and softly caressing her back and shoulders, and the tender skin between her breasts.

The depth of Lorren's sensual mental diversion startled her back to reality. She snapped her eyes open. *For Pete's sake! What's happening to me?* Turning off the water, she quickly stepped out of the shower and hurriedly dried herself with a thick velour towel.

First last night, and now this. It's bad enough being isolated out here with the man, without starting to have sexual fantasies about him. Girl, you better get your act together.

Stepping into her robe, she tightened the sash at the waist just as the doorbell chimed. She walked out of the bathroom to the living room.

"Who is it?" she asked, peering through the tiny glass peephole in the door. A hot ache grew in her throat. The flaps of a shirt gaped open and a dark, muscular, hair-covered chest dominated her view. She sucked in a quick breath. It was as if her fantasies had zapped Justin to her doorstep.

"It's me Lorren, Justin."

Lorren reached a trembling hand for the doorknob. Her palms became sweaty. Her mouth felt dry. Slowly, she opened the door.

Justin stood before her dressed in a pair of outlandishly sexy swimming shorts and a camp shirt. Somehow she managed to speak. "What do you want, Justin?"

Justin's gaze swept over Lorren. Even with her hair damp from a recent shower and her face scrubbed clean of makeup, she was breathtaking. He would bet the keys to his Vette she wasn't wearing anything under her robe. X-ray vision was something he'd give just about anything to have at the moment.

"Good morning, Lorren. I happened to be in the neighborhood," he teased as a smile touched his lips, "and was wondering if you'd like to join me in an early morning swim?"

Lorren looked at him, trying not to notice how the hair on his chest tapered down his sides, spreading out again along his navel until it disappeared beneath the waistband of his shorts. She marveled at the splendor of his trim flanks and long muscular legs. There wasn't an ounce of spare flesh on him.

"I—I can't," she stuttered, forcing her gaze from his body to his eyes.

Justin smiled. "What is it you can't do? You can't join me, or you can't swim?"

"I—I can't join you because I haven't had breakfast yet," Lorren answered, her tongue stumbling over the first excuse she could think of.

Justin's eyes twinkled. "Never fear, the doctor's here." From behind him, he produced a bag. "It occurred to me, since you'd just arrived yesterday, you hadn't had a chance to go to the grocery store. So being the friendly and considerate neighbor that I am, I decided breakfast would be my treat to officially welcome you to the neighborhood. With your permission, I plan to take your kitchen by storm."

Lorren had a feeling that wasn't the only thing he would take by storm if given the chance. Common sense told her to refuse his generosity. However, it suddenly dawned on her that common sense was something she seemed to lack around him.

Whether she liked it or not, he *was* living next door, so she might as well follow his lead and try to be neighborly. Besides, she really was hungry. "How can I reject such an offer?" she said, stepping aside.

A subtle hint of pure male, and the crisp, clean scent of after-shave, permeated the air as Justin swept past Lorren. He turned to face her, his gaze moving from the top of her damp head to the polished toes of her bare feet peeking from under her robe. His gaze slowly retraced its path. "I'll fix the main course."

Lorren nodded. "All right. And I'll make the coffee. I noticed a full can last night."

Justin followed Lorren into the kitchen. She tried to concentrate on taking the cups out of the cabinet. Spinning around and colliding with the hard wall of his chest, she slowly lifted her gaze to his. There was something about his features she hadn't noticed last night. His sculptured cheekbones added a greater dimension to his already dark handsome face.

"Sorry. I didn't realize you were so close," she said, swallowing hard. She turned to the sink to pour water in the coffeemaker. Even with her back to Justin, she was aware of his blatant scrutiny.

"Did you get a good night's sleep?" he asked.

Lorren turned around. "Yes," she lied. "What about you?"

"Best sleep I've had in a long time."

"Glad to hear it. Now, if you'll excuse me, I'm going to get dressed."

Justin blocked her way out of the kitchen and made no attempt to step aside. "Why? I like what you're wearing. The color peach looks good on you."

Lorren looked down at her robe. Although the thick material hid a lot from Justin's eyes, it wasn't the proper thing to wear when entertaining a male guest.

"Thanks, but I like the color I'm changing into even better," she said. "I'll be back in a minute. If you need anything while I'm gone, check inside the cabinets or the closet." She walked around him and out of the kitchen to the bedroom.

Lorren was slightly unsettled getting dressed. After blow-drying her hair and applying light makeup, she headed back to the kitchen. The rich aroma of eggs and bacon filled the air.

She paused at the kitchen's entrance. Justin had evidently searched the place and found a hand-crocheted cotton lace tablecloth. The table was set and there was also a beautiful bouquet of bluebonnets for the centerpiece. He was leaning over the stove, tending to a tray of pancakes.

She was amazed. "I wasn't gone that long. How in the world did you accomplish all this in that short time?"

A gleam shone in Justin's eyes. "I work fast. I don't believe in beating around the bush or taking things slow."

Lorren knew he was talking about more than his cooking abilities. "Well, your swiftness at getting things done is appreciated this morning. I'm starving." She crossed the room to the counter.

Justin's gaze followed her movement. The soft material of her blue romper did more than hint at the feminine curves it covered. He watched her hips sway provocatively with each step, enticing him with an allure that was as old as mankind. She turned around to face him.

"How do you like it?"

Justin blinked twice. He swallowed hard. "Excuse me?" he asked huskily.

"Your coffee. How do you like it? Or should I ask, how do you take it?"

He cleared his throat and said the first words that came to his muddled mind. "Black and hot."

"What?" Lorren stared at him dumbfounded.

"Oh, I meant black with sugar. Sorry."

Lorren poured the steaming hot liquid into a cup, then added a spoon of sugar. Walking over to him, she handed him the cup, careful to avoid touching him. It was bad enough keeping her gaze from roaming over his physique.

"Thanks." His gaze scanned her outfit. "I take it you've decided not to go swimming with me this morning," he said, disappointed.

"Afraid so. I still have a lot of unpacking to do. I hope that doesn't mean you won't be feeding me after all."

Justin laughed. "No, but it does mean you owe me a rain check."

"I told you last night, I don't give rain checks," she said, smiling, and finding herself relaxing in his company in spite of her apprehensions.

Justin smiled. "Then I'll be your first." He gave her a teasing wink. "Come on, let's eat."

Lorren eagerly escaped to the table and sat down. Justin sat across from her and began spooning hefty servings of scrambled eggs, bacon, and pancakes onto her plate.

"Thanks." Lorren dug hungrily into the meal. "Justin, this is wonderful. I haven't eaten food that tasted this good in a long time. You're definitely full of surprises."

Justin watched as she parted her lips and small white teeth bit down on a piece of crisp bacon. Slowly, she chewed the piece of meat, savoring the taste. A crumb clung to the corner of her mouth. A knot rose in his throat. He was tempted to sweep the crumb away with his tongue.

"Who taught you how to cook, Justin?"

Justin shifted in his chair as he experienced a tremor in his stomach— well, not quite in his stomach. Actually, it was a little lower. He took a calming breath before answering her. "I'm the oldest of six kids, so I was the one who had to learn everything. I enjoyed helping my mom in the kitchen as much as I enjoyed performing surgery on my sisters' baby dolls."

Lorren couldn't keep the amusement out of her voice. "You didn't really do that to their dolls, did you?"

He chuckled. "Afraid so. It got so bad they would hide them from me. I tried convincing them I was just making the dolls better, but after a while, they didn't buy it." He laughed. "I grew out of it when my parents started using my allowance to buy new dolls."

She smiled. "So you always knew you wanted to be a doctor?"

"Yes, I think so. I've always cared for people and wanted to help others. What about you? Did you always want to become a writer?"

"No," she replied softly, remembering the first story she'd written at the age of nine. "After my parents' death, the courts assigned Mama Nora and Papa Paul as my foster parents. At first it was quite an adjustment for me, and I wanted to be left alone. Mama Nora discovered I liked to read and gave me a lot of books to occupy my time. Soon I was writing my own stories. I would give them to her for safekeeping, not knowing of her plans to submit them to a publisher when I got older. She did, and in addition to becoming a published author, I received a four-year scholarship to attend college in California. I've been writing ever since. My books are specifically designed and written to commemorate our ethnic heritage, as well as to entertain and enlighten children."

Justin nodded. He wondered how her parents had died, but didn't want to ask her about it. He of all people knew how hard it was losing a loved one. In her case, she had lost two. But she'd still made something of her life. He was impressed. "That's quite a success story."

"You think so?" Lorren's voice clearly reflected her surprise with Justin's comment."

"Of course, don't you?"

It had been a long time since she'd considered any part of her life as being successful. The guilt of a failed marriage had overshadowed any such thoughts. But now, hearing Justin's words made a part of her feel good inside. "I guess I don't think about it. Writing stories is something I enjoy doing."

Justin knew he was probably about to tread on dangerous ground with his next question. "Did you meet your husband in California?"

Justin's question brought back memories of the day she and Scott had met. It had been one morning in a small café across the street from the newspaper publisher where she worked. Having graduated from college only a few months earlier and landed her first job as an editorial assistant, she'd been experiencing her first real taste of independence.

The first things she'd noticed about Scott were how handsome, well dressed, and sophisticated he was. Three years older than her, he worked as a project consultant for a major television network. For their first date, he'd taken her to an elegant restaurant in LA. On all their other dates, he'd made her feel special and important . . . and loved.

Scott had pursued her for more than six months before finally accepting that she would not agree to sleep with him or any man before marriage. Not engaging in premarital sex was a decision she'd made years earlier because of the good Christian upbringing Mama Nora had given her. But that decision had been reinforced after seeing what Syneda had gone through.

Syneda's father never married her mother, and, knowing she was dying of breast cancer, Ms. Walters had written to the man who had fathered her child, asking that he come and get their ten-year-old daughter and provide a home for her. Syneda's mom, who had never stopped loving the man, had died believing he would come. She had also convinced Syneda that the father she never knew would come for her, thus giving Syneda something to look forward to. Syneda's father never came.

Even believing that Scott actually loved her had not been enough to change Lorren's mind about sleeping with him before marriage. At first, he had continued to hound her about it, but on that issue she had stood her ground.

It was only after her marriage to Scott, which came exactly eight months to the day after they'd met, that Lorren discovered just how self-centered, overambitious, and controlling he was. After she had thoroughly disappointed him in bed on their wedding night, he'd been bent on making her life with him miserable.

But he would keep her anyway, he'd told her, and had further elaborated that he believed in time she could develop technique and finesse a little more to his liking. Besides, he'd added, even with her shortcomings in the bedroom, she had other things going for her—looks and a promising career.

It didn't take her long to realize that he really didn't need a wife, but a hostess for when he entertained his colleagues and associates. He'd told her countless times it was her duty as his wife to help advance his career.

The only reason she'd stayed with him those two years, aside from her deep belief in their commitment, was that she hadn't wanted to be a failure by giving up on their marriage or on him.

In the end, all she'd gotten out of her marriage with Scott was the stripping away of her pride and confidence. That was the price she'd paid for loving him.

Bringing her thoughts back to the present, Lorren responded to Justin's question. "Yes, I met my ex-husband there." She quickly changed the subject, not wanting to talk to Justin about Scott.

"What brought you to a small town like Ennis? I would think this place is rather boring to someone from Houston."

Taking the hint she didn't want to discuss her ex-husband, Justin answered, "I'd lived in a big city all my life and wanted to try a small town." He smiled. "Senator Malone and my father attended Morehouse together, and when Ms. Nora told him about Dr. Powers's retirement, and that the town was in need of a general practitioner, he contacted me to see if I was interested."

A wry smile curled up the corners of Lorren's mouth. She could just imagine the single women's reaction to the town's new doctor. Especially one as handsome as Justin. Her smile faded when she remembered all the pain she'd endured after being taken in by a handsome face. She was determined not to get sucked into that kind of hurt and heartbreak again.

"I feel stuffed. Breakfast was really good. Thanks." She stood and began clearing the table.

Justin picked up on the sudden change in her. She acted as if she was in a hurry for him to leave. For some reason, the amiable time between them had ended. "I'll help with the dishes."

She shook her head. "There's no need. I'm probably one of the few women alive who enjoys doing dishes. When I lived with Mama Nora, I used to make money off the other kids when it was their week for kitchen duty."

Justin grinned. "As much as I like cooking, I've never developed a fondness for washing dishes. And washing pots is really the pits." He stood. "At least let me help you clear the table."

The two of them removed the dishes from the table, then Justin took his leave. As they approached the front door, he asked, "Are you sure you won't change your mind about going swimming?"

"Yes, I'm sure."

Justin studied her face for a moment. "How about dinner tonight? I know of this swell restaurant in Dallas that serves wonderful seafood. Then afterward I can take you dancing. There's this nice—"

"Justin, I won't go out with you." Lorren paused as she formulated her words. "It was fun sharing breakfast with you, but I don't think we should overdo it."

Justin rested against the closed door. "What do you mean?"

"We shouldn't make it a habit, spending a lot of time together. The fewer personal things are between us, the better off we'll both be. We're like oil and water. We don't mix. I'm a realist and you're a dreamer."

"Why? Because I believe in fate?"

"Yes, which means you probably believe there's a pot of gold at the end of the rainbow. You think every marriage should be like the one you had—made in heaven. I found out the hard way that's not true. No one gets married expecting doom, but it happens to the best of us. Unfortunately, statistics have proved it happens to most. I believe true love and a happy marriage are things only shared by a select few."

"I happen to disagree with that assessment," Justin replied, his voice low and sexy. "Sounds like you have a case of divorcitis," he said, smiling mischievously, daring her to smile with him. Reluctantly, she did.

Lorren wondered what there was about Justin that made just looking at him pleasurable, notwithstanding the ability to send her emotions into overdrive. "Divorcitis? Oh my gosh, Doctor. What's that?" she asked teasingly, sounding like a frantic patient.

The soothing rays of the early morning sun came through the window and shone on Lorren's face, giving it a velvety brown softness. Justin thought she looked even more beautiful than last night. He cleared his throat and spoke in a professional tone. "It's a condition that plagues divorcees when, for whatever reason, they refuse to accept the fact there's life after a divorce. They seem to equate a divorce decree with a death decree. And you, Lorren Jacobs, have the usual symptoms."

Lorren decided not to tell him a death decree was not what she equated with her divorce. She'd considered her divorce a rebirth. "I gather a loss of appetite isn't one of the symptoms," she said, laughing at the ridiculousness of their conversation.

Justin grinned. "Nope, your appetite isn't affected; however, at times your peace of mind is. Since I've diagnosed your condition, and free of charge I might add, I don't want to waste any time before starting to treat you. Time is of the utmost importance when handling a condition like yours."

"You don't say, Doc?"

"Oh, I do say," he assured her with a smooth smile. "To leave it untreated could be detrimental to your well-being. However, when given the proper attention, the prognosis is excellent. And with the right dosage of tender, loving care, you'll be good as new in no time."

Lorren's laugh was soft. "Good as new? Really?"

Justin's smile widened. "Yeah, really."

"And just who'll be giving me this TLC?"

"I will."

"Ummm. To be on the safe side, maybe I should obtain a second opinion."

He leaned toward her. "A second opinion in your case isn't necessary. I'm the only one who can diagnose your condition. And more importantly, I'm the only one with a cure. I'll start you off with a mild dosage," he said, his mouth inches from hers, "and when I think you're ready for something stronger, I'll see that you get it."

Lorren felt her heart skip a beat. Was Justin going to kiss her? Did she want him to? No! She had to keep her head on straight. But he had the most sensuous mouth. What would his lips feel like on hers?

She crushed the thought and stepped back. "I think we've played this game long enough, Justin. Weren't you about to leave?"

Justin moved, closing the distance between them, He was so close, the tip of his shoes touched the tip of her flats. "I've changed my mind."

His voice had deepened and thickened. "I want to do something I could barely refrain from doing last night."

Justin's lips brushed against hers as he spoke.

A wild shudder of pleasure touched Lorren's body. Blood coursed through her veins like a raging river. Succumbing to curiosity and the attraction she had fought since first meeting him, her lips parted.

A groan rumbled in Justin's throat as he closed his mouth over hers. He made sure his kiss was gentle, yet seductive. Her taste was sweet, hot, sensuous. He hungered for her and relentlessly explored her mouth, demanding a response and enticing her tongue to mate with his.

Not only was he kissing her, Lorren thought, but he was encouraging her to participate, something Scott never did. He'd said hugging, kissing, and caressing weren't a necessary part of lovemaking.

Heat throbbed deep within Lorren as Justin's thrusting tongue dueled with hers in a slow, sensual motion. She wound her arms around his neck and arched against him, quivering, as hot waves of desire consumed her. Sliding her hands over his rib cage, she felt the hardness of his muscled body through the material of his clothing.

This was better than anything she had ever experienced before. The times she and Scott had kissed had never excited her this way, so completely, so thoroughly.

Her senses pulsated with the strength, feel, and scent of Justin. These new sensations stirred passion, the likes of which she'd never known, to rage within her. Operating purely on instinct, her body leaned into him, intensifying the kiss as she slanted her mouth against his.

Lorren's barrier of self-protectiveness should have had her turning from any intimate contact with a man. Instead, she automatically rose on tiptoe to follow Justin's mouth when he unexpectedly pulled away.

With a fevered moan Justin lifted his mouth from Lorren's to draw much-needed air into his lungs. "I can't handle too much more of this," he whispered roughly, burying his face in her neck and breathing a kiss there. "I just knew it would be like this. I just knew we'd be good together."

His words zapped Lorren back to reality. No! They wouldn't be good together. After what had just happened between them, there was no doubt in her mind he'd be better than good. But she knew with that same certainty, she'd be a disappointment to him. How could she have forgotten that one elemental fact about herself?

Suddenly anxious to escape his presence, she twisted out of his arms, taking a deep breath. "I'm sorry if I gave you the wrong impression, Justin, but I don't sleep around."

Justin's eyes grazed a path from Lorren's swollen lips to the stubborn set of her chin. The woman had transformed the act of kissing into a work of art. At the beginning she'd seemed unsure of what to do, which he'd found strange for someone who'd been married before. But in no time at all she had him indulging in pleasure so wonderful, it felt almost sinful. She had enjoyed their kiss just as much as he had. But he had picked up on the fact that what he'd seen in her eyes was more surprise at the effects of the kiss than recognition of the results of it. If he didn't know better, he'd think she had never been properly kissed before.

"And I don't sleep around either, Lorren," he said quietly. "As a doctor, I know just how rampant AIDS is. I'm a firm believer you should think twice before going to bed with just anyone." He took a step forward. "While I don't go in for one-night stands, I don't have anything against an affair."

A lean, dark finger caressed her cheek. There was such an awe-inspiring beauty about her, with her mouth slightly swollen from his kiss and her face tinted with desire. "I think we may be headed for one," he said softly.

"No." The response was fast from Lorren's lips.

Justin's reply was even quicker. "Yes." His dark eyes held hers. "You're attracted to me just as much as I am to you, whether you're willing to admit it or not. Think about it."

"There's nothing to think about," she replied curtly.

"I believe differently."

Turning, he walked out the door.

CHAPTER 3

"Why do men think they know everything?" Lorren asked Syneda as they sat at a table in Sophie's Diner.

Syneda looked up from her meal. "I guess it's a man thing." She raised a brow. "Is there a particular reason for this little episode of male-bashing? You've been on a roll since we got here."

Lorren took a sip of her soft drink, then regarded her friend through lowered lashes. "No reason."

The look Syneda sent her was pointed. "Let's not get cutesy, Lorren Nicole Jacobs. We've been through too much together. The disappointment of my father not coming for me, your schoolgirl infatuation with Carlos Nottenkamper, and last, but not least, your bummer of a marriage to Scott."

Lorren raised her eyes heavenward. "Thanks for reminding me of that last one."

Syneda smiled sweetly. "Couldn't pass up the chance. So, are you going to tell me what's bothering you, or will you keep me guessing?"

Lorren tried pulling her scattered emotions together. When she spoke, her voice was low and unsteady. "I'm attracted to Justin Madaris."

"For crying out loud, Lorren. Tell me something I don't know. Have you forgotten that I'm the one who called a cab for you the other night. It was obvious at Mama Nora's party the two of you were attracted to each other."

Lorren shook her head. "No, Syneda. You don't understand. I mean *deeply* attracted, to the point that I've felt things." She dropped her voice lower, her words barely more than a ragged whisper. "Physical things."

Syneda stared at her friend for a moment. She would have grinned at the bewildered expression on Lorren's face had she not known the depth of her anxiety. "Oh, Lorren," she said softly, a tender smile dancing across her lips. "Honey, you're supposed to feel physical things when you're attracted to someone."

"I didn't feel anything physical like this for Scott."

Syneda sighed. "Then *that* should tell you something, shouldn't it? When will you realize that Scott Howard didn't walk on water? In my opinion, he didn't walk on land either. He crawled around on his belly like other snakes." She smiled. "So, you're really attracted to the good doctor, uh? Well, hallelujah! It's about time you're attracted to someone. Now maybe you'll stop overprotecting yourself because of what Scott put you through and get on with your life."

"You act as though I haven't dated at all since my divorce. I've gone out with numerous men."

"Numerous men?" Syneda asked, drawing out the words slowly. "Don't make me get hysterical. What you dated were numerous wimps. The only competition you got was from their mamas. Face it, honey, Justin Madaris is no wimp."

Placing her elbows on the table, Syneda laced her fingers under her chin. "Why are you fighting your attraction to Justin, Lorren?"

Lorren took a deep breath before answering. Syneda was one of the few people who knew most of the details of her breakup with Scott. "You know Scott's accusations. You know all the things he said about me."

"Yes," Syneda answered softly. "And I've told you a million times not to believe any of it. He said those things to hurt you. Hurting you was the only way he could cover his own feelings of inadequacy."

Lorren took another sip of her drink before responding. "I really wish I could believe that."

A wry smile tilted the corners of Syneda's mouth. "Do more than believe it, Lorren. You can prove Scott was wrong."

Lorren's brow shot up. "And how am I supposed to do that?"

"You know the answer to that. The way I see it," Syneda continued, "there's only one thing left for you to do. Sleep with Justin."

Lorren's mouth dropped open at the calm, easy way Syneda had made the suggestion. "Syneda Tremain Walters! Are you out of your cotton-pickin' mind?"

"No, but you'll be if you don't make an attempt to find out the truth once and for all. So what's the problem?"

Lorren glanced at her friend sharply, wondering if the onion burger Syneda had just eaten had gone to her head instead of her stomach. Syneda didn't believe in casual sex any more than she did. "For your information, Syneda, Justin Madaris *is* the problem. He's not the type of man I want to get involved with. It's bad enough he's my neighbor, but I simply refuse to let—"

"Whoa, whoa, whoa. Back up a minute. Did you just say Justin's your neighbor?"

Lorren shifted uneasily in her seat. "Yeah, but that doesn't—"

"Hold it right there. Let me get this straight, girlfriend. Justin's out there with you, all alone, in no-man's-land?"

"It's not no-man's-land."

Syneda gave her a half smile. "All right, all right, so it isn't no-man's-land. The two of you are out there all alone in the boondocks?"

Lorren raised her eyes to the ceiling. "Evidently there's a point to all of this. If so, please make it."

"The point is, I think Justin Madaris is exactly what you need, a man with experience."

"Syneda, a man with experience is the last thing I need. His expectations would be too high. I couldn't handle it if another man was to tell me how worthless I am in bed."

Smiling through the sadness she felt for her friend, Syneda said, "As far as I'm concerned, the person who told you that lie wasn't a man, but a snake. Now tell me, what have you and Justin been doing out there all alone?"

Lorren took another sip of her drink. She hadn't seen Justin since the morning he had prepared breakfast for her. That had been two days ago. She'd expected him to show up uninvited again with the pretense of wanting to go swimming, or being a good neighbor by checking up on her. When he didn't, she'd become confused at her mixed feelings of both relief and disappointment.

"We haven't been doing anything," she finally replied. "I haven't seen him much."

"Well, don't look now, but the good doctor just walked through the door. He's seen us and is headed this way. My-oh-my, it should be against the law what that man does to a pair of Levi's jeans."

When Lorren turned to look at Justin, she had the irrational urge to bolt out the door. She felt trapped, and a shiver swept down her spine. The mere sight of him did strange things to her.

"Good afternoon," Justin greeted, stopping at their table.

"Justin, what a pleasant surprise. Come join us," Syneda said, a smile curving her lips.

He returned the smile. "Thanks." He sat down in the chair next to Lorren. A waitress came to take his order. "Hi, Sunnie. Just give me the usual."

Justin and Syneda went into a round of topics, ranging from the weather to foreign affairs. Lorren contributed to the conversation only when asked a direct question. For the most part she tried ignoring Justin's presence. However, every time his gaze lingered on her, she was reminded of his parting words to her the other day.

"We'd love to. Wouldn't we, Lorren?" Syneda asked.

Lorren blinked. "What? I'm sorry, I'm afraid I wasn't listening. My mind was elsewhere."

"Justin invited us to a cookout Thursday night, and I've accepted," Syneda said, giving her a meaningful look. "That will be great since that's when I'm staying overnight with you."

Lorren shrugged. "Fine."

The waitress reappeared at their table. Lorren and Syneda declined dessert, but Justin ordered a slice of strawberry shortcake.

"There's nothing like an onion burger from this place to set you back. I'll probably have indigestion for weeks. Any good advice, Doctor?" Syneda asked, grinning.

Justin smiled. "A teaspoon of baking soda mixed with water. It's a homemade remedy that works."

"I'll give it a try," Syneda said before glancing at her watch. "Well, I hate to run, but I've got to go."

Lorren looked up startled. "Go where?"

"Shopping. But there's no reason for you to leave, too," she replied, with eyes twinkling in devilment.

Syneda turned to Justin. "Thanks for the invitation to the cookout."

Justin stood when Syneda got out of her chair. He smiled. "My pleasure, and don't worry about your bill. I'll take care of it for both you ladies."

"Thanks. That's kind of you. I'll see you guys later."

Lorren felt abandoned and thoroughly set up by her friend. Looking across the table, she found Justin's eyes on her as he sat back down.

"How have you been, Lorren?"

"Fine."

"Are you almost all settled in?"

"Not quite."

Justin held her gaze with his for a few moments. "So you decided to go swimming the other day after all." It was a statement, not a question.

Lorren's eyes widened. "How did you—" she began, then broke off as she realized what the only possible answer to her unfinished question could be. He'd been at home. "I, ah—"

"You what, Lorren?"

She hesitated before answering. "I didn't know you were home. Your car wasn't parked out front. I assumed you had gone somewhere."

Justin leaned back in his chair. A slow smile touched his features. He sensed her nervousness. "Most of the time I keep my Vette parked in the back, under a shed. Texas weather can be murder on a good paint job.

And to answer the question you didn't complete, the reason I know you went swimming is because I saw you."

And what he'd seen had been a sight to behold. He'd been sitting at his kitchen table, which overlooked the lake, reading an informative but boring medical journal article. For some reason he'd glanced up and caught sight of her. Whatever information he'd been reading abruptly faded from his mind when he'd received the jolt of his life. Of course, he'd known she had a shapely figure. The black dress she'd worn at Ms. Nora's party had clearly emphasized that. But the swimming suit she'd been wearing had knocked the breath out of him. All he could do was stare. He couldn't pull his gaze from her. He had all but devoured the vision of her wet curvy body, admiring every inch of it.

Lorren shifted her chair. "I, ah—" she swallowed. "After you left, I changed my mind and thought the swim would relax me."

Justin studied Lorren's well-manicured hand tightening around the glass of soda. "Did it?"

Lorren lifted a brow. "Did it what?"

"Did the swim relax you?"

She shrugged. "Yeah, pretty much."

He smiled. "I'm glad."

Lorren's throat suddenly felt dry, and she took a huge swallow of soda. Justin seemed amused, not irritated, that she'd gone swimming alone, less than an hour after turning down his invitation to go swimming with him.

"You have nice strokes."

Lorren almost choked on her drink. "Excuse me?"

"Your strokes are nice. You're a good swimmer."

She studied him intently. "You must have seen a lot that day."

Smiling, his teeth flashed white against his dark skin. "Yeah," he said huskily. "I saw enough. And I was very impressed with everything I saw. Every bit of it."

Lorren bridled at the double entendre.

Before she could dissect his words, he bailed himself out. "With your swimming, of course." He grinned lazily, certain she knew her aquatic ability had nothing to do with his remarks.

"Of course," she returned stiffly.

"Have you given any thought to what I asked you the other day?"

He saw her tense at his question. Her eyes met his candidly. "As I told you, there's nothing to think about." She stood. "Well, I'll be seeing ya."

"Where're you headed?"

"Fred's Garage. I had my car shipped here from California. It arrived this morning with a flat tire."

"Wait up and I'll walk with you partway," Justin said, signaling the waitress for the checks. "My next patient isn't due in the office until three."

Lorren glanced around the crowded diner, with its clinking dishes, faded wallpaper, and aromas of home-cooked meals. Over the years, it appeared very little had changed, including Sophie's clientele. There were still the truck drivers, senior citizens, and some of the younger locals who enjoyed Sophie's down-home country breakfast in the mornings, her mouth-watering lunch at noon, and her delectable soulful spread at dinnertime. Her sweet potato pie was worth dying for.

"Ready?" Justin broke into her thoughts.

"Yes. I really don't need an escort," she said to Justin when he ushered her out of the restaurant.

"I know, but I need to walk off lunch anyway."

They were both quiet as they strolled along the sidewalk. More than once she was drawn closer to his side in order to let people pass. And each time she was acutely aware of him holding his ground so their bodies would brush against each other.

Lorren tried concentrating on her surroundings. Some years ago the citizens of Ennis had decided to preserve their historic downtown. As a result, after extensive development, renovation, and restoration, the numerous buildings lining Main Street had undergone some degree of revitalization, preserving a bit of the historical nostalgia of her favorite part of town. It had become the central business district.

"Here we are," Lorren said, upon reaching Fred's Garage. "That's my car over there," she stated, pointing to the dark blue Camaro. "It should be ready now. It's been here since this morning."

Justin nodded. "Even so, you'd better check to be sure. I've discovered punctuality and timely service aren't Fred's strong points."

Lorren couldn't help the smile creeping into her features. "You're right. I guess some things never change."

"And some things will in good time," he replied, his eyes fixed on her. The true meaning of his words was all too clear. "If your car isn't ready, let me know. I'll be glad to give you a lift home."

"Thanks, but that won't be necessary."

"How about going swimming with me this evening? The only patient I have is the one scheduled at three."

Lorren hooked her thumbs in the pockets of her jeans and met Justin's gaze. An idea began forming in her head. What if she agreed to become involved with him? Or at least let him think she had. How would he handle it if her preaffair requirements were more than he was willing to agree to? Would he suddenly back off? Was she brave enough to pull off such a stunt? The thought was insane, but if there was a possibility it might work and get him to leave her alone, then . . .

A huge smile appeared on Lorren's face. "I'd love to go swimming with you, Justin. I owe you a rain check anyway."

A look of surprise registered on Justin's chestnut features. "I thought you didn't give rain checks."

"You'll be my first."

He studied her, his eyes dark and intense. "Are you sure?"

She knew he was referring to more than just swimming. "Yes, I'm sure."

"Okay, then I'll see you later. I better get back to the office. Remember the offer still stands if you need a ride home."

"Thanks. I'll do that." Lorren watched as he turned to walk away, suddenly feeling in control. "Justin?" she called after him.

He turned around. "Yeah?"

With dazzling determination she decided she might as well go for the gusto. "Don't worry about dinner. It'll be my treat this evening after our swim," she said breezily. "It's the least I can do after your terrific breakfast."

He stared at her. "Thanks."

She watched him until he was no longer in sight.

Had she bitten off more than she could chew?

Upon arriving at the office, Justin discovered that Mrs. Breland, his three o'clock appointment, had canceled. *Just as well,* he thought. His mind was definitely not as focused as it should be. All his mental activity was concentrated on one person—Lorren Jacobs. The woman had him more confused than ever.

Why had she suddenly accepted his invitation to go swimming *and* invited him to dinner? Had she decided an affair with him wasn't such a bad idea? He had gone to bed last night thinking that a woman like Lorren was the last thing he needed in his life right now.

But the last thing he had been prepared for were dreams of her. The sweet image of her curvy body had tortured him in sleep. In his dreams he had tasted her, soothed her, and gently destroyed her defenses. But his torment hadn't stopped there. He'd also dreamed of holding her tightly in his arms as he made love to her, sinking deeper into her body, inhaling her fragrance as his body vibrated with a fever that . . .

There was a sudden knock on the door. He jumped at the sound. "Come in."

Sandra Dickerson, a middle-aged woman who doubled as both his receptionist and secretary, peeked around the half-opened door. "Your mom's on the line," she said, smiling. "And I'm out of here until morning."

"Have a good evening, Sandra. See you then."

"Okay, see ya," she said, waving and closing the door behind her.

Justin took a long steadying breath before picking up the phone on his desk. "Mom? When did you and Dad get back?" His parents, both college professors at a university in Houston, had been visiting friends in Atlanta for the past two weeks.

"We got back this morning and right in the nick of time. Dex called within twenty minutes after we returned."

Justin's smile widened at the mention of the brother he hadn't seen in quite some time. Dex was working in Australia as a geologist with a major oil company.

"How is he?"

Marilyn Madaris released an excited breath. "You'll find out soon enough. He'll be here for Christy's birthday party."

"Wonderful! Is he coming home to stay?"

"Let's hope so."

Justin heard the deep longing in his mother's voice. In his mind he could envision her, a Nancy Wilson look-alike, sitting at the kitchen table wearing a smile only mothers wore when they thought of their children returning home. He had seen that same motherly smile on Ms. Nora's face when she'd told him that Lorren was his neighbor.

"And how have you been, Justin?"

"Fine, Mom."

"Have you been seeing any nice girls lately, dear?"

Leave it to his mom not to beat around the bush at anything, he thought with a smile. That was Marilyn Madaris's style. After a brief hesitation, he replied, absently fingering the medallion around his neck. "I do my share of dating."

"Really? As far as I'm concerned, they're all faceless women since your family hasn't met any of them. It's hard for a mother with three sons to accept the fact that none of them have marriage on their minds."

Justin grinned. "I'm sure you can forgive Dex for his lack of enthusiasm. His divorce from Caitlin nearly tore him apart. And you can definitely forget Clayton. He claims the only men that aren't fools are bachelors."

"Humph," she snorted. "And what about you?"

"I'd remarry in a heartbeat if the right woman came along, Mom, you know that," he chuckled.

"Do I, Justin? I'm beginning to think this fate song you've been singing over the years is for the birds. A part of me can't help but wonder if perhaps you're only fooling yourself."

"Fooling myself? About what?"

"About ever wanting to marry again."

Justin raised his eyes to the ceiling. "Mom, if it's meant for me to marry again, I will. Now tell me how the rest of the family is doing."

CHAPTER 4

I must be out of my mind, Lorren thought as she drove through the residential streets of Ennis toward Mama Nora's house. How could she have convinced herself to try and pull a fast one on Justin Madaris? Syneda was right. The man was no wimp. There was no doubt in Lorren's mind that he was way out of her league. But it was too late to back out of it now. She would have to go through with it and pray that somehow her plan worked.

What do I have to lose if it doesn't work? she asked herself as she pulled into Mama Nora's driveway. She dredged up a wavering smile. *Probably my peace of mind. Not to mention my sanity.*

"So . . ." Mama Nora poured herself a cup of coffee and sat at the table to join Lorren. "Have you finished unpacking?"

Lorren nodded. "Yes, except for the boxes that arrived this morning. I really appreciate your letting me use the lake house while I finish working on my book. The seclusion helps me concentrate."

"Mmmm." Mama Nora sipped the coffee she had poured into the cup. "And just how long will it take you to finish this book?"

"No more than two to three months at the most. Then I'll begin looking for a place to live somewhere in town before beginning a new book."

Mama Nora nodded. "I'm still not crazy about you being out there alone. But I feel a lot better, though, knowing Justin isn't far away."

Lorren leaned back in her chair. "You really like him, don't you?"

"Who? Justin? Sure I do. I've known the Madaris family for a long time. They're good people. Roman and Justin's daddy were roommates in college." Mama Nora took another sip of coffee before she continued. "Justin turned out to be a fine young man, even with all the pain he's suffered. He's worked hard over the years to mend that hole in his heart."

"Did you know his wife?"

"No, but I understand she was a sweet little thing, and that he simply adored her. It was sad how she died and so young." She shook her head. "I can remember his mama telling me how hard Justin had taken her death. For a while his family thought he'd never recover, that he had hardened his heart and would be a loner forever. But he pulled himself together and came around." Mama Nora swept a strand of gray hair over her left ear. "Yep, there's no doubt in my mind that one day he'll remarry."

Lorren refrained from making eye contact with Mama Nora. Instead, she fingered the pattern of the tablecloth. "Yes, he's said as much," she replied softly. "He certainly has an optimistic view on life. He claims he's waiting for fate to bring this special woman to him."

Mama Nora took another sip of coffee. "So I've heard. I hope it happens soon, and he gets just the kind of woman he needs. A good man like him shouldn't go to waste."

Lorren's head shot up. "Surely you don't believe in this fate stuff?"

"Me? Naw. But evidently Justin does, or at least he's convinced himself he does. People who have encountered pain in life will use just about anything as a safety net." She stared at Lorren. "You and Justin are alike in a way. Both of you are people made for love."

"Love? Me? Not hardly. I prefer just living, and to me living and loving don't necessarily go hand in hand. This business of love and marriage may be a turn-on for Justin, but they're a definite turnoff for me. I don't think I'll ever fully get over what Scott put me through . . . supposedly in the name of love."

Mama Nora touched Lorren's hand. "Believe this, child, all our hearts have been wounded in some kind of way. A person has to be able to dust herself off after a fall and move on. Somehow you got to get on with your life and not look back."

The words penetrated Lorren's mind. That was the whole idea of her moving back to Ennis—to get on with her life. And a man like Justin Madaris was too dangerous to the life she wanted. Whenever she was around him, she found herself thrown into one episode of blank-minded tizzies after another. He had the ability to stop her from thinking straight. She was determined more than ever to get him out of her life.

* * *

"Mmmm. Something smells delicious," Justin said, entering the house carrying a bottle of wine in one hand and a gym bag in the other.

Lorren's pulse quickened and her stomach fluttered nervously as she gazed up at him. Could she pull off what she'd planned? If so, before the evening was over she would scare the pants off him. Well . . . she really didn't want to go that far. The thought of Justin without pants was too much to think about. "It's gumbo. My roommate in college was from New Orleans and introduced me to Creole cooking. I hope you like it."

Justin broke into an open, friendly smile. "I'm sure I will."

Lorren couldn't help smiling back at him. Hurrying home from her visit with Mama Nora, she had dug through a box containing old magazines that had been delivered with her other stuff that morning. Rummaging through the box, she'd found an old magazine which contained the article, "Ways to Send an Overeager Male Running for Cover." She hoped the author of the article knew her stuff.

"Thanks for the wine, Justin. You can go on ahead. I'll join you after making sure everything's taken care of in the kitchen."

She tried not to give an overinterested glance at him. In swimming shorts, his physique was so well sculpted. Each muscle in his hard body was defined.

Justin pulled a towel out of the gym bag. "Oh yeah, will you go to the movies with me tomorrow night in Dallas?"

At any time she would have refused his invitation. But since chances were after tonight he would be avoiding her like the plague, she agreed to go for appearances' sake. "Sure, I'd love to."

Justin gave her a smile that sent her pulse racing. "Great!"

Lorren took a deep breath when Justin left. *Get your act together, girl, and don't screw up.*

When she reached the lake Justin was already in the water. The only part of him visible was his naked brown chest. She slowly disrobed, revealing her two-piece swimming suit, fully aware his eyes were on her.

Calling out to him, she asked, "How cold is the water?"

"It's not cold at all, which is surprising for a day in April," he answered, taking in every detail of the exotic orchid print bathing suit that was molded to all her curves. "Come on in," he invited.

Lorren couldn't help noticing the interest he was showing in her outfit.

"You look absolutely sensational, Lorren."

She smiled. "Thanks." She then dived down deep into the water, resurfacing seconds later. She pushed the wet hair from her eyes. "Justin Madaris! I thought you said the water wasn't cold! It's freezing in here!"

Justin laughed a throaty laugh. "No, it's not," he said, swimming toward her. "Just relax. You'll get used to the temperature."

"I—I doubt it," she muttered in a chattering voice.

"Oh, come here, you big baby, let me warm you." Before she could react, he was wrapping his arms around her. "Does that feel better?"

Lorren nodded, unable to speak. His arms were holding her gently. The motion of the water nudged them together from breast to thigh. She was aware of Justin's solidly built body. The water pushed them even closer, and her breasts brushed against his chest. The muscles of her abdomen quivered.

Justin felt Lorren's breasts swell against him. He ached to remove her top and rub his thumb against their taut tips. How many times had he fantasized about holding her like this, so achingly close to his aroused body? Even now, he could smell her perfume, an alluring scent that made him want to . . .

Suddenly, with trembling hands, he released her. He had to resist temptation. "That should warm you up some," he murmured huskily. "Come on. Let's swim for a while."

Lorren nodded. His touch hadn't just warmed her; it nearly had her in flames.

They swam, hard and fast, their arms splashing vigorously through the water, trying to channel their powerful heat for one another into playful activities. For an entire hour they had a gung ho time treading water and engaging in water wars. Twice when he caught her trying to cheat during a race, he grabbed her and pulled her under. Once, after making it to the other side and resting on the edge, he jumped out of the water and tossed her up in the air and out over the water.

"Justin Madaris! You're going to pay dearly for doing that!" she screamed.

He threw his head back, releasing a great peal of laughter before diving in. Coming up beside her, his arms wrapped around her waist. "Threats!" he teased.

In spite of herself, Lorren joined him in laughter. They trod water some more before swimming to the other side again.

"If we don't get out of here soon, we'll start looking like prunes," she said. "Besides, it's almost dinnertime."

Justin gave her a devastating smile. "My stomach agrees with you." He got out of the water. "I really enjoyed myself, Lorren. You're a lot of fun."

"I had a great time, too," she replied, getting out of the water and toweling herself. *Too great a time,* she thought, grabbing her robe. A feeling of happiness rose inside her, making her feel lighthearted and relaxed. This was the most fun she'd had with a man in a long time.

"Allow me." Justin took the robe from her fingers and held it out so she could slip her arms into the sleeves. His hands smoothed the fabric around her shoulders, down her back, and over the curve of her hips. He was tempted to go farther, to run his hands lightly up the insides of her thighs, to make her ache for him as much as he was aching for her.

Lorren's head was whirling. How could his touch have this effect on her? His arms were now around her waist, forcing her against his body so she could not ignore his want of her. She closed her eyes. She couldn't give in. "Thanks, Justin," she whispered.

"You're welcome." His hot breath caressed her ear. "Are you ready?"

His husky voice reverberated through her body. "Ready?"

Justin turned her around to face him. His hand moved caressingly along her side. "Yeah. Are you ready to go?"

Unable to speak at the moment, Lorren nodded.

They walked back to the lake house. Justin drew her closer to his side, making her aware of the strength radiating from him as well as the power of his body. When they entered the house, she attempted to breathe normally. It wasn't easy. His proximity had nearly stolen the air from her lungs.

"Is the spare bedroom okay?" Justin asked.

His question startled her. "For what?"

"To change clothes."

"Oh. Sure," she replied, embarrassed that she'd jumped to conclusions. "I'll meet you back here in a few minutes."

They returned to the living room about the same time. Lorren had changed into a pair of shorts and a T-shirt, and Justin was wearing jeans and a sweatshirt. She noticed the gold coin medallion around his neck. "That's a nice medallion, Justin."

"Thanks," he replied, unconsciously tucking it inside his sweatshirt. "Do you need help preparing anything?" he asked.

"No thanks. Just make yourself comfortable. It'll only take a few minutes to warm up everything," she replied, rushing off to the kitchen. The man was too sexy for words.

Back in the kitchen, she busied herself with dinner, trying not to think about the man in the other room. The gumbo's spicy aroma helped clear her mind.

In the living room, Justin glanced up at a huge painting Lorren had hanging on the wall. It was a painting of two African children, a boy and a girl. Both were dressed in their native apparel. "Who are they?" Justin asked, turning in Lorren's direction and asking the question across the open breakfast bar separating the kitchen from the living room.

Lorren glanced up and saw him standing in front of the painting. She smiled at him. "Evidently you've never read any of my Kente Kids books, Justin," she said teasingly. "Or you would know that's Suma and Zakiya, my two original Kente Kids. They are everybody's favorites. Suma is a male African name which means the first one, and Zakiya is a female African name which means smart and intelligent. Every so often, I introduce a new Kente Kid in one of my books. That's what I'm doing in the book I'm presently working on. There are now a total of six Kente Kids."

"And who's the new kid?" Justin asked, grinning.

"A little boy by the name of Mukasas. His name means giver and provider."

"That's interesting." He turned his head back to the painting. "I wouldn't mind having a copy of this painting for my very own."

Lorren grinned. Like Justin, most people were immediately taken with her Kente Kids. "Sorry, that painting is one of a kind. It was painted by a friend of mine from college and given to me as a gift."

Justin nodded as he glanced around the room. He noticed a stack of boxes sitting on the floor in the corner. "You're still unpacking?"

"Yes. Those boxes arrived this morning. I'm not sure whether or not I'll be unpacking all of that stuff. Other than the items I need for my writing, I'm going to wait until I'm settled into my own place before unpacking most of it."

"Will you be moving into town?"

"Yes, but I'm in no hurry. I like the privacy and the seclusion this place provides. I wish I could talk Mama Nora into selling it to me. It's just what I need. I don't want anything too big. It's perfect."

Justin walked into the kitchen as Lorren was making the salad. "Why don't you ask her?"

She shook her head. "I can't do that. She loves this place as much as I do."

Justin nodded. "How would you like leasing the one I'm in?"

Lorren looked startled. "Where're you going?"

Justin's mouth curved into a smile. "I'm buying the Taylors' place. In fact, I'm meeting with the attorneys tomorrow to sign the final papers. That's the reason for the cookout on Thursday. It's sort of a celebration. I've been negotiating with the seller for over four months now. We've finally reached a satisfactory agreement."

"You bought Taylor Oaks?" she asked, totally surprised. In her early days in Ennis, Taylor Oaks had been one of the largest spreads in the county. Sam and Holly Taylor had been members of Ennis's elite society. Their beautiful cattle ranch had also been the sight for breeding thoroughbred horses. It was situated on over three hundred acres of land encompassing the most beautiful oak trees found anywhere. That ranch had been Lorren's dream home since the time she'd first attended the Taylors' annual barbecue. She used to envision herself living there.

Mama Nora had informed her last year of the Taylors' deaths when their private plane had crashed. Because they left no children, the ranch became the property of a wealthy distant relative. Uninterested in the ranch, he had put it up for sale.

"Yes, I bought Taylor Oaks." Justin leaned proudly against the kitchen door. "It cost me a bundle, but I think it's a worthwhile investment. I knew I wanted it the moment I saw it."

"But it's so huge. Isn't it too big for one person?"

Justin smiled. "I plan on closing my office in town and moving it to the ranch. I'm converting a section of the house downstairs into an office and examining rooms. And I do plan on remarrying one day and want a large family, so the size of it will fit perfectly with my future plans."

"When will you be moving?"

"Not for a while. I'm going to have the place completely renovated. It's been empty for over a year."

"That's wonderful, Justin. Congratulations."

"Thanks. Are you sure you don't need any help?"

Lorren smiled. "Positive. Everything's all set."

During dinner Justin told her some more about his family and his childhood escapades.

"My goodness," she said, filled with laughter. "You and your siblings were definitely a rowdy bunch. It's a wonder your parents didn't snip your ears."

Justin laughed. "Believe me, there were moments when they were tempted. My two brothers and I used to fight like hell among ourselves, but when it came to protecting each other against some outsider who tried to bother any one of us, we stuck together like glue."

Lorren smiled. "Where's your family now?"

"In Houston. Both of my parents are college professors at Texas Southern. My youngest sister, Christy, will be sixteen next month. She claims being the youngest in the family isn't much fun with three over-protective older brothers. My other sisters, Kattie and Traci, are both married. Neither of my brothers is married. Dex is only eighteen months younger than me. He was married for a short while, but things didn't work out. He works for a major oil company in Australia. We're expecting him back in the States any day, and I'm looking forward to it. I haven't seen him in almost two years. My brother Clayton is three years younger than me, and is an attorney in Houston. He's flying in for the cookout, so you'll get to meet him then."

Lorren's eyes sparkled with admiration for the obvious warmth and affection Justin felt for his family. "Any nieces or nephews?"

Justin grinned. "Not enough according to my parents. Kattie and Traci both have two kids each, all boys. My parents are anxiously awaiting their first granddaughter. Since Kattie and Traci claim they're not having any more kids, my parents aren't too pleased with the marital status of me and my brothers."

Lorren smiled as Justin finished off the last of the gumbo soup she'd served with a tossed salad. She removed their dishes from the table to the sink. "Go on into the living room. I'll bring dessert right out."

She came into the living room a few minutes later, carrying a tray with cut slices of apple pie which she placed on the coffee table.

A big smile covered Justin's face as he tasted the pie. "This is delicious. Is it homemade?"

Lorren grinned. "Thanks, and yes, I made it myself. Everyone who lived with Mama Nora left with a degree in baking."

Awhile later Lorren gathered their dishes and took them into the kitchen. When she returned she switched on the tape player sitting on a nearby table. The soft melodic sound of Michael Bolton filled the air.

"Dinner was great, Lorren."

"Thanks."

"Come here." Justin's voice was husky as he patted the spot next to him on the sofa.

As much as she hated doing so, especially when she was enjoying his company, the time had come to send Justin running for cover. Taking a deep breath, she joined him on the sofa. "Would you care for some more wine, Justin?"

"No, this is fine." He spread his arms out along the back of the sofa, then slipped his hand to the nape of Lorren's neck.

She turned toward him slightly, clearing her throat. "Did you have a busy day?"

He rubbed his finger against her cheek. "No busier than most."

"Oh," she replied as she watched him drink his wine, thinking how sensuous his mouth was. She couldn't help remembering the feel of that mouth on hers. How he had run his tongue over her lips. How his tongue had parted her mouth and slipped inside to . . . *Good grief! What's wrong with me?* she shifted frantically in her seat. She felt Justin's hand move from her cheek to her shoulder. His fingers traced a heated path down her arm.

Lorren bolted from her seat.

"Justin, there's something I'd like to give you."

Confusion appeared on Justin's face when he watched her lift the sofa pillow she'd been sitting on and pull out an envelope, dropping the pillow back in place.

"Here."

Justin eyed the envelope she held out to him. His gaze returned to her, bewilderment evident in his features. "What is it?"

"Read it and see."

Justin stood and, taking the envelope from Lorren's hand, opened it. A legal-looking document was inside. He pulled it out and glanced at it, then looked back at her. "A preaffair agreement?"

"Yes, it's the latest thing. Isn't that neat? It spells out all my requirements."

"What requirements?"

"The requirements you have to agree to before I'd consider having an affair with you."

Justin stared at her in disbelief, then back at the paper he held in his hand. A shudder slithered down his spine. How could he have been so wrong about her? Not in a million years would he have thought there was a conniving bone in her body. Had this evening been nothing but a setup?

A part of his mind sent him an entirely different message. His expression suddenly turned thoughtful as his gaze moved over Lorren's features. She glanced nervously around the room, refusing to look at him. Justin backtracked his thoughts to earlier that evening. Memories tugged at him—their swim and how much fun they'd had, the expression on her face when he'd told her about his family, how she'd listened and the smile she'd worn. A part of him simply refused to believe this entire evening had meant absolutely nothing to her but a ploy to put him on a leash. Still, the piece of paper in his hand proved otherwise.

What were these requirements Lorren wanted? And did she really expect him to go along with them? He doubted it, which meant she knew he wouldn't. Was that what she was counting on? There was only one way to find out. He glanced down and briefly read the typewritten, legal-looking document. A few minutes later he glanced up at her, shaking his head. "Is this a joke?"

To Lorren's surprise, Justin sounded amused, not angered. "No."

"Your first requirement is unlimited use of my Vette?"

Lorren raised her chin. "That's right. Hopefully, I won't need to use it often, but I want to know if I ever needed to, there wouldn't be a problem. I detest a man who thinks more of a piece of tin than he does the woman in his life."

She saw a flash of disbelief cross Justin's face. "My Vette is not a piece of tin, Lorren. Can you handle a Vette?"

Lorren lifted a dark brow. "Justin, we're talking about a car, not a spaceship. What's there to handle? If you've driven one automobile, you've driven them all. I could never understand why some men think car manufacturers make certain vehicles just for them. There's not a car on the road that a woman can't handle."

Justin shook his head. He didn't have the time to disagree with her. He looked back down at the paper. Moments later his head shot up. "Your second requirement is that your name be added to my checking account?" he asked incredulously.

Lorren smiled. "Yeah. I thought that was a great idea. You wouldn't believe just how stingy some men are. Any man I become involved with will have to make sure I never run out of money. I'm sure being a doctor pays well, so you won't have a thing to worry about. Any money you make will be our money."

When Justin spoke his tone was dry. "No kidding? And what about the money you make?"

Lorren chuckled. "Any money I make will be *my* money, of course."

"Of course. How foolish of me to think otherwise."

"What do you think of my final requirement? Of course it's nothing you can do right away, but as long as you'll agree to it, that will be fine." Lorren took a deep breath. This one was a doozy.

"Let me make sure I understand this correctly," Justin said moments later, his voice low and dangerously controlled. "You want a child . . . out of wedlock?"

"Yes. As I've told you before, I've no intentions of remarrying, but I do want to have a child before I'm thirty. I'll have full custody; all you have to do is provide me with generous child support payments."

Justin looked at her intently. "You aren't serious about these requirements, are you?"

"Yes. I'm dead serious."

"And you won't agree to an affair until I've agreed to them?"

"That's the bottom line, Justin."

Lorren smiled sweetly. She could just imagine the thoughts tumbling through his mind. Her requirements were ludicrous. He would never agree to any of them. No man would. According to the magazine article, not too many men willingly turn over their prized autos to a woman. Very few of them parted easily with their hard-earned dollars, and what man wanted to pay through the nose for child support payments? Being caught in that sort of a trap was something they tried to avoid.

Justin watched a satisfied smile quirk the corners of Lorren's lips. She was having her laugh, or so she thought. Now he would have his.

"Well, there's nothing else for me to do, Lorren."

Lorren's smile widened. She watched as he fished in his pocket for his keys.

Her brow arched in confusion. He hadn't driven over, he'd walked. What on earth did he need his keys for? As she continued watching, he took a key off the ring and placed it on the table.

"That's the key to the Vette. I'll use the spare I have at home."

Lorren stared at him with openmouthed shock, totally speechless. She then watched him reach into his back pocket and pull out a checkbook that looked like it had seen better days.

"I'll add your name to my account first thing in the morning, as soon as the bank opens. You can use these until new checks arrive."

When in one swift motion he stripped his sweatshirt off over his head, Lorren found her voice. "What are you doing!"

Justin looked at her. A huge grin touched his mouth. "Getting ready to give you that baby you want before you're thirty. I know you have a few years left before then, but practice makes perfect, you know." He almost laughed out loud at her look of amazement.

Lorren's heart jumped in her chest. What had she gotten herself into?

Justin, bare-chested except for the medallion around his neck, and a sexy smile, took a step toward her.

She took a step back, rubbing her hands together. "It—it was a joke," she managed to get out.

Justin smiled, taking another step forward, covering the distance between them. "What was a joke?" he asked in a deep, sexy voice. He stood before her appearing completely relaxed.

Lorren cleared her throat. "I got this stupid idea and it was supposed to work." Justin didn't comment, which struck Lorren as strange. He just continued looking at her. "You weren't supposed to agree to my requirements," she continued.

She tried not to focus her attention on his shoulders. They were broad and powerful. She suspected those shoulders would feel massive against the palms of her hands. She drew a very slow, very deep breath, trying to put a halt to where her thoughts were headed, praying they hadn't shown on her face.

"And just what was I supposed to do, Lorren?"

She tried to ignore the fluttering in her stomach produced by the deep, husky sound of his voice. She had gotten herself in enough trouble. "You were supposed to be scared off."

Justin's shoulders moved in a dismissive gesture. "I don't scare easily." He took another step forward, bringing him directly in front of her.

Lorren's eyes fastened on the play of rippling muscles across his chest. Heat flared in the pit of her stomach. The look in his eyes was dangerous. The air surrounding them seemed to thicken. She lifted her chin. "I can see that."

"But what I do, Lorren, is get even."

She swallowed hard. "Get even? How?"

"A number of ways. But this way is just for you." He leaned forward, his breath misted across her mouth. The touch of Justin's lips was gentle. His tongue playfully massaged her lips, seeking entry.

"Open your mouth to me, Lorren."

The plea whispered softly against her lips had a hypnotic effect, and, taking a deep, unsteady breath, her mouth formed the word "no," but instead she did as he requested. His tender caresses destroyed her last thread of resistance. She surrendered completely to his masterful seduction and placed her arms around him.

His mouth, wet and hot, nibbled at hers with a hunger that was mind consuming. The burning sensation flooding through her was unbearable.

The kiss grew hotter, hungrier.

Lorren could feel every hard-muscled inch of Justin, including evidence of his desire for her. A powerful tremor swept through her body as she fought for control. The little bit she had took a nosedive when she felt his hand move underneath her top. She shuddered involuntarily at the multitude of emotions overwhelming her with his touch. Deep in the recesses of her mind she wanted to put a stop to what they were doing, but couldn't find the strength to do so.

When his arms tightened around her, prolonging the kiss, she melted into him. An indescribable sweetness flared in her belly, stripping away the last of her defenses. Releasing a soft moan, her tongue met his, stroke for stroke.

Without any control she slid her hands between them to rub his chest. The feel of his chest hair against her palms made her entire body tingle. Her hands brushed against the medallion. His body instantly stiffened. He pulled his mouth away.

Lorren was breathless. Confused. Why had he stopped kissing her? Before she had time to think about it, he leaned down to brush his lips against her cheek. Then his mouth was on hers again and all thoughts flooded from her mind.

Capturing her hands, he pulled them around him, coaxing her arms to wrap around his waist as she pulled herself closer to him.

Their kiss intensified. She could feel the pressure of his other hand in the curve of her back, drawing her closer to him, urging her more intimately into the fit of him. For the first time in her life, she knew how it felt to become insane with the need of someone.

Justin released her mouth. His voice was thick with desire. "Baby, let's finish this in the bedroom."

His words intruded like a blast of cold air, snapping Lorren back to reality. She jerked away from him and began straightening her clothes. She struggled to hide her confusion over what she'd felt—an upsurge of devouring yearning. It was an emotion too new to her. Disconcerted, she crossed her arms and pointedly looked away from him. What had gotten into her? Why had she let him kiss her like that, knowing nothing would come of it? Why on earth did she enjoy his kisses so much?

Out of the corner of her eye she saw Justin fighting for control. His breathing was deep and rapid. He would want answers, but she wouldn't give him any. She couldn't.

"Lorren?"

Unlike earlier, he said her name in a voice with a cutting edge to it. If he was upset with her, that was too friggin' bad. She could deal better with his anger than his disappointment. Never again would she see the look of total sexual letdown on the face of another man.

Still she couldn't bring herself to look at him. How could she face him?

"Lorren, look at me!"

She flinched at the hardness of his command. No matter what, she wouldn't look at him. "Please leave, Justin. Tonight was a mistake."

Justin frowned. There was something about the tone of her words that cooled his anger. Her voice sounded tired and laced with hopelessness.

With a sense of purpose he didn't understand, he walked over to her and took her into his arms. She tried pulling away, but he wouldn't let her. She still refused to look at him. "What's wrong, Lorren?"

"Nothing's wrong. And no matter what you think, especially after tonight, I'm not easy, Justin." The words were spoken barely above a whisper.

Justin lifted her chin, forcing her eyes to meet his. The depth of pain he saw confused him. The pallidness of her nutmeg skin disturbed him. He touched a finger gently to her swollen lips, sealing off any further words of protest. "I don't think you're easy, Lorren. In fact, I think you're complicated as hell."

Lorren pulled away from him.

This time Justin let her.

"Please leave, Justin. I want to be alone."

He hesitated before speaking. "All right. If that's what you want. I need to get my bag out of the spare bedroom."

Minutes later he returned to find her standing by the door as if anxious for his departure. "Are you sure you're okay, Lorren?"

She nodded. "You can have these back," she said, handing him the key and his sweatshirt and checkbook, being careful not to touch him. "As I said, Justin, I did it as a joke."

Justin reached out and took her hand. She tried pulling away, but he held on to her wrist. Their gazes held as his hand slipped from her wrist, and he threaded his fingers through hers. "Someone once told me years ago that no matter how painful your yesterdays were, there's always tomorrow. I'm passing that same message on to you. Think about it."

With those final words, he released her hand, squeezing it gently before letting go. Turning, he walked out into the warm Texas night.

CHAPTER 5

Moonlight sliced a thick silver path across the water, bathing the lush grasslands in a magical glow.

Emerging naked from the waters of the lake, Justin shivered in the cool, damp air. With a grimace, he pulled on his pants over his wet skin.

Gathering up the rest of his clothing, he started walking back to his house. He glanced toward the house where Lorren was probably sleeping and slowed his steps. His eyes didn't blink for the longest time as he stared at the outline of the structure through the trees.

He stopped walking as thoughts of Lorren consumed his mind. There was no mistaking the woman had a problem. And it was deep enough to drive her to the point of pulling a stunt like the one she'd pulled tonight. What exactly had her ex-husband done to make her feel the need to protect herself so fiercely? What had he done to put that tone of hopelessness in her voice, that look of sadness in her eyes? He wondered if she'd ever really experienced a loving relationship at any point during her marriage.

The enormity of those questions propelled him forward toward his place, wondering where he could find some answers. Would Ms. Nora tell him if he asked? What about her friend, Syneda?

Unlocking his door he stepped inside, allowing his eyes to adjust to the room's darkness. He closed the door behind him, then leaned against it. What was there about Lorren that made him even care enough to want to know?

That's an easy question, man, his mind replied. *The woman's kisses have only whet your appetite. Her resistance has only increased your determination. And surprisingly, though it seems otherwise, it's not all about sex. She's the first woman who's actually gotten next to you, really next to you, since Denise.*

Justin was grateful the door supported his back as the realization hit him full force. He ran a hand over his unshaven chin. The last thing he needed in his life was any complications.

He laughed. *Think again, bro. Lorren Jacobs is clearly a complication.*

There was a lot about her he didn't know, a lot he didn't understand. But then there was something he did know, and that was that whatever problems she'd had in the past, the last thing she needed was a man who'd allow her to wallow in self-pity; a man who'd easily give up on her and her cynical facade. What she needed was someone willing to explore the woman hidden underneath her hard shell—no matter what road-blocks she tried putting in his way. She needed a man capable of giving her tender, loving care.

Point-blank, she needed him.

Everyone was entitled to experience a loving relationship at least once in a lifetime. Even one with no strings attached. As far as he was concerned, Lorren's time had come.

After a sleepless night, Lorren got out of bed early to start writing. She hoped it would erase Justin from her mind. How could she have been so stupid to think she could stand a chance against him?

Hours later she sat at her personal computer in deep concentration, keying her thoughts into it. She was having fun writing about Mukasas, her newest Kente Kid. Her agent was presently negotiating a deal with a major toy manufacturer, who was interested in transforming her ethnic book characters into cute, cuddly, and culturally rich toys. Lorren felt very excited about the project that would introduce her "kids" into even more households. She was so involved in working on her story that the ringing of the telephone startled her.

"Yes?"

"Good morning."

The husky, sensuous sound of Justin Madaris's voice filtered through the telephone lines. Lorren's stomach twisted in knots. Had he called to gloat about last night?

"What do you want, Justin?"

Justin clenched his hands into fists inside his pockets. He wondered if her mouth was swollen from his kisses of last night. Thinking about it made his blood race. He took a deep steadying breath. "Tsk, Ms. Jacobs. You were a lot more neighborly yesterday."

Lorren glanced at the computer monitor before her. The characters seemed to darken before her eyes. She knew it wasn't the monitor, but her mood. "So I'm fickle. Sue me."

"I'd rather make love to you," Justin replied, his voice low, deep, and sexy.

Lorren was glad she was sitting down. Sensational shivers streaked through her body. She'd recognized desire in his eyes before, but until now, he'd only hinted at wanting her. She had never expected him to actually say the words, and his doing so now had her gasping for air. "Don't say that," she whispered through jagged breaths, her words soft.

"Why not? It's the truth, and we both know it. Don't you think it's time we began being honest with each other?"

Lorren closed her eyes, trying not to conjure up visions of them last night, wrapped in each other's arms, kissing. He'd desired her last night—she might be a novice in some things, but that much she was sure of. However, would his desire have slowed to a fizzle once he'd gotten her in the bedroom? She didn't know and wouldn't give herself a chance to find out.

"Why're you calling, Justin?" she asked curtly. "Don't you have patients to see, examinations to perform, sinusitis or arthritis to cure?"

"The reason I'm calling is to find out what time you want me to pick you up tonight."

Lorren's brow lifted. "Pick me up? For what?"

"The movies. Have you forgotten our date?"

Lorren groaned inwardly. She'd only agreed to go out with him because she thought her plans to get him out of her life were a sure thing.

"And don't try getting out of it, Lorren. You said you'd go with me, and I took you at your word. Besides, if nothing else, you have to admit we do enjoy each other's company."

Lorren sighed. His words held the truth. She'd had more fun with him yesterday than she'd had in a long time. Her ability to laugh seemed to blossom around him. And if she was completely honest with herself, she'd have to admit she couldn't really blame him for the fact she had made a complete fool of herself with the stunt she'd pulled.

She stared pensively into space. She hadn't been to a movie in years, which in itself was unusual for someone who lived in Los Angeles. Besides, one thing Mama Nora had always taught them was to face any problems head-on, no matter how big or small. And with Scott, she'd done just the opposite. Now she was making the same mistake with Justin. Instead of standing up to him, she'd been retreating.

It was obvious he had no intentions of leaving her alone, and she refused to spend the rest of her days living in Ennis avoiding him. He was a problem she would have to deal with directly. Pretty soon he would tire of pursuing her. Then, like all the others, he'd leave her alone and move on to some other viable conquest.

"How about it, Lorren? Are you still going?"

Silence hung in the air. "Yes, I'm still going."

"Is seven o'clock okay?"

Lorren took a deep breath. "Yes, seven o'clock is fine. I'll be ready."

"Why are we here, Justin?"

"I thought it was a lovely night to park awhile. Don't you like the view?"

"I'd rather go home." Lorren sighed. Up to now the evening had gone the way she had hoped. Justin had arrived at precisely seven, dressed in a pair of snug-fitting jeans and a white cotton shirt. And, as usual, he looked devastatingly sexy.

She'd worn a denim wrap skirt and a loose white pullover shirt. A pair of flat slingbacks adorned her feet. A necklace of graduated bone-colored wooden disks graced her neck with coordinating earrings for her ears. Justin had taken one look at her and his mouth had fallen open. The expression on his chestnut face had been purely comical.

"Well, Justin. Are we going to the movies or are we going to miss most of it while you stand there gawking?"

The movie had been a comedy, and they had shared laughter the entire time. After the movie they'd gone to a café in the West End Market Place for coffee. On the way home he had taken a sharp turn off the highway, heading toward Bristol Trail, a wooded area reputed to be a nighttime hideaway for lovers.

Lorren's mind returned to the present as Justin shifted positions in the car seat. He turned to her and openly studied both her and the outfit she wore. His eyes boldly scanned her from head to toe. She tensed under his close examination, suddenly feeling underdressed. His gaze locked with hers, as if trying to penetrate every defense she had. And to her dismay, it was beginning to work.

"Take me home, Justin. We're a bit too old for this sort of thing."

A slow smile tilted Justin's lips. "You're never too old for lovers' lane."

Lorren shook her head, more than slightly annoyed. "That's your opinion. I happen to disagree."

"Did you enjoy the movie?"

"Yes. Thanks for taking me. Now take me home."

"I brought you here to ask a favor of you."

She raised a suspicious brow. "What kind of favor?"

"How would you like to go camping with me this weekend?"

"No, I *don't* think so."

Justin smiled. "Relax. We won't be alone. In fact, you'll be the only female with me and five other guys."

Lorren's eyes widened. "You can't be serious!"

Seeing the look of shock on her face, Justin laughed. "On the contrary, I'm completely serious. But before you get all bent out of shape, I'll level with you. The other guys are between the ages of five and ten."

Lorren frowned, her eyes puzzled. "I don't understand."

"I'm a volunteer at the Children's Home Society. A group of the little guys and I are going camping this weekend. The Society has a policy that there has to be at least two adults for every five kids. My usual partner can't make it, so I'm asking you to fill in as his replacement."

"And I'll be the only female?"

"Yeah, for my group. Friends of mine from Dallas—John and his wife Juanita—will be camping in the site next to us with another group."

"What happens if you can't find a replacement?"

"Then I won't have any other choice but to cancel the trip. And I'd hate to do that. The boys have been looking forward to this outing for quite a while."

Lorren sighed. Should she consider going? She would hate for the little guys to be disappointed if the trip had to be canceled. Growing up in a foster home, she knew how important outings were.

"Are you sure there's no one else you can ask?"

"Yeah, I'm sure. There's no one else I can ask at this late date."

"Will the boys have any qualms about a woman tagging along?"

"Erick will probably have something to say at first, but he'll get over it. He still classifies girls in the same category as spinach. Yucky, yuck."

A smile touched Lorren's lips. "What you're doing with the boys is real special, Justin. One of the things I appreciated most when I lived with Mama Nora was the people who unselfishly gave their time to us."

Justin noticed how her face became even more beautiful when she was pleased with something. "Then you'll go?"

"Yeah. I'll go."

"Great. My parents' friends from Dallas let me borrow their recreational vehicle whenever I take the boys camping. I'm picking it up late Friday afternoon. We'll leave around six o'clock Saturday morning."

Lorren nodded, a smile pursing her lips. "You didn't have to bring me to Bristol Trail to ask me about the camping trip."

She glanced toward the rear of the car. "I guess I should be glad your Vette doesn't have a back seat. I wouldn't want you to get any ideas," she said, grinning, beginning to feel relaxed.

There was teasing laughter in Justin's eyes. "Shame on you. You're behind the times. No one uses a back seat anymore."

Lorren tried suppressing a giggle. "No? What're they using now?"

"The hood."

Lorren couldn't help herself as she burst out laughing at Justin's reply. Justin found himself joining her infectious laughter.

Suddenly, their amusement died simultaneously. All traces of humor were replaced by raw desire. Their gazes held. Their breathing quickened in unison. Concurrent shivers surged through their veins.

Justin slowly leaned forward, his eyes focused on Lorren's mouth. She felt paralyzed under his intense gaze. Her pulse became erratic.

He touched her forearm. The heat of the caress made Lorren feel dizzy. Warmth radiated in her throat. Liquid heat raced from her head to her toes—and he hadn't even kissed her yet.

Her breath sharpened painfully as his mouth came closer; the manly scent of his cologne was overwhelming. A soft groan escaped her throat. Her mouth burned with anticipation. Desire bubbled within her like a geyser, filling her with a strange inner excitement.

Justin flicked his tongue over her bottom lip, making her shiver. His tongue leisurely outlined her upper lip. She melted. Lorren felt the thrusting pressure as his tongue entered her mouth. She died a slow, erotic death as their mouths mated, hotly, hungrily.

He pulled her across the seat and into his lap, cradling her intimately, crushing her breasts against his chest. He kissed her with searing intensity, with heated longing, with unconcealed wanting. The kiss was greedy, sensuous, deep. His hands moved in provocative caresses over her back and down her legs.

Lorren clung to him, as a hot glowing ache began radiating from the very core of her. Sinking even deeper into his arms, her body responded to his seduction, slow and hot.

A loud crash jarred them from the heated moment, and they parted quickly.

"What the . . ."

"What was that?" Lorren's voice was slurred with passion, her lips wet from his kiss. She moved from Justin's lap and back into her seat, straightening her clothing.

Justin shook his head, his breathing coming in short gasps. "I don't know, but I intend to find out. It sounded like an accident or something."

Backing his car out of the secluded spot, he headed toward the highway. They hadn't driven far when they spotted an overturned vehicle on the road. Reacting with undaunting speed, Justin used his cellular phone to call for help. Then, grabbing his medical bag from the back of the car, he ran toward the vehicle. Chills swept over Lorren's body as she followed him to offer her assistance.

"Go back, Lorren," he ordered, taking immediate charge of the situation. "This car might blow any minute. There're two people inside. I have to get to them and check the extent of their injuries. Call 911 again and tell them to get a chopper in here fast. It looks pretty bad, and I can't risk moving them."

Lorren did as Justin instructed, moving swiftly. When she returned moments later, he had crawled through a broken window and was inside the car, administering medical aid to the victims. She noticed they were teenagers, a girl and a boy.

Standing a safe distance away, she watched Justin. Gone was the taunting gleam in his eyes and the suggestive smile tilting his lips. Both had been replaced by frowns of deep concern and compassion. She fought back the bile threatening to rise in her throat at the sight of the teenagers' physical condition. She felt faint. "Justin, are they—"

"They're alive, Lorren, but barely. I hope the chopper gets here soon. They need to be transported to the hospital immediately. Both have extensive injuries."

A few minutes later the sound of a chopper could be heard overhead and the loud squeal of sirens followed. Shortly thereafter, the area was swarming with help.

Justin beckoned to her when both victims were being loaded in the chopper. "I'm going with them to the hospital. It was touch and go there for a while with the girl, so say a prayer for both of them. Drive the Vette back to your place. I don't know how long I'll be, so just leave the keys under your mat."

"How will you get home?"

"I'll get one of the officers to drop me off." He quickly brushed her lips with his. Then, turning, he ran toward the chopper.

Lorren got in Justin's car. Before starting the ignition she bent her head and said a prayer.

Lorren threw off the bedcovers when she heard the sound of a car pulling into the driveway. Not bothering to slip into her robe, she quickly went into the kitchen and turned on the coffeemaker. A quick glance at the kitchen clock indicated it was almost three o'clock.

Peeping out the window, she saw Justin get out of a patrol car. He headed toward the porch to retrieve his keys from under the mat. She opened the door. "Justin?"

Justin came toward her, then stopped. Hooking his thumbs in the waistband of his jeans, he cocked his head to one side. "What are you doing up?"

"I couldn't sleep." She moved aside, holding the door open for him. "Come in. I've made coffee."

Inside, in full view of the lights, she saw lines of strain and fatigue etched on his face. Without further thought, she took his hand and led him into the kitchen. She poured a steaming cup of coffee and gave it to him.

Justin gazed into the dark murky substance before lifting the brew to his lips. He raised his head and met her eyes, knowing the questions lodged there. "They're in critical condition. Let's pray they make it."

He let out a deep breath, and his eyes bored into Lorren. "They had a high alcohol level, way over the limits. Can you believe that? The boy is only seventeen and the girl is sixteen. And to top if off, neither of them were wearing seat belts. It's a wonder they weren't killed instantly. If we hadn't heard the crash, there's no telling what would've happened. That stretch of highway is pretty much deserted after midnight."

His voice crumbled slightly. "They're just kids, Lorren. Kids who should have a full life ahead of them, going swimming, skating, dancing. Kids who should not have been drinking. The girl is just a few months older than my baby sister."

Instinctively, Lorren put her arm around Justin and pressed her head against his chest. He was a man who had dedicated his life to helping others, but he was also human. And at the moment, the human side of him agonized over a senseless accident. His hold on her tightened, and she knew he was trying to come to grips with what he'd witnessed tonight.

She pulled back and gave him a quick kiss on the cheek. "You did all you could, Justin. And you may have saved their lives. You even risked your own life by getting inside that car to help them. The car could have caught fire at any moment. I was so proud of you tonight."

Justin slipped an arm around Lorren and drew her back against the hard warmth of his chest. She became confused with the feelings of warmth and protectiveness he was stirring in her. The thought that she could protect him from anything was absolutely ridiculous. But still, she couldn't help feeling she was comforting him in some way.

Lorren intended to place another kiss on his cheek, but he turned and caught her lips with his. Her mouth responded to the gentle probing of his tongue. He drew her closer to him. She moved her hips and gasped when she felt his hardness pressed against her.

Justin gently caressed her mouth with slow moist strokes, building pleasure inside of her with each second that ticked by. He thoroughly explored the insides of her lips, drawing one into his mouth, sucking on it. She groaned at the sensations churning inside her.

"Let me love you, Lorren. Please." His plea, spoken huskily in her ear, sent shivers down her body. He hadn't demanded anything from her with dirty words, as Scott had always done. His words were soft and sensual. And he wasn't handling her roughly either. He was touching her as though she were a fine piece of china. She shivered as his caresses became more sensual, more heated through the fabric of her nightgown. Her breathing quickened along with his. She knew where they were headed if she didn't stop him. But for the life of her, she couldn't.

And deep down, she didn't want to.

Please let all of Scott's accusations be lies. Please don't let me disappoint Justin.

More than anything else in the world, tonight I want Scott to be wrong about me. Please let it be so. Please.

"Please." Her lips whispered the words in his mouth. Slipping her arms around his neck, she melted into his embrace. "Please."

Justin's eyes smoldered with desire when he raised his head. In one smooth movement he swept Lorren into his arms. She closed her eyes and brushed her face against his throat as he carried her from the kitchen to the bedroom. Once there he gently placed her on the bed in the tangle of bedcovers, then joined her, pulling her into his arms.

His lips again took hers, his tongue probing the soft sweetness of her mouth. She melted against him. Justin's hand traced a path down her waist, toward her thigh, then stopped. A part of him held back as sanity returned. *What am I doing? The last thing Lorren needs is for me to take advantage of her. We're both in a highly charged emotional state as a result of the auto accident. I won't be able to handle it if she regrets our lovemaking in the morning.*

Reluctantly, Justin broke off their kiss. "No," he whispered raggedly, forcing his head up. "This is no good."

Misunderstanding his words, Lorren's body stiffened. She pushed herself away from him and his rejection. Humiliation swept through her. She was lying in bed, with her nightgown up, and he didn't want her.

Scott had been right about her.

A fresh wave of pain swept over Lorren. She pushed her gown down and turned away from him. She couldn't look at him. "Please leave," she managed to say, her voice shaky.

Justin got off the bed, straightening his clothes and cursing under his breath. "Lorren, I'm really sorry about—"

"Just leave, Justin." She couldn't handle any words of pity he was about to say.

He hesitated before speaking again, rubbing the palm of his hand across his haggard face. "I think we need to talk about—"

"No. There's nothing to discuss. Just go."

When Lorren heard the door closing behind Justin, she collapsed on the bed, giving in to her tears.

CHAPTER 6

Justin stood at the grill and basted the ribs. Looking up, he smiled. "Syneda, I'm glad you could make it." He glanced around the patio. "Where's Lorren?"

"She's not coming."

Justin's smile vanished. "Did she say why?"

"She said something about feeling a little under the weather."

Justin cast a sidelong glance through the trees, to the house where Lorren was staying. "Oh, I see."

Syneda was silent for a long moment. As an attorney she'd become very adept at judging people's characters. She felt she'd done a pretty good job of summing up Justin Madaris. He came across as a very caring man, one who would never intentionally hurt a woman. And the bottom line was that Lorren was hurting because she was convinced that, like Scott, Justin had rejected her. Lorren had told her what had almost happened last night, and how Justin had stopped and walked away. She believed he had done so because he'd realized she wasn't worth the bother. But Syneda believed he'd acted the role of a gentleman, and had stopped himself from taking advantage of the situation. Nothing she could say would convince Lorren of her theory. Now Syneda wondered how she could get Justin to succeed where she had failed, without betraying her friend's confidence.

Justin cleared his throat. Syneda was staring at him silently, her sea green eyes oddly speculative. "Is something wrong, Syneda?"

Syneda gazed up at him, her decision made. "Yeah. I have this problem, and I'm hoping you can help me with it."

Justin raised a brow. "Oh, what sort of problem is it?"

"Strictly professional, involving one of my clients. It may be a little out of your expertise, but at times another ear helps. And I'm hoping, with your medical background, you can possibly steer me in the right direction."

"All right. I'll try."

Syneda took a deep breath. "I've been working with this client who's been abused by her husband."

"Physically abused?"

She squinted up at him. "No, emotionally abused."

Justin nodded knowingly. "Sometimes that's even worse. Cruel words can hurt just as deeply as any physical blow. Physical wounds can heal pretty quickly. Mental wounds can fester for years."

"I agree, Justin. My client and her husband have been married a couple of years, and he's managed to tear down her self-confidence as a woman by convincing her she's sexually worthless."

"And she believes him?"

"He's the only man she's ever been involved with, so yes, she believes him. And because he's been successful in convincing her of this, she feels threatened by any other man who tries to get too close."

"In other words, she's built a wall around herself."

"Precisely."

"Sounds like your client has one hell of a problem, Syneda. Have you advised her to seek professional help?"

"Yes, I've tried, but she refuses to listen," Syneda admitted softly. "To be totally honest with you, Justin, I'm not sure professional help is what she needs right now."

Justin lifted a brow. "What do you think she needs?"

"Someone caring and concerned enough to prove her husband wrong."

"Matchmaking isn't within your profession, but if you feel strongly that's the answer, I suggest you do your damnedest to get her out of her present situation by speeding up her divorce. Hopefully she'll be able to rebuild her life. Eventually she'll meet someone who'll realize just how special she is."

Syneda smiled. "Perhaps she has already. She recently moved back to her hometown and has a doctor living close by. In fact, he's her only neighbor, for miles. The good doctor appears to be interested in her. I just hope he's smart enough to key in on the fact she needs his help."

She paused before continuing. "I've met him and, although I really don't know him that well, both my mind and my heart are leading me to believe that he's a good person, and that he won't ever intentionally hurt her. I think he's exactly who she needs now."

She reached out and touched Justin's shoulder. "Thanks for being a captive audience. It felt good to talk to someone else about it."

Justin thought for a long moment before giving her a crooked smile. "You're welcome. You can bend my ear anytime."

Syneda nodded. Satisfied. "Now if you'll excuse me, I'm going to mingle. I see a few people I know over there." She turned to leave.

"Syneda?"

She looked back over her shoulder. "Yes, Justin?"

His eyes met hers directly. "This, ah, client of yours. She sounds like someone who's really a special person."

"She is, Justin. She's a very special person."

"I hope she knows just what a true friend she has in you."

"No, Justin, it's the other way around. I know just what a true friend I have in her. Long ago she was there for me when I was going through a difficult time in my life. And now, I can't stand to see her hurting any longer."

It was strange how things worked out, Justin thought when Syneda walked away. Just a few nights ago, he'd wondered who could provide him with answers to his questions about Lorren. And without even asking, Syneda, in a roundabout way, had told him basically all he needed to know—at the moment. Anything else would have to come directly from Lorren. What he'd found out had explained a lot, especially some of her behavior.

Justin drew in a deep breath. Lorren was the most sensuous woman he'd ever met. How could she discount her worth as a woman? Her ex-husband had really done a number on her.

He leaned against the wooden post and thought of the times he and Lorren had spent together since meeting at Ms. Nora's party—especially last night. When he'd arrived back at her place from the hospital, she had stood in the open door for him. Somehow, she had understood how he'd felt. It was as if she had read his inner thoughts, had known his inner feelings, and had responded to them by offering him comfort and compassion.

He couldn't remember the last time he'd freely taken either of those things from a woman. But he had accepted them easily from her. By being there for him, she had shared a part of herself, a major concession on her part, and deep down he knew it. He also knew she'd been willing to go further last night. But, somehow, he had found the strength to walk away from her and the complete surrender she had offered.

He had walked away . . .

Justin took a sharp intake of breath. Did Lorren see his walking away as another rejection? Did she realize that he'd done them both a tremendous favor by pulling back?

He heaved an exasperated sigh. No, she wouldn't realize it. Not in her present frame of mind. She would definitely see it as a rejection.

He ran his hand across his chin. He had to convince Lorren that he hadn't rejected her. Somehow he had to make her understand.

The night air was unusually cool, Lorren thought, stepping out onto her porch. The heavy aroma of smoked spareribs and well-seasoned steamed blue crabs floated on the breeze. The tantalizing smell was coming through the trees from Justin's place.

She should have stayed inside. Unable to concentrate on her writing, she should have done something else, like read a book or watch television. She didn't particularly want to think about Justin tonight; she wanted to think of other things.

But she had nothing else to think about.

Even while sleeping last night, thoughts of him had plagued her. Desire for him had hummed through her body, causing her to shift restlessly in bed, aching for his touch.

A touch she would never feel again.

Smoothing her skirt, she sat down on the bottom step, stretching out her legs. Someone once said, "the truth shall set you free." Well, in her case, learning the truth had placed her in even more bondage. For the first time, she was beginning to think moving back to Ennis had not been such a good idea after all.

She had been a fool to think she could start over. No matter where she went, she couldn't run away from the truth of who she was and what she was. She was a woman with the inability to take care of a man's physical needs. Therefore, she would never be able to share a serious relationship with any man.

Long ago she had learned the best way to protect herself was to stay away from any sort of involvement and to maintain an emotional distance as a safety precaution. She had let her guard down with Justin and was paying for it now. She would have to be more careful in the future. Her peace of mind depended on it.

Justin leaned against the oak tree, glad Lorren hadn't noticed him yet so he could study her. Just looking at her gave him such a sense of pleasure. Lorren Jacobs and her eyes, the color of rich caramel, demanded a second look, and a third. A man would have to be a fool not to appreciate her beauty.

And a man would have to be far worse than a fool not to appreciate her as a woman. Her touch was fire. It rushed through him like a brush blaze caught by the wind. The times they'd kissed, desire, the likes of which he'd never known, pulsed through him, making his need for her insistent and monumental.

But it didn't just stop there. He knew there was more to her than just sensuality and physical beauty.

Lorren was different from any woman he'd been involved with since Denise. From their initial meeting that night, there had been something about her that had drawn him to her like a moth to a flame. And whatever it was, it still held him captured, entranced.

Now, knowing a little about her past life, he could just imagine the pain she had gone through; the misgivings and uncertainties she still felt. For some unexplainable reason, he felt attuned to her and sensitive to her feelings. And he knew, without a doubt, he would not be completely satisfied until all her barriers were gone.

Sighing deeply, he moved away from the tree and began walking toward her.

Lorren sensed someone's presence in the woods and drew in a quick, startled breath.

"I didn't mean to frighten you," Justin said, coming forward.

"Justin?" She sat up straighter, feeling somewhat nervous. "What are you doing here? Why aren't you at the party with your guests?" she asked in a strained voice.

Justin sat down beside her on the wooden step. "Everyone has left except for my brother Clayton and Syneda. And they're too engrossed in a discussion of law to notice my absence. You can't imagine how dull it can be when two attorneys get together."

"Why are you here?"

"I heard you were a little under the weather. Thought I'd drop by to see if there's anything I can do."

"No. I'm fine."

"About last night, Lorren."

"I'd rather not talk about it, Justin."

"That may be true for you, but I need to talk about it."

Lorren stood. "Then talk to yourself, because I don't intend to listen."

Justin reached up and gently touched her arm. "Please, let's talk."

She frowned. This didn't make sense. Why was he here? Now that he knew the truth, he wasn't supposed to come back.

"Please, Lorren," Justin repeated quietly. He wanted to hold her in his arms and protect her from the pain of the past. But first, he had to straighten things out between them.

Something in Justin's voice pulled at Lorren. She stared at him for a moment before finally giving in and returning to the seat beside him. She firmed her lips. If he wanted to talk, she would let him. For once she wouldn't run away. There was nothing he could say that would be worse than what Scott had already said.

"I owe you an apology for last night, Lorren. I almost pushed you into doing something you weren't ready to do. We were both upset about the accident, and were going to use sex as a way of comforting each other. And as much as I wanted you, that wouldn't have been right. No matter what you might think of me, I would never deliberately take advantage of you. I'm glad we stopped when we did, and I'm sorry I lost control of the situation."

Justin's words left Lorren more than a little stunned. Her lashes flickered, and a cord in her throat tightened. She didn't know what to say. He hadn't pulled away because he'd found her lacking? He had pulled away to not take advantage of her? He had actually wanted her?

"But I thought—"

"Yes? What did you think, Lorren?"

"Nothing. It's not important."

Neither of them spoke for several minutes. Lorren fingered the fabric of her skirt, knowing she should say something. Justin spoke before she had a chance to. "Will you forgive me, Lorren?"

She shrugged. "There's really nothing to forgive, Justin. What almost happened was just as much my fault, too. As you said, we were both upset and feeling kind of down over the accident. It was just a natural reaction to turn to each other that way."

Lorren felt Justin's arms go around her, and in one smooth sweep, he moved her to his lap. Taken by surprise, she opened her mouth to say something. She couldn't recall what she'd wanted to say when Justin tenderly nestled her in his strong arms.

She could hear the sound of his heartbeat against her face, and could smell the manly scent of him. His chin rested atop her head, his arms wrapped securely around her. His tender hold and the soft stroke of his fingers on her arm were caring. The tensions caused by her jumping to conclusions slowly began leaving her body, and she surrendered to the protectiveness of his embrace, feeling warm and contented.

For a long moment Justin continued to hold her, rocking her gently in his arms. Never before had any man shown her so much tenderness. Never had anything she wanted to feel so wrong felt so right. The feeling was wonderful, but at the same time terrifying. She was attuned to his closeness, his strength, and the hardness of his body. She threw her head back and their eyes met and held. She was startled by the warmth displayed in the depths of his eyes.

"I should go in now, Justin," she whispered. "It's getting late."

Reluctantly, he released her, allowing her to stand. Lorren smoothed down her skirt and straightened her blouse. When she had finished, Justin rose to his feet in a swift, seamless movement and gently pulled her to him. His lips moved in a soft caress, tracing a path across her forehead, the tip of her nose, then across her cheek and to the base of her neck. Leaning over slightly, he touched her mouth very lightly with his.

Lifting his head, he looked down at her. His gaze was gentle. "You do know things aren't completely settled between us, don't you?"

Lorren swallowed and shifted her eyes downward a little. "What do you mean?"

"As I told you before, I'm not into one-night stands. And I'm not interested in a casual entanglement either."

"What exactly are you interested in, Justin?"

"For now, I want to spend some time with you. I want us to get to know each other without your putting up a wall. If you'd like, you can call the shots. We won't do anything you don't want to. I'm willing to take things slow."

Lorren swallowed again. The last thing she needed was to become involved with Justin. But somehow, she felt involved with him already. He was the first man who made her blood race, whose touch stole the very breath from her lungs, and whose kisses made her entire body burn. And he had admitted he wanted her. For those reasons, shouldn't she try discovering more of him? And along with him, shouldn't she try discovering more of herself?

"All right." She trembled when she finally said the words.

Justin's embrace tightened, drawing her closer. "You won't regret it." He wanted to say more, but he didn't.

"So, how was the cookout?"

"It was okay, but you were missed. I know it's kind of late, but I'd like you to meet Clayton. Will you walk with me over to my place?"

Lorren felt tension seep out of her, leaving her oddly relieved and feeling closer to Justin. "Sure, why not. Besides, if we don't put an end to your brother and Syneda's conversation, it might go on forever. She gets kind of fired up whenever she discusses law."

Justin laughed. "So does Clayton. But when I left them, they weren't discussing it, they were debating it. They couldn't seem to agree on any of the issues."

Lorren stuck her hands into the pockets of her skirt as they started walking back toward Justin's place.

Never had she felt this sense of serenity with anyone since her divorce, a sense of well-being Justin could instill so effortlessly.

Wrapping an arm around her shoulder, he pulled her closer to his side. They began walking toward the front of the house. Taking the path through the trees, they headed toward the spot where Justin's brother and Syneda stood in deep conversation.

Lorren could no longer deny she drew comfort from the strong arms around her.

CHAPTER 7

"**S**he's a girl, Dr. J.!" The little boy with a mop of curly black hair snarled.

"You must be Erick," Lorren replied, trying to hide her grin. Upon opening the door, she'd found Justin with five youngsters surrounding him.

"No, she's not," a brown-eyed boy with toasted skin answered beboppingly. "She's a knockout."

Lorren laughed. "Thanks. And who are you?"

"I'm Charlie. The C in my name stands for *cool*."

"Oh, all right, Charlie," Lorren said, grinning and turning her attention to the remaining three youngsters. "Now who do we have here?"

"I'm Derick, ma'am. Erick's twin brother," a third little boy answered. "But we're not identical twins," the youngster with close-cropped, curly black hair said shyly.

In more ways than one, Lorren thought, gazing at the mild-mannered Derick, then back at Erick, his surly twin brother, who was eyeing her with distaste.

"I'm Conan," the fourth little boy replied. His oval face was cocoa in color, and his gorgeous ebony eyes matched his tight curly hair. "My friends call me the 'Barbarian.'"

"Oh," Lorren answered as a smile touched her lips. "I'll try remembering that. Who're you?" she asked the remaining little boy with dark brown curly hair who was clinging shyly to Justin's hand. It was obvious he was the youngest of the group. His small bashful face held the innocence of an angel. She fell in love with him at once.

"That's Vincent, ma'am," Derick answered. "He doesn't talk much. He's only five, but Dr. J. always invites him along with us big guys."

Lorren's smile widened. "Hello, Vincent. How are you?"

The little boy cast Justin an uneasy look. Justin nodded his head, then the boy answered softly, "Fine."

"She's not even ready, Dr. J.!" Erick stormed. "Just like a girl to make us have to wait."

"You're wrong, Erick," Lorren chuckled. "I'm ready. I just need help getting my things to the car."

"We don't have a car. Dr. J. brought an RV," Conan quickly corrected her.

"That's right," Lorren replied. "He did mention he would."

"I bet she's bringing a whole bunch of stuff we won't be needing. Girl's stuff. We're going to be crowded out, Dr. J.," Erick stated in disgust.

Lorren tapped her finger thoughtfully to her chin. "In that case I may as well leave behind the huge container full of homemade brownies and cookies I was bringing along."

That statement captured the boys' attention. Justin, who had been quiet all this time, released a hearty laugh. "I was wondering how long it would take you to wrap them around your finger."

Lorren smiled up at him. She hadn't seen him since the cookout Thursday night. He looked handsome as ever. She had never seen such beautiful thick eyelashes on a man before. They were lashes a woman would kill for.

"Hey you guys, this is Lorren Jacobs. She's a friend of mine and will be our special guest for the weekend."

"We've never taken a girl along before, Dr. J.," Erick replied, not bothering to hide his displeasure. "Why is she coming? What makes her so special?"

Complete silence fell upon the group. They eyed both Lorren and Justin speculatively, waiting for Justin's answer. Lorren noticed even Vincent had emerged from his hiding place behind Justin to analyze them.

"First of all, she was kind enough to fill in for Mr. Bob. He couldn't make it this trip. Now, let me see what makes her so special."

Justin then tipped his head to one side as if studying Lorren. "Ummm . . . she's pretty. Real pretty. She can cook. She understands and likes children, because she writes books especially for them to read. And when you guys get older you'll discover all men like having a girl around every once in a while to keep them in line. I guess all those things make her special."

Lorren felt herself tint from Justin's statement, feeling just as special as he'd made her sound.

"You keep Dr. J. in line?" Charlie asked, as if the task was a monumental undertaking.

Her eyes squinted with laughter. "I try my best."

"Wow!" the boys exclaimed in unison.

Justin laughed. "Come on, you guys. That's enough questions. How about grabbing those things over there and heading on out to the RV. And watch your step."

When the boys were out of hearing range, Justin turned to Lorren. His gaze held her so intently she was only vaguely aware his arm had slipped around her waist. He pulled her against his chest, resting his chin on the top of her head. "Are you ready to have a terrific weekend?"

Lorren took a step back and gazed up at him. "I'm more than ready."

Justin smiled. "Good. John and Juanita should be there with their group about an hour after we arrive." He extended his hand to her. "Let's go. The guys are waiting."

"Is this a recreational vehicle or an apartment on wheels?" Lorren asked, stepping on board the huge RV and glancing around.

Talk about going camping with all the necessities! It was equipped with a refrigerator and stove, private toilet and shower facilities, a game table, enough room to sleep at least six people comfortably, a disc player, a television and VCR.

Justin chuckled. "I ask myself the same question whenever I'm using it. You may as well make yourself comfortable and enjoy the ride. It'll take a couple of hours to get where we're going."

"When can we start eating the goodies?" Erick asked excitedly licking his lips, his discontent with Lorren's gender suddenly forgotten.

"Not for a while yet. You just finished breakfast. Besides, it's too early for sweets," Justin answered, getting behind the steering wheel and snapping his seat belt in place. "Try keeping yourselves busy until snack time."

"When is snack time?" Charlie asked eagerly.

"Not for at least another hour or so," Justin replied, grinning. Now he understood what his mother meant when she claimed he and his brothers almost ate her out of house and home when they were kids. Little boys seemed to have bottomless pits instead of stomachs.

Apparently satisfied with Justin's answer, the boys, with the exception of Vincent, went toward the back of the RV. Vincent, Lorren noticed, had curled up on one of the sofa-sleepers and was going to sleep. "Vincent isn't very talkative, Justin. Are you sure he's feeling well?" she asked with concern.

"That's just the way he is. He's the newest member of the group, and is still somewhat shy. He's only been with the Society a little over a year, and during that time he's come a long way. He's the lone survivor of an automobile accident that killed both his parents and little sister."

Lorren shuddered as painful memories resurfaced. Her own parents had been killed in a car accident. She would never forget how she, at the age of eight, had taken a final stroll with her parents when she'd walked behind their caskets up the aisle of the church.

"And to make matters worse," Justin continued, "Vincent had no other family. When he first arrived he was scared and withdrawn. He's slowly coming around. I spend more time with him than I do the other boys. He still has a few medical problems as a result of the accident."

"Nothing serious, I hope."

Justin shook his head. "Not anymore. He's coming along nicely."

Lorren met his gaze. "I'm glad you get to spend a lot of time with him, Justin. The worst thing anyone can do is let him continue to withdraw. I went through something similar when I first went to live with Mama Nora and Papa Paul. If it hadn't been for their love and patience, I don't think I could have survived emotionally. It's very hard to adjust when you've lost everyone you've ever loved."

They remained silent for the remainder of the trip until the boys interrupted them for a snack.

They finally reached the campgrounds of Davy Crockett National Forest. Justin delegated the boys the task of unpacking the smaller items from the RV. To Lorren's surprise, the five of them worked well together.

John and Juanita Graham arrived with their group within the hour. Lorren took an immediate liking to the attractive woman who was married to Justin's old college friend.

Juanita had smooth almond skin, high cheekbones, ebony eyes, and a bubbly and friendly smile. Her short curly hair fit almost caplike around her head, emphasizing the beauty of her features and giving her a dark, sultry look, even while dressed in a pair of jeans and an oversize T-shirt.

John, Lorren learned, was a Texas Ranger and was nearly as handsome as Justin, with maple skin and tawny-colored eyes. Before the Grahams left for their own camping site, they had talked Justin and Lorren into making plans for the four of them to get together for dinner sometime in the near future.

It was wonderful to get away and enjoy the solitude of the wild, Lorren thought. To her dismay, she discovered tremendous pleasure in watching Justin take charge. Dressed in a pair of well-worn jeans that fit his body snugly, and a short-sleeved blue shirt, he looked perfectly at home in his surroundings.

As he worked diligently getting camp set up, Lorren's gaze encompassed his sleek body, the perspiration-sheened brown skin of his bare back after he'd removed his shirt, and the play of muscles across his torso whenever he reached for something.

A couple of times he caught her looking at him and gave her a huge arrogant grin, as if reading her thoughts. She quickly turned her head, embarrassed at being caught, but glanced back at him minutes later.

They spent the rest of the day exploring the park and taking hikes with John, Juanita, and their group. Later that day, Justin, Charlie, and

Erick went fishing for their dinner. When they returned Lorren was delegated the task of cooking their catch. She became the hit of the day when she surprised them with a hidden dessert she'd brought along, a huge chocolate cake.

Justin insisted Lorren sleep inside the RV, but she had other ideas and started to protest until Charlie mentioned certain unmentionables, like snakes, bears, and mosquitoes. Justin and the boys really roughed it by bedding down on the ground in sleeping bags with the stars for their roof and a pile of leaves for their pillows.

By the time Lorren settled into the RV that night, every muscle in her thighs ached, her backside felt sore and her feet were tender. No sooner did her head touch the pillow than she went quickly to sleep.

They awakened early the next morning to Justin's breakfast of biscuits and sausage, hot chocolate for the boys, and coffee for them. It was another full day of vigorous activities. By four o'clock that evening, they were all packed to return home.

Lorren had thoroughly enjoyed herself. The boys, to her surprise and utter amazement, turned out to be a bunch of darlings. They, along with Justin, catered to her every whim. It had been wonderful enjoying the simple pleasures of camping, such as singing songs and exchanging ghost stories over an open fire and hiking in the woods. The camping trip also afforded her an opportunity to see another side of Justin.

She realized just what a genuinely caring man he really was, and saw in him a sensitivity that overwhelmed her. It was evident he loved kids, and the boys adored him. His time had been their time, their survival, his, and their happiness, his enjoyment. She didn't miss the expressions of gaiety on Justin's face when Vincent and Erick recited poems they'd learned in school, or his expression of deep interest as he listened to Conan expound on his desire to one day become an astronaut.

He had hugged Derick with loving arms when he had caught the biggest catch of the day, and had gently but sternly scolded Charlie for his insistence that he be allowed to go spend some time with a group of Girl Scouts he'd discovered camping nearby.

Justin had made them laugh with his rendition of the Fat Albert character. Later, he pulled out a guitar and, ignoring the snickers and giggles from the boys, played her a beautiful love song.

Although there was sexual tension surrounding them on the camping trip, they were able to harness it, most of the time. However, more than once their eyes met over an open fire.

Later that night, when Justin took Lorren home after dropping the boys off, he helped her unload her gear into the house. They worked in silence until the job was done. Afterward, she walked him to the RV.

"Thanks for coming along, Lorren. You were a big hit with the boys, and I thoroughly enjoyed your company."

"Thanks for inviting me. I had a great time. The boys were wonderful, and John and Juanita are really super people."

Justin nodded. "Are you planning to go to the National Polka Festival?"

"Yes."

"Are you going with anyone?"

"No."

"Would you go with me?"

Lorren smiled. "Do you promise to bring me straight home afterward?"

Justin chuckled. "If you insist, but you have to admit our being at Bristol Trail may have been a blessing for those two kids."

Lorren shuddered slightly, remembering the accident. Earlier Justin had given her an update on the teenagers' conditions. Although improved, their conditions were still guarded. "Maybe it was at that."

"Well, I better get along. I need to return the RV tonight. I guess I'll see you later."

"Okay."

Justin stepped closer. Lorren gazed up at his face, just a couple of inches above hers. He gently pulled her to him. "How do you manage to stay slim and trim when you bake so well?" He placed his arms around her slender waist and drew her closer.

Her response was an amusing laugh. "I usually don't bake for myself. I enjoy baking for other people." She unconsciously wrapped her arms around his neck. He didn't seem as surprised at her boldness as much as she did.

"You can bake for me anytime," he said huskily, before bringing his lips to hers. His tongue sought hers, tentative at first, then with more assurance when he felt her response.

As their mouths clung together, his hands pulled her body closer to him. Moments later he reluctantly pulled away. "Yes sirree, you can bake for me anytime," he whispered in between quick breaths.

Lorren smiled. "I'll remember that."

"How about joining me in a late-night swim when I get back?" he suggested in a deep husky voice.

She moistened her lips with her tongue as a tingling sensation settled in the pit of her stomach from his touch. She shook her head. "I don't think that's a good idea."

His hand brushed her cheek. Dark eyes met hers. "I happen to think it's a great idea."

Lorren smiled, feeling the gentle pressure of his hand on her face. She was tempted to turn her head and touch the tip of her tongue against his fingers. Instead she said, "You would be the one to think so. If my memory serves me correctly, the one and only time we went swimming together, you didn't play fair."

Justin laughed. "*I* didn't play fair? Lady, *you* give a whole new meaning to the word cheat."

"I do not."

"Oh, yes you do."

Lorren stuck her tongue out at him. Justin quickly captured it with his mouth, all firm with need. Lorren felt fire race down to her toes and back, settling in the core of her.

She moaned deep in her throat as she gave herself up to Justin's touch and taste. His hand wandered up and down, caressing first her hips through the fabric of her shorts, then her bottom.

The kiss continued for a long moment until, breathless, Justin drew back. "Lorren Jacobs, you're going to be the death of me yet."

She gazed up at him with eyes alive with desire. "Why do you say that?"

"Because I want you so much I could die."

"Oh, Justin." Lorren curled into him, wrapping her arms around his waist and resting her head upon his chest. "You really mean that, don't you?" Disbelief, then acceptance, was in her voice.

Her words, spoken in a heartfelt whisper, tore through Justin. It was hard to believe that a woman so beautiful and desirable could harbor insecurities about herself and her ability to be wanted by a man.

"Yes, baby. I really meant it. Trust me."

He pulled Lorren closer in his embrace until every inch of his body touched every available inch of hers. His body shook with the intensity of the emotions he felt inside. They stood that way for an endless length of time.

"Lorren," Justin breathed, lifting her face with one of his fingers under her chin, "I told you the other night I was willing to take things slow. I meant it then, but now I want to say the hell with slowness. And unless you're in agreement with me, I suggest you go on into the house."

Lorren pushed away from Justin's chest and looked up into his eyes. Without saying anything, she slowly turned and walked away. When she got halfway to the door, she turned around. Justin was leaning against the RV, with one foot crossed over the other at the ankle and folded arms across his chest. His eyes were directly on her, watching her intently.

She knew her lips were swollen and must look a sight, but nonetheless, she tilted them in a smile. "Justin?"

"Yes?"

"There's always tomorrow."

Justin nodded, returning her smile. He dared not hope her words were hinting at possibilities of things yet to come.

Lorren turned and hurried on inside.

Justin kept his gaze on Lorren until she'd entered the house and locked the door behind her. He took a deep, calming breath before reaching for the doorknob on the RV.

"Yeah, there's always tomorrow," he said softly.

CHAPTER 8

L orren couldn't sleep.
The soft spattering rain could be heard beating gently against the window, and not too far away the sound of distant thunder rumbled across the sky. However, it wasn't the weather keeping her awake. She couldn't get Justin out of her mind.

Sighing, she slid out of bed and crossed the room. Turning on one of the small lamps on the dresser, she stared at her reflection in the mirror. She looked, she admitted, like the same woman who had arrived in Ennis a couple of weeks ago. But she realized something was different, something not showing that was deep within.

She had fallen in love.

Lorren had sworn after her experience with Scott, she would never fall prey to that emotion again, but somehow what she'd merely shrugged off as a physical attraction to Justin had been transformed into love. Genuine love. And with that startling clarity, she could now admit that what she'd felt for Scott was nothing compared to what she was feeling for Justin.

Straightening, she switched off the lamp and got back into bed. Lying in darkness, she gazed up at the ceiling, reflecting on her relationship with Justin. In a little more than a few days she had gained so much insight into who he was as a man, a doctor, and a person. She had dated Scott for eight months before they had married, and had never really known him or what he'd been capable of doing until it had been too late.

Her ragged sigh echoed in the quiet stillness of the room. Even though Justin had admitted he believed in love, he didn't love her. Lorren knew she was merely someone he was spending time with while waiting patiently for that special woman he believed fate would deliver to him.

She had been hurt too deeply in the past to allow herself to assume that, although Justin enjoyed her friendship, company, and the growing passion between them, he wanted more. She was determined never to make the same mistake with him that she'd made with Scott by assuming too much.

A lone tear fell from Lorren's eye, making its way down her cheek. Would love always be something she could touch but never hold on to?

The gentle sound of the rain soon lulled Lorren. Her lashes fluttered against her cheeks as the heaviness of sleep touched her.

The roar of thunder grew louder. Lorren awoke, startled, hearing the torrential rain pounding against the window. Lightning flashed everywhere.

Gripping the bedcovers, she battled with fear, not of the storm but the memories it seemed to evoke. Severe thunderstorms often made her remember the night her parents had gotten killed. And tonight, the memories were stronger than ever.

Drawing the covers around her, she scrunched deeper into the pillows. Howling winds beat against the windows and jagged streaks of lightning tormented the sky. Lorren covered her ears with her hands to drown out the perilous noise. She didn't want to remember.

Justin's words filtered through her mind. *Don't forget I'm next door if you need anything. No matter how late it is . . .*

Unable to confront the memories any longer, she jumped out of bed, shoved on her slippers, and grabbed her robe. Dismissing the danger, she ran from the house into the pouring rain to the one person she needed most.

She ran to Justin.

Justin groaned as he pulled the pillow over his head in an attempt to drown out the incessant knocking at his door. He was too absorbed in his dream to be distracted.

. . . Silken arms reached up to encircle his neck as he captured eager lips in a seductive kiss. He released her mouth momentarily to drink in the beauty of her naked brown body. Desire surged through him each time he looked at her. Caramel-colored eyes, aflame with a heated hunger, gazed back at him. He rose above her, proud and powerful, wanting to be tender, yet desperately wanting to be inside her . . .

The knocking became more persistent as reality invaded the deep recesses of his mind and abruptly ended his dream. Struggling to throw off the covers, he groped for his pajama bottoms and hurriedly put them on. Who in their right mind would venture out at this ungodly hour of the night and in this wretched weather? He left the bedroom and muttered an obscenity when his toe came in contact with the coffee table, Limping, he finally reached the door and yanked it open.

"Lorren!" His surprise was immediately replaced by concern. Her nightclothes were drenched, and she shook from head to toe. At first he thought the cause was the chilling rain, then he saw the terror in her eyes and face.

"What's the matter? Baby, what's wrong?"

Petrified caramel eyes pleaded understanding. "I—I . . . the storm . . . I don't want to remember," she answered incoherently. Her voice was a mere whisper before the flash of a jagged spear of lightning and the sound of a mighty roar of thunder propelled her into his arms.

Justin held her tight against him, not caring he was getting soaked in the process. Cradling her tenderly in his arms, he picked her up. After kicking the door shut, he carried her into his bedroom. Gently placing her in a huge recliner near the bed, he knelt beside her. Softly stroking wet hair from her face he said, "It's okay. You're here with me. You're safe."

Her eyes fluttered open. She gazed down at him.

"Are you all right, Lorren?"

She closed her eyes, remembering another time when she had run out into the storm at night. She nodded weakly, still trembling.

"You need to get out of these wet things, take a hot shower, and dry your hair. Do you think you can manage by yourself, or do you need my help?"

Their eyes met. Justin's expression was one of genuine concern and caring. Lorren's lids lowered. "I—I can manage, but . . . " She swallowed deeply. "I don't have anything else to put on."

"Don't worry about that. I'll find something." He tenderly caressed her cheek. "Everything's going to be all right."

The touch of Justin's finger on her skin brought a sensation of warm security. His eyes held hers with mesmerizing intensity.

"I'll leave you alone. Everything you need should be in there," he said, indicating the bathroom.

She nodded.

"I'll be right outside the door if you need me." He stood and walked out of the room, closing the door behind him.

Lorren felt totally drained, both mentally and physically. Justin's voice had been kind, almost loving. Sighing deeply, she stood to go into the bathroom.

In the living room, Justin paced the floor from one end to the other.

After a while, he sat on the sofa, with his elbows resting on his thighs and his hands clasped loosely between his knees. He stared thoughtfully into space.

What was there about the storm that had frightened her so much to have driven her out into it? And what was it that she didn't want to remember?

When he heard Lorren moving about in the other room, he decided to fix something hot and soothing for her to drink. She'd need it after being out in the weather.

Lorren came out of the bathroom, securely wrapped in one of Justin's oversize bath towels. She was glad the storm had subsided. Entering the bedroom, she saw a Houston Oilers T-shirt lying on the bed. Discarding the towel, she slipped into the big shirt. Her slender form was swallowed by it as it fell past her knees.

She glanced around the room. Shades of sable brown, black, and tan filled it with masculine strength and sensuality.

Above the king-size bed hung a colossal African painting depicting intricate expressions of cultural pride. Numerous pieces of artwork by various African-American artists adorned the other walls in the room. A tall bookcase stood on one side, neatly filled to capacity with books, carvings, and figurines.

Like a kid turned loose in the toy department, she padded barefoot to the bookcase for a closer look. She was impressed with Justin's collection of Buffalo Soldier figurines honoring the elite band of black soldiers who served in the Union Army over a century ago. She could tell the figurines had been skillfully hand-painted.

Lorren knew she should go out to the living room and face Justin. But at the moment she couldn't cope with an explanation. She wondered what he thought of her? Did he think she was a madwoman for being out in the storm? A soft knock sounded on the door, interrupting her thoughts.

"Lorren?"

"Yes, come in. I'm dressed."

Justin entered the room. "I've brought you something hot to drink, love." He handed her the cup.

Love? Lorren tossed the word of endearment about in her mind. *Love, baby, honey, sweetheart, sugar, darling*—all were words Scott had used all the time without any particular significance. "Thanks, and I know you're wondering why I was out in the storm . . ."

"We'll talk later. Right now I want you to take a swallow of that. It'll warm you up a bit."

Nodding, she took a sip, then frowned.

Justin grinned sheepishly at her. "I put some whiskey in it. After being out in this weather, you need it."

Lorren smiled back, then took another sip.

"You should try to get some sleep. I'll be out in the living room."

"I can't take your bed. I'm all right now. I'll go back to—"

"No. You're more than welcome to stay here. The sofa will do me just fine. Try getting some rest. We'll talk some more in the morning." Turning, he started out of the door.

"Justin?"

He turned around. "Yes?"

"Thanks."

He smiled. "Anytime." He closed the door behind him.

Lorren finished the rest of her drink and placed the cup on the nightstand. She then pushed the covers back and slid into the roomy bed, settling comfortably. The clean masculine scent of Justin clung to the sheets, pillows, and bedcovers. She found safety and warmth in the manly fragrance. Shifting her head on the pillow, she was soon sound asleep.

Lying on the sofa in the darkened living room, Justin studied the closed door. "I'm glad one of us can sleep," he muttered, shifting positions again. He tried not to think about the transparency of Lorren's wet nightclothes when she'd first arrived, or her in his bed with his T-shirt as her only piece of clothing. Much to his dismay, the thoughts made his pulse race, and a shiver rippled through him.

His mind then voiced the questions it had earlier. What had driven her out in the storm? And what was it she didn't want to remember? Did either have anything to do with that creep she'd been married to? Whatever was bothering her, she was enduring her own private storm.

Justin willed himself to be patient. He would get answers to his questions tomorrow. Pounding his pillow into a more comfortable shape, he turned over, hoping he'd be able to get some sleep.

In the deep recesses of her dream-ravaged sleep, Lorren struggled to free herself from her dream, crying out at the fear holding her in its grip. Thrashing about, she kicked her covers aside.

"Lorren," a gentle masculine voice called out to her. She felt strong arms engulfing her. Slowly her heart slowed its wild race. Forcing her eyes open, she saw that Justin was with her. He was half-kneeling, half-bending at her bedside. Tightening her arms she clung to him, her body ripped by uncontrollable spasms.

Justin's hands stroked her hair, back, and shoulders. "It's all right, sweetheart," he whispered softly as she became calmer. "You were having a bad dream. It's okay. I wasn't far away."

Lorren tried to stop trembling. Tonight she'd had a full-blown replay of that night eighteen years ago, when her world had come to an end. "Oh, Justin," she whispered against his throat. "I relived that night."

He kissed the tears from her eyes. "What night?"

"The night my parents left me." Her voice broke slightly. "It was a night very much like tonight. We were having the worst thunderstorm I'd ever seen. I was eight years old and had gone to bed. My parents had gone out for the evening and had left me in the care of a baby-sitter."

She paused to catch her breath. "The thunder couldn't smother the sound of the doorbell ringing later that night. I got up and saw two police-men talking to my baby-sitter. I overheard them telling her my parents had been killed in a car accident on the way home."

She trembled at the memory. "I screamed and, before anyone could stop me, I ran out into the storm."

Justin tenderly stroked her hair. His heart went out to the child who'd overheard such shocking news. He could just imagine her emotional tur-moil. "Where did you go?"

She shrugged. "Nowhere in particular. I just kept running and run-ning. It seemed I ran forever before one of the policemen caught up with me."

Justin held her tighter in his arms. "But tonight, when you ran out into the storm, you went somewhere, Lorren. You came here to me." He made a move to stand. "You should try sleeping now."

Lorren's hold on him tightened. "Don't . . . don't leave me, please, I don't want to be alone. Not now."

Justin only hesitated a moment before slipping into bed beside her, gathering her into his arms. "Go on and get some sleep. I'm here with you."

Releasing a sigh, she let her eyes flutter closed, feeling safe in the arms of the man she loved.

Justin forced himself to remain still while he held Lorren. Perspiration formed on his forehead. He was fighting a feverish desire to make love to her. The memory of the erotic dream he'd been having moments before she'd arrived didn't help matters.

A moan got trapped in his throat when she shifted positions in his arms, bringing a firm flat stomach and full breasts against him. His fin-gers itched to lift up the T-shirt and explore every part of her body, be-ginning with the very essence of her womanhood.

He closed his eyes, as if doing so would shut her from his mind as well as from his sight, and would bring his thoughts under control. Even though this was definitely the place for what he longed to do to her, now was certainly not the time. The last thing she needed was to be taken ad-vantage of.

He opened his eyes seconds later. Tonight would be a long night. *A very long night.*

* * *

Consciousness slowly infiltrated Lorren's mind, and her eyes gradually opened. Justin was lying next to her, asleep. His hand was resting on the curve of her hip, and her head was cradled against his shoulder. She could feel the taut hardness of one of his legs, which was thrown over hers.

She lay perfectly still for a moment as memories of her dream came flooding back. The last thing she remembered was falling asleep in Justin's arms.

Swallowing nervously, she fixed her eyes on the man who held her securely in his warm embrace. To wake up in his arms gave her a deep feeling of warmth and contentment, but it didn't completely erase her uneasiness.

Justin stirred slightly. His eyes suddenly flickered open and held hers. That one instant of eye contact jolted Lorren, making her heart take a perilous leap, and spurring a heated sensation in the pit of her stomach. He continued to stare at her, his fixed gaze like a soft caress. She could feel the touch of that gaze and tried to throttle back the dizzying current racing through her.

Desire, the likeness of which she'd never known, rose in her like the hottest fire, clouding her mind and heating the soft core of her body. It was as if his eyes were casting a spell on her, bewitching her senses. She was transfixed, mesmerized by a fascination so overwhelming, so overpowering, it acted like a catalyst destroying her self-restraint.

Accepting her dilemma was both frightening and exhilarating, and with the steamy mist floating around her, from whence there was no escape, she faced the truth. She wanted to make love with him. All her uncertainties melted into a driving need to discover what lay ahead in an intimate union.

They continued to stare at each other it seemed for the longest time. Then Justin's mouth captured hers. He kissed her softly at first, a series of slow, shivery kisses. Suddenly, he began smothering her lips with demanding mastery and pulled her closer to him.

Her mouth opened invitingly, accepting his probing tongue. Her surrender was instantaneous as she returned his urgent searing kisses. She kissed him in all the ways he had ever kissed her.

Justin inwardly berated himself for coming on so fast and so strong, but he didn't want to give her the chance to think about anything except what was taking place between them.

His hands sought the hem of the oversize T-shirt, and, breaking the kiss, he gently pulled it up and over her head, removing it completely. He quickly resumed kissing her.

Lorren moaned in his mouth when his finger traced a line around her navel before slowly moving upward to her breasts. His hands tenderly cupped their fullness. In one smooth movement, his tongue replaced his fingers on her breasts, bringing their dark tips to crested peaks.

Moments later, she uttered a small cry of pleasure when his hands were on the move again, gliding over her, as though obsessed with knowing every line of her body.

He stroked her back and shoulders, squeezed her behind, and spanned her waist and thighs. When his hand moved lower to the very essence of her, little whimpers of pleasure escaped her throat, only to be captured by his mouth.

Lorren's mind was whirling. Sensations she'd never felt before tore through her body. All she could think about was the feel of his sensual mouth and hands on her, making her tremble with a foreign need.

She became totally lost in a blaze of passion and gave herself over to all the things he was making her feel. She forgot everything except Justin and his touch. She couldn't think of anything else.

"Stop me now if you don't want things to go any further. Because if you don't, I won't be able to stop later. I want you too much, Lorren."

Each word he spoke sounded like a caress, an erotic stroke. Lorren wanted him, too. She couldn't deny she was aching with a need to be possessed by him.

"Tell me, Lorren. Tell me what you want me to do."

She answered, whispering in his ear, "I want you to make love to me."

Justin didn't realize until that very moment how much he longed to hear those words from her. Standing, he removed his pajama bottoms, his eyes never leaving hers.

Moments later he was completely naked. His rich brown body was totally male, totally splendid, and, at the moment, totally aroused . . . for her.

He sought out her lips when he rejoined her in bed, pulling her to him. "I've wanted you for so long, Lorren. From the first moment I saw you that night, I wanted you," he breathed hotly against her ear.

He kissed and caressed every inch of her body. She became a writhing mass of red-hot passion from the heat his touch generated. He was losing himself in a sensual whirlwind, but knew he had to take the necessary steps so there wouldn't be any regrets later. He tore his lips from hers. "Baby, are you protected?"

She shook her head, answering in a breathless whisper as shivers coursed through her. "I—I, there was never a need . . ."

Justin reached into a drawer of the nightstand and withdrew a small foil packet. "I'll protect you," he said huskily.

Lorren trembled with the force of her emotions as she watched him prepare himself for her. A short while later he came back to her. Their limbs automatically tangled, all control lost.

Lorren's passion-engulfed mind felt his knees nudge open her thighs, his hand parting her, his body moving over her, and the hardness of him probing at the heat of her, pressing downward and slowly penetrating her. She sucked in her breath at the sheer size of him.

She cried out his name the moment their bodies became one. The fullness and strength of him was deep inside her, and she curved her body receptively.

"Are you all right, love?" he asked tenderly, giving her body time to adjust to him. Her body felt hot and tight.

She smiled up at him, her face damp with perspiration. "I've never felt so alive, so filled with wanting, so filled with need . . ."

"Neither have I," he rasped.

Placing a kiss on her lips, he slowly and gently began moving within her, setting an erotic rhythm.

Lorren wrapped her legs around him. Her lips moved reflexively, keeping time with his movements as he burrowed deeper and deeper inside her. His tongue, seeking hers, matched the rhythm of their bodies.

Justin murmured softly in her ear with each sensual stroke into her body. He told her how good her mouth tasted, how wonderful she felt to him, and just how incredible she was making him feel.

"Explosive," he breathed against her lips. "You're explosive, sweetheart. I can't get enough of you. Baby, you are completely blowing my mind."

The feel of Lorren moving beneath him brought on memories of the night of Ms. Nora's party, when he'd watched her on the dance floor, moving her body to the sound of the music. He could feel the increasing tempo of her hips moving to meet his every stroke, beat for beat. Her sighs and moans were music to his ears, a sensuously sweet melody that caused one feverish sensation after another to overtake him.

"I don't think I can handle too much more of this," he said, groaning, fighting for control. He pushed harder and deeper into the moist, clinging heat of her. "Baby, you're too much."

Lorren's senses were on overload and his words, spoken in a guttural groan, pushed her over the edge. She gripped his shoulders and dug her nails into his skin, feeling his muscles strain and tighten against her hands. With all the strength she could muster, she kept up with him and his vigorous pace. Each hard, powerful stroke into her body was intense, ecstatic, complete. She gave just the response his body demanded, making their movements more wild and feverish.

"You're perfect." Justin breathed the words into her mouth as he surged forward one last time. His cry of satisfaction muffled against her mouth the moment his body bucked and spasmed with his release.

Their passion encompassed them. Together they scaled the heights of ecstasy, becoming one in body and soul.

Lorren cried.

She couldn't stop the tears flowing down her cheeks and the hard sobs shaking her body.

Justin cradled her face between his hands, alarmed. "Baby . . . Lorren, sweetheart. What's wrong? Did I hurt you?"

Lorren lifted her tear-stained face to meet him. The expression in his eyes showed such open concern and tenderness. It made her cry even more.

He gathered her closer to him as she wept, crying her heart out in harsh, racking sobs that shook her body.

"Please, Lorren. Answer me. Did I hurt you?"

"I—I never . . . I never knew anything could—could be so . . . so beautiful," she cried brokenly. "I never knew I—I could feel that way. Or that—that I could make anyone feel the way you—you said I made you feel." She turned her face into his bare chest. "Oh, Justin, I never knew."

Justin expelled a ragged breath. He was glad her tears weren't from any physical pain he'd inflicted. But he knew of the emotional pain Syneda had hinted at—the one caused by her ex-husband. He wanted her to share that pain with him, so he could help rid her of it.

"Talk to me, Lorren. You've been married before. How could you not have known?"

Lorren raised tear-filled eyes to him. "Scott told me I—I was a failure in bed. He said I was lacking. And until a few minutes ago," she whispered brokenly, "until we made love, I—I was certain it was the truth. But he lied, Justin. He lied to me. How could he have hurt me that way?"

Justin hugged her tightly to him. "Oh, sweetheart, the only one who has an answer to that question is him. Chances are he lied to hide his own feelings of failure. It wasn't you who was lacking, but him. Instead of admitting that to himself, he found it easier to cast the blame on you."

He rested his cheek on the top of her head. If her ex-husband was around this very minute, he would do the man in for what he'd done to her.

"He lied to you, Lorren. Trust me." Justin shifted positions, and she could feel the heat of him, rigid from wanting her again. "See how quickly and easily my body responds to you. Feel pride in your power as a woman, your ability to bring pleasure this way. You did more than just live up to my expectations. You went above and beyond my wildest dream. Nothing could have prepared me for what we shared. Nothing. I feel like I've been to heaven and back. It's not the act of lovemaking itself that makes it special, but the person you share it with. Making love with you was special. It was earth-shattering, and something I could never forget."

Lorren knew she would never feel more like a woman or love Justin more than she did at that very moment. In his arms she had learned what it was to make love, truly make love.

Their eyes met and held for a long, silent moment before Justin leaned over, parted her lips with his tongue, and eased inside. Her arms went around his neck as she drew his tongue deeper into her mouth, then gave hers to him.

Love, strong and deep, swelled within Lorren, and Justin once again went about transporting her to a world of indescribable beauty and passion.

The moon reached out and grappled a dark cloud for possession of what remained of the night.

The storm was over.

Justin drew a long breath and slowly expelled it. Lorren was nestled up against him, asleep in his arms. He gazed down tenderly at her, studying the warm sensual glow of peace on her face. With care, not wanting to wake her, he slid his arms around her, gently bringing her closer to him.

He stared at her in awed wonder. Never in his life had making love with anyone been so powerful, so magnificent, so intoxicating, so satisfying.

Never.

He turned his head away—from looking at her with the admission that that included his lovemaking with Denise.

The truth hammered into him with all the force of a tidal wave. What he'd always believed to be the ultimate in sexual fulfillment in the arms of the woman he'd loved and married didn't come close to what he had experienced tonight with Lorren.

And that realization shook him to the core, because he didn't know if perhaps his lovemaking with Denise wasn't as exciting as it could have been, or if making love with Lorren was going far beyond anything he thought possible.

He had loved Denise, both physically and emotionally, in a gentle kind of way. The passions he'd shared tonight with Lorren had been wild and feverish.

A knot formed in his throat as he looked down at the gold coin medallion resting on his naked chest. It was his visible, tangible bond to Denise.

In sleep, Lorren's tousled head lay against the medallion. Earlier, her tears had bathed it when she'd cried. A part of him had known the exact moment of contact.

It was that part of him that had reached out to Lorren when she had needed to be comforted.

It was that inner part of him no other woman had touched since Denise.

It was his heart.

CHAPTER 9

Pulling on a pair of jeans, Justin couldn't help gazing down at Lorren, asleep in his bed, bathed in the warm glow of the morning light. A mass of glossy dark brown hair framed her face and shoulders, making her even more beautiful.

His gaze lingered on the dark tips of her bare breasts for an instant, before leaning over to cover her completely with the bedspread.

He left the bedroom for the kitchen. After a night of vigorous love-making, he had a ferocious appetite. It took only a few minutes to get the coffee started, then he went back and checked on Lorren. Finding her still asleep, he returned to the kitchen to phone his office, hope riding high on this call. His first patient, Mrs. Breland, was due in the office at eleven, but was notorious for last-minute cancellations.

Moments later, Justin hung up the phone, smiling. Mrs. Breland hadn't failed him. His first appointment was not until one o'clock. That would give him extra time to spend with Lorren before he'd have to leave.

There were a lot of questions concerning their relationship floating around in his mind. He needed answers. He'd lain awake most of the night, trying to figure out what sort of relationship he wanted with Lorren and what sort of relationship she would agree to. All he was sure of at the moment was that he wanted her.

And he wanted her badly. He was afraid to look at the possibilities beyond that one emotion.

* * *

The smell of coffee brought Lorren instantly awake. Opening her eyes, she found herself in bed alone. She sucked in a deep breath as memories of Justin's lovemaking filtered through her mind. It had been the most beautiful thing she'd ever experienced.

On her wedding night, Scott's performance should have forewarned her of his downright selfish nature. The lovemaking had been rushed and totally unfulfilling for her. It had left her wondering what all the fuss over making love had been about.

Now she knew.

Justin had been right. It wasn't the act itself that made it special, but the person you shared it with.

The thought that she'd pleased Justin filled her with a multitude of emotions—joy, delight, and relief. The sexual gratification he'd experienced with her had been real, and she was still in awe of it. His body had been warm and hard, and his whole being had vibrated under her touch.

He'd burrowed deeper and deeper inside of her, whispering words in her ear, letting her know just how good she made him feel. He'd released a loud moan before climaxing with her name on his lips. They'd made love over and over, their hunger for each other insatiable.

"You look like you belong in my bed."

Lorren turned her head in the direction of the deep, sexy masculine voice. Justin stood shirtless in the doorway of the bedroom. Lorren's mouth went dry as her gaze raked his dark muscular body. He was such a good-looking man—in or out of his clothes.

Sauntering over to the bed wearing jeans that clung to his body like a second skin, he knelt on the bed, drawing her to him. His long hard kiss left her weak, filled with need and desire. She wrapped her arms around his neck when he pulled her closer to him.

"We need to talk, Lorren. About us."

Lorren nodded, unable at the moment to say anything. Held within the circle of his arms, she gazed into his dark eyes. She felt too weak after the kiss they'd shared to speak.

A fresh jolt of sensual shocks raced through her when Justin's fingers threaded through the thickness of her hair, tightening around the silken strands.

"I want you, Lorren. I want you to be mine," he whispered. His hand leisurely stroked her body, sensitizing every inch of her skin.

Lorren sucked in her breath sharply at the feel of his hands on her. She allowed her mind to zero in on the words he'd spoken. He wanted to claim her as his. But not forever, and not as the woman he loved or wanted to marry. He wanted her to be his, the woman he could share his passion with.

Tell him you love him, an inner voice urged. *Tell him you're no longer afraid to want all the things he believes in. Tell him how he's single-handedly destroyed your resolve against love and marriage. Tell him you're no longer confused about what you want in life, as long as that life includes him.*

Another part of her mind screamed, *Girl, don't be a fool! He hasn't said anything that should make you think he wants more than what he's asking for. All he wants is an affair, not a lifetime commitment. And if he thinks you're getting too attached, he may back off. Then you'll be alone again. Remember what he told you. Even though he sanctions love and marriage, he believes in fate, and that one day the special woman he's holding out for will eventually come into his life. He hasn't given any indication that he thinks you're the one, so just appreciate the time the two of you'll share until things come to an end.*

Justin stilled Lorren from any further thoughts when he captured her face in his hands, making her gaze into his eyes. The look in them was a mixture of passion and tenderness.

"I have to know you *won't* put roadblocks between us again tomorrow. I need to know for sure, Lorren."

The force of Justin's gaze swept through Lorren, making her want to scream out the depth of her feelings for him. Speechlessly, breathlessly, she shook her head.

"Say it, Lorren. I want to hear it from your lips. Tell me you're mine."

Mixed emotions filled Lorren. He was asking for a commitment. A commitment without a future. A commitment until he had his fill of her. Could she handle that? She would be entering into a relationship with him with both eyes wide open and her heart on a platter.

Moving her fingers gently over the slight roughness of his unshaven jaw, with her heart in her throat she answered, "Yes, Justin. I'm yours."

Justin hadn't realized he'd been holding his breath until Lorren's words were said, her commitment to him spoken. He pulled her to him, sealing their mouths together.

Lorren was instantly lost, as she became wrapped up in the feel of his mouth on hers. Uttering a soft moan, she kissed him back, meeting his tongue, tasting him, and drawing him into her more deeply, hungrily.

He slowly released her and stood back from the bed. Lorren watched as he unzipped his pants and slowly began removing them.

"Aren't you going into the office today?" she asked in a whisper of her own voice, watching him discard his jeans.

"My first appointment isn't due until one. If an emergency comes up, Sandra will call me." He smiled down at her. "Let's forget about everything and just concentrate on us."

Lorren returned his smile when Justin came back to the bed. Tossing the covers aside, he slipped in next to her, gathering her in his arms.

"Oh, Justin. I feel so wonderful. It's hard to describe in words just how I feel. Years ago, the Stylistics came out with a song titled, 'You Make Me

Feel Brand-New.' That's a perfect way to describe just how you've made me feel, brand-new."

Justin leaned over and gave her a kiss . . . and more.

Hours later, Lorren's mouth curved into a lazy, satisfied smile. "What time is it?"

Justin pulled up his jeans and turned around. "Close to eleven."

"I've never stayed in bed this late."

Justin laughed in sheer joy at the expression on her face. "Maybe you never had a reason to before. I'm going to fix a light brunch. That should hold us both over until we go out tonight."

Lorren raised a brow. "We're going out?"

"I thought it'd be nice. There's a super restaurant in Dallas I'd like to take you to. But if you'd rather, we could stay here and get into other things," he hinted suggestively, coming to stand before the bed.

Lorren shifted slightly in bed and moistened her swollen lips with her tongue. "Going out tonight will be fine. I'd like to take a shower now. Do you have another T-shirt I can borrow?"

"Yeah. There should be another one in that top drawer over there. How do you feel?"

"Sore," she answered honestly.

"That's understandable. We'll have to do something about that. Go on and take your shower. I'll have brunch prepared by then." He left the room.

Lorren had been in the shower for a few minutes when the shower door opened, exposing a completely naked Justin. "Justin! What are you doing?" she squealed.

In answer, he stepped into the shower, closing the door behind him. He cornered her nude body between his and the shower wall, pressing her against the ceramic tile, and pulling her into his arms.

"I'm going to make love to you, here in the shower. The use of your muscles, together with the warm water, will work the soreness out of your body," he answered, reaching behind her to retrieve the soap from its compartment.

Lorren's eyes widened. "Make love in here? But how?"

"Like this." He proceeded to do wonderful things to her body as he introduced her to the various ways of lovemaking. Ways Lorren didn't know could be done in a shower or anywhere else.

The restaurant Justin had chosen for dinner was an elegant establishment that spared no expense in creating an atmosphere catering to the tastes of the affluent. They were shown to a table that had a fantastic view of downtown Dallas.

"Justin, you didn't have to go out of your way for dinner tonight," Lorren said after the waiter had taken their order.

A grin tilted his lips. "I want tonight to be just as special as today was. This is just an example of the many things to come. I would, however, like to ask a favor of you."

Lorren lifted an arched eyebrow as a smile touched her lips. "Another camping trip already?"

Justin laughed. "No, not another camping trip. Do you remember my mentioning I'd purchased the Taylors' place and was completely renovating it?"

"Yes, I remember."

Justin took a sip of his wine. "Well, I seem to have encountered a little problem."

"What?"

"The interior designer dropped by the house with catalogs of material and fabric samples before I picked you up. I'm at a loss as to what to select. So I was wondering if you'd help me out."

"How?"

"I'd like you to meet with the interior designer for me and give her some suggestions."

Surprised by his request, she said, "But I don't know what you may or may not like."

One corner of Justin's mouth lifted in a satisfied grin. "I'll like whatever you select."

Absorbing his words, she bit her lower lip. How could he ask her to help decorate a house he would one day share with Ms. Fate, his future wife? A woman she'd already begun to hate. "I don't know, Justin. Did you think of asking one of your sisters, or maybe your mom?"

Justin sensed her hesitation. "Why can't you do it?"

"Why can't one of them?"

"I'd like you to."

Lorren sighed heavily. "I don't think that would be fair to the woman you'll one day bring there as your wife. How would she feel, knowing her home had been decorated by a woman with whom you once had an affair?" There, she'd said it. She had to be realistic that one day their relationship would end.

Justin started to tell her the reason he wanted her to do it was because he desired something of her in his home, something to remind him daily of her. But he couldn't bring himself to say the words. "If she has a problem with it, she can redo it."

Lorren lowered her lashes. She couldn't let him know how much his words had pierced her heart. Those weren't the words she had wanted to hear. "All right. If you really feel that way about it, I'll be more than happy to meet with the interior designer for you."

He smiled. "Thanks, Lorren."

There was little conversation between them when Justin drove her home. It seemed they were both deep in their own private thoughts. Every so often he would give her a smile, bestowing upon the car's interior a challenging intimacy.

The evening had made Lorren realize just how tenuous and fragile a relationship with Justin would be. At any time he could end it. How long would it last? A few more nights? A week? A month or two? Until fate intervened?

Torn by this uncertainty, she questioned why she was clinging to him when there was no future? Why prolong the agony of a final good-bye? *Because you love him,* her heart answered. *You can't fight your love for him. How could anyone fight love?*

They finally reached the lake house. Justin was silent while opening the door, letting her enter. He followed, closing the door behind them. Wordlessly, they stared at each other. He then began undoing the buttons on his jacket.

"Go on and get ready for bed, sweetheart. I'll turn off the lights and lock up for you," he whispered softly.

Justin got detained when he had to return a call to one of his patients. When he finally appeared at the bedroom door, Lorren was curled up in the middle of the bed asleep. She was wearing a white satin sleep shirt, delicately designed with lace at the neck. She looked sensuous, but at the same time, innocent.

Justin walked over to the bed and stood gazing down at her. He shook his head. How could any man in his right mind not appreciate her? Only a fool would put her through what she'd suffered in her marriage. No woman deserved that. Especially not her.

A fierce surge of protectiveness, so intense it made Justin's legs shake, swept over him. He stepped away from the bed and began removing his clothes. He ached with the need to have her in his arms, and to hold her against him all through the night. He knew she still had a lot of inner healing to do, and he wanted to be there for her. He wanted to put more laugh lines in her face, and more joy and pleasure in her voice.

Climbing into bed beside her, he pulled her soft body to him. Sliding his arms around her waist, he buried his face in the curve of her neck.

Moments later, he joined her in sleep.

"Who'd ever have thought I'd actually enjoy spending time with my nose stuck in a decorating book?" Lorren asked herself.

Sitting on a kitchen stool and leaning over the breakfast counter, she paged through the huge catalog of fabrics Justin had given her nearly two weeks ago. A catalog of carpet samples lay tossed on the floor nearby.

She'd finally narrowed down the carpet selections to five colors she really liked. Now, if she could find colors for the draperies to complement her selections, she'd be pleased with herself.

She would be meeting Justin in town for lunch and wanted to advise him of her choices. And later, when he arrived home, she'd show them to him. She planned to meet with the interior designer again later in the week.

The past weeks had been absolutely wonderful. She and Justin spent most of their time together. In the afternoons, she worked on her writing, and he worked on finishing the charting of his patients. Then at night, they worked on each other. Waking up every morning in each other's arms, as the first rays of sunshine came through the bedroom window, had quickly become the norm.

Lorren smiled. There was no doubt in her mind that Justin Madaris was an extraordinary man. Not only was he successful in a profession he loved—the healing of the human body—he was also a man gifted in the art of healing the soul.

Her soul.

She'd come home to Ennis with barriers erected, an understandable means of protection after her marriage to Scott. No one, not even Syneda or Mama Nora, knew the emotional stress, the mental anguish she had battled. But like a beam of light, Justin had come into her life and gone about changing that. Like a fierce and mighty African warrior, he'd not only made her battle his, but with a sharp, pointed spear in hand, he had taken on the demons that haunted her.

Justin had done so many things. Simple things. Things like holding her hand whenever they went places together. Asking her opinions on various topics. Complimenting her often on her dress and looks.

They were simple things that Scott had never bothered doing. He'd said putting fanciful ideas in her head wasn't good, and he didn't believe in public displays of affection of any kind.

Then there were the special things Justin did. Things like holding her in his arms a long while after they made love. The sharing of his thoughts, his needs, his feelings with her. His ability to boost her spirits after she'd had a long, tiring, and unproductive day at writing.

Lorren couldn't help but think about the gifts he'd given to her for no reason at all—stuffed animals, flowers, candy—and then there were the candlelight dinners he prepared occasionally.

Simple things. Special things. All of them had meant so much to her. And all of them had shown her how much he cared. But still, she continued to be cautious in their relationship. She refused to let herself put too much stock in Justin's solicitous actions. Although there was no doubt in her mind that he cared, he still hadn't given her any reason to believe that she was the woman he loved and wanted to marry and have his children with. As far as she was concerned, he was still waiting for Ms. Fate.

The loud, piercing ringing of the telephone interrupted her thoughts. "Hello?"

"Ms. Jacobs? This is Sandra Dickerson, Dr. Madaris's receptionist."

"Yes, Ms. Dickerson?"

"Dr. Madaris asked me to call and let you know he won't be able to meet you for lunch. It seems we have a little virus going around town and our office is swamped with patients. However, he hopes to leave here by four and was wondering if you could meet him at his ranch around five?"

"Sure," Lorren replied. "That won't be a problem." In fact, she thought, it would be perfect. Then she could go over the selections she'd narrowed down.

"Dr. Madaris left a key for you on the ledge above the front door."

"Okay. Thanks for calling, Ms. Dickerson." Lorren heard the click on the other end. But she continued to hold the phone in her hand, deep in thought. If Justin would be skipping lunch, he'd probably be starving by the time he met her at Taylor Oaks. An idea came into her mind. She would prepare something special to take to him when they met later.

Lorren cast her eyes on the massive ranch-style structure before her, and the tranquil beauty of the surrounding land of Taylor Oaks. No matter how often she came to this place, the view had always been simply breathtaking and had always held her spellbound.

Her favorite aspect of the house was its air of openness and warmth. Nearly every room overlooked a large enclosed patio, which featured a one-of-a-kind swimming pool. The pool had an unusual zigzag shape that was emphasized at night with some sort of special lights the Taylors had had installed. She remembered how the lights' soft glow subtly illuminated the patio and pool area after dark. It was a unique change from the harsh glare created by many other types of traditional pool lights.

She glanced around, not seeing Justin's car anywhere. Retrieving the key from its hiding place, she opened the door and entered the house. Her insides twisted in knots, knowing Justin would one day share this house with the woman he loved.

The foyer was completely empty. Only one rug adorned the floor. Moving farther inside she found the other rooms just as bare. She glanced around the living room. Justin would pay a pretty penny to completely refurnish this place, she thought, as the resinous smell of fresh paint teased her nostrils.

She visualized how she would decorate the house if it were hers. The house consisted of a huge living room, an enormous dining room, a spacious kitchen with bright countertops, a massive family room with a fireplace, an ample-size study, six bedrooms, a master suite with a fireplace, and five bathrooms.

The kitchen would have bright-colored appliances to accent its countertops. Except for the kitchen's polished tile floor, she would let the remaining floors of the house retain their dark oak. She wouldn't dare cover them up with carpet as Justin had suggested doing.

Along with the rustic walls, the oak floors bestowed upon the dwelling a bit of Western flare. Mrs. Taylor had told her all of the oak wood used throughout the house had come from the numerous oak trees that had been chopped down to clear way for the house.

On impulse Lorren walked into the spacious kitchen. Outside the kitchen window a particularly large oak tree provided shade for the kitchen and a couple of the bedrooms. Its lower limbs dipped and curved, nearly touching the ground. She remembered climbing that tree on a dare many years ago. It had been quite an experience, one that had gotten her a scolding from Mama Nora when she'd returned home with a soiled and torn skirt.

She placed the picnic basket on the long kitchen counter. It was at that point she heard the sound of shoes clicking loudly on the wooden floors.

"Lorren? Where are you?"

"In here."

Justin came into the kitchen. The sight of Lorren caused his heart to race and his entire body to react. Her hair hung in a single French braid. He wanted to loosen it and let her hair fall unhindered about her shoulders.

She wore a pair of jeans that hugged her thighs and bottom enticingly. He could barely refrain from staring at her. She was staggeringly beautiful. He smiled. "Come here, Lorren." His voice was low and deep.

Lorren returned the smile, tilting her head to one side. "Pardon me, Doctor Madaris. I don't recall hearing you say please."

Justin watched as she pretended to dismiss him and went about the task of spreading a blanket on the kitchen floor. She grabbed the picnic basket he noticed for the first time. Leaning against the counter, he watched her empty the basket of its contents.

A platter of different cheeses, a bowl of salad, two large apples, a container of fried chicken, a small basket of grapes, rolls, a handful of napkins, some plastic utensils, wineglasses, and, last but not least, a bottle of wine, chilled California Chablis. He watched as she sat cross-legged on the blanket, her eyes shining, a bright smile on her luscious mouth. "The spread awaits you, sir."

Justin took a few steps and stood towering over her. He reached down and unceremoniously pulled her up into his arms and carried her to the counter. He set her down atop it.

"This," he murmured, "is what I want now. Food can wait a moment. This is what I've been starving for all day." He gently covered her mouth with his, his tongue stroking her lips to grant him deeper penetration. She willingly parted her lips.

Once inside her mouth, his tongue tangled with hers. His hands caressed her back, and he gently pulled her closer, feeling a gnawing ache in his loins. He'd thought about savoring the taste of her tongue in his mouth all day. He tore his mouth from hers.

"I needed that," he said huskily, pulling in quick intakes of air. "Now we can eat."

He gathered her in his arms and carried her back to the blanket. Placing her on it, he joined her. They ate in silence. He watched her every movement; how she bit into a big apple and the way her mouth widened to cover it; how she devoured the cheeses slowly, one at a time, as if savoring each slice; the grapes, and how she licked her lips after each one.

But it was her eating of the chicken that pushed him over the edge. He watched as she again licked her lips before biting into a chicken leg, taking little nibble bites before taking a miniature plug out of it . . . then a little bigger plug . . . then another . . .

"That does it!"

Lorren's eyes widened when a half-eaten chicken leg was abruptly snatched from her. She was suddenly pulled into Justin's strong arms. "What's wrong with you?"

"Like you don't know," he muttered, stalking out of the room with her in his arms. "I've warned you about tempting me."

"I didn't tempt you." She laughed.

"Oh, yeah, you did. You had me actually envying your food, Lorren." He gently placed her on the lone rug in the foyer, staring down at her with an intensity that made a passionate chill flow down her spine. One look at the huge bulge pushing against his metal zipper said it all.

A sensuous grin appeared on Justin's face as he began unbuckling his belt. "We do *this* first, then we'll eat."

A smile touched the corners of Lorren's lips. "Fine with me. I wasn't all that hungry anyway. At least not for food."

The sound of Justin scrambling about on the floor beside her woke Lorren. He was naked on his hands and knees, searching for something.

Lorren couldn't believe she'd actually fallen asleep on the floor in the foyer not wearing a stitch of clothing. Her hair was no longer in a neat French braid, but hung in disarray around her shoulders. *Hell's bells! What if one of the workers had returned unexpectedly and walked in on them!* "Justin, what on earth are you looking for?"

He glanced at her. "Sorry. I didn't mean to wake you."

Lorren sat up. A grin touched her lips. "I can't believe I actually fell asleep after we, uh, you know." Her eyes wandered over Justin's body. The sight of him naked on all fours sent her blood racing. She cleared her throat. "So, what are you looking for?"

"My medallion. I seem to have lost it around here someplace. I know I had it on when I brought you in here."

"It'll turn up. Come on, let's go back in the kitchen and finish eating. I'm starving. You should be hungry yourself after that workout you just had." She stood and began dressing. "After we eat, I'll help you look for it."

Justin continued on with his purpose, ignoring her offer to help later. "Naw, I can look for it myself. I don't intend to leave until I've found it."

Lorren snapped her jeans. Her hands stilled at the waistband as she considered Justin's words. There was an urgency in his voice she'd never heard before.

"Justin, what's so special about the medallion? I noticed you wear it all the time. Is it some sort of fraternity memento from college?"

He looked up at her. "It was a gift. Denise gave it to me on our wedding night."

Lorren felt as though she'd been slapped. *He was frantically searching for something he'd received from his dead wife . . . and just moments after they'd made love!* "Oh, I see. Then by all means I hope you find it," she snapped, before turning and walking off toward the kitchen.

"Lorren, what's wrong with you? Come back here."

Justin stood. Quickly pulling on his pants, he followed her. By the time he caught up with her, she was on her knees repacking the basket.

"What's the matter with you, woman?"

She stood and faced him. "You got some nerve asking me that."

"Forgive me if I seem a little dense here, but I don't know what you're upset about."

"Then by all means, let me spell it out for you, Dr. Madaris. What's bothering me is the fact you've never mentioned the significance of the medallion."

Justin frowned. "And just what was I supposed to tell you? Have I ever asked for an accounting of every piece of jewelry you own? I really don't understand what the big deal is here."

"The big deal is you're still wearing a keepsake given to you by your wife, who's been dead ten years. As far as I'm concerned, wearing that medallion is no different from you wearing your wedding ring."

"For crying out loud. Why are you making such a big deal out of this?"

"Because any woman you become involved with has to compete against your wife's ghost, or what you perceive as the perfect memory, the perfect love." *Which is exactly what I've been doing without even realizing it.* "Whoever told you there's always tomorrow evidently forgot to tell you to let go of yesterday. And Justin Madaris, you haven't done that."

Grabbing her purse from the counter, she walked toward the door. Before reaching it, she turned back and gave him the same parting words he'd often given to her.

"Think about it."

Lorren walked out the door. She was nearly to her car when she heard Justin call her name. Ignoring him, she kept walking. Opening the car door, she slid inside, started the ignition, and drove off. Tears dimmed her vision. She wiped them away from her eyes.

With agonizing slowness, she recalled touching the medallion once or twice, and how Justin's body had stiffened in response to her contact. At the time she'd been too caught up in what they were doing to really think much about it. Now she did, and the thought made her cringe—even from the grave, Denise held Justin's heart captive.

When Lorren reached the lake house, she went inside and sank into the softness of the sofa. Her heart ached, and she was unable to control her tears any longer.

Justin continued to stare in the direction Lorren's car had taken, even when it was no longer in sight.

"Let her go," he angrily told himself, going back into the house and slamming the door closed behind him. "I don't need this," he muttered, pacing the floor between the kitchen and the foyer, looking for his medallion. "I should never have gotten involved with the woman. She's . . . she's . . ."

He stopped talking to himself, unable to complete the sentence. When he did moments later, the words echoed loudly in the room. "She's the first woman to bring some real happiness into my life since Denise."

Justin took a deep breath and slumped against the wall. He was stunned at the confusing feelings he was experiencing. Lorren couldn't be more wrong in what she'd said. He had let go of yesterday. But he could see why she thought he hadn't. He had to talk to her and make her understand.

He turned to leave and his gaze caught sight of the medallion on the floor near his feet. He reached down and picked it up. Several emotions passed over him while he looked at it—love, joy, pain . . . and fear. The first three emotions had been for Denise. The last one, for Lorren.

He was suddenly afraid that she had just walked out of his life.

Lorren jumped when she heard the sound of the doorbell. She stood. Her muscles were stiff and cramped. Glancing at her watch, she saw an hour had passed since she'd come home. She'd been sitting on the sofa all that time. Walking to the door, she opened it.

Justin stood in the doorway with the picnic basket in his hand. "May I come in so we can talk?"

Lorren drew in a shaky breath. She'd known she was going to have to see him sooner or later, but a part of her wished it could be later. Much later.

She wasn't sure if she was ready to hear whatever it was he wanted to say right now. He looked tense and exhausted, and his voice sounded ragged. She relented.

"Yes, come in," she replied, trying to keep her voice neutral, but knowing she'd failed miserably. She took a step backward and Justin entered the house, closing the door behind him.

Lorren walked across the room and sat in the wing chair. After placing the basket on the table, Justin stood with his back to her, gazing out the window at the lake. It seemed he stood that way for hours instead of minutes. When he finally turned around, his eyes were glazed with remembered pain. He stared at her, studying her, before he began speaking.

"It seems I'd known Denise forever, when actually we first met in high school. Her parents moved to Houston from Dallas in our sophomore year. Even then, I knew there was something special about her. We dated through high school and decided to wait until we'd finished college before marrying. She got a scholarship to Spelman in Atlanta, and I attended Howard."

There was a pause before he continued. "During the time we were apart, we were miserable. One day I couldn't take it any longer and purchased a plane ticket to Atlanta. When I got there, I asked her to marry me. Since there's no waiting period in Georgia, we got married that same day. Our parents, though surprised, were very supportive. Denise completed her semester at Spelman, then transferred to Howard to be with me. We got a small apartment near campus. It was hard at first, but we had each other and plenty of love."

Justin took a deep breath. "She'd finished college and was working at an accounting firm when her headaches began. At first we thought they were the result of stress. She'd been doing a lot of heavy studying for an upcoming CPA exam. But when she began having dizzy spells, we became alarmed and had her checked by a doctor. A CAT scan revealed an inoperable turmor at the base of her brain, and she was given less than six months to live."

Lorren watched the man she loved in the grip of emotional pain, reliving his tortured memories. A part of her wanted to put her arms around him and comfort him. However, she didn't move. She sat still while he continued.

"For us it was a lifetime of happiness and dreams to be snuffed out in less than six months." Justin paused suddenly, sucking in a deep gulp of air.

"Toward the end, she wanted to talk about my life without her, but I couldn't. For the first time in my life, I felt completely helpless. With all my medical knowledge, I could do nothing to prevent the inevitable. I felt like I had failed her somehow. I even began questioning whether I wanted to continue in the medical field. But Denise refused to let me blame myself and give up. She said life was too short for regrets."

He cleared his throat. "Although I knew the cold, hard facts surrounding her condition, a part of me kept hoping, kept praying. Deep down she understood what I was going through. The only thing she asked was that her last breath not be taken in the sterilized confines of a hospital. She wanted to be at home with me. During her final days, her body had weakened from the chemo treatment, but she maintained her good spirits until the end. We spent our days and nights together—alone. We wanted it that way, and, thankfully, our families understood."

The sound of Justin's voice became more hoarse. "She died one night while I held her in my arms. With the very last of her strength, she clutched my medallion and held it in the palm of her hand."

Lorren felt heartsick. The pain he'd endured watching the woman he loved die must have been devastating for him. Just like her parents' death had been to her. Fighting back tears, she stared at him and saw misty, pained eyes staring back into hers.

"Losing Denise," he continued, "was the hardest thing I've ever gone through. We shared so much. And I feel I lost so much."

He sighed deeply and walked over to the chair and knelt in front of Lorren, gripping her hand. "Whether or not I wear the medallion won't change the fact that I respond to you in ways I've never responded to any woman, including Denise. I never thought the void left in my life after her death would be filled. But you're doing it, Lorren. I just can't make any promises about anything right now."

New tears welled in Lorren's eyes as she tried to hold back her emotions. After hearing his story, her love for him gave her the strength to accept things as they were for now, and pray one day a change would come. She knew there was a chance he would never love her. There was a very strong possibility that the only woman he would ever be capable of loving had died ten years ago.

"Thanks for sharing that with me, Justin. It explains a lot of things."

He stood and nervously rubbed the palm of his hand over the back of his neck. "So, where do we go from here?"

A wry smile touched Lorren's lips. She wanted things back the way they'd been between them, and he was letting it be her decision. "Why don't we finish eating. I'm starved."

Justin stared down at her. His expression was one of heartfelt relief and thanks. A smile curled the corners of his mouth. "Me too."

Lorren's gaze traveled over his handsome features and saw the sparkle had returned to his eyes. She stood. "So, did you find your medallion?"

He hesitated before answering. "Yes, I found it."

"Where is it?"

"Here." He touched his pants pocket.

She took a step toward him and reached into his pocket, pulling out the medallion. Accepting the reason why it was so special to him, she stood on tiptoe and placed it around his neck. "Now it's back where it belongs until you decide differently."

Justin grabbed her wrist. "You don't have to do this. If you prefer that I not—"

"No, it's okay. I'm fine now."

"Are you sure?"

"Yes, I'm sure." *I'm doing the right thing,* she told herself. *The decision to stop wearing it has to be his.*

When Justin gently pulled her into his arms, she reminded herself she was nothing more to him than the woman he enjoyed sharing his passion with, the woman who was helping him decorate the house he'd ultimately share with someone else.

And unknown to him, she was also the woman who loved him.

CHAPTER 10

"**Y**ou better have a darn good reason for pulling me over," Justin said to the tall, handsome man wearing a huge grin on his face and a badge of the law on the blue shirt covering his broad chest.

"I believe I do," the man answered lazily, leaning down and resting both elbows in the car's open window. A wan shaft of sun struck his hair and it gleamed like dark gold. His grin broadened and his ocean blue eyes shone mischievously. "I have a deep appreciation for beautiful women, and the one sitting next to you looks too stunning for words."

"You haven't changed a bit, Roderick Clark," Lorren said, laughing. "You're still quite a character. Becoming sheriff hasn't changed you at all."

"Sure it has. Now I'm giving the tickets to speeders instead of getting them all myself. The reason I stopped you guys is because of Rhonda. That wife of mine sent me on a mission. She ordered me to find you, Lorren, and invite you over for dinner Friday night. We were out of town the night of Ms. Nora's birthday party and missed Justin's cookout because of Rod, Jr.'s little league game. Rhonda is determined for the two of you to get together so she can bring you up to date on the latest gossip in Ennis Place," he said jokingly. "It'll be a small gathering of a few couples." Then, seemingly as an afterthought, he added, "I guess that invitation also extends to you, Justin," he teased.

Lorren smiled. "That sounds like a great idea. I'd love seeing Rhonda again." She turned to Justin. "Is Friday night okay with you?"

"Sure. I wouldn't miss the chance to sample some of Rhonda's peach cobbler."

Rod raised a brow at his friend. "What makes you so sure she's making peach cobbler that night?"

Justin laughed. "Your wife wouldn't miss the chance to serve her prize-winning cobbler. I'm depending on you to keep her in a good mood till Friday. You know how testy pregnant women can get at times."

"Rhonda's pregnant?" Lorren asked, breaking into the men's conversation.

Rod beamed proudly. "Yep. She's pregnant with child number four, and the doctors have already said it's a boy." He checked his watch. "I'd better get going. I'll see you guys Friday night around seven."

"All right, Rod," Justin answered. "See you then."

The sound of loud music and laughter could be heard as Justin and Lorren walked up the sidewalk to the Clarks' home. Numerous cars were parked in the driveway.

"I thought Rod said this was to be a small gathering with a few couples," Lorren whispered to Justin when they reached the front door.

Justin chuckled. "If you know Rhonda well enough, you should know her small gatherings often get out of hand, especially where the number of people are concerned. She loves people and, because of it, she loves to entertain," he said, pressing the doorbell. "I met Rod a few years ago, when he worked with John a short while as a Texas Ranger, before becoming sheriff. A couple of weeks after I arrived in town, Rhonda invited me to dinner. She failed to tell me that half of Ennis would also be there. Her small dinner party turned into a full-scale welcome-to-town affair."

Amusement lurked in Lorren's eyes. "Remind me to tell you about the time Rhonda gave an all-girls party one night. You won't believe how it turned out.

Before Justin could ask for the details, the door opened and they found themselves greeted with hugs from a very pregnant woman.

"Lorren! Justin! I'm glad you made it," she said, pulling them into the house.

Justin and Lorren had been right. This was no small party. As Lorren looked around she eyed all the other guests. Some of them she recognized, and some she did not. A good number of them were crowded around a table laden with food.

"Let me take a look at you, Lorren Jacobs. I can't believe it. You haven't changed a bit. I bet you can still fit into your cheerleading outfit."

Lorren laughed. "Don't count on it. But what about you, busy lady?

Three kids and a fourth on the way," she exclaimed with an I-don't-believe-it look. "What happened to your plans after high school to take Hollywood by storm?" Rhonda Clark was indeed a beauty, Lorren thought. She was a Meg Ryan look-alike and appeared even more radiant pregnant.

"What happened is a man by the name of Rod Clark. Surely you remember him," she teased. "I don't think anyone who has ever lived in Ennis could forget him. He's the guy who used to ride that Harley-Davidson motorcycle and wear that black leather jacket. He's also the guy all the mothers used to warn their daughters about."

She laughed. "Well, somehow he managed to put a ring on my finger and an even bigger one in my nose. The next thing I know, my plans of becoming an actress were history. What I do now, in between babies, is teach drama at the University of Texas in Dallas."

"It's about time the two of you got here," a loud male voice boomed from behind them. Wearing a huge grin, Rod walked up to greet the latest arrivals. He leaned down and gave Lorren a peck on the cheek and Justin a warm handshake. "I was just about to send my deputy out to find you."

He turned to his wife. "And what's this nonsense about mothers trying to keep their daughters from me?" He pulled her into his arms. "If that's true, your mom didn't do such a good job, did she, honey?" he drawled lovingly.

Rhonda giggled. "See what I mean, Lorren. I'm putty in this man's hands."

Love clearly shone in both of their eyes, Lorren thought, looking at the two individuals. She was touched by their warm, open display of affection.

"If the two of you are going to get mushy, Lorren and I will leave." Justin grinned.

"Why, Justin. We never get mushy." Rhonda laughed "Come on, let's pah-tay."

The four of them were still laughing when they were joined by the other guests. After quick introductions to the people Lorren didn't know, Rhonda proceeded to be the perfect hostess. Lorren was also introduced to the Clark clan. The two boys were clones of their father, and the little girl looked just like her mother. Lorren thought it was cute that all the family members' names began with "R." Rod and Rhonda's daughter's name was Rochelle, and their sons were Rod, Jr., and Randle.

An hour or so later, Lorren and Justin found themselves in the kitchen, escaping the crowd. They were enjoying the party but decided to sneak away for a moment of privacy. Justin had just reached out to take Lorren into his arms when the kitchen door flew open and Rhonda walked in.

"Not in my kitchen, you don't. Now who's getting mushy?" she teased, opening the refrigerator to take out another tray of food.

"Where's Rod?" Justin asked.

"He's somewhere out in the backyard showing David Myers his skill at gardening. He has a little vegetable garden on the other side of the house away from the pool."

"Rod's growing a garden? This I gotta see." Justin gave Lorren a quick kiss on the lips before going out the back door in search of his friend.

"I think I'd better open the windows," Rhonda said jokingly. "I don't know if I can stand the heat the two of you generate."

Lorren almost choked on the punch she was sipping.

"Don't you dare get embarrassed, Lorren Jacobs," Rhonda said sternly. "You're in the home of friends. Besides, you and Justin deserve to be happy. Everyone knows he's a widower, and news about your divorce got around pretty fast. I think the two of you getting together is pretty neat."

"But it isn't what you think. Justin and I are just friends," Lorren protested.

"Wow! Some kind of friendship," Rhonda said as her eyes lit up. "It hasn't slipped by me that this is the first time Justin's let you out of his sight all night, and I bet he'll be back in here before you know it."

No sooner had the words been spoken than Justin reentered the kitchen. Lorren met Rhonda's teasing I-told-you-so eyes from across the room before their laughter broke to the surface.

Justin looked at them both curiously. "What's so funny?"

"It's a private joke, Justin," Rhonda said teasingly, wiping the tears coursing down her cheeks.

"That could be dangerous, knowing the two of you."

Rhonda grinned. "Relax, Doc. We're completely harmless."

Justin extended his hand to Lorren. "Let's rejoin the party."

"All right." Lorren enjoyed being around him. His presence was like a safety net and she felt thoroughly entwined in it.

When they rejoined the others, she couldn't help noticing they were the object of a lot of people's curious stares. Although Justin joined in the conversations around them, he never once left her side for long. And when he did, she was always within range of his watchful eyes.

"Enjoying the party, baby?" he asked, when they found themselves alone on the patio overlooking the pool.

"Yes. What about you?"

Justin stared at her for a moment. "I'm having a blast, but wish I was someplace else right now," he said softly.

Lorren was entranced by his chocolate-colored eyes. "Oh? Where?"

"Your bed."

A soft gasp escaped her with his words. There was a tingling in the pit of her stomach. "I wish you were someplace else, too," she whispered, her heart fluttering wildly in her breast.

Justin's gaze was soft as a caress. "Where?"

"Deep inside of me."

For a long moment neither of them spoke. They gazed into each other's eyes, their breathing becoming heavy.

Justin's words broke their silence. "Shall we find Rod and Rhonda and tell them good-night?"

Lorren nodded. "Yes. That's a good idea."

Later that night, Lorren sat in the dark watching Justin. From the way he was breathing, it was evident he was very deep in sleep. He hadn't even stirred when she'd left the bed.

She pulled the spread around her naked shoulders to guard against the late-night chill that crept through the room. Leaning back in the chair, she felt moisture gathering in her eyes.

"You're a very special man, Justin Madaris," she whispered softly. In his own unique way, using what he'd often referred to as tender, loving care, he had helped her overcome the sexual inhibitions that had been deeply rooted inside of her. Thanks to his patience, understanding, and tender, loving nature, she no longer felt panicky whenever she recognized her body's need for him, those tremulous sensations within her that were still new and unfamiliar. Like the ones she'd experienced tonight at the party that had made her bold enough to say what she'd said to him.

Justin had repeatedly shown her that the driving, physical longings she felt were a natural, normal, and healthy reaction to the attraction between them. Yet at the same time, he had unknowingly proved that her desire for him wasn't the only thing she felt. Her love grew stronger each day.

Lorren knew in her heart she had never known or truly loved a man until him.

Main Street was lined with people eagerly waiting for the parade to begin. Each year, on the first weekend in May, the township of Ennis and its neighboring counties came together for a jam-packed weekend of laughter and fun, highlighting the National Polka Festival. The festivities began Saturday morning with a giant parade. It was a sunny morning with hordes of people and children.

Justin and Lorren were dressed in shorts and festive T-shirts commemorating the event, and had conveniently found a shady spot under a huge oak tree, providing them a good view of the coming procession.

With a camera firmly in her hand, Lorren began snapping pictures as the gaiety and excitement made her relive some of her most cherished memories of living in Ennis.

Participants in costumes, bands from various schools, and floats from numerous organizations dazzled the spectators. A giggle of excitement bubbled up in Lorren's throat when the float from the Children's Home Society came by.

"Look, Justin!"

"I see it, baby," he answered. "That's a nice-looking float. The kids really did an outstanding job putting it together."

Lorren twisted her head to smile at him, not realizing because of the crowd, they were standing so close. Another inch and their lips would have made contact. Not giving in to the temptation, she simply turned her head back to watch the float. The feel of Justin's arms around her waist tightened and sent her a message that he understood.

"Later," he whispered for her ears only.

After the parade, they wound their way through the crowds of people. They walked hand in hand, darting along paths, around babies in strollers, and stopped at various booths to try out a variety of treats.

"I want some popcorn, Justin," Lorren said, pointing to a nearby vendor.

Justin dug a bill from the back pocket of his shorts. "For a woman who usually doesn't eat much, you're costing me a bundle today," he teased. "What do I get in return?"

"Are you being obnoxious?" she asked, as a grin tilted her lips.

Reaching across her to share some of the popcorn, he whispered in her ear, "I refuse to answer that. Just wait until I get you home, lady. For punishment, I'm going to make love to you over and over again."

Lorren slid her gaze to his. "Promises, promises."

They came to a group that was watching boys and girls perform precision gymnastics routines. She leaned back against Justin, letting her head rest intimately on his chest.

"What time is it?" she asked silkily, raising her eyes to his.

Justin checked his watch. "Almost three. The Festival dance starts at four. Do you want to hang around until then?"

"No."

"Where would you like to go?"

Lorren shrugged sheepishly. "Pat's Bookstore."

He lifted a brow. "The bookstore? Why?"

Lorren smiled. "My books are arriving today."

Justin returned her smile. "Then by all means, let's go check them out, Ms. Famous Author." They began walking hand in hand away from the crowd.

"Dr. Madaris! Yoo-hoo, Dr. Madaris!"

They turned to the short, bald man racing toward them. "Hello, Mr. Coleman," Justin greeted.

"Hello," he replied, and acknowledged Lorren with a nod when Justin made the introductions. "I was wondering if I could ask you a couple of questions about the medicine you mentioned that would work wonders for my back pain. You don't mind if I borrow him for a few minutes, Ms. Jacobs?"

"No, not at all. I'll just browse through that little shop over there," Lorren replied, giving Justin a smile of understanding.

He pulled her to him and brushed her lips with his, not caring they had an audience. "Don't go far."

Lorren entered the art shop, which was adorned with many gift ideas. She was staring at some beautiful ebony art figurines that she thought would be perfect to add to Justin's collection when a man's deep voice spoke from behind.

"Hello, Lorren. It's been awhile. How have you been?"

She whirled around, recognizing that voice anywhere. It belonged to the man who had caused her so much heartache, shame, and misery. He was the one man she had never wanted to see again. The shock on her face extended to her eyes.

"Scott! What are you doing here?" Standing just under six feet tall, he stood smiling down at her as if they were the best of old friends. He had lost a few pounds since she'd seen him last but, other than that, he looked the same. She used to think he was a handsome man. And there was no doubt in her mind that some women would still think so. His golden-colored eyes, strong jaw, and the cleft in his chin were features most would consider striking. But those were things people saw on the outside. On the inside, he had everything it took to make up a sleazy human being.

"I was hoping I'd run into you."

Anger flared in Lorren's eyes. "Why?"

"So we could talk."

"There's nothing we have to say to each other, Scott. We said it all the day of our divorce." Bitterness laced her every word. How could she have ever thought she loved him? How could she have ever thought at one time he was special? And how could she have tolerated the pain he'd caused her for two years?

She sighed deeply. How many times during her marriage had she gone to sleep crying from his cruel words? And how many times had he apologized for his ill use of her, and she'd forgiven him?

"Baby, surely you don't mean that."

Lorren flinched at the endearment and threw her words at him like stones. "I mean every word. We have nothing to say to each other. Goodbye."

He was silent for a long moment and she could tell he was controlling his anger. He was known to have a quick temper when things weren't going his way.

"All right, Lorren. Now isn't a good time to talk. You're upset, I can see that, and it's understandable. I treated you badly while we were married, and I regret it. I've missed you, baby."

She laughed in his face. "Missed me? Give me a break, Scott."

His smile faded. "I've given you more than a break, Lorren. I've given you a year. Don't forget we still have some of the same friends. And according to what I've been hearing, you haven't been doing a whole lot of dating since our divorce. And that can only mean one thing. You haven't gotten over me. What other possible reason could you have for moving back to this dreary little town?"

Lorren was speechless at Scott's incorrect assumptions.

"I'm willing to take you back, baby," he continued, as if he had walked out on her instead of it being the other way around. "I'll even agree to go with you to counseling sessions for that little problem of yours. This time, we'll work things out together. But like I said, now isn't a good time to talk. I'm going to hang around town for a few days. When I think you're ready to see me, I'll give you a call. See ya."

Lorren watched as he turned and walked out of the shop, becoming lost in the crowd. She was still too stunned to speak. Of all the nerve! Scott Howard had just proved beyond a shadow of a doubt that he was a conceited jerk. And it only made her feel just that much more ashamed of how stupid she'd been to have ever gotten involved with him.

"See anything you like?"

Lorren turned when she heard Justin's voice. He slid his arms around her waist.

"Lorren, what's wrong? You're shaking."

She inhaled deeply. Should she mention seeing Scott to Justin? No. There really was no need. Contrary to what Scott thought, she wasn't pining away for him. She was free of him, and he couldn't hurt or humiliate her anymore. And if he did try contacting her as he claimed he would do, she would refuse to talk to him.

"Lorren?"

Bringing her thoughts back to the present, she met Justin's concerned gaze. "I'm fine, Justin. And no, I didn't see anything I liked. Besides"— she forced a smile—"as you reminded me earlier, I've spent enough of your money for one day."

Justin grinned. "Go ahead, woman, and break me. I'm enjoying every minute of it. Are you ready to go to the bookstore?"

Her smile widened. "Yes, let's go."

CHAPTER 11

There was a slight breeze coming in off the lake, and the scent of blue-bonnets was heavy in the air. Dusk crept through the trees and surrounded the land in a purple mist.

Justin and Lorren stood on the porch and watched as night came. Its arrival beckoned the moon and stars to show their faces.

Lorren's arm was around Justin's waist as she nestled her head against the broad expanse of his chest. She was unusually quiet, and had been since they had returned home from the Festival.

"Lorren?"

"Ummm?"

"A penny for your thoughts."

Lorren shifted slightly. *You're better off not knowing them.* She felt Justin's cheek resting on top of her head. His arms felt warm and strong as they caressed her back.

She turned her head slightly and looked up at him. There was no way she could tell him that she'd been trying to convince herself that she really hadn't seen Scott in Ennis that afternoon; and that she really hadn't talked to him.

But the truth of the matter was she had, and she couldn't help but remember his words . . . *"When I think you're ready to see me, I'll give you a call. . . ."*

Lorren turned back to look at the lake and decided not to share with Justin her present thoughts, but to share with him some of her earlier ones.

"I was just thinking how wonderful this day has been and how I hate to see it come to an end."

She felt Justin smile against her temple. "Do you know what my favorite part of the day was?" he asked.

She laughed softly, giving her head a nod. "I think I have an idea, but tell me anyway."

"Our visit to the bookstore." He laughed as he pulled her closer to him. "It's nice to know a celebrity."

Lorren's mood lightened with Justin's teasing. When they had reached the bookstore, she'd discovered she wasn't the only person who had anxiously awaited the arrival of her books. The store had been swarming with a crowd of children and their parents, who wanted to purchase the newest Kente Kids book.

She soon found herself surrounded by the children, who wanted her to autograph their books. Justin had found the scene rather amusing and had waited patiently, something Scott would never have done, while she accommodated each and every child. He didn't like kids—something he hadn't bothered to mention until after they'd gotten married. Besides, Scott had always been slightly jealous of her work.

Justin, on the other hand, seemed immensely proud of her. He'd even taken the time to keep some of the smaller children occupied by gathering them in a group and reading some scenes out of her book to them. He had kept them entranced with the words that flowed from his mouth. His deep voice made the characters in her book come to life, and the African names rolled easily off his tongue.

She had been so rapt as she watched him thumb through the pages, reading to the children. He truly loved kids, and it showed. She could envision a little boy with Justin's strong features, and a little girl with her daddy's heartwarming smile.

Lorren noticed some of the parents had also gotten caught up in Justin's recitation. He was so compelling, his magnetism was so rich. His vitality completely captivated everyone around him.

She tipped her head back to look at him. She was driven to ask the one question that amazed her about him ever since he'd told her about his wife's death. "How did you do it, Justin? How were you able to bounce back after suffering so much pain?"

For a long moment he didn't say anything, and for a while she thought he was not going to answer. He was overcome with emotion when he finally spoke. It was evident his composure was under attack.

"I'd be a liar if I said it was easy. Because it wasn't. But somehow, at some point in time, you learn not to let the pain destroy you, and not let the hurt haunt you every waking moment. You have to believe it'll go away eventually . . . if you let it. But," he went on, "not before you ask yourself a thousand times, why me? What did I do to deserve such heartache, such misery, such pain?"

He took a deep breath before continuing. "Pretty soon you get tired of looking for answers that won't come. You finally make up your mind to leave behind the thing you can't change—your past, and concentrate on the thing that you can—your future."

Lorren wished she could have taken that attitude when she'd become engulfed in her pain. She had gotten so wrapped up in the hurt, she hadn't been able to see beyond it. Even now she hurt when she remembered how things had been between her and Scott, and the lies he'd told.

She wondered how long it would take before her pain completely faded. At what point would she stop looking for answers to questions regarding Scott's treatment of her? One thing was for sure, she thought, as a smile tugged at the corner of her mouth. Justin had become the best pain reliever around.

"While I have you exactly where I want you, Lorren, there's something I'd like to ask you."

"What?"

"I'm going home to Houston in a few days. My parents are giving my baby sister a sweet sixteen party. The entire family will be there, and I'd like you to go with me."

Lorren twisted in his arms so that she could see his face. She didn't want to read more into his invitation than was really there. But a part of her couldn't stop the happiness that flowed through her. "Will it be okay with your parents if I were to come?"

"Sure. My parents, especially my mother, will be ecstatic. She's dying to meet you."

"In that case, I can't disappoint her, can I?"

Justin laughed. "No, you can't. And believe me, you won't."

Later that night Lorren sat at her desk, working on an outline for a new book. The ringing of the telephone interrupted her thoughts.

"Hello?"

No one answered her, although she heard a deep, breathing sound on the other end.

"Hello?" she repeated.

A quiet click sounded in her ear when the caller hung up on her.

Lorren took a deep breath. Common sense told her the caller evidently had gotten a wrong number, or it had been a bored teenager with nothing else to do on a Saturday night but play games on the telephone.

But another part of her, the one that dealt more with caution than common sense, couldn't help wondering if . . .

"Was that a wrong number, Lorren?"

Lorren looked up. Justin had completed his shower and stood in the doorway of the bedroom with the towel wrapped around his waist. His upper body gleamed a golden brown in the soft light, and the beads of water on his shoulder shimmered like jewels.

There was a tremor in her voice when she answered. "Yes, apparently." She found it difficult to draw air past the heaviness unfolding in her chest.

"Are you coming to bed now?" he asked huskily, walking toward her, his gaze never leaving hers.

All thoughts of completing the outline for her book were lost. "Yes, I think I will."

Justin gathered her into his embrace. "Good. I'd be lonely in bed without you."

Lorren rested her cheek against his damp chest, feeling his strength and the very essence of him. His iron-muscled thighs felt warm against the soft cotton of her shorts. All thoughts of the phone call left her mind.

She stepped back out of his arms. Without taking her eyes off his, she began removing her clothes. "The last thing I want is for you to be lonely."

Lorren lifted her eyelids slowly, trying to ignore the sunlight dancing along the windowsill and sliding into her room. She didn't want to wake up just yet.

"Uhmmm," she moaned, closing her eyes again. The memories she encountered when shutting them made the very air around her seem electrified. All during the night and the early morning hours, Justin had loved her.

Their bodies had come together with the reverence of intense hunger and the promise of total fulfillment. And it had continued until Justin had received an emergency call and left.

The warmth of the bedroom as well as the clock on her bedside table told Lorren it was well into the morning. Eleven o'clock to be exact.

She was about to get out of bed when the telephone rang. Thinking it could possibly be Justin or Mama Nora, she quickly picked it up.

"Hello?"

"Are you in a better mood to talk to me, sweetheart?"

Lorren's shoulders stiffened and her fingers tightened their grip on the phone. "Why are you calling, Scott? I've told you, we have nothing to say to each other."

"But we do. I want us to get back together. Baby, I admit I was wrong and want to make it up to you. Just give me a—"

Lorren pushed the button, disconnecting the call. She placed the phone back on the receiver, not wanting to hear anything he had to say.

The telephone rang again. She flinched at the sound. She refused to answer the phone. There was no way she would believe Scott wanted a reconciliation with her. There had to be another reason for his sudden interest after a year.

She would bet any amount of money that he'd heard about her pending business deal with Corvel Toy Company. If everything worked out, that deal would become a very profitable venture. Scott was a big enough jerk to try to woo her back just to be able to cash in on her success.

The phone stopped ringing and Lorren took a deep breath and tried to relax. She got out of bed and started for the bathroom. She stopped in the doorway when the phone began ringing once again. Biting her lips, she entered the bathroom and closed the door, shutting off the shrill tone of the ringing phone.

"Why didn't you answer the phone?"

Lorren spun around from the kitchen counter at the sound of the welcome voice. Her gaze traveling the length of him, Lorren thought just how good Justin looked dressed in a pair of jeans and a pullover shirt. "What?"

He walked over and hugged her, then held her away. "I asked why you didn't answer the phone, baby. I tried calling you a couple of times from the hospital."

"Oh. I may have been in the shower, or I may have been outside," she replied half-truthfully. "What did you want?"

Justin pulled her back into his arms. "I thought I'd let you know that I ran into Rod at the hospital, and he told me Rhonda delivered last night. They have another son."

Lorren glanced up, happiness for their friends shining in her eyes. "Oh, Justin, that's wonderful. Give me all the details."

Justin laughed. "Of course Rod says the kid looks just like him. He weighed nine pounds and twelve ounces. Both mom and baby are doing fine. Rod claims his newest son will be ready to play for the Cowboys in twenty-two years." Justin shook his head. "Poor kid. Who would want to play for the Cowboys?"

Lorren flashed him a piqued look. "Watch it, Justin. You're really asking for trouble." She grinned. "What are they going to name him? I'm sure whatever it is, it'll begin with the letter 'R.'"

"They're naming him Royce."

"Royce? I like that," Lorren replied, nodding. "It's a pretty name."

"Wrong."

Lorren raised a brow. "Wrong?"

"Yes, wrong. Boys names aren't pretty. Girls names are."

Lorren smiled. "That sounds a little chauvinistic, but I guess I really can't expect much better from an Oilers' fan."

Justin laughed, then placed a kiss on her lips. "How would you like to go out to dinner, then drop by the hospital to see Rhonda and the baby?"

Lorren's smile widened. She needed to get away from the house for a while to get her muddled thoughts together. "I'd really like that."

It was nearly seven in the evening when Justin and Lorren returned. Dusk was just beginning to settle in.

"Sandra cleared my calendar for tomorrow, and I was wondering if you wanted to leave for Houston earlier than we'd planned?" Justin asked as they entered Lorren's house.

"That'll be fine," Lorren replied. She was anxious to get away for a while. All during dinner, her nerves had been stretched to the limits, not knowing if Scott was still hanging around. She didn't want to run into him again. Hopefully, while she was out of town, he would give up his insane idea of their talking and return to California.

"Let's dance, Lorren."

"What?" She looked up at Justin, a bit confused.

"I said let's dance."

Lorren's ears suddenly picked up the soft sound of Toni Braxton as it floated through the room. Justin must have turned on her CD player while her thoughts had been a million miles away.

"Sure," she said, going into his outstretched arms. He pulled her closer to him, and she drew comfort from his hard body as they slowly swayed to the music.

Lorren knew in reality that Justin wasn't actually dancing. What he was doing was holding her so that every inch of her body felt every hard inch of his. Evidently he'd sensed something was bothering her, and, in his own special way, he was giving her a portion of his inner strength.

Resting his cheek against the top of her head, he swayed gently from side to side, holding her close. His arms tightened around her.

"What's bothering you, baby?" Justin murmured against her ear. "I'm a good listener if you want to talk about it."

Lorren took a deep breath. He was giving her the perfect opportunity to open up to him, to tell him about Scott's calls. Deep down she wanted to, but to confide in him about it also meant telling him about the last night she'd spent with Scott. She'd told no one about that night, not even Syneda, although Lorren was sure Syneda had an idea of what might have happened to make her finally leave Scott.

She shuddered with shame each time she thought of how naive she'd been. Would Justin understand anyone being that stupid and gullible? His marriage had been perfect, free of blemishes. Would he comprehend the nature of a troubled marriage?

Because of her uncertainties, she couldn't bring herself to talk about Scott to him. At least not yet.

She raised her head to look up at him and decided to talk about something else that had been on her mind. "I'm a little nervous about meeting your family."

He grinned down at her. "Don't be. They'll love you."

Lorren smiled. "You think so?"

"Baby, I know so. Trust me."

Justin pulled his Corvette to a stop in front of the spacious, two-story house. Coming around to the passenger side of the car, he opened the door for Lorren, linking his arms through hers. "We'll get the bags later." He bent down, brushing his lips to hers. "Still a little nervous?"

She grinned. "Should I be?"

"It depends on how brave you are. There're fourteen of us, counting spouses and nephews. We can be a pretty rowdy bunch when we all get together. You've already met Clayton, and he's the worst one of all."

Lorren laughed. "I found your brother to be very charming."

Justin chuckled. "Don't let the charming act fool you, honey. Clayton is a smooth operator," he said, ringing the doorbell.

The front door opened and a pretty teenage girl with dark eyes, toasted almond skin, and vibrant reddish brown hair stood in its frame.

"Justin!" she squealed, throwing her arms around him.

Justin returned the hug. "This is the birthday girl," he said to Lorren, drawing her inside the house. "Lorren, I'd like you to meet my baby sister, Christina Marie Madaris, but we call her Christy."

"Hi," the girl smiled, offering Lorren her hand in a friendly handshake.

Lorren returned the smile. "Hi, and happy birthday."

"Thanks." Christy then turned to Justin. "Where's my birthday present?"

"The girl has no tact."

Lorren's head whipped around at the deep masculine voice. Leaning against a wall was a tall handsome man with charcoal gray eyes, dark wavy hair, and nut-brown skin. His sculptured mouth curved into a smile as he straightened his stance and came toward them.

"Blame it on Clayton," Justin jokingly replied, giving the man a hearty bearhug. "Christy convinced Mom and Dad to let her go live with Clayton a few weeks last summer while the folks were vacationing in Florida. Would you believe I haven't been able to de-Claytonize her since?"

Justin turned to Lorren. "My brother Dex." To Dex he said, "I'd like you to meet Lorren Jacobs."

Lorren found her hand resting in the man's firm grip. His eyes bored into hers assessingly. "You wouldn't happen to have any sisters, would you?"

Lorren laughed. "No. I was an only child."

Dex chuckled. "Too bad."

"But she has a close friend who most assuredly has got it goin' on," a third masculine voice intruded. Lorren turned and gave Clayton Madaris a smile as he entered the foyer to join them. Like the other two Madaris men, he was devastatingly handsome. He had dark hair, soft sable skin, and brown eyes the exact color of Justin's.

"I'm disappointed you didn't bring Syneda with you," Clayton said.

Justin lifted eyes heavenward. "I'm sure you'll get over it. Where there's a woman concerned, you usually do."

Clayton chuckled. "I don't know about that, bro. It's not too often I meet a gorgeous woman who enjoys discussing Roe versus Wade as much as I do."

Justin grinned. "It sounded as though the two of you were debating the case more than discussing it."

Clayton smiled, shaking hands with his brother. "We did seem to have a little difference of opinion." His smile widened as he turned to the woman at his brother's side.

"Lorren, it's good to see you again. I'm glad you could make it. You'll bring beauty and warmth to our dreary family gathering as we come together to celebrate the birthday of the milkman's kid."

Justin and Dex laughed at his statement. "I think you've lost me," Lorren replied, smiling. She gazed from one brother to another, totally confused.

"Don't mind them, Lorren," Christy said, coming to her aid. "My brothers have this thing about me being the milkman's kid since I have reddish hair. The truth of the matter is our paternal great-grandmother also had natural reddish brown hair, so I inherited my hair coloring from her."

Clayton laughed throatily. "Christy's been telling people that story for years. I know for a fact our great-grandmother's hair was just as black as mine."

"Cut it out, Clayton," Dex admonished playfully. "We don't want to upset the birthday girl too much. Did anyone tell big brother that little sister is going out on her first date tonight?"

Before Justin could open his mouth Christy rushed in. "The rest of the family is waiting for us in the den. They can't wait to meet you, Lorren."

Justin put his arm around Lorren's shoulders as they began to walk down the hall. "What do you think so far?"

Lorren laughed. "Like you said earlier, you're a rowdy group, but so far I feel right at home."

Moments later Lorren felt even more at home. She was overwhelmed by the friendliness of Justin's family. His father, a larger model of Justin, gave her a hug as if she wasn't a stranger but a family member. His mother, an elegant-looking, petite woman, with dark hair and charcoal gray eyes, smiled with genuine delight at meeting her. Now Lorren knew where Dex had inherited his eye color.

"It's nice to finally meet you," Marilyn Madaris said. Her warm smile and welcoming gaze put Lorren completely at ease. "I'm glad Justin brought you home with him."

"Thanks for having me," Lorren replied. "It's a pleasure to meet you, too. And you have such a lovely home."

Justin's other two sisters, Kattie and Traci, were very attractive and friendly. They pulled her from their big brother's side the minute they were all introduced. Their handsome husbands gave her smiles and warm hellos.

Lorren was even more surprised to learn she had a fan club of two with Justin's older nephews, both seven, who told her they'd read all her Kente Kids books and asked for her autograph. The little boys said they couldn't wait to go back to school and tell everyone that Lorren Jacobs, the writer and creator of the Kente Kids, was their Uncle Justin's girl-friend.

Lorren smiled, knowing this was the beginning of a glorious weekend.

The three Madaris brothers sat around the table playing cards. Their parents and Lorren had retired hours ago.

"Lorren's a nice girl, Justin."

Justin smiled, pulling another card off the desk. "Thanks, Dex. I have to agree with you."

"Is there something we should know, Big Brother?" Dex asked, as a smile touched his lips. "If my memory serves me correctly, you've never brought a lady friend home for us to meet since Denise died. Although I've been in Australia for two years, I'm sure I would have heard about it through the family grapevine if you had. Is there some meaning in this?"

Justin met his brother's gaze. "She's special."

"We guessed that much, Justin. How about telling us something we don't know," Clayton said, throwing a card out.

Justin shrugged. "There's nothing to tell. She's just special."

A huge grin covered Clayton's face. "Special as in marriage?"

Justin gave him a hard glare. "Special as in special, Clayton. Don't read more into it than that. Lorren's been married before, and the experience wasn't good. She's been left with a deep scar."

"I know exactly how that can be," Dex said dryly.

Justin looked long and steady at his brother, who sat studying his hand. "Dex, have you tried contacting Caitlin since you've been back in the States?"

Dex's head snapped up sharply. His eyes locked with his older brother's. They stared at each other for a tense moment. Complete understanding flowed between the three men at the table. They were not only linked together by blood, but also by deep concern and love for each other.

"No, I haven't, and I don't intend to either. Caitlin made it very clear that our marriage was over. I've accepted that."

Justin nodded. "All right," he replied, not missing the anguish he heard in his brother's words. Then a smile touched his lips. "Since we've discussed my love life and yours, I guess it's time to discuss Clayton's. Has anyone told you about the woman he was dating last winter?"

Dex shook his head. "No. What about her?"

"Don't you dare remind me about that woman, Justin," Clayton bellowed.

Justin laughed. "I thought she was rather a nice girl. I especially thought she had a nice set of teeth."

Dex raised a brow. "Then what was the problem?"

Clayton answered, smiling. "Her nice set of teeth was the problem. She got turned on from biting her dates. She was a regular Miss Vampire. At first her bites seemed harmless enough, a little nibble here and a little nibble there. Then suddenly her nibbles became full-fledged bites. I had the good fortune of having her teeth print on my rear end for at least a month. Talk about a very sore behind."

Roaring laughter engulfed the table, and the card game was momentarily forgotten.

Dex shook his head. "It seems, kid brother, you still have a penchant for the unusual."

That night Lorren had trouble sleeping. She and Justin had been given separate rooms, which made her acutely aware of how long it had been since she'd slept alone. They had been sharing a bed continuously since the night of the storm over a month ago.

The evening had been full of fun and excitement. Justin had been right. He had a warm, loving family who did get a little rambunctious at times. A smile quirked her lips as she remembered the hard time the three brothers had given Christy's date, Michael. One would have thought the Madaris brothers worked for the FBI with the interrogation they'd put him through.

Once Michael had been introduced to everyone, the three brothers had huddled him off in a corner. Lorren only hoped Christy had warned

Michael beforehand what to expect from her brothers. She hadn't seemed the least annoyed or upset with their behavior. Evidently she was used to their high degree of overprotectiveness.

Michael, on the other hand, was a nervous wreck when the brothers all but read him his rights, with Clayton using legal jargon, Justin using medical terms, and Dex using no terms at all but giving the young man bold eye contact.

The Madaris clan had dined at a restaurant where a section had been reserved just for them. After dinner the family surprised Christy when the owner of the establishment, along with a few of the waiters, had sung happy birthday to her and brought out a lovely cake adorned with sixteen candles. After cake and ice cream had been served and adequately eaten by all, Christy and Michael stood to leave. They'd made plans earlier to join friends for a movie.

"Don't forget our discussion, Michael," Clayton said easily, not bothering to lower his voice. "Remember what I told you about justifiable homicides."

"And don't forget what I told you about how many bones there are in the human body, and how painful it feels if any of them are broken," Justin added pointedly.

Lorren looked at Dex to see what friendly reminder he would offer Michael. Evidently the other family members had the same inclination, for all eyes turned to him. He gave them a lazy smile, then said to Michael in a voice that was deep and deadly, "One wrong move, kid, and I'll personally boil you in oil."

After dinner the rest of them had returned to the Madarises' home. The men played a friendly game of cards, the kids retired to the family room to watch a Disney movie, and the women sat around discussing changing trends in fashion, movies, and assorted other topics of feminine interest.

Lorren had thoroughly enjoyed their company. More than once she'd looked up to find Justin's eyes on her.

The house was quiet. Justin's sisters and their families had left for their own homes, and she and Justin's parents had gone to bed shortly thereafter, leaving Justin, Dex, and Clayton up playing cards as they waited for Christy's return from her date.

Tomorrow would be another day full of activities. Justin's sisters and his mother had invited her to go shopping with them. Afterward, she and Justin would leave to return to Ennis.

She took a deep breath. Why had Justin brought her here? She had turned that question over in her mind since he'd issued the invitation. One of his sisters had mentioned that Justin had not brought a woman home for them to meet since his wife's death. Lorren could only hope he was considering a meaningful, long-term, committed relationship with her. She didn't know how much longer she could deal with not knowing how long their relationship would last.

She couldn't help wondering when Ms. Fate arrived, where that would leave her.

Why did he bring Lorren here?

The question plagued Justin. His mind replayed all the scenes that had taken place since he and Lorren had arrived. Just as he knew they would be, his family was completely taken with her. And every chance they got, they made sure he knew it.

And he wasn't sure just how he felt about that.

He was beginning to get annoyed with his family's hints that "It's about time" and "She's the girl." They couldn't seem to understand that his life wasn't being governed by the ticking of some internal biological clock. He still wanted the usual things in life. He wanted to remarry, have a bunch of kids, and watch them grow while living on the ranch he'd bought.

Years ago he'd chosen to leave his future to fate. And although he enjoyed his relationship with Lorren, he had no reason to believe she was the woman he'd been waiting for.

For starters, she didn't believe in love and marriage. She'd said so the night they met. And although he knew she'd been spending a lot of time with Vincent ever since the camping trip, he didn't really know how she felt about having kids of her own someday.

Besides those things, she hadn't given him any reason to believe she would put down her roots in Ennis permanently. For all he knew, she'd only moved back to lick her wounds.

Then there was the main reason that stood out. She was totally different from Denise in a number of ways, especially one in particular. Denise had always been soft and gentle, and he'd always treated her that way, even while they made love.

Lorren, on the other hand, wouldn't accept gentleness. She could fuel a want and need in him until he took her with a force that stunned him. Even now, he had to grind his teeth to hold back a deep, rough groan threatening to escape him just from thinking about her.

"Couldn't you sleep?"

Justin turned from staring out the kitchen window. His mother's question had invaded his thoughts. "I should be asking you the same thing."

Marilyn Madaris smiled. "I wish I could go to sleep, but your father's snoring tonight is worse than ever. It must be from the excitement of having all of his children home," she said, unhooking two coffee cups from the cup rack and filling them with the coffee Justin had made. She handed him a cup.

"Oh, by the way, Justin. I think Lorren's a lovely girl."

He took a sip of coffee. "So what else is new?"

Marilyn Madaris stared at him. "Why are you getting upset? Don't you think she's a lovely girl?"

"Of course I do. I just don't want the family reading more into my relationship with Lorren than what's really there."

"Then you tell us, Justin. How should we read this? She's the first woman you've brought home since Denise died."

"But that doesn't necessarily mean she'll be the last. That's all I'm saying, Mom. I like Lorren. I like her a lot. We enjoy each other's company but . . ."

Marilyn Madaris raised a brow. "But what?"

"Nothing." He set his cup of coffee on the counter. "Good night, Mom."

Marilyn Madaris watched her oldest son walk out of the kitchen. It was her guess that his "song singing days" were coming to an end. She couldn't help but wonder how he would handle it when that fact hit him?

Justin slid into bed after doing one hundred push-ups and just as many jumping jacks. He really hadn't expected to get much sleep, especially since he wasn't sharing a bed with the one person he wanted to sleep with.

His mother had put Lorren down the hall in one of his sister's old rooms, and the thought that she was so close yet so far irritated him. He tossed and turned most of the night.

He arose at the crack of dawn and went downstairs for coffee and was surprised to find Clayton and Dex already up, drinking coffee and eating toast. Clayton was the first to speak.

"What in the world was happening in your room last night, Justin?"

Confused, Justin a brow as he poured himself a cup of coffee. "Nothing that I know of."

Clayton grinned. "Then that explains why you were making all that racket working off your frustrations. Leave it to dear old Mom to put Lorren in the bedroom next to theirs, out of your reach."

Clayton plopped the last piece of toast in his mouth and washed it down with coffee before adding, "Whatever it is you're afflicted with, you got it bad, Big Brother. And I hope it's not contagious."

Justin shot Clayton a dark look. He refused to ask him what he meant by that comment. He then threw a thunderous gaze in Dex's direction.

"Don't look at me, Justin," Dex said, grinning. "I haven't said a word."

"Good. And see that you don't."

Justin was still in a testy mood when the rest of the family came down for breakfast a little while later. He found himself staring at Lorren as she made her way around the kitchen, helping his mother prepare breakfast. The sight of her dressed in something simple, like a denim wrap skirt and peasant blouse, made his entire body ache. His hands felt damp and a film of perspiration began forming on his upper lip.

And to make matters worse, he found his two brothers watching him and grinning from ear to ear. They didn't seem the least bit threatened when he shot them a murderous look.

That afternoon didn't come fast enough for Justin. Although he had enjoyed the time he'd spent with his family, he was more than ready to leave. Bidding them farewell, he loaded both the luggage and Lorren into the car in record time and headed back to Ennis.

He kept a firm grip on the steering wheel and fought the temptation to reach out and run his hand over Lorren.

He took a deep steadying breath. They couldn't get back to Ennis quick enough to suit him.

Closing her eyes against the surge of fierce pleasure clutching her, she urged him deeper into her, absorbing the tremors of rapture that flowed through her body.

"Lorren!" Justin breathed her name sharply in her ear at the same time he drove them both over the edge.

Lorren woke early the next morning, sprawled across Justin's chest and securely cradled in his embrace.

Last night they had made love with a hungry intensity she'd never imagined possible. It was as if they couldn't get enough of each other. His body had claimed her as firebolts of desire raced through her.

Her body had understood his rhythm and, instinctively, arched to meet his steady thrusts of possession. The fires burning between them had somehow gotten out of control, becoming a fiery blaze of ecstasy. After their hunger had been temporarily satisfied, they'd slept, then wakened and made love again and again.

Justin stirred slightly. Lorren slowly eased off him, not wanting to wake him. "Where're you going?" he murmured, pulling her back firmly against him.

An easy smile played at the corners of Lorren's mouth. "To make coffee and get something to eat. We sort of skipped dinner yesterday."

Her eyes glowed with playfulness as she continued. "So let me go, Justin Madaris, or suffer the consequences. You know how testy I get whenever I'm hungry."

Lorren felt the pressure of his hands loosen some. "All right, baby. I'll let you go, but only if you promise you'll come back."

She smiled down at him, marveling at the handsome features looking back at her. His dark eyes were soft with slumber. She took his face in her hands and kissed his lips. "I promise."

He released her completely then and, when she stood, rolled onto his stomach and buried his head in the pillow.

Lorren took slow steps to the bathroom. The tenderness in her thighs and deep in her body reminded her of the strength of Justin and the intensity of their lovemaking.

After taking a shower and changing into a pair of shorts and a T-shirt, she went into the kitchen and put on a pot of coffee. Opening the pantry, she took out a box of cereal and opened the refrigerator for the milk when the phone rang.

She answered it absently. "Hello."

"Where have you been the last couple of days, Lorren? I needed to talk to you."

Lorren immediately recognized the voice, and her body stiffened as rage engulfed her. "You just wait one minute. I don't owe you an expla-

CHAPTER 12

"Aren't we going to bring in our bags?"

"Later," Justin muttered, guiding Lorren through the door and locking it firmly behind them. He didn't waste any time pulling her into his arms. "Do you have any idea how much I want you? How much I need you?"

Not as much as I want you to want and need me, Lorren thought, seeing the heavy look of male hunger in his eyes.

Justin kissed her, and she arched herself against him, forgetting everything except the touch of his lips, the taste of his mouth, and the feel of his hands moving over her body.

In one smooth motion he picked her up in his arms and carried her to the bedroom. Lorren felt the heat of his gaze touch every part of her skin as he undressed her.

Then he quickly removed his own clothes and took time to prepare himself for her, to keep her safe.

Wordlessly, they stared at each other. She wanted to tell him she loved him, but knew she couldn't. Instead, when his mouth met hers again, she kissed him with all the longing in her heart.

Lorren put into action what she dared not say in words. Letting her love for him be a guide, she gave to him a passion the likes of which she'd never before given, wrapping him in the sensuous warmth of her feelings. She became bold, she became daring, she became a tormentor, and, in the end, she became a pleaser. She would always remember the exact moment their bodies became one, fitting together perfectly.

nation about anything. I don't want to talk to you, and if you call here again, I'll notify the police. There are laws against harassment. Do you hear me?"

The only response Lorren received was a click in her ear. She placed the phone back in the cradle and leaned against the counter to catch her breath, fighting to control her shaking body.

"Do you want to tell me what the hell is going on?"

Lorren whirled around to find Justin leaning against the kitchen door. He was completely awake now, and he wasn't smiling.

When she didn't answer him, he walked over to her and put his hands on her shoulders, gently squeezing. "Who was that on the phone, Lorren?"

Somehow she found herself leaning against him, absorbing the strength that was an innate part of him. "It was Scott."

Justin muttered a soft curse. The arms that surrounded her stiffened. "What did he want?"

"He wants to talk."

His mouth tightened. "Has he called you here before?"

Lorren nodded. "Yes. He's called a few times since the day I saw him—"

"Saw him?" Justin asked, easing her away from him, cutting off her words. "You saw him? Here in Ennis?"

"Yes."

"When?"

Her voice was quiet. "At the Polka Festival last week."

Justin exhaled through clenched teeth. "Why didn't you say something?"

She cast her eyes downward. "Because I didn't want to bother you. It was my problem."

Justin lifted her chin with his finger so their eyes could meet. "Baby, your problems are my problems. Don't you know that?"

"No, and it really doesn't matter. I've brought enough emotional garbage into this relationship without adding more."

"Emotional garbage? What are you talking about? You had a bad first marriage, but you're not the first and certainly won't be the last. There are problems in every marriage."

A part of Lorren didn't want Justin's tenderness and understanding at the moment. It was the part of her that couldn't forgive herself for being a fool and staying with Scott as long as she did. That part of her wanted to lash out, and, unfortunately, Justin was the target.

Her eyes flashed with fire when she looked at him. "What do you know about problems in a marriage? Yours was perfect. You got the person you wanted and the two of you would have lived happily-ever-after had she not died."

Lorren's eyes filled with tears as she continued. "You don't have any idea how it feels to believe you've chosen the perfect mate, and then have that person turn on you and try to destroy your self-respect and dignity. You can't begin to imagine how it feels when your inability to pleasure him in bed becomes something he belittles you with, day and night."

Justin reached out. She moved a few inches away from him. "No, you can't imagine any of those things, Justin, because your marriage was perfect. It was made in heaven. All of us aren't that lucky."

The last thread of Lorren's composure crumbled, and she gave in to her tears. She was powerless to resist Justin when he picked her up in his arms and carried her to the living room, while she sobbed into his chest.

"That's right, baby. Get it all out. Let yourself cry. Get rid of the anger, the frustration, and the hurt. And after you've finished, I'll give you as much tender, loving care as anyone could possibly receive. I will make you feel loved, and I'll show you just how special you are."

"But you don't understand," she got out between sobs.

Justin sat on the sofa and cradled her in his lap. "Baby, I *do* understand. Nobody's marriage is perfect, and I'm sorry I gave you the impression that mine was. Denise and I disagreed about a number of things. But we didn't allow our disagreements to come between us."

He placed his lips against her cheek, kissing away the tears there. "You don't have to experience pain firsthand to understand it, Lorren. Someone I love and respect very much, my brother Dex, met and fell in love with Caitlin at a time when all of us thought he never would. He had promised himself years before that he would never give his heart to a woman after a close friend of his committed suicide after receiving a 'Dear John' letter."

Justin's thumb absently traced circular motions on Lorren's arm while he continued. "Greg and Dex were as close as brothers since the time they were kids. They attended Morehouse together. Greg met and fell in love with someone who attended a neighboring college."

Justin pulled Lorren closer. "To make a long story short, the girl broke things off. Dex was the one who found Greg when Dex went back to their apartment in between classes. Greg had shot himself in the head. He left Dex a note that said . . . 'Don't ever fall in love. It hurts like hell.' . . ."

Lorren drew back, remaining absolutely motionless as she absorbed Justin's words. Her heart went out to the man who had taken his life on account of love. "But Dex eventually fell in love, didn't he?"

"Yes, nearly twelve years later. He met and fell in love with a younger woman, a lot younger. Caitlin was barely twenty-one and fresh out of college when Dex married her at thirty-two. They met when she came to work at my uncle's ranch for the summer. Dex and Caitlin fell in love immediately, and were married in less than two weeks. The company Dex worked for was sending him to Australia for two years."

Justin's hand slowly stroked her back. It was a soothing feeling. "Caitlin was to join Dex in Australia."

"Did she?"

"No. What she did was send him a 'Dear John' letter along with divorce papers and her wedding ring. None of us really knows the complete story, and Dex refuses to talk about it."

"It must have been awful for him."

"Yes, it was, and he still hasn't completely gotten over it. He was in a foreign country without his family and friends for support. He had to go through that painful period in his life alone."

Justin gave her a level look. "So you see, Lorren, I *do* understand the depth of your pain, just as I understand Dex's. You aren't the only person whose life was nearly destroyed by falling in love. Even I was hurt by love, but in a different way."

Lorren knew Justin was right and her anger began dissolving. She appreciated him for sharing Dex's story with her. It made her realize she wasn't in a class by herself. Pain hadn't singled her out for attack as she wanted to believe at times.

"Lorren?"

"Ummm?"

"What are you planning to do about your ex-husband?"

Lorren's eyes met Justin's, then glanced away. She wondered how much of her phone conversation with Scott he had overheard. "Hopefully, I won't have to do anything. I'm praying that he finally realizes I won't talk to him and leaves town."

"And if he doesn't?"

Lorren turned to face Justin again. She stirred uneasily at the thought of Scott remaining in Ennis, trying to persuade her to talk with him. "I really don't know, Justin. I'll probably talk to Rod to see what can be done to stop him from calling me. Legally, Scott is out of my life."

"Do you have any idea why he's here?"

"He claims he wants a reconciliation, but of course I don't believe that for one minute. It's my guess that he's found out about my possible deal with Corvel Toys and wants a piece of the action. I can't believe he thinks I'll be stupid enough to take him back. There's no way I'll ever do that."

Justin was quiet for a moment before he spoke. "There's more to it than what you're telling me, isn't there?"

She swallowed. "What do you mean?"

"What did he do to you to make you afraid of him? I can detect it in your voice."

She shrugged. "You know that already. He tried convincing me that as a woman I was worthless."

"No. I think there's more to it than that. What aren't you telling me, Lorren?"

She chewed on her lower lip as she looked at him. "What makes you think I'm not telling you something?"

"Just a hunch."

He saw the wary look in her eyes. "Knowing about the emotional abuse you endured while married to him, I can understand your anger at him for being in town. I can even understand your being furious at the thought that he's contacting you, wanting the two of you to get back together. But I can't understand your being afraid. Unless . . ."

"Unless what?" she asked uneasily.

Justin didn't reply for a long time. Lorren knew he was seriously considering what he was about to say. "Unless he was physically abusive to you as well. That would explain your fear."

Lorren looked away from Justin quickly. She tried to move away. His hands tightened around her waist. When he spoke again, his voice was velvet edged with steel. "Was he, Lorren?"

"I'd rather not talk about it, Justin."

"Tell me. Did he hit you?"

Every fiber in Lorren's body shook with the anger she heard in Justin's voice and the hardened look in his features. He rested his hand lightly against her chin, his voice husky with tenderness when he said, "I have to know."

His touch acted like a catalyst that destroyed the last of the self-protective shield surrounding her. She loved him and wanted to share everything with him. Even if it was a part of her life she'd rather not remember.

"Yes. He hit me, but only once. That was the night I finally left him."

She wished she could expunge the memories of that night from her mind. "He'd been out with his friends, and I gather I'd been the topic of their conversation for the evening."

"He discussed your personal lives with his friends?" Justin asked, his voice incredulous with rage.

"I found out later that night that he had. They had given him advice on how to whip me into shape. And he came home and tried to do just that, literally. My only advantage was that Syneda had talked me into taking a self-defense course after there had been a series of rapes in the LA area. I effectively used the right maneuvers to defend myself from his attack and get away from him."

Her eyes were misty. "But he did manage to hit me a few times, since he'd caught me unawares. I'd been asleep when he'd come in. He jerked me out of bed and began whipping me with his belt. I got a few bloody cuts from the buckle and had to get medical attention."

Justin's eyes conveyed the fury within him. She tried ignoring it as she continued. "That night I saw a different side of Scott. It was a side I'll never forget. I knew then that, when pushed to the limit, he was capable of anything. That's why I don't want to talk to him."

Justin combed his fingers through Lorren's hair. A part of him wished it was her ex-husband's neck instead. "Why haven't you told me about this before?"

She drew a deep breath. "Because I felt ashamed at having let him do that to me, and for being naive enough to marry him in the first place. I should have known what he was capable of. I should not have given him the opportunity to make my life a living hell. But I did, all in the name of love."

Justin's eyes softened as he gazed into her tear-stained face. "You have no reason to be ashamed, Lorren. He is the one who should be ashamed of what he's put you through. Was last week the first time you've seen him since the divorce?"

"Yes."

He pulled her closer. "I think we should pay Rod a visit and make him aware of what's going on."

"All right." Lorren sighed, pressing closer to Justin. She hoped the phone calls would be reason enough for Rod to ask Scott to leave town.

"What do you mean he agreed to leave town voluntarily?"

Justin leaned against the desk with his arms folded across his chest as he waited for Rod to answer his question. A dark scowl covered his face.

He and Lorren had driven into town earlier that day and met with Rod. He'd sat and listened while Lorren had given Rod her account of the calls she'd gotten from her ex-husband. Afterward, they'd left to visit awhile with Ms. Nora. Then Justin had dropped Lorren off to visit Rhonda and the baby. He had returned to talk to Rod alone.

Rod eyed his friend. "Just what I said. He left town voluntarily. I didn't have to throw him out. After you and Lorren left, I paid the guy a visit. He was staying at Cullers Inn and was already packing to leave when I got there. Since we always have a number of strangers lingering around after the Festival, no one in town gave his presence much thought."

Rob took a sip of coffee. "He comes across as a likable guy. There doesn't appear to be a mean streak in his entire body. In fact, he appeared rather pleasant."

"A likeable guy? Pleasant? Hah! If you believe that, I have some prime vacation land to sell you in Alaska."

Rod grinned. "I said he *seemed* to be a likable and pleasant guy, Justin. In this business, I discovered a long time ago people aren't always what they seem to be. Besides, I've known Lorren since grade school, and I have no reason not to believe her story about him."

Rod leaned back in his chair. "I talked with him for over half an hour. He said he came to Ennis to talk Lorren into giving him another chance. He hadn't intended for his phone calls to upset her. Since he now knows she's against the idea of the two of them getting back together, he's willing to leave her alone."

Justin arched a brow. "He actually told you all of that?"

"Yeah."

"Sounds like the two of you got rather chummy."

Rod chuckled. "Not hardly."

"Are you sure he's left town?" Justin asked.

"I gave him personal escort service into Dallas myself. I also told him that if he ever came back to Ennis and tried contacting Lorren, I'd arrest him."

Justin sighed as he fished in his pocket and pulled out his car keys. "I should have gone with you to see him."

"No, you did the right thing by letting me handle it, Justin. You're too close to the situation, too close to Lorren. Things could have gotten a little messy with you there." Rod's eyes sparkled teasingly. "I take that back. Things could have gotten a whole lot messy with you there. When you came into my office this morning with Lorren, you were out for blood. I had to talk you out of going looking for him yourself. You were like a lion out to protect his lioness—at any cost."

Justin met his friend's stare. "I don't want him to ever hurt her again, Rod."

"I understand that," Rod replied, tipping his head back to look up at Justin. He saw the anger flaring in Justin's eyes. He hoped, for Lorren's ex-husband's sake, the man had the good sense to stay away from Ennis and leave Lorren alone. Rod wasn't sure if Justin even realized it, but he was wearing his heart on his sleeve.

Rod stood. "Just to be on the safe side, I'm going to keep a close eye on things in town. And I plan to have one of my men cruise the area around Elliot Lake more often for a while, just to make sure Mr. Howard doesn't change his mind about revisiting Ennis."

"Thanks, Rod, I'd appreciate it."

"Tell Lorren if she receives any calls that sound even remotely suspicious to let me know."

Lorren placed the last of the dishes in the sink before turning around to Justin. "But I don't understand why Rod wants a police car cruising the area when Scott has left town."

"It's a safety measure in case he didn't quite understand he's not welcome in Ennis."

Lorren turned back to the sink. Reaching up, she opened the cabinet and placed a bowl inside. Justin's eyes were drawn to the soft material of her skirt as it clung to her bottom. When she lifted her arms, his gaze zeroed in on her fine hips and shapely thighs as the material stretched upward. His body immediately hardened.

"Don't do that, baby," he said huskily.

Lorren turned around and gave him a strange look. "Don't do what?"

"Don't reach up like that."

Their eyes held. Then Lorren's lips curved into a mischievous smile when understanding dawned. "Oh, you mean don't reach up like this?" she asked, deliberately reaching up farther this time.

"Woman, you're really asking for it," Justin said, his voice strained.

"Asking for what?"

"You know what," he muttered, getting out of his chair and walking toward her.

Lorren laughed when she saw the evidence of his desire straining against his jeans. "You always want me."

"Yes, I always want you," Justin agreed, placing his arms around her waist.

"That makes me feel good," she said, leaning into him. "For so long I considered myself undesirable."

Justin pulled her closer. "Oh, but you are desirable, baby. Too desirable for your own good," he said, as he began fumbling with the buttons on her blouse. "And mine."

CHAPTER 13

A week later, dressed in shorts and a knit top, Lorren leaned back from the papers spread across her desk. She had been up since sunrise, putting the finishing touches on her book, and hadn't eaten breakfast. A cup of coffee was all she'd had, and now her stomach was rebelling.

Glancing around the room, she felt Justin's absence. He'd gone into the office to work half a day and had invited her to join him for lunch at Sophie's Diner.

The tile floor felt cool under her bare feet as she walked into the kitchen. Even though it was still early, she had about two more hours of writing time left before joining Justin for lunch.

By eleven o'clock, she had completed her writing, showered and changed into a challis print skirt and silk blouse, and was ready to leave. She had just grabbed her car keys off the table when she heard the doorbell.

Lorren gasped when she looked through the peephole in the door to see who was on the other side.

Scott!

What was he doing back in Ennis after Rod had warned him against returning?

For a few moments, she stood with her hand on the doorknob, trying to decide what to do. She squared her shoulders when her internal fuming had reached the boiling point. She'd had enough of Scott.

Snatching open the door, she confronted the man who was standing before her dressed impeccably in a tailored suit. "What are you doing here, Scott?"

He reached into his jacket pocket and pulled out a small gift-wrapped box. "I bought you a gift. It's sort of a peace offering."

Lorren couldn't help remembering the other times he'd caused her pain, then brought her gifts to make up for it. In the past, she had fallen for such gestures. But not anymore.

"No thanks. I don't want it."

"You're really going to like this, Lorren," he continued, ignoring her remark. "It cost me a bundle, but you're worth every penny. I really should be angry with you for sending that small-town cop after me. But I know you're still upset about how things ended between us."

He held the gift out to her. "Take it, Lorren. I got it especially for you."

Lorren's eyes narrowed. "I don't want it, Scott. Understand? Things are over between us."

Scott hesitated, then stuffed the box back into his pocket. "I don't believe that, and neither do you. You love me too much."

The corners of his mouth curved upward. "Besides, what other man would put up with you and your problem, baby?"

"That does it!" Lorren tried slamming the door in his face, but Scott, suspecting what she was about to do, blocked its closing with his foot and pushed his way into the house.

"Forceful entry is against the law, Scott. You're already in hot water for even being here. I would advise you to leave. Now!"

He shrugged his shoulder, walked into the center of the room, and glanced around. "Nice place, but it's not where you belong. You belong back in California with me. There's nothing for you here in this little depressing town."

Lorren continued to stand by the open door, determined to keep distance between them. "I happen to disagree. Everything I've ever wanted is here."

"You're just not thinking clearly, sweetheart." His voice softened cajolingly. "I know that while we were married I wasn't the perfect husband, but I promise to do better. I even plan to help promote your career more. I've heard about your deal with Corvel, but I've got even bigger plans for you. How does the idea of the Kente Kids going to television grab you?"

Scott leaned against the bookcase with his arms crossed, a satisfied grin on his face, and contintued. "I've run the idea of the Kente Kids becoming a Saturday morning cartoon show past my boss, and he absolutely loves it. He believes they'd be a smash hit. Just think what that could mean. There haven't been all-black cartoons on television since Cosby's Fat Albert series. I can just see all the bucks rolling in, not to mention the recognition the network will give me as the creator of the series."

Lorren stared at him. It was hard to believe she hadn't seen through his self-centered, smooth-talking, scheming ways before they had married. But she hadn't. Would she ever be able to get over her faulty judgment in choosing him for a husband?

Anger, the likes of which she'd never known, ripped through her. She slowly left her place near the door and walked a little farther into the room.

"You've got it all worked out, haven't you?" Lorren asked, her voice as chilling as her expression.

Scott didn't pick up on it either. He smiled, obviously thinking Lorren was giving him a compliment. "Yes, baby. I do."

Lorren laughed. "Well, I hate to disappoint you, but you've evidently forgotten one major detail."

His smile faded. He raised a brow. "What?"

"Me, and how I would feel about your whole scheme of things. I wouldn't take you back, Scott Howard, if you were the last man on earth. Thanks to God, you're not. And I certainly wouldn't let you manage my career. My agent is doing a remarkable job, and I have no complaints. In fact, another network has already made us a similar offer, which I'm seriously considering at the moment. So forget it, Scott. I'm not interested in you or your deals. So get out."

Something cold flashed in Scott's eyes. His lips drew back in a snarl and he took a step toward her. "You little—"

"Don't even think about touching her."

Scott halted, going instantly still at the sound of the low, lethal, masculine voice. His gaze flew to the man who stood just inside the doorway. "Just who the hell are you?"

Justin ignored Scott's question, and instead spoke to Lorren in a controlled voice. "Come here, baby."

Scott's eyes narrowed when Lorren didn't waste any time going into Justin's outstretched arms.

"You okay?" Justin asked her softly, placing his arms securely around her waist.

Lorren nodded. "Yes, I'm fine. But how did you know about—"

"The police cruiser. I was at Rod's office when one of his men radioed in that he had seen a rental car in the area, and that the driver fitted this man's description."

Scott, obviously unnerved by the sight of Lorren in Justin's embrace, spoke up. "Look you. I don't know who you are, but you can't just barge in here. This is between me and my wife."

Justin's eyes darkened, and Scott had the good sense to take a step back. "Don't ever refer to Lorren as your wife. She was, and still is, too good for you."

Scott laughed viciously and sneered. "Too good for me? Is that what you think about that cold, empty woman standing next to you? Boy are you in for a surprise. She's nothing but a beautiful shell."

Justin took a step forward. "Why you—"

"All right, that's enough!" A uniformed Rod Clark walked into the house. He first fastened his level gaze on Justin. "I'm going to give you a ticket for speeding, Justin. You were doing every bit of ninety in that Corvette getting here."

He then turned his attention to the other man. "And you, Mr. Howard, evidently don't understand simple English. I thought I made it clear just a few days ago that you weren't welcome in Ennis."

Scott's shoulder lifted in a dismissing shrug. "This is a free country, Sheriff, and I can go anywhere I please."

Rod squinted at the ceiling for a moment, then looked at Scott again. "Not in my town, and not when it involves harassing one of the citizens I'm duty bound to protect."

Rod turned to Lorren. "How do you want me to handle this? Just say the word and Mr. Howard will be my guest for a few days in the Ennis Park Suite Jail, cell number ten."

Lorren clasped her hands in front of her, squaring her shoulders. "He's leaving, Rod, and he's not coming back. I think Scott has finally realized there's nothing here in Ennis for him. And since he claims he came here on behalf of the network where he works, I'm sure the president of that company would not take too kindly to one of their up-and-coming junior executives behaving in such a despicable manner. I don't want to, but if I have to, I *will* cause trouble for him. I have both the means and the funds to do it now."

She turned to Scott. "Do you understand what I'm saying, Scott?"

He glared at her and the two men. "I understand."

"Then I would suggest that you get in your car, leave, and don't come back."

Scott threw them all one last disapproving glance, then strode through the doorway. Rod and Justin followed behind him.

He had made it to the porch and was just about to walk down the steps when he whispered sneeringly to Justin. "Man, you're making a big mistake if you're thinking about making her your woman. She ain't worth your effort in bed."

By the time Lorren reached the porch, she found Scott sprawled on his face in the front yard. "What happened?"

Justin shrugged. "He slipped."

"I did not," Scott yelled, pushing himself up on his elbows. "You tripped me."

"Your word against mine."

"Sheriff, you saw him," Scott said, getting to his feet and wiping dirt off his expensive suit. "He tripped me."

"Sorry, I didn't see a thing, Mr. Howard. The sun temporarily blinded me. Are you sure you weren't just a little clumsy?" Rod asked, grabbing Scott's arm and leading him over to the rental car.

"I'm going to waste the taxpayers' money one more time and escort you across the county line. If you come back again, causing problems, I'll make sure you find out just how mean I can be when my patience is tried."

Rod yanked open the driver's door to the rental car and shoved Scott inside. He then walked casually around the vehicle to his patrol car.

"Don't think I'm going to forget about that ticket, Justin," Rod said, before getting inside the vehicle.

"I didn't think for one minute that you would," Justin replied. He walked over to Scott's car to have a few words with him. He lowered his voice to a deadly tone.

"Just thought I'd tell you before you go, Howard, just in case you're thinking about returning—Lorren belongs to me. And what's mine I keep and protect. If you ever try contacting her again, you'll have me to deal with. Just remember that."

An angry Scott nodded before starting the engine and pulling away, with Rod following behind.

When the two vehicles could no longer be seen, Justin walked back up to the porch.

"You sure you're okay?"

Lorren nodded as Justin followed her back inside the house and closed the door behind them.

"Yes, I'm all right. Scott forced his way inside here and there was nothing I could do," she replied, kicking off her shoes and walking into the bedroom.

Justin followed.

Mindless of the fact that she'd just gotten dressed to meet Justin for lunch moments earlier, Lorren began stripping off her clothes and re-hanging them neatly in the closet. She didn't want thoughts of Scott to consume her. He had been a big mistake in her life, but she had to accept that and move on. But he had taught her a very valuable lesson—all that glittered was not gold.

Lorren shuddered and forced herself to clear her mind. Right now she only wanted to concentrate on the man leaning against the bedroom door, watching her. He was the man she loved more than anything, and at this very moment she needed him to make her feel whole.

"You're one tough lady, Lorren Jacobs. I was proud of you today."

She frowned slightly, feeling somewhat undeserving of his words. "I was scared, Justin. But I couldn't let Scott know it. For once, I wanted to stand up to him."

"You did, and I really don't think you'll hear from him again."

"I hope not."

Lorren backed up a few steps until the back of her legs touched the side of the bed. "Love me, Justin," she whispered. "Please love me. Now."

Justin straightened his stance and walked toward the woman standing next to the bed, wearing a lacy black bra and a black half slip.

"We're missing lunch," he said huskily, coming to stand in front of her. "And we'll probably miss dinner, too."

Lorren framed his face with her hands, pulling him to her. "Right now, I have a totally different type of hunger. One only you can feed," she said, moments before his lips covered hers.

Beautiful.

The fragrance Lorren wore and the scent of their lovemaking combined forces and retriggered primitive yearnings deep within Justin. However, he refused to give in to the urge to make love to her again . . . at least, not yet.

It was late afternoon and dusk was slowly approaching. They had only been out of the bedroom once, and that had been when Rod had dropped by to deliver the speeding ticket.

He and Lorren had used that time to grab something to eat, only to return to the bedroom. Now she lay snuggled against him, asleep. Her soft curves molded to the contours of his body. He allowed his gaze to travel over her face.

Beautiful.

There was no other word he could think of that would describe not only her, but also what they had shared that afternoon. Their lovemaking had spiraled to new heights.

Some sort of desperation had driven both of them, had consumed them. It had made them so wild and out of control that the bed was a complete mess because of it. The bottom sheet had somehow worked its way to the top; pillows and the bedcover were strewn on the floor.

Justin breathed deeply. The truth of the matter was that, even with the hot, fiery turbulence of their mating, he had felt something beyond just satisfying their bodies. He'd felt an inner contentment he hadn't felt in a long time.

How had Lorren accomplished something in a couple of months that other women hadn't been able to achieve in ten years? How could she make him feel so complete? So whole?

He continued to hold her as his thoughts shifted to Denise. She had been his first love, and he appreciated that fact. Through her, he had been able to grow and mature.

He could now admit that after her death he had compared every woman he would meet to her and none would measure up. It hadn't dawned on him until much later that there was not another Denise Wakefield Madaris out there, and it wouldn't be fair to her memory to try to find one. Deep down he never thought he'd get lucky enough to find the kind of happiness he and Denise had shared a second time.

Then he'd met Lorren.

From the first moment he'd seen her that night, he had wanted her, needed her. With Lorren he was a different person, which proved that over the years he had changed in many ways. He couldn't help but wonder had Denise lived, if she would have been able to adjust to those changes.

He now admitted he'd reached an age where a totally different type of woman appealed to him. A woman glowing in the image of fire and passion. A woman capable of stimulating him physically as well as mentally.

A woman like Lorren.

He stroked the length of her back, holding her closer to his body, and even closer to his heart. It was an act of emotion-filled possession. An act of love.

The thought hit him full force. He loved Lorren. She was the woman of his fate.

And with that realization came something else, ice-cold fear. He was scared to death of loving someone again and losing her. He was frightened of experiencing more pain, and he wasn't sure he was ready to give up his heart again, so totally and completely.

Fear's icy grasp tightened. Loving was for a lifetime. Loving was forever. Love meant emotional vulnerability. He had discovered the hard way that there was pain in loving someone, and what he felt for Lorren was stronger and deeper than what he'd felt for Denise.

A conversation he'd had with his mother a few months ago filtered through his mind . . .

"I'd remarry in a heartbeat if the right woman came along, Mom, you know that," he chuckled.

"Do I, Justin? I'm beginning to think this fate song you've been singing over the years is for the birds. A part of me can't help but wonder if perhaps you're only fooling yourself."

"Fooling myself? About what?"

"About ever wanting to marry again. . . ."

His mother had been right. He'd only been fooling himself.

He suddenly came face-to-face with the reality of the lie he'd been telling himself, his family, and everyone around him for the last ten years. Waiting on fate had just been an excuse not to get deeply involved with anyone, not to give up his heart.

And now he was faced with the hard fact that fate had done exactly what he'd claimed it would do. It had given him a woman he couldn't imagine living his life without. And that in itself was his greatest fear.

No! I can't handle this. I need time to think. I need time to work this out. I need time to make sure.

But still, even with all his uncertainties, he knew he had to be fair to Denise's memory and the love they'd once shared. Although Denise would always hold a special place in his heart, he loved Lorren now. Reaching up, he removed the medallion from around his neck. Being careful not to awaken Lorren, he opened the drawer to the nightstand next to the bed and placed it inside. Tomorrow he would take it home and put it in the small trunk where he kept his other cherished possessions.

Somehow he had to deal with the problem he was faced with—the fate he wasn't quite ready to accept.

He needed time.

CHAPTER 14

Lorren leaned against the kitchen counter and braced herself for the question she knew Mama Nora was about to ask. It would be the same question Rhonda and Rod had asked her at the beginning of the week when she'd stopped by their house to see the baby. It would be the same question Syneda had asked when she'd flown in for a brief visit a few days ago.

"Where's Justin?"

Misery welled up inside Lorren and she brushed away tears that clouded her eyes. She'd sworn she wouldn't cry. But here she was doing just that, partly because she didn't have an answer to the question. The truth of the matter was that she didn't know exactly where Justin was. For the past week, he'd been avoiding her like the plague.

It had started the day after the incident with Scott. That morning, instead of staying and having breakfast with her as he usually did, Justin had told her he needed to go back to his own place to do a few things before leaving for the office. And then, later that day, he'd called to say he had too much paperwork to complete for them to have dinner together.

That day had established a pattern that would be repeated for the rest of the week. She knew he would leave his house before she would awaken in the morning, and would return home from work late at night. He had completely stopped coming over to her place.

At first she had thought his withdrawal had something to do with the incident involving Scott, but now she wasn't certain of anything.

"Lorren? Child, what's the matter?"

Lorren sniffed and brushed her hand across her face again. "I'm sorry, Mama Nora. I didn't invite you to dinner to—"

She couldn't finish what she'd been about to say when she found herself enveloped in the older woman's warm embrace.

"Come on, baby, let's go in the living room and sit a spell. Dinner can wait. I want you to tell Mama what's wrong."

"But that's just it. I don't know what's wrong. All I know is that Justin is putting distance between us and I don't know why. He didn't give me a reason." She then told Mama Nora how Justin had begun avoiding her.

Lorren sniffed again when they reached the living room and, together, they sat on the sofa. "But then an explanation really isn't necessary, is it. He no longer wants me. There were never any promises of forever. I knew that and loved him anyway."

"So you do love him?"

Lorren looked stunned. "Of course I love him. He's the kindest, most tenderhearted, loving man I know. It's not his fault that I read more into our relationship than what was really there," she said through her tears. "I'm just not the woman he needs. I'm not the woman he's been waiting for."

"Have you thought that maybe there's another reason why he's avoiding you?"

Lorren frowned. "What other reason could there be?"

"The boy just might be scared, Lorren. Maybe you are the woman he's been waiting for, and he just can't deal with it."

Confusion showed in Lorren's face. "I don't understand."

Mama Nora hugged Lorren tenderly. "Have you ever heard the old saying—'Be careful what you ask for, you just might get it'?"

Lorren nodded.

"I think Justin has gotten just what he asked for, and now he can't deal with having it. But you shouldn't give up on him, baby. The boy will come around when he realizes how much he loves you."

He missed Lorren.

Justin had a hard time sleeping—waking often, tumbling about. Even after a week, he still missed the feminine body he'd grown used to sleeping next to.

Tired of tossing and turning, he rose from the bed and pulled on his jeans. In the living room he sat down on the sofa and reached for the small framed photograph Clayton had taken of him and Lorren after the cookout. Gazing at the picture, memories tugged at him.

They were memories of the night he had seen Lorren for the first time at Ms. Nora's party, the shocked look on her face when he'd told her he was her neighbor, and an even more shocked look when he had agreed to go along with her preaffair agreement.

He would never forget the sight of her standing in the doorway when he'd returned to her house the night of the car accident. And he would always have memories of the time they had spent together on the camping trip, the night she had run to him in the storm, and the first time they had made love.

Closing his eyes, he recaptured the look of impassioned surrender on her face whenever his body joined hers, and her expression of utter satisfaction when their bodies climaxed simultaneously.

A deep groan escaped his throat. He reopened his eyes and was filled with wonder at the enormity of all the things they had shared. His fingers gripped the frame until they hurt. Carefully, he relaxed his hand, but not his mind. It was still in turmoil. He replaced the photograph on the table.

Standing, he walked to the window and gazed out at the lake. Moonlight brought a magic aura to the water, and the tops of nearby trees stirred with the whisper of a warming breeze. His hand stroked the windowsill as he stood in deep thought.

He knew he'd hurt Lorren by pulling away without giving her a reason, but what excuse could he have given her? . . . *I know I love you and that you're my fate but I'm too much of a coward to face it . . .*

Justin heaved a heavy sigh. He was getting the time he'd felt was needed to work things out within himself. But it didn't keep him from missing her, needing her, loving her. Why was their separation causing him such misery? Such pain?

He walked back into his bedroom. Since sleep was out of the question, he decided to go swimming.

So close together but yet so far apart, Lorren thought, entering the house after returning from taking Mama Nora back home after dinner. Justin's car was parked in front of his place, which meant he was home.

Should she go over and confront him? No. He was the one who had put distance between them without giving her an explanation. If he wanted to talk, he knew where to find her.

She couldn't buy Mama Nora's theory that she was Justin's fate, and he was running scared. It just didn't make sense.

Locking the door behind her, she went into the bedroom to get ready for bed. After taking her shower, she returned to the bedroom and glanced around, wondering where she had put the envelope she planned to mail to her agent. She checked atop the dresser, then pulled open the drawer of the nightstand next to her bed.

"Oh." Lying on top of the envelope she'd been looking for was Justin's medallion.

She fought for control of her muddled emotions. What was Justin's medallion doing in her nightstand drawer? When had he taken it off and placed it there?

Lorren forced herself to remember the last time they had shared her bed. It had been the day Scott had shown up. All that afternoon and night they had made love.

A thrill raced through her as she tried to come to grips with what Justin's removing the medallion could possibly mean. Could Mama Nora be right? Had he actually realized he loved her, and that she had taken Denise's place in his life? Was that what he was fighting?

Lorren replaced the medallion in the drawer. She needed to talk to Syneda. Her friend had always been a good listener. Hurrying to the living room, she placed a phone call to New York.

A sleepy, feminine voice on the other end returned her hello.

"Syneda?"

"Lorren, is that you? What's wrong? Has something happened to Mama Nora?"

Lorren dropped down on the sofa. "No, Mama Nora is fine. She had dinner with me tonight."

There was a pause. "Then what's going on?"

Lorren felt an instant knotting of her stomach. As casually as she could, she asked, "Are you alone?"

Syneda chuckled. "Funny you should ask. I have Mario Van Peebles sleeping right beside me."

Lorren smiled. She knew of her friend's fascination with the handsome model turned actor. "Hmmm, Mario Van Peebles? You don't say?"

"I do say." Syneda giggled. "Shape up, sister-girl, of course I'm alone. What gives?"

Lorren leaned back onto the cushions and picked up a plump pillow. Her fingers traced the patterns of its floral design as she held it close to her. "Justin's still avoiding me."

"Then you need to confront him and find out why."

Lorren caught her lip between her teeth. "Mama Nora has formed her own opinion as to why he's staying away."

She then told Syneda about the conversation she'd had earlier with Mama Nora, and about finding the medallion in the nightstand.

"Ummm, in that case, Mama Nora just might be right, Lorren. Everyone who has ever seen you and Justin together knows how much he adores you, and you of all people know how much that medallion means to him. There has to be a reason why he took it off."

"I hope so."

"If you truly love him, Lorren, you'll fight for him."

"Fight whom? Or what?"

"Whoever or whatever is standing in the way of your having him. You can do it, Lorren, you're a fighter. Go for it."

Lorren drew in a long weary breath as she stood from her seat. She wished she were as convinced of her abilities as her friend. "But what if we're wrong? What if he doesn't really love me?"

"I believe with all my heart that Justin loves you Lorren, and if you'd take a minute to think about it, I know you believe it, too."

"I want to, Syneda."

"Then do it. Justin is nothing like Scott. He's the kind of man dreams are made of. But like all of us, he probably has a few demons to face. Just remember that being in love with someone means helping him through rough times."

"For someone who has never been in love, you sure seem to know a lot about it."

"I read a lot of those romance novels," Syneda teased. "Now can I get back to Super Mario?"

Lorren grinned. "I suppose so."

Syneda laughed. "Gee, thanks. And Lorren, good luck."

A bird chirping outside Lorren's bedroom window awakened her the next morning. Opening her eyes, she knew what had to be done if she wanted to spend the rest of her life with Justin. Deep down she'd known all along.

She would fight for him.

Not because Syneda thought she *should,* but because she believed she *could.* Never before had Lorren possessed so much confidence in herself. She was not the insecure woman who had come to Ennis three months ago. Nor was she the weak woman who'd allowed Scott to brainwash her into believing she was anything less than she was.

She was a woman with guts, strength, and determination. She was a woman who believed in herself, and come hell or high water, Justin would find out that she was not a woman a man could take lightly—or disregard.

He was about to discover that, whether he liked it or not, he had finally met his fate.

"Why do I get the feeling you aren't glad to see us?" Clayton asked his oldest brother as he and Dex sat at the kitchen table watching Justin prepare them breakfast.

"It's all in your mind, Clayton," Justin responded, as he continued scrambling the eggs.

"Is it? Then what's the reason for your funky mood?" Clayton grinned. "It can't be because Dex and I showed up this morning on your doorstep."

Justin eyed his brother crossly. "I'm not in a bad mood," he snapped. "And the two of you don't need an invitation to visit."

Clayton chuckled. "That's good to know. Oh, by the way, where's Lorren?"

Justin sat the plate of eggs in the center of the table. "Home, I'd imagine. Lorren and I aren't seeing each other anymore."

"Why?" Clayton and Dex asked simultaeously.

Justin took his seat at the table. "Why all the interest?"

Dex answered. "I guess we all thought you and Lorren were pretty tight."

"Well, you all thought wrong."

Clayton smiled and rubbed his chin. "So, in that case, you won't have a problem with me, ah, checking her out myself?"

Justin stared at his younger brother. "It won't work, Clayton. I know what you're trying to do, and it won't work."

"What am I trying to do?" Clayton asked innocently.

"You're trying to pull the same stunt on me that you pulled on Dex and Caitlin when they first met. You're going to pretend to be interested in Lorren to make me jealous. Forget it. That stunt may have worked for Dex and Caitlin back then, but it won't work for me."

"Why?" Clayton asked, running the risk of being told it was none of his business. He shrugged. It wouldn't be the first time, and he seriously doubted it would be the last.

"Because Lorren is my fate."

Clayton frowned. "Your fate? That woman you've claimed to have been waiting for all these years?"

Justin nodded.

Clayton shook his head. "Damn, that's scary. All this time I thought you were giving us a bunch of bull about that fate stuff." He took a huge swallow of orange juice.

"Hey, wait a minute," Clayton said moments later. "Then what's the problem if Lorren's your dream girl?"

"The problem is that I don't want to give my heart to anyone completely and totally, ever again. I don't know if I could handle it if I were to ever lose another person. The love I feel for Lorren is a hell of a lot stronger than what I felt for Denise. And you're right, it is scary."

"But think about what you're saying, Justin," Clayton implored. "If Lorren's the woman you've been holding out for all this time, you can't just turn your back on her."

"I'm not turning my back on her, Clayton. I'm just giving myself time to come to terms with it."

"And what's Lorren supposed to be doing while you're taking the time to think things through?"

"Look, Clayton, I really don't expect you to understand any of this. Until you've gone through the pain of loving someone and then losing her, you won't understand."

Clayton Madaris always enjoyed a good argument. And he had no qualms about engaging in one now, especially if it would make Justin see the mistake he was making.

"You aren't thinking straight, Justin. Hell, bro, you're not thinking at all. No man in his right mind breaks up with the woman he loves, especially if it's the woman he's been waiting ten years for." From the expression on Justin's face, Clayton knew Justin had heard his words, but was refusing to let them sink in.

Justin eyed Dex, who had been quiet all this time. "Aren't you going to contribute your two cents, Dex?"

Dex met Justin's glare. "No. We came here to check out this monstrosity of a house you bought, Justin. We aren't here to stick our noses where they don't belong. *Are we,* Clayton Jerome?" he asked his younger brother pointedly.

Clayton smiled. Any other man would have felt outnumbered, but he didn't. He really wasn't surprised by Dex's attitude. He was still hurting from a failed marrlage. lt was bad enough to have one brother suffering from heartache, Clayton thought. He sure didn't want to add Justin to the "pain and suffering" list with Dex, but it appeared that's just where he was headed. Clayton was glad his motto in life was—the only men that aren't fools are bachelors. He was doing the right thing playing the field. This falling in love stuff was far more trouble than it was worth.

"I guess not, Dexter Jordan," Clayton finally replied, grinning at the two brothers he loved and respected. "But I hope the two of you understand that the attorney in me can't resist giving a closing argument. And I promise to make it brief."

Clayton then gave Justin his full attention. "The way I see it, not accepting Lorren as your fate is the same thing as losing her. Either way, she's out of your life forever."

He spooned a hefty serving of eggs onto his plate before continuing. "For ten years you've been tempting fate, and it's time for you to pay up. You're a smart man, Justin, you'll come to your senses and work things out with Lorren when you've had enough. Hopefully, by then, it won't be too late."

CHAPTER 15

Three days later

Justin had had enough.

Last night had been another sleepless night. He wondered at what point he would stop thinking of Lorren and start sleeping again. When would the memories of the time they'd spent together stop slipping into his thoughts?

Wearily, he slumped back in his desk chair and closed his eyes. Was it possible for someone to escape the world as he knew it and create one of his own—a perfect world? A world free of injustices, disappointments, heartaches, and pain? A world where everything lasted forever?

His eyes flitted open. There was no such thing as a perfect world. The real world was filled with imperfections. Life held no guarantees. You had to take chances.

But if you chose to do so, you could live each day of your life to the fullest, appreciating the time you shared with that special person.

In the real world only the strong survived.

He straightened in his chair. Was he such a weakling that he was willing to let his fear of the unknown destroy him and what he could have with the woman he loved? The woman he'd been waiting for.

Justin inhaled sharply, finally able to confront his fears. Clayton had presented a good argument. Would not accepting Lorren as his fate make the pain easier to bear when he lost her?

No! He needed her like he needed the very air he breathed. He loved her too much to let his fear keep them apart.

Now that you've finally gotten your act together, there's something you need to think about. You love Lorren, but she may not love you. She's never said she did. In fact, she said she stopped believing in love and marriage a long time ago.

He stood quickly. No matter what his mind was saying, Lorren loved him. Over the past months, she'd said it in every way but with words. He'd felt it every time he held her in his arms and when his body joined with hers. No woman gave herself to a man the way she'd given herself to him without love. Lorren was a woman made for love, his love. She was the woman he'd dreamed of finding for ten lonely years.

Picking up a slip of paper from his desk, he quickly scanned it. Lorren had called earlier while he was with a patient. She'd left a message asking him to meet her at Taylor Oaks at four o'clock.

He smiled. He was giving up his fight with fate, accepting defeat graciously. And he would thank God every day for bringing Lorren into his life.

The builders doing the renovations had finished for the day and were leaving when Lorren arrived at Taylor Oaks. The carpenters had already arranged a portion of the downstairs, converting it into Justin's medical office. She'd been thrilled that he had agreed with all of her suggestions and decided not to cover the beautiful oak floors with carpeting.

Lorren paced the floor, nervously waiting for Justin to arrive. "Too late to get cold feet now," she muttered to herself. But she couldn't help the fluttering of her heart when she heard his car pull up.

Justin entered the house, closing the door behind him. He found Lorren in the living room, enclosed by crates and boxes and looking completely out of place in the chaotic surroundings.

She was dressed in a peach-colored suit made of soft silk and matching heels. The outfit was stylishly sculptured to fit the curves of her body. The straight skirt hit her knees, showing long, beautiful legs. He'd known the first time he'd seen her—the night of Ms. Nora's party—that her legs were perfect. That everything about Lorren was perfect. And he'd discovered just how right she was for him in every way.

A fancy peach-colored wide brim cuff hat adorned her head. She wore a diamond necklace and matching diamond stud earrings. She looked stunning, and the sight of her nearly took his breath away.

"You look sensational, Lorren. Where're you going?"

Lorren's pulse quickened upon seeing Justin. "To a wedding." Her nerves tingled. She had to be strong. Their future depended on it. "The reason I asked you to meet me is because there's a couple of things I'd like to say to you, Justin."

He gazed at her. "There's a few things I'd like to say to you, too, Lorren."

"I'll go first, if you don't mind."

"All right." Justin leaned against the wall. He watched Lorren pace the floor a few times before coming to a stop in front of him.

"I'd like to return this," she said, handing him the medallion. "You left it at my house the last time we were together."

She hesitated for a brief moment before continuing. "On the night we met, Justin, you said you believed in fate and that one day fate would bring this special woman to you. At the time, I thought you were living in a dream world, and I was realistic enough to know things just didn't happen that way. And I believe that deep down, you knew that, too. You just didn't want to admit it."

She paused for a moment. "I now realize that you were still hurting that night, just as I was. You just developed a different way of dealing with the pain, which was convincing yourself that one day you could love again, and that you *would* love again. You conveniently left your future in the hands of fate."

Lorren frowned up at him. "The only problem with that, Justin Madaris," she said, tapping the point of her well-manicured finger several times on his chest, "is your refusal to accept your fate when it came knocking on your door. You may have believed in love and marriage as you claimed, but you never had any intentions of involving yourself with either one again."

"Lorren," Justin broke in, taking her hand in his before she tapped a hole in his chest. "Lorren, I—"

"I'm not through saying what I have to say, so please don't interrupt."

She took her hand from his and looked deep into his eyes. "Well, I've got news for you. I love you, Justin, and I intend to spend the rest of my life loving you. I won't let you go. And if there's anything I've learned about myself in the last few months, it's that I go after what I want. And once it's mine, I'm not about to let go.

She poked his chest once more with her finger. "So take a good look, Justin. Take a real good look because, as far as I'm concerned, I'm your fate whether you like it or not."

Lorren sighed deeply. There. She'd said what was on her mind. Now for the really daring part. She pulled an envelope out of her purse.

"This is for you," she said, handing it to him.

Justin's brow lifted as he eyed the envelope she held out to him. His gaze returned to her, confusion revealed clearly in his features. "What is it?"

"Read it and see."

Justin remembered another time they'd shared a similar scenario. He opened the envelope and pulled out an elegantly designed card and read it.

His head shot up. He stared at her. One look at her face was enough to assure him this was not a joke this time.

He was invited to a wedding. Theirs.

Lorren awoke the next morning, cradled in Justin's arms. Last night he had carried her to thrilling heights during their lovemaking. He'd fulfilled her every dream and had lavished her with the most secure feeling of belonging and love she'd ever known. She smiled as she lay contented in his warmth, knowing she was truly and completely loved.

Justin roused himself from blissful slumber and shifted his gaze to Lorren. Her smile widened when their eyes met.

"Good morning, Mrs. Madaris." Raising his hands, he captured a mass of silky brown hair and brought it to his lips.

"Good morning," she replied in a voice barely above a whisper. "Did you sleep well?"

Justin's eyes turned a deep brown as he ran a hand along Lorren's body. "I didn't sleep at all. I've been taking little catnaps. I have this demanding wife who married me for my body."

Lorren leaned upward and placed a kiss on his jaw. "Oh, yeah? And what did you marry her for?"

His expression became serious. Lorren drew a steady breath when she saw the intense look of love in his eyes. "For all the love the two of us will share forever."

"Ummm, that sounds wonderful."

"It *is* wonderful," Justin replied, pulling her atop him. "It's undeniably wonderful."

She took his face in her hands. "I hope you don't feel you were forced into marrying me yesterday. You handled it admirably, though, and didn't seem at all upset to discover I had a wedding service all planned."

"I had no reason to be upset. I was elated." He grinned. "I'm just glad you timed the ceremony to at least let me shower and change first," he said, placing a kiss on her cheek.

She smiled. "Only because Syneda's plane was late."

He chuckled. "I'm a bit curious as to how you pulled it off so quickly?"

Lorren grinned. "Clayton was real eager to help. He said with you happily married off, he'd only have Dex to deal with on the 'pain and suffering' list." She lifted her brow. "I gather that's a 'male thing' and you understand what he means by that?"

At Justin's nod, she continued. "Well, anyway, Clayton basically took care of everything, especially pulling the strings for the quickie marriage license. He has friends in high places who were willing to make a few exceptions here and there."

Justin laughed, thinking those friends of Clayton's were probably all females. "A few exceptions? Honey, it seemed to me like quite a number of exceptions were made. But I don't care as long as everything's legal."

"Trust me. Everything's legal. We're very much married." She gazed at the sparkling diamond ring on her finger and the matching wedding band. Justin had surprised her with both at the ceremony. She'd been knocked off her feet when he'd told her he had stopped by a jewelry store on his way out to Taylor Oaks for their meeting. He had accepted her as his fate and had every intention of asking her to marry him once he got there. His other surprise was changing the name of the ranch from Taylor Oaks to Lorren Oaks. A new marker had been ordered already.

"Thanks to you, Lorren, I don't have any fears of my tomorrows," he said huskily. "In fact, I'm looking forward to them."

"And thanks to you, Justin, I'm cured of divorcitis."

In a smooth movement he shifted positions and rolled her beneath him. He smiled. "I told you from the beginning all you needed was a dose of tender, loving care."

Lorren's arms locked around his neck. She breathed in the tantalizing male scent of him. "You may have given me too much TLC, Dr. Madaris. I think I'm addicted. I hope you're prepared to feed my habit." She nuzzled her face against his neck. "I may as well warn you, I'm plagued with a new condition."

"Oh?" Justin asked, pulling her closer to him. "And what condition is that?"

Lorren gazed into the eyes of the man she loved. "Happyitis," she replied silkily. "Is there a cure?"

His eyes met hers. Love shone through in them. "No, sweetheart, there's no cure for happyitis," he answered, brushing his mouth across hers. "It's terminal."

EPILOGUE

A Year Later

"You're doing great. Just continue to breathe deeply, love."

Lorren bit her bottom lip and breathed as her husband instructed. She sighed with relief as the pain ebbed.

Justin wiped his brow. "I never thought the day would come when I'd be delivering my own child."

"You're doing a great job, Doc," Lorren assured him, just before another hard contraction hit her.

"Hold on, baby. It's almost over." Justin's hand pressed her stomach. "Give me one final big push."

Lorren pushed at the same time grinding agony tore into her. She felt the baby's head slip from her body and into its father's waiting hands. A split second later, the sound of a wailing baby rent the air.

"It's a girl, Lorren! We have a daughter and she's beautiful!"

Justin held their daughter and grinned proudly, tears misting his eyes as he placed their newborn child on Lorren's chest. He gazed down at his wife with a soft look of love on his features. "Now will you tell me the name you've decided on?"

Tears shone in Lorren's eyes as she held in her arms the product of her and Justin's love. "Yes." She smiled up at him. "Because I know our daughter will be her daddy's girl, it seems fitting to name her after you. Her first name will be Justina. And for her middle name," Lorren said softly, "I want to name her after a person I've never met, but one I've grown to admire and respect. She's a person I owe a lot to for having a hand in making you the man you are today. I'll always be grateful to her for giving you a reason to believe in love and marriage, and for you caring enough to make me believe in them again, too. Her middle name will be Denise. Our daughter's name will be Justina Denise Madaris."

Justin wiped the moisture from his eyes, tears of joy and happiness. "Thank you, baby, for proving there's always tomorrow."

He smiled warmly as he lovingly touched his wife's cheek and gazed down at the gift of love she had just given him. He also thought about Vincent, the little boy they had adopted not long after he and Lorren were married, who was now their son. Justin was overwhelmed by the intensity of emotion he felt for his wife, his daughter, and his son.

His gaze moved from his daughter and fastened intently on Lorren. She was his, to love and to cherish. And he would always do both. He knew his forever had begun the night he'd met his fate.

WHISPERED PROMISES

Acknowledgments

To the 1971 Class of William M. Raines High School, Jacksonville, Florida. Twenty-five years of excellence. And to Raines Vikings everywhere. Ichiban!

To Debbie Bowen, Rosemarie Baker, Mary Anne Coursuti, and Marge Smith (aka Elizabeth Sinclair) for their invaluable critiquing.

To Brenda Arnette Simmons for her helpful feedback on the finished product.

To my family and friends for their continued support.

To all the readers who fell in love with the Madaris brothers. This one is for you.

Love knows no limit to its endurance,
no end to its trust,
no fading of its hope; It can outlast anything. Love never fails.

—I Corinthians 13: 7–8

Taken from the *New Testament in Modern English*

CHAPTER 1

"Girl, take a look at the brother who just walked in."

"He's definitely a good-looking man."

"A real work of art."

"Handcrafted in all the right places."

"I wonder who's the lucky sister meeting him here."

"Wished it was me."

Feminine whispers rippled through the restaurant as a number of heads turned, and admiring eyes glanced toward the man entering the establishment.

Dex Madaris was oblivious to the attention he was getting. His gaze roamed the room before zeroing in on the dance floor. A few couples were dancing, locked in each other's embrace, slowly moving to the soft sound of the jazz music being played. No doubt they were caught up in their own private world, sharing whispered promises of love like he and Caitlin had once done.

Caitlin.

He took a deep breath. Everyone was entitled to at least one mistake in life, and Caitlin had been his.

"Welcome to Sisters. Will you be dining alone?"

A soft voice broke through Dex's reverie. He glanced down into a hostess's smiling face.

"I'm meeting my brother here. I believe he made reservations."

"What's the name?"

"Madaris."

The woman's smile widened. "So you're Clayton's brother?"

Dex raised a brow. "Yeah, one of them. I gather you know Clayton." It was more a statement than a question. He knew there weren't too many females in Houston who didn't know his younger brother, the confirmed bachelor.

A soft chuckle erupted from the woman's throat. "Oh yes, I know Clayton."

He slanted her a curious look, not failing to notice the light dancing in the depths of her dark eyes. He couldn't help wondering just how deep her acquaintance with his brother went.

"Clayton hasn't arrived yet, but if you'll follow me, I'll show you to your table."

She led the way to a table overlooking downtown Houston. Sitting down, Dex couldn't help noticing the number of females that were either dining alone or together in groups.

Sisters.

It suddenly dawned on him the connection between the name of the restaurant and the number of women that were there. Although quite a few men were in attendance, they were outnumbered by the women two to one. Evidently this restaurant was a meeting place where the sisters came to hang out and bond.

"Would you like to order now, or do you want to wait until Clayton gets here?"

"I'll wait."

"All right." A grin curved the woman's lips. "Clayton has told me a lot about you."

Dex gave her a dry look. "Really? And just what did he tell you?" Evidently Clayton hadn't told her just how much Dex enjoyed his privacy.

"He said you're a workaholic and somewhat of a loner."

Dex moved his shoulders in a noncommittal shrug. *A workaholic and a loner.* He knew in all honesty there was more than a little truth to Clayton's claim. Since his divorce from Caitlin four years ago, he had drowned himself in his work. He'd volunteered for longer hours, and had taken on projects other geologists with Remington Oil hadn't wanted to be bothered with. Since returning to the States from Australia, he had formed his own company, Madaris Explorations, almost a year ago. He worked day and night to assure its success, and to prevent his mind from idle wandering to the past. The memories were too painful, and work, he'd discovered, was the best antidote for a distracted mind.

The waitress had said something.

"What?" Dex shook himself out of his distraction and back into awareness.

"I said Clayton's here. He just walked in. I'll be back to take your order."

Dex glanced around and watched with amusement as Clayton stopped at a number of tables to greet the ladies. Dex shook his head as he reflected on just how different the three Madaris brothers were. Justin, his older brother by eighteen months, was considered the warm, loving, sensitive one. After suffering the pain of losing his first wife nearly twelve years ago, he was a happily married physician living near Dallas.

Dex knew that he himself was often viewed as a true-blue Scorpio man—deep, complex, intense and as serious as a heart attack. He was the Madaris not to cross.

Baby brother Clayton, two years younger, was a prominent attorney here in Houston and a womanizer of the third degree. Outgoing and friendly, the only time he was completely serious was in the courtroom. Unfortunately, he was also a notorious busy-body. He acted as if it was his God given right to stick his nose into his brothers' affairs whenever he felt it was necessary.

"Sorry I'm late," Clayton said sitting down. A mischievous grin played at the corners of his mouth. "So what do you think of this place? Have you ever seen so many gorgeous sisters under one roof before?"

The glint in Clayton's eyes confirmed Dex's suspicion that his brother was up to something. "No, can't say that I have."

Clayton leaned back in his chair. "Did you get the chance to check out any of the ladies?"

Dex decided to sidetrack Clayton's question. "And how was your day?"

"It was just another day. And don't change the subject. Did you get the chance to check out any of the ladies?"

"No."

"But you will."

Dex gave an exasperated sigh as he picked up his menu. "Maybe."

Clayton rolled his eyes. "Can't you get excited about anything other than rock formations and soil samples?"

Dexter Madaris stared long and hard at his brother. "Like I said, maybe."

Clayton snorted in frustration. "You're a hopeless case, Dex."

"Does that mean you're finally giving up on me?"

Clayton chuckled. "It would serve you right if I did. But I won't let you off that easily. When was the last time you were with a woman?"

Dex raised a brow. "*That* is none of your business."

A burst of laughter exploded from Clayton's throat. "Hey, man. Come on. You can level with me. I'm blood remember," he said when his laughter had subsided to a chuckle. "It's been that long, huh?"

Dex grinned and shook his head. "The last time for me, I'm sure, was probably not as recent as for you."

"Probably not," Clayton responded, scanning the menu. "So what's the problem?"

"There isn't one. You may find this hard to believe, but there're more important things in life than sex."

"Really?" Clayton exclaimed in a tone of total disbelief. "Name one."

Hearty laughter escaped from Dex's lips. It was a rare occurence. "Now *I* happen to think you're the one who's a hopeless case."

Clayton smiled. "If I am, you better believe I'm definitely a very satisfied one. How about letting me fix you up with Cocoa over there. She's just what you need."

Dex's gaze followed Clayton's to the lone diner sitting across the room. The attractive woman was smiling at him. The meaning behind her smile, and the look she was giving him were obvious. But he refused to acknowledge or accept her open invitation. "Thanks, but I'll pass."

Clayton looked intently at Dex. "When will you bury the past?"

"I have."

"I don't think so. You're still carrying a torch for Caitlin."

Dex gave Clayton a scathing look. "I hate to disappoint you, bro, but you're wrong."

"Am I?"

"Yes, you are. Caitlin's history."

"Then prove it. Let me introduce you to Cocoa."

"Clayton . . ." he began.

"You need a woman, Dex, and Cocoa is just the person for you. She'll make you think about something else besides work. Don't you know that all work and no play makes Dex a dull boy?"

Dex frowned. "Dull, huh? Then it's a good thing I won't be wasting Hot Chocolate's time."

"Her name's Cocoa, and she has a knack for undulling people."

"Yeah, I bet she does. Maybe some other—"

Dex suddenly stopped talking when his ears picked up the sound of the music being played. It was the song that had been playing the last time he and Caitlin had danced together. Even after four years, he could still remember the warm, soft feel of her in his arms; her body so close to his as he held her tight, not ever wanting to let go.

"Dex? Is something wrong?"

Dex took a deep calming breath before answering, forcing the memory to pass. "No, there's nothing wrong. Let's go ahead and order. I need to make a stop by the office tonight. There's some work I need to finish up."

Long hours and hard work helped him to forget the things he didn't want to remember.

200 miles away

Caitlin Madaris stood near the window gazing at the beauty of the skyscrapers that spanned the moonlit sky. In the distance below, specks of light could be seen reflecting from the blue waters of the San Antonio River.

A tremor shuddered through her as she desperately tried to appreciate the night's allure. It was useless. Her thoughts were miles and miles away. Drawing in a deep breath, she inhaled the disinfectant smell of the visitor's waiting room and swallowed the lump in her throat.

Fear and grief surged through her. Biting her lower lip, she clenched her hands together. She wanted to scream out her pain, yell out her anguish and tear the inner turmoil from within her. Unfortunately, she couldn't. She could not lose control. Not now, not ever. She had to be strong. There were no family members she could turn to. Both of her parents had been the only child of their parents. There weren't any grandparents, aunts, uncles or cousins. There was no one to share her anguish.

The sound of footsteps echoed softly on the tiled floor. "Caitlin?"

Bracing herself, she turned around. Fighting back tears, she faced Dr. Flores. "How is he?" she asked, her voice remarkably steady. She searched the face of the gray-haired man wearing a white lab coat. He was not only her father's physician, but an old family friend as well. Seeing his sullen expression, any hope she harbored vanished. Nevertheless, she willed herself not to panic.

Dr. Flores placed a gentle hand on her shoulder. "Your dad's condition is stable for now, and he seems to be resting comfortably. Although his medication has worn off and he's in pain, he refuses to swallow another dose until he speaks to you."

A terrifying weakness paralyzed Caitlin. Her father had always been a healthy man, except for a light heart attack a few years back from which he'd fully recovered.

"You can only visit him for a few minutes, Caitlin. Then I need to sedate him so he can rest comfortably through the night."

A sense of despair washed over her. Her dark eyes burned with fatigue brought on by a sleepless night. "So nothing has changed." It was more a statement than a question.

Dr. Flores hesitated before answering. "As I explained over the phone this morning, we diagnosed his condition over eight months ago. Since the tumor was discovered, its malignancy has spread very rapidly. Chemotherapy would have been useless. I advised him to tell you about his condition but he refused. He didn't want you to know he had prostate cancer until it became absolutely necessary."

Caitlin nodded, then asked the dreaded question she had to have answered. "How much longer?"

Louis Flores shrugged. "A matter of days, maybe a week. It's hard to say at this point. There's really nothing we can do for him, other than making him comfortable. He doesn't want you to see him this way, but has no choice."

Dr. Flores paused and then went on. "And another thing, Caitlin. Don't question anything he tells you. The reason he won't let me sedate him just yet is because he wants to be completely coherent when he talks to you. Don't think what he's saying is prompted by the medication."

Caitlin's instincts sensed a warning in Dr. Flores' words; a warning that went beyond mere medical advice. She lifted her eyes to his face, letting her gaze run over the distraught features he arduously shielded behind a cloak of professionalism. "Dr. Flores—"

"No, Caitlin. Whatever Halston has to say he'll tell you himself." An expression of tenderness softened his face. "Let's not keep him waiting."

A short walk down the hall brought Caitlin to her father's room. Inhaling a deep breath, she walked over to the bed where he lay with his eyes closed. Taking a seat in the recliner next to the bed, she studied her father's pallid face. As if sensing her presence, a weak smile touched his mouth. His eyes opened slowly.

His gaunt appearance looked nothing like the robust man she'd always known and loved. Sickness had aged him beyond his fifty-eight years, and he'd lost an enormous amount of weight. Caitlin had to bite back a strong urge to cry out in agony. Instead, she remembered Dr. Flores' words and took her father's hand in hers. Immediately, she sensed his loss of strength. Her heart ached.

Halston Parker forced out a ragged breath. "Caitlin?"

"Yeah, Dad. It's me. Don't try to talk now. I'm here, and I'm not going anyplace."

He closed his eyes, then reopened them. A hint of a smile barely touched his mouth. He stared at her. Caitlin wondered if he saw her or was visualizing her mother whom she favored, his beloved Catherine, who'd died eight years ago. He had taken her mother's sudden death from a ruptured appendix extremely hard, never fully recovering from it. It had been during that time their already close relationship had become even closer. He had devoted all of his time and attention to his only child. It was as if Caitlin had become the only thing that had kept him going in a world filled with extreme loneliness.

Caitlin sighed, remembering how six months ago, he had encouraged her to accept a job offer that required a move to Fort Worth. He'd known about his condition and had sent her away to spare her the anguish of seeing him suffer. If only she had known . . .

She reached out, and with an unsteady hand, wiped beads of moisture from his forehead.

"Dex."

Caitlin's hand stopped moving, hanging in midair. Her eyes widened. Surely her mind and ears were playing tricks on her. Her father couldn't have spoken the name of the only man she'd ever known him to despise . . . and the only man she'd ever loved. "Dad?"

Halston Parker stared at his daughter through glazed, dark eyes. "Call Dex. I need to see him."

His words, although wrested from his lips, sounded clear and precise. Silently, Caitlin stared at him. She moistened her dry lips remembering Dr. Flores' words, ". . . *don't question anything he tells you . . .*" but with her father's strange request, she couldn't help asking, "Why would you want to see Dex, Dad?"

Pain clouded Halston Parker's eyes, making them appear more deepset. His craggy jaw was covered lightly with a day's growth of gray whiskers. His once rugged features now looked muted and frail. New lines, a result of some emotion Caitlin couldn't name, creased across his cheekbones. His nostrils flared slightly from labored breathing. "Tell him to come before . . ."

His words drifted off as his eyes closed slightly. He forced them back open to gaze at her. "Call Dex, Caitlin," he pleaded raggedly in a voice so low Caitlin had to lean over to catch the words. He closed his eyes again.

Caitlin forced back a rush of tears. Why would her father want to see her ex-husband? She'd decided four years ago Dex would no longer be a part of her life. Since that time she'd managed to move ahead and not dwell on the love she'd given up. She couldn't say she hadn't looked back, because a few times she had. No, she confessed, more than a few times. A familiar twist of pain unfolded within her. It had been a decision she'd made and stood by.

Seeing that her father had lapsed into a deep sleep, she rose from the chair and went to the window. Could she do what her father had asked? Could she handle seeing Dex again? Would he come even at a dying man's request?

She took a deep breath as numerous questions flowed through her mind. No matter what her father's reasons were for wanting to see Dex, no matter what the chances were of her wounds being reopened, she would do as her father had asked. Telling Dex her father wanted to see him didn't necessarily mean he would come. Why should he?

Walking out of the room, she went to use the pay phone in the lobby. She wasn't even sure if Dex was in the States. The last she'd heard, he was still out of the country. Minutes later, she dialed the residential telephone number in Houston that had been given to her by the operator.

After three rings, she found herself listening to Dex's answering machine. The sound of his deep masculine voice nearly made her jump. It had been four years since she'd heard it. A sensation she thought had dissolved long ago crept down her spine. Even over the phone lines Dexter Madaris had the ability to make her knees weaken, her pulse escalate and her breathing thicken.

She quickly hung up the phone, deciding not to leave a message. She would try contacting him again later. A sigh whispered through Caitlin's lips. Time hadn't totally destroyed the effect Dex had on her. This unexpected revelation struck her suddenly. After four years, she still couldn't force the strong-jawed, dark handsome face with its sensuous voice out of her mind . . . and completely out of her heart.

But she had to. She couldn't afford to go back and dwell on the past. But still, she couldn't stop her mind from drifting back to that beautiful day in late May four years ago, when she and Dex had met . . .

Caitlin Parker had a hard time believing her eyes when her gaze settled on the handsome man who'd just entered the cafe. He moved with the grace of a black leopard, reflected in the powerful movement of his shoulders and muscles. There was a smooth leanness in his tall form, reminding her of a spirited athlete combined with a laid-back silent manner.

His jeans molded to his firm thighs and long legs, while his white shirt stretched tautly across his broad chest. When he removed the Stetson from his head, she saw that his naturally wavy black hair was cut short in what she considered a blatantly masculine style. His nut brown features, bluntly strong and sensuous, seemed carved into his firm jawline, high forehead, and straight nose. However, it was his eyes that took Caitlin's breath away. There was something very cryptic about the charcoal gray eyes scanning the room before coming to rest on her. After mumbling a few words to the waiter, he moved in her direction.

Caitlin was caught up with the handsome man's approach to her table. Her grip tightened nervously around the glass of ice tea she held, attempting to control the trembling in her body, beginning with her fingers. It didn't work. All attempts at control failed when he stood before her.

"Caitlin Parker?"

The sound of his deep voice nearly undid Caitlin, causing her to nod in mute silence.

"I'm Dexter Madaris. My uncle, Jake Madaris, had planned to meet with you but, unfortunately, he had to fly to Wyoming unexpectedly on business. He won't be back for several days. As a favor, he asked me to come meet with you to discuss the summer job you've applied for. May I sit down?"

Caitlin could only stare, hypnotized by the man standing before her. He had to be without a doubt, the sexiest man she'd ever seen.

"Miss Parker?"

At that moment, Caitlin realized she hadn't answered his request.

Heat flushed her face and her lips trembled slightly with embarrassment. "I'm sorry, Mr. Madaris. Yes, please have a seat." She watched as he settled his lithe frame into the chair.

"How old are you, Miss Parker?"

"What?" Caitlin whispered, caught off-guard by the question. His voice echoed a Texas drawl that made her breath lodge in her throat. Masculine and distinct, it conveyed a strength and an endurance all its own. Together, his eyes and voice were a deadly combination.

Dex smiled in a way Caitlin thought enhanced the fullness of his sensual mouth. "I asked how old you are?"

Caitlin cleared her throat. "I'm twenty-one. Why?"

"Because you look rather young for the job. By the way, you can call me Dex. Do you mind if I call you Caitlin?"

"Not at all." She nervously lifted the glass of tea to her lips and asked, "And how old are you, Dex?"

He shot her a surprised glance before answering. "I'm thirty-two."

The waiter came and took Dex's order. Caitlin used the interruption to contain her breathing. Dex's presence had her heart beating at an alarming rate.

"What about you, Caitlin? Can I order something for you?"

"No, thanks, I'm fine."

Dex nodded then dismissed the waiter. "I understand you graduated from college a few days ago. Now that school's over, why do you want to spend your summer working when you could be celebrating by heading for the beach, or the border like most of the other graduates?" he asked.

Caitlin looked away then returned her gaze to his. "In the fall I'm going back to college to begin a Masters program. I really don't consider what I'll be doing this summer as work. I'll get to do something I enjoy."

"Working with computers?"

"Yes," Caitlin replied, tensing under Dex's direct stare. Somehow she managed a smile. "Besides, I've always wanted to spend some time on a real ranch." She didn't add that she'd often heard about the handsome cowboys and bronco-busters that worked there. If he was a sample of what the place had to offer, then what she'd heard had been true.

"Oh?" Dex laughed softly. "And how does your family feel about that?"

"My mother died a few years ago, so it's just me and my father. Although he's not thrilled with the idea, I convinced him it would benefit me in the long run to gain a degree of experience in my field of study. But to pacify him, I've agreed to return to San Antonio for a while before going back to school in September."

"San Antonio? Is that your home?"

"Yes."

He studied her intently. "Do you always give in so easily?"

Caitlin lifted her brow, unsure whether he was referring to the incident with her father or something else. "No. I'll stand my ground when I believe what I'm doing is right."

The waiter interrupted them when he served Dex his drink. Caitlin watched as he took a sip and thought it was the most sensuous gesture she'd ever seen. She tried to submerge the heat flaring in her stomach as she watched the way his mouth touched the rim of the glass of wine, tipping it up to his lips, savoring the taste as it slowly slipped down his throat. She felt a strange ache in her limbs when he ran his tongue over his lips in appreciation of the wine's fruity taste.

"Tell me a little more about your background, Caitlin."

Caitlin tore her gaze from his mouth and directed her attention to the scented candle burning in the middle of their table. She cleared her throat. "I graduated from the University of Texas," she said, "with a degree in Computer Technology and a minor in Accounting. For the past three years, I've been part of the work study program on campus, working in the computer department."

Dex swirled the liquid around in his glass. A faint sparkle lit his eyes when he spoke. "Uncle Jake's business is livestock. He raises cattle and horses and then sells them to farms all over the country. His reputation as an excellent stock breeder has spread, and over the years his business has grown tremendously."

"I think everyone in Texas has heard of the Whispering Pines Ranch and Jacob Madaris," Caitlin said.

Dex took another sip of wine. "Fortunately, he wants to upgrade his billing system. The system he's using now is really outdated. What he wants you to do is to analyze his present setup and come up with some suggestions on computerizing his business accounts."

Caitlin nodded. "Smart idea."

"I agree, however, I may as well warn you that the person who does the bookkeeping, Delane Ormand, has been there for ages and detests change. According to Uncle Jake, she doesn't feel comfortable working on a computer, since she doesn't know anything about them. Think you can handle setting up the program and selling the idea of computerized accounting to Delane?"

There was a determined gleam in Caitlin's eyes. "Yes," she said with easy confidence. "Once Ms. Ormand realizes how much easier her work will become with a computer, she'll love it." Caitlin paused for a moment before asking. "Do you work at the ranch, too, Dex?"

He smiled. "No, I don't work there, although I used to during summers and vacations while in high school and college. Right now, I'm just visiting my uncle. I'm a geologist in oil exploration. My company has transferred me to Australia for two years. I'll be at the ranch for the next three weeks for some rest and relaxation before leaving the country."

Caitlin hoped her face didn't show her disappointment. She swallowed against the fullness in her throat. The intensity of Dex Madaris' eyes stirred her insides. He had a way about him she was sure attracted numerous women. He was dangerous, not in the normal sense, but instead dangerous to one's common sense.

She didn't doubt for a minute he had the ability to make the most sensible woman throw all caution to the wind for an opportunity to get to know him intimately. Her cheeks heated from her candid thoughts. She twisted slightly in her chair.

"Is there something wrong, Caitlin?"

Her gaze flew to Dex's face. She felt her body stir under his intense scrutiny. She suddenly realized she was dealing with a man with the ability to strip away any emotional barriers with one smoldering look.

"Caitlin?"

She inhaled deeply and forced herself to shake her head. "No, nothing's wrong."

Dex took another sip of his wine. "The pay is twelve dollars an hour and includes your room and board. Uncle Jake figures the project shouldn't take any longer than four to six weeks. Are you absolutely sure you want the job?"

"Yes, I'm positive."

"Then it's yours."

Joy swept through Caitlin. "Thank you."

A widened smile touched Dex's lips. "How soon can you begin?" . . .

"Caitlin?"

The soft, gentle voice brought Caitlin's thoughts back to the present. She immediately recognized the person standing before her. "Reverend Timmons. I'm so glad you came . . ."

By the time Dex crawled into bed that night, he was bone tired. Before returning home from the restaurant, he'd stopped by his office, and he and his project foreman and good friend, Trevor Grant, had worked well past midnight going over an important job proposal.

The ringing of the telephone interrupted what he'd hoped to be the beginning of a good night's sleep. Reaching over to the night stand, he picked up the phone.

"Yeah?" When Dex didn't get a response but heard the faint sound of breathing on the other end, he became annoyed. "Who the hell is this? State your business or hang up."

"Dex?"

Dex frowned, trying to recognize the voice. "Who wants to know?"

There was a pause. "It's Caitlin, Dex."

The words were a hard blow to Dex's firm stomach. He rubbed the bridge of his nose finding himself drenched with first disbelief, then a surge of renewed anger. There was a tightness in his throat. "What do you want, Caitlin?" His words were clipped and devoid of any emotion except one. Bitterness.

"I'm calling for my dad. He's very ill and wants to see you. I don't know why, but he's asking for you. Please come, Dex."

Dex's jaw stiffened and his eyes hardened like ice. The urge to tell her father where he could go—in not so nice words—was on the tip of his tongue, but he hesitated. He wasn't that heartless. Besides, Caitlin sounded scared, and he heard the pain and anguish in her voice.

"What's wrong with your old man this time, Caitlin? The last time I saw him he wasn't doing so hot either. If my memory serves me correctly, it was the news of our sudden marriage that sent him to the hospital with a heart attack. Have you decided to marry again and Daddy Dearest can't handle it?"

"Dex, please. Don't. My—my father is dying of cancer and wants to see you."

"I'm sorry to hear that. However, he and I aren't the best of friends. What's this all about?"

"I don't know. But he wants to see you. Please come see him. P-please." Her tearful plea came through the phone lines.

A tightness squeezed Dex's chest and instead of his anger intensifying, he found his heart losing some of its hardness with her plea. He loathed himself for allowing her to get next to him after all this time—after she had turned her back on him and his love. But something was happening to him he hadn't counted on, something he didn't understand. Even after four years of hurt, she could still arouse a degree of protectiveness in him.

A natural instinct to protect her from any type of pain kept his bitterness in check. Her words penetrated his mind. Her father was dying? Then he could just imagine the depth of her agony. He, of all people, knew just how much the old man meant to her. He hesitated briefly before answering. "Where is he?"

"Baptist Memorial Hospital, the eighth floor."

Dex took a deep breath. "I'm on my way."

After hanging up the phone he let his head fall back against the pillow. He stared at the ceiling. Could he handle seeing Caitlin again? He didn't love her anymore, but the pain she'd caused him was like a wound that wouldn't heal. Her decision to end their marriage before giving it a chance was an act he could never forgive her for.

His heart felt like it was ready to explode in his chest. In a short space of time, she had become his life, his very reason for existing.

He should never have let it get to that point. After all, he had seen first-hand what falling head-over-heels in love with a woman could do.

His best friend, Greg, had taken his own life over a woman while they were in college at Morehouse. Dex had vowed never to become a victim of love to that extreme. And he had kept his vow—until he had met Caitlin.

His mind reflected on their first meeting. He'd fallen in love with her the first time he'd seen her that day in the restaurant. Her beauty had nearly taken his breath away. She had eyes the color of dark coffee. Her face, burnished bronze in color, had sharp high cheekbones, a perfectly shaped mouth and a flawlessly aligned nose. Silken strands of jet black hair had fallen in soft curls around her shoulders. Each attribute had added radiance to her warm unblemished features.

The timing had been awful. He was to leave the country within three weeks. Besides, she was young—eleven years his junior. But those things hadn't kept him from wanting her, from loving her.

In the beginning, for the first couple of days after she'd come to work at his uncle Jake's ranch, he'd kept his distance. Then Clayton had arrived and had immediately set his sights on their uncle's newest employee.

Convincing himself he was saving Caitlin from the clutches of his womanizing younger brother, Dex began pursuing her himself. It was only later that he'd discovered Clayton had somehow picked up on his intense but unacknowledged attraction for Caitlin, and had played devil's advocate, propelling Dex into action. What followed had been a whirlwind romance between him and Caitlin.

After spending time with her, he had felt that although she was eleven years younger than him, she was a young woman who knew her mind. She had acted more mature than her twenty-one years. The more time he had spent with her, the more he became sure that he wanted her as the woman in his life—forever. He couldn't handle the thought of going to Australia and leaving her behind. There were a number of good universities in Australia where she could obtain the additional education she wanted to pursue. When he had asked her to marry him, she had readily accepted.

Within two weeks, they were married in a rushed ceremony at Whispering Pines ranch with just his uncle and Clayton present. It was only when they were on their way to meet each other's families, that he had an opportunity to dwell on her reluctance to notify her father about their marriage.

Although surprised by his unexpected marriage, his parents and siblings accepted Caitlin into the family with open arms. But nothing, Dex thought, could have prepared him for the horrible scene they encountered upon arriving at Caitlin's home and announcing their marriage and her plans to accompany him to Australia.

Halston Parker had gone into a rage, which subsequently doubled him over clutching his chest. After he was rushed to the hospital, Caitlin had been told he'd suffered a mild heart attack.

She had been upset and besieged with guilt. Dex had spent his last day in the States pacing the waiting room of the hospital with her. He'd somehow managed to convince her to come back to the hotel with him. Once there, she had found comfort in his arms. He'd made love to her to erase her fears. The next morning, he had felt her withdraw from him, and wondered if their newfound love could withstand the external pressures.

Before catching a cab for the airport, he had literally begged her to join him in Australia as soon as her father recovered. She had promised him she would.

As the weeks passed and she'd begun avoiding his nightly phone calls, he'd made arrangements to return to the States on an emergency leave. The day he was to depart, he received the divorce papers and Caitlin's wedding ring. She wanted out of their marriage.

According to the brief letter she'd enclosed with her ring, she claimed she loved him, but her father needed her more and she couldn't leave him. She thought it best they end their marriage.

The impact of her decision had hurt deeply. Deeper than any pain was supposed to hurt. He had always known and understood the internal war he had fought since Greg's suicide. He had waged such a fierce battle against ever falling in love that when it happened, he had been totally consumed by it. Caitlin had been everything he had ever wanted and desired in a woman. And when he had fallen for her, he'd fallen hard. No one, and that included his family, had understood the depth of his bitterness after his breakup with Caitlin. Considering her age when they had married, and the brief period of time they had known each other, Caitlin's actions, as far as his family were concerned, had not been surprising.

Unfortunately, he did not share their reasoning. The way he saw it, Caitlin had said her vows and had made promises, and neither was meant to be broken.

Sighing deeply, Dex reached for the phone and began dialing.
"Hello?"
"Clayton, I'm leaving tonight for San Antonio."

CHAPTER 2

The antiseptic smell of the sterilized facility stung Dex's nostrils the minute he walked into the hospital's lobby. Stepping into the elevator, he punched the button for the eighth floor.

It seemed like an eternity before the elevator door finally opened. Stepping out, he dismissed the interested looks he received from a couple of nurses and walked over to the nurses' station. A middle-aged woman stood behind the counter with her head bowed, reading a patient's chart.

"Excuse me. I'm here to see Halston Parker."

The woman lifted her head and smiled at him kindly. "Are you a member of the family?"

The question was a common one to ask, but Dex couldn't help but flinch. "No," he answered curtly. "I'm not, but I was asked to come here by Caitlin Parker."

The woman gave him a bemused glance although her smile continued to be friendly. She glanced down at the chart she pulled from a nearby rack. "Caitlin Parker?" she questioned.

"Yeah. Caitlin Parker. Halston Parker's daughter," he replied glancing around the nurses' station.

"You must mean Caitlin Madaris."

Dex's head whipped around sharply. "What did you say?"

"I said Mr. Parker's daughter is Caitlin Madaris."

"I'll take care of this, Diane," a deep voice said behind Dex.

Dex turned around and came face to face with a man he remembered as being Halston Parker's physician.

"Mr. Madaris, welcome back to San Antonio."

Dex nodded tiredly and rubbed his temples. The nurse had referred to Caitlin as Caitlin Madaris? Why was she still using her married name? His name? Why had she kept the name when she'd rejected the man who'd given it to her? He stared into the doctor's face. It had aged considerably in the last four years. "This isn't a pleasure trip, Doctor," he said, shaking the hand the man offered.

Dr. Flores nodded his head. "You're right, it's not. Did you have any problems getting here?" he asked politely.

"No. I caught a cab from the airport."

The older man lifted a brow. "Your luggage?"

"I didn't bring anything but what you see here," Dex said, indicating the overnight bag he carried. "I don't plan on staying long," he added in a clear firm voice.

Dr. Flores looked at him for a moment. "Oh, I see. Did you know that Caitlin isn't living here in San Antonio, Mr. Madaris? She moved to Ft. Worth six months ago."

Dex looked at the older man in complete surprise. "No, I didn't know that." Heat stained his cheeks and his eyes narrowed "But then I haven't had a reason to keep up with my ex-wife over the past four years. Where she lives is no concern of mine."

The doctor appeared slightly flushed. "I'm sorry, my mistake."

Dex nodded. "No sweat. We all make them." He glanced around. "Where's Caitlin?"

"She's resting. I gave her something to relax her. It's been a very trying time for her. I'll go get her now."

Dex grabbed the man's arm when he turned to walk off. "Don't bother. Whatever Halston Parker has to say, he can say to me alone. There's no need to involve Caitlin."

The older man shook his head. "Halston wants to speak with both you and Caitlin."

Dex studied the doctor for a moment. "Do you have any idea what this is about?"

"Even if I did, I'm not at liberty to say, Mr. Madaris. If you would like to wait in a private waiting room, I'll get Caitlin."

In the waiting room, Dex stood at the window looking down at the smaller office buildings below. His body tense, his senses alert, he knew the exact moment Caitlin quietly entered the room. He turned slowly to face her.

Their eyes connected immediately. Dex dragged his gaze over her. Even with tired lines etched around her eyes, her hair in disarray and her dress slightly wrinkled, as far as he was concerned, she still looked utterly beautiful. His heart felt like it was about to explode in his chest. How could he find her desirable after the hell she'd put him through? He resented the fact that his strong attraction to her was still there. His reaction to her sparked his temper.

"Hello, Dex."

"Caitlin," he acknowledged curtly. "I'd like to see your father as soon as possible, so he can say whatever it is he wants to get off his chest."

"We can go see if Dad's awake now. If you don't mind coming with me," she said, opening the door.

"You go ahead. I'll catch up in a minute." He needed time alone to regain his composure. Seeing Caitlin again had brought a greater reaction than he had expected. Unwanted memories had coursed through him.

Caitlin nodded and closed the door behind her. A shiver passed through her body. The memories she had carried of her ex-husband were nothing in comparison to the masculine, virile reality she'd just seen. Strength and power emanated from him. He was still the handsome Texan she'd fallen in love with four years ago. His features were rugged and strong, and his nut-brown skin had darkened to a coppery-brown from hours undoubtedly spent in the sun. Dexter Madaris was still the most attractive man she'd ever seen. A sudden feeling of dread washed over her when she remembered something else about him. He was a man who didn't forgive easily. She'd discovered that the hard way when he had not responded to her letter.

Her hands were numbed with cold when she found Dr. Flores at the nurses' station. They were as cold as Dex's attitude had been toward her. "Dex wants to see Dad now, Dr. Flores. Is he awake?"

The older man searched her eyes. "Are you all right, dear?"

She swallowed hard before forcing a smile. "Yes. I'm fine. Can we see my father now?"

"Yes."

They turned upon hearing footsteps approaching on the tile floor. Dex came to stand before them. "I'm ready."

Dr. Flores gently placed his hand on Caitlin's arm to restrain her when she turned to leave. "Please keep in mind at all times how much your father loves you, Caitlin." He then walked off.

Caitlin frowned, pondering the doctor's words. Did he know why her father had summoned Dex?

"Let's get this over with." Dex's biting words intruded into her thoughts.

"This way," she said, leading the way to her father's room. She wished she could ignore Dex's obvious signs of anger, but he was definitely a brother with an attitude. When they reached her father's room, without a single word, Dex pushed the door open and walked into the room past her.

Dex sucked in his breath. Nothing could have prepared him for the sight of the man he saw lying in the hospital bed. The shriveled up man caused a sick feeling to engulf him. Halston Parker was almost unrecognizable.

He stood back and watched Caitlin square her shoulders and approach the bed. Her face didn't reveal a flicker of emotion, but her eyes did. The pained look in them was unmistakable. Losing her father was affecting her more deeply than she was letting on. He knew she would have done anything to prevent that kind of loss. He continued to watch as she drew her hand across the bed, smoothing the wrinkles in the hospital blanket. She bent over the frail body and whispered. "Dad. Dex's here."

Dex was suddenly filled with compassion when he could no longer retain his distant attitude. He was again confused by the betrayal of emotions he had held in check for so long. As if by some connective power Caitlin's pain became his. He was suddenly struck with a return of the urge to shield her from what she was going through. More than anything she needed support. Support from family, friends or someone who cared, but right now she was all alone. All alone except for an ex-husband, who wished more than anything he was someplace else.

With a heavy sigh, he leaned against the back of the closed hospital door and continued to stare at her. Could he somehow find it within himself to give her the support she desperately needed after what she'd done to him? Could he put all his bitterness aside and reach out and give her someone to lean on? Forgiveness wasn't one of his strong points. His family had told him countless times that he could hold a grudge longer than anyone they knew.

"Dad, did you hear me?"

Dex noticed the head of the frail body in the bed nod. Caitlin looked up at Dex, her dark eyes misty with tears, assessed his expression. Coming forward, he nodded his understanding. Looking down into the deathlike face, he watched as Halston Parker's eyes slowly fluttered open. For a brief second he stared up at the both of them, seemingly in tremendous pain—both physically and mentally.

"Caitlin. Dex. You're here," Halston Parker whispered hoarsely, a weak smile touching his lips. "I have the two of you back together again."

Caitlin could feel a sudden sharp chill in the air from her father's words. "Dad, Dex can't stay long," she rushed in. "You wanted to see him, and he's here."

Halston Parker's eyes shut for a moment. He reopened them and stared intently at Dex. "Legally, Caitlin's still your wife."

Caitlin stared at the deathlike face lying against the white pillow. "I don't understand what you're saying, Dad. Dex and I aren't married. Don't you remember? I filed for a divorce a month after he left for Australia. The papers were sent to him and he signed them."

Halston Parker nodded, oblivious to the tension in the room. "Yeah, he signed them and your attorney got them back a couple of months later. But I told him you'd changed your mind about the divorce and not to file them with the courts. I've had them in my possession ever since. They're in a trunk in the attic."

Caitlin's glance flew to Dex with her father's revelation. His chin twitched. His eyes darkened. He gazed speechlessly down at her father. She could feel the anger radiating deep from within him. When he spoke, his voice, although low, conveyed blatantly all the anger he felt.

"You had no right to do that, Mr. Parker. You had no right to interfere."

Halston Parker's breathing became labored. "I did what I thought was best, under the circumstances."

"That doesn't make sense. You didn't approve of my marriage to your daughter. Why would you stop our divorce from becoming final?"

The older man tried responding, but couldn't. It was a brief moment later before he found the strength to speak. "In the beginning, I was only thinking of myself. I didn't want to lose her. I didn't want to be left all alone. Please try and understand, son, she was all I had. I couldn't let you take her away. I know I was wrong, and I've asked you here for your forgiveness and to set matters straight. I know you could have taken advantage of Caitlin four years ago, but you didn't. You did the honorable thing and married her. But at the time, I couldn't accept the difference in your ages. I thought she was too young for marriage, especially to you. I didn't want to see her get hurt."

A number of questions flooded Dex's mind. He still didn't understand why Halston Parker had stopped their divorce. He watched the older man try to raise his hand up to him. Dex knew the attempt was draining on him, so he took the frail hand in his.

"Regardless of whether the divorce is valid or not, it was Caitlin's decision to end our marriage, Mr. Parker, not yours. You didn't do anything to me personally so there's no reason for you to ask my forgiveness," Dex replied harshly.

Halston Parker shook his head weakly. "I made her choose between the two of us, and I never should have done that. I used her one weakness, her love for me, to turn her away from you. Don't you understand? I pressured her."

"But the decision was still hers, not yours," Dex stated sharply. A part of him hardened at the man's words. What was Caitlin's father driving at? Why was he attempting to find excuses for the decision his daughter had made? As far as Dex was concerned, there was no acceptable excuse.

Halston Parker removed his hand from Dex's and offered it to Caitlin. She tenderly took his outstretched hand. She had been standing quietly by Dex's side as tears streamed down her face. "Will you forgive me for being so selfish and for thinking more of my happiness than of yours, Caitlin?"

Caitlin's breath caught her in throat making speech difficult. "Dex's right, Daddy. It was my decision so don't ask either of us to forgive you. I love you very much."

"And I love you, baby-girl. I don't want to leave you alone," he said, his voice taut and thick with emotions and worried concern.

"I won't be alone, Dad. I have Jordan."

A lone tear fell from the older man's eye as he slowly nodded. "You've been the joy of my life. Every man should have a daughter such as you to love. No man should be cheated out of that." He turned his attention back to Dex. "Promise me you'll take care of Caitlin. Please take care of my baby for me. Promise me."

Dex had not been prepared for this request and his gaze quickly flew to Caitlin. She refused to meet his eyes, and he couldn't help but see the way she was clenching her teeth to keep from crying out. Her body began trembling as silent tears continued to stream down her face. This was an enormous ordeal for her. How would she feel if he were to make a promise like that to her father? And who on earth was Jordan? Was he a new man in her life? If so, why was her father asking him to come back into her life when it appeared she was involved with someone else? Was Halston Parker trying to manipulate his daughter's life even now with one foot in the grave?

Dex gazed down in the older man's face. Glassy eyes watched him, waiting for his answer. He didn't have to be a doctor to know the man's condition was going downhill and fast. He was fighting just to keep his eyes open. The man lay facing imminent death, and more than anything he needed the assurance that his daughter would be taken care of.

Without any further thought Dex answered, "I promise to take care of Caitlin and to do what I can for her, Mr. Parker."

Halston Parker released a long ragged breath, accepting Dex's promise. He closed his eyes and moments later, his breathing became deep and even. Wordlessly, Dex and Caitlin sat in the chairs next to the bed.

Seconds became minutes. Minutes ticked into hours. Before the dawning of a new day, Halston Parker's breathing stopped.

He was gone.

CHAPTER 3

The sun was shining bright in the midmorning sky when Dex and Caitlin walked out of the hospital. It wasn't even ten o'clock yet, but already the day promised to be miserably hot, which wasn't unusual for a day in mid-June.

Caitlin squared her shoulders and tried to keep all the grief of losing her father at bay, but found she couldn't. Swallowing, she blinked back a surge of fresh tears.

"I'm driving you home, Caitlin. Where're you parked?"

The touch of Dex's arm around Caitlin's shoulder penetrated deeply. Sniffing, she angled her head to look up into his eyes. To her surprise, they were filled with compassion, something she hadn't expected. Feeling a lump form in her throat, she answered in a choked voice. "My car is parked over there."

When they arrived at her father's home, Caitlin covered her face with her hands and began crying openly in heart-wrenching strangled sobs. Dex turned off the car's ignition, pushed the seat back and gently pulled her into his lap.

"That's it, get it all out. Everything's going to be all right, Caitlin. Your father isn't in any more pain. He's at peace," Dex whispered softly, tenderly cradling her in his arms.

When her sobs turned to soft whimpers, she lifted her tear stained face to his. "Dad didn't get a chance to see Jordan for the last time," she said brokenly.

Dex's hand stopped stroking Caitlin's hair and back. His eyes darkened. "I gather Jordan means a lot to you."

Caitlin frowned at his words. She then began swiping her eyes with trembling hands. "Of course. Jordan is my life."

Dex felt a surge of renewed pain and anger. He had to clamp down on his teeth to keep from lashing out at the thought of her deep feelings for another man. He stared hard at her. "Since he's your life, why hasn't he made you his? I would think under the circumstances, he'd be here for you."

Confusion covered Caitlin's face. "What are you talking about?"

Dex's voice was as hard as his eyes and held a steely edge when he continued. "I'm talking about this person named Jordan. Never mind, he's your problem, not mine. My only concern is the promise I made to your father, and I intend to keep it. I'll not leave before the services. After that, I have no intention of staying a minute longer. I'll contact Clayton to fly in as soon as the services for your father are over. If your father's claim is true, and there's a possibility that we're still married, I'll make sure Clayton does whatever has to be done to legalize our divorce. Then you can continue your life with Jordan."

Caitlin's eyes grew wide with startled surprise with Dex's words. He acted like he didn't know who Jordan was? But how could he not know? She had written to him so he had to know. But, if he really didn't . . .

Panic seized Caitlin when she thought of that possibility. She skittered away from Dex and quickly got out of the car.

Dex raised a questioning brow. He watched Caitlin at her front door fumbling nervously with her keys, before opening the door and going inside the house.

He tilted his head back against the car seat and closed his eyes, totally bewildered. *What in the world was going on?* When he'd mentioned the other man, Caitlin had acted as though she was having an anxiety attack. Something wasn't right, and he intended to find out what was going on.

Dex sighed deeply. He wondered if her actions had anything to do with the letter Dr. Flores had discreetly given to him at the hospital. It was a letter Halston Parker had asked Dr. Flores to give to him. No doubt it was another chunk to add to this bizarre puzzle which only Caitlin's father had all the pieces. Instead of reading the letter when Dr. Flores had handed it to him, he had stuffed the envelope in his pocket to read later. He wasn't ready to read anything Caitlin's father had written to him. He was still trying to recover from the old man's claim that he and Caitlin were still legally married.

Fury almost choked Dex. He was tired of playing games. He wanted answers and wanted them now, and he intended on getting them from Caitlin. He got out of the car, and walked up to the house.

Caitlin had left the door open, and Dex walked inside. He heard her sobs and took the stairs two at a time, following the sound of her voice.

He entered the bedroom at the precise moment she reached for a tan-colored jacket that was tossed across a chair. The masculine decor of the room, smelling of pipe tobacco, had been her father's. Clutching the jacket to her chest, her shoulders began to shake.

Dex swiftly crossed the room and gently pulled Caitlin into his arms. Once again the need to protect and shield her from pain overwhelmed him.

She tried pulling herself out of his arms, but his hold on her tightened. "You don't have to take care of this now, Caitlin. Come downstairs and let me get you something to eat before I leave to go check into the hotel."

She trembled in response to the tenderness in his voice and shook her head against his shoulder. "I—I need to tell you about Jordan, Dex."

Dex attempted to control the anger renewing itself within him at the mention of the man's name. "Not now, Caitlin. We'll talk later. I'll come back, after you've rested."

"No, Dex. We need to talk now. Jordan is . . ."

Caitlin didn't finish the statement. She felt Dex's body push away from her. Gazing up into his face, she saw a nerve in his jaw twitch. Harsh lines etched his face. Her gaze followed his and came to rest on the picture frame sitting on her father's dresser.

A suffocating sensation overtook Caitlin. She stepped back out of Dex's arms. She watched as he walked over to the dresser and picked up the frame. Her breath caught in her throat when he stood studying the pho-tograph of her and the little girl who sat in her lap. He turned to her, his expression stony, his eyes narrowing. "Who's this in the picture with you?"

Caitlin's voice was barely a whisper when she responded. "Jordan."

Dex stared at her in both shock and surprise. Jordan wasn't a man but a little girl? He gazed at the photograph he held in his hand, closely ex-amining the face of the little girl. He studied the abundance of black wavy hair entwined into two fat braids, the shape of her nut-brown face, the curve of her eyebrows, the thick lashes fanning her eyes and the full-ness of her lips. But what really caught his attention was the color of her eyes. They were charcoal-gray. The photographer's camera had picked up the color perfectly.

A heaviness erupted in his chest. "How old is she, Caitlin?" His ques-tion thundered loudly in the room.

Caitlin's voice was filled with apprehension when she answered. "She turned three on March first."

Dex's gaze never left Caitlin as he stared in disbelief. He began doing calculations in his head. If she was born the first of March then she was conceived the end of May, during the first week of their marriage.

Dex's jaw hardened as his anger escalated. He knew without a doubt he was looking into the face of his child. A child he'd known nothing about. He also had a sinking feeling as to why Caitlin's father had gone through so much trouble to preserve their marriage, and why Caitlin still used his name.

"Why didn't you tell me?" he asked in a voice that shook with rage. "How could you not let me know I had a child? What kind of a woman are you to keep something like that a secret? It was just fine and dandy that you didn't want me, but you had no right keeping the existence of my daughter from me. You had no right at all, lady!"

Anger washed over Caitlin. She stood facing him, her body stiff with indignation. "I didn't try keeping anything from you. I didn't find out that I was pregnant until after I'd filed for divorce, Dex. But I did write to you when I found out. How could you think I wouldn't tell you? She belonged to you as much as she belonged to me. I would never have kept her existence from you. Never."

A quiet uncertainty lingered in Dex's stare as his hard gaze touched Caitlin. "I never got a letter from you, Caitlin."

"But I sent it, and you never responded," she said louder than she had wanted.

Her statement slashed through him. "I didn't answer because I didn't get a letter. If I had, I would have responded." Dex couldn't help but wonder if the envelope in his pocket, the one given to him by Dr. Flores, contained the missing letter. How far had Halston Parker gone to keep him away from Caitlin and from ever finding out about his child? Caitlin should have come to him in Australia like she'd promised. He could never forgive her for not doing so.

"For the sake of argument," Dex said in a controlled tone. They weren't getting anywhere raising their voices at each other. "Let's say you did send the letter. Weren't you concerned when I didn't write back or call?" he asked curtly.

"No. I assumed you hated me for choosing to stay with my father instead of coming to you. I thought you—"

"You thought I didn't want my child?" Dex thundered. An incredulous look of disbelief crossed his face. He quickly strode across the room. Snatching her wrist, he pulled her closer to him. "What kind of man do you think I am?" he asked, his dark eyes blazing with fury. "How could you think what happened between us could've had any bearing on how I felt for my child, my own flesh and blood?"

Caitlin snatched her hand from him. She tilted her chin and glared up at him. "I wrote you."

"I have no proof of that. Besides, if I didn't reply to the first letter the decent thing would have been to write again or even call. They do have telephones in Australia, and you had my number. Something that important deserved a phone call. Your flimsy excuse won't wash with me, Caitlin. And what about my family? If you couldn't reach me, all you had to do was get in touch with them. Any one of them would have been more than happy to hear from you."

"I'd met them only once. I thought they wouldn't want to have anything to do with me. We were no longer married, and I'd hurt you. I thought they despised me for what I'd done to you. When I didn't hear from you, I assumed the worst."

Caitlin struggled mentally for a few seconds, telling herself she needed to make Dex understand. "Can't you see I had my doubts, Dex? You're right. I should have known you better. But as far as I'm concerned, you should have known me just as well. The truth of the matter is that we really didn't know each other at all. Everything between us happened so fast. We got caught up in a whirlwind romance that quickly moved into marriage."

"If you felt that way, why did you marry me? Why didn't you turn me down when I asked you to become my wife?"

"Because I wanted to be with you. You swept me off my feet, Dex, and at the time, nothing else mattered; not the short time we'd known each other, or how my father would react to the news of our hasty marriage. There were so many things we didn't know about each other."

Dex's jaw hardened. "We knew enough. You should have known the most important thing about me, Caitlin. You should have known how I felt about you. I didn't want an affair with you for those three weeks. I wanted more, I wanted forever. I made the mistake of thinking that you did too."

"No, Dex. You didn't make a mistake. I did want forever. But after you left for Australia, I began having my doubts about a lot of things. And when you didn't answer my letter, I accepted what I thought was your decision not to want your child. I continued on with my life. But I never once gave up hope that one day you would want to see her. I've not once kept Jordan in the dark about you, even when I thought you didn't want her. She began asking questions about her daddy when she noticed all of her friends had fathers and she didn't. She knows all about you. Although I didn't have any pictures of you to show her, Jordan knows who her father is."

Dex frowned. She was right about not having any pictures. There hadn't been a lot of time for any. The only photo of them together had been the one his mother had taken when he'd taken Caitlin home to meet his family.

He moved toward the window. He looked below at the empty street. "And just what did you tell my daughter about me? That I didn't want her? That I deserted her? That I deserted you?" he asked coldly.

Caitlin folded her arms tightly in front of her. "No," she replied softly.

"I never gave Jordan the impression you were a terrible person, or blamed you because the three of us weren't together. When she began asking about you, I told her you worked in a country far away, and that maybe you'd come back to see her one day. She accepted that."

Dex took a minute to put a cap on his anger before turning to face Caitlin. "And when she got older, and I didn't show up, what lie would you have told her then?"

Caitlin met his cold gaze head on. "Whatever was necessary."

A strained silence saturated the room as Dex stared at Caitlin. "Where's she now?"

Caitlin took a deep breath, her thoughts in chaos. She looked at him. "She's with Marsher Logan, Dad's neighbor. She took Jordan with her to visit her own little granddaughter who lives in the country. They'll be back tomorrow."

Dex thought about Caitlin's response. He would get to meet his daughter for the first time tomorrow. He continued looking at Caitlin. His anger escalated. She had stripped him of three years of his daughter's life because she hadn't chosen his love over her father's. Angered beyond control, he stormed past her and out of the room.

Caitlin blinked rapidly, losing control of her emotions. She bit her lower lip as Dex's words came back to haunt her. He was right. She should have known he would not have turned his back on his child. But then, he should have known she would not have deliberately kept their daughter's existence from him

Leaving her father's room, she closed the door behind her and went into her own bedroom. Once there, she began pulling off her clothes. She felt tired, drained and depleted of all strength and logical thought. And to make matters worse, her head had begun to ache. Emerging from the shower minutes later, she slipped into a nightgown. Her father was gone, her daughter was away, and the only man she had ever loved totally despised her.

Once again she succumbed to her tears.

Dex paced the living room in quick angry strides. Coming to a stop, he pulled the letter Dr. Flores had given him from his pocket. Opening the envelope, he was surprised to find not the missing letter—the one Caitlin claimed she'd written to him about his child—but another letter. It appeared to have been written by Halston Parker and was dated over a week ago.

Moments later, after reading the letter, Dex's jaw tightened. If Caitlin's father's words could be believed, there was a possibility that Caitlin could be in some kind of danger.

The letter stated that Halston Parker owned a piece of property near

Eagle Pass; land that had been in the Parker family for generations. Halston had recently received offers on the land, which he'd repeatedly turned down. Not long after that, things began happening to him that had vindictive overtones. He'd reported the incidents to the police, but after the police's investigation turned up nothing, they'd dismissed them as teenagers' mischief.

The letter further stated Caitlin didn't know anything about what had been going on since she'd been living in Fort Worth. But there was little doubt in Halston Parker's mind that whoever had been after him to sell would now begin harassing Caitlin. He had ended the letter pleading with Dex to protect her.

As Dex refolded the letter and stuffed it back in his pocket, he couldn't help wondering if any of what he'd read in the letter was true, or was it just another ploy by the old man to get him and Caitlin back together. As soon as he had some free time, he would pay a visit to the local police to see if there had been an investigation as Halston Parker had claimed. But first he had to make a telephone call.

Dex picked up the receiver of the phone that sat on a nearby table and punched in a few numbers. He needed to talk with Clayton. Hopefully, he would be able to give him some legal advice. The phone was answered on the second ring.

"Hello."

"Clayton. It's Dex."

"How are things going?"

"Not too good. Caitlin's father died a few hours ago."

"I'm sorry to hear that. Please convey my sympathy."

"You can do that yourself," Dex replied bitterly. "I need you here as soon as possible. There's a legal matter I need to discuss with you."

"Oh? What's up?"

"According to Mr. Parker, the divorce papers Caitlin and I signed four years ago were never filed with the courts."

"What? I don't understand. Why?"

"He told the lawyer that Caitlin and I no longer wanted a divorce."

"If what you're telling me is the truth, you and Caitlin may still be married."

Dex sighed deeply. "I was afraid of that."

"If you still want to end your marriage, it won't be a problem since you haven't lived together in four years. Under the circumstances, a judge may agree to make it effective the day of the original divorce."

"There may be a problem with that. There's something else I think you should know."

"What?"

"Caitlin found out she was pregnant a couple of months after I left for Australia and she'd filed for a divorce."

There was a pause. "What are you saying, Dex?"

Dex beamed proudly. It was late in coming but he was announcing the existence of his daughter to his family for the first time, and he felt every bit a proud father. "What I'm trying to tell you is that our parents have another granddaughter. And you, Clayton, have another niece."

"What! I don't believe it."

"Believe it."

"I take it you didn't know about her."

"Of course I didn't know about her!"

"All right, all right, just take it easy, Dex. Did Caitlin say why she didn't tell you?"

"She claims she wrote me when she found out she was pregnant."

"And I take it you don't believe her."

"I didn't get a letter, Clayton."

"But that doesn't necessarily mean she didn't send one just because you didn't get one. You yourself have complained about how lousy the mail service was in Australia. Just give her the benefit of the doubt."

Dex's frown deepened. Clayton always had had a soft spot where Caitlin was concerned. "I don't know if I can do that. Because of her, I may have lost too much already."

There was a brief silence. "Just don't be so hard on her, Dex. She's going through a lot right now. The last thing she needs is for you to make things worse. What she really needs is your support, not your anger. Lighten up. Now tell me about my niece? What's her name?"

Dex was glad to get off the subject of Caitlin. "My daughter's name is Jordan."

"Jordan? Caitlin named her after you?"

Clayton's question caught Dex by surprise. He'd been so upset, he hadn't made the connection. Jordan was his middle name, and he had to admit it was a very unusual name for a girl. Had Caitlin named his daughter after him? "I don't know, Clayton."

"Ummm. That's interesting. If she did, I wonder why?" Clayton asked, seemingly more of himself than of Dex.

Dex frowned. He couldn't help wondering what Clayton was driving at.

"How did Jordan take to you, Dex?"

"I haven't actually seen her yet. She went on a little trip with a friend and won't be returning until tomorrow. But I've seen a picture of her and she's beautiful."

Clayton laughed. "She must be Caitlin's little look-alike."

Dex chuckled. "I hate to disappoint you, little brother, but she's the spittin' image of me. She has my eyes, my nose and those Madaris lips. She couldn't look more like me if I had given birth to her myself."

"I thought you said she was beautiful. Everyone knows what an ugly cuss you are," Clayton replied jokingly.

"Keep talking, bro, and I may be tempted to break your nose when I see you. But seriously, there's a lot I need to discuss with you. I desperately need legal advice."

"No problem. I'll be there as soon as I can."

"There's something else that's bothering me, Clayton."

"What's that?"

Dex proceeded to tell Clayton about the letter Halston Parker had left him and what it said.

"Have you told Caitlin about it?"

"No. She's pretty shaken up over her father's death. And until I'm sure what's in Halston's letter is legit, I don't want to say anything to her about it."

"When will the services be held?"

"The day after tomorrow. I'll put off going to the police until that's over . . . and Clayton?"

"Yeah?"

"How about dropping by my place and packing a few things. It seems I may be here awhile."

"What's the name of the hotel where you can be reached?"

"Until I find out what's going on, I'm staying right here with Caitlin. I blindly promised her father I would take care of her, and I'm going to keep my word."

"Will Trevor be running the business while you're away?"

"Yeah," Dex replied. "He's the best project foreman there is. Madaris Explorations is in good hands. I'll give him a call later to let him know where I am, so he'll know how to reach me."

"I'm going to catch the first available flight out in the morning, Dex. I'll call you from the airport for directions to Caitlin's father's home. I'll see you then."

Caitlin heard someone knocking on her bedroom door in the deep recesses of her mind. She opened her eyes. Moaning, she shifted her head on the pillow. Good . . . the sound had stopped. She felt completely awful, and in an attempt to find relief she sank back against the pillow and closed her eyes.

The knocking started again. She opened her eyes and blinked once sluggishly. Slowly pulling herself out of bed and putting on a robe, she nearly stumbled over her shoes which were tossed carelessly on the bedroom floor. Making her way to the door, she snatched it open and found Dex standing there with concern etched on his face. She thought he'd left.

They regarded each other silently. His rough and chiseled features did nothing to downplay his handsomeness. Instead they placed a greater emphasis on his detached emotions. "What are you doing here, Dex? I thought you had left."

Dex didn't respond to Caitlin's statement. Instead, he took a good look at her appearance. He had begun worrying when she hadn't come downstairs. Studying her intently, he took in the unhealthy pallor of her skin.

"You're ill, Caitlin." It was a statement and not a question.

"What?" Caitlin asked. Tearing her gaze from his, she crossed her arms over her abdomen, chasing away a chill.

Seeing her tremble, Dex entered her room. "I said you're ill."

Caitlin shook her head. "I'm not ill, Dex, just tired."

He wasn't easily convinced. "Maybe you should see a doctor."

"I don't want to see a doctor. All I want is to be left alone."

"Sorry, that's not an option." With a quick movement, Dex swept her off her feet into his arms.

"What do you think you're doing? Put me down this minute!"

"You're too weak to argue with me, so do yourself a favor and save your strength. I've made lunch, and you're going to eat it."

"I don't want to go downstairs. I'm too tired."

"I can believe that. When was the last time you ate anything?"

Caitlin glared up at him. "I don't remember. Maybe yesterday, I don't know."

Dex swore through gritted teeth. He carried her over to the bed and placed her on the comforter. "Where are the serving trays kept?"

"I don't remember," she snapped.

A slight frown touched Dex's features. "Since you aren't cooperating, I'll find them myself. I'll be back in a minute." He left the room.

Standing, Caitlin took off her robe and tossed it on the chair across from the bed, then got back into the bed. She felt as weak as a newborn baby, and all she wanted to do was to go back to sleep. The next thing she knew, Dex had returned carrying a tray with food on it.

The aroma of the vegetable soup teased her nostrils and her stomach began growling. Sitting up, she took the tray he offered. "Thanks."

Dex sat in a chair at the foot of her bed and watched through hooded eyes as Caitlin quickly consumed the meal he had prepared. He couldn't help but remember another time he'd served her in bed. It had been the morning after they had gotten married. His pulse began racing at the memory of them together. He never knew how truly wonderful love between a man and a woman could be until he'd made love to her. But then . . . his thoughts reminded him, he'd also found out later just how painful love could he.

When Caitlin had finished eating, he removed the tray, pleased that she had eaten everything. "Now try and get some rest. I'll be downstairs if you need me."

Caitlin yawned, fighting sleep. "Downstairs? When are you leaving?"

"I'm not."

Caitlin blinked. "What do you mean, you're not. I don't remember inviting you to stay here."

"You didn't." He was not ready to tell her about the contents of the letter her father had left for him. "I've decided to stick around to make sure you're all right."

Caitlin frowned. "I appreciate your concern, but I'm capable of taking care of myself."

"Evidently your old man didn't think so," Dex said, gently pulling the comforter and going about tucking her in. "I made him a promise, Caitlin, and I intend to keep it."

Caitlin yawned again. "I don't need you here."

"Go to sleep, Caitlin."

"No. I'll be fine. My father always thought of me as his little girl, Dex. You're the one who thought of me as a woman," Caitlin said sleepily, barely able to keep her eyes open. "Don't you remember, you made me a woman."

Despite his anger, a part of Dex could never forget. "Yeah, Caitlin. I remember, now go to sleep. I'll be downstairs if you need me."

"Mmmm . . . ," she replied, drifting off into sleep.

Dex's eyes softened as he watched her fade into blissful slumber. Reaching out, he removed a wayward strand of hair from her cheek. Her earlier words assailed him with pleasant memories. "You're right, I made you a woman. *My woman.*"

He went to the foot of the double bed, deeply disturbed by the strong emotions stirring within him. His gaze took in the feminine body nestled beneath the bedcovers. He fought a sudden wild impulse to climb into the bed beside her.

Glancing around the bedroom, his eyes caught sight of a brass picture frame on Caitlin's dresser that held a copy of the same photograph in her father's room. Moving to the dresser, he picked up the frame and again studied the photograph. Emotions welled deep within him. His daughter, a part of him and a part of Caitlin.

He couldn't help but think about the things he had missed out on. Things like watching Caitlin's belly swell while carrying his child. Being a doctor, his brother Justin had delivered his own daughter a few months ago. Although Dex knew that he himself lacked the medical qualifications needed to accomplish that same feat, nothing on earth would have prevented him from being in the labor room with Caitlin, and to have been present when Jordan was born. He wished he could have heard his daughter's first words and seen her take her first steps.

A faint noise drew his attention back to Caitlin. She had turned in sleep, facing him. Compelled by a need he didn't understand, Dex moved to stand by the bed again. Without conscious thought, he reached out and traced his finger across Caitlin's brow, cheek and chin, feeling the velvety softness of her brown skin and being careful not to wake her.

Suddenly, he snatched his hand back. He wouldn't allow himself to get burned by love again. His life had not been the same since the day he'd met her. How much pain and heartache could one man endure before learning a valuable lesson in life?

He had learned his lesson well. No matter what, Caitlin would never get close to his heart again.

Never.

CHAPTER 4

Dex tossed aside the magazine he'd been reading when the sound of the doorbell vibrated through the room. Moving quickly, he made his way to the door. Caitlin was upstairs sleeping, and he didn't want her to awaken. She needed the rest.

He blinked, surprised at what he saw upon opening the door. An older woman stood before him holding a sleeping child in her arms. Dex's throat suddenly felt tight and dry. He knew without an introduction who the woman was. And he also knew whose child she held in her arms.

His.

"You must be Ms. Logan?" he said, smiling against the sudden lump in his throat. "Please come in."

The woman's thin mouth curved into a smile as she stepped inside. Her eyes reflected surprise as they swept over him. "Yes, I'm Mrs. Logan." She gazed at him with thoughtful curiosity. "You seem to know who I am, but I can't recall ever having met you before. Although you do look familiar." She looked down at the sleeping child in her arms and then back at Dex. "Oh," she said making the connection. "Jordan looks so much like you. Caitlin always said she looked a lot like her father. You must be Caitlin's ex-husband."

Dex nodded. *Or her current one,* he thought. "I'm Dexter Madaris," he said, offering the woman his hand in a warm handshake. "Caitlin said Jordan wouldn't be back until tomorrow."

"Yes. That was our plans, but . . ."

The woman's cheerful chatter faded into oblivion as Dex's gaze was drawn to his child asleep in Ms. Logan's arms.

"Mr. Madaris. Are you all right?" The older woman's eyes, reflecting concern, reminded Dex she'd been talking to him.

"Yes, I'm sorry. What did you say?"

She looked at him closely. "I said Caitlin wasn't expecting us back until tomorrow, but Jordan began missing her mommy. I see Caitlin's car in the driveway. Is she home?"

"Yes, she's upstairs sleeping."

The woman nodded. "I'm surprised she's here and not at the hospital. How's Mr. Parker?"

"He died this morning."

Ms. Logan's smile was replaced with a sympathetic frown. "I'm so sorry. My husband and I moved into the neighborhood a couple of years ago. Mr. Parker was such a nice man. How's Caitlin doing?"

"As well as can be expected, under the circumstances."

Ms. Logan nodded. "Please convey my condolences to Caitlin and tell her if there's anything my husband and I can do to let us know." She transferred the bundle from her arms to Dex's.

"The drive back tired Jordan out. Tell Caitlin if she needs me to babysit tomorrow, I'll be more than happy to. Goodbye, Mr. Madaris. I'll let myself out."

"Goodbye." Dex's palms began perspiring as he stared down at his child. Tightening his arms, he cradled her closer to him. His composure crumbled. His surroundings became nonexistent. He was aware of nothing except the sleeping child he held—his daughter, his own flesh and blood.

Seeing her for the first time had a devastating impact on him. Because of his preoccupation, he was not aware of another presence in the room.

"Dex?"

He looked up to find Caitlin standing on the bottom stair. Her nap seemed to have renewed her. Her hair fanned softly about her face and shoulders. Her eyes were minus the traces of puffiness beneath them. Her skin had a satin gloss and appeared to be as smooth as the skin of the child nestled in his arms. She was wearing a cream-colored velour robe and looked absolutely beautiful and seductively innocent.

"I heard the doorbell," she said, coming toward him.

Dex expelled his breath slowly. "Ms. Logan said Jordan missed you."

A smile touched Caitlin's features. "That doesn't surprise me. Jordan and I are seldom apart, except for when I'm working." She reached out to take their child from his arms.

Dex stared down at Caitlin's outstretched hands. He then looked up and met her gaze. "No," he said in a deep husky voice that did little to hide the deep emotions he felt. "I want to hold her for a while."

Turning, he went to the sofa and sat down. Tenderly, he cradled his daughter in his arms, holding her close.

Caitlin took a deep breath to ease the awful ache in her chest after witnessing this first-time meeting of father and daughter. She started back up the stairs, but stopped when she heard the sound of her name from Dex's lips. She turned around. Dex was staring at her over Jordan's head and was holding his free hand out to her.

A warm feeling touched Caitlin with Dex's offer of a temporary truce. She walked over to the sofa and placed her hand in his. Gently pulling her down on the couch next to him, he drew her against him.

"She's beautiful, Caitlin, and I want to thank you for her."

"You don't have to thank me, Dex."

"Yes, I do. There were other options you could've taken. And I'm glad you didn't choose any of them."

Her gaze held his. "Jordan has been my joy, Dex. There was never a question that I wanted her."

Dex's expression remained neutral, although Caitlin could feel his body stiffen when he said, "But there was a question in your mind whether or not I did."

Caitlin wished she could deny his accusation, but could not. She felt a tightening in her throat. Seeing Dex hold their daughter made her realize Jordan's loss the past three years. Caitlin's biggest regret was that Jordan was growing up without being a part of a loving, close-knit family. Some of Caitlin's fondest childhood memories were those of her parents and how much they had loved each other, as well as how much they'd loved her.

She also knew that Dex had had a similar childhood, although he hadn't been an only child. There were six Madaris siblings, three of each. When he'd taken her to his family home, it was obvious the Madaris family was a close one.

Caitlin glanced at Dex. To her surprise, he had drifted to sleep holding Jordan with one hand and her with the other. "It appears I wasn't the only one tired," she said softly. Her worries, tears and confusion were momentarily forgotten. Snuggling comfortably against Dex, she closed her eyes.

Dex didn't know how long he'd slept, but when he awoke his gaze locked with miniature eyes that were a mirror image of his own, staring at him curiously.

He sensed numerous emotions flowing through his daughter's small body. She looked as though she didn't know what to make of this strange man holding her in his arms. Her gaze moved from him to Caitlin, whose head rested on his shoulder as she slept.

Dex began to panic when he saw the curiosity and confusion in his daughter's eyes being replaced with sprouting tears. The last thing he wanted was to make her cry.

He nudged Caitlin and whispered, "She's awake."

Dex's words stirred Caitlin from a sound sleep. A smile touched her lips as she straightened in her seat. "Hi, Jordan."

"Mommy!" The little girl squealed in delight, eagerly scampering from Dex's lap into her mother's outstretched arms. Her chubby arms fastened themselves around Caitlin's neck.

Caitlin laughed. "Whoa. Not so tight, baby. Don't choke Mommy." She was not at all surprised at Jordan's lack of acceptance of the man she'd never seen before. Except for Caitlin's father and the fathers of her playmates, Jordan wasn't used to much male company.

Jordan loosened her hold on her mother slightly. Turning, she looked at Dex from beneath dark lashes. "What's your name?" she asked him in a voice matching the suspicious glint in her gaze.

Dex held his breath, taking in the beautiful darkness of his daughter's eyes, so like his own.

Jordan folded her arms over her chest and stuck out her lower lip when she mistook Dex's silence as a refusal to answer her question. "I'm Jordan," she lifted her chin and unceremoniously announced.

A smile tugged at the corners of Dex's mouth. She was definitely a Madaris. The females in his family were notorious for pouting which could usually be soothed by kind words or actions. "That's a pretty name."

Dex's comment awarded him a softening of his daughter's features.

Caitlin, who had been watching the exchange, decided to use this time to prove something to Dex. "Jordan?" She spoke softly to her daughter. "Who's your daddy?"

Jordan turned her head and looked at her mother. The expression on her small face indicated she didn't know what to make of her mother asking such a ridiculous question. Nevertheless, she answered anyway, in a clear voice. "My daddy is Dexter Jordan Madaris."

Jordan then turned her full attention back to Dex. "My daddy's named Jordan, too."

A heartfelt emotion welled in Dex's chest and threatened to burst. Caitlin hadn't lied to him. Even when she had believed he had rejected his daughter, she had told their child about him. His daughter knew his name and seemed awfully proud she shared part of it. He couldn't help the smile that stole over his lips, or the joy he felt inside.

"What's your name?" Jordan asked Dex again.

Dex met Caitlin's gaze over the head of their daughter, and she nodded briefly. The time had come for him to answer her question. "My name is Dexter Jordan Madaris."

Jordan's cherub face became confused. She looked at him then shook her head vigorously. "No. That's my daddy's name."

Dex extended both arms out to her. "I'm your daddy, sweetheart."

"No!" Jordan said glaring at him defiantly. "My daddy's in Azalea."

Dex couldn't hide the smile touching his lips with his daughter's mispronounciation of Australia. Understanding the depth of what was taking place between them, he didn't want to confuse Jordan, but he felt it was important that she knew who he was. And the sooner, the better. "I am your daddy, Jordan."

Jordan turned to her mother for support. She was not ready to accept this stranger's claim. "My daddy's in Azalea, isn't he Mommy?"

Caitlin swallowed. She was prepared to say the words she often wondered if she would ever get the chance to say. Not knowing what Dex's future plans were regarding their marriage, she wanted Jordan to know Dex was her father, but didn't want to give the impression he would be a permanent fixture in their lives.

"He *is* your daddy, Jordan. And he's come to see you."

A small frown appeared on Jordan's face. She turned back to Dex, and sized him up once more.

Dex held his breath, hoping and praying that his child would accept him as her father. He could tell that her young mind was trying to absorb the words her mother had just told her. He watched as the expression in her eyes changed from confusion to comprehension, and then acceptance. A smile spread over her features, and she moved from her mother's lap and into his outstretched arms.

Dex kissed his daughter lightly on the forehead, snuggling her closer to him, to his heart. His voice was choked when he spoke. "Your daddy loves you, Jordan."

Caitlin shivered at the deep emotions Dex's words of love to his daughter caused. It took every ounce of restraint she could muster not to let those emotions rip her in two. She was more than a little surprised when Dex suddenly released one of his arms from around Jordan to pull Caitlin closer to him. She accepted his embrace and rested her head on his shoulder.

Jordan lifted her head from her father's chest. Looking into her mother's misty eyes, she let out a happy chant. "Daddy's home, Mommy! My daddy's home from Azalea!"

Caitlin awoke the next morning as the sound of her daughter's laughter filtered through her sleepy mind. Shifting her head on the pillow, she remembered how hard it had been for her to go to sleep, knowing Dex was sleeping in the guest bedroom across the hall.

Getting out of bed, she headed for the bathroom. As she began to dress after taking a shower and blow-drying her hair, she remembered Jordan's excitement that her daddy was home. To celebrate, Caitlin had ordered Jordan's favorite food, pizza.

It was a little past nine by the time Jordan had gotten bathed and in her pajamas. After her bath she'd grabbed her favorite doll and had gone looking for her daddy. She had found him sitting quietly on the sofa. Dashing across the room to him, as though it was the most natural thing, she crawled into his lap. Dex had wrapped his arms around his daughter and hugged her with fierce tenderness and open affection. The touching scene had nearly brought tears to Caitlin's eyes.

She had found it difficult to tear her gaze away from them. Somehow she had forced her attention to things she needed to do like preparing the guest room for Dex.

It was only when she had come back into the living room that she noticed a confused expression on Jordan's face.

"Jordan, what's the matter?"

Jordan looked up at her mother. "Where's Grampa?"

Jordan's question made Caitlin go still as pain tore through her. She had wondered how long it would take for her daughter to notice her grandfather's absence. The two of them had been very close. From the time she had brought Jordan home from the hospital, they had lived in this house with her father. Moving to Ft. Worth six months ago had been hard on all three of them.

"Grampa's gone away, honey," she finally whispered to her daughter.

Jordan seemed to ponder Caitlin's words. "To Azalea Mommy?"

A lump formed in Caitlin's throat. She had been unable to reply. She was grateful to Dex for coming to her rescue by answering for her. "No, Jordan. Your Grampa hasn't gone to Australia. He's in heaven."

Jordan turned wide dark eyes on her father. "He's up there with the angels?"

"Yes, sweetheart," Dex replied smiling tenderly, pulling his daughter closer to him. "He's up there with the angels."

A pleased smile spread over Jordan's face. "They'll give him some wings."

It wasn't long afterwards that Jordan began getting sleepy. Together, Caitlin and Dex had taken her upstairs to tuck her in. They had listened as she said her prayers, saying a special prayer for her grampa in heaven, and thanking God for sending her daddy home to her and her mommy.

Listening to Jordan's prayer had made Caitlin's throat constrict. It had taken all the strength she could muster not to fall apart right then and there. After letting Dex know the guest room had been prepared for him, she had quickly said goodnight and escaped to her own bedroom.

The sound of Jordan's laughter brought Caitlin's thoughts back to the present. Sighing, she glanced at her watch. The services for her father were tomorrow, and there were a number of things she needed to do before then.

Following the sound of cheerful loud voices, she wondered if the truce between her and Dex was still in effect. Taking a deep breath, she pushed open the kitchen door and walked into the room.

Dex's gaze met hers when she entered. He was standing near the kitchen table. The collar of his shirt was unbuttoned and the sleeves were rolled up on his forearms. "Good morning, Caitlin."

At the mention of her mother's name, Jordan, who had been on her knees in a chair leaning over the kitchen table, squealed with glee when she saw her mother. "Mommy!"

Dex quickly helped his daughter down from the chair when it appeared she would jump. Running over to Caitlin, Jordan leaped into her mother's outstretched arms. "Mommy! We're making you breakfast!"

Caitlin smiled at her daughter. "Really? What're you making?"

Jordan turned to her father. "What's it called, Daddy?"

Dex's laughter filled the room. "If we told her, sweetheart, it wouldn't be a surprise."

"Oh," she replied to her father. To her mother she said, "It's a surprise, Mommy." Then in the same breath she exclaimed. "I'm going to see the world today."

Caitlin raised a brow. Her lips formed in a grin. "You're what?"

There was deep amusement in Dex's eyes when he glanced at Caitlin. "What she's trying to say is that she is going to Sea World today. If that's all right with you, that is. Ms. Logan called and invited Jordan to go with her and her granddaughter."

"Yes, it's all right with me."

"She also told me to tell you that she'll be happy to keep Jordan for you tomorrow."

Caitlin nodded. She was grateful for Ms. Logan's kindness. She put Jordan down. "Have you had breakfast yet?"

Jordan nodded her head. "Daddy said when you got up we would give you your surprise."

"Oh, he did, did he?" Slowly being pulled in the excitement and conspiratory merriment surrounding father and daughter, Caitlin turned to Dex. "What's this big surprise for breakfast?" She sniffed the air, bringing forth giggles from her daughter. "I don't smell bacon or eggs or anything like breakfast."

"Come see for yourself," Dex invited. He couldn't help noticing the style of Caitlin's hair. It was arranged in a bevy of soft curls that dipped over her face and shoulders. He thought the stylish cut provided her with a totally different image than the one she had worn four years ago. This new style gave her a look of an even higher level of maturity and sophistication. Even dressed in a pair of well-worn jeans and a T-shirt, she looked nothing like the little slip of a woman that he had married.

Caitlin walked over to the table where Dex was putting the finishing touches on a concoction she didn't recognize. She looked from father to daughter. "I give up." She raised a brow. "What is it?"

Jordan laughed. "Tell Mommy what it is, Daddy."

"It's a Rice Krispies Ice Cream Float with berries, nuts, chocolate syrup, and whipped cream," Dex said chuckling. "This one is for you. We ate ours already. They were delicious."

"Would you like some more?"

Caitlin pushed herself away from the table. "I think I'm going to be sick," she said rubbing her stomach.

Dex grinned. "No one forced you to eat it, Caitlin."

She moaned. "How could I not eat it? Jordan was so excited about helping you prepare breakfast, I didn't have the heart not to eat all of it. It's a good thing Ms. Logan came when she did, or Jordan would have wanted me to have seconds." Caitlin smiled. "If I've gained weight from eating that thing, it's all your fault. I feel fat."

He smiled easily. "Relax. You're not fat. You're as beautiful as you were the day I first laid eyes on you."

The lighthearted remark sent panic racing through Caitlin. *Please don't bring up the past. I couldn't handle it if you did,* her mind screamed. Not wanting to bring up their past, she took the initiative to change the subject. "You did say Clayton was coming today?"

Dex met Caitlin's direct gaze. "Yes. He should be here sometime this morning."

She regretted asking about Clayton the moment the question had left her lips. She knew why he was coming. Dex had summoned his attorney brother to do whatever was necessary to undo what her father had done. He wanted to make sure he was free of her as quickly as possible. However, there was the issue of Jordan. She wasn't certain what Dex's plans were regarding their daughter, but she was more than sure he wouldn't be one of those fathers who would be satisfied with just seeing his child whenever the mood struck. He had been cheated out of three years already, and she had a gut feeling that was the limit. What she wasn't sure of was just how far he would go to be a part of Jordan's life. Would he try to get full custody of her? Not wanting to even think of that possibility, Caitlin decided to stay clear of any conversation concerning Clayton's visit, too.

"How's your brother Justin?"

Dex smiled. "Justin couldn't be better. He's married with two kids and lives in Ennis, Texas. His wife, Lorren, is the author of the Kente Kids books."

"Really? Jordan has all of those books, and the Kente Kids Show is her favorite Saturday morning cartoon."

Dex nodded. He then brought her up to date on his other family members. Caitlin couldn't help noticing that Dex's love for his family ran deep. It showed in his discussion of them.

"I understand you're no longer living here in San Antonio, Caitlin."

She leaned back in her chair. "I moved away six months ago. I was offered a teaching job in Fort Worth."

"I'm surprised your father didn't try and convince you not to go."

She inhaled deeply, hearing the sarcasm in his voice, but deciding to ignore it. "He actually encouraged me to take the job. I should've known then that something was wrong. He was dying and he didn't want me or Jordan around to watch. According to Dr. Flores, it was too late for chemotherapy. Unfortunately, the disease hadn't been diagnosed early enough. By the time Dad began experiencing symptoms, the cancer had already spread to other parts of his body. He and I talked on the phone often and not once did he tell me about his condition. I can only imagine what it cost him to pretend nothing was wrong so I wouldn't find out."

"When did you find out?"

"A few days ago. Dr. Flores called and told me. By that time Dad had been in the hospital a week already. He had ordered them not to contact me until it became absolutely necessary."

Caitlin signed heavily. "He was a wonderful father and I loved him dearly. What you told him at the hospital was true, Dex. It was my decision to remain here in the States with him and not join you in Australia. I couldn't turn my back on him."

Dex stared at Caitlin through narrowed eyes. "But you could turn your back on me, is that it? What about the vow you made during our wedding ceremony to forsake all others? And the one you made on our wedding night, Caitlin? Didn't they mean anything? And let's not forget the big one. The promise you made the last night we spent together. You promised to come to me in Australia after your father got better."

"Dex, try and understand. I was placed in a position that I shouldn't have been placed in. I had to choose between the two of you. Dad was pulling me one way, and you were pulling me another. During the day Dad would lecture me on all the reasons you and I shouldn't be married, and then at night when you would call from Australia, just hearing your voice reminded me of all the reasons we should be married. But that didn't stop the turmoil. It only added to it. Finally, I had to make a choice."

"And we both know what choice you made, don't we?"

"Yes." Caitlin tore her gaze away from his. He would never believe how difficult it had been for her to make that decision or how totally alone she felt after making it. He would never understand the happiness she felt when she discovered she was pregnant and knowing that although she no longer had him, she had been left with a part of him.

Jordan became a constant reminder of the one man she had truly loved, and the only man she would ever love. During the brief time of her marriage to him, Dex had touched her in a way no man had touched her since. Her daughter had been the physical link she needed to keep Dex alive in her heart. It was only after Jordan was born that she truly understood how alone her father must have felt after her mother's death.

"I did what I thought was best. My father needed me, Dex."

"And you think I didn't?"

She forced herself not to react to the anger in Dex's voice. How could she explain to him how the thought of her leaving had nearly destroyed her father?

Misinterpreting Caitlin's silence, Dex's gaze seated her with its intensity, and anger seemed to radiate from every masculine pore. "Your promises didn't mean a thing." He pushed his chair back and stood. "So much for whispered promises."

He turned and walked out of the kitchen.

Duncan Malone knew something was wrong the minute his nephew walked into his office at Malone Land Developers. More than once over the past few months, he'd cursed the day he'd decided to bring his deceased brother's son into the business. Walker Malone had proven to be irrational, short-tempered and something of a hothead. The only reason he had kept him on was because, like it or not, he was family.

Duncan pushed himself away from his desk and stood. "What is it, Walker?"

Walker Malone quietly closed the door behind him. "I just received word, Uncle Duncan, that Halston Parker has died."

"He did what?" Duncan asked with disbelief etched on his face.

"I said . . ."

"Never mind, don't repeat it. I heard you." He sucked in his breath sharply. "How did he die?" Duncan's eyes narrowed suspiciously as he looked at his nephew. He knew Walker had been putting the squeeze on the old man by trying to scare him into selling. He wasn't all that keen on the use of scare tactics, but Walker had assured him that no one would get hurt. "I asked how he died."

"He died of cancer."

"Cancer? You mean to tell me the man was terminally ill, and we didn't know it."

"Apparently not too many people knew it."

"Well, it's part of your job to know everything, Walker," Duncan replied as his jaw tightened, his hands doubled into fists and his eyes burned with rage. "I've already told Remington Oil that Parker was willing to sell. If we've lost the chance to get that land, I'll—"

"We haven't. According to my sources, Parker's survived by a daughter. His death may be a blessing for us. She may be more cooperative than he was."

"And if she isn't?" Duncan asked tersely.

The younger man's face was perfectly calm when he spoke, but his eyes had a look that was chilling. "Then we'll have to convince her otherwise."

CHAPTER 5

Caitlin glanced around the room. Most of the people had left. She'd tried as best she could to prepare herself for the continued flow of condolences from those who had dropped by the house after the services.

Her gaze found Dex. He stood across the room talking to Mr. Burke, the man who owned the drug store located next to her father's printing shop. Mr. Burke and her father had been good friends for a number of years. Undoubtedly he was sharing some fond memory with Dex.

Caitlin found herself staring at Dex, fascinated by his clothing. It was the second time she'd ever seen him dressed in a suit. The first time had been at their wedding. And now, like then, she couldn't help but admire what she saw. The dark suit he wore made him even more handsome.

She couldn't help noticing the interest he drew. At first, she'd been unsure how she should introduce him to everyone, but he had taken the decision out of her hands by simply introducing himself as her husband. When he'd met her gaze evenly, it reminded her that legally, he could be just that.

At least now there was a face to go along with the name Dexter Jordan Madaris. Caitlin knew deep down some people had seriously doubted she had ever married. There were a few who had not easily been convinced, and believed her marriage had been fabricated to give her daughter a name and to retain her respectability.

A flood of heat suffused Caitlin's cheeks when she realized while her thoughts had momentarily taken her miles away, Dex had been watching her. She blinked self-consciously under his concentrated gaze, but continued to hold his stare. His eyes had lost the coldness they had acquired over the past couple of days, and now appeared warm and caring. Not once had he left her side during the entire service. He'd been there for her just like he had promised her father.

She watched as Dex excused himself from Mr. Burke's company and headed her way. She couldn't help studying him, and a sinking feeling swept over her. She'd given up a man most women would have given their right arm for.

"I think you should go lie down for a while, Caitlin," Dex said, in a gentle voice when he stood before her.

She met his dark eyes. "There're people still here. I can't just leave them, Dex."

"Yes, you can. I'm sure everyone will understand."

"But what about Jordan? She'll be home any time now, and I need to straighten this place up after everyone—"

"All you need to do is to take care of yourself. You can begin by going upstairs to rest. Don't worry about Jordan or this house, I'll take care of everything."

Rather than argue, Caitlin relented. He was right. She was tired. The funeral service had taken its toll on her. She felt depleted of strength, logical thoughts and resistance. "Are you sure? I feel like I'll be deserting you."

Something flickered through his expression. "You won't be . . . deserting me."

Though spoken soft, his words carried a definite barb. Although he hadn't made a comeback to her statement, Caitlin knew he was probably thinking deserting him was something she was pretty good at.

"Go ahead and get some rest, Caitlin."

She turned and started up the stairs.

It was two hours later before Caitlin returned from her nap. She had showered and changed into a pullover white blouse and a matching flowing gauze cotton skirt.

"You're beautiful as ever, Caitlin, and I still think you married the wrong brother," Clayton Madaris said.

A smile touched her lips as she met Clayton's gaze. All the guests had gone and the living room was as neat as a pin. Clayton and Dex had removed their jackets and were sitting lazily in chairs sipping drinks. They stood when she entered the room.

She studied Clayton's handsome face. Like Dex, he had nut-brown colored skin, but where Dex's eyes were charcoal-gray, Clayton's were a deep rich brown.

She had wondered what Clayton's attitude would be toward her, and had been slightly nervous when he'd arrived the day before. To her surprise, he had greeted her like an old friend. It didn't take long for her to discover Clayton Madaris was the same witty and utterly charming man she'd met four years ago. She had felt comfortable with him immediately.

Smiling at Clayton's offhanded comment about her marrying the wrong brother, she walked over to him and gave him a light kiss on the cheek. When they had met four years ago at Whispering Pines, Clayton had tried coming on to her. She had later found out his actions had been to make Dex jealous. Dex, who had been ignoring her up to the day Clayton had arrived, suddenly began showing interest in her.

"I happen to think she married the right one, Clayton," Dex said, glaring at his brother.

Clayton chuckled, pulling Caitlin close to his side. His eyes were brimming with devilishment. "If you hadn't come to your senses when you did, you may have been the one who ended up as her brother-in-law. I would've been her husband. Does that thought bother you, Dex?"

Caitlin's heart lurched at Clayton's question. She wondered why he was baiting his brother. She also wondered how Dex would answer the question, if he responded at all. She was surprised when he did.

"Yeah, Clayton. The thought of Caitlin with any other man bothers me."

Caitlin took a deep breath, not sure how she should take Dex's response. The set of his jaw was stern and the slant of his eyes was hard, dispassionate, almost angry. She was frozen in place under his forceful gaze.

She jumped when she heard a door close upstairs. Turning around, she realized Clayton had left them alone. She turned back to Dex. "Why did Clayton leave?"

Dex shrugged. "Just ignore him. Clayton's into playing games these days."

She lifted a brow. "Oh? And what game is Clayton playing?"

"Patchup. For some reason he thinks all our marriage needs is patching up. I tried telling him it's beyond repair, but he won't believe me."

"I see," she replied softly. Although she knew he was telling the truth, his words had hurt. "Where's Jordan?" She glanced around the room. "Hasn't Ms. Logan returned yet?"

Dex nodded. "She brought Jordan home around five o'clock. I gave her a bath then put her to bed a few minutes ago. She wanted to see you after her bath so we sneaked into your room. She gave you a good night kiss."

Caitlin frowned. "I must have really been sacked out. I don't remember the two of you coming into my bedroom."

I certainly do, Dex thought as his mind conjured up the image of Caitlin lying in bed. She had removed the black dress she'd worn to the funeral, and was sleeping atop the covers in a sexy black teddy. His eyes had devoured her long smooth, shapely legs, her small waist, the fullness of her curvaceous hips and the firmness of her breasts.

No longer did she have the figure of a young girl, but possessed the enticing shape of a woman. All of which he knew had come about as a result of giving birth to their child. He hadn't wanted to want her, but he had. He had felt a throbbing ache within him so keen that he'd been tempted to remove her scanty clothing and run his hand over her body, reacquainting himself with it. Jordan's presence had been the only thing that had prevented him from doing just that. His desire for Caitlin hadn't changed. The past four years hadn't been able to erase that. If anything, the years had sharpened his hunger and desire for her.

"Did Clayton get a chance to look at the divorce papers?"

Caitlin's question brought Dex's mind back to the present. He closed his eyes momentarily in an overwhelming sense of relief. His wayward thoughts were destined to get him in trouble. "Yes," he replied.

She turned to stare at him. "And?"

Dex shrugged. "We don't have to go into this tonight, Caitlin. You've been through enough for one day. Let's just wait until tomorrow to—"

"No, Dex. I'd like to know now."

Dex's eyes narrowed like dark slits. "Why the rush?" he asked harshly. "Is there someone waiting for you in Fort Worth that you're anxious to get back to?"

"Of course not."

Dex eyed her speculatively to determine the truth of her answer. The thought that she might be involved with someone else made his guts twist into knots. "Since the issue of our marital status isn't a pressing concern tonight, let's discuss it tomorrow. Goodnight, Caitlin." He stared at her for another second before turning and mounting the stairs two at a time.

Hours later, Dex was still wide awake, his body was consumed with anger. Forcing air out of his lungs, mounting fury stole its way over his body. He closed his eyes in an attempt to stop it.

In frustration, he snatched his eyes back open. All he could see when he had closed them was Caitlin in another man's arms, being touched by him, being kissed by him and being caressed . . .

He gritted his teeth. "Calm down, man. No woman is worth this much trouble, this much pain."

He turned his head toward the window. The full moon's glow was shining through and illuminated the room in a pale luster of light. A sudden shiver ran through his tall frame as memories flooded his mind. There had also been a full moon in the sky on their wedding night. A night that had been full of so much joy, love, and promises.

During the midnight hour and early morning he'd awakened and had reached out for Caitlin. Again and again she'd come to him willingly, satisfying him more than any woman he'd ever known.

But then, no other woman had given him such pain, something he could never forget. Clayton had tried to convince him that time would ease the pain and soften the anger. But there was something time could not do, and that was to turn itself back. Nor could time restore his bruised male ego her rejection had caused.

In the morning, they were to sit down with Clayton and discuss the state of their marital status. Married or divorced, their daughter would always be their connecting link, and they would never really be free of each other.

Dex's mouth tightened. Who was he kidding? Had he ever really been free of Caitlin? Over the past four years he'd thrown himself into his work until exhaustion racked his body. And no matter how much he'd tried, he hadn't been able to completely exorcise her from his mind. He admitted he hadn't lived a celibate life since they'd been apart, but there hadn't been anyone he'd gotten serious about. All his affairs—if you wanted to call them that—had been casual. Any woman he'd become involved with had known the relationship was a dead end. And deep down a part of him blamed Caitlin for it.

Dex took a deep breath. There was no use trying to sleep. It was out of the question tonight. Getting out of bed, he slipped into a pair of jeans and went downstairs to catch a late night movie on television.

Caitlin sighed looking into her cup of warm milk. Tonight she couldn't sleep. A knot formed in her throat as she glanced around the huge, spacious kitchen. Even when her mother had been alive, the kitchen had been her father's domain. He enjoyed doing all of the cooking, and they'd enjoyed eating all of the dishes he had prepared.

"Is something wrong, Caitlin?"

Caitlin jumped, almost spilling the milk on herself. Her heart started beating wildly and a funny feeling settled in the bottom of her stomach when she turned to face Dex. He was watching her curiously through dark eyes.

"No, nothing's wrong. I just had a hard time sleeping."

Dex stood paused at the doorway, his tall frame almost filling it. "What're you drinking?"

Caitlin's fingers tightened on her cup. "Warm milk. Would you like some?"

"No," he answered stiffly. "I prefer something stronger."

Caitlin nodded. "Couldn't you sleep either?"

Dex's gaze rested on her. His face expressionless. "No."

Caitlin began to feel ill at ease. They were acting like polite strangers. She was suddenly struck with the realization that they were two strangers.

She turned her head to take a better look at him. He was wearing a pair of jeans that rode low on his hips, and his dark chest was bare. As she continued to stare at him, her mind replayed memories. Memories of his touch, his taste and how he had taught her the physical meaning of love. She squeezed her eyes shut trying to blot out the memories from her mind.

"Caitlin, are you sure you're all right?"

She forced herself to look back at him. She saw concern on his face. "I'm fine. I think I'll go back to bed now." She stood to leave.

"No, don't go yet."

Caitlin didn't miss the husky timbre of his voice or the hot glow of desire shining in his eyes. She watched him slowly advance toward her and gasped at the tingling sensation spreading through her body. The next thing she knew he was standing directly in front of her.

Dex gently cupped her cheek and ran his thumb over her bottom lip. Caitlin retreated but he took a step forward recovering the distance. She caught her breath when his thumb parted her lips. His eyes held hers.

"I'll never forget the day I opened that packet and saw those divorce papers and the box with your wedding ring. It tore me in two," he whispered hoarsely.

His gaze moved from hers and directed their full attention to her lips. "After reading your letter, I knew your decision was final, and there was nothing I could say or do to make you change your mind. I felt totally and thoroughly rejected. But most of all I felt downright betrayed."

A lump formed in Caitlin's throat. She stared into the darkness of Dex's eyes and saw pain and anger completely exposed. The emotions displayed there said it all. He would never forgive her for not coming to him in Australia.

"I'm sorry," she whispered, her eyes glazed with tears. "I know an apology is worthless now, but I never meant to hurt you. Please believe I never meant to hurt you."

Dex stared down at her. His gaze took in the sight of her breasts partially visible above the low cut of her lacy white nightgown, a part her robe didn't hide.

"But you did hurt me, and you're right, an apology now is worthless," he said huskily, removing his hand from her mouth to touch the center of her back. "But this isn't."

Then with the slightest of pressure there, he pulled her to him. Her body was warm against his and the smell of her perfume was heady. Beautiful, his mind declared as his eyes consumed her. Her brown face, scrubbed clean of makeup was fresh and lovely. Dex reached up with his free hand and touched her face. "You're beautiful."

Caitlin looked up at him. Her mouth throbbed for his. She wanted him to kiss her, to remove all her lingering doubts about the future, the pain she was feeling for the present and the guilt she held of the past. She wanted all of those things destroyed under the onslaught of his kiss.

Dex read her eyes and what he saw in them made his breathing quicken. The look in them was the sign of imminent surrender.

His gaze moved to her mouth. It was a mouth begging to be kissed, and he intended to give it just what it wanted.

Slowly, he lowered his head to hers. Their lips touched; cautiously at first, withdrawing slightly, then touched again. Caitlin felt desire flood her body when Dex took control. His tongue hungrily stroked the insides of her mouth.

Passion consumed Dex like a lit explosive. He knew at that moment he would never be free of Caitlin. She was in his blood and in his mind. But he was determined to never let her find a way to his heart again.

Dex pulled his mouth away. He allowed Caitlin a quick breath, then once again captured her lips, dominating her mouth in a relentless assault of his tongue. A faint groan escaped her throat as he made a thorough exploration of her mouth, while his hand boldly caressed her through the soft material of her robe.

The deep recesses of Dex's mind declared kissing her was not enough. He wanted to bury himself deep within her body. He wanted to make love to her all through the night, wake up with her in his arms and make love to her again in the bright morning light. He wanted to touch her every hour on the hour.

But then another part of his mind, the one that dealt with reality, was determined to shield him from further pain. It reminded him of what she'd done to him four years ago. How she had taken the love he had never given another woman and had made a mockery of it; how she'd rejected him. Those thoughts sharply cut into his passion. Suddenly he stopped kissing her and stepped backward.

"Go to bed, Caitlin." Dex's words were sharp and cold. They sent a chill through her body. Her questioning eyes met the icy glow in his.

At that precise moment the kitchen door swung open and Clayton walked in. His eyes registered surprise at seeing them in the kitchen at such a late hour. "Sorry. I didn't know the two of you were still up."

Caitlin spoke, her voice shaky, her eyes filled with tears. "Don't apologize, Clayton. In fact your timing was perfect. Goodnight." Noiselessly, she swept by Clayton and out of the kitchen.

Clayton watched her fleeing back. He then turned to his brother, a dark scowl on his face. "What was that all about?"

Dex leaned against the counter. "I don't know what you're talking about."

"Don't fake innocence with me. I'm talking about Caitlin's tears, not to mention swollen lips belonging to a mouth that's been kissed. Just what kind of game are you playing with her?"

Dex's eyes narrowed. "Stay out of this, Clayton. It doesn't concern you."

Clayton stared at his brother, attempting to control his anger. "You're right. It really doesn't concern me other than the fact Caitlin is family. And you know how protective Madarises are when it comes to family."

Dex picked up Caitlin's cup of unfinished milk. Turning to the sink he poured the contents out, rinsed the cup and placed it in the dishwasher. Slamming the dishwasher closed, he turned to face his brother. "Family? Would you care to explain that remark?" he asked harshly.

"Not at all. Like I told you, there's a good chance that legally Caitlin's still your wife whether you like it or not. I think once you finally get over your bitterness, and all this anger you've been carrying around for the last four years, you'll realize that other than Jordan, she has no one. With her father's death, she's all alone now."

"And you expect me to cry about it? It was her choice, Clayton," Dex snapped.

"Yeah, and one you'll undoubtedly hold against her for the rest of her life. You don't know how to forgive or let go of past hurts. I think it's time you tried."

"Damn it. How can you even think I should forgive her for what she did to me, and what she put me through? I believed in her, Clayton. I trusted her with my heart, I loved her with my entire soul, and I had faith that her love for me would survive the test of time. I was the biggest fool when she chose to stay here with her father and end our marriage. Once destroyed trust, love and faith can't ever be recaptured or replaced. It's impossible for me to ever share those same feelings with her again. There will always be doubt, resentment and heartache no matter what," he stated in a gruff voice.

Dex let his fist hit against the counter. "I don't want to care for her again, Clayton. I don't want to ever love her again. Can't you see that? The pain went too deep. Caitlin and I can't ever go back."

Hearing his brother's pain so deeply expressed, Clayton felt Dex's innermost agony. It wasn't clear to him why he was so obviously sticking his nose where it didn't belong other than he believed reuniting Dex with Caitlin was the key to his brother's future happiness. Dex had always been a person who did not do anything half-measure, and that included falling in love. Hopefully, when he put his trampled pride aside, he would realize that deep down he still loved Caitlin. Otherwise, why would there be so much pain, even now? As far as Clayton was concerned Dex needed Caitlin in his life. But right now, the concepts of forgiving, letting go of the past and moving ahead were foreign to him.

Clayton gave Dex a half-hearted smile. "I know the two of you can't go back, and as far as I'm concerned you shouldn't even try. What I suggest is for you and Caitlin to just start over. You have a second chance to start fresh. Get to know her, Dex. Court her properly and build a life with her again. Just put the past behind you once and for all and start over."

Just start over . . .

Clayton's words rang in Dex's ears. Discarding his jeans he climbed back into bed. Could he and Caitlin actually pull it off? Was there a chance the past could somehow be buried and the future built anew? Did he even want to try? Did she? Could he erase that uneasiness that comes when one's trust in another has been damaged?

Numerous questions flooded his mind. He knew he couldn't consider a future with Caitlin until he was able to deal with his inner turmoil and doubts, but most of all, his anger. His thoughts went to his daughter, his beautiful little girl. He knew he owed her a chance to have a normal family life, which meant some sort of reconciliation with Caitlin.

A whispered sigh escaped Dex's lips. There were a lot of things about his relationship with Caitlin that he'd never dwelled on before. Caitlin was right when she'd said they really didn't know each other. Yes, they had married . . . and as it turned out probably still were, and they had conceived a child. But they really didn't know each other. He didn't know her favorite color, hobbies, type of music or her favorite food; the things married couples should know about each other.

Had they really known each other four years ago, they could have been spared a lot of pain and anguish. He would've been better able to deal with her emotional upheaval brought on by her father's nonacceptance of their marriage. And he would have known that because of Caitlin's close relationship with her father, she would have been driven by both guilt and loyalty, and would have felt compelled to stay with Halston at least until he had recuperated. And during that time, she could have somehow convinced her father to accept her love for her husband.

But instead, because she'd been so sure Dex wouldn't understand and allow her the extra time she needed before joining him in Australia, she'd opted to turn her back on their love and sacrifice her own chance at happiness.

And it appears he may have been slightly mistaken about Caitlin's level of maturity four years ago. When they had met, she had been a recent college graduate, somewhat naive in the ways of the world, and had just landed her first job away from home. She'd been inexperienced as far as men were concerned and had been forced to choose between the love of a man she'd just met, and that of a loving father who represented the only security she had ever known.

Thinking back now, Dex could almost sympathize with the situation she'd suddenly been placed in. And with belated hindsight, he could see how it had happened. However, he still wasn't sure a part of him could ever forgive her for not living up to his expectations and for not keeping her promises. But he owed it to their daughter to try. Trying to rebuild their marriage would take a lot of effort on both of their parts, but he was willing to give it his best shot if she was.

If they decided to give their marriage another try, there would only be one of two possible endings; they would either move forward together, or they would allow the pain from the past to consume them, and their marriage would become a living hell, one they would both come to regret.

CHAPTER 6

Caitlin regarded both men through lowered lashes. Clayton was sitting across from her in what used to be her father's favorite recliner. Dex stood gazing out the living room window. However, his expression was a dead give-a-away that any objects outside the window were not where his concerns were. She was more than sure that like her, he was very interested in what Clayton had to say.

Nervously, she locked her fingers together and rested her hands in her lap. Jordan was spending some time with Ms. Logan and her granddaughter, so there were only the three of them in the quiet house. Except for the shuffling of the papers Clayton was studying, and for the ticking of the grandfather clock across the room, no noise broke the strained silence.

Clayton looked up and met Caitlin's worried expression with a reassuring one. "We might as well get this over with," he said smiling. "As much as I have enjoyed all of your company, especially that of my darling niece, I do have a job to return to. My plane leaves this afternoon." He gave her a wink. "Don't look so nervous, Caitlin. This is all very informal. I'm merely here as a neutral party."

Dex made a loud noise that sounded suspiciously like a snort.

Clayton laughed. "It seems my brother obviously thinks otherwise. Dex, how about joining us," he called over his shoulder.

Caitlin watched Dex turn from the window and walk toward them Surprise flickered in her eyes when instead of taking the chair not far from where Clayton was sitting, he came and sat next to her on the sofa.

He sat so close, the material of his jeans pressed against her thighs not covered by her shorts. Her heart skipped a beat. His nearness was having an arousing effect on her. The palms of her hands were damp, and a tingling sensation began spreading throughout her entire body.

"Now then," Clayton said eyeing them both speculatively. "Your father was right, Caitlin. Legally, you and Dex are still married. Therefore, to deal with your situation the two of you can either continue on with your marriage by picking up where you left off four years ago, or contact your own attorneys and file for a divorce. However, if you do decide to file for a divorce it won't be as cut and dried as the last time because of Jordan. There will be the issues of child support and custody rights to deal with."

Caitlin spoke softly. "I don't want to cause any unnecessary problems. There's no need for much child support. The sale of Dad's printing shop should bring in enough money for me and Jordan to live comfortably. And I do have a job in Fort Worth to return to in the fall."

She shifted nervously in her seat. "And as far as custody rights, I'll agree to whatever visitation privileges Dex wants. I'd never do anything to deliberately keep him and Jordan apart."

Clayton nodded. He then fixed his gaze on his brother. "And just what is it that you want, Dex?" he asked.

Dex stood slowly and walked back to the window. Caitlin had addressed the issues that would only be pertinent if they chose to get a divorce. "It would probably be a lot simpler if you were to ask me what I didn't want, Clayton."

Clayton rolled his brown eyes to the ceiling. "Very well, what is it you don't want?"

Dex turned. His gaze held Caitlin within its dark scope. He couldn't help noticing a slight shiver pass through her body with his close scrutiny. She looked as beautiful and radiant as the morning sun. The velvety softness of her cheeks reminded him of an African violet. The lips that he had so thoroughly kissed last night were now parted slightly as if in an open invitation for him to do so again. Her hair hung loose about her shoulders, and she looked incredibly sexy in the outfit she was wearing. He walked toward her slowly, coming to a stop directly in front of her.

When he finally spoke, his words came out clear and firm. "What I don't want is a divorce."

Shocked into silence, Caitlin's eyes widened. "B—but why? What possible reason could there be for you to not want a divorce? Just last night you said our marriage was beyond repair."

Dex's gaze slid from Caitlin to his brother. "If you don't mind, Clayton, I'd like a few words alone with my wife."

Caitlin was stunned at the possessive tone of Dex's voice when he referred to her as his wife. Although it appeared that legally she was, she never expected him to ever say it like he didn't mind it. She thought he would be upset upon finding out they were still actually married.

"In other words, Dex," Clayton chuckled, breaking into Caitlin's thoughts. "You want me to get lost for a while."

A smile curved Dex's lips. "Your ability to figure things out amazes me."

A few minutes later Clayton had left them alone to go upstairs to pack. Caitlin watched as Dex sat in the chair his brother had vacated minutes earlier. He stretched his long legs out in front of him, and leisurely crossed them at the booted ankles.

"Now to answer your question, Caitlin, there're numerous reasons why we shouldn't get a divorce, and the foremost one should be obvious, our daughter. Staying together wouldn't be for either one of us, it would be for Jordan. I think we owe her that. She's too young to understand what's going on. All she knows at the moment is that I'm here. In her mind, my appearance into her life is permanent. She doesn't have the faintest idea what a divorce means. But we do, don't we? Although neither of us came from broken homes, we've heard numerous stories about the scarring of children that do. I don't want that for our daughter. Do you?"

Caitlin shook her head as her hope sank dejectedly. Dex didn't want them to continue their marriage because of any feelings he still had for her, but because of their daughter. "A child is no reason for two people to remain married if they don't love each other, Dex."

Dex's eyes narrowed. "I disagree. If both individuals want what's best for their child, they'll be willing to sacrifice just about anything. Even their own happiness."

Caitlin sighed. He was admitting that he was willing to sacrifice his happiness by remaining married to her for Jordan's sake. "It won't work."

"It'll work, if we make it work. You've had Jordan for three years. All I'm asking is a chance to be a part of her life. Maybe four years ago we did act hasty and rushed into things, but now the situation is different. We have a child, Caitlin, a child that one way or another, I'm going to be a father to. I don't want to be a part-time dad, but a full-time one, and I won't settle for anything less."

Gazing directly into his eyes, Caitlin drew a deep breath and asked, "And just what are you proposing?"

When he spoke Dex's voice was deeper and huskier than before. "What I propose is that starting today we put the past behind us and start over. There's no way we can pretend that part of our life didn't happen, but we can move on and not look back."

Stunned dark eyes held Dex's gaze. "That's impossible! You hate me."

A deep scowl settled over Dex's features. "That's not true. I don't hate you."

Caitlin stood. Placing hands on her hips, she glared at him. "You may as well. You still harbor resentment for what I did. How can you expect me to give our marriage another try when I know how you feel? No matter what you say, Dex, I know the anger and hurt is still there. Those feelings couldn't have dissolved overnight."

Dex sighed, rubbing his fingers to his temple. "My feelings are something I have to deal with. In time, I'll come to terms with what happened between us."

"And what if you can't? You said I'm the woman who betrayed you, remember? As far as you're concerned, I'm the one you feel rejected you, and the one who made promises of love and commitments, then broke them all. I'm also the woman who had your child and, according to what you believe, didn't have the decency to contact you to let you know I was pregnant. Knowing what you think of me, how can you expect me to live with you again as your wife?"

Dex pushed himself to a standing position and faced her. "I'm not promising miracles, Caitlin. But I am willing to give our marriage another chance, if you are. I can honestly admit the blame of our breakup wasn't entirely your fault. I've been too hurt and angry to realize that I, in part, was responsible for what happened between us. We had met less than two weeks before we married. There were a number of things that I could've done, like being more supportive and less pushy. I could've weathered your father's disapproval of me more diplomatically by understanding you were his only child, and that his life had been centered around you. I could have taken it less personal."

He pushed his hands deep into his pockets. "We can both look back and say if only we had handled things differently, but doing so won't turn back the hands of time. I believe we can make another go at things because we have something very special going for us. We both love our daughter very much and want what's best for her. And we can use our time together and get to know each other without feeling rushed." Dex hesitated, then smiled smoothly. "That kiss last night proves we're still attracted to each other. So what do we have to lose?"

Caitlin shook her head, fighting the urge to grab Dex and shake him. Didn't he know that sexual attraction was no basis to continue their marriage? A marriage had to be based on love. A lot of marriages failed when held together merely for the sake of a child. And to make matters worse, she knew at that very moment she still loved Dex, and had never stopped loving him.

When she decided to end their marriage, she'd also ended her only chance at happiness, because he was the only man she could and would ever love.

Pain darkened her expression. Telling him how she felt was the last thing she would do. Doing so would have her heart at his mercy, and she didn't want that. It hurt her to know he was only willing to continue their marriage because he felt an obligation to see that Jordan got a normal family life.

"Well, what's it going to be, Caitlin?"

She frowned. "If I agree to continue our marriage, just what will you expect from me?"

Dex's eyes continued to hold hers. "I'll expect no more from you than I'll expect from myself. Marriage is like a partnership. The both of us should give everything we have to make it work."

"Will it be a marriage in name only?"

"No. I want you to be a wife to me in every way, and that includes sharing my bed. We should resume our marriage with the full intentions of things working out. Therefore, neither of us should hold back on anything. We're both adults, with normal, healthy physical appetites."

Caitlin's stomach began doing somersaults. Their steamy kiss last night had made her realize just how much she ached for Dex. Long after she had gone up to bed, her body still longed for his touch. He had stirred up memories inside of her. Now the thought that he wanted them to plunge head on into physical intimacy, made the ache inside of her that much more urgent and made her doubts and fears that much more acute. There would be passion in their marriage, but not love. Could she live with him from day to day, sharing his bed, knowing how he really felt about her? And that the only reason he remained married to her was because of their child?

Caitlin released a heavy sigh. What choice did she have? By being Jordan's father, Dex had certain rights. He had made it clear that he intended to become deeply involved in his daughter's life, which meant technically, he would also be involved in hers. If she refused to go along with what he was proposing, would he take her to court to gain custody of Jordan? Could she risk the chance of him doing that? Besides, wasn't it time for Jordan to have her father in her life?

"All right, Dex," she said, meeting his gaze. "I'm willing to give our marriage another try."

Dex nodded. "You do understand that we'll both have to make concessions, especially about where we'll live. I'm willing to move to Fort Worth if living there is important to you."

Caitlin was surprised by his offer. She knew how close he was to his family. He had told her when they'd first met that one of the things he regretted about going to Australia was the time he would be away from them. "No. Living in Fort Worth isn't important to me. I can find a teaching job just about anywhere."

"Does that mean you're willing to move to Houston with me?"

"Yes."

"And are you willing to be my wife in every way?"

She knew what he was asking. "No."

Dex's brows lifted. "No?"

"No. I don't think we should rush into anything. Especially the part about us sharing a bed. I want the decision of when we resume the intimate part of our marriage to be mine, and not yours."

Dex stared at her. He started to disagree, then changed his mind. If that was what she wanted, he would go along with it. But after the kiss they had shared last night, he wondered how he would handle being around her and not being able to touch her. "All right, Caitlin. It will be your decision when we sleep together again."

Caitlin was glad he hadn't fought her on that. She would need plenty of time to get adjusted to the idea that Dex was still her husband.

"Now that we have all that settled, let's seal our agreement with a kiss," Dex said.

Caitlin saw a smile tugging at the corners of his mouth and knew he thought he had her just where he wanted her. But she had news for him. He would soon find out she could play just as hard as he did.

"All right," she said blandly. She walked up to him, but before he could reach out and touch her, she gave him a chaste peck on the cheek.

Dex grabbed her arm. "Hey, that's not what I wanted, Caitlin."

"But that's all you're getting, Dex Madaris," she countered, giving him an all-accusing glare.

Dex's eyes widened in surprise at how she had just stood up to him again. During the two weeks that they were together at Whispering Pines, she had been accommodating to his every whim. He couldn't retain the grin touching his features. Sometime during the past four years, Caitlin had grown into a gutsy woman. He had a feeling she wouldn't be as accommodating as she used to be. He would just have to work on that, and would enjoy every minute breaking down her resistance. He was looking forward to seducing his wife.

Wrong, Caitlin," he said, pulling her closer. "That's not all I'm getting."

Before she could react, Dex's mouth covered hers. His kiss was urgent. It was warm and demanding as their tongues met in an exchange so stimulating, so frenzied, Caitlin was immediately consumed with desire. Her lips moved eagerly beneath his, and she lifted her arms and encircled his neck. Dex pulled her closer to his hard frame, his hand gently pressing her more intimately to him.

Somewhere in the back of Caitlin's mind she remembered they still had a guest in the house who, like last night, could pop up anytime. She pushed herself out of Dex's arms.

Dex lifted his head and looked down at her, his eyes glazed with desire. He shook his head, clearing it. He'd been completely held captive by the sweetness of Caitlin's mouth. The taste of her would remain with him the rest of the day. Reaching up, he touched her swollen lips with the tip of his finger.

"Your mouth can't handle too many of my kisses can it?"

Caitlin's gaze rested on his lips, and without thinking, she replied saucily, "My mouth can handle as many kisses as you care to give it."

Dex chuckled at her sassy words of confidence. "You think so? Would you care to prove it?"

Caitlin took a deep breath. She was slightly dismayed at how easily Dex could arouse her to the point of making her forget that beside being physically attracted to each other, they had nothing going for them other than the love of their daughter. That wasn't completely true. Unknown to him, he still had her love; a love that unlike his, had survived the test of time.

"Maybe some other time, Dex."

Dex's mouth curved upward. "Is that a promise?"

Caitlin stiffened at his words. "Haven't you learned by now that I break any promises I make?"

The smile on Dex's face vanished instantly. He cupped her chin roughly with his hand. "Why can't you just leave well enough alone?" he asked sharply. "There's nothing wrong with making promises as long as you intend to keep them."

He quickly released her then regarded her resignedly. "How can you expect me to put the past behind us when you can't?"

It was only after Caitlin had heard the door slam behind Dex, that she realized she'd screwed up what had started out as a promising new beginning.

Corinthians Avery nervously sat in the plush reception area on the executive floor of Remington Oil. Although she was looking forward to the meeting with the company's board of directors, she couldn't stop the butterflies floating around in her stomach.

Her gaze skimmed approvingly over her outfit. Knowing she had this early morning meeting, she had taken the extra time needed to look her best, conveying an aura of total professionalism. She knew the navy blue tailored suit, with its straight skirt did wonders, and outlined the slimness of her five-foot eight inch figure. Her legs and feet were encased in ultra sheer black hose and navy leather pumps.

Her hairstylist had given her hair a totally new look. Gone was the long thick black hair that she often wore in a French braid. Instead, she had a chic short style that was curled around her chocolate-colored face. Her makeup was flawless, thanks to the teachings of her best friend, Brenna, who was a former model.

Satisfied with her appearance, Corinthians slanted the man sitting next to her a sidelong glance, wondering if he shared her nervousness. She inwardly laughed. Adam Flynn, senior exploration manager for Remington Oil, had been in the business much too long to get nervous. It was well known that he had worked for the company a lot longer than her age of twenty-nine years. It was also a known fact that he was a personal friend of S. T. Remington.

Corinthians shifted in the leather chair, making another attempt to downplay her nervousness. It wasn't the idea of attending a board meeting that made her anxious—she'd done that several times before; it was anticipation of the news she hoped the members of the board had for her and Adam. Specifically, she wanted to hear that the Leabo Project was a sure thing.

The Leabo Project was her baby. As one of the top geologists with Remington, it had been her untiring research—not to mention Adam's belief in her uncanny sixth sense when it came to playing hunches, and her intense analysis of core samples that had produced the detailed report. Her studies had discovered some promising geological anomalies located in an isolated area not far from Eagle Pass, Texas. Based on her report, the executives at Remington Oil were moving quickly to acquire all the land in the area for exploration.

Although no one would admit it, there was little doubt in everyone's mind that the possibility of locating a major oil field in the area existed.

"Ms. Avery. Mr. Flynn." The secretary's soft voice captured Corinthians' attention. "The members of the board are ready now."

Corinthians tightly grasped the portfolio she held in her hand as she stood.

"Don't you dare get nervous on me," Adam Flynn said as a smile flitted across his face. His blue eyes gleamed bright as he heaved his huge muscled framed to an upright stance.

Corinthians returned the smile to the man who had been her immediate boss since the day he had interviewed her just weeks before graduating from Grambling. Remington Oil had sent him and a team of company recruiters to the university, and they had made her an offer she couldn't refuse—a chance to work as a geologist with one of the nation's major oil companies. That had been nearly eight years ago, and since then, Remington Oil had made good on all its promises.

As a geologist, she had received a top salary, had done extensive traveling to all corners of the globe, and had worked with a number of well known scientists and researchers. During all that time, the older man standing before her had been her mentor, her teacher and most of all a friend. He was a man she highly respected.

"Let's not keep the old boys waiting," Adam said, taking a firm grip on her arm and leading her out of the reception area toward the meeting room. "The question is no longer 'if', Corinthians, but it's 'when'. As soon as all the land in the area is purchased, Remington will make their move."

She nodded as Adam swung open the huge ornate door to the board-room, to let her enter. The members of the board were already seated around the table. She and Adam moved toward the vacant chairs left for them. Seconds later, S. T. Remington, president of the company, entered the room through double doors at the opposite end of the room and took his place at the head of the table.

With a cursory nod to everyone in the room, Mr. Remington brought the meeting to order. Corinthians nervously listened as items on the agenda were dealt with one after another, which to her way of thinking seemed to take forever.

"The next item on the agenda is the Leabo Project." Mr. Remington's gaze moved to her. "Corinthians, I know I express the sentiment of every man here by saying your research for Leabo was outstanding and is to be commended. We're lucky to have you as a member of R O's team. I hope your recent promotion to head geologist indicates how much we value you and your services."

Corinthians' smile lit up the entire room. "Thank you, Mr. Remington, and it does." Adam gave her hand an I-told-you-so squeeze.

"Now," S. T. Remington continued, "Edward, can you give us an up-date on the land purchase?"

Edward Wilson stood. "As you know, gentlemen, to date we have pur-chased quite a number of landholdings in the area for the Leabo project. However, as you can see from my report in front of you, there is one tract that isn't marked with our ownership. This, gentlemen, is a very impor-tant parcel that has not yet been purchased. Although Corinthians' re-port doesn't indicate this tract of land contains any promising formation, without it, there can be no Leabo."

Boisterous conversation rumbled around the table after the man's statement. Mr. Remington had to use his gavel several times to get order restored. "Edward, would you please explain why this parcel is so impor-tant?"

"The tract which is registered as Shadowland encloses the area of Leabo on three sides. Therefore, without it, we have no way of getting our equipment on Leabo."

"You said this tract only surrounds Leabo on three sides. What about the fourth side?" a board member asked.

"The fourth backs up against a small pool that's filled with some sort of rock formation. Without Shadowland, our only other alternative would be by air. And that too, gentlemen, is impossible when you think of the equipment we'll be using."

"Have we made an offer to the owners of Shadowland?" S. T. Remington asked.

"Yes, and according to Malone Land Developers, the company we're using to handle the negotiations, they were just about to close the deal with the owner when he suddenly became ill and died. Mr. Malone is to meet with the man's daughter, after a reasonable period of mourning has passed. He doesn't foresee any problems. The deal on the land should be finalized by the end of the month."

"Good." Mr. Remington's gaze then swung to Adam Flynn. "Adam, have you selected an exploration company for the project?"

Adam stood. "Yes, S. T., I have. The company I've chosen is relatively new but they have completed a number of smaller projects for us. I think they're ready to take on something of this magnitude." Adam smiled at the men sitting around the table. "There's no doubt in my mind the owner of the company will do an outstanding job, basically because I'm the one who taught him a lot of what he knows. He's a former employee who went into business for himself. I've decided to offer the job to Dexter Madaris of Madaris Explorations. Unless, however, there're some objections."

Corinthians felt a sharp jolt at the mention of Dex's name. She glanced up at Adam, clenching her hands together, trying to concentrate on her surroundings and not on the name she had just heard. But she couldn't.

Dex was back in the States and had formed his own company? If that was true, then Adam was right. Dex was the best man for the job. In her personal opinion, Dex Madaris was the best man for anything.

She swallowed with difficulty as memories assailed her. Memories of her love for a man who had never returned it. Dex had been one of Remington Oil's top geologists when she'd been hired on after college. He had taken her under his wings, showing her the ropes. During that time, they had become close friends, but not as close as she'd wanted. Before she had been given the chance to push for more, he'd been transferred to Australia. She had heard through the company grapevine that he'd gotten married and had later divorced. For the life of her, she couldn't imagine any woman not wanting him. He was hard-working, intelligent, well-mannered and as handsome as sin.

Corinthians unclenched her hands and relaxed her muscles when none of the board members opposed Adam's choice. As head geologist for Leabo, she and Dex would be working closely together again.

Determination grew like a flame within her. This time she would have the intimate relationship she'd always longed for. Dex didn't know it yet, but she was the woman for him and had always been. She was exactly what he needed, a woman who would appreciate him for the man he was.

She lifted her chin, her dark eyes cool and calm as her decision was made. Dexter Madaris would one day be hers, and this time nothing would stand in her way of having him.

"When will you be contacting Mr. Madaris?" Mr. Remington's question jarred Corinthians' attention back to the meeting.

"I'll try reaching him later today," Adam said.

Mr. Remington nodded. "Fine. That concludes our business. Good day, everyone."

With solid conviction and a made up mind, Corinthians slipped out of her chair and stood. A bright smile covered her face as she walked briskly from the room.

"Mommy! Mommy! My daddy's back from taking Uncle Clayton to the airport. I heard the car outside!"

Caitlin was standing at the kitchen cabinet lining the shelves with fresh contact paper while Jordan jumped up and down beside her. Her daughter's face was filled with excitement. Caitlin couldn't remember ever seeing her in such a happy mood. In just four short days Dex had managed to capture a special place in his daughter's heart.

A slight tinge of jealousy touched Caitlin. Before Dex's appearance she'd been the most important person in her daughter's life. It amazed her how children could accept changes so easily. She bent down on one knee so that she could face Jordan on her level. "You like your daddy a lot don't you, darling?" she asked smiling.

Jordan's dark head bobbed up and down and her eyes lit up. "Yes, Mommy. I like my daddy a lot." Her cherubic brown face took on a serious expression. "You like my daddy, too, don't you, Mommy?"

Caitlin cradled her daughter to her. Like wasn't a strong enough word to describe what she felt for the man who was her husband and the father of her child. "Yes, baby, Mommy likes your daddy a lot. An awful lot."

"That's good to hear," a deep masculine voice said from the doorway.

Caitlin jumped. She hadn't heard Dex enter.

"Daddy!" Jordan broke from her mother's embrace and raced straight to her father, who reached down and picked her up in one smooth sweep. His eyes met Caitlin's over Jordan's head. She noticed the anger that had penetrated their depths earlier that day had disappeared and in its place were traces of tenderness and warmth. Not understanding what had prompted his change in attitude toward her, Caitlin's gaze fell away from his.

"Daddy, do you like my mommy?"

Jordan's innocent question made Caitlin gasp in silence. She quickly turned to the cabinet presenting her back to her husband and her daughter. However, that did nothing to stop Dex's response from reaching her ears. "Yes, Jordan. I like your mommy. I like your mommy a lot, too."

For the rest of the evening Caitlin watched from a distance as Jordan and Dex spent time together. He read her a story from one of her Kente Kids books, and helped her put a puzzle together. He even watched her favorite Disney video with her twice.

Caitlin kept busy so she would not intrude on father's and daughter's time together. Hours later, after a quiet dinner and Jordan's bath, she and Dex put her to bed. When Jordan said her prayers for the night, once again they included her grandfather and special thanks for her daddy coming home. She also thanked God for her Uncle Clayton and for having a mommy and daddy that liked each other so much.

Dex grabbed Caitlin's arm when she tried backing out of the room after Jordan had fallen asleep. "Not so fast, Caitlin," he said, pulling her out into the hall and closing Jordan's door behind them. "I believe there's some unfinished business between us."

A quick stab of desire settled in the pit of Caitlin's stomach with Dex's touch. "I don't know what you're talking about," she replied breathlessly.

Dex pressed her against the wall. "I'm talking about a statement you made earlier today that your mouth can handle as many kisses I care to give it."

Heat stained Caitlin's cheeks. "I don't remember saying that."

"Don't you?" Dex rasped hoarsely as his finger traced the base of her throat. A smile touched his lips. "I'm going to enjoy starting over with you again, Caitlin."

"Why?" There was a hint of alarm in her voice.

"Because all afternoon I've been remembering just how things used to be between us. Especially on our wedding night. That's the night I discovered that you're a woman who was made to love a man."

A knot in Caitlin's stomach tightened when Dex ran his hand gently against her arm. "You're full of it, Dex. I didn't know the first thing about pleasing you." Her voice was a dazed whisper. "You were the one with all the experience."

Dex took another step forward, making any retreat impossible. "You were perfect. I'll never forget the first time I saw you without any clothes."

Caitlin's face flushed. She lifted her head a fraction to gaze into the dark eyes that held hers. What was Dex trying to do to her? Did he have any idea what turmoil this topic of conversation was causing? She was beginning to ache for him again.

"You walked out of the bathroom wearing the sexiest nightie I'd ever seen. You looked so shy and so unsure of yourself." Dex's finger gently traced a path up Caitlin's arm causing every cell in her body to vibrate. She silently held back a groan as he continued.

"Your hair was pulled up away from your face and you wore diamond stud earrings in your ears. You looked so beautiful and so sensuous, yet you were so innocent. I wanted you in a way I'd never wanted anyone else, and I soon realized you were not like anyone else. I could never compare you to anyone. You were in a class by yourself."

Dex's finger left her arm and moved across to her breasts. Caitlin's nipples grew taut beneath his touch, and her legs felt like jelly. He moved his body closer. She was unable to move or breathe. The only things she could do were inhale the manly scent of him, and feel his arousal pressed against her stomach.

Dex's breath was hot against her ear as he continued. "I remember coming toward you in a daze and slowly undressing you. I remember the trust in your eyes. I also remember the shocked expression on your face when I whispered just *what* I was going to do to you, *how* I was going to do it and *when* I was going to do it. Before the clock struck twelve, I had made you mine, Caitlin. I made you my woman. Do you remember?"

They gazed at each other, their thoughts victims of the past. "Yes," Caitlin whispered. "I remember."

"Do you also remember when I carried you to the bed, placed you on it and stretched out beside you? Do you remember me kissing you all over then—"

"Why are you saying these things? Why are you bringing all of this up?" Caitlin asked, her eyes dark with sensual memories. She couldn't look away from him. Her voice was soft and husky, her breathing uncontrolled. "Don't you understand we can't pretend we haven't been apart these last four years?"

"I don't recall asking us to."

"You might as well be, Dex. You're expecting us to pick up where we left off four years ago, and that's not possible."

Dex gave Caitlin a long assessing look. "We're not picking up where we left off. What we're doing is starting over. There is a difference." His hand moved lower to her stomach and a small gasp escaped her lips.

"And," he added, "the reason I'm saying all those things and bringing up all those memories is because I want you to remember how good things were between us." His hand moved even lower and Caitlin thought she wouldn't be capable of ever breathing again.

"I don't ever want you to forget how it was between us."

Caitlin's mouth fell open. "You said it would be my decision when . . ."

Dex leaned closer, his lips mere inches from hers. "When what, Caitlin?"

"When we sleep together again."

Dex's hand touched Caitlin intimately through her shorts, and she silently groaned at the multitude of feelings his boldness caused. He was being deliberately provocative as his fingers unbuttoned her shorts. He stared down into her eyes. Slowly, he slipped his fingers through the shorts' opening. Caitlin's breath lodged in her throat when his fingers came into contact with the silky material of her panties.

"I haven't gone back on my word. It will be your decision. I won't go any farther than you let me," he said in a deep hoarse whisper.

"But you're trying to seduce me," she implored with the barest of breath.

Dex smiled. "You're damn right, I am," he confessed huskily. His lips came down on hers gently and swiftly. His tongue thoroughly swept the insides of her mouth. Caitlin's body jerked with desire as devastating sensations flowed through her.

Suddenly Dex broke the kiss and quickly released her. He then refastened her shorts. "Goodnight, Caitlin, sleep well."

A speechless Caitlin watched as he walked away whistling. She began wondering if she had somehow imagined the whole thing. But with her heart pounding loudly and her body trembling, she knew she hadn't. She closed her eyes and inhaled a deep breath.

Caitlin had thought she could play just as hard as Dex did, but now it was quite obvious to her that Dex Madaris didn't play fair.

CHAPTER 7

"Mr. Madaris, please come in and have a seat. I'm Lt. Williams." Dex closed the door behind him. Crossing the room he extended his hand to the tall, muscularly built man standing behind the desk. The man accepted his hand in a firm handshake. "I was just about to have a cup of coffee. Would you like some?"

"Yes, thanks," Dex said, settling his frame into the chair across from the desk.

After pouring two cups of coffee, Lt. Williams presented Dex with his cup before taking a seat behind his desk. "So what is it you want to know about the Parker investigation?"

A funny feeling unfolded in Dex. "So, there was actually an investigation?"

Lt. Williams eyed Dex over the rim of his coffee mug. "Before I answer any of your questions, I'd like to know what's your interest, Mr. Madaris?"

After taking a sip of coffee, Dex lifted his head and looked directly at the police officer. "My main interest at the moment is his daughter, Caitlin Parker Madaris. She's my wife. Since Halston Parker's death I've—"

"Death? Halston Parker died?" Lt. Williams sat up, immediately alert.

"Yes. He died a few days ago."

Lt. Williams came around and sat on the edge of his desk. "What was the cause of death?"

"He had terminal cancer."

The lieutenant's body relaxed. "Please accept my condolences. This is all very surprising since I just saw Mr. Parker a few weeks ago, and he appeared to be in good health."

Dex nodded. "It's my understanding his condition suddenly took a turn for the worse. A lot of people, including his daughter, didn't know the extent of his illness." He thought that was putting it mildly since Caitlin hadn't known about her father's condition at all.

"I see. So, I suppose the reason you're here is because of Mr. Parker's allegations against Malone Land Developers?"

"Yes. Halston left a letter for me to read after his death. The letter really didn't give any specifics, other than claiming someone was trying to buy land from him and had begun using unsavory tactics to coerce him into selling. He was extremely concerned for my wife's safety. I was hoping you could shed some light on exactly what this is all about."

"Did you bring the letter with you?"

"Yes."

"Do you mind if I take a look at it?"

Dex pulled the letter out of his shirt pocket and handed it to the lieutenant.

Lt. Williams scanned the letter before giving it back to Dex. He then went to a filing cabinet in the corner of the room, and after flipping through various folders, pulled one out. He returned to sit behind his desk.

"Mr. Parker called my office several times within the last couple of months with complaints of harassment by Malone Land Developers. It's my understanding they approached him about some land that's been in his family for a number of years. Each time I checked into Mr. Parker's allegations, I couldn't find anything to link Malone to the incidents taking place."

Dex sat back. A number of questions were buzzing in his mind. "Exactly what sort of incidents were there?"

"Besides the harassing phone calls Mr. Parker claimed he was receiving late at night," Lt. Williams said, going through the folder. "He also reported being followed in his car a few times, his business was vandalized once, and his car was broken into twice. All within a two week period."

Dex tilted his head to the side and looked at Lt. Williams with a curious expression on his face. "Why was my father-in-law so convinced Malone Land Developers were behind any of those things?"

"He claimed he received threatening phone calls about his land after each incident. That wasn't much for us to go on, and after talking with Duncan Malone, who denied that he or anyone in his office made such calls, it was Mr. Parker's word against his. So frankly, without any proof, there wasn't anything we could do."

Dex nodded in understanding. "I see."

"Right now the case is closed. However, if for any reason you feel it should be reopened, let me know."

Dex stood. "I'll do that. And I really appreciate the information. Thanks for taking the time to see me." He turned and walked out of Lt. Williams' office.

"I'm so sorry I can't be there with you."

Even over the phone lines, Caitlin could hear the sadness in her best friend's voice. The unexpected call had been just what she'd needed. She had awakened that morning feeling slightly depressed.

"That's all right, Bev. I know you'd be here if you could." Caitlin sat down on the sofa. "Under the circumstances, it's probably for the best that you didn't make it to Dad's funeral. Dex is here."

"So I've heard. Dad told me. What's going on?"

The question placed a placid smile on Caitlin's face. She and Beverly Burke Garrett had been best friends since grade school.

Caitlin sighed. She then told Beverly about her dad's confession, the promise Dex had made to her father, him finding out about Jordan and their decision to remain married.

"Maybe I should catch a plane and come home. Chase will understand."

"Whether he does or not isn't important. You can't go flying around the country in your condition."

"I guess you're right. That's the price I have to pay for falling in love with a man whose job takes him all over the world. Although I have to admit, London is beautiful this time of the year." There was a pause. "So tell me, how's Dex Madaris? I imagine he's every bit as sexy as he was the time I met him at the hospital after your dad's heart attack."

Caitlin's voice cracked somewhat when she answered. "He's even more so." As far as she was concerned, Dex's very presence in her home was causing her to short-circuit. The smell of his cologne, clean and masculine, was a seductive aroma that permeated the entire house.

"Oh, Bev. What am I going to do? The only reason Dex wants to stay married is because he feels obligated."

"Stop it right there, Caitlin Shi'Larie Madaris. Don't you dare start feeling sorry for yourself. Up to now you've accepted what happened between you and Dex and moved on with your life. Don't you dare start wallowing in 'what could have been'."

"Give me a reason why I shouldn't. Thanks to me, my daughter didn't know her father for three years." Caitlin stood and went to the window. She could see Jordan playing in the backyard with Ms. Logan's granddaughter, while the older woman worked nearby in her flower garden. Caitlin was all alone in the house. Dex had left right after breakfast saying he was going out and would return in a couple of hours. She couldn't help wondering where he'd gone.

"You did write to tell him about your pregnancy."

"I doubt he believes me. You ought to see him and Jordan together, Bev. Each day they're growing closer and closer. I keep thinking things could have been different if I'd joined Dex in Australia like I had promised. Even you thought I should go."

"But you didn't and you can't change things, so move on. I know you're probably feeling depressed over losing your dad and you're still grieving, but the last thing you should do is let Dex take advantage of your vulnerability now. Please, whatever you do, don't start thinking that you're lucky he wants a reconciliation. Instead you should feel he's the one lucky that you agreed to it."

"But—"

"But nothing. Give yourself credit for something. You've raised Jordan for the past three years, without any help from Dex Madaris. Being a single parent isn't easy. Don't ever take what you've done for granted."

Caitlin sighed. "But what about a life filled with love and happiness?"

"You and Dex have another chance at that, Caitlin. What you should do is turn whatever setbacks you've encountered into victories. Don't focus on what you didn't do, but on what you can do now."

Caitlin chuckled softly. "You sound just like a philosopher."

Beverly laughed then spoke in a teasing British accent. "It must be the English air I'm breathing. But seriously, stop trying to cast Dex in the role of a perfect man."

"I never said he was perfect."

"Well, don't. He has faults just like everyone else. And to be quite honest with you, he thoroughly disappointed me by not taking the first plane out of Australia when you filed for a divorce. I really had expected him to come after you. One of the reasons I had liked him right away was because he was a lot older than you, and he appeared to be a man who wouldn't hesitate to fight for what was his. I think he gave in to your father too easily."

Caitlin frowned. "Aren't you being a little bit hard on him, Bev?"

"I'm being no harder on Dex than you're being on yourself. I'm your friend remember. Your very best friend. I want things between you and Dex to work out. Not just for Jordan's sake, but especially for yours and Dex. More than anything, I want you to be happy. Just give your relationship with him some time, and don't expect miracles overnight. The best relationships are those that grow from the knowledge that we're more than worthy of the best that life can offer."

"Oh, Bev, I want to believe that."

"Then do believe it. I wish you and Dex the very best of luck. Although it was a whirlwind love affair, I believe it's the quality of time and not the quantity of time that's important. Call me a romantic if you want to, but I think you and Dex had something very special four years ago. And I truly believe something that special can't die or isn't easily destroyed. Just follow your heart, listen to your mind, stand behind your convictions and don't be afraid to take risks. The only failure lies in not trying."

"You make it sound so easy."

"No, it's not easy, but it's well worth the effort."

Caitlin took a deep calming breath. "You could always do this to me."

"Do what?"

"Show me the errors of my ways."

"No more than you could help me see mine. You were right there cheering Chase on whenever I got a streak of stubbornness. If it hadn't been for you, love would have passed me by, and I'd still be an unhappy pharmacist working in my dad's drug store. Chase and I will be forever grateful to you for prodding me in the right direction. If one of the twins is a girl, I'm going to name her after you."

"Twins! What twins?"

Beverly roared with laughter, unable to keep her secret any longer. "I found out this morning. We're having twins!"

Dex walked into the kitchen and found Caitlin bending over while unloading the dishwasher. He paused in the doorway to watch her, enjoying the way the shorts she wore outlined her shapely bottom. His pulse quickened. He would love to fill his hands with her incredible softness, to pull her against him and . . .

He shook his head to clear his thoughts. The last thing he needed was to begin seeing Caitlin as only a sex object. She was, after all, the mother of his child and by law, his wife.

His wife, Dex thought again. In that case, according to the minister who married them four years ago, she was his—to have and to hold—and at this very moment he ached to do both.

"Get a grip, Madaris," he muttered to himself.

Dex's muttering caught Caitlin's attention. She turned around. "Oh, I didn't hear you come in."

Straightening, she closed the dishwasher door. "How long have you been back?"

"Not long," he answered. No way he was going to tell her that he had stood in the doorway a good five minutes ogling her body.

Caitlin's gaze held Dex's for a fraction of a second too long before she looked away quickly. "I wasn't sure if you would be back for lunch so Jordan and I went ahead and ate."

"That's fine," Dex replied absently. He watched Caitlin move around the kitchen gathering up a few of Jordan's toys that were scattered about. It was obvious he made her nervous.

"Where's Jordan?" he asked, breaking the silence that had descended upon the room.

"She's taking a nap."

Dex nodded. He knew Caitlin was probably wondering where he'd been. On the return drive back, he had decided not to tell her about his meeting with Lt. Williams. Since there had been no proof to Halston's allegations, it would be best to let the matter drop.

"Dex, I almost forgot. You got a call from someone by the name of Trevor Grant. He said it's important that you call him back. If you need privacy to make the call, I'll go—"

"No. Trevor's my project foreman," Dex said, picking up the phone.

Caitlin was aware of her sweaty palms as she rummaged through the refrigerator looking for a carton of orange juice. She didn't have to guess the cause of her body's warmth—or more specifically, *who* was the cause of it. She knew that even now while he talked on the phone, Dex was watching her every movement.

She found the item she'd been looking for and closed the refrigerator door. In a way she felt awful that she'd completely forgotten Dex had a company to run—a company he was neglecting while being here with her.

When she heard Dex let out a loud whoop, she swung around quickly, almost dropping the carton of juice out of her hands. Nervously she placed it on the counter. Before she could ask Dex what was going on, he rushed across the room and captured her in his arms, giving her a big bear hug.

"Dex, what in the world is going on?" she asked, staggering to keep her balance when he released her.

"We got it!"

"Got what?"

Dex laughed exuberantly as he gave Caitlin another crushing hug. "Madaris Explorations has been offered a chance to handle this big project for Remington Oil. I don't have all the specifics, but according to Trevor, we may be talking mega-bucks. This is a dream come true. It's more than I could have ever hoped for."

Caitlin smiled, sharing his happiness and excitement. "Congratulations, Dex. I'm really happy for you. You know, it just occurred to me just how little I know about what you do now that you're in business for yourself. When we first met you were working for Remington Oil."

Dex's gaze was drawn to Caitlin's legs when she reached down to pick up an item off the floor. She had beautiful legs, long, smooth and shapely—majorette legs. He didn't think he would ever tire of seeing her in any outfit that showed them. He forced his mind away from her legs and back to the comment she'd just made.

"To be quite honest with you, Caitlin, I should thank you for Madaris Explorations."

Caitlin's brow raised as she looked at him. "Thank me? Why?"

Dex sat on a stool at the counter. His gaze fixed on hers. "While in Australia trying to get over you, I became a workaholic. I took on jobs other geologists weren't interested in. Sometimes, I worked from daybreak to sundown, weekends and holidays. My work became my life. I learned all sorts of new jobs, and I met a lot of interesting people. They were people who didn't mind my eagerness to learn, and people who didn't mind sharing their knowledge with me. By the time I left Australia to return to the States, I was ready to start my own explorations company. It's something I wanted more than anything."

Caitlin glanced down at the floor, unable to meet his gaze any longer. The idea that she had driven him to such a state didn't make her feel good at all. "I'm glad at least something worthwhile was happening for you then."

Dex nodded. "And I also have Clayton and Justin to thank. No man could ask for better brothers. Without as much as blinking an eye, the two of them provided the financial backing I needed to begin my company. They proved just how much they believed in me."

Caitlin nodded. She'd known the three Madaris brothers were close but their gesture of love to Dex had proved just how close they actually were. She'd never had any siblings to share such special closeness with.

She walked across the room to the window. A group of kids were playing a game of kick ball in the street. They seemed to be having so much fun being part of a group. She knew from experience that being an only child could be lonely. She wondered if Jordan would be the only child she and Dex would ever have together.

She glanced around when she heard Dex move off the stool. He came to stand beside her.

"Justin and Clayton are really special, Dex," she said softly. "In fact, I think your entire family is. That's the main reason I couldn't contact them when I found out I was pregnant. They were so kind to me when you took me to meet them, especially your parents."

Dex smiled warmly. "Yeah, Mom and Dad are super people. My father has always been there not only for his sons, but for practically every fatherless boy who lived in our community when I was growing up. During my teen years Dad was the principal at our high school. He used to always stress the importance of getting a good education. He drilled it into our heads that we couldn't just give one hundred percent in what we did, we had to give one hundred plus."

Caitlin nodded. She could just imagine the older Mr. Madaris trying to prepare his sons for the harsh realities of life. "What about your mom?"

Dex chuckled. "Mom was just Mom. Also being an educator, she was just as tough on us as Dad. Justin, Clayton and I participated in a lot of sports while in school, but Mom's top priority for us was a good education. And she strongly encouraged us to learn as much about our heritage as possible. During the summer months, all of us were required to read a certain number of books written by black authors. She believed that the more you knew about yourself, the more you would be able to love and appreciate not only yourself, but also those around you."

Caitlin's eyes twinkled. "Your mom's a smart woman."

"No argument from me." Dex couldn't help wondering if their discussion about his parents had made Caitlin think of her own. He knew the pain of losing her father was still fresh. When she turned to look back out the window his gaze played over her profile.

What sort of future were they bound to have together? She had hurt him deeply once, and he knew he would never give her the chance to do so again. That meant he would always be on his guard around her. That also meant that he would never be able to share a really close relationship with her, not even for Jordan's sake.

"I'm sure the people at Remington Oil want to meet with you. When will you be leaving?" Caitlin asked suddenly, her dark eyes darting up to him.

"They want me in Austin by Friday to brief me on the project," he said hesitantly. "But Trevor can go in my place."

"I'm sure they'll prefer discussing things with you personally, Dex. If you really need to be there, then there's no reason why you shouldn't be."

Dex caught Caitlin's chin in his fingers and tilted her face up to his. He smiled slightly, his eyes falling to her moistened lips and then back to her eyes. "Are you trying to get rid of me, Caitlin?"

She shrugged her shoulders. "No, of course not. I just don't want you to feel like you have to stay here because of any obligation to me and Jordan. We'll be fine."

He withdrew his hand from her face. "And how will you explain my leaving to Jordan?"

"I'll tell her the truth. That you had a job to do and you'll be coming back."

Dex frowned thoughtfully. A part of him didn't want to leave Caitlin and he wondered why. Could it be because the last time he'd left her behind in San Antonio, he had ended up losing her? He quickly reminded himself that at the time, he'd been deeply in love with her. But now she was a woman he no longer loved, and could never love again.

"Are you sure you'll be all right?" he asked, taking a step back.

"I'm positive. I've accepted Dad's death. I'll miss him deeply, but I have to get on with my life." Caitlin studied Dex's features. His eyes appeared clouded, making it difficult to tell what was going on behind them. She had no idea what he was thinking.

"How about if we go out to dinner tonight to a really classy restaurant and celebrate my good news."

Pleasure grew within Caitlin with the thought that he wanted to take her out to celebrate.

"Oh, Dex, that sounds like a wonderful idea. I'm sure Ms. Logan wouldn't mind watching Jordan for a few—"

"Jordan's coming with us."

An embarrassing tint spread across Caitlin's features. "Oh. I thought it would be just . . ." She quickly looked away. "Nothing. It's not important. My mistake."

Dex touched her hands and she looked up at him, meeting his gaze. "You thought it would be just the two of us," he finished softly. His eyes filled with absolute understanding after she hesitantly gave a slight nod.

"There will be other times for us. Tonight I want the three of us to celebrate together as a family."

"Yes, of course."

"Caitlin, I—"

"No, you don't have to explain. I shouldn't have jumped to conclusions." She racked her brain for an excuse to flee from his presence. There wasn't any need hanging around and making another complete fool of herself. "I better go check on Jordan."

She turned and quickly left the room.

Corinthians pulled off her reading glasses and pinched the bridge of her nose. She'd been working on a report since early that morning, unintentionally skipping lunch. And now it was three o'clock already. The report would be the one presented to Dex when he met with them on Friday. It would be so good seeing him again.

She smiled as she pushed herself out of the chair and stood staring around her plush office. She had come a long way since that day eight years ago when Adam had escorted her from the personnel department and up to the tenth floor. There he had shown her her working area or more precisely—her space. It hadn't been much larger than the smallest closet in her apartment.

Corinthians left the office to get a drink of water from the water cooler in the reception area. Darcy, Adam's personal secretary, was still at it, typing furiously, trying hard like everyone else to get prepared for Friday's meeting.

Returning to her office minutes later, Corinthians went to the window and stared out at downtown Austin. She wrapped her arms around herself, a habit of hers whenever she was happy about something. She wondered if Dex was as happy as she was. He wouldn't be told the full extent of the Leabo project until the last piece of land had been purchased. Only then would he realize just what a very lucky man he was.

Walking away from the window, she had seated herself behind the desk again when the buzzer sounded. She reached over and pressed the button of her intercom. "Darcy, I thought I asked you to hold all my calls for the remainder of the day."

"I know, Ms. Avery, but Dexter Madaris is on the line. Before he left, Mr. Flynn told me to put Mr. Madaris through to you if he called."

"Yes, of course," Corinthians said, drawing air deep into her lungs. The mere thought of talking to Dex made a warm feeling pass through her. "Please put him through."

"Dex? Hi. This is Corinthians. How are you? You're right, it's been a long time." *Too long* "I understand congratulations are in order." She smiled as she slipped off her shoes and snuggled deeper into the comfortable chair.

"Yes, I know all about the project," she said grinning, deciding not to tell him just how much she actually knew and how close she was to it. "And no, I'm not telling you a thing about it. My lips are sealed. But I will tell you this, Dex, it's big. Bigger than anything you could imagine."

Corinthians laughed. "When will you be arriving? Not until Thursday afternoon?" She tried to keep her voice from exposing her disappointment. She'd hoped he had planned on arriving sooner.

"I have an idea. How about if I go ahead and make reservations for you to save you the trouble." She looked only slightly sheepish. "No, it won't be any bother at all, in fact it'll be my pleasure."

Corinthians' smile widened. "All right, I'll see you when you get here. Bye, Dex. Take care."

She had barely hung up the phone, then she jumped up from her desk and wrapped her arms around herself. Moments later she picked up the phone to call the hotel. Her solemn expression didn't mask the sparkle in her eyes.

Dex wouldn't know what hit him until it was too late.

CHAPTER 8

"Do I look pretty Daddy?"

Dex tossed aside the magazine he'd been reading. Jordan stood on the next to the last stair dressed in a pink dress trimmed with ruffles and lace. Pink and white ribbons were in her braided hair and small pearl earrings were in her pierced ears.

A proud smile tugged at his mouth. He reached his hand out to help her down. "Yes, sweetheart, you look very pretty."

Jordan gave him a dazzling smile, obviously pleased with his response. She leaned closer to him. "As pretty as Mommy?" she whispered.

"Yes," he admitted with a soft chuckle. "You look as pretty as your mommy." Dex glanced up the stairway. Caitlin was coming down and look absolutely gorgeous dressed in a tailored pant suit. The scent of her perfume seduced him. He inhaled it and recalled the first time he'd met her and how even then, that same fragrance had captured him.

When Caitlin reached them, Dex extended his hand to her. "I'm a very lucky man to have two such beautiful ladies with me tonight." He took Caitlin's fingers and pressed a light kiss on them.

"You can kiss my fingers, too," Jordan exclaimed, presenting her hand to him.

Dex gave in to a low laugh before leaning down and kissing his daughter's hand. "Are you ready?"

Jordan bobbed her head excitedly.

Dex chuckled. "Then let's go."

Dex had taken Caitlin and Jordan to an elegant restaurant where both the food and the service had been outstanding.

On the ride back, the car's interior was quiet except for the soft music playing on the radio. He glanced back in the rearview mirror and saw that Jordan had fallen asleep.

When he stopped the car at a traffic light, he glanced at Caitlin. She was sitting beside him with her eyes closed. The car was flooded with moonlight, and he could see the perfection of her features. Her brown skin glowed like smooth satin, and a few strands of her hair whipped around in the wind coming through the car's window. He couldn't help staring at her lips, thinking how good they looked and knowing just how good they tasted.

Dex turned his gaze back to the road when the traffic light changed to green. But he couldn't stop the outpouring of memories that hit him—memories of that night long ago when, thanks to Clayton, he'd had to admit to himself that he loved Caitlin.

After hiring her to work at his uncle's ranch, he'd kept his distance, especially after discovering he was attracted to her in a way he'd never been attracted to any woman before.

Dex fought back a smile. He'd been doing a pretty good job avoiding her until Clayton had shown up. Even now, he could remember that short conversation with his brother in his uncle's barn like it had been yesterday . . .

"Dex?"

"Yeah?"

"Are you, umm . . ." Clayton looked at him speculatively. "Is something going on between you and Caitlin Parker?"

"No," he replied tersely. "Why?"

"Because," Clayton smiled faintly. "If you're not interested in her, I'm sure I can be."

He gave his brother a hard glare. "What's that supposed to mean?"

Clayton laughed. "Don't be dense, Dex. You know how attracted I am to beautiful women."

He caught Clayton's arm in a hard grip. "Stay away from her. She's not that kind of girl."

Clayton raised a brow. "Give me less than a day and I'll find out just what kind of girl she is."

For the first time in his life, he wanted to beat his womanizing baby brother to a pulp. Instead, he gave him a hard look that spoke volumes. He tightened his grip on Clayton's arm. "I mean it. Stay away from her." He released Clayton and with fury in his eyes, he walked out of the barn . . .

* * *

Dex shook himself, bringing his thoughts back to the present. These insistent memories were making his life a living hell, he thought, pulling the car into the driveway of Caitlin's father's home.

He never got the chance to find out if Clayton would have heeded his warning, because from that night on, Dex stopped avoiding Caitlin.

Dex looked over at her when he brought the car to a stop. No woman should be this beautiful, he thought, letting his gaze move over her. She looked so damned desirable, he'd do just about anything to make love to her again.

"Caitlin, wake up. We're here."

Dex's voice sounded oddly tender, Caitlin thought, slowly opening her eyes. Her gaze locked with his. The look in his eyes made her breath catch. It was the same look of desire she'd seen in them last night, and the night before that.

Somehow she managed to tear her gaze from his and straightened in the seat. "Sorry, I didn't mean to snooze on you," she said, unbuckling her seatbelt. "I guess I wasn't much company was I?"

"You were a lot of company," he said, reaching across and caressing the side of her face. "Asleep or awake, you're all the company I need."

Caitlin didn't want to read more into his words than were actually there. "Why? Because we're celebrating tonight?" she asked in a whisper, not even daring to look at him. She was too afraid to do so. When he didn't answer her immediately, she took a chance and looked at him. He'd been waiting for her to do just that, she thought, because he was looking intently at her.

His gaze held hers for a long, taut moment, warm and sensuous. Then he smiled and Caitlin was aware of nothing but his gaze, his smile and the irregular beat of her heart.

Dex's fingers, which had been caressing the side of her face, moved to her lips. Slowly, tenderly, he outlined her upper lip with his thumb, then moved down to her lower lip.

"No, it's not because we're celebrating." When he'd finally answered her question, she had to think hard to remember just what she'd asked him.

"It's because I want you," he continued, leaning toward her. "Plain and simple."

Her lips parted when she saw the deliciously male mouth slowly coming toward hers. She felt the delicate tip of Dex's tongue touch her. She took it into her mouth, joining it with hers. He continued to kiss her slowly, thoroughly. Instinctively her hands reached up and touched his shoulders, then curled around the back of his neck.

Dex finally drew his mouth from hers, and brushed back a wisp of hair from her face to gaze into her eyes. "I think we should go inside, put our daughter to bed then finish this. I don't like the idea of giving the neighbors something to talk about, sweetheart."

"I know," she said softly, tracing his handsome face with her eyes. It had completely slipped her mind as to where they were. "Kissing in a parked car while our daughter is asleep in the back seat is kind of crazy, isn't it?"

"Depends on how you look at it," Dex whispered. And then he was kissing her again, more passionately than before.

"I think we'd better go inside," Caitlin murmured against his mouth a minute or two later. Her gaze was pinned to his lips that were still hovering close over hers.

"Yeah, I guess we'd better," he said, slowly pulling away from her. "I'll carry Jordan inside. Just remember what I said, Caitlin. This is far from finished tonight."

He got out of the car whistling the old Temptations' tune, *Get Ready, Cause Here I Come.*

CHAPTER 9

Caitlin stood awkwardly at the bottom stairs watching Dex carry Jordan up to bed. She should help him with Jordan, but for now she just wanted to stay in place and get her bearings. Dex had a way of rocking her precariously balanced emotions.

She should never have allowed things to get so far out of hand with him tonight. No doubt he expected them to finish what they had started in the car. But she wasn't ready to renew the intimate part of her relationship with him. She still felt uncertain and insecure about a number of things, especially his feelings for her.

She finally walked up the stairs, too confused and too filled with doubt to think straight. When she entered the room, Dex was removing Jordan's shoes and socks. She joined him and together they finished undressing Jordan and got her into her pajamas and under the covers.

Needing to get away from Dex, Caitlin quickly left the room, leaving him standing beside the bed watching their daughter sleep. Walking across the hall to her bedroom, she turned on the light and closed the door behind her. She paced the room for several minutes before hearing the faint knock on the door. "Come in."

Caitlin met Dex's gaze when he entered the room, closing the door behind him. She could feel the sizzle of sexual awareness and attraction between them. She forced the thoughts from her mind of just how good he looked standing there, leaning a shoulder against the closed door with his hands thrust into the pockets of his pants. He stared at her with eyes that could melt her very soul, not to mention her resistance.

"Why are you acting so skittish, Caitlin?"

"I'm not acting that way."

Dex straightened from his position against the door. He walked farther into the bedroom. "Yes, you are. Do you want to talk about what's bothering you?"

"I think you already know what's bothering me," she informed him in a brisk tone. She came to stand in front of him. For a while, she was unable to continue speaking. From where she stood, the heat of his body was warming her. His scent was all male, a combination of clean, masculine freshness. "You're doing it again, Dex," she accused.

He looked at her and smiled slightly, acknowledging that he knew exactly what she was talking about. "Trying to seduce you?"

"Yes." Her voice was hoarse when she answered.

Dex's smile widened. "I plea guilty as charged."

She lifted her brow. He hadn't tried denying it. "Well, stop it."

"Yes, ma'am."

They stood motionless in the silent room, facing each other for an eternity. The slow, even rhythm of Dex's breathing was all Caitlin could hear. She refused to acknowledge the hard pounding sound of her own heart beating rapidly.

Suddenly, Dex leaned close and put his mouth against her ear and whispered, "You need relaxing."

There was more silence for a moment, then Caitlin's trembling voice replied. "No, I don't."

He reached out and touched her hand, feeling her tremble with his touch. "Yes, you do. Go ahead and take your shower. By the time you're through, I'll be back with just what you need."

"Dex, I don't think—"

"Have I ever forced myself on you, Caitlin?"

She looked at him without comment for a moment, then shook her head. "No."

"And I don't ever plan on doing so. I'll be back in a little while. Enjoy your shower." He then turned and left the room, closing the door behind him.

Worry lines knitted between Caitlin's delicate brow. She shook her head, clearing her mind. Four years ago, it had never occurred to her that Dex was too much for her to handle. At twenty-one she had felt completely at ease and comfortable around him, even when he was helping her to realize, acknowledge and accept the full extent of her sexuality. During those two weeks before they had married, he had taken the time to actually court her properly. She would always remember their daily horseback rides, their occasional picnic lunches and the times he had taken her dancing at a country-western dance club not far from Whispering Pines. At no time had he come on too strong. His kisses had always been passionate, leaving her breathless, wanting more. But he'd always stopped before things got too out of hand. And he had never forced himself on her. They had made love for the first time on their wedding night. What she had experienced in his arms had been so beautiful, it had brought tears to her eyes. He had not just made love to her, he had used his body to cherish her. She smiled, remembering those heated nights after they had married. The memories were electrifying, and for a moment Caitlin couldn't catch her breath for the force of them.

But what about now, Caitlin? Can you handle Dex Madaris now? Her mind screamed. She shook her head. For some reason, she wasn't as sure of herself as she had been at twenty-one. She felt completely out of her element with Dex. He was more sensuous, more rugged, more appealing, and if possible, more male.

Caitlin shivered, then realized she was standing in the same spot where she'd been when Dex had left the room. Sighing, she went into the connecting bath to take her shower. Dex had said he would have something to relax her. She couldn't help wondering just what that was.

During her shower, Caitlin forced herself to focus her thoughts on other things, like how Dex's family would react to the news of their reconciliation, and what would they think of Jordan.

Stepping out of the shower, she toweled herself dry. After lotioning her body, she slipped into her nightgown. When she heard a knock at her bedroom door, she grabbed her robe and hurriedly put it on. As she approached the door, she held her breath, not certain what to expect. Slowly, she opened the door.

"I told you that I had just the thing to relax you."

Caitlin smiled. Dex stood in her doorway carrying a serving tray that held a teapot and two cups. "Tea? Is it too much to hope that it's Whispering Pines' own special blend?"

Dex grinned. "No, it's not too much to hope at all."

"Then by all means, Mr. Madaris, please come in."

Caitlin closed the door behind him and wondered why she hadn't figured it out earlier. While working at Whispering Pines that summer, she had acquired a taste for a delicious tea that Jake Madaris made each night. He'd claimed its special ingredients of herbs and spices was a secret recipe that could only be shared with the men in the Madaris family, but only after they had reached their thirty-fifth birthday. Her smile widened as she also remembered how, after a week of working at Whispering Pines, she had discovered it would not be as easy as she had thought to convince Delane Ormond that a computer would make her job easier. By the end of each work day, Caitlin found herself ready to pull her hair out. To help her relax each night, Dex would serve her a cup of tea before she retired to bed.

"Does this mean that you know the secret recipe?" she asked.

Dex turned after placing the tray on the table next to the bed. He chuckled. "Yes, I know it, and like the other Madaris men before me, my lips are sealed. Uncle Jake would kill me if they weren't."

Caitlin grinned. "And just how is Jake Madaris?" She had liked Dex's uncle, and had been surprised upon meeting him to discover how young he was. Jake Madaris, Dex's father's youngest brother, was only seven years older than Dex. He and Dex looked more like brothers than uncle and nephew. She became amused each and every time Dex and Clayton had called him "Uncle Jake." She often wondered if they did it out of respect or to needle their young uncle.

Dex began pouring the tea into the cups. "He's fine. But he's still angry with me for stealing his employee. You never did finish that job you know."

Caitlin laughed as she accepted the cup of tea from Dex. The aroma of it filled the room. "No doubt Ms. Ormond was overjoyed."

"If she was, it didn't last long. Uncle Jake hired someone else to take your place, and they finished the job."

"I don't envy that person at all."

Dex sat down in the wing back chair. "What you should do is pity him. I understand he had become an alcoholic by the time the job was finished."

Of course he was joking, Caitlin thought. His dark eyes were sparkling with laughter. And she couldn't help but laugh with him. It felt so good to laugh. "Thanks, Dex," she said when their laughter finally stopped.

"For what?"

Caitlin moved to the bed and sat Indian-style in the middle of it. "For helping me relax tonight."

Dex nodded, and a mellow silence followed while they both sipped their tea. Dex was the first to speak. "Did you ever get the chance to go back to school?"

"Yes, after Jordan turned six months old. Dad watched her while I attended classes at night."

Dex nodded. "Do you like teaching?"

Caitlin shrugged. "It's all right, but one day I want to have my own company."

"A computer consulting company?"

"Yes. It's nothing I want to get into right away, of course, but I've been thinking about it a lot lately. How do you like being your own boss?"

Caitlin listened while Dex told her a number of things about being self-employed. They then talked about recent books they had read and movies they hadn't seen.

"I can never find time to go to the movies. My work keeps me pretty busy," Dex said, not adding that he had preferred it that way.

"And I never wanted to leave Jordan with a sitter for long," Caitlin said, finishing off the last of her tea.

"Maybe, when we're all settled in Houston, you and I can do stuff like that, go to movies and go out dancing. Any member of my family would be more than happy to look after Jordan for us."

She stared at him, somewhat surprised. He was suggesting that they begin spending time together. "I'd like that."

Dex nodded as he stood. "I think it's past your bedtime," he said. The clock on the wall indicated it was after midnight. He picked up the serving tray.

Caitlin stood and placed her empty cup on the tray. "Thanks again, Dex."

Dex lowered his head. Just before his lips lightly touched hers, he whispered, "Don't mention it." He straightened. "Goodnight, Caitlin. I hope you sleep well."

She watched him open the bedroom door and walk out. Caitlin sighed deeply. Being with Dex tonight, talking to him while they sipped tea, reminded her of how things had been before, peaceful and loving. But she was realistic enough to know that although he was making every effort to make their marriage work, they were still together for all the wrong reasons. He may care for her as the mother of his child, but he didn't love her.

Caitlin forced that thought from her mind, not wanting to ruin what she considered a nice ending to a perfect evening. Instead, as she prepared for bed, her thoughts were focused on what a sexy and good-looking man she was married to.

Dreams swirled around in Caitlin's mind, making her hot with desire even while she slept. She could feel Dex's hand on her, pulling her to him in an embrace. She was pressed so tightly to his naked body that she could feel every part of him as she became enveloped in his seductive masculine heat.

The strength of him throbbed against her and the muscular sculpted hardness of his chest pressed against her breasts. In the deep recesses of her mind she could feel his massive upper arms and broad shoulders. Her fingers burned as they trailed a path over his body, well-defined and taut.

When his warm lips moved across her forehead and cheeks before finally claiming her lips, she melted. His mouth was seductively firm and bittersweet. A tortured sigh from four years of celibacy, escaped her, followed by another filled with blatant need. The kiss was one of sensuality and one of deeply held passion. It filled her with escalating sensations.

The ringing of the telephone jarred Caitlin awake. Startled, she sat up in bed. Her breathing was irregular, her heart beat was hammering in her ears. The gown she wore was slightly damp from the heat her dream had generated. She quickly picked up the phone.

"Hello? "

"I hope you're a lot smarter than your old man was, lady," the muffled voice said. "Take any offer that's made and sell that land of yours."

Clutching the receiver in trembling hands, Caitlin asked, "Who is this?"

"Just sell that land near Eagle Pass and no one will get hurt."

"Who is this?" The only response she received was a click followed by the buzzing of the dial tone. Placing the telephone back in the cradle, she sank against the bed.

Land near Eagle Pass? Was someone interested in Shadowland?

Fury made her heart pound. How dare that person call and threaten her. No one could force her into selling Shadowland, the land that had been in her family for generations. Evidently her father had received a similar threat.

Disturbing emotions sparred inside her. She shuddered at the threat the caller had made. Should she tell Dex?

Taking a deep breath, she knew she had to deal with her own problems. She didn't want to give Dex any reason to feel responsible for her. Somehow she would handle this without his help.

CHAPTER 10

"When will we be leaving for Houston, Dex?"

Dex gazed across the breakfast table. The shadows under Caitlin's eyes indicated she'd had a sleepless night. His mouth tightened. "Does your eagerness to leave San Antonio have anything to do with the phone call you got around three this morning?"

Surprise flared in Caitlin's eyes. She set her coffee cup down. She hadn't wanted Dex to find out about that call and wondered how he had. Him knowing would only compound the problems already existing between them.

"How do you know about the call?"

The kitchen grew tense and silent. Caitlin couldn't help noticing the angry lines creasing Dex's forehead and mouth.

"I couldn't sleep and was up watching television. I picked up the phone the same time you did," Dex replied. He would not mention the reason he hadn't been able to sleep was because he couldn't get her off his mind. He'd lain awake remembering how long it had been since he'd been intimate with a woman. But his body hadn't wanted just any woman, it had wanted her. And it still did, which wasn't helping his attitude toward her this morning.

"Were you going to tell me about the call, Caitlin?"

Caitlin met Dex's gaze as his question hung in the air between them. There was a certain coolness in the charcoal gray eyes staring at her. She immediately picked up on the dark brooding hard-edginess of his mood.

"No, I wasn't going to mention it to you. I have to fight my own battles."

Dex laughed harshly as he stood. "And just when did you begin fighting your own battles, Caitlin? I was under the impression you totally enjoyed being told what to do and when to do it. You must have done a hell of a lot of growing up over the past four years."

Outrage flushed Caitlin's cheeks as she stood. Her chin lifted and she met his blazing gaze head on. "You're right. I have done a lot of growing up over the past four years. And I won't let you or anyone else push me around. I meant what I said, I don't need you to fight my battles."

Dex couldn't help noticing the fire in Caitlin's eyes and the way she had straightened her spine and placed her hands on her hips. If ever he'd seen a woman who was ready to draw blood, this was the one. But he had no intentions of letting her fight anything alone.

He closed the distance between them. "As your husband, I have certain rights and obligations. One of which is to protect you from any type of harm or danger. You're my wife, and I won't take threats made to you lightly."

There was a tense silence as they stood staring at each other. Dex spoke again, this time his tone was somewhat gentler. "As long as there is breath in my body, Caitlin, nobody will threaten you and get away with it." He took her face in his hands and leaned toward her, capturing her mouth with his.

A hot rush of desire surged through Caitlin when Dex's mouth took hers, making her melt under the heat of his passion. Her arms crept around his neck at the same time she opened her mouth to him. Fire leaped into her veins and a shiver coursed through her body as Dex deepened their kiss.

Caitlin was fully aware that his hand was moving, pulling her even closer to him. Her body, with a will of its own, arched closer, not wanting the moment to end. She was glad Jordan, who'd gone to bed later than usual last night, was still asleep.

Caitlin whispered Dex's name when he trailed his mouth across her face and kissed her eyes. He pressed her head against his neck.

"I'm sorry for losing it and blowing up at you like that," he said in a husky voice. "But when I listened in on that call, I got madder than hell. And knowing he's probably the same guy who harassed your father, made me—"

Caitlin pushed herself out of Dex's arms. "What do you mean he's probably the same person who harassed Dad? What do you know about this, Dex?" Sparks suddenly flared in her eyes. "And if you do know anything, you should have told me. You have some nerve getting mad with me for not telling you about that phone call, when you're keeping things from me."

"Look, Caitlin, You had enough to deal with. I didn't want to—"

"You didn't want! Who made you an expert in knowing what's best for me? I'm not some damsel in distress. I happen to be a very strong woman who doesn't need you in my life to survive. Jordan and I were doing just fine without you."

Dex frowned. "There's no need for you to cop an attitude."

"Cop an attitude?" she repeated in a low, lethal tone. "You want an attitude, Dex Madaris, then I'll show you an attitude."

Dex shook his head. He had to constantly remind himself that the woman standing before him was not the meek and mild twenty-one-year-old he'd left in San Antonio four years ago. She was a twenty-five-year-old woman who didn't mind showing him how stubborn she could be, nor how independent. He had to force himself to admit that he actually found the new fiery Caitlin more intriguing, and she looked so sexy when she got angry.

"We can stand here and argue till night, and the only thing we'll accomplish is waking up Jordan," Dex said in a calm tone. "I suggest we go in the living room and discuss this like two adults, and I'll tell you everything I know."

Caitlin hesitated briefly before following him. Together they sat on the sofa. Dex then told her about the letter Dr. Flores had given him, and about his visit to the police station. He saw a lone tear flow down her cheek. She quickly wiped it away.

"I can't believe anyone would be that cruel, that heartless. My father was a sick man. He didn't need that kind of aggravation in his life."

Dex pulled her into his arms. "I know, baby." After a while he said. "Tell me something about this property Malone Land Developers are interested in."

"Shadowland is property that's been in my father's family for generations. His great-great grandfather was Blaze Abrams, a Black Seminole Indian and a scout for the United States Army. Blaze fell in love with Vashti Randolph, the niece of a retired Buffalo soldier. Vashti's uncle Robert had been like a father to Blaze and when Robert Randolph died, he willed Shadowland to Blaze and Vashti in hopes they would marry one day."

Caitlin smiled. "I remember the stories my grandmother used to tell me. They were stories about the Black Seminoles and how they helped the government keep law and order along the Mexican border."

Her smile widened. "But my favorite story was of Blaze and Vashti and the rocky romance between them, and the love and happiness they shared when they eventually married. As you know, following the Civil War, many blacks in these parts owned land. And there were a number of prosperous all-black communities in the area as well. There were a number of land-grabbers who tried to say as an Indian, Blaze couldn't inherit land, but he and Vashti were able to hold on to it. Each of their descendants since then have promised never to sell Shadowland and to keep it in the family. There's a lot of history behind Shadowland; rich history that my parents and I have always been proud of."

Caitlin's eyes reflected the depth of the emotions she felt. "There's no way my father would have ever sold it, and I feel the same way. It's part of my heritage, and now Jordan's. Shadowland has been in my family for over five generations, and I intend for it to remain there for many more."

Dex thought of his Uncle Jake and his huge ranch, Whispering Pines. Just like Shadowland had been in Caitlin's family for generations, Whispering Pines had been in the Madaris family for just as long.

"You said Shadowland's located near Eagle Pass?"

"Yes It's out in the middle of no where. Why anyone would be interested in it is beyond me."

"I'd like to see it. How do you feel about me, you and Jordan taking a little ride?"

"But I thought you had to get ready to fly to Austin for your meeting on Friday."

"Caitlin, there's no way I'm going to Austin now. I'll contact Trevor to go in my place."

"I don't want my problems to interfere with your job."

He smoothed back a stray tendril of hair from her face. "They won't and they aren't your problems, they're our problems." Dex stood. "How soon can you and Jordan be ready to leave?"

"In thirty minutes or so."

"Good. I need to leave for a while. I'm going to pay a visit to Malone Land Developers. I'll be back shortly."

"You've got to be kidding, Corinth. Please tell me you aren't serious about buying anything out of this place."

Corinthians' dark brown eyes sparkled. She glanced around the posh room filled with scantily dressed mannequins wearing all types of sexy lingerie. "I most certainly am serious, girlfriend, and I didn't bring you along to try and talk me out of it. I need help picking out a few items."

Brenna stared at the mannequin in front of them wearing a sheer short nightie. The outfit brought a blush to her light brown cheeks. "I hope you know what you're doing."

Corinthians frowned. "Of course I know what I'm doing. I'm doing what I should have done years ago. I'm going after the man I love. Of all people, I thought you'd be happy for me."

Brenna turned to face her. "I don't have a problem with what you're doing, Corinth, but I do have a problem with how you're going about it. Blatant underhanded seduction isn't your style."

Corinthians lifted her chin. "And just what's wrong with me finally taking the initiative and going after who I want? He's free and so am I. I'm also older and more self-assured than before. The timing is right."

"Don't you dare get an attitude with me, Corinthians Avery. I'm your best friend remember. All I'm saying is that you haven't seen Dex Madaris in over four years. He may not be the same man you remember—the same man you supposedly fell in love with."

"And why wouldn't he be?"

"People change. You've even said he's been married and divorced since you've seen him last. A bad marriage changes some people. I just don't want you to get hurt. All Dex Madaris ever wanted from you is friendship. How's he going to feel if you suddenly force yourself on him?"

Corinthians tried concentrating on a matching edible pair of panties and a bra, and not on what Brenna was saying, but couldn't. The two of them had been friends since grade school, and deep down she knew Brenna had her best interest at heart.

"I'm not forcing myself on him," Corinthians finally said, as they continued walking around the store. "All I'm doing is letting Dex know I want more than just friendship."

"But what if he doesn't want more? That will place a strain on the relationship the two of you already have. No man likes to feel cornered."

"I have to take that chance, Brenna."

Brenna shook her head. "I just hope you know what you're doing."

"I do." Corinthians stopped in front of a mannequin dressed in a sexy black lace merrywidow stretched over a G-string bikini. Garter straps held up a pair of black stockings.

Corinthians waved a well-manicured hand toward the outfit. "Well, what do you think?"

"I think you've lost your mind." Brenna smothered a laugh. "And I think the person who sees you in that is in big trouble."

Duncan Malone looked uncomfortable as he gazed up at the man standing across from his desk. The man's eyes were dark and piercing and appeared to be the color of smoldering ashes.

Duncan was baffled by the man's apparent enmity. Was he someone he should know? His secretary had indicated a Dexter Madaris had wanted to see him and that he did not have an appointment. He had just finished telling her he was not taking any unscheduled appointments when the man had barged into his office with his frantic secretary running behind him.

"Should I call security, Mr. Malone?"

Duncan Malone sat upright, refusing to stand for his intruder. He cleared his throat. "No, Lynn, I'll handle this."

When his secretary left the two of them alone, he turned to the man. "Mr. Madaris, what can I do for you?"

Dex met Duncan's intense stare before the man lowered his eyes. "I want you to stop harassing my wife, Malone."

Duncan shifted uneasily in his chair. "Look, mister, I don't know you, and I don't know what you're talking about. I want you to leave my office."

"Does the name Caitlin Parker Madaris sound familiar? She's Halston Parker's daughter, and I believe there's a piece of property you're interested in buying from her."

Dex's ever-observant eyes took in the expression which Malone unsuccessfully tried to hide.

"Mr. Madaris, you've been misinformed. I'm sure this has been a rather dramatic time for your wife, with the recent loss of her father and all, but I assure you, no harassment has been going on—at least not by me. Although we would like to acquire the Parker land, we will never resort to such crude tactics. I have not spoken with Ms. Parker to see whether or not her decision will be any different than her father's."

"The lady is Mrs. Madaris and her decision won't be any different. She's not interested in selling."

Duncan nervously ran his fingers through his hair. "That's too bad."

Dex gave the man a hard look. "Yeah, I'm sure for you it is. And I'm curious as to how you found out Halston Parker had died."

The man actually reddened. "I—I read about it in the papers."

Dex had a feeling he was lying. He leaned on the desk and stared straight at him. "I don't want to leave here with any misunderstandings. The land is not for sale, now or ever. If you or anyone associated with this outfit as much as picks up a telephone to call my wife, or look her way, there'll be hell to pay and you, Malone, will have to deal with me personally."

"Is that a threat, Mr. Madaris?"

Dex shook his head. "I don't make threats, Malone. That's your game. What I do is state facts. For your continued good health, you best remember that."

A frown covered Duncan's face. He watched Dex turn and walk out of his office just as boldly as he had walked in. He punched the intercom on his desk. "Lynn, find Walker, and find him now!"

Halston Parker's pickup truck bounced to a halt in front of a homemade sign posted on a large oak tree that read PRIVATE PROPERTY—NO TRESPASSING.

Caitlin was glad the ride had ended. The last thirty minutes had been the most discomforting ride she'd ever taken, thanks to the rough road. Once they turned off the main highway, their taxing journey had begun. Only Jordan had taken the bumpy ride in stride and had looked upon each jounce with merriment. Caitlin was glad for Dex's decision to take her father's truck instead of her car.

"That ride was fun, Daddy. Let's do it again."

Dex and Caitlin exchanged amused glances before their laughter broke to the surface. "We will, soon enough," Dex replied, looking around the wooded area.

"You're right, Caitlin, there's really not much out here. Let's take a look around," he said, getting out of the truck. He grinned as he thumped the fender on his way around to the other side of the vehicle to open the door for Caitlin and Jordan. Jordan immediately jumped into her father's arms, leaving her mother to carry the picnic basket Caitlin had packed.

"If I remember correctly, there's a path near here that leads to the center of the property," Caitlin said as they began walking.

"When were you here last?"

"The month before my mom died. My parents used to keep a trailer here. We would come up occasionally just to get away from the city."

"Did you enjoy it?"

Caitlin smiled. "I enjoyed the time I spent with my parents, otherwise, I thought this place dull, so far from civilization. There wasn't even a McDonald's close by."

Dex chuckled. "McDonald's? You're definitely a city girl."

"Yeah, I guess I am at that. It was nice getting away once in a while, but I enjoy being close to neighbors and the golden arches."

Dex shook his head grinning. "I have one girl who's addicted to Big Macs and another who's addicted to pizzas." He then bounced Jordan in his arms. Her squeal of delight echoed in the silence of the surrounding woodland. They walked the path through the trees.

"The trailer should be just around the bend," Caitlin said.

"It's still here?" Dex asked, shifting Jordan in his arms.

"Yeah, but I don't know what shape it's in. For a while Dad didn't come up here at all after mom died, but I recently found out from Dr. Flores that he came up here pretty often after I began college. He liked to fish and there's a small stream not far from here," she said, as they walked across the uneven ground, devoid of any kind of growth.

"There it is," Caitlin said, pointing toward a trailer sitting in the clearing. "And it looks like it's in pretty good shape."

Upon reaching the trailer, Dex tried the door. "It's locked. Do you know anything about the key?"

"No, but I'd imagine it's on my father's key ring."

After trying a few keys they found one that worked. Their luck hadn't come too soon as far as Caitlin was concerned. Jordan had just whispered in her ear that she needed to use the bathroom.

Inside the trailer was a small living area with a galley kitchen. There were two bedrooms across one end, a small hallway and closet and a nice bath area. The entire unit appeared compact and neat as a pin. Caitlin could tell by the stuffy smell the place had been locked up tight for quite some time.

While Dex took a look around, Caitlin rushed Jordan off to the bathroom. The diversion gave her an opportunity to deal with the sudden rush of grief the memories of the place caused.

When they returned, Dex had the air conditioning going full blast. "This is a neat little set up. Your father even had his own generator installed out here. Seems like everything is pretty much in working order. I'm gonna take a look around on the outside. Since it's so hot, I suggest we have our picnic in here instead of outdoors."

"That's fine with me. I would hate to have an uninvited lunch guest like a snake or something."

Dex laughed. "This is pretty much like a wilderness out here, isn't it?"

"Yes, and I'm questioning the sanity of any developer who wants to put anything out here."

Dex nodded. "So am I."

"You wanted to see me, Uncle Duncan?"

Duncan looked up from the papers he'd been reading. "I want you to back off on Halston Parker's daughter. No one told you to put the squeeze on her without consulting me. The police are already suspicious. What are you trying to do, get me thrown in jail or something?"

Walker picked up a paperclip off the desk. "Of course not. What I'm trying to do is get results."

Duncan pushed his chair back; his face appeared stern. "Your results can put the both of us in prison, if not in the hospital first. Her husband paid me a visit today, and he's meaner than hell. Leave Halston Parker's daughter alone. I don't want word of this getting back to Remington Oil. It could mess up future relations with them."

"It's going to mess up future relations with them anyway, when you can't deliver a signed contract for that land. You told them it was almost a done deal. What does Remington Oil want with the land anyway?"

"I don't know and I really don't care. All they've hired us to do is to make sure the land is purchased for them, and not to get into their business."

"Well, the way I see it," Walker said, "you really don't have a choice but to force Parker's daughter into selling you that land, if you want to continue doing business with Remington Oil."

"Forget it," Duncan said, slicing one hand through the air. "There has to be another way. The last thing I want to do is tangle with that husband of hers, not to mention having the police breathing down our necks."

"So what do you suggest?" Walker asked, giving his uncle a hard glare.

"Damn, I don't know," Duncan said rubbing his forehead. "I need to think about this," he replied, staring into space.

A slow sadistic smile formed on Walker's lips. "Yeah, you do that. And I'll think of something, too."

"Hello."

"Clayton, sorry to call so late. This is Dex."

"What's up, bro?"

"I need your help. Caitlin received a threatening phone call last night about her land."

"What? Do you think it's the same person who tried dogging her father. out?"

Dex's features hardened. "Yes, I do."

"Did you report it to the police?"

"I went to the police yesterday to check out Halston's story. But I haven't reported the call Caitlin received last night to them yet."

"Why? What are you waiting for?"

"I'd like Alex to do some investigative work first." Alexander Maxwell was the brother of a close friend of Clayton's and a top notch private investigator.

"What kind of investigative work?"

"I went out to Caitlin's property to take a look around. And to be quite honest with you, I can't find any reason why anyone would be interested in it, especially for any type of major development. Although there's over eight hundred acres of land, the terrain is rocky and the soil isn't of good quality. Plus, it's in the middle of no where. I'm curious why Malone Land Developers want it."

"Malone Land Developers?"

"Yeah. Ever heard of them?"

"The name doesn't sound familiar, but I'll have Alex check them out. If there's something about them that we need to know, he'll find out what it is."

"Thanks, Clayton."

"And Dex, I understand congratulations are in order. I ran into Trevor today, and he told me the good news about Remington Oil's offer. Congratulations."

Dex smiled. "Thanks. I was going to call you and Justin with the news, especially since the both of you are my financial backers." His smile faded. "But I got sidetracked with this thing about Caitlin's land. I have a feeling something's going on and that Malone Land Developers are right smack in the middle of whatever it is. I'll bet my oil rig on it."

"When will you be going to Austin to meet with Remington Oil?"

"I'm supposed to meet with them on Friday, but I don't feel comfortable leaving Caitlin and Jordan now. I'm sending Trevor in my place. He's making a pit stop here in the morning to deliver some papers that need my signature."

"If there's anything I can do, just let me know, Dex."

"I will."

"I'll put Alex on this right away. Hopefully, he'll have some information for you in a few days. I'll keep in touch."

CHAPTER 11

"You're Dex's ex-wife?"

Caitlin studied the handsome, ruggedly built man standing before her in the open doorway. She raised a brow, not certain she liked what he'd said or the way he'd said it. Something bordering on disbelief was etched on his face. He stood several inches over six feet with curly close cropped black hair and dark piercing eyes. His dark coffee-colored face encompassed high cheekbones, a straight nose and a strong jawline. She had a gut feeling he was the type of man a person would have to be crazy to even think about tangling with.

"No, I'm not Dex's ex-wife," she responded. "I'm his wife."

Trevor Grant was lost for words. "Sorry ma'am. You're not what I expected."

"Oh? And just what were you expecting?"

Trevor shrugged, grinning sheepishly. "An older woman. A bigger woman. A less prettier one. Hell, I don't know. I just wasn't expecting you."

Caitlin could not prevent herself from softly biting down on her bottom lip to prevent a smile. "Well, you're in luck since I *was* expecting you."

She stepped aside. "Please come in, Mr. Grant. Dex's upstairs. He'll be down shortly. Won't you have a seat?"

Before Trevor could sit down, Dex came down the stairs with Jordan trailing behind him.

"Trevor, it's good seeing you, man." The two men clapped each other on the back. "How was your flight?"

"So-so," Trevor replied looking curiously at Jordan. "And who do we have here?" he asked. Although his gaze was on Jordan, his question was directed to Dex.

"This is my daughter. Jordan, sweetheart, say hello to Mr. Grant."

Trevor's head snapped up. He barely heard the little girl's greeting. "You've only been gone a week and already you got a kid? That's pretty fast work, bro."

Dex laughed and gave Trevor a wink. "Yeah, tell me about it." He then turned to Caitlin. "Guess the two of you have met already."

"Yes, we have," Trevor said raising a brow. "And I think you and I have a lot to talk about."

Dex grinned. "I guess we do at that. Did you bring the papers that I need to sign?"

"Yep."

"Good." Dex motioned for Trevor to follow him. "Come on. We can use the kitchen table."

"Dex, I'm going to take Jordan to the park for a while. We'll be back later," Caitlin said, taking Jordan's hand in hers. "It was nice meeting you, Mr. Grant."

"Likewise and please call me Trevor."

Caitlin smiled. "All right, Trevor." She turned and walked out the door, unaware of the subtle swaying of her hips.

Trevor watched her departure, not realizing that his mouth hung open. Dex placed his forefinger beneath Trevor's chin and closed it.

"You're drooling over my wife, Trev."

Trevor couldn't help but laugh. It was a lucky thing for him that his and Dex's friendship went back a long way. "Don't expect an apology from me, Dex. Damn it, man, she's gorgeous. But she looks so young. Just how old is she?"

"Caitlin's twenty-five."

"Twenty-five! Gee, man, I didn't know she was that young."

Dex knew there were a lot of things about Caitlin that his good friend didn't know. It had been much too painful to ever talk about her. "She was twenty-one when we married."

"And the kid, man," Trevor said, shaking his head. "It's obvious she's yours but where did she come from?"

Dex grinned. "It's a long story. Come on. I'll fill you in over a can of beer."

"Do you mind if I share this bench with you?"

Caitlin's gaze flicked up from the book she'd been reading and into the smiling face of the man who'd asked the question. "Sure."

She shifted on the park bench to allow him room to sit down. She couldn't help noticing the sketch pad in his hand. "Are you an artist?"

"Sometimes," he answered, fixing her with a friendly look. "For me it's a great stress reliever from the hustle and bustle of the business world."

They sat in amiable silence for some time. Caitlin would glance up from her book a few times whenever he would flip a page to his sketch pad to start on another subject.

"Mommie, see the pretty flower." Jordan, who'd been playing in the sandbox with some other kids, had come over to the bench.

"Yes, baby, it's pretty," Caitlin said, reaching out and taking the flower from Jordan's hand. She gave her daughter a big hug. "Are you ready to go?"

"Not yet, Mommie. I want to play some more." Before Caitlin could respond, Jordan raced back toward the other children.

"She's a pretty little girl. Is she yours?"

Caitlin smiled. "Thanks, and yes, she's mine."

"I think she'll be a joy to capture on paper."

Caitlin watched as the man sketched Jordan's likeness on his pad. He showed her the finished product. "What do you think?"

She smiled. "Why that's beautiful. You're very talented."

He returned her smile and tore off the sheet containing Jordan's likeness. "Here, you can have this."

"Thanks." Not one who would routinely converse with strangers, Caitlin accepted the drawing and tucked it in the back of her book. She then focused her attention back to her reading. The guy seemed nice enough, she thought, but so had Ted Bundy, the serial killer.

"I prefer sketching people more so than objects," the man said a short time later.

Caitlin looked up from her book. "Really? Why's that?"

"They're more interesting."

Caitlin noticed that while he'd been talking to her, he'd quickly captured on his pad a very good likeness of her. He showed it to her. "I think once again you've done an outstanding job," she told him.

"Thanks." He checked his watch. "Gosh, it's later than I thought." He stood. "Enjoy the rest of your day in the park. Goodbye." He quickly turned and left.

It was only after he was gone did Caitlin realize he had not offered her the picture he'd drawn of her. She shrugged. He was in such a hurry to get back to work he probably forgot to do so, she thought, returning to her book.

"Let me get this straight, man. You actually weren't divorced all this time? And Caitlin found out she was pregnant after you'd left for Australia?"

"That's about it, Trev."

Trevor shook his head. "Talk about a rather interesting story. You could have found yourself in one hell of a mess had you married someone thinking you were divorced. It's a good thing you never got involved with anyone."

"I never wanted to get involved with anyone."

Trevor knew that Clayton had tried fixing Dex up with a number of nice-looking sisters, and he'd never shown an interest in any of them. Dex's work had been his constant companion. "Why? Because you've never gotten over Caitlin?"

"No, because getting hurt once was enough."

"Then pardon me for asking, but why are you here now? Seems like the two of you are pretty much back together."

Dex took another swig of beer before answering. "Caitlin and I have decided to try and make a go of things for Jordan's sake."

"For Jordan's sake? Yeah right, man," Trevor said grinning. "I saw the way your woman was looking at you, and I also saw the way you were watching her. And I guess you want me to believe your decision not to go to Austin has nothing to do with leaving her behind."

Dex frowned. "My decision not to attend Remington Oil's meeting has everything to do with Caitlin." He then told Trevor everything, beginning with Halston's letter and ending with him having Alex investigate Malone Land Developers.

"Is the man crazy or what?" Trevor asked, shaking his head. "People can't go around forcing others to do anything against their will. Doesn't Malone know a contract isn't binding if either party was forced into it?"

"I really don't know what the man knows, except the fact I made it absolutely clear he was to leave Caitlin alone. The land is not for sale and that's final."

"Still bro, if I were you I'd be careful. Some people don't get messages, even clear ones. Did you report the telephone call to the police?"

"Yeah, I spoke with a Lieutenant Williams yesterday and again this morning. He's reopening the case." Dex didn't add that the officer hadn't been too pleased that he had taken matters into his own hands by confronting Duncan Malone.

"Lieutenant Williams and I have decided the best way to handle things is to keep a low profile since I'm moving Caitlin and Jordan to Houston in a few days. I told him that I've hired a private investigator to do some checking into Malone Land Developers." Dex smiled inwardly. Lt. Williams hadn't liked that move on his part either.

"But enough about my personal woes, Trev. Are you ready for your meeting with Remington Oil tomorrow?"

"Yeah. I'm flying directly to Austin from here. I should get there this afternoon around six. I'm going straight to the hotel from the airport."

"My reservations are at the Hilton," Dex said. "Since you're taking my place tomorrow, the hotel accommodations and the rental car are yours, courtesy of Remington Oil."

"Did you let the people at Remington Oil know of the change in plans?"

"Yes. I spoke with Adam today. Corinthians took the day off so I didn't get a chance to talk with her."

"Who's Corinthians?"

"Corinthians Avery is a geologist with Remington Oil. And according to Adam, she's now the head geologist. We used to work together a few years back." Dex smiled. "She's a real nice lady, man."

Something about Dex's voice when he'd made the last statement made Trevor raise a brow. "Was there something between the two of you once?"

Dex shook his head grinning. "No. There's never been anything between Corinthians and me other than friendship. I always considered her like one of my own sisters. She's someone with easy charm and polished manners; a real prim and proper, well-bred sister. She's nice. You'll like her."

"Corinthians. Ummm," Trevor said, taking his index finger and running it alongside of his cold can of beer. "Sounds like her name was taken straight from the Good Book."

Dex chuckled. "It was. Corinthians' father is a Baptist minister, and he named his son and daughter after books in the Bible. I'm sure you've heard of her brother, Senator Joshua Avery."

Trevor's smile faded. "Who hasn't heard of Avery and his aspirations to one day become Texas' first black governor."

"Do I detect you have a slight problem with that," Dex said, eyeing his friend.

"Let's just say, I think Avery has his priorities screwed up. He's a prime example of a brother who's so focused on where he's going, that he's forgotten where he came from."

Dex nodded. "Well, enough of politics. Give me those papers you have for me to sign. I don't want you to miss your plane to Austin."

Trevor laughed. "Are you trying to get rid of me before your gorgeous wife gets back?"

Dex joined him in laughter. "That hadn't crossed my mind, but now since you've mentioned it, that's not such a bad idea."

Walker rapidly strode down the long hallway to his office. When he reached his destination, he grabbed the knob and opened the door, letting himself inside.

He removed his jacket before sinking into the well-padded chair behind his desk. A grin tugged at the corners of his mouth.

He fully understood the unique nature of running a land development company. He'd discovered that most people didn't know their own minds, and the majority of their decisions could be made more quickly with other people's help and influences. A prime example was the Parker deal. Halston Parker had claimed he hadn't wanted to sell the land. He'd also said he hadn't had any plans to develop the property himself. That didn't make sense. Why would anyone in their right mind let a piece of land just sit there when it could bring them a bunch of money?

And as far as Walker was concerned, his Uncle Duncan had become soft in his old age. It was time for him to retire and let Walker take over. He was certain he could get the Parker's land for Remington Oil if he could do things his way, without any interferences from his uncle.

He smiled and began flipping through the pad he'd placed on his desk. He stopped when he came to the likeness of the woman he'd drawn that afternoon in the park, Halston Parker's daughter. He'd been parked outside her house since morning and had followed her to the park.

His smile widened. Once he used a few more scare tactics on her, she'd be glad to get rid of that land. Unlike his uncle, he wasn't afraid of her "wanna-go-for-bad" husband. If he had to, he would deal with him later.

While his uncle continued to sit around pondering what to do, he would have already finished the job.

"How was your afternoon in the park?"

Caitlin smiled as she loaded the last plate in the dishwasher. "It was nice. Jordan got plenty of playtime, and I got to do some reading. How was your meeting with Trevor?"

"Okay."

Caitlin sat down at the kitchen table across from Dex, "I'm sorry that I've placed you in an awkward position with your friends, Dex, with you having to explain our marriage and all."

Dex leaned back in his chair. "Don't worry about it."

Caitlin cleared her throat before continuing. "I know Clayton knows, but have you told the rest of your family yet?"

"No."

"I see," she said quietly.

A shadow of something Dex couldn't quite put a name to flickered across Caitlin's face, then was gone. It had happened so quickly, he wondered if he'd imagined it. "My parents are vacationing in the Bahamas. And I haven't gotten the chance to talk to Justin or my sisters."

Dex paused for a moment, then went on. "My family will be happy about Jordan. And I have a feeling they'll be even happier to know that we've gotten back together."

Caitlin picked up an empty coffee cup off the table, and slid her chair back to stand up. "What makes you think that?"

"Because I know them."

"But they won't know the truth, Dex. The truth that we really haven't gotten back together at all. The real truth is that we're farther apart than before."

Dex stared at Caitlin for a moment. "I disagree. We're getting along just fine."

"That's your opinion."

"And what's yours?"

"There's no love in our marriage, Dex." Caitlin regretted saying the words the moment they had left her lips. He was looking at her, fixing her with an angry stare.

"Aren't you forgetting something, Caitlin?" he said finally, in a deceptively calm voice. "You're the one who took my love and threw it back in my face. I can't believe you have the nerve to even talk about love."

"Because of what you consider as my one big mistake?"

"No. Because of mine," Dex answered. "I should never have fallen in love with you. I should've known better."

"Why?" Caitlin was baffled by his bizarre statement.

"My best friend killed himself over a woman while we were in college."

She heard the pain in Dex's voice. It filled the hushed quiet of the room. "But what does that have to do with us?"

"After seeing how Greg suffered over a woman, I vowed never to fall in love. Then I met you and did the one thing I vowed never to do."

Caitlin shook her head. "You never gave us a chance, did you?"

His gaze narrowed. "What do you mean?"

"Because of what happened to your friend, we were doomed from the start. You took a chance and fell in love but you never actually believed in what we shared. A part of you had expected to get hurt. That's why you gave up on me so easily."

Rage swept through Dex. He stood. "What do you mean I gave up on you? Have you forgotten it was the other way around? You're the one who called it quits, Caitlin. You're the one who wanted out."

"Yes, but you never should have given up on me."

Fingers of steel closed around Caitlin's arm as Dex pulled her to him. "What did you expect me to do?"

"You should have come for me," she said softly. "I was your wife."

"A wife who didn't want me," he grounded out through clenched teeth.

"But I did want you, Dex. Had you gotten that letter I sent telling you about Jordan, you would have known that."

"What are you talking about?"

Caitlin sighed. It wouldn't do any good to tell him that once she'd discovered she was pregnant, she had wanted to come to him and hoped he would take her back. She had written him telling him about her pregnancy and asking if he was willing to give their marriage another try. When she didn't get a reply to her letter, she had assumed he hadn't wanted her or his baby.

"It doesn't matter now, Dex. It's all in the past."

"Daddy! Daddy! See my picture!"

Dex released Caitlin's arm when Jordan raced into the room with a piece of paper in her hand. He caught Jordan up in his arms, taking the paper from her. "What's this?"

"It's a picture of me. Isn't it pretty, Daddy? The nice man also drew a picture of Mommy, but he kept it."

Dex lifted a brow. "What nice man?"

"The one in the park today, Daddy."

He frowned as he placed Jordan down out of his arms, and watched as she raced back out of the room to finish watching her Disney video.

Dex turned to Caitlin. She was wiping off the kitchen table. "Who was the man in the park?"

She shrugged her shoulders and continued with her task. Her earlier conversation with Dex had taken a toll on her. "Some guy. I think he did a real good job, don't you?"

"Why didn't he give you the one he did of you?"

"He was kind of rushed for time and left before thinking about it."

Dex shook his head. "Caitlin, has anyone ever told you never to talk to strangers?"

She stopped wiping the table. Her gaze shot sparks at him. "I'm not some little child. The park was crowded and there was no other place for the man to sit except next to me. There's nothing wrong with me being friendly."

"Look, all I'm saying is—"

The sound of Jordan calling for her daddy to come and watch the video with her, interrupted what Dex was saying. "We'll finish this conversation later."

He turned to leave, paused and turned back around. "Going back to our earlier conversation, Caitlin, just for the record, when you began avoiding my calls from Australia, I figured out what your father was probably trying to do. I put in for an emergency leave with my job to come back to the States to get you. I was walking out the door on my way to the airport when the postman arrived with the divorce papers and your ring."

He turned and walked out of the kitchen.

CHAPTER 12

Dex had been coming back for her . . .
Caitlin leaned back in the kitchen chair as thoughts of what Dex had said ran through her mind. She closed her eyes and remembered when she had begun avoiding his nightly calls from Australia. At the time, she'd been filled with so much doubt and uncertainty, that she couldn't think straight. Instead of telling him over the phone of her decision regarding their marriage, she had taken the coward's way out and had sent him a letter; a letter that had accompanied divorce papers and her wedding ring.

And he had received them on the same day that he had been coming back for her.

Caitlin reopened her eyes as tears rolled down her cheeks. What she had done had hurt him deeply. But there was one thing she hadn't realized until this afternoon. Her actions had also trampled his pride.

She rose out of the chair and went to stand before the window. She could smell the fragrance of the bluebonnets that grew around the back porch. But even that didn't have her full concentration. Her thoughts were on the man she had met in a cafe four years ago; a very proud Texan whom she had fallen deeply in love with. Of all of the things she had doubted and been unsure of, it had never been about her love for him. There had never been any question in her mind that she loved him. But in the end, her love for him hadn't been strong enough. And because of that, she had let him down.

"Caitlin?"

She shivered upon hearing her name from Dex's lips. She hadn't heard him reenter the kitchen. Turning around, she looked at him. Intense dark eyes held hers. "Yes?"

"I told Jordan that I'd come ask if you wanted to watch the next video with us."

Caitlin swallowed. "I'd love to."

He turned around to leave.

"Dex?"

He turned back around. "Yes?"

There was a moment of charged silence. "Dex. I . . ."

He took a hesitant step toward her. "Don't, Caitlin. It's in the past. Just let it go." He turned and walked out of the room.

Caitlin took a deep breath. She wondered if he would ever realize that he had just asked her to do the one thing that she couldn't do.

"We hope your stay at our hotel is a pleasant one, Mr. Madaris."

Trevor was about to tell the hotel clerk he wasn't Dex then quickly changed his mind. If he told them he was not Dex, there would probably be some paperwork required for the change, and he was too tired to deal with any type of hassle now. Because of thunderstorms, his flight into Austin had been delayed an hour. All he wanted to do was to go to his room, take a shower and go to bed. He needed to be well-rested for his meeting with Remington Oil tomorrow.

"Thanks. I'm sure it will be," he replied to the perky hotel clerk.

Upon reaching his room, Trevor was pleased to see that Remington Oil had reserved Dex a suite. He immediately went into the bathroom and turned on the shower. He came back out and noticed the message light flashing on the telephone. Picking up the phone, he dialed the hotel operator. A message had been left for Dex from Corinthians Avery telling him she'd be joining him for dinner at eight.

Trevor frowned, glancing at his watch. It was a little past six now. Dex hadn't mentioned anything about having a dinner date with Ms. Avery. Undressing, Trevor went into the bathroom to take his shower, closing the door behind him.

"This is Ms. Avery. I'd like to know whether or not Dex Madaris has checked in yet. Yes, I'll hold."

Butterflies floated around in Corinthians' stomach and had been ever since she thought she had heard movement in the room adjacent to hers. "Yes? Oh, he has? Thanks for taking the time to check."

Corinthians smiled nervously. Dex had arrived.

When she'd made plans for the evening, everything had seemed simple. Now she was becoming a nervous wreck and was having second thoughts about pulling off what she'd planned. When she'd made reservations for Dex, she'd also reserved the suite next to his. And since Remington Oil was picking up the tab, she had been given access to both. Her plans were for them to have dinner together. But what Dex didn't know was that she intended on being the appetizer.

She took a deep breath, deciding to make a move before she lost her nerve. Her breath caught in her throat when her ears picked up the sound of the shower running in Dex's room.

Corinthians opened her robe and looked at herself in the mirror. Her outfit looked more scanty on her than it had on the mannequin yesterday. She felt awkward wearing it, having never dared pulling such a stunt like this in her life.

She touched the silk material of the outfit, liking the way it felt against her skin. How would Dex handle seeing her in something so outlandish? There had never been anything romantic between them before. Would he want to begin a different sort of relationship with her? Or would she scare him away like Brenna had suggested?

A number of uncertainties crept into her head. Quickly closing her robe, she walked to the connecting door. Before opening it, she checked the pocket of her robe for the packs of condoms she'd purchased earlier that day. Taking a deep breath, she opened the door and walked into Dex's room.

Trevor stepped into the shower. The warm water felt good against his skin and soaked his aching muscles. He inhaled deeply, feeling somewhat revamped. He began to relax, not feeling as tired as he'd been just moments earlier. There was nothing like a good shower to get a person stimulated again.

He raised a brow, thinking he'd heard a sound coming from the bedroom. With the shower going full blast, he could have been mistaken. But he'd always been credited with having good ears.

He shrugged. Maybe it was housekeeping delivering more towels or something. But still, he didn't like the idea of some stranger in his room. He left the shower running and quickly stepped out.

Good. Dex was still in the shower, Corinthians thought, still hearing the sound of the shower going. She quickly moved around the room, dimming the lights before taking off her robe and neatly placing it across a chair. She tried quenching her nervousness by studying the picture on the wall.

"Who the hell are you?"

The sound of the unfamiliar voice made Corinthians turn around quickly. Her eyes locked first on the stranger's dark handsome face, then drifted down to his bare wet chest, before moving downward to the white towel covering his middle . . . barely. Her gaze flew back up to his.

Her throat suddenly became dry but somehow she was able to conjure up a voice. She cleared her throat. "You're not Dex." She quickly snatched her robe off the chair, shielding herself from him.

The man merely stared at her without comment. The only sign he gave that he'd heard her was the sudden lift of his brow. When seconds ticked by he finally spoke. "I know who I am, but who the hell are you?"

The man's rudeness, as far as Corinthians was concerned, was totally uncalled for. And it didn't help matters that he'd seen her outfit. How embarrassing! Could she have made a mistake and entered the wrong room? No! She'd made the reservations with the hotel herself. She and Dex were to have connecting rooms. So who was this man?

"I'm a friend of Dex's. Where is he?" she asked, suddenly feeling light-headed.

Trevor's gaze took in the woman standing before him who'd been dressed in what he thought was the sexiest getup he'd ever seen on a woman before. Too bad she had put her robe on. She had to be the most gorgeous woman he'd ever laid eyes on. He couldn't help wondering who she was. Was this some sort of joke Clayton was playing on Dex? It wouldn't have been the first time Clayton had gone a little overboard by sending one of his numerous female friends to liven up what he considered as Dex's dull and boring life.

"Did Clayton put you up to this?"

Corinthians frowned. "What?"

"I asked if Dex's brother, Clayton, put you up to this. If he did, you're out of luck. He forgot to cancel you out."

"What are you talking about?" Corinthians straightened her shoulders and met the stranger's gaze head on. She tried putting out of her mind just how handsome he looked.

"You're looking for Dex, right?"

She nodded. "Yes. Where is he?"

The man continued to stare at her, seemingly totally nonchalant with *his* state of half-nakedness, but definitely not with hers. His gaze moved over her from head to toe, occasionally lingering in certain places. He acted as if he had x-ray vision and could actually see through her robe. "Dex's home with his wife," he said bluntly.

His statement came as such a shock that Corinthians had to lean against the bedpost. "You're lying. Dex isn't married."

Trevor frowned. Not too many people called him a liar and got away with it. "Look. I don't know who you are or what you're doing in my room, but you're going to tell me, or you'll have a lot of explaining to do to security. You have no right to be in my room."

Corinthians could feel her head spinning. This couldn't be happening to her. Everything was going wrong, and this man claimed Dex was married.

"I know Dex got married a few years ago. But he got a divorce a short while later. Are you saying he got married again?" she asked him dazedly.

Trevor saw the bleakness in her face. It was obvious that whoever she was, she wasn't taking the news of Dex's marriage very well. He began having doubts she was someone Clayton had sent, but was someone who knew Dex personally. He came to stand before her.

"Dex got married, but he never got divorced. He and his wife were separated. Now they're back together. All three of them," he said.

"All three of them?" she asked softly.

"Yes, all three of them. Dex, his wife and daughter."

The next thing Trevor knew, the woman had fallen in dead faint at his feet.

"What happened?"

"You fainted."

Corinthians looked up at the man towering over her. He was still dressed in that darn towel. It took only a few seconds to realize she'd been placed on his bed. She made a move to get up.

"Lie still."

Ignoring his command, she sat up. This evening had become a nightmare, and it would be even more of one if what this man had told her about Dex was true. She suddenly noticed she wasn't wearing her robe and quickly jumped under the covers. "Where's my robe? Why did you take it off?"

"It's over there," he said, indicating the back of the chair. "I took it off after picking you up off the floor. I was concerned and thought that perhaps you had some sort of identification in your pockets. Instead, all I found were these."

Corinthians tinted when he held up the packs of condoms. She wished there was a way for her to crawl out of the bed and under it. This was getting more embarrassing by the minute. "Please hand me my robe. I want to leave."

"Lady, you're not going anywhere until I get some answers. Now who are you and what are you doing in my room?"

Corinthians closed her eyes and inhaled deeply. She reopened them. "I've told you. I thought this was Dex's room. I'd planned to spend an evening with him."

"Sounds kind of cozy for you and a *married* man."

Her eyes flashed fire. "I didn't know he was married. I talked to Dex a few days ago, and he didn't mention a thing about being married and having a child."

"And the two of you made plans to spend an evening together?" Trevor asked with disbelief in his voice.

"No. Dex didn't know anything about this evening. It was going to be a surprise."

"Aha! Clayton Madaris *did* put you up to this."

Corinthians became so mad she forgot just how skimpy her outfit was and angrily got out of bed. The next thing she knew, she was facing him, fuming. Her scantily clad body nearly touched his. All she could think about was the outrage she felt. This man was deliberately making things difficult for her. He had to be the most despicable man she'd ever met.

"I don't know what you're talking about. Clayton Madaris didn't put me up to anything. I don't even know Dex's brother that well. I only met him once."

"Then you have a lot of explaining to do. I want a name."

Corinthians' anger reached boiling point. "Why should I give you my name when you haven't given me yours?"

Trevor was stunned by her statement. "I don't have to tell you who I am. This is my room, not yours. You're the one who shouldn't be here."

Corinthians took a step forward, bringing her even closer to Trevor. The anger in her eyes grew. "Wrong, brother. My room is right through that door. We have connecting rooms and my company is paying for both. This room was strictly reserved for Dex Madaris and you aren't him. So you're the one out of place."

"I'm Dex's replacement."

"What?"

"I said I'm Dex's replacement. The name's Trevor Grant. I'm project foreman for Madaris Explorations. Dex couldn't make tomorrow's meeting, so I'm here in his place. All of this has been cleared with Adam Flynn."

Corinthians' anger drained abruptly. Complete humiliation took its place. She tried to take a step back, but Trevor Grant wouldn't let her. He placed his hands around her waist. "Take your hands off me, Mr. Grant."

Trevor gave her a crooked smile. "No-can-do. I won't run the risk of you fainting at my feet again. Now, where were we? Ahh, yes, introductions." Trevor's gaze held hers intently. "I'm still waiting on a name."

"Then wait on."

A mirthless smile curved Trevor's lips. "All right, so you want to play hard ball. I think I'll just call the head honcho at Remington Oil and find out what the hell is going on. Maybe he'll be able to explain why some half-dressed woman entered my hotel room wearing a robe full of condoms, claiming to be an employee of Remington Oil."

Trevor's eyes darkened. "You can tell me who you are, or you can explain your actions to Mr. Remington himself. Got it?" he growled.

Corinthians glared up at him. "Yes, I got it." She then swallowed deeply. "May I have my robe first please?"

Trevor's brows narrowed. He gazed at her thoughtfully before saying, "No. I happen to like what you're wearing." He continued to stare at her. "And don't pull some sort of stalling act. I'd like to have a name before midnight."

Corinthians knew from this moment on, she would despise this man forever. "I'm Corinthians Avery."

Trevor was completely stunned. "Corinthians Avery?"

Corinthians became livid. She leaned toward him with hands on her hips, and her dark brown eyes flashing. "Mr. Grant, I'm leaving whether you like it or not." With that said and done, she walked around him, grabbed her robe off the chair and put it on.

The quiet seductive rustle made by the silk material she wore echoed in the room. Trevor thought his eyes were going to pop out of his head when she had stomped across the room for her robe. She had the best shaped behind he'd ever seen. Hell! She had the best shaped everything! Before she reached the connecting door, he called out to her.

"Aren't you forgetting something?"

Corinthians turned around. "What?" she snapped.

"These." He held up the packs of condoms.

She tinted furiously, but not to let him get the best of her, she lifted her chin and gave him her most haughtiest glare. "You can have them."

Trevor smiled and Corinthians thought she would melt then and there. He had the sexiest smile.

"Thanks," he said. "I'll be saving them to use one day. Maybe when I see you again."

Corinthians knew an overwhelming urge to use her fingernails to claw Trevor Grant's face up. Never before had one man driven her to such anger. "Don't hold your breath."

Trevor's smiled widened. "Goodnight, Ms. Avery."

Without responding, Corinthians went into her room, slammed the door behind her and locked it.

Trevor's laughter could be heard throughout the suite. He sobered somewhat when he remembered the words Dex had used earlier that day to describe Corinthians Avery. He'd said something about easy charm, polished manners, real prim and proper, well-bred, nice and likable.

As Trevor made his way back to the bathroom, he couldn't help wondering when Dex had last seen the wench.

Caitlin was on her hands and knees, looking under the bed for her missing bedroom slipper, when she heard a soft tap on her door. She took a deep breath, knowing it had to be Dex. "Come in." In her position on the floor, she had to tilt her head back slightly in order to look up at him when he entered the room.

"What are you doing, Caitlin?"

She shrugged, coming to her feet. "I was looking for my bedroom slipper."

He nodded. "I made some more tea tonight. I thought maybe you'd like a cup."

She noticed he wasn't carrying the serving tray of tea but held a single cup. "Yes, thanks," she said, taking the cup he was handing to her.

"Be careful, it's hot."

A corner of her mouth lifted. "Just the way I like it. Where's yours?"

"I had a cup already, downstairs."

"Oh." Evidently he hadn't wanted to share her company over tea like he had done the other night. Confused lines etched her brow when he made no effort to leave the room. "Would you like to have a seat?"

"Nah, thanks anyway. But we do need to talk about a few things."

"A few things like what?" she asked sitting down on the edge of the bed and sipping her tea.

"The movers for starters. I wasn't sure how you wanted to handle things regarding your move from Ft. Worth. We can leave here and go there and get you all packed before heading to Houston."

"Hmm, what do you suggest?"

"Whatever you want to do is fine with me."

Caitlin nodded. She was aware of the fact that unlike her job that was out for the summer, Dex had taken the last few days off work to be with her and Jordan, not to mention that important business meeting he wouldn't be attending in Austin tomorrow. She couldn't ask him to make those kinds of sacrifices any longer. "I live in a leased furnished apartment, so other than clothing and a few personal belongings, there's really not a whole lot to be moved. I have another three months before my lease expires so there's no hurry for me to pack up things in Fort Worth. If you don't mind, I'd rather we go on to Houston. I can go back to Fort Worth later. I brought enough clothes, so Jordan and I have plenty to last us for a while."

"All right. What are you going to do about this place?"

Caitlin's emotions suddenly reeled under Dex's question. It had been one she'd avoided asking herself. Things had been different when she had left to move to Ft. Worth. But now with her father gone, leaving here would seem so final. So permanent.

"Caitlin?"

She met Dex's gaze, hoping he wouldn't see the tears she felt misting her eyes. "I'm going to start packing Dad's things up tomorrow, but I don't think . . ."

Dex came and sat next to her on the bed. He took the cup of tea from her trembling hands and placed it on the nightstand. He gathered her in his arms. "Hey . . ." His voice was soft, gentle. "It's okay. You don't have to do anything you don't want to. You've had a lot to deal with this past week. If you need more time to take care of things here, we can delay leaving for Houston for a while."

"No. I'm fine," she said, giving him a shaky smile. "I just haven't decided what I'm going to do with this place yet. I guess I can sell it, rent it out or lease it."

"You don't have to make any decisions now. Give yourself time to think about it."

She stared at him. Considering their history she was overwhelmed by his kindness and understanding. "Thanks, Dex. You've really been understanding about everything. Your being here has helped me get through a very difficult time."

"You don't have to thank me." He looked at her, and an unwanted familiar emotion gripped him. It was an emotion he fought each and every time he was around her. He wanted to make love to her so badly that he ached. He wanted the feel of her mouth under his, and the feel of her body beneath him. There was only so much a man could take. "Caitlin," he said, his voice deeper, husky with desire.

"Yes, Dex?"

His gaze flicked to her mouth and back up to her eyes. He shook his head to clear his mind. She didn't have the faintest idea of what he was going through; what he'd been going through the past few days. It wasn't just about getting her into his bed. It was about getting her there and keeping her there. But the decision of when that would be was hers. A part of him hated the thought of how much he wanted her. The last thing he needed was to allow Caitlin to become enmeshed in his emotional needs. Needs he'd been able to contain for the past four years.

"Dex?"

He stood. "Nothing. You better get some sleep. I hope the tea relaxes you. I couldn't help noticing how tense you were at dinner."

Caitlin stood. "I had a lot on my mind."

Dex nodded. "Good night, Caitlin."

Her gaze fastened on his. "Good night."

Ever so slowly, Dex bent his head and touched his lips to Caitlin's in a kiss intended to be chaste. But the feel of her warm mouth beneath his, was too much for him. His mouth settled on hers, moving very slowly, sensuously, coaxing her lips apart. He then deepened the kiss, his tongue stroking her, tasting her, fueling her passion and igniting his own.

A throaty groan escaped Caitlin's lips as she accepted the deep exploration of Dex's tongue inside her mouth while he held her body firmly against his. Her hands went around his neck, pulling him closer. She could feel the rapid beat of his heart as her breasts were flattened against his chest. His musty masculine scent intoxicated her, and a throbbing ache began growing deep within her. She burned from the heat, leaning into him for support.

Caitlin felt herself being lifted into Dex's strong arms. With their mouths still joined, their tongues still hotly mating, he placed her on the bed then joined her there. Stretching out next to her, he untied the belt at her waist and slid one hand inside the opening of her robe, feathering his fingertips across her bare skin left exposed by her short, skimpy gown. Her skin tingled from his touch, and the desire within her began leaping out of bounds. She fought for control. Her upbringing dictated that sharing a bed with someone involved love and commitment. And although she and Dex were legally married, until she felt their marriage was on more solid ground, she couldn't be intimate with him. She pulled away. "No, Dex, I can't—"

Dex gently pulled her back into his arms. "Shh, it's all right, baby. I won't do anything you don't want me to. Just let me hold you. I need to hold you for a while."

Caitlin heard the deep longing in Dex's voice. She heard the need in it too. It was so deep, so intense, it almost shattered her resolve, broke her resistance. But a part of her held back. It was the part of her that believed in the true meaning of making love. She couldn't give in to him just to satisfy their sexual hunger, their body urges and their rampant desires. There had to be more between them, something a lot deeper and more meaningful than mere lust.

Dex tenderly held Caitlin in his arms. Although at the moment he was totally frustrated, a part of him admired her and respected her decision to hold back. His hunger for her went deep, but he wouldn't be completely satisfied until he possessed all of her. And he couldn't do that as long as she couldn't fully accept the way the relationship had to be between them. She wanted something from him that he could not give her again. The pain went too deep. There could never be promises of love between them. Not ever again.

After moments of contented silence with Caitlin in his arms, Dex leaned over and kissed the tip of her nose, her lips, and the side of her mouth. "No matter what, Caitlin, I will be a good husband to you, and a good father to Jordan."

Caitlin heard Dex's words and knew them to be true. From the moment they had met, he'd come across as a man of honor. He had proven it countless times during their brief courtship. At no point had he tried taking advantage of her innocence. He'd always been the perfect gentleman, always treating her like "his lady." And now she knew that with that same sense of honor, he was accepting what he felt to be his obligation to her and Jordan. He was not a man to turn his back on his responsibilities.

Dex Madaris was a man who took care of his own. A part of Caitlin believed that in the end, her father had known that.

"I believe you, Dex," she said softly as he continued to hold her.

They were silent for several minutes, and then Dex spoke again. "I better go." He pulled himself up and sat on the edge of the bed.

Caitlin also sat up. "Dex, I . . ."

"It's okay," he assured her, whispering against her forehead. He slid his arm around her waist, and she leaned against him. "Everything's going to work out all right, Caitlin."

"I hope so," she replied.

"It will. We're in it for the long haul. We have the rest of our lives."

She nodded, yawning.

Dex stood. "You're tired. You need to sleep, and I've kept you up long enough." He drew her up gently into his arms. "Goodnight, Caitlin," he whispered before kissing her on the cheek. "Sleep well." He then turned and walked out of the bedroom.

Corinthians threw the overnight bag on her bed and immediately went to the telephone. She had to dial the number twice. Her nervous fingers just didn't want to cooperate.

"Hello?"

"Brenna, can we talk?"

"Corinth? Where are you?"

"I'm at home."

"At home? What's wrong? I thought you'd made plans to spend the night at the hotel."

"Oh, Brenna, tonight was a total disaster."

"What happened, girl?"

Corinthians settled down on her bed. She should have taken Brenna's advice, then none of this would have happened. But, no, she thought she'd had everything under control, only to have things blow up in her face.

"Dex didn't show," Corinthians said.

"He didn't show? And you went to all that trouble buying those outfits and making arrangements to get connecting suites."

"Brenna, Dex didn't show up, but someone else did. Dex sent his project foreman in his place. I didn't know about the change and . . ."

"And what?" demanded Brenna.

"He saw me, Brenna. This other guy saw me the way Dex was supposed to see me."

Corinthians heard her best friend's sharp intake of breath. "This man saw you? He saw you dressed in that black thing?"

"Yes."

"Girl, get outta here. Tell me you're lying," Brenna said before bursting into full-fledged laughter.

It's not funny," Corinthians shouted. "It was a totally embarrassing situation for me. I'd appreciate a little bit of sympathy from you."

"Oh, I'm sorry," Brenna managed between giggles. "But as far as I'm concerned you got just what you deserved. I told you from the get-go that your plan to snag Dex was a bad one. Now tell me what happened. Don't you dare leave out a thing."

Corinthians gave Brenna the story blow by blow, pausing occasionally to allow Brenna's outbreak of laughter, especially the part about her fainting and him finding the condoms.

"So after I made it back to my own suite, I quickly dressed, packed my bags, checked out of the hotel and came home. I'm embarrassed to death. How on earth can I possibly face this guy at the meeting tomorrow?"

"Umm, Corinth?"

"What?"

"You say this brother is fine?"

Images of Trevor Grant wearing nothing but a white towel covering his middle flashed across Corinthians' mind. "Yes, he's fine, but that's not the issue here. Didn't you hear what I said? Dex's married and has a child. How could that happen?"

"The usual way I guess. What part don't you understand? The wedding or the conception part?"

"Brenna! Get real. You're making fun of this."

"You're right, I am. Face it, Corinth, Dex Madaris is no longer a viable candidate for your affections. He's a married man. We both know you aren't a home-wrecker, so I suggest you get over him and move on to someone else. And I got just the person for you."

"Who?" Corinthians asked, sounding totally defeated. She didn't want anyone else.

"The fine brother who saw you in that call-girl outfit tonight."

"Never!" screamed the voice on the other line.

CHAPTER 13

Caitlin spent the next day preparing for her move to Houston. The re-
altor had phoned that morning to let her know that already he had
found a buyer for her father's print shop. After her talk with Dex last
night she had decided not to do anything regarding her parents' home
for now.

She glanced at her watch as she carefully sealed the cardboard box containing the last of her father's things that were being donated to charity.

It was a little before noon. Dex had taken Jordan to a morning movie
matinee. He had invited her to come along, but she'd refused because
she still had a lot to do before they left for Houston tomorrow.

That morning at breakfast, things had been slightly tense between her
and Dex. She couldn't rid herself of the memory of him in her bed, holding her in his arms last night. The mere thought had stimulated a fierce
ache within her. And what made it even more unbearable was that she
had a feeling Dex was experiencing a similar ache. More than once, over
the breakfast table, his dark eyes had sought her out. Jordan's ever joyful
presence had served as a buffer for their sexual frustrations. Frustrations
Caitlin knew were taking their toll on her. She had to do something to
burn off some of her nervous energy.

She left her father's bedroom and entered her own. Removing her
jeans and blouse she replaced them with her white jogging pants and a
blue t-strap top. Shoving her feet into a pair of Reeboks, she raced downstairs and quickly scribbled a note to Dex. She stuck it on the front of the
refrigerator with a magnetic holder.

Once Caitlin's feet touched the earth, she broke into a run. It was a lovely summer day, not as hot as the others had been. Her destination was the park a few blocks away. She ran until perspiration soaked her entire body and until the muscles in her legs throbbed. She ran until she couldn't possibly take another step, and collapsed on the first park bench she came to. Her whole body heaved as she fought for breath, and at the same time she silently berated herself for running hard without warming up first.

Minutes later after her body had relaxed, she hauled herself to her feet and stretched her taut muscles. Her body was, for the moment, rid of the frustrations and tensions that had plagued her since awakening that morning. Taking a deep breath, she headed toward home, walking at a slow pace.

She couldn't help wondering how things would be for her in Houston. Would Dex's family forgive her for the pain she'd caused him? She and Dex had been apart for four years. Had he been involved with someone during that time? He was a very handsome man, and she was sure he'd been dating while they'd been apart.

"Look out, lady!"

Caitlin found herself being jerked backward by big strong arms and collided with a hard solid chest. If it hadn't been for the support of the arms holding her, she would have lost her balance and fallen. "What's going on?"

She turned to the heavyset man dressed in a jogging suit. "That car nearly ran over you!" He pointed toward a dark-colored sedan that was rapidly disappearing down the street with the roar of its engine fading into the distance.

"It was probably some crazy kid who shouldn't even be driving yet," the man muttered, releasing her. "Are you okay?"

"Yes, I'm fine."

"Sorry I had to grab you so hard like that, miss, but that car was zoomin' up real fast."

"Please, don't apologize," Caitlin protested. "I should've been watching where I was going. I appreciate what you did. Thanks."

"Don't mention it. I jog this way everyday. There's always some nut who wants to be a show-off on wheels." He laughed loudly. "Enjoy the rest of your walk. See ya later."

Caitlin watched as the man jogged off. "Thanks again," she called out to him.

He threw up his hand in a wave.

Caitlin resumed her walk, a little shaken over her near mishap. She'll have to be more careful in the future and pay more attention to where she was going. She'd been walking with all of her thoughts on Dex.

When she turned the corner of her block she saw that her car was parked in the driveway, which meant Dex and Jordan had returned.

"Did you have a nice run?"

Upon entering the house, Dex's question made Caitlin whirl around. He was standing in the kitchen doorway.

"Yes, but I may have overdone it a little," she replied, deciding not to mention her near accident to him. The last thing she needed was for him to know how careless she'd been. She stared at him. He was dressed in a pair of jeans and nothing else, and as usual they revealed just how masculine he was. When she remembered just how wonderful his bare chest felt caressing the nipples of her breasts, a deep sensation erupted in the pit of her stomach.

"Have you heard anything from Trevor about the meeting with Remington Oil?" she asked.

"No. Unless there's some major development, I probably won't hear from him until much later."

Caitlin nodded. "Where's Jordan?"

"Taking a nap. She barely made it through the entire movie before falling asleep."

An easy smile played at the corners of Caitlin's mouth. "Are you hungry? If so, I can fix you something for lunch."

Dex stood very still. His eyes moved slowly over Caitlin. "Yes. I'm hungry, but not for food."

She blinked at his words. If his statement was meant to shake her up a bit, he had succeeded.

"What about you? Are you hungry?" he asked, giving her a smile that made her breath catch in her throat. His dark eyes were as velvety as his voice. "And I don't mean for food."

Caitlin couldn't help the shiver passing through her body. Her mind screamed not to ask, but she couldn't help herself. "Hungry for what?"

The slow smile that spread over Dex's face increased Caitlin's anxiety. "Hungry for me."

Regaining the breath that had been knocked out of her with Dex's response, she made an attempt to make light of what he'd just said. "Dexter Jordan Madaris, you're awful."

Dex chuckled wryly. "How would you know? You haven't tried me in four years," he teased in a low, caressing tone. "And if I remember correctly the last time you did, you thought I was pretty good."

For a while neither spoke when the meaning of Dex's words sank in. Caitlin watched him walk slowly toward her. The teasing glint in his eyes had been replaced by smoldering desire. Her breathing quickened. He stopped directly in front of her.

Dex gently pulled her closer. His hands moved down her back and over the slope of her backside. "Ask me what I'm hungry for," he taunted.

There was tension virtually cracking in the air surrounding them. "What are you hungry for?"

He looked down at her. "For starters this." He lowered his lips to hers. His tongue swept the insides of her mouth mating with hers in a sensuous duel. Caitlin let his magic engulf her as he took her mouth fiercely. He showed no mercy. His hands moved to her face and cupped the sides of it.

He suddenly broke the kiss. "Take a deep breath, baby."

Caitlin obeyed his command mere seconds before his mouth came down fiercely to take possession of hers again. His hands left her face to again move to her behind, pulling her closer to him and letting her feel his deep desire for her.

His mouth moved to the side of her neck placing fleeting kisses there. She clung to him, unable to stand on her own. His kisses had snapped her of any strength.

"Ouch!"

Dex lifted his head. "What's wrong?"

She saw concern in his eyes. "My leg. It's hurting. I think I may have pulled something during my run."

Before she could say anything else, she found herself swept into big strong arms. "Dex! Put me down. I can walk."

Ignoring her words, he carried her up the stairs. Without pausing, he took her to her bedroom and gently placed her on the bed. "Take your pants off."

"What?"

"I said take off your pants. I want to take a look at your leg."

"T—that's not necessary, Dex. It's probably nothing more than—"

Before Caitlin could react, he leaned down and quickly removed her shoes and socks. He then grasped the elastic waistband of her jogging pants and pulled them down slowly.

Caitlin's breath caught in her throat. She found herself held motionless by the look in Dex's dark eyes. As he tugged her jogging pants past her thighs, his eyes left hers to look down at her body. She lifted her hips slightly, and he completely removed her pants. Her cheeks were flushed when she lay before him wearing only her top and white bikini panties.

Dex dragged in a large breath. "Which leg?"

His question, asked in a low husky tone, made Caitlin's skin burn. "This one," she answered. Her eyes held his as she slowly lifted her left leg to him.

When he reached out and touched her leg, there was a slight tremor in Dex's hand. His fingers tightened around her leg as he gently massaged it. He pressed down with his thumbs, gently moving up the back of her leg in circular motions, tenderly kneading each muscle with long, soothing strokes. A fine film of perspiration formed on his brow. "Does it feel better, baby?"

His term of endearment sent Caitlin up in smoke. *Yes, it feels better but I'm replacing one ache with another.* Unable to speak, she merely nodded in response to Dex's question. She was slowly floating on a wave of sensuous pleasure. The workings of his fingers on her leg reminded her of the workings of his fingers on other parts of her. She noticed his fingers were slowly inching their way upward, toward her inner thigh. Her eyes met his. The smoldering look of desire and longing in them made a quiver surge through her body. He leaned toward her. His fingers moved erotically closer and closer to . . .

"Whatcha doing to Mommy, Daddy?"

Caitlin snatched her leg from Dex at the precise moment he drew back and stepped away from the bed. Jordan entered the room wiping sleep from her eyes.

"Mommy's leg hurts a little, Jordan. I was trying to make it feel better," he offered.

"Oh," Jordan said, as if understanding completely. She looked at her mother with sympathy in her eyes. "Why don't you kiss it, Daddy? That makes the pain go away."

A glint of amusement shone in Dex's eyes. He gave Jordan a sparkling smile. "You don't say? Why, I think that's a great idea. I don't know why I didn't think of it myself." He took a few steps back toward the bed.

Caitlin immediately straightened. "No. That's not necessary. My leg feels better already."

"But he has to kiss it, Mommy," Jordan exclaimed. "You always kiss whatever makes me hurt. It'll make the pain go away."

"Yes, Mommy," Dex said with hidden laughter in his voice. Reaching out, he gently grabbed Caitlin's leg. "I'll kiss it and the hurt will go away."

He leaned down and gently lifted Caitlin's leg to his lips, placing a kiss on it. Caitlin thought she would faint when she felt the tip of his tongue caress her smooth skin.

"And just to be on the safe side," Dex said to Jordan who was wide-eyed. "I'd better do it twice."

Jordan bobbed her head in complete agreement. "That's a good idea, Daddy. Isn't that a good idea, Mommy?"

Caitlin gave her daughter a forced smile, then gave Dex a disapproving look. "Yes, darling," she answered through clenched teeth. "That's a good idea."

Dex winked at Caitlin before kissing her leg again. She closed her eyes. The heat flowing through her was overwhelming. She opened her eyes. He backed up slowly from the bed and stared at her as she pulled herself up in a sitting position. His gaze roamed over her, and she knew she hadn't been the only one affected by the kisses.

"Can we have pizza for lunch?" Jordan's question reminded her parents they were not alone.

Dex made a face at his daughter. "Pizza! Is that all you ever want to eat? Maybe your Mom and I should send you to live at a pizza restaurant, then you can eat pizza every day," he teased, reaching out and grabbing her into his arms. He lifted her high on his shoulders.

Jordan. "But I don't want to live with anyone else but you and Mommy.

I like living with the both of you. It's just like Faye's house now. I have a mommy and daddy, too."

Caitlin and Dex exchanged glances. Their daughter, in her own way, had just let them know she wanted the three of them together as a family. Dex bounced Jordan on his shoulders. "Let's go downstairs and raid the refrigerator."

Caitlin watched Dex and Jordan leave. Getting off the bed, she closed the door behind them. After taking a shower, she put on a pair of beige slacks and a yellow blouse.

As she applied light lip color to her lips and blush to her cheeks, she noticed her reflection in the mirror. She felt nervous. Once again she had come close to losing control and throwing all caution to the wind. That was something she couldn't do with Dex.

The three of them would spend a perfectly normal evening together, which would include a special dinner she was preparing. What really worried her was what would happen later that night after Jordan went to bed and she and Dex found themselves alone.

She quickly decided as soon as Jordan went to bed, she would avoid Dex by going to bed herself. After all, she did need a good night's sleep for the drive to Houston in the morning.

Taking another deep breath, she left her bedroom to join Dex and Jordan downstairs.

"Trevor, you're early. The meeting doesn't start for another hour."

"I know, Adam," Trevor said, glancing around the huge conference room. "I was hoping to get a chance to speak with Corinthians Avery before the meeting."

"She hasn't arrived yet, but I expect her any minute. Would you like to wait for her in her office?"

"If it's okay."

"Sure. Come on, I'll take you there."

Minutes later, Trevor was pacing the confines of the plush office. He wasn't as alert as he wanted to be. He had spent most of the night thinking about Corinthians Avery. The woman had truly gotten next to him. Visions of the chocolate-colored woman had danced through his mind all night, along with mental images of silk sheets and naked bodies. Last night her velvety smooth dark skin had glowed in the hotel room's soft lighting, and she had smelled so good when he'd picked her up off the floor after she'd fainted. And that sexy black scrap of nothing she'd worn would forever be carved into his memory. The enticing piece of lingerie had showcased her small waist, firm breasts and shapely hips.

Trevor sat down in the leather chair in front of the large oak desk. He reached for one of two framed photographs sitting on it. The first one was a group picture of Corinthians, an older couple and a man. The man he recognized immediately from seeing his picture in the newspapers a number of times. He was Senator Joshua Avery. Trevor could only assume the older couple were Corinthians' parents. A younger looking Corinthians stood next to her parents and brother, wearing a black cap and gown. Evidently the photo had been taken on her college graduation day. He placed the picture back on the desk and picked up the other one.

The other framed photograph was another group picture and one person he recognized immediately was Dex. He was standing next to Corinthians, at what appeared to be a job site, with his arms around her shoulder. Everyone in the group was smiling for the camera. Everyone but Corinthians. Her smile wasn't directed at the cameraman, but at the man standing next to her.

Trevor's eyes darkened. Dex had told him that he and Corinthians had never been romantically involved, and that he thought of her as one of his sisters. Trevor had no reason not to believe him. Evidently during the years of Dex's friendship with Corinthians, he'd never picked up on the fact that she had wanted more. Or to put it more bluntly, Dex had no idea that Corinthians Avery was in love with him.

Trevor couldn't help wondering what were Corinthians' plans now that she knew Dex was married. Would she try and get over Dex or would she pursue him anyway? Was she one of those women who thought nothing of breaking up a marriage? The kind of woman who had ruined his own parents' marriage.

He placed the photograph back on her desk at the same exact moment Corinthians entered her office. He watched her walk into the room, unaware of his presence. She closed the door behind her.

Trevor's breath caught in his throat. Today with the bright sunlight shining through the blinds, she looked just like the woman Dex had described her to be: someone with easy charm, polished manners, prim and proper, well-bred, nice and likable. He also knew by the outfit she was wearing this morning, a conservative dark two-piece suit, that she was totally professional. She looked nothing like the alluring seductress who had been in his hotel room last night.

"Hello, Corinthians."

Corinthians stopped dead in her tracks when she heard the low, husky voice. It was the same voice she'd heard countless times in the deep recesses of her mind during her sleepless night. "What are you doing here, Mr. Grant?" She watched his gaze travel swiftly from the crown of her head to the black pumps on her feet and back up to her eyes. She hoped just from looking in her eyes, he could tell just how furious she was at seeing him.

Trevor smiled as he stood. It was a slow smile that showed perfect teeth, straight and pearly. It was also a smile that nearly took Corinthians' breath away.

"After last night, I'm sure we can dismiss with formalities and be on a first name basis. Especially considering our friendship," he said.

Corinthians felt the heat of anger filling her head. "We're not friends." She couldn't help but study him. Unlike last night when he'd been wearing a towel, he stood before her fully dressed in an expensive suit. She had to hand it to him, the brother was well put together. Her gaze returned to his face to find him watching her close scrutiny of him. The hard line of his mouth curved into an even wider smile.

She cleared her throat. "I'm going to repeat myself, just in case you weren't listening. We aren't friends."

"Oh, but we are, Corinthians. Mainly because we share a secret."

Corinthians came closer into the room, walked over to her desk and placed her briefcase on it. She then faced Trevor with a deep frown. "We do not share a secret."

"Are you suggesting what happened last night shouldn't be kept between the two of us?"

She straightened her shoulders. Of course she didn't want anyone to know she'd made a complete fool of herself. She had told Brenna, but she wouldn't dare tell anyone else. Her eyes narrowed. Would Trevor Grant mention it to anyone? Possibly even Dex? The thought of Dex finding out was too humiliating to think about.

"I'm not suggesting anything."

"Then we do share a secret?"

Corinthians knew he had her cornered. She folded her arms across her chest and glared at him. "Yes." She was literally boiling on the inside. No man had ever gotten on her last nerve like Trevor Grant was doing, not even her brother who could be a monumental pain at times. She quickly did a mental comparison of Dex and Trevor Grant. She remembered Dex as being a perfect gentleman, a man who always treated her like a lady. But she had a gut feeling that Trevor Grant would never treat her like a lady. He would treat her like a woman. He would make her feel hot, sexy, sensual, desirable . . .

Corinthians reared up in shock at the way her thoughts were going. "I would appreciate it, Mr. Grant, if you left."

Trevor stared at her. She was beautiful. A fierce rush of desire surged through him. Although she was a possible home-wrecker, not to mention a woman pining for his best friend, he still wanted her. "I'll see you at the meeting."

With those final words, he crossed the room, opened the door, then walked out of her office.

"Dex? Hey, man, can we talk?"

"Yeah, Caitlin and Jordan are next door. What's up, Clayton?"

"Are you standing or sitting?"

Dex frowned. "Why?"

"You might want to sit."

Dex leaned against the kitchen counter and adjusted the telephone to his ear. "I take it you found out something."

"Yep. Alex has given me the report on Malone Land Developers."

"And?" he asked quietly.

"After careful and thorough digging, Alex was able to come up with information which indicates that Malone Land Developers is an undercover land buying agent for Remington Oil.

Dex slammed his fist down on the table. The sound traveled through the telephone line.

"I didn't think you'd be happy about it; especially since they just chose Madaris Explorations for a major project."

Dex rubbed his forehead. He suddenly felt a strong headache coming on. "Are you sure about this, Clayton?"

"Yeah, man, I'm positive. There's been a massive land buy in the area near Eagle Pass, and as usual, everything is pretty hush-hush. However, I'd bet my Porsche that Remington Oil isn't aware of the tactics Malone Land Developers are using to coerce people into selling their land. I believe S. T. Remington would denounce such actions."

"I agree," Dex said, deciding to sit down after all. He felt a deep sense of loyalty to the company he'd worked for for twelve years. Remington Oil was one of the largest oil companies in the United States, and S. T. Remington, as far as Dex was concerned, was an honest and fair man.

Since Dex had started Madaris Explorations, he had gotten a number of smaller contracts with the company and now he had been offered the opportunity to head up a major project. He knew Caitlin's refusal to sell to Remington Oil would place him in a precarious position with them.

He also knew it was not uncommon for a major oil company who was interested in a certain piece of property, to obtain the property through different land brokers and camouflage their intentions so as not to tip off their competitors. That way, no one would know of their plans to go into an area with a massive exploration program. It would be imperative to their well-planned strategy to keep everything quiet and deflect curiosity and unnecessary problems. And because he was a former geologist, Dex understood the driving force behind an oil company wanting to be first with any discovery. He knew if Remington Oil was interested in Caitlin's land, there was a very good reason for it.

"Dex?"

"Yeah?"

'There's something else I got to tell you. You better sit this time for real."

Dex leaned back in his chair. "I *am* sitting, Clayton. What else is there?"

"That major project you're suppose to do for Remington Oil—what do you know about it?"

Dex frowned, wondering about Clayton's question. "Not a whole lot. Adam can't go into any specific details until one loose end has been tied up. He said something about a piece of property they were negotiating on. It's called the Leabo Project. Why do you ask?"

"Caitlin's land is part of the Leabo Project, Dex. It's the final piece of property Remington Oil needs. Evidently Malone Land Developers led them to believe Halston Parker was willing to sell. Caitlin's refusal to co-operate has put them in a tight squeeze. No wonder they're desperate. You and I both know how much oil companies pay their land buying agencies. Malone Land Developers could lose a bundle if Caitlin doesn't sell, not to mention them losing face with Remington Oil."

Dex said nothing. He was shocked. When he finally spoke, his voice was weary and downcast. "Are you absolutely sure about this?"

"You know Alex, Dex. He's very thorough. Two things I never question about his reports; how he gets his information and the validity of it."

Dex sighed defeatedly. Madaris Explorations' golden opportunity hinged on Caitlin. "I guess we may as well kiss our deal with Remington Oil good-bye. Caitlin has no intentions of ever selling that property."

"I 'm sorry, Dex. I guess this doesn't help you and Caitlin's already delicate relationship does it?"

"No, it doesn't."

"Are you sure she won't sell? Maybe if she knew the position you'd be in, she might change—"

"No. That property has been in her family for generations. It's all she has left of her parents. It's her legacy, and I won't influence her in any way."

"Will you tell her what's going on so she can make the choice?"

Dex couldn't help but remember the last time Caitlin was faced with making a choice involving him; the one between him and her father. In the end, Dex had lost out. He didn't want to think about the outcome if she had to choose between him and a piece of land.

"No. I'm not telling her anything. Whatever happens or doesn't happen between me and Remington Oil is my business."

"I think you're making a big mistake, Dex. You should at least talk things over with her and see if perhaps—"

"No. There'll be other projects. If not with Remington Oil, then with some other oil company."

After several moments of silence, Clayton said. "When will you and Caitlin be leaving for Houston?"

"We're leaving in the morning. And, Clayton, I want your word that you won't say anything to Caitlin or the rest of the family about this."

Clayton hesitated a second before saying. "You have my word. But I still think you're making a big mistake."

* * *

"How's your leg, Caitlin?" Dex asked when they were seated at the dinner table.

Caitlin glanced up from her meal and looked at him. Ever since she and Jordan had returned from visiting Mrs. Logan, Dex had seemed preoccupied about something. She wondered if he'd heard from Trevor. Had something gone wrong at the meeting with Remington Oil?

"My leg is fine," she answered. "Thanks for asking."

"See, Daddy. Your kisses helped."

Dex smiled at his daughter. "They sure did, honey." He cast an amused glance at Caitlin. "You wouldn't happen to have any more aches and pains would you? I would just love kissing them to make them better."

Caitlin tinted. "No, but thanks anyway."

When dinner was over, Dex helped Caitlin clean up the kitchen. Afterward, he read Jordan a story. Caitlin used that time to do some last minute packing.

Later that night, before putting Jordan to bed, a few of the neighbors dropped by to say goodbye and to wish them well. It was late when the last of their company had left. Dex had taken Jordan up to bed hours earlier.

Caitlin had been tempted more than once during the course of the evening to ask Dex what was bothering him. But each time, she changed her mind.

Even now, he stood looking out the window at the darkness. He appeared entrenched in deep thoughts. She tried not to notice how good he looked wearing scuffed black boots, a white shirt and faded skin-tight jeans. The sight of him sent a surge of desire through her.

"I think I'll go on up to bed now," she said, breaking the silence. "I'm feeling sleepy. I guess it's because I ran today. I'm going to have to jog more often. I'm definitely out of shape."

Dex turned around to face her. A smile touched the corners of his lips. "You're rambling, and I happen to like the shape you're in."

Caitlin lowered her lashes. Should she try to find out what was bothering him? Could she handle it if he were to tell her it was none of her business? For all she knew his mood may have nothing to do with Remington Oil. Suppose he had been seeing someone special in Houston, and with plans of taking her there in the morning, he was beginning to have second thoughts about continuing their marriage.

She lifted her gaze to his. "Dex, is something—"

"Goodnight, Caitlin," he cut in before she could finish her question. "Sleep well."

And every time you say that to me, I usually don't, Caitlin thought, turning to go up the stairs.

CHAPTER 14

". . . here's another soft favorite for your listening pleasure. This sound is going out to all the frustrated drivers caught in Houston's noontime traffic. This number has just the right touch to add a bit of magic to your afternoon. It's a golden hit from the Supremes titled, Where Did Our Love Go?"

The disc jockey drawled the words over the radio in a velvety masculine voice, and the sound of the Supremes followed, bathing the car with their soulful Motown sound.

Where did our love go? Caitlin tried keeping her mind on the scenery outside the car window, and not on the question being asked in the song playing on the radio.

The long drive from San Antonio to Houston had seemed endless. Each road sign they'd passed, and the small and sparsely populated towns and cities in between, had brought her closer to the city and her new home.

The dashboard clock indicated it was a little past noon. Jordan slept peacefully in the back seat while Dex maneuvered the vehicle expertly through the freeway traffic.

He suddenly broke the silence when they came to a stop at a traffic light. "I spoke with my parents before we left this morning. I finally reached them in Freeport."

Caitlin turned to find him staring thoughtfully at her. "And?"

He reached over and gently touched her hand, then squeezed it reassuringly. "They are happy about our news. They are very, very, happy."

Caitlin nodded. "About Jordan?"

Dex smiled. "Yes. They're ecstatic to find out they have another grand-daughter. It took me a full half hour to convince them not to cut their trip short and return home. I assured them Jordan wasn't going any place and that she would be here when they return two weeks from now."

Caitlin removed her hand from his. "I see."

"My parents are also thrilled that you and I are back together again."

Caitlin moistened her lips with a nervous sweep of her tongue. She wondered if that was something Dex knew for sure, or something he was hoping for. Although she knew Dex to be his own man and a person who made his own decisions, she couldn't help wondering if the Madaris family would resent her because of the pain she'd caused him.

It wasn't long before they arrived in Dex's neighborhood. He'd told her he had poured all the money he'd made over the past four years into purchasing a home a few months ago in a nice area of Houston.

Caitlin's eyes widened at the house. Dex's home was a stately stucco house that rose two stories with a large meticulously well-tended lawn on a tree-lined street.

The car stopped at the end of a long driveway. Dex rested one arm on the steering wheel and with the other, he reached out and cupped Caitlin's chin. "We're home."

Upon entering the house, they moved through a wide foyer that led into the living room. The house was spacious and the decor had the pro-fessional touch of an interior designer. Most of the contemporary-style furniture appeared new and obviously expensive.

"What do you think so far?" Dex's voice cut into Caitlin's close study of his home. She turned to him. He was holding a sleeping Jordan in his arms.

"I think if I'm not too careful, I could really fall in love with this place. It's beautiful, Dex."

"I'm glad you like it."

"Where will Jordan be sleeping?" Caitlin asked. "It'll be a lot easier on you to lay her down."

Dex laughed. "You may be right. She's carrying all that pizza weight. Come upstairs with me."

"What about our luggage?"

"I'll bring it in later."

Caitlin followed Dex up a long winding staircase to the second floor and into a room obviously decorated for a teenager rather than a little girl. The colors in the room were so vivid Caitlin had to blink twice. There were numerous framed photos and posters of various R and B groups dominating the walls.

"We'll use this bedroom for now. There's a couple of empty rooms up here, and I'm sure one will be fine for Jordan," Dex said. "You can redec-orate it any way you like."

He smiled. "I let Christy talk me into doing her own thing in this room. I agreed since this is where she sleeps whenever she comes to spend the night."

Caitlin smiled as she watched Dex place Jordan on the bed. Christy was Dex's baby-sister. She had been only thirteen when Dex had brought Caitlin to meet his family four years ago. By the look of the room, Christy was now an older teenager who was very much into music and bright colors.

Dex took Caitlin's hand in his. "Come on, let me show you the rest of the house." He strode out of the bedroom and led her to another one across the hall. "This is the guest bedroom." Jacquard woven drapes and valances of floral design graced the windows. A matching quilted comforter covered the queen size bed.

"Oh, Dex. It's lovely."

After showing her two more bedrooms, each with their own private bath, he led her to another bedroom at the far end of the hall isolated from the others. Double doors led to a huge room which housed a massive four poster bed and a fireplace. Long ceiling to floor windows completely covered the facing wall, while French doors opened onto a balcony overlooking a courtyard and swimming pool.

"And this is *our* room."

Caitlin didn't miss the emphasis Dex placed on the word "our."

"Now for the downstairs," he said, leading her back toward the stairs.

A huge living room, a formal dining room, a family room with another fireplace, a library, a study and two bathrooms made up the house's downstairs. While Dex was giving Caitlin a tour of the immaculate country kitchen, the phone rang.

"Hey, Trevor. Yeah, man, we just got here. When did you get back?" Dex rubbed the top of his head. "I see." There was a pause. "All right. I'm on my way."

He hung up the phone. "This is a lousy way to start things off, but something urgent has come up at the office," he said apologetically.

Caitlin smiled. "Don't worry about it. I know you have a business to run. I'll spend the rest of the afternoon unpacking."

Dex nodded. "I'll call Gwen. She can come over and fix you and Jordan some dinner."

Caitlin's brow lifted. "Gwen?"

"My housekeeper and cook."

"That's not necessary, Dex. I can fix us something."

"Are you sure?"

"I'm positive."

"Okay then, I'll bring in the luggage."

A few minutes later, he was back. "When Jordan wakes up, tell her that I'll be home as soon as I can. If I get detained, I'll call."

"All right."

"The two of you may want to try out the swimming pool while I'm gone."

"That sounds like a great idea. I think we will."

Dex started for the door. He stopped, turned around and walked back over to Caitlin. Leaning down, he brushed his lips against hers. "See ya, baby."

Caitlin watched as he walked out of the door. She knew that wherever he went, he was taking her heart with him.

"Excuse me, ma'am. I'm looking for the lady who lives next door."

Ms. Logan turned to the nicely dressed handsome gentleman. "You mean Caitlin?" At the man's nod, she said. "She's moved."

Surprised flickered in the man's eyes. "Moved?"

"Yes, son. She moved this morning. Is she a friend of yours?"

The man smiled. "Yes, ma'am, she is. I heard about her father and wanted to stop by and offer my condolences. I've been out of town. Do you have any idea how I can reach her? Do you happen to have her address?"

"No, I don't have her address. She's going to write me and give it to me soon, though."

"Do you have any idea where she moved?"

"Yes, she moved to Houston. That's her husband's home."

"Do you know his name?"

"Yes," Ms. Logan replied, continuing to pull weeds from her flower bed. "Her husband's name is Dexter Madaris."

Walker Duncan's smile widened. "Thanks, ma'am. You've been a big help."

Miles away in Ennis, Texas

Justin Madaris lay propped up in the king-size bed listening to the sound of the thunderstorm that had hit the area that afternoon. He smiled remembering a similar night nearly two years ago when Lorren had run to him in a storm with bad memories chasing her. By the next morning, her bad memories associated with thunderstorms had been replaced with good memories to last a lifetime.

"A penny for your thoughts."

He glanced in the direction of the familiar voice. Lorren his beautiful wife, stood leaning next to the bedroom door. She was wearing the most seductive gown he had ever seen. To anyone else the gown would probably be considered plain and simple. But to him, on Lorren, it was utterly seductive. His breath caught in his throat. He'd been blessed with finding true love twice in his life. Some people never found it once. He frowned when his thoughts shifted to his brother Dex.

"Sorry I asked about your thoughts," Lorren said, coming over to stand next to the bed.

Justin raised a brow, knowing she had seen his frown and had mistaken its meaning. "Come here. I missed you." He pushed the covers aside. "The frown wasn't for you, although it should be. That stallion I bought the other day is a mean one, and I don't want you around him again until after Grady breaks him in."

Lorren slipped in bed beside Justin, going straight into his arms. "All right, I admit it was foolish of me to think that he would accept my kindness. I won't do it again."

"Good."

She snuggled closer to him. "Well, if the frown wasn't for me, who was it for?"

Justin kissed the tip of her nose, and gave her playful nips around her mouth. "I was thinking about Dex. He and Caitlin should be in Houston by now. I hope everything's all right."

"Why don't you call?"

"According to Clayton, Dex doesn't want the family to call or come by for a couple of weeks. He feels he and Caitlin need an adjustment period without visits from anyone. He wants time to bond with his new family."

Lorren nodded. "I bet it was hard finding out that not only did he still have a wife, but also a child he hadn't known about. Can you imagine not knowing about Justina or Vincent?"

Justin smiled at the mention of his daughter who had turned four months old that day. He also thought of Vincent, the son they had adopted. He loved them both deeply. "No. I can't imagine something like that. And that's one of the reasons I'm worried about Dex."

Lorren's brow furrowed. "I think Caitlin is the one we should be worried about."

"Why?"

"Because Dex is a Scorpio."

Justin's eyebrows raised inquiringly. "Meaning what?"

"Meaning Caitlin has her work cut out for her. Scorpios are unforgiving. They can hold a grudge forever. They only see things as black or white. There's never room for gray."

Justin chuckled. "That sounds like Dex all right."

Lorren shifted in her husband's arms and looked up at him. "Justin, how do you feel about Caitlin?"

Justin shrugged. "I only met her that once, right after they married. I thought she was kind of young at the time. All of us did."

"All of you except for Dex?"

Justin nodded. "He was too deeply in love. To him that was all that mattered. When we heard about the divorce, none of us were really surprised. She hurt him deeply and I guess a part of me resents that. But I keep thinking of Christy. You know how overly protective we are of our baby sister. What if that had been her instead of Caitlin? There's no way we would have accepted her marriage to an older man, especially one eleven years older. And for that reason, I don't hold anything against Caitlin. None of us in the family do."

"Did you try explaining the analogy about Christy to Dex?"

"Yeah, but he wouldn't listen. He couldn't see beyond the pain."

Lorren gazed deeply into Justin's eyes. "Do you think they'll be able to work things out between them?"

"I don't know, baby. I hope so."

"Me, too. It's hard being part of a loveless marriage."

Justin knew Lorren was thinking about her first marriage and the pain it had caused her. "I don't want to talk anymore," he said.

She smiled. "Oh? What do you want to do?"

His arms slid around her waist and lifted her atop him. "This," he whispered before giving her a very heated kiss.

It was well past midnight before Dex returned home. He found Caitlin sitting in the middle of the living room floor sorting through several small boxes. She glanced up and smiled, then moved the boxes out of her way before standing. "Hi."

He returned her smile, letting his gaze roam up and down her small shapely figure that was covered by a white ballerina-length nightgown. "Why are you still up?"

Caitlin met his gaze. She thought she saw annoyance in their dark depths. She'd tried convincing herself she should be in the guest room asleep when Dex came home, but for some unexplainable reason, she had waited up for him.

Tearing her gaze away, she looked down at the boxes sprawled by her bare feet. "I was trying to organize some of your papers that I found tossed on the desk in your study. I hope you don't mind."

Dex shrugged. "Why should I mind? I've been meaning to take care of them and kept putting it off. Thanks for doing it, but you really didn't have to."

Caitlin smiled. "I didn't have anything to do after Jordan went to bed. Have you ever thought about putting this stuff on computer? It would save you a lot of time and space."

Dex's eyes reflected amusement. "Probably would, but if you're suggesting I do it tonight, forget it."

Caitlin laughed, then her expression became serious. "You look tired."

Her whispered evaluation of his physical state brought a wry smile to Dex's lips. "Yeah, I am. The meeting lasted longer than I expected," he said, taking her hand and leading her toward the sofa.

Dex thought about his meeting with Trevor. They had made a conference call to Adam and Corinthians. As best as Dex could, he had explained the situation to them. Everyone was totally surprised Caitlin was Halston Parker's daughter and didn't want to sell Shadowland. Adam had been extremely upset with Malone Land Developers' handling of things, and had indicated that he would be speaking directly to S. T. Remington about it. He was more than sure that Remington Oil would sever all ties with Malone Land Developers.

When they sat down on the sofa, Caitlin relaxed against Dex, letting her head rest on his chest. "How did Trevor's meeting go with Remington Oil yesterday?"

"Remington Oil changed their mind."

Caitlin lifted her head to meet his gaze. A look of confusion covered her face. "What do you mean?"

"They've changed their mind about the entire project. And without the project, there's no need for Madaris Explorations' services." He decided not to tell her everything.

"Oh, Dex. I'm sorry. I know how much getting that project meant to you."

"Don't worry about it. There'll be other projects." He stood. "If you don't mind, I prefer not discussing this anymore."

"All right, I understand."

"I take it Jordan went to bed long ago."

Caitlin smiled. "Yes. Your phone call earlier this afternoon pleased her immensely. When she first woke up from her nap, she thought you had gone back to Australia. She tried waiting up for you tonight, but couldn't. She had a lot to tell you."

"Oh? Such as . . . ?"

Caitlin's smile widened. "For starters, she just loves our new home and has found the perfect tree out back for you to build her a tree house. She wants it to be a smaller version of this house."

Dex laughed.

"That's not all, Dex. She thinks the back yard is plenty big enough for her horse."

Dex raised a brow. "What horse?"

"The one she's going to try and convince you she needs."

Dex roared in laughter. "Is there anything else?"

A resigned smile curved Caitlin's lips. At first she had decided against telling Dex about Jordan's third request, in hopes that Jordan would forget it. But Caitlin knew just how persistent Jordan could be and felt at least he should be prepared when he saw Jordan in the morning.

Dex noted Caitlin's hesitancy. "What else does she want?"

Caitlin took a deep breath. "She wants a baby sister or a baby brother."

Dex's dark-eyed gaze pierced her intently. "You may have a problem with that, Caitlin, but I don't," he said more harshly than he intended. He rubbed the back of his neck. "Look, I didn't mean to snap at you, but I have a lot on my mind right now. If you'll excuse me, I'm going to take a shower and then go to bed. Goodnight." He left the room and headed up the stairs.

Caitlin straightened her spine as she watched his departure. Standing, she walked over to the window and stared out into the darkness as she thought about her relationship with Dex.

Suddenly, Bev's words came back to her in a rush . . . *"Don't be afraid to follow your heart, listen to your mind, stand behind your convictions, and don't be afraid to take risks. The only failure lies in not trying . . ."*

She released a heavy sigh knowing what had to be done before she and Dex could rebuild their marriage. He needed a lesson in forgiveness, and the way she saw it, the best person to give it to him was the one he couldn't forgive.

"I love you so much, Dex," she whispered, inhaling slowly. "And I will use my love to fight you and to break down your defenses. I have to believe that love draws love."

Dex's exhaustion vanished under the hard, steamy spray of water that ran through his lathered hair and soaked into his skin. He turned his face into the nozzle as the hot water rushed down the curve of his back, then trickled down his legs.

Minutes later, he stepped out of the shower and dried off with a thick velour towel. Leaving the bathroom, he entered his semidarkened bedroom. A faint movement near the vicinity of the bed caught his attention. Caitlin stood there looking innocently seductive. The vision before him was like something out of a dream. It beckoned him to come closer.

But he didn't.

"Caitlin?" Dex asked in a whisper.

Caitlin found her gaze locked with Dex's. He stood in the middle of the room wearing a towel wrapped around his waist and another draped around his neck. He studied her with dark compelling eyes, making her pulse race.

Her breath caught in her throat. Deep within her a spark of desire was ignited by the look in his eyes. His gaze was reaching out and touching her. A ripple of excitement surged throughout her body. Silence between them was so thick in the room it could have been cut with a knife.

"It's my time to serve the tea. I think you're the one who needs relaxing tonight," she finally said, indicating the serving tray holding the cup of tea she'd placed on the nightstand. "I may as well warn you it's not Whispering Pines' finest, but it was the best I could do."

"Thanks, it smells good." He walked over and picked up the cup. "Where's yours?"

Caitlin sat on the edge of Dex's bed. "I thought we would share."

Dex turned and fixed a surprised gaze on her face. "All right." He picked up the cup. "Here, you can take a sip first."

Caitlin shook her head. "No, I made it for you. You can go first."

Dex nodded and took a sip. He smiled. "Not bad." Being careful of the hot liquid, he held the cup while Caitlin took a sip. His stomach clenched deep inside when she deliberately found the place where his mouth had touched on the cup, placed her mouth there and took a sip.

"You're right, it's not bad. But I can think of something better," she whispered, holding his steady gaze. "To relax you."

"Something like what?" Dex asked, his voice husky. He placed the cup back on the tray.

"Mmm," she said, as her gaze scanned him from head to toe, letting him know she was very aware of the fact that he was standing before her semi-nude. She looked up and met his gaze once again. "Me. Tonight I'm serving tea and . . . me."

Dex stared down at her, hoping he had heard her correctly. "Tea and you? That's a mighty hot combination, Caitlin. Are you sure?" he asked, his voice raspy, husky.

A smile tilted Caitlin's mouth. "Yes, I'm sure. I'm ready for a real marriage, Dex. I know what my feelings are for you. I've been dealing with them since the day you returned. I love you. I always have, and I always will."

Dex stood very still, stunned by her words. Her voice was soft and breathless, and her eyes were filled with the love she'd just proclaimed. Reluctantly, he pulled his gaze from hers. He wanted her, but a part of him couldn't place his heart in her hands again. And it was only fair that he let her know upfront just how he felt. He met her gaze again.

"I care for you, Caitlin, but—"

"It's okay, Dex. I have enough love for the both of us right now." She reached out her hand to him. Dex gazed at her outstretched hand. His hand was unsteady as he took it into his, their fingers joining. He gently pulled her to him.

Standing on tiptoes she wrapped her arms around his neck. Her smile was soft and sensual. "Thanks for bringing me home, Dex."

He cupped her face and lowered his head. He had meant for his kiss to be gentle, soft, tender. But it was none of those things. It was hard, fierce, aggressive. It unleashed all the passion and desire that had been dormant the past four years. Those emotions had been untouched and unconquered by any other woman. Caitlin had a patent on them. They were hers and hers alone.

He reached out and gathered her into his arms and placed her on the bed, kissing her uncontrollably. His tongue stroked hers over and over again. She brazenly returned the kiss, igniting his passion and feeding his fire.

He reached out and touched her, letting his fingers follow the path of his heated gaze. "I want you so much." He braced himself on his elbow to stare down into her eyes. Memories filled his mind of how things had been for them the first time they had made love. He wanted their coming together now to be as special as it had been then. Already he was burning for her with a need that went beyond anything he'd ever known. All he wanted to do was to feel her beneath him like he'd fantasized this past week. But first, there was something he had to do; something he wanted to do.

Dex stood and walked over to the dresser and opened the top drawer. Coming back to the bed, he placed a velvet box in Caitlin's hand.

A lump caught in her throat. Without opening the box she knew what was inside. Her wedding ring. Nervously, she lifted the lid to gaze down at the beautiful gold band embedded in white velvet.

"It was hard for me to remove this ring from my finger," she said softly Shadows of pain and regret haunted her eyes.

Dex removed the ring from the box and placed the wedding band on her finger. "And it was just as hard for me when I got it back." He gazed into her eyes as he lifted her hand to his lips. "Now it's back where it belongs."

He straightened, slowly removing his towel. The hungry look in his eyes told Caitlin just how much he wanted her. His aroused body showed just how much he desired her. Her eyes took in the magnificent build of him. She watched him through passion-glazed eyes as he slowly came to her.

"My memories didn't quite do you justice," he said, slowly removing her gown. "You're more beautiful than I remembered." An arousing glow lit his gaze as it fell upon her naked body. He wanted her desperately.

"There's something you should know, before you go any further," Caitlin said breathlessly, encircling his neck with her arms.

"What should I know, sweetheart?" he asked, leaning down. His lips placed small kisses on her neck and the side of her mouth, while his fingers stroked lightly along her inner thigh.

She met his gaze. "I'm not protected."

Deep emotions shone in Dex's eyes. "Neither am I, Caitlin. I've been unprotected since the moment I first laid eyes on you."

Caitlin's heart swelled with love for him. They were referring to two totally different things. He was admitting that with her, he was vulnerable,
unguarded.

"Love me, Dex. Please make love to me."

"I will, baby." He kissed a path down her neck, moving lower. Her skin
felt soft and smooth, and he wanted to taste every inch of her.

Her nails dug into his shoulder blades as he sweetly tormented her. It
seemed every fiber in her body was responding to him. The molten ache
he had created inside of her was almost unbearable. She let out a little
cry; his name escaped her lips; her sensual pleas begged for fulfillment.

He whispered soft words in her ear as he continued to build the fire
between them. She clung to him, quivering with a turbulent need as he
continued to touch her. His hands moved over her body, stroking her,
gently kneading her, and making her breast swell even more fully in his
palms.

Dex's stomach muscles tightened with anticipation. He was going
through sheer torture and couldn't deny their heated desires any longer.
Positioning himself between the dark, soft thighs, he pulled her tightly to
him. He slipped his hands beneath her, lifting her hips to receive him
and entering her in one smooth thrust. Planted deep within her, he
filled her completely. Her tightness encompassed him, and he could tell
no other man had made love to her since him. That realization almost
made him lose control.

His mouth caught hers in a deep kiss that fired their passions into glorious splendor. He began moving against her, taking her with slow, deep
and gentle thrusts.

Caitlin arched against him, caressing his strong body, reacquainting
herself with him as he moved inside her. Her nails bit into his back and
shoulder as he drove deeper and deeper. She wrapped her legs around
him, stroking him with her hips as the slow erotic rhythm he'd set earlier
increased. Dex began moving more rapidly, more urgently. His thrusts
became harder, stronger. Her breath came in short gasps and her body
was strung to its maximal cord.

"You're mine, Caitlin. You've always been mine. You'll always be mine,"
he whispered hoarsely.

She knew Dex's words of possession were the closest to any thing endearing he would give her. He kissed her then, long and hard. The rhythmic mating of their tongues matched his every thrust as his hips drove
repeatedly into her, flooding her with intense pleasure. She clung to him
as powerful rapturous waves increased and touched her body. She shuddered, clinging to him, moaning his name again and again as he filled
her completely.

With one final thrust, Dex cried out her name in his own shattering release, exploding inside of her. They continued to shudder together uncontrollably. He pulled her closer, and Caitlin automatically locked her legs around him drawing him even farther into herself.

Ever so slowly, the stormy reuniting of their bodies left them both weak with passion spent, but at the same time, overwhelmed, consumed and pleasurably satisfied.

In each other's arms, they were home.

The glitter of sunlight filtered through the room and cast its radiant beam upon the man sleeping peacefully in the bed. Caitlin lay propped up on her elbow totally absorbed in watching Dex sleep. How had she turned her back on such a gorgeous brother? How could she have given up a man who was filled with so much passion? Even in sleep his entire being called out to her, making her ache for him, making her blood burst into flames. If only he loved her as much as she loved him. If only he trusted her as much as she trusted him. If only he would have as much faith in her as she had in him.

Leaning over, she planted small kisses on the sweeping lashes that fanned his cheeks, on his firm cheekbone and the angular jaw covered with a bit of morning stubble. She then leaned down and kissed his chest. It had been so long since she had felt so alive, so contented and so tired.

Their hunger had been profound. It had mounted and demanded release over and over again. All through the night and early morning Dex had made love to her. Their lovemaking had been unlimited. It had been deeply passionate, and it had been wonderful. His musky, masculine scent still clung to her body.

Caitlin gently eased from the bed. When she got to her feet she winced at the unexpected soreness, proof of the intensity of their lovemaking. She took a deep breath and headed for the bathroom knowing the soreness would remain for a day or two. But its presence would be a welcome reminder of a night spent making love to her husband.

As she began to dress after her shower she knew they had crossed one hurdle, but there were still more to overcome. Her love for him would give her the strength to endure the days ahead.

Dex was awakened by the sound of his daughter's laughter floating lazily through his hazy mind. Shifting his head on the pillow, he remembered his dream. It was strange how dreams could almost seem real.

Suddenly the reality of last night struck him. He came wide awake. It had not been a dream. The intimacy he and Caitlin had shared had been real. The heat-wave of passion totally consuming them had been mind-shattering and earth-moving. He had kissed her senseless, and she'd encouraged him with her groans of pleasure and her shivers of delight.

Dex closed his eyes, remembering her beneath him. Her silken thighs wrapped firmly around his waist in a tight grip while he stroked the fire within her. Each time he'd entered her, she'd arched against him pulling him deeper and deeper inside of her. He had tried being gentle. He had tried being tender. But his control had faltered. She had returned his tempestuous, intense and moving passion, making him burn for her. It was as if she had deliberately tried stealing his soul, his mind and . . . his heart.

Never had he felt such stirring, inspiring and stimulating surrender. He felt completely drained yet totally renewed. As he lay there, he knew the project he'd lost with Remington Oil wasn't important. What was important to him was Caitlin. She was the only thing that mattered.

Minutes later, Dex found himself whistling in the shower. Anxious to see his wife and daughter, he finished showering and hurried with his dressing. Slipping into a pair of jeans and a short sleeve knit shirt, he walked briskly down the hall and stairs toward the kitchen where his daughter's laughter could be heard.

The scene that awaited him took his breath away. Caitlin was sitting at the table with Jordan. Their heads were close together as they excitedly put together a puzzle.

Dex found himself staring at them. He released a long deep sigh of both pleasure and satisfaction that caught his daughter's attention.

"Daddy!" Jordan's bright cheery smile indicated she was very glad to see him. He would never get tired of seeing her happy. Dex walked over to her and picked her up. He gave her a gentle yet fierce hug and at the same time, he placed a warm kiss on his wife's lips.

"How's daddy's princess today?" he asked Jordan who'd been so absorbed in giving her father a hug that she completely missed her parents' kiss.

A dimple formed in Jordan's chin. "Fine, Daddy. Mommy said I couldn't wake you. She said you needed to sleep and you were tired." She gazed up at him curiously. "Were you?"

Dex caught Caitlin's eyes. "Yes, Jordan. Daddy was very tired."

"Why?"

Dex cast Caitlin a deep smile. "I worked very hard yesterday, especially last night."

"Oh," Jordan replied. She then shifted positions in her father's arms. "Daddy?"

"Yes, baby?"

"Will you build me a tree house just like this house?"

Dex smiled. "Yes, but I don't think you'll need one quite as big as this one."

Jordan nodded. "Will Uncle Clayton help you?"

"Yes, I think he'll help if we ask him."

"Daddy?"

"Yes, sweetheart?"

"May I have a horse to keep in the back yard?"

Dex laughed. "I don't know if our neighbors will like that very much, Jordan. But I'll get you a horse, and since your Uncle Justin's yard is so much bigger than ours, and he doesn't have any neighbors, I think we should let him keep it for us. How's that?"

"Who's Uncle Justin?"

"He's your other uncle whom you haven't met yet. He's real nice and has a little boy name Vincent who has a horse, too. In fact Uncle Justin has a lot of horses at his ranch, and I'd bet he'll be glad to take care of yours. I'll take you to see him often so you can learn to ride."

A smile covered Jordan's face. She was completely satisfied with her father's answer. "Daddy?"

"Yes, Jordan?"

"Can I have a baby sister or a baby brother?"

"Do you really want one?"

Dex chuckled as his daughter's head eagerly bobbed up and down. He met Caitlin's gaze again. The dark circles under her eyes reminded him of their night together and how little sleep she'd gotten. Her words that she was not on any type of birth control came back to him. "I think that's possible one day, Jordan."

"Do I have any more uncles, Daddy?"

"Yes, you do," Dex answered, thinking of his two brother-in-laws. "Why do you ask?"

"Since Uncle Clayton is going to help build my tree house, and Uncle Justin is going to keep my horse for me, will my other uncles help you and Mommy get our new baby?"

Dex's laughter filled the room. "No. That's something Mommy and I can handle all by ourselves. We won't need any help. No help at all."

CHAPTER 15

Dex spent the following week in total awe of how wonderful Caitlin felt in his arms every night, and how right she felt in his life. They were taking each day one at a time and so far, everything was going smoothly. She had turned his house into a home, and had made his infrequent smile a permanent fixture on his face.

The sensual attraction between them had not lessened any, nor was their lovemaking confined strictly to the bedroom. They thoroughly enjoyed the stolen moments they shared while Jordan napped or the long pleasurable hours wrapped in each other's arms after their daughter had been tucked into bed for the night.

During the past week, they'd not had any company. Dex had asked his family to stay away to give him and Caitlin time to scale the barriers between them and to adjust to their life together. His family had understood and had honored his request, but he knew he couldn't keep them at bay much longer. He stared down at the letter that had arrived that morning.

> . . . *Dex, the nineteenth of July is Lorren's birthday and I'm giving her a birthday party here at Lorren Oaks. I would like the family to come prepared to stay the entire weekend. I think it would be a great time for the family to get reacquainted with Caitlin and for all of us to finally meet Jordan. I've spoken with Mom and Dad and they will be arriving here from their trip. There's plenty of room for everyone. I sure hope all of you can make it. Best Regards, Justin* . . .

Dex left the kitchen and went looking for his wife. He found her as he knew he would, in his study bent over his computer system entering data into it.

Caitlin had taken on the project of organizing his files. She'd declared with the two of them working on it during their free time they could have the task completed in a couple of days.

Dex had found himself less than enthused with the idea. Unlike her, fiddling around with a computer was not his favorite pastime. Her knowledge of them and her ability to work with them were amazing. He would watch in utter fascination as she effortlessly plowed through stacks and stacks of paperwork, entering them onto the system in a logical way for him to retain and have easy access to information about locations of various drilling sights and oil formations. Although her dedication had been appreciated, he had other ideas on how they could spend their free time.

Suddenly aware she was being watched, Caitlin swiveled the chair around just in time to see Dex enter the room and lock the door behind him. He leaned against the door with his arms folded across his chest staring at her. His expression was gentle and warm. They continued to regard each other in silence for a minute. Then Dex spoke. "Are you having fun?"

Caitlin smiled. "Sure, I'm having a blast. However, if I remember correctly this was supposed to be a team effort."

Dex grinned. "You're doing just fine without me." He came farther into the room. "This arrived earlier." He handed her the letter.

Caitlin read it. Her brows furrowed. "Why didn't he just call?"

"I told my family not to bother us."

"Why? I was wondering why none of them had dropped by. I know how close you all are."

"I did it for purely selfish reasons. I wanted you and Jordan all to myself for a while. I'm not ready to share the two of you yet," he said, pulling her up from the chair and into his embrace. "We needed time alone," he murmured against her throat.

Caitlin arched her body to him when his arms urged her hips against his. "Where's Jordan?" she asked breathlessly.

"She's taking a nap."

Caitlin's hand traced lightly upon the warm skin of Dex's arm. Her pulse accelerated madly. "It's time for me to take a break."

Dex's eyes darkened. "I totally agree."

Caitlin placed her hand against Dex's cheek, touching the lines of his brow and detecting deep concern there. "Dex, is anything wrong?"

He hesitated before replying. "How do you feel about seeing my family again, Caitlin?"

She shrugged her shoulders. "I can't avoid them forever. I know because I've hurt you, I'm probably not their favorite person."

"Don't feel that way. Believe it or not my family understood what you did."

His words surprised her. "They did?"

Dex nodded. "They thought you were too young at the time to really know your own heart. They actually accused me of rushing you into a situation you weren't quite ready for. According to my dad, if Christy had been in your place and had left for a summer job and returned less than a month later with a husband, especially one eleven years older, who had plans to take her out of the country, he would have been upset about it."

He chuckled. "Justin and Clayton, on the other hand, would have been more than upset. I can see them taking the man apart piece by piece. They take their roles of big brothers seriously." He reached out and took her hand in his. "I have to constantly remind myself you were barely twenty-one when we married. Compared to me, you were a mere child," he teased.

"I was not," Caitlin said as a grin spread across her face.

"Yes, you were. You've grown up a lot over the years in more ways than one. I left you a blushing bride and now you're a very mature woman and a wonderful mother."

Neither said anything else for a few minutes then Caitlin spoke. "Thanks for your concern regarding your family but I'll be okay. Actually, I'm looking forward to seeing them again, and I'm especially looking forward to meeting Justin's wife, Lorren."

Dex pulled Caitlin closer into his arms. "You'll like Lorren. She's a sweetheart and just what Justin needs. He loves her very much."

Caitlin stirred against Dex as she considered his words. "Lorren's a very lucky woman to have the love of her man."

Dex tensed at her words. "Caitlin?"

"Yes?"

"I do care for you. You know that, don't you?" Dex's breath was warm against her cheek and he tightened his arms around her.

Caitlin had to close her eyes at the tears that stung them. She shifted slightly and pressed closer to him. Caring wasn't the same thing as loving. She lifted her head and looked up into his eyes. "Yes, I know you care for me."

Dex leaned down and kissed her. Caitlin's response to him was immediate, it was spontaneous, it was urgent. Their heat was ignited by their passion, their sensual demands unleashed by desire. One kiss led to another and another, each one deeper, more greedy and more intimate than the others.

A smile touched Dex's lips seconds before they sank to the plush carpeting. Within minutes they had removed every stitch of their clothing. Caitlin took Dex's face into her hands. "I'm not protected, Dex."

Dex gathered her closer to his naked form. His forehead dropped to rest against hers. "Neither am I, baby. Neither am I."

His hands cupped the sides of her face and when his mouth touched hers it put an end to all conversation. The only sounds echoing in the room were the sounds of their heavy breathing, their moans of delight, and their groans of pleasure as they shared total fulfillment.

Dex was driven by a raging need, and a desire to communicate physically just how much he wanted and needed her. His mouth became more demanding, his body greedier, and his movements harder, fiercer.

Caitlin used her hands to cherish him, she used her mouth to entice him, and she used her body to please him. She wanted to prolong what they were sharing, but couldn't.

The first rush of ecstasy touched them simultaneously. Their hold on each other tightened as Dex drove hard inside of Caitlin, filling her completely with his release at the same time she found her own. Tortured cries were rung from their lips as they were overtaken by an all-consuming climactic force that left neither of them protected.

"What do you mean we were dropped by Remington Oil?" Walker asked, looking at his uncle. "I don't understand."

"Well, you should understand," Duncan Malone shouted. "Since it's all your fault. I never should have gone along with your scheme to harass Halston Parker. Now look what's happened. Remington Oil knows everything."

"But how can they? No one knows of our connection to Remington Oil. How could they have found out?"

"Halston Parker's daughter," he growled. "That man she's married to used to work for Remington Oil. Somehow he figured out what was going on."

"But how?"

"I don't know." Duncan Malone snorted derisively. "All I know is that I got a call from the top brass at Remington Oil who said my services were no longer needed, and I was told why. Do you know what that means? Do you have any idea how much money I'll be losing? They were my biggest client."

He flung a large hand toward his office door. "I want you out of here, Walker. Maybe with you gone, I'll be able to salvage a little of the good name I used to have. If word gets around about what happened, other companies will stop doing business with me, too. Then I'll lose everything, all because of you."

Walker saw his chance to one day run Malone Land Developers crumble before his eyes. "Where will I go? What will I do?"

"I don't care," Duncan Malone thundered. "Just clean out your desk and get out of my sight before I forget we're related. And don't come back."

Less than an hour later, Walker Malone had loaded his belongings in the car. His fingers tightened on the steering wheel as he drove around town with no particular destination in mind.

When the car came to a stop at a traffic light, he glanced down at the sketch pad in the seat beside him. His stony gaze slid over the paper he'd drawn of the woman who was the cause of all his troubles. His hard muscled arms and strong hands gripped the steering wheel tighter.

"You're going to pay, lady. I'll make sure of it."

Corinthians gave the young woman who opened the door a forced smile. "Ms. Madaris. I'm Corinthians Avery from Remington Oil. May I come in?"

"Yes." Caitlin moved aside to let Corinthians enter. She then gestured toward the living room. "If you're here to see my husband, Ms. Avery, he's not home. Dex's at a job site and probably won't be back until late tonight."

"I'm not here to see your husband, Ms. Madaris. I'm here to see you."

Caitlin looked back at the sharply dressed woman who was following her into the living room. "Me? Why would anyone from Remington Oil want to see me?"

Yes, why indeed? Corinthians thought as she sat down on the sofa. She'd been so curious to get a chance to see for herself the woman who'd stolen Dex's heart, that she had volunteered for this mission. But whatever prior images she'd had of the woman had faded the moment she'd opened the door. Caitlin Madaris appeared to be a vibrant and friendly person. And she was indeed pretty. No, pretty wasn't a strong enough word. Drop-dead beautiful was better.

Corinthians could immediately see how Dex had fallen in love with her. Even dressed in a pair of cut-off jeans and a T-shirt, there appeared to be a certain softness about her. And she was so young. Corinthians had oftentimes wondered if the seven year difference in her and Dex's ages had been the reason he'd never had a romantic interest in her. Evidently age hadn't been a factor, since the woman he'd eventually married looked to be around twenty-four or twenty-five. That meant there was at least an eleven to twelve year difference in their ages. There also seemed to be some sort of strength surrounding her. But the strength did not lessen her femininity. When she walked, she moved like a model or a dancer.

"Can I get you something to drink, Ms. Avery?"

"No thanks, and please call me Corinthians. May I call you Caitlin?"

"Sure. And Corinthians is a pretty name."

Corinthians settled back in her seat. "Thanks. My father is a minister and couldn't resist naming me after his favorite book in the Bible."

"Which one, First Corinthians or Second Corinthians?"

Corinthians grinned. "I believe both."

A smile creased the laugh lines beside Caitlin's mouth and eyes. "My father's favorite book in the Bible was Psalms, especially after my mother's death," she said. "I believe the scriptures gave him the strength he needed to face each day without my mother. With them he found peace and comfort."

She also had sought solace in the scriptures, Caitlin thought. While she was pregnant with Jordan, she'd selected a verse out of the Book of First Corinthians. That passage had given her strength each day for the past four years. And even now, being back with Dex, she depended on it even more. She had to believe its words—*Love knows no limit to its endurance, no fading of its hope. It can outlast anything. Love never fails . . .*

"I think I'd like that drink after all," Corinthians said, interrupting Caitlin's thoughts. "A cola will be fine if you have one. Then I'd like to explain to you why I'm here."

Caitlin stood. "All right. I'll be back in a minute."

While Caitlin was gone, Corinthians glanced around the room. It was a really nice place. She suddenly wondered where Trevor Grant lived and what his taste in decorating was like. After the meeting on Friday, he'd quickly left the building, which at the time had been just fine with her. All during the business meeting he'd kept her within the scope of his relentless gaze. It had been totally unnerving to have him sit across the conference table and stare at her most of the time. She had wondered if he was remembering what she'd been wearing the night before. She was more than certain an embarrassing blush had been on her face during the entire meeting.

"Here you are," Caitlin said, returning with a glass of Coke on ice. She handed the glass and a napkin to Corinthians.

"And like I told you earlier, Corinthians, I really don't understand why you want to see me. Dex is the one whose company was going to head up some major project with Remington Oil."

Corinthians took a sip of her soda. "Yes, he was."

"It's my understanding," Caitlin continued, "that the project has been cancelled."

"I wouldn't go that far," Corinthians said, smiling. "Let's just say the Leabo project has been placed on hold for a while. And I for one hope it's only temporary since I'm the one who did all the research for the project. I'm a geologist for Remington Oil."

"Really? Dex used to be a geologist for them a few years ago. Did you know him?"

"Yes, Dex and I used to work together. We're good friends."

Something about the tone of Corinthians' voice when she made the statement caused Caitlin to lift a brow. "Oh, I see."

Corinthians met Caitlin's inquiring stare. "Dex trained me when I first started working at Remington Oil, and we continued working together until he was sent to Australia. I haven't seen him since then."

Caitlin sat back in her seat wondering just how good of friends Corinthians and Dex had been. Had they been lovers? She wasn't naive enough to think his life before marrying her hadn't included women. But still, she couldn't help the tinge of jealousy that suddenly struck her that perhaps she and this woman had something in common—Dex.

"Why are you really here?" she asked, suddenly feeling there was more to the woman's visit then she'd let on.

Corinthians picked up on the change in Caitlin's tone. It was still friendly, but cool. "I told you the truth, Caitlin. I'm here to discuss Remington Oil." She shifted positions in her seat so she could face Caitlin squarely. "Before we go any farther, I think we should clear the air about something. What I said a few moments ago is the truth. Dex and I are friends. But that's it. He's like a brother to me. But I'm going to be completely honest with you and give it to you straight. I've always wanted more than just friendship between the two of us. But he never knew it. He thought of me as one of his sisters."

"And what about now, Corinthians?"

Corinthians had no doubt that Caitlin was staking her claim and she liked that. "Now Dex is a married man, and I have no reason to think he's not a happy one. I believe strongly in the marriage vows. I would never try to come between you and Dex."

"Do you still love him?"

Corinthians smiled. Lately, she hadn't been doing a whole lot of thinking about Dex. There was another brother who'd begun occupying her thoughts—Trevor Grant. "Had you asked me that same question a few weeks ago, I would not have hesitated in saying yes. But now, to be quite honest with you, I don't know. I've talked to Dex on the phone a couple of times," at the lift of Caitlin's brow, she rushed in, "all business-related conversations. I haven't actually seen him in over four years. So I don't know how I feel right now."

Feeling secure in her love for Dex, Caitlin replied. "Until two weeks ago, I hadn't seen Dex in nearly four years either. But there was never a day that went by, while we were apart, that I didn't know I loved him. At times, that was the only thing I was completely sure about."

"In that case, Caitlin, maybe what I've always thought I've felt for Dex hasn't really been love after all. Maybe it's been some sort of hero-worship or infatuation." Corinthians grinned. "Although you would think at the age of twenty-nine I'd know the difference. But what I do know, is that I want the very best for him. He's a good man. It's not very often that a brother gets an opportunity to succeed in his career like Dex has. His time has come, and it couldn't have happened to a more deserving man. Dex works hard and plays by the rules."

"I really don't understand why you're telling me all of this. I'm very supportive of his career. I was very happy for him when he was chosen by Remington Oil to head that project. And I was very disappointed with their decision to abandon it."

"You left us no choice."

Confusion clearly shone in Caitlin's eyes. "What do you mean I left you no choice. That's crazy. I had nothing to do with it."

Corinthians frowned. Something wasn't right here. Caitlin acted as if she didn't know a thing about her involvement in the Leabo project. If that was the case, why hadn't Dex told her?

Corinthians stood and began pacing the room, fully aware that a confused Caitlin watched her. If Dex hadn't told his wife anything, what right did she have to? But, if Caitlin didn't know, didn't she deserve to? Corinthians took a deep breath. She was in a quandary on how to proceed.

"I'm going to ask again, Corinthians. What do you mean I left you no choice?"

Corinthians stopped pacing and faced Caitlin. "What has Dex told you about the Leabo project?"

"Nothing, and until a few moments ago, I never knew the name of the project. Dex refuses to talk about it. I just assumed Remington Oil's decision to stop the project was too much of a disappointment to him, and he wanted to get beyond it."

Corinthians took her seat on the sofa again. "Well, I'm going to tell you a little about the project, and I hope in the end you'll understand why I'm here."

She then told Caitlin about the project, beginning with her research and ending with Remington Oil's failure to secure possession of a final parcel of land needed for the project.

"That parcel of land that's vital to Leabo is land you own, Caitlin. I understand it's land that's been in your family for generations."

"Shadowland?"

At Corinthians nod, Caitlin flew out of her seat and began doing what Corinthians had done moments earlier, pace the room.

"That's crazy. I've never heard anything about Remington Oil wanting to buy Shadowland. I'm well aware that some land developing company by the name of Malone Land Developers tried forcing my father into selling it, and even made an harassing telephone call to me. But no one ever said anything about Remington Oil."

"Malone Land Developers were working for us, Caitlin, although we had no idea they were harassing you or your father. Duncan Malone had us convinced you and your father had agreed to sell Shadowland. We

were taken back when Dex told us you didn't want to sell, and that neither you nor your father had ever wanted to sell."

"When did you talk to Dex about this?"

"Last week. And he made it pretty clear that Shadowland was not for
sale and there would not be any further discussion on it."

Caitlin's head began spinning. Why had Dex risked losing out on a
major job that would have boosted his career? Why? Even as she asked
herself the question, deep down she knew the answer. Because he hadn't
wanted to place himself in a position where she would have to make a
choice again. The last time, she'd chosen her father over him. Did he actually think she wouldn't choose what was best for him over a piece of
land? Granted, she loved Shadowland, it held deep ties for her, but she
loved Dex even more. Didn't he know that?

"Caitlin, are you all right?"

"Yes, I'm fine." She wasn't at all sure of that now. It hurt to know that
Dex still didn't have faith in her love for him. He still hadn't let go of the
past and probably never would. She had lived each day since he had returned hoping and praying, but now it seemed, there would never be
love, trust and faith in their marriage. Those things would be there, but
only from her. But considering the pain he'd suffered when his friend
had died as a result of love, and the hurt she'd caused him, did she really
expect him to be any different?

"The reason I'm here," Corinthians continued, "is to first apologize on
behalf of Remington Oil for the actions of Malone Land Developers.
Since finding out about what they did, Remington Oil has severed all ties
with them."

Corinthians stood. "The other reason is personal. I had to see the
woman who had captured Dex's heart. And after meeting with you today,
I can see why. Goodby, Caitlin. It was nice meeting you. I'll let myself out."

"Wait, before you go," Caitlin said, coming to stand before the woman.
"How much time do you have today?"

Corinthians lifted a brow. "I have all the time in the world. I flew in
from Austin on the company's jet. It'll take off whenever I'm ready to
leave. Why?"

"I'd like to read whatever reports you have on the Leabo Project. If the
project is as important to Remington Oil as you claim, I would like to
make them a counteroffer."

Corinthians smiled. "I think they'll be receptive, depending on what
you'll be wanting, Caitlin."

"Good, and I'd feel a whole lot more comfortable if an attorney was
here to help draw up a proposal."

Caitlin went over to the telephone and began dialing. "Hello, Clayton.
This is Caitlin. I need your help in working up a land deal."

* * *

"You're what!"

"I'm selling Shadowland. Clayton is helping me draw up the papers to make Remington Oil a counteroffer."

Dex's mouth hung open at Caitlin's casual statement as she moved around their bedroom, packing for their trip to Justin's and Lorren's home. He had been gone all day at a job site and had been in the house only long enough to shower before she'd dropped this little bombshell. No, he corrected, this big bombshell.

"Caitlin, will you please stay in one place long enough to tell me what the hell is going on," he thundered.

"Dex, please. You don't have to yell."

Dex crossed the room in great strides, coming face to face with his wife. His patience was wearing thin. He gritted his teeth. "What's this nonsense about you selling Shadowland?"

"It's not nonsense. I'm selling Shadowland to Remington Oil. It seems you forgot to tell me that Malone Land Developers were working for them and my refusal to sell jeopardized your position with the project." She moved around him.

Dex grabbed her wrist, and brought her back to him. "Who told you?"

Caitlin glared up at him. "You didn't, that's for sure." She snatched her hand from him. "Corinthians Avery came here today to apologize on behalf of Remington Oil for Malone Land Developers' actions. Can you imagine what a fool I felt like when I had no earthly idea what she was talking about? You should have told me."

"I thought it best that you not know."

"There you go again, thinking you know what's best for me. Didn't it matter to you that you were losing the project?"

"I don't care about losing this project. There will be others."

"But none of this magnitude, Dex. I read the report. This job can make you millions."

Dex didn't know how long they stood there, staring at each other, before he spoke. "Money isn't everything."

"You're right. But love is. Besides Jordan, you're the most important person in my life. Shadowland is just a piece of land. It's cold, hard, rocky soil. You're a man. The man I love. The man who gave me a beautiful little girl. The man who starts my blood racing with a smile, a word, a touch. And you're right, Dex, money isn't everything, but my love for you is."

With a low groan, Dex pulled Caitlin into his arms and began showering her with kisses. With a flick of his wrist the sash around her waist came undone and the front of her robe fell open. He picked her up in his arms and carried her to the bed then placed her on it. He tugged the towel from around his waist. With a swipe of his hand, he removed Caitlin's robe and nightgown. His gaze met hers.

"Caitlin, I—I love—"

Caitlin's breath was held suspended in her throat.

". . . looking at you," he finished.

Caitlin pushed her disappointment aside. Love draws love. She had to believe that.

Dex lay with Caitlin sleeping in his arms. Her head was tucked under his chin and her leg rested between his muscular thighs. The passion they'd shared earlier that night had been shattering and gratifying. Even now, his heart was beating erratically inside his chest. He pulled her closer to him. Her eyes were closed but he couldn't stop staring at her.

Tonight she had shown just how much she loved and trusted him. And the truth smacked him dead in the face that she'd been doing that all along. She had named his daughter after him, even when she hadn't been sure of him. And even when he'd not made her any promises, she had freely given him her love, faith and trust.

She had not given up on him like he had done on her. What she'd told him a couple of weeks back had been true. Deep down he never really gave them a chance. To his way of thinking, she had lived up to his expectations, exactly what Greg had prepared him for—the pain of falling in love. Instead of giving up, he should have fought for her and her love. He should have come after her, even after receiving the divorce papers.

He leaned down and kissed her softly on the lips. As much as he didn't want to, he needed her and despite everything, he still loved her. And if he was completely honest with himself, he had to admit, he had never stopped loving her. He had been too bull-headed to see it until now.

Dex knew at that moment that all the hurt and anger he'd harbored in his heart for the past four years had crumbled under the onslaught on Caitlin's undying love and trust. The emotions consuming him were too powerful to ignore, and at the moment, too new to share with her. Blinking rapid, he fought the stinging in his eyes. Caitlin was just where she should be, where she belonged. She was in his arms, next to his heart.

And he would never let her go.

CHAPTER 16

"Jordy!"

Upon recognizing a familiar face standing next to the tall stranger who'd opened the door, Jordan Madaris's face broke into a huge smile.

"Uncle Clayton!" She squirmed out of her father's arms and ran straight to the outstretched ones of her uncle who knelt down for her.

"I think I'm jealous," Justin Madaris said, greeting Dex with a firm handshake. "Your daughter is already playing favorites. That puts the rest of us at a disadvantage."

Dex laughed at his brother's remark. "You of all people should know just how much of a ladies' man Clayton is. Every female around is open game, except for Lorren and Caitlin of course."

"Of course." Justin eased his mouth into a smile. He turned his attention to the beautiful young woman at Dex's side. He didn't miss the way his brother's arm was possessively wrapped around her waist. "Caitlin, it's good seeing you again." He leaned down and kissed her cheek.

Caitlin's entire face spread into a smile for her brother-in-law. Like Dex and Clayton, Justin Madaris was a very handsome man with chocolate-chip colored eyes and a chestnut-brown complexion. "Thanks, Justin. I understand congratulations are in order. First on your marriage and then for your son and daughter. You've been a very busy man."

Justin laughed. "Yes, I've been very busy and very happy. Everyone is out back. I put Dad and Jake to work grilling the ribs with Mom supervising. Traci and Kattie are in the kitchen fixing a salad, and Lorren and

Christy went to the airport to pick up Syneda. They should be back at any time."

"Who's Syneda?" Caitlin asked curiously. She didn't remember the name when she'd met Dex's family four years ago.

Justin's smile widened. "Syneda is Lorren's best friend and is like a member of the family. She's an attorney in New York, and there's never a dull moment when she and Clayton get together. You can always count on them to have different views on various issues, and usually all of us have to suffer through their opposing summations."

"Syneda and I keep these dreary family gatherings lively," Clayton bellowed, placing a bubbly Jordan on his shoulder. He leaned down and boldly gave Caitlin a kiss on her lips. "I still say you married the wrong brother."

"Who's that?" Jordan asked curiously, eyeing Justin Madaris.

"I'm your Uncle Justin." Justin smiled up at the little girl who looked so much like his brother it was uncanny.

"Oh goody. You're the one who's gonna take care of my horse for me," Jordan replied happily.

Justin raised an amused brow. "I am?"

Jordan bobbed her head up and down and gave her newest uncle a radiant smile.

"I can't turn down such a beautiful young lady," Justin replied, chuckling. "And you're in luck. If Spitfire cooperates, her baby will be arriving before you leave."

Jordan frowned. "Who's Spitfire?"

"Spitfire is your Aunt Lorren's horse. She's a beauty and I think she'll have a beautiful baby colt. And if she does, it's all yours."

"Goody," Jordan exclaimed, clapping her hands. Now I'll have two babies."

Justin's and Clayton's eyebrows raised inquiringly. "How will you have two babies, Jordy?" Clayton asked grinning.

"Uncle Justin is giving me his baby horse, and my mommy and daddy are giving me a baby sister or brother."

Caitlin's face tinted. Dex merely laughed. "That's wishful thinking on Jordan's part, you guys. Caitlin's not pregnant so don't go spreading rumors, Clayton."

Clayton looked aghast. "Would I do something like that?"

Justin and Dex answered simultaneously. "Yes."

Caitlin couldn't help laughing. The three Madaris brothers were close, and didn't mind anyone knowing of their fondness for each other.

"Come on, let's join the rest of the family," Justin said. "Don't worry about your luggage. I'll send Clayton back for it later."

A frown covered Clayton's face. "Why me?"

"Not being married, you need all the exercise you can get to stay in shape," Justin answered, giving Caitlin and Dex a wink.

"That's not necessary, Big Brother," Clayton answered, grinning. "There are more enjoyable ways for a single man to stay in shape."

"Not in front of the child, Clayton," Dex admonished with a grin. "Not in front of the child."

The dark blue sedan turned off the highway into a heavily tree-lined street. Instead of pulling into the driveway leading to Lorren Oaks, the driver parked the car, hiding it from view among a cluster of trees.

He had followed the light-colored Camry undetected for over three hours, wondering where it had been heading when it had left Houston. Seemed like someone was having a big cookout. The huge ranch-style house was sitting too far off the road for him to get a good view of the people.

He slammed his fists against the steering wheel wondering when he would get the chance to make his move. There was no way he would leave Texas without first teaching the woman a lesson. He intended to make her sorry she'd refused to cooperate. Thanks to her, he'd lost everything.

Walker Malone opened the car door and got out. He would check out the place and wait for the perfect opportunity. Opening a gate, he slipped onto the property without being seen.

"You and Justin have a lovely home, Lorren."

"Thanks. I'm very proud of it, especially since I helped with the decorating. And that was before I had any idea Justin's and my relationship was serious. I knew I loved him, but had no idea how he felt about me."

Caitlin's arched brows raised slightly. "I don't understand."

Lorren grinned. "It's a long story but one with a very happy ending, just like your's and Dex's. I've never seen Dex laugh or smile so much. I'm glad everything has worked out for the two of you."

Caitlin couldn't help smiling at Lorren's words. She didn't have the heart to tell her that she had very little to do with Dex's improved demeanor. Jordan was the main reason for his happiness.

"I think the two of you make a beautiful couple," Lorren added.

Dex had been right, Caitlin thought after thanking Lorren for her compliment. Lorren Madaris was a sweetheart whose husband loved her deeply. It was evident in Justin's loving attitude toward his wife and his casual touching of her, whether it was placing his arm around her shoulder, holding her hand or sitting close beside her. Caitlin envied the open display of genuine affection. And it was obvious Lorren was deeply in love with her husband as well.

Lorren was also a beauty, Caitlin thought. Her caramel colored eyes, dark brown hair and high cheekbones were a perfect combination with her nutmeg complexion.

"Do Clayton and Syneda debate often?" Caitlin asked. She couldn't help observing the couple standing on the other side of the patio who were in a very deep discussion about the upcoming presidential election. Caitlin thought Syneda Walker was a gorgeous woman with her long luxurious golden bronze curls and an attractive light brown face.

"They really don't debate all the time, just ninety-nine percent of the time," Lorren grinned. "They get a kick out of verbally sparring with each other. We're all used to it."

Caitlin nodded. Her gaze then came to rest on some of the other guests. Dex's family had welcomed her with open arms and had been completely taken with Jordan. All of them had acted as if her and Dex's long separation had never happened, and as far as they were concerned the past was dead and buried.

Dex's sisters, Kattie and Traci, offered to take her on a shopping spree to show her how to spend their brother's money, and Christy offered to keep Jordan if she ever needed a sitter. Dex's parents had smothered her with hugs. They told her they wished they could have been there for her when her father had died, and that they were glad she and Dex were back together.

Tall, handsome Jake Madaris had said basically the same thing. He even offered to give her an opportunity to come back to Whispering Pines to update his computer system. Granted she was willing to take his bookkeeper, Delane Ormond, on again. Caitlin had quickly turned down the offer, causing Dex to burst out laughing.

Caitlin also got a chance to meet Nora Phillips, Lorren's foster mother, as well as a couple who were good friends of Justin and Lorren by the name of Rod and Rhonda Clark. Rod was the sheriff of Ennis, and Rhonda worked as a drama professor at a university in Dallas. Rhonda, a blond beauty with gorgeous blue eyes, was the mother of four. And to Caitlin's astonishment, was considering a fifth.

Caitlin glanced around for her husband and didn't see him anywhere.

"The guys are probably out near the corral," Lorren said smiling, noticing Caitlin's roving eyes. "Justin purchased a wild stallion a few weeks ago and the guys are probably checking him out. That horse is a mean one. He hasn't been broken in yet."

Caitlin nodded. "I'd like to see this animal. I need to walk off some of this food anyway."

"Just follow the path over there and you'll come to the corral. It's half a mile from here. I would walk with you, but I promised the children I'd read them a story."

Caitlin smiled. "You have a beautiful son and your baby daughter is just adorable. She reminds me so much of Jordan when she was a baby," she said.

"Thanks." The beginning of a smile tipped the corners of Lorren's mouth. "Is it true that you and Dex are thinking about having another baby?"

Caitlin's face split into a wide grin knowing where that rumor had come from. "That's wishful thinking on our daughter's part."

Minutes later following the path Lorren told her about, Caitlin headed for the corral.

The men had ridden their horses to a meadow not far from the ranch. A cloister of tall oak trees surrounded the glen and hid a stream of clear water. It was a beautiful private place and Dex knew immediately that before he and Caitlin left to return home, he would bring her to this spot of ground. He would try and talk her into going skinny-dipping with him. He glanced around. All the oak trees that enclosed the meadow would assure them complete privacy.

"Did Caitlin tell you what she's decided to do about Remington Oil, Dex?"

Dex's gaze turned to Clayton who was leaning back against a tree. Justin and Rod had ridden a little further, leaving Dex and Clayton behind to water their horses. "Yeah, she told me."

"I think her mind is pretty much made up." Clayton tossed a couple of twigs into the stream.

"Speaking of minds," Dex said, slanting his brother a curious look. "What's on yours? It was obvious you wanted to get me alone for some reason. What's up?"

Clayton gave in to a low laugh. "I was that easy to read?"

"Only when you suggested that we go riding. Everyone knows how much you hate riding a horse. That's how Justin and I used to keep you in line when we were kids. All we had to do was threaten to take you horseback riding with us whenever we visited Whispering Pines."

Clayton couldn't help himself. He laughed loudly at the memory. "You were a mean cuss even back then, Dex."

Dex smiled. "If you say so. Now tell me what's up."

"Caitlin . . ." Clayton began, and with obvious reluctance, he met his brother's quick frown.

Dex turned and stared out over the stream. "What about her?"

"She loves you, man. Once she found out that Shadowland was a part of the Leabo project, she took steps to protect you and your company, Dex." Clayton's gaze lingered on his brother's profile for a full minute before he continued. "Did you know that when she found out she was pregnant she not only wrote to you telling you about it, but in the same letter she also asked you to take her back and give your marriage another try?"

Dex turned and looked at him. "She told you that?"

"Yes."

"When?"

"Yesterday. After Corinthians Avery left, Caitlin invited me to stay and join her and Jordan for lunch. We talked about a number of things. I wanted to make sure she understood what selling her land to Remington Oil meant if that's what she wanted to do. Somehow we got to talking about Jordan. That's when she told me about the letter and what was in it. According to her, she found out she was pregnant a couple of weeks after she had sent those divorce papers to you. She had made up in her mind that she wanted a life with you and the baby, and had even told her father of her decision. She mailed you that letter and waited for you to call to tell her it was okay to come to Australia."

Dex crouched down in front of the stream and threw a pebble in it. "I never got that letter."

"I know, and what really happened to it will always remain a mystery. We'll never know if it got lost in the mail or if it was destroyed by Caitlin's father. The important thing is that she now knows you didn't get it. But at the time Jordan was born she didn't know that. She thought you were rejecting her like she'd rejected you." Clayton threw another twig in the stream before continuing.

"But still, believing that you didn't want her didn't stop Caitlin from keeping your child, naming it after you and telling her about you. From the way I see it, there was never a question that Caitlin loved you. Everybody makes mistakes. She's made hers and you've made yours."

Dex had to swallow to find his own voice. "Yeah, I have, and these past couple of weeks have made me realize just how many mistakes I've made with Caitlin. I love her, Clay."

"I know that, Dex. But you're telling that to the wrong person. The reason I wanted to talk to you is because I couldn't help noticing how Caitlin's been watching Justin and Lorren with wistful eyes. It's plain to see Justin proudly wears his heart on his sleeve for Lorren. Maybe it's time you let your woman know that you love her just as much."

A grin appeared on Dex's face. "I can't believe I'm getting advice on how to handle my wife from you of all people, Houston's number one womanizer."

"Well? Are you going to take my advice?"

Dex stood when he heard the sound of Justin and Rod returning. "Yep, so do me a favor and make sure this place is vacated when I get back. There's a special young lady I want to bring here."

Clayton laughed. "Sure thing." He then watched as Dex mounted his horse and rode off.

"Where's he going?"

Clayton turned to Justin. "He's doing something he should have done four years ago."

Justin raised an inquiring brow. "What?"

"He's going after his wife."

Walker couldn't believe his luck when he saw Caitlin walking away from the house alone. He figured her destination was the corral. He'd checked it out earlier. A group of men had been there a while ago, but had left on horseback a few minutes earlier. He knew this would be his only opportunity. He wanted revenge, and he would get it.

Careful to avoid being seen, he made his way back toward the fenced yard where a stallion was being kept. Just from looking at the huge animal he could tell he was a mean one. After sliding the latch from the gate, he got out of the way.

It didn't take the horse long to sense freedom. He tossed his head back, snorted angrily and headed toward the open gate.

From a distance, Dex saw a man running away after opening the corral gate. Then he saw the black flank of the horse as it charged through the opening and take off in the direction of a lone figure who was unaware of the pending danger.

Caitlin!

Dex's breath caught in his throat, and a chill of fear and dread swept up his spine. Gathering speed with his mount, he sprinted forward, hoping he would reach Caitlin in time. The fierce rattle of hooves sounding not far behind him indicated Clayton, Justin and Rob weren't far behind and were aware of the situation.

Dex was pushing his horse forward at such a fast rate of speed, that it seemed the animal's hooves were barely touching the grassy ground. He called out Caitlin's name, hoping she would hear him and get out of the stallion's way.

A cluster of oak trees and thicket lined the path leading to the corral. Caitlin was enjoying her walk. She stopped occasionally to breathe in the clean fresh air and to give a concentrated look of admiration at her surroundings. She was so involved in the beautiful scenery, she did not hear the deep stampering sound of horse hooves imprinting the hard earth. Nor did she notice the trail of billowy dust following in the animal's wake.

But she did look up in time to see the black, fiercelooking steed heading directly in her path at breakneck speed; his deep nostrils flaring in anger, his dark eyes enraged. Fear crawled up Caitlin's spine. She screamed seconds before jumping out of the animal's way. Stumbling, she fell to the hard ground. She could hear the faint sound of Dex screaming her name mere seconds before her mind and senses succumbed to total blackness.

Dex launched himself from the horse's back the moment he reached Caitlin. She lay flat on her stomach, unmoving. It was only after he'd gathered her in his arms that he'd realized he had been holding his breath.

"Give her to me, Dex. Let me check her over."

Dex turned to see that Justin was kneeling beside him. Clayton and Rod had ridden on ahead in an attempt to apprehend the runaway horse before it did any more damage.

"Give her to me, Dex. I need to check her," Justin said with more force.

Dex shook himself to clear his mind and released Caitlin into his brother's care.

"Who in the devil opened that gate?" Justin grumbled as he checked Caitlin to see if anything was broken. Her groan indicated she was slowly coming around.

"One of your men."

Justin glanced up sharply from his task. "None of my men are working today."

Dex stared long and hard at his brother. His face became a glowering mask of rage. He stood and quickly remounted his horse.

"Dex! Where are you going?"

Walker Malone thought he was home free as he made his way toward the cluster of trees where his car was parked. He smiled, thinking to himself that the woman had gotten just what she deserved.

He had nearly made it to his car when suddenly, the sound of a horse and rider made him turn around. Before he knew what was happening, the rider propelled himself from the horse's back and right at him, knocking him to the ground.

Although it appeared that the man equaled him in both height and weight, Walker knew he didn't stand a chance.

This man was ready to fight. The look in his eyes was chilling, and Walker knew without a doubt that he had met his match. He tried whirling away in an attempt to reach his car but failed. The man proved to be too quick.

Walker felt his first taste of pain when the man sent a fist smashing into his face, knocking him backward and again to the ground.

"Get up!"

He never had the opportunity to stand completely. The man hurled himself down at him, slamming him back to the ground and hitting him with hard, punishing, and relentless blows. Walker tried fighting back but it was useless. The man's rage was too great.

"Stop it, Dex! Get off him! Let him up!"

Dex struggled against the fury that raged through him. Clayton's sharp words penetrated his wrath.

"Dex, for pete's sake, let him up. Rod's here. Let the law handle this. Caitlin needs you, man."

The mention of his wife broke through Dex's raging haze. He had to get to Caitlin.

"Are you absolutely sure she's all right?"

Justin gave his brother a reassuring smile. "I'm positive, Dex. Caitlin will be just fine. There are no broken bones. The only injury she received was to her side and that was slight. She jumped out of the way before the horse touched her."

Dex released a deep sigh of relief. "I thought that blasted animal had trampled her, Justin. I've never been so scared in my life. I thought I had lost her again."

"She'll be fine. I've given her something to make her sleep through the night. Try and persuade her to stay in bed an hour or so longer in the morning and fill her with fluids to counteract the dosage of the medicine I've given her. By midmorning, she'll be ready to party like the rest of us."

Dex nodded.

"It's a good thing Rod and Clayton got to you when they did. You almost beat that poor guy to a pulp. I've never seen you that angry before. Who is he?"

Anger crossed Dex's eyes and hardened his features. His face was a glowing mask of rage. "According to his drivers license, he's Walker Malone of Malone Land Developers. He's the man who harassed Caitlin's father, and who had started in on Caitlin," Dex answered, rubbing his bruised knuckles. "I can't believe he would go so far to try and hurt her."

"Greed makes some people do strange things, Dex. The law will make him pay for what he did." Justin placed an assuring hand on his brother's shoulder. "I'll go let the family know Caitlin's all right. By the way, where's Jordan?"

"She's with Mom and Dad. They're keeping her busy with all her new presents. She asked me about her mommy a little while ago, and I told her she hurt her side and you were making it better." A slight smile touched Dex's lips. "She asked if you were kissing it better."

Justin grinned. "What did you tell her?"

"I told her absolutely not. I'm the only one who can do that to her mommy." Dex sighed deeply. "Thanks, Justin, for everything."

Justin smiled warmly. "Don't mention it. That's what brothers are for."

A while later Dex entered the room where Caitlin lay sleeping. She didn't hear Dex when he entered the room. Nor was she aware of the chair scraping the floor as it was dragged closer to the bed; or the sounds of his boots hitting the oak floor as he removed them from his feet. She didn't feel the tender kiss placed on her lips; nor hear the whispered promises that flowed from her husband's lips.

When Caitlin awoke the following morning, she felt groggy and her side ached slightly. She closed her eyes before cautiously shifting her body. She squinted against the sun's brightness that flowed into the room through the window. Turning her head slightly, she saw her husband asleep in the chair next to the bed. Had he slept there all night? "Dex . . . ?"

Her call got Dex's immediate attention, and he dropped to his knees beside the bed. "Good morning, sweetheart," he said in a deep husky voice.

Caitlin reached up and touched the stubble on his chin. "Where's Jordan?"

Dex took her hand and kissed it. "She's with my parents. They're spoiling her rotten."

Caitlin smiled then frowned. "And the horse . . . ?"

"They caught that blasted animal before he could do any more harm." He decided to wait before telling her about Walker Malone's part in it. "I thought that horse had trampled you."

"I got out of his way in time, but fell on my side."

"How do you feel now?"

"A little groggy but other than that, I feel fine."

Dex lay down beside Caitlin and gently gathered her against him. "I thought I had lost you," he said in a whispered voice.

He lifted her head with trembling fingers and touched her cheek so their gazes could meet. What Caitlin saw in his eyes took her breath away. They reflected his pain, his agony and his fear. And unless she was mistaken, mistiness was welling within his eyes. She fought to control her emotions, deeply touched that he cared so much. She swallowed against the tightness in her throat, then whispered huskily. "Thanks for your concern, Dex, but I'm fine now. Really I am."

Dex covered her mouth with his fingers, stopping any further words. He looked down at her. His voice was a forced whisper when he spoke. "I've been a fool, Caitlin. I've been such a fool. The pain of our breakup was so great, I was totally consumed by it. It was so overpowering, I denied myself the one thing I wanted more than anything, and that was you."

Caitlin looked up at Dex. Her dark eyes widened with uncertainty. "What are you saying?"

He reached down and tenderly touched her bruised temple. "What I'm trying to say is that I love you, Caitlin. I truly love you. And for as long as you live, you'll never have reason to doubt my love ever again. My life would be nothing without you in it. I love you so very much."

A sob escaped Caitlin's lips. She covered her face with her hands trying to control the sobs that racked her body.

Dex pulled her closer to him. This wasn't exactly the response he'd expected or had hoped for. "Caitlin, darling, what's the matter? What's wrong?"

Caitlin removed trembling hands from her face. Tear-glazed eyes met Dex's inquiring ones. "I thought I'd never hear you say those words to me again, Dex. I didn't think I'd ever hear you say them again. I wanted to believe that one day you would love me again, but I wasn't sure it would happen."

There was so much anguish in her voice it tore Dex in two hearing it. He gave her a reassuring smile. "Come on now, Caitlin, you've known from the jump you've owned my heart ever since I first laid eyes on you. I never realized how much I loved you until you told me about your decision to sell Shadowland. It hit me in the face just how much you were willing to sacrifice for me. Your love and trust in me was unwavering. I knew then that I loved you beyond anything else. I can't imagine my life without you. You are my life, and you are an essential part of my existence."

Dex's fingers moved tenderly along Caitlin's tear-stained cheeks. "I want to spend the rest of my life loving you, sharing all the joys of watching Jordan grow up. I want to be there with you when our other children are born, and go to sleep each night with you in my arms. I want to wake up every morning with you beside me. I need you in every way that a man can possibly need a woman."

Dex took a deep breath. "There's something else I need to tell you about Shadowland. I looked over the proposal you and Clayton drew up for Remington Oil. You don't know how much it meant to me for you to work out a deal stipulating that Madaris Explorations be used exclusively for a number of their major projects. I was deeply touched with the extent of your loyalty and faith. But I can't let you sell Shadowland. Not even for me."

Caitlin shifted in bed. "But, Dex, you mean more to me than Shadowland does."

"I know that, and that's why I can't let you do it. You don't have to prove your love for me. You've done it countless times already. Your first act of love was wanting to keep my baby."

"But what about the Leabo project?"

"I talked with Adam yesterday morning about the possibility of Remington Oil only leasing Shadowland for a number of years instead of actually buying it. That way you'll retain complete ownership of Shadowland."

Caitlin's eyes gleamed with hope. "Do you think they'll go along with it?"

"Yes. Leabo is very important to Remington Oil, and it would be in their best interest to make a move on it as soon as possible. Adam's going to present the offer to the board at a special call meeting this week."

Dex saw the love and trust shining in Caitlin's eyes. He pulled her closer into his arms. "What did I do to deserve a woman who loves and trusts me so much?" he asked huskily. He sought Caitlin's mouth. It parted willingly.

Caitlin was thrown into turbulent emotions, fueled by an agonizing hunger only Dex had the power to ignite.

He moved his body against hers, trying to fuse their two bodies into one. She wanted the feel of his naked skin against hers, she wanted the feel of him inside of her. "Make love to me," she pleaded, reaching out and unbuckling his belt.

Dex released a ragged sigh, and with a massive effort he grabbed Caitlin's wrist, stopping her from going any further. "Have you forgotten about your side?"

"My side isn't what's aching, Dex," she answered in frustration. "This is." She arched her body up against him as an exquisite fever ignited within her.

Dex stood and slowly began removing his clothes. His smile was intoxicating and touched Caitlin intimately. His eyes were filled with love and desire and held promises. "Justin did mention I was to keep you in bed a while longer this morning and to fill you with plenty of fluids." A seducing smile touched his lips. "And I plan on doing just that although, I have other things to fill you up with."

Caitlin reached her arms out to her husband. "Just remember that I'm not protected," she said seductively as an alluring smile touched her lips.

Dex returned her smile as he came back to her. Unfastening the back of her gown, he lifted it over her head. "Neither am I but it doesn't matter. The only thing that matters is our love for each other. We are protected by our love and it will survive the test of time."

"Yes," Caitlin said, her gaze melting to his. "Love can outlast anything."

As Dex took Caitlin into his arms, more words of love were exchanged and whispered promises were made.

EPILOGUE

Eight Months Later

The awards banquet was packed, and all eyes were on the master of ceremonies who had just finished announcing the nominees for Houston's Businessman of the Year award.

Caitlin's heartbeat accelerated as the man's hand began opening the envelope. Slightly turning her head, she smiled warmly at Dex sitting next to her. As far as she was concerned, he was a sure winner.

Two months ago, Madaris Explorations had made history when it located the first major oil field in the United States in fifty years.

"And the recipient of this year's award is," the man said, glancing down at the paper in his hand. A huge smile spread across his face—"Dexter Jordan Madaris of Madaris Explorations."

It seemed to Caitlin's ears that the entire room exploded with applauses. The entire Madaris family was there. Corinthians Avery, Adam Flynn and Trevor Grant were also present.

Dex stood and pulled Caitlin into his arms, giving her a huge kiss before walking toward the stage. Pride and love swelled inside Caitlin as she watched her husband, who looked smashing in his black tuxedo, move forward to accept his well-deserved award.

The room got quiet when Dex stood in front of the podium. He looked down at the plaque that had just been presented to him. After a brief moment, he looked back over the audience to give an acceptance speech.

"There are a number of people I'd like to thank for this, but due to time I won't be able to thank them all. But I would like to send special thanks out first and foremost to God, from whom all blessings flow. To my wife Caitlin, who believed in me and was willing to sacrifice a piece of land that was dear to her so that I could fulfill my dreams. I want to thank her for giving me her love, unconditionally. More love than any one man could possibly ever deserve." He found her tear-glazed face in the audience. "I love you, sweetheart." A huge smile touched his lips. "And I want to thank her for giving me another special gift tonight, one that's priceless. She told me just minutes before we arrived here that I'm going to be a father again. So I have two reasons tonight to be a very proud and happy man."

The roar and cheers from the crowd with Dex's announcement were almost deafening. When the audience quieted down, he continued. "I'd also like to thank my parents who have always instilled in me deep values and a sense of pride for my heritage."

Dex looked in the direction where Corinthians and Adam were sitting. "And to Remington Oil, for being a company that believes in equal opportunity for all people. I want to thank them for giving Madaris Explorations the opportunity of a lifetime."

Dex's gaze found those of his two brothers. "To my two best friends, who just happen to be my biological brothers. Thank you for your faith and support. You two are the greatest. And last but definitely not least, to my project foreman, Trevor Grant, and the entire Madaris Explorations' crew whose hard work and dedication made all this possible. To all of you I give my sincere thanks."

Dex's smile widened. "Now it's my turn to make a presentation," he said, pulling an envelope out of his pocket. The room got quiet as the audience wondered what was going on. This was not a part of the program.

"Not long ago, Texas suffered a great loss with the passing of Barbara Jordan. She was a tower of spiritual and political strength who fought passionately for her race and nation. I stand before you proud that because of my mother's long and close friendship with her, I was given the middle name of Jordan when I was born. And because of my deep respect and admiration for Ms. Jordan, I'd like the presidents of the University of Texas and Texas Southern to come forward."

When the individuals had reached the stage, Dex continued. "Because of your universities' close ties with such a magnificent woman, on behalf of Madaris Explorations and Remington Oil, I would like to present both universities each with a check for a million dollars to be used for the establishment of the Barbara Jordan Scholarship Fund. These funds are to be used to help deserving students continue Barbara Jordan's fight in defending the Constitution, the American dream, and the common heritage and destiny all of us share.

Dex presented the checks to the individuals then walked off stage.

Everyone in the room rose to their feet, giving him a standing ovation. Striding swiftly back toward his seat, his eyes locked with the woman he loved. Moments later, he walked straight into her outstretched arms.

"I love you, Caitlin," he whispered. "I will love you forever."

His words were both a pledge and a promise.

ETERNALLY YOURS

*Clayton Madaris's time has come, and this book
is dedicated to all my avid readers who agree with me.*

SPECIAL THANKS

To my family and friends for their continued support.

To Denise Coleman, Lynn Sims, and Chimeka Hodge, who helped with my Christmas shopping so I could meet my deadline.

To Brenda Arnette Williams for her feedback on the finished product.

To Attorney Cecil Howard of Tallahassee, Florida, who took precious time from his busy schedule to talk to me and helped me to understand the fundamentals of family law.

To a very special and dear friend, Syneda Walker. I appreciate the friendship and most of all, the laughs and good times.

And last but not least, to my Heavenly Father, who makes all things possible.

To every thing there is a season, and a time to every purpose under the heaven:

Ecclesiastes 3:1
King James Version

There is a right time for everything.

Ecclesiastes 3:1
(Taken from *The Living Bible*)

CHAPTER 1

"Your bed or mine?"

Clayton Madaris glanced up from his meal and gazed into the eyes of the woman who'd asked the question. She was beautiful, and her sensuous proposition was something any man would jump at. No hot-blooded male in his right mind would ever think of turning it down.

So why was he contemplating doing just that?

An impassive expression masked his handsome features. His hesitation had nothing to do with the fact that he'd just met her that morning. Like him, she was an attorney attending a convention in D.C. He had come to enough of these conferences to be prepared for the expected. One would be surprised just how many unmarried, as well as married people took advantage of the three day convention to engage in short, no-strings-attached affairs. In all his thirty-five years, there had never been a time when he'd been hesitant about making love to a willing woman, granted the situation wasn't a risky one.

So what was wrong with him tonight?

His dinner companion undoubtedly was wondering the same thing and had no plans to stick around and find out. He sensed her agitation with his silence. Her eyes narrowed. "I won't make the same offer twice," she said quietly. There was a feverish edge to her voice.

Clayton nodded slowly, his eyes never leaving her face. He knew her type. She was a woman hungry for physical intimacy. Her eyes had sent him silent, intimate messages all day. There was no doubt in his mind that although he'd just disappointed her by not jumping at her offer, she wouldn't give up on him. She *would* make the offer again.

His smile was slow. "Sorry. Not tonight . . ."

Evidently not happy with his response, she pushed her plate aside and stood, giving him a measured look. "Perhaps another time, then?"

Clayton stared up at her before answering. "Perhaps."

After she left he simply sat, quietly eating the rest of his meal and drinking his coffee.

A short while later, after taking care of the dinner bill, he rode up the elevator alone to the fifth floor. During the ride he tried coming to terms with his sudden lack of interest in an affair. It wasn't like him to turn down any woman's advances or not make a score or two of his own. It definitely wasn't his style. Enjoying the opposite sex was something he had been overly fond of doing since his first time with Paula Stone when he'd been sixteen.

So what was his problem now?

The huge metal elevator doors swooshed open. Taking a deep breath he stepped out and began walking down the long hallway leading to his room. Opening the door to his suite, he walked into the sitting area, then through open double doors to the large bedroom.

He leaned his shoulder against the doorjamb, looking at the king-size bed. No one, especially those who considered him a player of the third degree, would believe he'd actually slept in the huge bed alone. And definitely not by choice.

He smiled as he pushed himself away from the door. There's a first time for everything, he thought, removing his tie and jacket and going into the bathroom. Peeling off the rest of his clothes, he stepped into the shower, dismissing the fact he'd taken a shower just before dinner.

Since becoming an attorney over ten years ago, he'd discovered his most soothing moments were in the shower while warm water caressed his skin. It was during that time he possessed the ability to blank out any thoughts other than those needing his undivided attention. In the end, whatever plagued his mind was usually put in perspective. At the moment, he needed to think about why he'd just refused an offer of no-strings-attached sex.

Adjusting the water, he picked up the scented soap and lazily lathered himself as he mentally analyzed the situation.

For some reason, he was becoming bored with the way his life was going. Somehow he was getting tired of his routine of chasing and bedding women. He twisted his lips in a wry grin. Now that was a laugh, especially since the main reason he had constantly shunned any sort of commitment with a woman was the fear of that very thing—boredom. He was the type of person who found any kind of routine deadly. He'd always been afraid of committing himself to someone only to lose interest with that person and ending up feeling trapped.

His thoughts fell on his two older brothers, Justin, the physician, and Dex, the geologist in oil exploration. Both were happily married and neither appeared bored. If anything they seemed to be having the time of their lives with their wives, Lorren and Caitlin. Was it possible he'd been wrong? Was there a woman out there somewhere who could forever excite, stimulate, and amuse him?

He shuddered at the way his thoughts were going; shocked that he could even consider such a thing. His credo in life for the longest time had been ". . . the only men who aren't fools are bachelors . . ." But he couldn't help wondering why lately he had been subconsciously longing for more than a little black book filled with the names of available women.

As the water from the shower pounded his body, he tossed the problem around in his mind, pulling it apart, analyzing and dissecting it. By the time the hot water began turning cold, he still hadn't come up with any answers.

With a groan he turned off the water and grabbed a towel. Stepping out of the shower, he began drying himself off. There were a lot of questions to which he needed answers. And he knew those answers wouldn't come from taking just one shower. The main problem might be that he had been working too hard lately. Too many court cases and too many late nights spent poring over them. A tired body occasionally filled the mind with foolish thoughts. And what could be more foolish than the notion that he was longing for a steady relationship with a woman?

Clayton shook his head to clear his muddled mind. What he needed was to get away for a while. He had some vacation time coming up. And it was time he took it.

Syneda Walters looked across her desk at the elegantly groomed woman sitting in front of it. She schooled her expression not to show her irritation and annoyance—or her pity. Bracing her elbows on the arm of the chair, she leaned forward. "Ms. Armstrong, I hope you'll reconsider your decision."

"But he has told me he's sorry about everything and really didn't mean to hurt me. He's been under a lot of stress lately. He loves me."

Syneda sighed, letting her well-manicured fingers run agitatedly over the desk surface. She could barely restrain herself from calling the woman all kinds of fool for letting a man abuse her. Yet the woman sat defending a man who evidently got his kicks using her as a punching bag.

Rubbing the ache at the back of her neck, Syneda stared beyond the woman and out the window. It was a beautiful day in early May. The midday sun slanted across the sky and reflected off another building. Its golden rays gleamed brilliantly in the blue sky. She watched as a flock of birds flew by and wished she could somehow fly away with them.

"Ms. Walters?"

Syneda's eyes again rested on the woman's tear-stained face. The bruises hadn't quite faded and were not adequately concealed with the use of makeup. "Yes?"

"You just don't understand."

Syneda allowed her eyes to close for a moment. Then pushing her chair back she rose and sat on the edge of her desk facing the woman. "You're right, Mrs. Armstrong, I don't understand," she replied quietly. "I don't understand several things. First, how can a man who claims he loves a woman physically hurt her the way your husband has repeatedly hurt you? Second, how can a woman who cares anything about herself let him do it and get away with it?"

Mary Armstrong blew her nose in a well used napkin. "But he's my husband," the woman implored, pleading understanding.

Syneda didn't give her any. "He's also your abuser. Look, Mrs. Armstrong, you've only been in the marriage for three years and he's doing this to you now. What do you think he'll be doing to you three more years from now?"

"He'll change."

"That's what you said a few months ago." Syneda gave a disgusted shake of her head. "It's time for you to make changes. Don't live under a false conception you're worth less than you really are. Don't ever believe you deserve to be beaten. No one deserves that. And please stop thinking you're nothing without him."

There was a moment of silence in the room. Then the woman spoke. Her voice quivered with indecisiveness. "What do you suggest I do?"

"As your attorney I suggest the first thing you should do is get some counseling. And I highly recommend that you bring charges against your husband."

"Will he be arrested?"

"That's a good possibility."

The woman's face paled. "What will happen to his practice? He's an outstanding member of the community."

Syneda let out a huff of breath that was more disgust than anger. "He's also an abuser. As far as his medical practice is concerned, if I were you I'd let him worry about that."

"He loves me, and he's sorry that he's hurt me. I can't let him lose everything. I can't do that to him."

Syneda stood. "Then there's nothing I can do. We'll be more than happy to help you, Mrs. Armstrong, when you're ready to first help yourself. Good day."

Syneda continued to gaze at the closed door after Mrs. Armstrong had left. She let out a deep sigh of frustration. She was not having a good day. To be more specific, it had not been a good week. It had started with the case she'd lost on Monday, and the week had gone downhill from there.

She rubbed her forehead, trying to relieve the throbbing at her temples. Even after five years she often wondered about her decision to practice family law. But then, she silently admitted, the profession she had chosen was important to her because she'd always managed to feel she had somehow made a difference in someone's life; whether it was getting them out of a hellish marriage, taking on their fight for custody rights, or in a case like Mary Armstrong's, helping them to realize options in life other than one filled with physical abuse.

A quick knock sounded at the door. "Come in."

The door opened and her secretary stuck her head inside. "I'm leaving for lunch now. Do you have anything you want me to take care of before I go?"

Syneda shook her head. "No, Joanna. There's nothing that can't wait until you return."

Joanna nodded. "All right. And Lorren Madaris called while you were with Mrs. Armstrong."

"Thanks and enjoy your lunch."

"I will," Joanna replied, closing the door behind her.

Syneda picked up the phone and began dialing. Lorren Madaris was her best friend. Both of them had grown up as the foster children of Nora and Paul Phillips. "Lorren? How was Hawaii?"

"It was great. Justin and I had a wonderful time."

"I'm glad."

"What about you? What was the outcome of that case you were working on?"

Syneda studied her manicured nail for a long moment before answering. "We lost." She shook her head and tried shrugging off her disappointment. "As far as I'm concerned the judge's decision was wrong. No one can convince me that Kasey Jamison should have been returned to her biological mother. Where was the woman when Kasey really needed her? If you ask me she showed up five years too late. You of all people know how I feel about parents who desert their kids."

There was a slight pause before Lorren replied. "Yes, I know. And you're thinking about your father, aren't you?"

Syneda's body tensed. "I don't have a father, Lorren."

Lorren said nothing for a while, then broke the silence. "So what're your plans now about the case?"

"For one thing, I won't give up. I feel like I've let Kasey down, not to mention her adoptive parents. I plan to appeal the judge's decision."

"Don't let things get you down. You did your best."

"But in this case, my best wasn't good enough." Syneda stood. She let out a deep sigh of frustration, not wanting to talk about the Jamison case any longer, not even to her best friend. "Lorren, I'll get back with you later. I need to get prepared for my next client."

"Okay. You take care."

"I will."

As Syneda hung up the phone, a part of her mind slipped into a past she had done everything in her power to forget. Eighteen years ago this week, at the age of ten, she had received her mother's deathbed promise that the father Syneda never knew would be coming for her.

Syneda sighed deeply, remembering how her mother had died of an acute case of pneumonia. Even after the juvenile authorities had come and taken Syneda away because she'd had no other relatives, her mother's words, "Your father will come," had been her comfort and hope. Weeks later, after she'd been placed in the foster home with Mamma Nora and Poppa Paul, she still believed her father would come for her. She would never forget how she would stand in front of her bedroom window, watching and waiting patiently each day for him.

For an entire year she had waited before accepting he was not coming. She began pitying her mother for dying believing in the love and devotion of a man. If his actions were proof of the love two people were supposed to share, then Syneda wanted no part of love. As far as she was concerned, love was like a circle. There was no point in it. She swore to never blindly love a man and put her complete trust and faith in one like her mother had done.

Syneda's thoughts drifted back to the present when she heard a group of fellow attorneys conversing outside of her door. She quickly wiped away the tears that had filled her eyes and released a quivering breath. Just as she had told Lorren a few minutes ago, she didn't have a father.

"Hello."

"Clayton?"

"Lorren? Is anything wrong?"

"No. I'm glad I was able to reach you before you left the hotel for the airport. Will your flight make a layover in New York?"

"Yes, why?"

"I need to ask a favor of you."

Clayton Madaris smiled. "Sure. What is it?"

"Will you check on Syneda when you get to New York?"

"Why? Is something wrong?"

"I talked to her a few minutes ago, and she's down in the dumps. She lost an important case."

Clayton frowned. "I'm sorry to hear that. No attorney likes to lose."

"It wasn't about just winning the case, Clayton. This case was very important to Syneda."

He glanced at his watch. "All right, Lorren. I'll check on her when I get to New York."

"Thanks, Clayton. You're the greatest. Next to Justin, of course."

Clayton laughed. "Of course."

"By the way, how was the convention?"

"Not bad. I had a nice time."

Lorren laughed. "Knowing you, I'm sure you did."

Clayton chuckled. "I'll call you after I've seen Syneda."

"Thanks."

"Hold your horses, I'm coming!"

Syneda's nylon-clad toes luxuriated in the deep smoke gray carpeting as she made her way to the door. A smile touched her lips when she glanced through the peep hole. She quickly opened the door.

"Clayton! What on earth are you doing here?"

Clayton stepped into the room and turned to face the attractive light-brown-skinned woman standing before him. Thick, golden bronze hair fell to the shoulders of her tall and slender figure. She looked cute in a short sleeve blue blouse and a flowing flowered skirt. A wide smile covered her full lips and shone in her sea-green-colored eyes.

He returned her smile. "I'm here at the request of Lorren. You know what a worrywart she is."

Syneda laughed as she took Clayton's hand and led him over to the sofa. She always enjoyed seeing him. He was Lorren's brother-in-law and since their first meeting a couple of years ago, they had become good friends. The two of them were attorneys and somehow could never agree on various issues, legal or otherwise. They were both extremely opinionated and at times their different viewpoints led to numerous debates and sparring matches at the Madaris family celebrations and holiday gatherings. She had gone head-to-head with him on just about every topic imaginable, from the government's policy on illegal immigrants to whether or not there were actual UFOs.

"Can I get you something to drink, Clayton?"

"No, I'm fine."

Syneda sat across from him in a chair, tucking her legs beneath her. "Lorren was always the mothering type. Now you would think the kids would be enough. Don't tell me she sent you all the way from Houston to check on me?"

Clayton's attention had been drawn to three framed photographs that sat on a nearby table. One was of Justin and Lorren, their son Vincent and daughter Justina. Another photo showed Dex and Caitlin, with their daughter, Jordan. The last photo was of her foster mother, Mama Nora. He smiled at the photographs before turning his attention back to Syneda to answer her question.

"No, I've been in D.C. for the past three days attending the National Bar Association Convention. She knew my flight had a layover here and suggested I look you up."

"How was the convention?"

"Pretty good. I'm sorry you missed it. Senator Lansing was the keynote speaker and as usual, he kept the audience spellbound."

Syneda nodded. She knew the one thing she and Clayton did agree on was Senator Nedwyn Lansing of Texas. He was admired by both of them and had a reputation for taking a stand on more unpopular issues than anyone in Congress. "What was this year's convention theme?"

"Law and Order."

"Not very original was it?"

Clayton laughed. "No, not very."

Syneda smiled. "I know Justin, Lorren, and the kids are all doing fine. How's the rest of the Madaris clan?"

Clayton smiled "My parents are doing great. They're off again. This time the ever-traveling retirees are headed for the mountains in Tennessee."

He leaned forward in his seat. "Since Christy's home from college for the summer, she went with them," he said of his youngest sister. "Traci and Kattie and their families are doing all right. With me being their only single brother, they've been playing the roles of ardent matchmakers lately."

Syneda grinned. "How're Dex and Caitlin?"

"They're fine. The baby isn't due for another six months but Dex is coming unglued already. Since he and Caitlin weren't together when she was pregnant with Jordan, he's really into this pregnancy big time." Clayton laughed. "Sometimes I wonder who's really having this baby, him or Caitlin. He swears he's been having morning sickness." Clayton shook his head. "By the way, you missed Jordan's birthday party."

"Yeah, and I hated that. Unfortunately I was deeply involved in a case and couldn't get away." A cloud covered Syneda's features. "We went to court on Monday and lost."

Clayton noticed the shadow of disappointment in her eyes. "Do you want to talk about it?"

She nodded. She did want to discuss it. Maybe doing so would unleash all the frustration, anger and resentment that had plagued her since the judge's decision. Although she and Clayton usually took opposing sides on most issues, she knew that like her, he was a dedicated attorney, and hopefully on this one he would understand how she felt, even if he didn't agree with the position she had taken.

Syneda took a deep breath. "It was a custody fight. The natural mother gave the child up at birth six years ago. She fought the adoptive parents for custody . . . and won. That has happened a lot lately, and I don't like the message being sent to adoptive parents. They don't have any protection against this sort of thing under our present judicial system."

Clayton frowned. "In the last two cases that received national attention, I thought the only reason the child was returned to its natural parents was because the natural fathers had not given their consent."

"True, but in our case the consent was given. However, the biological mother claims that at the age of fifteen, she'd been too young to know her own mind and had been coerced by her parents to give up her child. She contends the contract was between her parents and the Jamisons, and that she wasn't a part of it. How's that for a new angle?"

Clayton shuddered at the thought of a fifteen-year-old giving birth. "You're right. That is a new angle."

Syneda leaned back in her seat. "As far as I'm concerned, the real issue is not why she gave up the child. No one seems concerned with what's best for Kasey. She's being snatched from the only parents she's ever known and is being given to a stranger. That's cruel punishment for any child, especially a five-year-old."

Clayton nodded. "Hopefully things will work out. But you can't allow what's happened to get you depressed."

"I know I shouldn't but at times I can't help wondering if what I do really makes a difference."

"Of course it does."

Syneda smiled. "Do you know this is the first time we've been able to talk about a case and not take opposing sides?"

Clayton chuckled as he rested back comfortably in his seat. "Just because I didn't oppose anything you said doesn't mean I fully agree. Tonight you needed someone to just listen to your thoughts and feelings, and not force theirs on you. I gave you what I thought you needed. But what I really think you need is a vacation."

"I took a vacation earlier this year."

"I mean a real vacation. You usually use your vacation time to mess around here and not go anywhere. You need a real vacation to get away, relax and do nothing. I'm sure you have the time available off your job if you need it, so what's the problem?"

Syneda shrugged. "There isn't a problem. I just never thought about it."

"Well, I'm giving you something to think about. What about going someplace with that guy you're seeing."

"Marcus and I are no longer seeing each other," she said slowly. "We decided it was for the best."

"Mmmm. Could it be you're also suffering from a broken heart?"

Syneda frowned. "Not hardly."

Suddenly Clayton sat up straight. His eyes beamed bright with an idea. Before checking out of the hotel, he had phoned his parents and asked their permission to spend a week at their time-share condo in Florida. They had given him the okay. "I have a wonderful idea," he said.

"What?"

"My parents own a condo in Saint Augustine, Florida. It's right on the ocean. I'm leaving next Sunday and will be there for a week. Come with me."

Syneda's brows arched in surprise. "Excuse me? Did I hear you correctly? You want me to go on vacation with you?"

A wide grin broke across Clayton's face "Sure. Why not? You need a rest and I think it's a wonderful idea."

She shook her head. "Clayton, get real. You know I can't go on vacation with you."

"Why not?"

"For a number of reasons."

"Name one."

"My work. I've appealed the Jamison case."

"So. It'll be a while before the courts reopen it. If you ask me, you need a vacation to deal with what you'll be up against when they do."

"True, but I still can't go anywhere with you."

"Why?"

Syneda refused to believe the man was so overlooking the obvious. It was rumored that no woman spent too many hours alone with Clayton Madaris and managed to keep her reputation clean. Although she considered herself a woman of the nineties, and in some people's opinion she carried her fight for sexual equality too far, she was cautious by nature in some things, although impetuous and aggressive in others. In this case, she needed to carefully weigh Clayton's invitation.

"What will people think, Madaris? Specifically, what will your family think?"

Clayton inwardly smiled. She always resorted to calling him by his last name whenever she was getting all fired up to stand her ground against him about something.

"If I remember correctly, my family has extended itself to become your family. They won't think anything of it. For pete's sake, Syneda, they know we don't think of each other as sexual beings, and they know we aren't romantically involved."

He chuckled. "If anything, they'll wonder how we'll spend a week together without doing each other in. We're usually completely at odds over just about everything."

Syneda laughed. "That's an understatement."

He grinned. "We aren't compatible. You know that as well as I do. There's nothing sexual between us. We're good friends, nothing more."

Syneda nodded in agreement. "But I wouldn't be any fun. What if you meet someone while we're there and want to get it on with them? I'll just be in the way."

"Women will be off limits to me that week. I'll be on vacation for rest and relaxation, nothing more."

"Maybe you should get away by yourself."

Last night he would have agreed with her, but now he didn't think so. He liked Syneda. She was intelligent, witty, highly spirited, and fun to be around even when she was giving him hell about something. Besides, he could tell by the tone of her voice when she had talked about the case she'd lost that she needed a vacation as much as he did.

"The beach isn't any fun when you're by yourself," he said. "I plan to unwind and relax and have a good time. I want to just chill and do whatever I want to do, whenever I want to do it."

"And you think you can do that with me?"

"Yep, just as long as we agree not to talk shop. For one week I don't want to be an attorney, a player, or anyone's lover. I don't want any worries or problems. We both need that. I think the two of us going away together is a wonderful idea."

Syneda still wasn't easily convinced. She gazed at the man sitting across from her who was impeccably dressed in an expensive printed tie, Brooks Brothers' shirt, and a costly dark blue suit.

Like his two older brothers, Clayton Madaris was a good-looking man who possessed sharply defined features. She had noticed those things the first time they had met. She'd immediately taken in his dimpled smile and dark brown eyes. A short beard—something he'd grown since she had last seen him—covered his nut-brown complexion, and his neatly trimmed mustache enhanced his full lips. His broad shoulders and towering height—almost six feet two inches—made him totally masculine. And his charismatic nature was like a magnet that attracted women to him in droves. But what he had said earlier was true. He wasn't her type, and neither was she his.

In Texas, Clayton had a reputation for being a lady's man. And according to his sisters, Traci and Kattie, he kept a huge case of condoms in his closet and used them with as much zeal and vigor as a shoemaker used leather. However, in spite of his more than active love life, she had to admit he did have a few redeeming qualities. He generously gave his free time helping others. He was an active member of Big Brothers of

America, and he spent a lot of time doing such noble community services as aiding senior citizens, the homeless, and underprivileged kids.
He was also a wonderful and adoring uncle to his nieces and nephews.

Clayton's sigh echoed loudly in the room. "I really don't understand
the problem. You and I both know that all the two of us can and ever will
be are friends. I think by getting away, we'll be doing us both a favor."

Syneda launched one objection after another and Clayton had a reason to shoot down every one of them. "Are you sure about this, Clayton?
I'd hate to be a bother."

"You won't be. The condo has two bedrooms and two bathrooms. It'll
be plenty big enough for the two of us. You can fly to Houston and from
there we can take a direct flight to Florida. Just think about the fun we'll
have spending an entire week on the beach of the nation's oldest city, not
to mention all the historical sites we can check out while we're there.
Come on, let's go for it."

A smile touched Syneda's lips. Clayton was right, she really did need to
get away for a while. And a trip to Florida sounded mighty tempting. "All
right, I'll go."

Clayton came over and pulled her into his arms and gave her a big
hug. "Great! We'll have a good time together. We won't argue at all about
anything. You'll see."

CHAPTER 2

Clayton and Syneda argued as they boarded the plane for Florida. Clayton had fronted the expenses and flatly refused to let Syneda reimburse him.

"I can afford to pay my own way, Madaris," Syneda said, glaring at him.

"I didn't say you couldn't. Just consider it my treat."

"But, I'd rather—"

"Let's drop it, Syneda," Clayton snapped.

Angry frustrations swept over Syneda's features. "Fine with me. It's your money," she replied curtly after they had taken their designated seats.

"I'm glad you finally realized that," he responded, getting in the last word.

Syneda decided not to respond. She didn't want to appear ungrateful, but she had a hang-up about a man doing anything for her. She had learned early in life not to depend on one.

After fastening her seat belt, she turned to Clayton. "What did your family say about us going away together?"

Clayton settled back in his seat. "They didn't have a thing to say."

Syneda raised a brow. "Not anything?"

"Not anything." He smiled. "Except for Dex."

She lifted her head. "Dex? What did he have to say?"

Clayton chuckled. "Dex didn't say anything. He just made the sign of the cross. I guess he thinks we're going to do each other in on this trip."

Syneda couldn't help but laugh. "Are we really that bad?"

"I guess, but we'll get along okay this trip. We did agree to be on our best behavior and not discuss any controversial topics. Remember?"

Syneda met his gaze then smiled slowly. "Well . . ." She dodged an answer, turning to look out of the window as the plane lifted off.

"Syneda . . ." Clayton said her name in a warning tone.

She turned back to him with her smile still in place. "Oh, all right. I remember, and I plan on keeping my end of our agreement. We'll get along just fine."

Dallas, Texas

The sun was setting in the afternoon sky when the man alighted from the parked car. Instead of being dressed in a business suit, which over the years had become his usual mode of dress while out in public, he had worn only a light-weight jacket and dress slacks. With the person he was going to visit, he could always be himself.

He crossed the dusty road and climbed the grassy hill before entering the meticulously cared for grounds. In his hand he carried two bouquets of mixed flowers.

The walk seemed to take forever as he weaved his way toward the hillside and the marked stone. He was fully aware of the tears that misted his eyes as he knelt to place the flowers next to the grave. The headstone, although worn with time, still clearly showed the name and inscription written on it.

JAN WALTERS—REST IN PEACE

A knot of pain and sorrow formed in his throat. He closed his eyes as poignant memories resurfaced. It had been exactly thirty years ago today that they had met. It had been a day that changed his life forever. It was a day that brought him here every year, after finding out about her death fifteen years ago. By that time she had been dead three years already.

His heart grew heavy when he thought about all the wasted years they could have had together. They had begun dating during their senior year of college. Then a few days after graduation, after he had left for the Air Force Academy, she had left town without telling him or anyone where she had gone.

He stood, straightening his tall frame. The woman in the marked grave would have his heart until the day he died. He also knew that he would continue to come here each year and share this special day with her. It was their day.

Tears gathered in his eyes and slowly spilled down his cheeks as he turned toward the direction where his car was parked.

Until next year.

"This view of the ocean is breathtaking, Clayton," Syneda said, leaning against the railing. From the balcony she watched the blue waters of the Atlantic Ocean ripple gently toward the shoreline of St. Augustine Beach.

"It sure is," Clayton replied, coming to join her. He handed her a glass of wine. "Compliments of the management. They also left some entertainment brochures as well as a visitors' guidebook to all the places to check out while we're here."

Syneda accepted the glass.

"Thanks." She looked out toward the ocean again. "I just can't believe all of this."

"All of what?" Clayton asked, sitting down in a patio chair.

"All of this! The ocean view, the size of this condo, the list of activities lined up for us, this city's history. Everything! And don't you dare sit there and pretend not to be moved by all of it. This place is wonderful, and I plan on enjoying myself immensely the next seven days. Thanks again for inviting me."

"You're welcome." He took a sip of his wine. "I told you what was Dex's reaction to us vacationing together. What did Lorren have to say about it?"

Syneda set her glass on a small table and reclined in a nearby lounger. "At first she didn't believe it. She couldn't imagine the two of us being anywhere together for too long without arguing about something. But after I explained we agreed to stay away from controversial issues, she thought it was a great idea. According to her, no one will think twice about us going away together. She said everyone knows the differences in our personalities and philosophies make the two of us ever getting it on impossible."

"See there. What did I tell you? You were worrying for nothing."

"Maybe, but a girl has to know when to safeguard her reputation." She grinned.

Clayton frowned. "You don't think your reputation is safe with me?"

Syneda smiled. "Let's put it this way, Clayton. Everyone knows about your womanizing lifestyle."

"Really? And what exactly do *you* know?"

Syneda gave him a rueful smile. "For starters, thanks to your sisters, I know all about that case of condoms in your closet. Do you deny it?"

He chuckled, thinking he needed to have a talk with his sisters for getting into his business. "No. I don't deny it. It's better to be safe than sorry."

"Have you ever given any thought of just doing without?"

He gave her a slow grin. "I've been doing without for a couple of months, and I don't like it too much."

She laughed. "Poor baby. What's the matter? The women are finally resisting that Clayton Madaris charm?"

Clayton laughed. "No, that's not it. Would you believe for the past couple of months, I've had a totally insane idea running through my head."

"What sort of insane idea?"

"I've been thinking that maybe it's time for me to stop playing around and get serious about someone."

Syneda almost choked on her wine. "You gotta be kiddin'. I can't imagine you ever getting serious about any woman."

Clayton grinned at the startled expression on her face. "Neither can I, and that's the reason I desperately needed a vacation. I needed to get away to rid my mind of such foolish thoughts. I must be going crazy to even consider such a thing."

"I totally agree."

He smiled. "I'm glad someone does. However, my family would disagree with you. They think it's past time for me to settle down."

Syneda shook her head. "The reason I agree with you is because I understand completely. Falling in love isn't for everyone. I know it's definitely not for me."

Clayton raised a brow. "Really? I thought most women dreamed of their wedding day."

"Well, I'm not like most women. I have no intention of ever falling in love," Syneda said matter-of-factly. She stared at him with eyes bright with curiosity. "What has held you back from ever getting serious with a woman?"

"Fear."

"Fear? Fear of what?"

"Fear of becoming bored with the relationship. Because of my parents' rather close relationship, marriage to me means 'forever after' and 'till death do us part.' The thought of spending the rest of my life with the same woman is enough to give me nightmares. I'd be afraid of eventually becoming bored with her and feeling trapped. For pete's sake, Syneda, forever after is a hell of a long time. Any kind of routine would drive me nuts."

He then smiled. "I enjoy spontaneity, creativity, and excitement. I don't want to be tied to a woman who would eventually have me settled into a dull life."

He lifted his dark brow. "What about you? What's your hang-up on falling in love?"

Syneda took a long deep breath before answering. She met his inquiring gaze. "As far as I'm concerned, falling in love means becoming dependent on that person for your happiness. I did that once and will never do it again."

She stood. "I think I'll go unpack and turn in early. Our flight wore me out. What would you like to do tomorrow?"

Clayton set his glass on the table next to hers and also stood. "How about if we go on one of those sightseeing tours around town."

"That sounds like fun. Well, good night, Clayton. I'll see you in the morning."

"Good night, Syneda."

Clayton watched as she walked off through the living room and toward the bedroom she had chosen to use. He couldn't help wondering about the man who had evidently hurt Syneda to make her feel the way she felt about falling in love.

Leaning against the balcony Clayton took his first sip of morning coffee and then released a satisfied sigh. "Ahh, good stuff," he commented as he looked out at the ocean to enjoy the early morning sunrise. He had gotten up before dawn to make coffee, and had tried to be quiet while moving around in the kitchen. He hadn't wanted to awaken Syneda.

Rest, unwind a bit, have some fun, and clear his overworked mind were the only things on his agenda this week. He turned and was about to go back inside when his gaze caught sight of a lone figure walking along the beach. The first thing he thought was that the woman, dressed in running shorts and a halter top, probably had the best body he'd ever seen. He couldn't make out her face because she was wearing a big straw hat and sunglasses, but he suspected any woman with a body like that had to have a terrific face to go along with it.

He stood transfixed, mesmerized, as she strolled along the beach apparently looking for sea shells. A fragment of something teased at his consciousness. Had he met her before somewhere? There was something about her walk that was familiar to him for some reason.

He momentarily closed his eyes thinking his mind was playing tricks on him. There was no way he could ever have met this woman and not remember it. He reopened his eyes in time to watch her lean down to pick up a seashell and put it in the basket she was carrying. From his position high on the balcony, he could see the shorts she was wearing, that were already cut close to her hip bone, had ridden higher and showed a very good-looking backside.

Clayton drummed his fingers against the railing. Perspiration began forming on his forehead. For crying out loud, he was on vacation to unwind and just looking at the woman had him all wound up. He wiped his forehead thinking this wasn't good. Women were supposed to be off limits to him this week.

He was just about to leave, when the woman turned and looked up in his direction and waved. He frowned, not understanding the friendly gesture. He had not known she had seen him watching her, and had definitely not expected her to acknowledge it. Not knowing what else to do, he waved back.

Only after she'd taken off her sunglasses and removed the big straw hat from her head did he recognize her.

The woman was Syneda.

Clayton turned and whispered in Syneda's ear. "Our tour guide has the hots for you. He's been checking you out ever since we boarded this train."

Syneda ungraciously shoved a handful of popcorn into her mouth, followed by a big gulp of Coke before responding. "You're imagining things."

"No, I'm not. I know when a man is interested in a woman."

Syneda giggled. "I guess you would, being an expert in womanizing and all."

Clayton frowned "It's not funny, Syneda."

"Yes, it is. Men have been girlwatching for ages. Will you stop being so uptight. What's wrong with you?"

Clayton took a deep breath. He was asking himself that same question. It had all begun that morning when he had seen her on the beach. Then later, things had gotten worse when they had decided to take an early morning swim before breakfast. She had joined him by the pool wearing the sexiest bikini he had ever seen. He had always thought she had a great pair of legs, and the bathing suit only made how great they were more obvious. His mouth, along with every male around poolside, had watered as they gazed at the sight of her delectable breasts swelling out of her bikini top, and her well-rounded hips filling the bikini bottom. For one brief moment, he'd experienced the oddest sensation—a heat flowing through his body and settling down toward his mid-section. He had also felt something else, too, possessiveness. He hadn't liked the idea of the other men looking at her. Then he'd shaken off the feeling, but now it was coming back. And he knew at that moment, without a doubt, he was in serious trouble.

"Clayton?"

Unwilling to consider just what was happening to him, he took a deep breath and met Syneda's bemused gaze. "What?"

"I asked what's wrong with you?"

"Nothing is wrong with me," he replied, placing a hand in the small of her back and leading her toward the Nation's Oldest Jail. "By the way. Where's the rest of your outfit?"

Syneda took a quick look at herself. She was wearing a printed backless skort set. The sides were held together in a few places by snaps. A wide-brimmed straw hat whose band matched her outfit covered her head. "What's wrong with my outfit?"

Clayton raised his eyes heavenward. It was obvious she wasn't wearing a bra and from the cut of the garment one would question if she was wearing underwear as well. He was tempted to ask her but thought better of doing so. "There's not much to it."

Syneda laughed as she eyed Clayton from under her hat. "That's the idea, Clayton. This is Florida. It gets too hot for a lot of clothes. The less the better."

"I'm sorry you feel that way," Clayton replied drily.

Syneda raised a brow. "Why?"

"I'm going to be spending all of my time keeping the men around here in line."

The guide led them back to the sightseeing train and then on to the next stop. After touring the Fountain of Youth, Zorayda's Castle and the Lightner Museum, they caught another bus to have lunch in a popular restaurant in the Lincolnville Historical District.

Lincolnville constituted the heart of the city's Black community. It was a large residential neighborhood whose occupants could trace their ancestors' origins to the city's sixteenth century founding.

After lunch they took a carriage ride through the Colonial Historical District before doing some extensive walking while touring the old homes along George Street.

It was midafternoon when they decided to call it a day. Clayton draped his arm across Syneda's shoulder as they walked from the bus stop in front of the condos.

At the door Syneda turned to face him. "I can't believe all the sights we took in today. There is so much to do and see here. And I can't believe how architecturally grand the buildings are. They were simply amazing."

"Yeah, amazing," Clayton replied feigning interest as he unlocked the door and ushered her inside. The only thing that had held his attention all day was her and that outfit she had on. He had been ever mindful of more than a few male stares sent her way. She hadn't noticed but he sure had.

Syneda dropped her purse onto the entry table. "Where do you want to go for dinner, Clayton?"

"I'll let you decide. The only thing I want to do right now is rest my poor aching feet."

Syneda laughed. "Aren't you used to walking?"

"No."

"How do you stay in such good shape?" she asked as she eyed his masculine body outlined in the shorts and top he wore. He was in great physical shape. "Surely all those nights spent in bed with women didn't do it," she teased.

Clayton gave her a wan smile. "I keep in shape in a lot of ways. I work out at least twice a week at the gym, and I play basketball with the guys every chance I get."

"Oh, I see." She looked down at her watch. "It's four now. How about if we go out for dinner around seven. That will give you a couple hours to rest up."

"That sounds good to me. What will you be doing while I'm resting up?"

"I think I'll go to the beach and build a sandcastle. The beaches around here have the whitest and silkiest sand I've ever seen."

Clayton frowned. "What will you wear?"

"Where?"

"To the beach."

"Clayton, that's a silly question. I'll be wearing a bathing suit."

"The one you had on this morning?"

"No, not that one," Syneda replied, turning toward the direction of her bedroom. "But it's one similar to it. Why?"

"Wait up. I think I'll build that sandcastle with you."

Syneda turned around and gave him a surprised look. "I thought you were tired."

"I've suddenly found myself with a new burst of energy."

Later that evening Clayton and Syneda entered a restaurant that the condo's management had recommended. It was a well-known place on Anastasia Island to dine for fresh seafood and tropical drinks. After enjoying a feast of assorted seafoods, they left the restaurant section of the establishment to enter its lounge. They were led by a waiter to an empty table in the back that had a wonderful view of the ocean.

After the waiter departed with their drink orders, Clayton rested back in his chair. "I'm curious as to where you buy your clothes."

Syneda raised a brow. "Why?"

"Just curious." In fact he was more than curious. He was having a difficult time keeping his eyes off her long, smooth legs that were showing from the outfit she had on, a mini length sundress with three tiers of ruffles on the hem. The outfit was blatantly sexy. Too sexy.

"I buy my things from a number of places. I don't shop at any one particular store. That reminds me. I need to go shopping while I'm here. I want to get something for the kids."

Clayton knew what kids she was referring to; his nieces and nephews who called her Aunt Neda. "Are you enjoying yourself, Syneda?"

"Yes. I'm feeling more relaxed than I have in days," she replied with a smile. "I want to again thank you for inviting me."

"My pleasure."

Syneda smiled. "When the waiter returns with our drinks I want to propose a toast."

"To what?"

"Our friendship."

Clayton swallowed hard. Friendship was the last thing on his mind and he felt guilty as sin. His mouth was watering over the sight of her, and she wanted to toast their friendship. And if her outfit wasn't bad enough, the perfume she had on was drifting around and through him. If only she knew how enticing the fragrance was. Her light makeup was immaculate and her hair appeared soft to the touch. He had taken this trip to clear his mind, but being around Syneda was beginning to turn his brains to mush.

"Do you want to dance?" he asked abruptly.

"The waiter hasn't returned with our drinks yet."

"He'll hold them," Clayton answered tersely, reaching across the small table and taking her hand. A slow-moving song was playing as he led her to the dance floor, which was crowded with other couples.

He knew it had been a mistake to ask her to dance the minute he took her into his arms and pulled her close. Her hands automatically folded loosely behind his neck, which caused her breasts to press against his chest.

Syneda tilted her head back and looked up at him. "What about you, Clayton? Are you enjoying yourself?"

Clayton looked down at her. She looked absolutely stunning. "Yes."

"Are you sure?"

"I'm positive," he replied pulling her closer.

They continued the dance in silence. He was so engrossed in the feel of having her in his arms that at first he didn't notice the tap on his shoulder. When he did, he turned and looked into the face of a man he'd noticed eyeing Syneda when they had first entered the lounge.

"May I cut in?" the man asked with a deep southern accent.

"No, you can't."

"Why not?" the man asked gruffly, obviously put off by Clayton's rudeness.

Clayton faced the man squarely. "Because I said so, that's why. Now back off."

"Clayton!"

"Excuse us," Clayton said to the man he'd been tempted to bring down a notch moments earlier. Taking Syneda's hand he led her back to their table.

"Clayton, what in the world is wrong with you? That was downright rude."

"I was protecting your sweet behind since you don't seem to notice it needs protecting. That guy's been drooling over you ever since we entered this place. He's just one of many men who are undressing you with their eyes."

"They're not!"

"They are, too! Just look at that outfit you're wearing. It invites stares."

Syneda stared at him with anger reflecting in her eyes and her mouth open. "I don't believe you, Clayton. There's nothing wrong with my outfit."

"Not if you're a woman looking for a pick up."

"How dare you—"

"You didn't want to come on vacation with me for fear of cramping my style. Maybe I should have made sure I wouldn't be cramping yours," he said curtly.

Syneda stood. "I'm leaving."

Throwing more than enough money on the table to cover the drinks they had ordered but not yet gotten, Clayton followed a fuming Syneda out of the door. Leaving the lounge, they rode in silence along the shoreline road that led back to the condos. As soon as he opened the door to the condo, Syneda entered and went straight to her bedroom, slamming the door behind her.

Clayton let out a disgusted sigh as he poured a drink and stepped out on the terrace. He stood seemingly transfixed for an hour or so looking at the ocean that was lit only by the moon's glow. He turned around when he heard a movement behind him. Syneda stood before him. She had changed into a night shirt.

"Clayton, I'm sorry. I can't believe we had an argument after agreeing not to."

Clayton held open his arms and she walked into them. He pulled her close to him. "I'm the one who should be apologizing, Syneda. I behaved like a jerk tonight and I apologize. There was nothing wrong with the way you were dressed. You looked sensational. I guess I'm so used to eyeing women myself that I know what goes through other men's mind when I see them doing it. And I don't want them thinking about you that way. I guess I've taken it upon myself to be your protector while we're here."

"Yeah, so I've noticed. But, Clayton, you don't have to protect me. I'm twenty-eight and old enough to take care of myself. Have you forgotten that I live alone in New York?"

Clayton smiled down at her. "Deep down I know you can take care of yourself, but that doesn't keep me from wanting to do it for you."

Syneda grinned. "I guess with three younger sisters you're used to it."

"Maybe so," Clayton replied, although deep down he had a feeling the root of his problem was jealousy, plain and simple.

Syneda stepped back out of his arms. "I'm really enjoying myself, but I don't think you are. Maybe I should leave tomorrow and return to New York. You're so busy looking out for me that you're not relaxing at all."

Clayton brushed a stray curl from her face. "No. I'm fine, and I don't want you to leave. I enjoy your company. Like today for instance. I had a great time building that sandcastle with you on the beach. And tomorrow is our day to spend shopping at the malls, remember."

Syneda smiled. "How could I possibly forget something as important as that?"

Encircling her with a protective arm, Clayton drew her closer to him. For a long moment there was no conversation between them. They just held each other. Clayton was going through pure torture. Everything about Syneda was sexy, and he felt a quickening in the lower part of his body. If he didn't separate himself from her, he couldn't be held accountable for his actions. "Syneda?"

"Umm?"

"I think we should call it a night, don't you?"

Syneda stepped out of his arms and peered up at him through a sweep of long lashes. A smile covered her lips. "Friends again?"

Clayton returned her smile as a surge of warmth passed through him. "Yes, friends again."

"Good. As much as we argue at times, I like having you for my friend."

"And I feel likewise."

Syneda leaned up on tiptoes and kissed his cheek. "Good night, Clayton."

"Good night, Syneda."

He watched as she turned to leave. He couldn't help but notice how the sleeper she wore clung to her body, accentuating her shapely hips and tiny waist. He had a feeling he was in for a long sleepless night.

CHAPTER 3

"**D**on't tell me we've finally done something that's tired you out," Clayton said grinning. He handed Syneda a cold can of soda. "I was beginning to think you were blessed with never-ending energy."

Syneda took the soda and flopped down in the nearest chair. "Shopping always tires me out," she replied after taking a sip of the drink. She set the can on a nearby table and began removing her sandals. "The stores at that mall were wonderful. Just look at all this stuff."

"I'm looking," Clayton replied, glancing around at the bags and boxes littering the floor. "Have you forgotten that I helped you carry most of it?"

Syneda smiled. "I really appreciate you being with me. I couldn't have purchased nearly as much stuff had you not been there."

Clayton glanced around the room shaking his head. "Yeah, your Master Card company should thank me profusely. I wonder if they'll be willing to give me some kind of a kick-back since you spent a fortune today."

Syneda laughed. "I doubt it." She stood to collect her boxes. "Do you mind if we order out tonight? I don't think I have the energy to get dressed to go anyplace."

"That's no problem. What do you have a taste for?"

"How about lobster?"

"That sounds good to me. I'll order delivery from a resturant nearby."

"Thanks, Clayton, you're such a sweetheart."

Less than an hour later, a just-showered Syneda stood leaning against the railing on the terrace enjoying the view of the ocean. Clayton had left her a note saying he was going downstairs to the pool for a swim.

From her position on the terrace she could see him below, and for some reason her eyes kept straying toward him. She became entranced by the movement of his muscular legs as he dived into the pool, by the firmness of his stomach beneath his swim trunks, and by the mass of dark hair covering his chest. He looked tough, lean, and sinewy. His powerful well-muscled toast-brown body moved through the water with easy grace.

"For heaven's sake, what am I staring at?" she exclaimed in dazed exasperation. "You would think I've never seen a good-looking male body before." And what really bothered her was the fact the body she was ogling belonged to Clayton.

She forced her gaze to move from the pool area back to the view of the ocean. But as if they had a will of their own, her eyes strayed back to Clayton time and time again, and each time she felt a flutter deep in the pit of her stomach. He might be downstairs swimming in the pool, but she was upstairs swimming through a haze of feelings and desires that were almost drowning her.

Knowing the only way she would be able to stay above water and stop looking at him was to move from her present spot, she walked over to stretch out on the lounger to take a nap.

Syneda had nearly dozed off to sleep when she heard Clayton return. She opened her eyes to find him standing next to the lounger. She couldn't help but let her gaze settle on the line of body hair that tapered from his navel into the waistband of his swim trunks.

"Did I wake you?" he asked, stretching down in the lounger opposite hers.

She pulled herself into a sitting position. "Not really. How was your swim?"

"Super. It relaxed me tremendously," he replied.

And it unsettled me, Syneda thought.

"What's on the agenda for tomorrow?" he asked.

Biting her lower lip, she looked away. "I thought I would give you a break and make it a do-your-own-thing day. That way you can be free of me for a while." *And I can be free of you to sort through all these strange feelings I'm beginning to have,* she thought.

"I like having you around."

"Oh," she replied. Her eyes were again drawn to the thick pallet of hair on his chest. Awkwardly, she cleared her throat. Her eyes met his. "Well then, let's not make any plans. We'll let it be a whatever happens sort of day."

"All right."

They spent the rest of the afternoon relaxing on the terrace enjoying the ocean's view and trying not to let it be obvious that they were also enjoying the view of each other.

Later that evening after enjoying a superb lobster dinner, they sat around on the floor drinking the remainder of the wine.

"You have butter on your nose."

Syneda twitched her nose. "I do?"

Clayton laughed. "Yes, you do."

When Clayton reached over to wipe it off, their gazes locked and held for several seconds. A mite too long to be at ease.

"Thanks, Clayton." Syneda said awkwardly, taking another sip of wine. Her mind was clouded with uneasiness. *For crying out loud, Syneda Tremain Walters, pull yourself together. You're acting like a bimbo. The man is Clayton for pete's sake. You know, Lorren's brother-in-law; the one who changes women as often as he changes socks; the one who has a case of condoms in his closet; and the one who is definitely not your type.*

"Here's something we can do tomorrow night."

Syneda glanced up to find Clayton looking in the entertainment brochure. "What?"

"Take a cruise around Anastasia Island aboard the *Rivership Romance.*"

Syneda almost choked on her drink. "A romance ship?"

"Yes."

"Why would you want to do something like that?" she asked. A shadow of caution touched her.

Clayton shrugged. "Because it sounds like fun, and we are here to have fun, aren't we?" he asked, his voice carefully colored in neutral shades.

"Yes, but we'll be out of place aboard that ship."

"Why?"

"Because most of the people there will either be married or lovers."

"And you'll feel out of place because we're not either of those things?" he asked, regarding her quizzically for a moment.

"Won't you?"

"Nope. It wouldn't bother me at all. But since it evidently will bother you, forget I suggested it."

Although her misgivings were increasing by the minute, Syneda felt like a complete heel. The last thing she wanted was to be a bore, especially after he had been nice enough to invite her on this trip with him. "We'll go."

Clayton shook his head. "We can do something else."

"No, I'm fine with going."

"Are you sure?"

"I'm positive."

"All right. I'll make reservations."

Syneda stood quickly, collecting her empty wineglass. She smiled down at him although inwardly she struggled with uncertainty. "Well, I guess I'll retire early. It was a tiring day."

Clayton couldn't help but look up at her. His eyes scanned her, beginning with the polished toes of her bare feet to the golden bronze hair atop her head. He met her eyes. He could almost drown in them and wondered why he had never felt like doing so before. Then there was that cute little dimple that appeared in her cheek each time she smiled. Why did he suddenly find it totally alluring? His senses began spinning. The scent of her perfume seemed to float around him. It was as sensuous as he found her to be. He inhaled deeply as a need as primitive as mankind touched him. "All right, Syneda. I'll see you in the morning," he replied huskily.

Syneda took a deep breath and feigned a yawn. "Not too early though. I can barely keep my eyes open so I may sleep in late tomorrow. If I'm not up by the time you want breakfast just go on without me. I'll grab something later. Good night." She hurried off to her bedroom.

As soon as she was in the privacy of her bedroom, Syneda rushed into the connecting bathroom. The reflection staring back almost startled her. Her features were basically the same, except she had gotten a little browner from the time she had spent in the sun. But that wasn't the only noticeable difference. Her eyes were glazed with a look that definitely spelled trouble. What bothered her was the fact Clayton Madaris was the one responsible for that look being there. And to make matters worse, she would be spending tomorrow night with him on board a romance cruise ship.

"Good grief! What am I going to do? I'm becoming attracted to Clayton Madaris!"

"Wake up, sleepyhead."

Syneda heard the deep masculine sound in her ear at the same moment she felt the warm breath on her neck. She opened one eye slowly, then another. Her eyes met the sparkling brown ones that held a flicker of mischief in their dark depth. She became instantly wide awake.

"Clayton! What are you doing in here?"

Clayton was lying down beside her, facing her. "I came to make sure you were still alive."

Syneda became aware of her state of dress and tugged her nightshirt down. "Of course I'm alive. I told you last night that I'd probably sleep through breakfast. Did you forget?"

He gave her a lopsided grin. "No, I didn't forget. I just didn't think you meant you would also sleep through lunch."

"Lunch! What time is it?"

"Around one thirty."

"One thirty! I didn't mean to sleep so late," she said, pulling herself up in a sitting position. She forced her gaze from his lips that were full and inviting. Somehow they had never intrigued her before as they were doing now.

"You must have really been tired."

"Yes, I was." She didn't bother to add that she had lain awake most of the night thinking about him. She suddenly felt uncomfortable from his closeness, and a confusing rush of desire whirled inside her. He was dressed in a blue pull-over shirt and a pair of white shorts. The masculine fragrance of his cologne was beginning to dull her senses.

She suddenly realized while she had been staring at him, he'd been doing likewise with her. "I need to get dressed."

"Don't let me stop you. Just pretend that I'm not here."

"Fat chance, Clayton Madaris!"

Clayton laughed throatily, and a disarmingly generous smile extended to his eyes. "I was afraid you'd say that."

Syneda watched him stretch his body before standing. "Okay, Miss Walters, I'll leave you to dress in peace. But if you're not ready to go in twenty minutes, I'm coming back for you."

Syneda watched as he left the room, closing the door behind him. She tried going back into her mind, into central control, to reset her emotions. She was not ready for the thoughts and feelings she'd begun having around Clayton.

"Senator, I'm glad you're back, sir. How was your trip?"

"The trip was nice, Braxter. It's always good to get away and spend some time with an old friend." Senator Nedwyn Lansing studied the young man in front of him. As a senator's top aide, Braxter Montgomery at the age of thirty was the best there was. A graduate of Georgetown University, he had begun working for him over six years ago, serving him through almost two full terms. During that time he had gotten to know Braxter as well as the other members of his immediate staff. They were people he could depend on. But only a few he felt he could trust completely. Braxter was one of them.

"Is something bothering you, Braxter?"

"There's nothing bothering me, sir. But there is something I'm concerned about."

"You worry too much."

"I'm supposed to. That's part of my job."

The senator nodded. "All right. Let's sit and talk."

The two men took seats that were facing each other. "Okay, let's have it, Braxter. What's so concerning that you've missed lunch?"

Braxter eyed the forty-nine-year-old, light-complexioned black man with hazel eyes sitting across from him. He was a man he highly respected. Most people did. Where most senators did good things for their image, Senator Lansing did good things for the people he represented. He was often referred to by the media as the "people's servant." His life was an open book.

It was a known fact he'd been a sharecropper's son from a small town in Texas not far from the border. His mother had died when he was five. With hard work and dedication, he had completed high school and because of his academic achievements, he had obtained a four-year scholarship to attend the University of Texas in Houston.

It was also well known that he had never been married, although he'd been steadily dating a law professor at Howard University for the past couple of years. The only thing that had always puzzled Braxter was the senator's annual trip to Texas this time every year; the one he had just returned from taking. It was a trip he never talked about, other than to say he had gone to visit a friend.

"What I'm concerned about, sir, is your blockage of the Harris Bill."

Senator Lansing raised a brow, "What about it? That bill needed to be blocked. I flatly refuse to support any legislation that proposes cuts in education."

"Yes, Senator, and I agree with you. But blocking that bill won't be a popular move on your part. Especially with certain people."

The senator nodded knowing Braxter was referring to the creator of the bill, John Harris, and a few other senators who were considered Harris's cronies. "I can't waste my time worrying about some people, Braxter. I want to do what's right for the majority of the people in this country, not just a limited socially acceptable few. Every child regardless of race, creed, color, or social standing is entitled to a good education."

Braxter smiled. He enjoyed seeing the senator fired up over an important issue. But his job as a senator's aide was to make him aware of what he could possibly be up against. Especially since the kickoff for his re-election campaign was less than two months away.

"I totally agree with everything you're saying. And according to recent polls, the American people are behind you all the way."

"Then I guess those people whose noses are out of joint will just have to get over it."

"I really don't know if they will, sir. By blocking that bill, you've stepped on a few toes. I have a feeling they'll step back."

Senator Lansing smiled. "Let them. I have nothing to hide."

"Do you remember the first time we met, Syneda?"

Syneda almost blushed under Clayton's warm stare. They were lying side by side on loungers at poolside. "Yes, it was almost two years ago, the night of Justin's cookout to celebrate his purchase of the ranch." A smile touched her lips. "He was very much interested in Lorren that night."

Clayton chuckled. "Yes, he was, wasn't he." Clayton thought about the night he and Syneda had met. When he'd first met her he had thought she was about as explosive as a stick of dynamite next to a blazing torch. Just about any controversial subject could set her off. She had disagreed with him on just about everything. It had been a first for him. Most women agreed with practically everything he said.

There was a brief moment of silence before Syneda spoke. "Clayton?"

"Umm?"

"Why did you ask me if I remembered when we first met?"

"I was just wondering."

Syneda gazed over at him but couldn't see his eyes behind the aviator-style sunglasses he wore. She wondered what his thoughts were and tried ignoring the funny, shivering sensation in her midsection just being near him was causing. Despite her best intentions, her eyes kept straying to him.

"Syneda?"

"Yes?"

"Did you bring a different bathing suit for every day?" he asked, lifting his sunglasses and squinting at her inquiringly.

She swallowed. Had he been checking her out like she had been doing him? "No, why?"

"Because I haven't seen you wear the same suit twice."

"Are you complaining?" she asked. The smile on his lips sent her pulse spinning.

He gave her body a thorough once over, which made Syneda's breath lodge in her throat. His gaze moved over her, traveling from her bare feet, up her thighs, past her waist. His gaze paused momentarily on her breasts, before moving to her face where it held hers.

"No. You won't get any complaints out of me. I think you look great. I don't know what happened between you and that guy you were seeing, but it was definitely his loss," Clayton replied huskily.

The dark brown eyes that held hers appeared to have darkened. What Syneda saw reflected in them made her lose all conscious thought. She read appreciation, attraction, awareness, and something she hadn't counted on, desire. Were those the things she saw in his eyes or the things she was afraid he saw in hers?

Stifling a low groan she quickly came to her feet when she felt an odd rush of heat flare in her belly before moving lower. "Thanks for the compliment, Clayton. I think I'll go back to the condo for a while. There's a book I bought yesterday that I want to start reading before we leave for the cruise tonight," she said hastily, pulling on her cover-up and grabbing her beach bag. "What time will we be leaving for the cruise?"

"Around seven," he answered, the huskiness lingering in his tone.

"Okay. I'll be ready. See you later."

Clayton watched Syneda walk back toward the condo. He took a deep breath with every step she took and with each sway of her hips. How in the blazes was he going to get through the evening pretending their relationship hadn't changed? How was he going to spend the rest of the week with her and pretend not to want her when he wanted her like he'd wanted no other woman before?

Going into her bedroom to wake her had been a *big* mistake. He had found her sprawled uptop the covers wearing a loose cotton nightshirt. Evidently sometime during her sleep, the sexy garment had risen to her hips revealing a pair of luscious thighs. And if that hadn't been bad enough, the first few buttons had been undone and had shown a hefty view of the slopes of her breasts.

Lunch with her had been even worse. He had sat across from her in a booth at a sandwich shop eating a submarine sandwich when he happened to notice the peaks of those same breasts poking through the front of her thin blouse. He had almost choked on the bite he'd just taken out of his sandwich. Desire, hot and rampant, had consumed him, had hardened him, and had made him fully aware of how much he wanted her.

Clayton sighed deeply. He would no longer fight the inevitable. He wondered how Syneda would handle the fact that he had every intention of getting close to her. Very close. He was a man who believed in going after what he wanted.

And he wanted her.

CHAPTER 4

"**I**'m ready, Clayton."

Clayton turned his attention away from the television to cast his gaze upon Syneda as she entered the room. He was utterly spellbound as he stood to his feet. She looked absolutely radiant.

While waiting for her he had begun watching a sitcom that he had found rather enjoyable. However, all thoughts of the television program left his mind when he saw her. He could only stare at the stunning woman standing across the room.

She was dressed in a fuchsia colored dress with a diagonal peplum that started at the side and dropped at the knee in a straight skirt. A stunning black bow added elegance from the bottom up.

A knot formed deep in Clayton's throat. He was totally captivated, and before he could stop his mouth from saying aloud his innermost thoughts, the words flowed from his lips in a voice rich with masculine magnetism and sensual appeal. "You look great, Syneda."

The dark intensity in Clayton's eyes touched Syneda to the core. The dress she had chosen to wear was one she had bought earlier that year to attend the law firm's annual get-together. The style of the dress showed off her figure to alluring advantage. She had made quite a hit in it at the party.

"Thanks, and you look pretty good yourself." She thought he looked particularly handsome dressed in a charcoal gray suit, white shirt, and printed tie.

Anxious to get away from Clayton, if only for a minute to get her bearings and to stop her senses from spinning, she said, "I think I lied earlier."

"About what?"

"About being ready. I left my purse in the bedroom. I'll be right back."

Clayton drew in a deep breath when Syneda turned to leave the room. His gaze traveled over her from behind. Her dress had a daring deep V-back that seemed to end at her waist. His skin felt flush, his tongue felt thick in his mouth, and his eyes felt swollen from expanding. He stared at her bare back, small waist, soft curves, and long shapely legs. He could feel the hammering of his heartbeat in his chest and was no longer stunned at the rush of pleasure that surged through him.

Syneda hurried off into her bedroom. Pausing just inside the door, she took a long, deep breath. What was happening to her? Clayton wasn't a man she had just met. Why was being around him affecting her this way? Why was every sensory nerve in her body sharpened with maddening awareness of him? With no answers but a determination to enjoy herself during the evening, she took another deep breath before snatching her purse off the bed. Moments later she returned to the living room where Clayton was waiting.

"I'm really ready this time."

"No more than I am," Clayton replied softly. Taking her hand he led her out of the condo.

"What a beautiful ship," Syneda said to Clayton as they boarded the *Oceanship Romance*. It was a one-hundred-and-ten-foot triple-decked catamaran that was positively elegant. On board was an interior of Tiffany lamps and plushly carpeted dining salons and lounge. The exterior contained promenade decks with seating that provided a stunning view of the ocean.

"Welcome aboard. I'm Captain Johnstone," a tall man dressed in a starched white captain's uniform greeted. "Tonight we're featuring live entertainment and a full cocktail service. Dinner will be served promptly at eight, and will include a selection of several mouth-watering dishes. Our crabmeat-stuffed white fish baked in parchment is usually a favorite."

"That sounds delectable," Syneda replied, flashing the captain a warm smile.

"It is and we're here to please. We want you to enjoy yourself."

"Thank you and I'm sure *we* will," Clayton replied, ushering Syneda on board. He hadn't liked the smile the good captain had given Syneda.

"Just as I thought," Syneda said moments later after grabbing a treat off the table of tantilizing hors d'oeuvres.

"What?" Clayton asked, also grabbing a plump chilled shrimp off the table.

"All the people here are paired off. And from the looks of things they're just as I predicted, either married or lovers. Just look at them."

Clayton did look. Most of the people were hugging and kissing, walking along the deck holding hands, or on the dance floor moving to slow music.

"Don't let it bother you, Syneda," Clayton said quietly, his eyes holding hers as he casually leaned against the ship's railing. "If you feel uncomfortable, you should consider the old cliché, when in Rome, do as the Romans do."

"Meaning what?"

"Meaning this."

Syneda didn't know what she expected, but it wasn't Clayton suddenly taking her into his arms, cupping her chin in one firm hand, tilting her head back, and lowering his mouth to hers. Her heart began pounding wildly as Clayton's tongue began an erotic exploration of her mouth. His hands massaged the center of her back, touching her bare skin.

Her body began to vibrate with liquid fire. She surrendered completely to his masterful seduction. A deep ache that began in her abdomen radiated downward, to the very core of her. The kiss was like nothing she had ever experienced, and she was shocked to discover she wanted more.

Clayton lifted his mouth from hers and looked into wide, amazed eyes. What he saw reflected in them almost took his breath away. He was too experienced not to recognize total desire in a woman. And he was inwardly elated to discover Syneda wanted him just as much as he wanted her. The burning question of the hour was where to go from here?

"Clayton, I—I . . ."

He silenced her by placing his finger against her slightly swollen and undeniably moist lips. "Don't say anything, Syneda. Not yet. We'll talk later. I think we have a lot to discuss." His body ached with the sweetness of taut sexual awareness. *Then maybe we shouldn't talk at all,* he thought, seeing signs of apprehension in her eyes.

After dinner the live band continued to provide the music. Clayton and Syneda walked along the promenade deck holding hands, not saying anything but very much aware of each other.

"Would you like to dance, Syneda?"

"Not if it's going to end like it did the last time we danced together a few nights ago," she replied teasingly.

"It won't. I promise." With deft fingers he led her onto the dance floor where couples were already moving slowly to the instrumental version of Billy Ocean's classic, "Suddenly." The music wrapped them and every other couple on the dance floor in a romantic web where everything else, except the person you were with faded into oblivion.

It was quite obvious most of the people there were in love, Syneda thought. She and Clayton began to slow dance. She felt his hand tighten around her, gathering her closer to him. A gust of desire shook her. She never dreamed his hands would feel so warm, so gentle, so hypnotic. In response, she moved her hips against his rock-hard thighs and heard his sharp intake of breath.

"You feel good," Clayton whispered, his warm breath hot against her neck. She felt so right in his arm, so perfect. It was as if she had been made just for him. "I can't believe we've never—" He cut off his words and began chuckling to himself. "The music they're playing is very appropriate for our situation."

Syneda lifted her gaze to his. "How so?"

"We felt pretty comfortable about coming on vacation together because there was nothing romantic or sexual between us. Then wammo, *suddenly*, after two years, I discover you're the sexiest woman alive. What do you think of that?"

Syneda gave her head a wry shake, feeling totally off balance. Passion was flowing through her entire body. "I really don't want to think anything about it, Clayton," she replied in a husky voice. To think about it would make her see reason and remind her that nothing had changed. She and Clayton were still not compatible. At the moment she didn't want to dwell on that. All she wanted was to share this special moment with him. But then again, maybe she should think about it. Them not being compatible just might be a plus. Clayton could very well be the type of man she needed to become involved with. Especially after Marcus.

She had explained to Marcus Capers when they'd first began dating that she wasn't in the market for a serious relationship. But as far as he'd been concerned, she was the perfect woman to settle down with and begin a family. He just couldn't get it through his head that she wanted no part of love and marriage.

After dating each other for a little over six months, he had proposed to her. She had turned him down. Syneda doubted she would have that kind of trouble with Clayton. Like her, he wanted no part of a commitment with anyone. He was a man who knew the rules and would play by them.

The band began playing another slow number, and Clayton pulled her back into his arms and held her close. He rubbed his hand, slowly, sensuously over her bare back, tracing erotic patterns with his fingertips. Again she felt passion rising in her like the hottest fire, clouding her brain.

Syneda was so close to him she could hardly move without her body moving both seductively and suggestively against his. She couldn't help but feel his virile response to her movements. For the first time in her life, she felt an aching emptiness in her that demanded fulfillment. Clayton's face was so very near that all she needed to do was to turn her head just a little to touch her lips to his.

Her pulse raced. The urge to do more than kiss Clayton was a physical ache deep within her, and her fervor mounted. "Clayton," she whispered. Her sea-green eyes held his dark ones.

"Yes? What do you want, Syneda?" he asked quietly, hoping it was the same thing he did.

They had stopped dancing and were standing in a secluded area of the dance floor. Syneda reached up and boldly traced his lips with her fingers. For a long while their eyes met and held. She drew a deep breath. She didn't understand what was happening to her, but she did know what was happening between them. Blame it on the magnificent sunrise she saw each morning upon wakening, or the plush condo and its gorgeous ocean view, or the cruise that was taking them around the island setting the mood for romance. No matter where the blame was placed, the result was the same.

She wanted him.

"What do you want, Syneda?" Clayton asked again.

The sexy huskiness of his voice made blood race through her body at a pounding speed. She attempted to calm herself down, discovered she couldn't and decided the devil with it. Why fight it anymore? Known to be upfront, candid and straight-to-the point in her dealings with anyone, Syneda slowly moved closer and whispered in Clayton's ear. "I want you, Madaris. Bad."

Clayton crushed her to him. Sharp needles of sexual excitement were pricking his every nerve with the five words she had spoken. It was impossible to maintain any semblance of control, physically or emotionally. He drew in a tremulous breath. "And I want you too, baby." He then leaned down and kissed her deeply, tasting her fully.

The hours didn't pass fast enough for either of them before the ship finally returned to dock. Clayton drove the rental car back to the condo. Neither said anything. However, Syneda couldn't help but study his profile, exalting at the male strength and beauty of him. She couldn't stop her gaze from lingering on his lips. Lips that had masterfully kissed her for the first time that night and had her own still quivering in desire. They were lips that had awakened a craving within her so strong it had literally transformed her into another person; definitely not the cool, calm, level-headed person she usually was.

She fidgeted restlessly in her seat, thinking about what would happen once they returned to the condo. She wanted the feel of Clayton's mouth on hers again. She wanted him to touch her all over. And more than anything, she wanted him to make love to her.

Sensing her anxiousness, a copy of his own, Clayton relieved one of his hands from the steering wheel and reached for her hand. Tenderly turning it over, he began tracing erotic circles in her palm. "This means I want you very much."

Syneda's breath caught in her throat. She was stunned by the wild and dangerous feelings coursing through her from his words.

"Here at last," Clayton said a few minutes later. At a brisk walk he came around to open the car door for her.

"Did you enjoy yourself tonight, Syneda?" he asked as they walked at a fast pace away from the car holding hands. Sexual tension between them was at its maximum. Small talk was the last thing either of them wanted to engage in.

"Yes, very much. What about you?"

His dimpled smile almost made her knees weaken. "I had a great time," he replied, increasing his pace. The door to the condo was now only a few feet away.

"I'm glad," Syneda said, almost having to run to keep up with him. Her heart was pounding with anticipation. When they finally made it to the door, he had the key in his hand. As they stood in front of the door facing each other, calming their deep, erratic breathing, Syneda gave Clayton a breathtaking smile.

He was surprised at his lightning quick reaction to that smile. Drawing her closer, he enfolded her in his arms. Leaning down, he touched his lips to hers, kissing her deeply, and simultaneously reaching for the door. Before he could use his key, the door was flung wide open.

"It's about time the two of you got back!"

Clayton and Syneda broke apart and stared in surprised shock at the couple standing in the doorway.

"Justin! Lorren!" Syneda exclaimed in astonishment. She quickly recovered and threw her arms around them.

"Did we surprise you two?" Lorren Madaris asked speculatively, eyeing Clayton and Syneda with a sort of stunned expression on her face. "We arrived a few hours ago. When we discovered the two of you weren't here, Justin used the spare key to get in."

Clayton hugged Lorren and shook hands with his oldest brother. Although he and Syneda had been well hidden in the shadows, it was apparent they had been doing a lot more than chitchating outside the door.

"Surprise is putting it mildly," Clayton muttered to them. His voice was as unwelcoming as his expression. "Your timing is lousy, Big Brother," he whispered for Justin's ears only.

Justin Madaris gave Clayton a hard look. "Apparently it was right on time," he whispered back.

"So what brings the two of you here?" Clayton asked entering the condo, still holding Syneda's hand. "Whatever the reason, I hope it's a short visit." He wasn't kidding. And to make sure Justin and Lorren knew it, the tone of his voice was deadly serious.

Evidently it wasn't serious enough. Both Justin and Lorren were smiling with a look that said, "Now that we see what you're up to, not on your life, Buddy."

After a moment of tense silence, Justin finally spoke. "Lorren has some news she just couldn't wait to share with Syneda. And your lack of phones in this condo made calling impossible."

"Our lack of phones was to assure complete privacy and avoid untimely and uninvited interruptions," Clayton replied, placing emphasis on the last part of his sentence. "So what's your news, Lorren, that was so pressing you had to deliver it in person?" His eyes fell on the sister-in-law he had come to love and adore, but at the moment wanted to strangle.

He couldn't help noticing her love-mussed clothes, tousled hair and slightly swollen lips. Despite not wanting to do so, he couldn't help smiling. Evidently Justin and Lorren had found a rather interesting way to pass the time while they had waited for him and Syneda to return.

Lorren's eyes sparkled with total happiness. "We're having another baby!"

"Lorren, that's wonderful! I'm so happy for the two of you." Syneda threw her arms around Lorren sharing her excitement.

Clayton couldn't help but roar in laughter. Now he had two pregnant sisters-in-law. Evidently his brothers had taken the Good Book's directive to be fruitful and replenish the earth rather seriously. "Somehow Lorren being pregnant again doesn't surprise me," he said. "It really doesn't surprise me at all."

Senator John Harris sat across the table from the other three men in the large conference room. They were all staring at him as if he'd lost his mind. He hated it whenever they stared at him like that.

Finally, one of the men, Senator Carl Booker, spoke. "I think you're taking all of this too personal, John."

"Because it *is* personal, Carl. Nedwyn Lansing and I have been at odds with each other since the first day we both arrived on Capitol Hill. The passage of that bill was important to me."

Matthew Williams, the oldest senator in the group spoke. "But it didn't pass, so I suggest you get over it. What you're proposing to do is crazy. I'm not all that fond of Lansing, none of us are, but I wouldn't deliberately do anything to destroy his political career."

"That's why you and I are different, Mat. I would destroy his career in a minute if I had the right ammunition. All I'm proposing is to get someone to dig into his past, just in case something is there. No one can be that squeaky clean. Even George Washington had skeletons in his closet."

"Forget it, John," Senator Paul Dunlap said. "If the media hasn't uncovered any dirt on Lansing, then there isn't any to be found."

The other men in the room nodded in full agreement.

Senator Harris fumed. "That's not necessarily true." One by one he looked in the eyes of everyone at the table. "No one has found out about that twenty-two-year old woman you've been two-timing your wife with for the past two years, Mat. Nor have they found out about your lovely teenage daughter's recent abortion, Paul. And last but not least, Carl, I really don't think anyone knows a thing about your son's drug addiction."

Senator Harris's eyes crinkled at the corners at the surprised look on each of the men's faces. He had just stated information they all thought no one knew. "And don't insult my intelligence by denying any of it. I have everything I need to prove otherwise."

"What do you want from us, Harris?" Dunlap asked in a voice with an edge to it. "It's getting late and I would like to make it home before midnight."

"I want all three of you to back me on this. Ruining Lansing has to be a group effort. And another thing, he has too many close friends who happen to be Fortune 500 CEOs. I find it hard to believe he's never accepted any type of kickback from any of them."

"I assume you're referring to Garwood Industries, Remington Oil, and Turner Broadcasting Corporation?" Carl said. "Everyone knows those three are loyal financial contributors to Lansing's campaign coffers."

"Yes."

"That can be explained," Paul replied. "Lansing and old man Garwood were friends since Garwood Industries opened their first Texas branch office. And since his grandfather's death, Kyle Garwood has maintained a close relationship with Lansing."

After taking a drink of water he continued, "As far as his association with S. T. Remington is concerned, it's my understanding they were roommates in college. And as for Ted Turner, they became good friends during the time Lansing was the mayor's assistant in Beaumont, Texas. He encouraged the school board to do an experiment using cable television as a teaching tool for elementary and secondary students. It was a project that proved to be very successful and got Turner Broadcasting much recognition."

"Besides," Mat contributed. "None of us can deny the fact that Lansing has done more for the interest of the oil and cattle industries than anyone in Congress. That's why he's always gotten such strong support from the oil companies and the cattlemen."

Senator Harris slammed his hand down on the table. "There has to be something in his past that will drop his popularity with the voters," he thundered. "And I plan on finding out what it is and destroy him the same way he destroyed my bill."

CHAPTER 5

"Clayton and Syneda. I don't believe it."

Justin Madaris shook his head as he whispered the words to his wife as she lay in his arms.

"They're the last two people likely to end up together. Who would have thought they would have stopped opposing each other long enough to get interested in each other," he added.

Clayton and Syneda had retired to their separate bedrooms, and Justin and Lorren had made the sofa into an extra bed.

"I can't believe Clayton," Lorren said tersely. A thundercloud of indignant frowns bunched her brows together. "The nerve of him hitting on Syneda."

Justin rolled his eyes heavenward. "Aren't you getting a bit carried away?"

Lorren lifted her head to glare down at her husband. "If I am, I have every right to. I don't want Clayton and Syneda involved with each other."

"Why?"

"He'll hurt her."

"Have you ever considered letting Syneda handle her own love life, Lorren? She's a grown woman, you know. Besides, don't you think you're being a little too hard on Clayton?"

"No. I love Clayton dearly, but he's a man who loves women. Lots of them. And I don't want him adding my best friend to his flock. Having a constant supply of willing women has spoiled Clayton. I know just how he operates, and I don't want him operating on Syneda."

Justin smiled. "Is that why you ignored his hints that we check into a hotel tonight?"

A satisfied glint appeared in Lorren's eyes. "You got that right. He was trying to get rid of us. As far as I'm concerned, we arrived right on time."

Justin laughed, pulling Lorren closer into his arms. His eyes glowed with amusement. "Clayton didn't think so."

"I'm sure he didn't. Especially when Syneda retired to her own bedroom."

"What happens when we leave the day after tomorrow?"

"Hopefully by then you'll have talked Clayton out of this foolishness."

"Me?"

"Yes, you." Lorren looked at her husband with appealing eyes. "You have to do something. You're his older brother. He might listen to you."

Justin laughed shortly and shrugged. "Lorren, I respect Clayton's privacy. Besides, it's none of my business and neither is it yours."

"But Syneda is my best—"

Justin didn't let her finish. "It isn't our business, Lorren," he repeated. "We should have enough faith in Clayton to believe he won't deliberately hurt Syneda."

He cupped his wife's chin with his hand and lifted her eyes to meet his. "Clayton loves you. He knows how close you and Syneda are. He won't ever do anything to ruin that."

Lorren took a deep breath. "I hope you're right Justin," she said softly in a voice that seemed to come from a long way off.

"I believe I am. Besides, I think you've over-looked one very important fact here."

"What?"

"One of the reasons Clayton and Syneda were never interested in each other was because neither was the other's type. Syneda is nothing like those women Clayton normally dates, flashy with no substance. She's an attractive, intelligent woman who has a lot going for her. I feel confident she'll be able to handle him."

Justin grinned. "In fact, you may be worried about the wrong person. I don't know if he realizes it yet, but I think Clayton has finally met his match. You just might want to take out the prayer book for Clayton."

"Where is everyone?"

Justin raised his head from reading the newspaper and met his brother's eyes. It didn't take much from Clayton's brooding expression to figure out he hadn't enjoyed sleeping in his bed alone.

"Lorren and Syneda aren't here."

"Where are they?"

"They went shopping."

"Shopping? That's crazy. Syneda and I went shopping a few days ago."

Justin chuckled. "Evidently like most women she enjoys it. Lorren said not to expect them back until dinner time. I guess we're stuck with each other until then."

Clayton gave his head a wry shake. "I could wring your wife's neck, Justin. She knew I was trying to get rid of the two of you last night, and she deliberately ignored my ploy. And now I have a feeling she's trying to keep Syneda from me today."

Justin smiled and shrugged his shoulders in mock resignation. "She feels Syneda needs protecting."

"Protecting?"

"Yes, protecting. Face it, Clayton, your reputation precedes you."

The two brothers stared at each other for a long time before Clayton finally looked away. He didn't need this, he told himself righteously. Why should he defend his actions to anyone, especially his family? He and Syneda were not teenagers, they were adults. They didn't need keepers, nor did they have to answer to anyone.

He let out a disgusted sigh before turning hard eyes to his brother. "I would never deliberately hurt Syneda, Justin."

"I know you wouldn't, Clayton."

A faint light appeared in the depths of Clayton's brown eyes. "Thanks," he said quietly. "I wish there was some way I could assure Lorren of that, but there isn't. Being attracted to each other was the last thing that Syneda and I planned on happening. It just did. The attraction became more than the two of us could handle last night."

"I gathered as much when I opened the door last night on you guys."

Clayton grinned. "Yeah, that was bad timing on your part. You and Lorren are welcomed to stay here for another day but then I want the two of you out of here. The last thing Syneda and I need is outside interference. We're going to enjoy the rest of our vacation in peace and quiet without you and Lorren acting as chaperones. Now with that out of the way, let's go grab some breakfast."

Justin chuckled. "I don't know if there's a need. You've just said a mouthful."

A spectacular view of the yacht harbor and intercoastal waterway was the setting for the Clam Shell Restaurant, a popular favorite with locals, yachtsmen and tourists. The restaurant was renowned for its luncheon specials, which were best enjoyed while sipping a cooling tropical drink.

Syneda and Lorren had chosen a table on the wooden deck that provided a breathtaking view of the Comachee Cove Yacht Harbor.

"Isn't the food terrific, Lorren? Clayton and I had lunch here a few days ago and—"

"Just what's going on with you and Clayton?" Lorren asked pointedly.

"What do you mean?" Syneda replied innocently.

"Don't act crazy, girlfriend. You know exactly what I mean. When Justin opened the door on the two of you last night, it was obvious we had interrupted something."

Syneda's lips broke into a wide grin. "Clayton and I could have made the same assessment about you and Justin."

"We are not discussing me and Justin. We're discussing you and Clayton."

Syneda sighed. "Clayton and I discovered that we're sexually attracted to each other, and both feel we should explore our attraction. There's nothing wrong with enjoying a sexual encounter for no reason beyond the physical pleasures it would bring."

Lorren didn't say anything for a few minutes, her expression was one of total shock and disbelief. Lately, Syneda's mood swings were extreme and unpredictable. "I don't believe what I'm hearing. You've never been a woman to let a man use her casually for a little quick, easy sex."

"And you think that's what he'll be doing?" Without giving Lorren a chance to reply, Syneda continued as her mouth curved into a smile. "Then there's no reason for me to feel guilty about using him as well."

For the first time since the conversation she had had with Justin the night before, Lorren gave serious thought to the possibility that Justin could be right. Her concern just might be directed at the wrong person. "What do you mean by that?"

Syneda leaned forward in her chair and met Lorren's leveled stare. "I've figured out what's been happening to me for the past few months."

"What?"

"I'm going through an emotional meltdown. Maybe it stems from the type of cases I've been handling lately or the fact that I'm approaching thirty in a couple of years. I don't know. All I know is that I'm sick and tired of being self-reliant, practical and levelheaded. This sister," she said, pointing at herself, "wants a new attitude."

"And you think messing around with Clayton is the answer?"

Syneda smiled. "No, but it's better than thinking seriously about getting my nose pierced, putting a tattoo somewhere on my body, or shaving my head."

Lorren couldn't help grinning. "Why not get married? You could have with Marcus. That's what he wanted."

"But that's not what I wanted. I don't love him. I'm not in love with any man, and I'm certainly not interested in getting married. I think of a wedding ring as a neon sign flashing the words, `you no longer have a life of your own.' "

"That's not true. Look at me and Justin, and Dex and Caitlin. No marriage is perfect, Syneda, and it sure doesn't make everything else in your life automatically fall into place. Nor is it a protection against career crises, economic disaster, or loneliness. But I wouldn't trade it for anything."

"Yeah, you say that now but I can remember a time when you wouldn't have. Your marriage to Scott was the pits."

"True, but it's the opposite with Justin. That just goes to show miracles can happen."

"But I don't want a miracle in my life, Lorren, nor do I need one. All I want out of life is happiness, namely mine. I don't want to be responsible for no one else's. Nor do I want a man to become my other half. I just want to become my entire whole, and I think I'll start with an affair."

Lorren sighed. "But why with Clayton?"

"Why not with Clayton? I like him, I trust him and I've recently discovered I'm attracted to him. Isn't that enough?"

"What do you think, Syneda? Will affairs be all you'll ever want?"

"Possibly."

"I don't believe this! You sound just like Clayton. His attitude on life seems to have rubbed off on you. I ought to say that the two of you deserve each other, but I can't. I want you to want more."

"But I can't allow myself to want more. Every time I feel myself wanting more, I remember Mama and how she died believing in a man who didn't come through for her or for me," Syneda replied quietly.

Lorren sighed deeply. She was among the few people who knew the situation regarding Syneda and her father. "All men aren't the same. For example, there's no comparison between Justin and Scott. One day you'll meet someone who's your soulmate, Syneda. Just like Adam was to Eve, like Ruby Dee is to Ozzie Davis, like—"

"Beauty was to the Beast?" Syneda cut in.

Lorren laughed. "Yes, just like Beauty was to the Beast. And like Prince Charming was to Cinderella, like—"

"I get the picture, Lorren."

"I hope you do, Syneda. I honestly hope you do."

Clayton glanced at his watch for perhaps the one hundredth time since he had awakened that morning to find Syneda gone. It was now four o'clock. Where were they? What he had told Justin earlier that day had been the truth. He could wring Lorren's neck.

He stood on the terrace drinking a glass of wine and staring moodily at the ocean. What would Syneda's attitude be toward him when she saw him again? Would she regret what had happened between them last night? Had Lorren convinced her she was making a mistake getting involved with him?

The sound of the doorbell interrupted his thoughts. Evidently Justin had returned. He had left a few hours ago to play a game of tennis with another physician he had met at lunch.

Leaving the terrace, he went to open the door.

"Telegram for Syneda Walters."

Clayton stared at the young man. "She's not here but I'll make sure she receives it," he said, taking the telegram and signing for it. He went into his pocket and handed the guy a bill that brought a bright smile to the his face.

"Thank you, sir!"

Clayton was staring blankly at the sealed telegram when the door opened again a few moments later. Lorren and Syneda walked in carrying a number of packages.

Clayton's eyes immediately met Syneda's. He was stunned by the rush of pleasure surging through him at the sight of her. His eyes wandered over her face for a long moment, and the slender hands holding the packages she placed on the sofa. She was wearing a printed romper and looked absolutely fantastic. The rare beauty of her sea-green eyes touched him. Her beauty was exquisite and overwhelming.

There was a noticeable pause in the room before Lorren cleared her throat. She couldn't help but pick up on the sexual magnetism radiating between Clayton and Syneda. At the moment, she wasn't quite sure which of the two individuals most needed her sympathy. "Hi, Clayton. Where's Justin?"

Clayton swallowed and forced his gaze from Syneda to his sister-in-law. All thoughts of wringing her neck were temporarily forgotten. "He's playing tennis with another doctor he met at lunch."

He then turned his sharp and assessing gaze back to Syneda. "How did shopping go?"

"It was okay," Syneda answered, almost unable to breathe. Clayton looked wonderful dressed in a pair of cutoff jeans and a tank top. He definitely had a monopoly on virility, she thought. His arresting good looks totally captivated her.

"I almost forgot. This came for you a few minutes ago," Clayton said.

Syneda forced her eyes from his to the item he was handing her. "A telegram?"

She tore into it and read it quickly. Regretful eyes met Clayton's. "It's from my firm. Something has come up and I have to get back to New York immediately."

"Why!" Clayton and Lorren exclaimed simultaneously.

"What's wrong?" Lorren asked as she threw her packages down next to Syneda's and gave her friend her absolute attention.

"A few weeks ago I was handling a case involving an abused wife. However, she wouldn't file for a divorce from her husband."

"Yes, I remember you mentioning it," Clayton replied, taking a step closer.

"She's been arrested."

"Why?"

"For shooting her husband. He's in critical condition."

"I don't understand," Lorren stated bemusedly. "Why would she be arrested? It was probably a case of self-defense."

"That has to be proven in a court of law," Clayton replied to Lorren's statement, taking the position of the attorney that he was.

"What does any of this have to do with you, Syneda?" he asked, his mouth set in a taut frown. "You're not a defense attorney."

"I know, but the woman asked for me and refuses to talk with anyone else. The firm has requested that I come back to New York as soon as possible," Syneda replied.

"But you're on vacation. Surely there's someone else who can help the woman until you return next week."

"Unfortunately there isn't. She feels comfortable with me. I have to go back." Syneda turned to Lorren. "Could you call the airlines for me and book me on the next available flight back to New York? There's a phone in the main office, which is located next to the tennis courts. I need to pack."

"Sure," Lorren replied and left immediately.

"I'll go back with you."

"That's not necessary, Clayton. You shouldn't ruin the rest of your vacation just because of me. Now if you'll excuse me, I really need to begin packing."

Syneda went into her bedroom leaving a disgusted Clayton standing in the middle of the floor.

A few minutes later, Clayton entered her bedroom. "Things aren't over between us, Syneda."

She looked up at him. "What do you mean?"

"I think you know the answer to that," he replied raspily. "Things can never go back to being the way they were between us—"

"Until we've satisfied this lust for each other that's wracking our bodies?"

Clayton took a step closer. "You think that's all it is?"

"Of course that's all it is. What else could it be? And I feel the best thing to do is to go ahead and get it out of our system."

Clayton's pulse raced. "What exactly are you suggesting?"

"Exactly what it sounds like."

Clayton raised a brow. "An affair?"

"Yes, an affair. A short, fulfilling, and mutually satisfying affair."

Clayton could not believe what he was hearing. Although he never had reason to inquire how serious they had been, he was well aware that since knowing her, she had been involved in a number of affairs. So why did her eagerness to engage in another surprise him? "Starting when?" he asked, studying her intently.

Syneda looked down at the bed. "Much to my regret, it has to be later. I have to return to New York."

Clayton couldn't shield the flints of desire and passion that shone in his eyes. "Can I visit you in New York?"

Syneda met his eyes. They touched her deeply. "Yes. You're welcome to come visit me anytime. You've always known that. Nothing has changed."

Clayton took a step closer. He took her hand in his. "Yes things have. My next visit will be in a whole new light, won't it?"

Syneda glanced down at the floor, deliberately avoiding his eyes. "Yes."

Clayton lifted her chin so their eyes could connect. "What about your concern regarding what the family thinks?"

Syneda hunched her shoulders. Deep down she knew that an involvement with Clayton was a bad idea. They were all wrong for each other but her mind was made up. What she had told Lorren at lunch was the truth. As far as she was concerned, she was going through changes in her life and needed something or someone to shake things up a bit, and Clayton would certainly do that.

Then she spoke softly. "Justin and Lorren already know what's going on, and they'll keep it to themselves. No one else has to know."

"Are you suggesting that we keep things a secret?"

Syneda nodded. "There's no reason for anyone else to know. It won't last that long anyway."

Clayton looked at her for a long while. "You sound so sure of that."

"I'm not entering into this relationship with any misconceptions, Clayton."

"Meaning?"

"I only want to finish what was started here. A serious relationship is the last thing you or I want."

Clayton pulled Syneda into his arms. "You think you know me rather well, don't you?" he asked in a husky voice. Cupping her chin in his hand, he tilted her head back and lowered his head to hers. When his mouth opened over hers, she welcomed it. She felt the probing of his tongue as it delved deep into the warmth of her mouth.

Her eyes fluttered shut as his tongue rubbed against hers, as their mouths sealed in a searing kiss.

Syneda's arms crept slowly around Clayton's neck as she strained toward him. A hot, heady rise of pleasure exploded deep within her, filling her with profound heat. And at the same time, a multitude of sensations coursed down her middle and her belly.

They were panting and breathless when Clayton slowly lifted his head. Syneda's lips were slightly swollen and her pupils were glazed with desire. She had the sexiest expression he'd ever seen, Clayton thought, gazing down at her. He then began wondering if a serious relationship was really, as she thought, the last thing he wanted.

CHAPTER 6

"I never did get a chance to thank you for coming back as soon as you did, Syneda. I hope I didn't ruin your vacation."

Syneda looked into the handsome face of the man sitting on the other side of her desk. Thomas Rackley, a widower in his early forties, was a well liked defense attorney who had begun working with the firm two years ago. She had often accompanied him to dinner and the theater until he began dropping hints of wanting a more serious relationship. To avoid the risk of hurting him by them becoming too involved, she had suggested that they begin seeing other people. Not too soon thereafter, she had begun dating Marcus.

"You didn't totally ruin my vacation." Syneda grinned. "But had it been anyone other than you, I would have given them hell."

Thomas let out a deep chuckle, fully believing she would have. Moments later his smile faded. "I ran into Marcus Capers at a baseball game while you were away. So I hope your friend didn't mind the interruption."

Syneda met his gaze. She knew the question that was on his mind. If he'd seen Marcus, it meant he knew they hadn't gone away together. He was curious to know if she had gone on vacation with a male or a female, but was too much of a gentleman to ask. She took a deep breath. It was time to bring to an end that part of her and Thomas's relationship forever. She didn't want him fostering any false hope; especially now since she was no longer dating Marcus.

They looked at each other for a long moment before Syneda answered. "He understood."

There was a pause in the room before Thomas replied. "I see."

Syneda decided to change subjects. "So how are things going with Mrs. Armstrong?" she asked quickly.

"Thanks to you, she has agreed to reveal the depth of her husband's cruelty. I believe once the prosecuting attorney reviews her case, the charges will be dropped. It was clearly a case of self-defense."

"And Dr. Armstrong?"

"His condition has changed from critical to stable. He'll live; however, he'll be getting quite a bit of bad publicity once the media gets a hold of what he's put his wife through.

"I'm just glad Mrs. Armstrong has finally realized she has other re-courses than remaining in a situation that has caused her to be painfully abused. No one should have to suffer the physical and emotional batter-ings she's gone through."

Thomas nodded in agreement. He continued to stare at her. "I hope he's what you want, Syneda. You deserve to be happy," he said, switching back to their earlier conversation.

Syneda's thoughts immediately fell on Clayton. She had no doubt he would certainly rock her world a bit. "I believe he is, and thanks, you've been a good friend."

Thomas looked at her. His eyes compelling. "I wanted to be more."

"I know, but it wouldn't have worked out between us."

"Because of our ages?"

Syneda shook her head. Although he was forty-three to her twenty-eight, their ages had never been an issue with her. "No, it wasn't that. I'm just not ready for what you want. I doubt if I ever will be. The love and marriage scene aren't for me."

He stood and held out his hand to her. "If you ever need a friend, I'm here for you."

Syneda accepted his hand and the offer of friendship that came with it. "Thanks, Thomas. I'll remember that."

When Syneda returned to her office from lunch, Joanna looked up from her desk. Her blue eyes were dazzling with merriment. "There was a delivery for you while you were out."

"Oh?" Syneda asked, pushing open the door to her office. The sight awaiting her was breathtaking. Four huge vases filled with roses sat in the middle of her desk. Speechless, she entered her office. The rose fra-grance was totally absorbed in the room.

"They're beautiful, aren't they?" Joanna asked, gazing at the four dozen peach-colored roses. "I wonder who sent them."

Quickly recovering from her initial shock, Syneda took in a deep breath. She hoped they weren't from Marcus.

"I placed the card on your desk next to your calendar."

"Thanks, Joanna. Please let Mr. Dickerson know I've returned, and I'm free to go over the Franklin case now."

Recognizing a dismissal, Joanna nodded and closed the door behind her.

Syneda walked over to her desk, picked up the envelope and pulled out the card. Her hand shook when she read the message inside. She couldn't help the smile that touched her lips nor could she prevent her heartbeat from quickening.

The card read . . . *A dozen roses for each day we spent together. Saint Augustine wasn't the same without you.* It was signed Clayton.

"Clayton." Syneda whispered the name as she leaned against the corner of her desk to slow down her breathing. Marcus hadn't sent the flowers as she had assumed. They had come from Clayton.

Nervously thumbing through the personal directory on her desk she located the numbers of her search. She picked up the phone and began dialing.

"Clayton Madaris's office."

"Yes, may I speak with Mr. Madaris, please?"

The woman's response was pleasant and businesslike. "I'm sorry but Mr. Madaris is unavailable. Would you like to leave a message?"

"Yes, please tell him Syneda Walters called."

"Oh, Ms. Walters. Mr. Madaris left instructions to put you through should you call. Please hold for a minute."

The secretary clicked off the line and Syneda nervously toyed with the telephone cord while waiting for Clayton to come to the phone.

"Syneda?" Clayton asked coming on the line.

Tremors raced through Syneda at the deep masculine sound of her name from Clayton's lips. Her hands on the telephone tightened as blood coursed hotly through her veins. Even over the telephone, he was reaching out to her and the sensations were like a soft caress. She tried to sound natural when she replied. "Yes, Clayton. The flowers are beautiful. You shouldn't have."

"I couldn't help myself," he said huskily. I meant what I said on the card. I want to see you, Syneda. Soon. This weekend. Is that possible?"

Syneda took a deep breath. "Yes."

"How about if I fly in on Friday afternoon?"

A lump formed in Syneda's throat. The silkiness of his suggestion touched her everywhere. "I'd like that."

There was a slight pause before he asked. "Are you sure?"

"Yes, I'm sure."

Another pause. "Do you want to go out to dinner when I get there?" he asked.

"If you'd like. Or we can have something delivered. Let's decide when you get here."

"Okay. I'll see you on Friday."
"Until then, Clayton."
"Yes, until then."

Clayton hung up the phone and glanced down at the legal brief he'd been working on before Syneda's call. He pushed it aside as he sat back in his chair.

He hadn't realized he'd been holding his breath until the plans had been finalized for his visit to see her. He had been in knots all week at the thought that after returning to New York, she would have had second thoughts about continuing what they had started in Saint Augustine.

He shifted uneasily in his chair wondering what had actually happened to bring him to such a state over a woman. There had never been a time when a woman had consumed his every thought. There were too many females out there to get hung-up on just one. Women had a way of making the most sensible man act foolish. So what in the world was happening to him?

After Justin and Lorren had left to return to Texas, he had tried resting, relaxing and enjoying his time alone. But he hadn't been able to do any of those things. Instead, he had thought of Syneda. He had spent an uncomfortable amount of time thinking about her and had begun feeling resentful. Resentful that any woman's overpowering allure could bring forth such a need in him.

So he had tried not to think about needing her, and wanting her. He had even made up his mind not to contact her when he returned to Texas from Florida. But something had happened to him that he hadn't counted on, something that had gone beyond any rational thought that he could have ever imagined. It was something that—after taking more showers than he could count—still had him mystified until he had finally faced the truth. Syneda had been able to do something no other woman had done. She had somehow exposed deep feelings within him.

Before the trip to Florida, his relationships with women had been uncomplicated. Over the years, he had dated a number of incredibly attractive women, but never did one have him thinking more about passion than winning court cases. Why was this thing with Syneda, of all people, different?

Why had kissing and touching her caused tremors deep within his body days after they'd parted? He shook his head thinking how in the last couple of days he'd lain in bed thinking about her and wanting her. It didn't take much for him to close his eyes and visualize her in every outfit she'd worn while they were in Florida. Right at this very moment, he would do just about anything to have her in his arms, with her soft, warm body pressed close to his.

He took a deep breath. It was an effort to breathe. A first for him. His features tightened at the thought that he was losing control. Again.

Clayton stood and moved to one of the windows facing downtown Houston. The only excuse he could come up with for his reactions was that it had been some time, sixty-four days to be exact, since he'd slept with a woman. Why was he putting himself through unnecessary misery? All he had to do was pick up the phone. He knew a number of women who'd be more than willing to take care of his needs. But for some strange reason not just any woman would do.

He wanted Syneda.

He again shook his head. He hoped Syneda was right when she said the two of them were dealing strictly with a case of lust. Pure and simple. A deep-throated sigh escaped him. He had a feeling anything involving Syneda wouldn't be pure and simple. And he had a sinking feeling that no matter what happened between them this weekend, his life would never be the same.

He frowned. That thought bothered him more than anything.

Later that day, Syneda sat at her desk going over her notes from her last appointment. Margie Sessions wanted a divorce from her husband of thirty-four years, a husband she claimed had been unfaithful.

Although the woman had tried not to show it, it was obvious she was deeply hurt. The pain was evident in her eyes, her speech, and in the way she had paced the room for nearly an hour while providing an account of how she had discovered her husband's infidelity.

Listening attentively while observing the woman, Syneda also found it blatantly obvious that even after discovering his unfaithfulness, the woman was still very much in love with the man.

Syneda had convinced the woman to think things through before making any hasty decisions. "If you decide to go through with this," she'd told her, "I hope you're prepared for the emotional pain you'll have to endure. That pain may be far worse than what you're going through now; although you may feel nothing is worse than finding out your husband has been unfaithful to you. The two of you share three children and six grandchildren, not to mention a wealth of cherished good memories."

"Are you saying I should just forget what he did? That I should let him get away with it and do nothing?"

"No, Mrs. Sessions, that's not what I'm saying. I just want you to be sure that you're ready to deal with the emotional turmoil this divorce may cause you. I have no qualms about representing you. I'm tough, and I fight hard for my clients. But there are some things you need to think about. During the years of your marriage, the two of you have accumulated a lot of possessions, so there's also the physical settlement to deal with. However, as your attorney I have a moral obligation to advise you to try and salvage your marriage before thinking of ending it."

"There's nothing to think about. I can't remain married to him. I can't stop loving him, but I'll never trust him again. A marriage can't survive without trust, Ms. Walters."

Margie Sessions's story wasn't a new one. Syneda had heard similar ones during the years since she had begun practicing family law. The anger, the hurt, the sense of betrayal, and the need for revenge were emotions most of her clients wanting divorces encountered.

Syneda had just reached for a small recorder to dictate her office notes when the buzzer sounded on her desk. "Yes, Joanna, what is it?"

"You have a call from Lorren Madaris."

"Please put her through."

A few seconds later she heard Lorren's voice, "Syneda?"

Syneda smiled. "Lorren. How are you?"

"I'm fine. I went to the doctor today and he said everything is okay."

"You mean Justin isn't going to deliver this baby? I thought he did a great job with Justina."

Lorren giggled. "Be sure to tell him that when you see him again. He said delivering Justina aged him about twenty years."

Syneda grinned. "So what do you want this time, a girl or a boy?"

"It doesn't matter. We have both already, so whatever we're having this time is fine with us."

Syneda sighed. She was completely elated with her friend's happiness.

"Syneda, have you talked to Clayton lately?"

Syneda tried detecting censure in Lorren's voice and didn't note any. "Yes, I spoke with him earlier today. He's flying in this weekend."

"So you haven't changed your mind about what we talked about in Saint Augustine?"

"No, I haven't."

There was a slight pause. "Promise me you'll take care of yourself."

"Lorren, lighten up. Clayton and I are two adults who can handle things. We're having a weekend fling. Nothing more. I'll be fine."

Braxter Montgomery saw the woman across the parking lot as she raised the hood of her car. Being the only son of a single mother and the brother of two younger sisters, he believed in assisting women in distress and began walking toward her.

Only after he had gotten a few feet away from her did Braxton discover he'd suddenly forgotten how to breathe. The woman, whose age appeared to be around twenty-five or twenty-six, was gorgeous.

"Do you need any assistance?" He finally found his voice to ask. His eyes scanned her slender figure before glancing under the raised hood of her car. She glanced up from her close study of her car's engine and smiled beautiful dark eyes at him.

"I think so. My car won't start. Do you know anything about cars, Mr. . . . ?" She glanced at the identification badge he wore on his suit. "Mr. Montgomery?"

He smiled. "A little. Let me take a look." Handing her his jacket and brief-case, he began rolling up his sleeves. "That is, if you don't mind, Ms. . . . ?"

"Rogers," she supplied, shaking his hand. "Celeste Rogers."

"And Ms. Rogers, do you work around here?" Braxter asked. His tone was polite as he began fiddling with some of the equipment under her car's hood. He couldn't help noticing she wasn't wearing a wedding ring.

"No, I don't work around here but a majority of my clientele do," she said, glancing at the Capitol Building in the background. "I own a travel agency and today is my day for deliveries." She looked down at her car and frowned. "At least it was until my car decided to give out on me."

Braxter nodded. "Now, Ms. Rogers, you can try the ignition."

She smiled. "Please call me, Celeste."

"Celeste," he said, liking the way the name sounded on his lips. "And I'm Braxter."

"All right." She walked around and slid into the car's seat. She smiled broadly when the car's engine roared to life. Getting out of the car she went back to where he stood, she smiled at him. "It's working again. What did you do?"

"It was just your distributor cap. It wasn't tightened enough." The ex-pression on her face told him that like most women, she knew nothing about what went on under the hood of a car.

"Well, whatever it was, I really appreciate you taking the time to help. How much do I owe you, Braxter?"

He checked his watch. "Nothing, but how about lunch? There's a great Chinese restaurant a few blocks from here. That is, if you like Chinese."

She hesitated a moment before answering. "I love Chinese and lunch sounds wonderful."

"Great, we can drive over in my car."

She shook her head. "I prefer if you lead in your car. I'll follow in mine."

"Okay." Braxter said smiling. He wasn't the least offended that she'd graciously refused his offer to ride to the restaurant with him. Evidently, she was a cautious woman by nature. He liked that.

Celeste watched the handsome man walk off, heading back toward his parked car. She then got into hers. As she followed him out of the park-ing lot, she picked up her cellular phone and punched in a few numbers. She waited patiently for the voice on the other end before saying, "Yes, this is Celeste." Her lips formed in a faint, victorious grin. "I've made my connection."

CHAPTER 7

Syneda glanced around her living room, nervously gnawing at her bottom lip. Clayton was to arrive any minute.

For the first time since her decision to have this weekend interlude with him, she was beginning to feel uncertain and apprehensive. Unnerved by those feelings, and unsettled by the novelty of the actions she was about to take, she uncomfortably ran a hand through her hair.

At the sound of the doorbell, she hesitated briefly before turning toward the door. Drawing in a deep breath, she made an effort to maintain her composure. Sharp needles of sexual excitement and anticipation pricked every nerve in her body. "Yes?"

"It's Clayton."

She slowly opened the door and smiled. "Hello."

Clayton smiled back at her. "Hello, yourself. May I come in?"

"Sure." Syneda couldn't help noticing how his dark form was silhouetted by the dim lighting flowing through the entrance foyer. Although she couldn't see his features clearly, she could tell he was dressed in a dark suit and white dress shirt. He must have left the office and gone directly to the airport, she thought, moving aside.

Clayton stepped inside the apartment. After placing his traveling bag down, he closed the door behind him. He stared at Syneda, suddenly realizing just how much he had missed her since she'd left him in Florida. He felt an overwhelming joy at seeing her again.

He was having a difficult time assimilating what he was feeling as he continued to stare at her. Air became trapped in his lungs, and his heart pounded in his chest. His mind tried reminding him, uncomfortably, that no woman had ever had this sort of effect on him. No woman had ever made him feel such joy, such desperation . . . and such panic.

A part of him—that part that had always been in full control where women were concerned—was wavering under the sea-green gaze that held him captive.

And that thought was frightening.

He suddenly felt a strong urge to protect himself by turning and walking back out of the door, and doing an easy escape before he got himself into something too deep, something he wasn't prepared for. But for the life of him, he couldn't make the move to retreat.

"Clayton? Are you okay?"

The sound of Syneda's voice was soft, smooth, sexy and concerned. Reaching out, he gently pulled her into his arms. "Yes, I'm fine," he said, lowering his mouth to hers.

Their contact was electric as Clayton ground his lips against hers with a hunger that could not be denied. Syneda opened her mouth to his immediately. Heat rose in her body and a tightening started in the pit of her stomach. She trembled all over, unable to believe what was happening between them. It had not just been Florida after all, because even here in smog-filled New York, the sexual chemistry between them was even greater than before. Breath rushed in and out of her lungs and she couldn't help wondering why no man before Clayton had ever made this kind of passion rise so quickly within her. It made her become urgent, wanting to hold back nothing, and lose control.

Clayton slowly raised his head and met dazed sea-green eyes. "You taste good," he whispered hoarsely against her lips. "I enjoy kissing you."

Syneda stared up into the dark eyes gazing down at her. The electric brown eyes were glowing like black fire. "You taste pretty good yourself. And I like kissing you, too."

Clayton grinned and kissed her again, long, deep, and hard. His hand lightly cupped her bottom. Syneda could feel the muscles in her body come alive with his intimate touch and she pressed herself closer to him. The powerful muscular build of his shoulders felt heavenly beneath her hands as he pulled her even closer.

He reluctantly broke off the kiss. His breathing unsteady. "What's planned for this weekend?" he asked huskily, planting butterfly kisses against the corners of her mouth.

He felt her facial grin underneath his lips. "If you don't know, I'm not telling."

Clayton's chuckle echoed deep in his chest where Syneda placed her head. He tightened his arms around her. "So, what's first?" he asked.

Syneda lifted her head and looked up at him. "First, we talk."

Clayton bent down and brushed his lips against hers. "Talk about what?"

"Rules."

He raised his head and looked down at her. "Rules? What rules?"

She smiled at him. "Rules I'm sure you've followed countless times and won't have any problems not breaking. In fact, I bet they're similar to the ones you've probably used in your relationships."

"What are they?"

Her eyes, he noticed, suddenly became set beneath a high, serious brow. However, she still managed to contain her smile. "The first and most important one being that we won't expect anything beyond what we'll share this weekend. And second, we must never, ever let ourselves think that what we're sharing is in any way, shape, form, or fashion associated with love."

She gave him a fierce hug. "See there, I told you they were probably similar to yours."

Clayton flinched. She was right, they were like some of his own rules. They were rules that had always governed his relationships with women and for the first time the thought of those rules bothered him.

"That's why," she continued, "I'm so excited about this weekend. For once I can let myself go without worrying."

He frowned. "Worrying about what?"

"About someone wanting more than I could possibly give, and trying to keep him at arm's length. I know how you feel about love and commitment. You don't want them any more than I do."

A tender smile danced across Syneda's lips. "And there's something else I guess I should tell you . . . about me."

"And just what could that be?" he asked. Taking her hand he led her toward the sofa. She only presented him with a surprisingly relaxed smile when he sat down and pulled her in his lap.

"It's nothing that's a big deal, but it's something I think you should know."

He lifted his brow. Despite her smile, he had a feeling there was something mysterious lurking deep in the back of the sea-green eyes staring back at him. "What is it?"

"I've never made love with a man before."

"What!"

If Syneda hadn't caught hold of the sofa, she would have fallen on the floor when Clayton unexpectedly jumped out of his seat.

"What do you mean you've never slept with a man before? That's stupid!"

Syneda stood then. The smile on her face was replaced with an angry frown. "What's stupid?"

"The notion that you're a virgin. That's impossible."

"And just why is it impossible?"

Clayton's eyes swept over Syneda as he tried coming to grips with what she was telling him. She stood before him as he'd seen her many times, with her hands on her hips, facing him squarely, ready to do battle. He met her glare head-on. He could believe a lot of things, but the thought that she had never slept with a man before wasn't one of them.

"I'm waiting for an answer, Madaris. Are you implying that all the time you've known me, you just assumed I've lived the life of some kind of slut?"

Clayton rolled his eyes heavenward. "I wasn't insinuating anything. All I'm saying is that you of all people would be the least likely candidate for a virgin." Clayton frowned wondering if the words he'd just spoken to clear himself had done more damage than good.

"What I mean," he said quickly, "is that you're twenty-eight—for heaven's sake, you live by yourself, you're a career woman, a professional. You went to college, and I'm sure you dated while you were there. You date men now, and you're a very sexy woman. Besides that, you have modern ideals."

Syneda shook her head at the mislogic in Clayton's way of thinking. "Let's get one thing straight. Having modern ideals doesn't mean you automatically toss aside old values. I control my own destiny and I've never depended on the smooth talk of some man to guide me. I make my own decisions when it concerns my body. I never felt compelled to give myself to a man to prove anything. And why do women have to prove anything anyway? Why can't a man do the proving for a change?"

Clayton folded his arms across his chest and leaned against a wall. He knew Syneda was on a roll. He glanced around the room for signs of her soap box.

"And another thing," she continued. "Most women have the good sense to know most lines men are feeding them are usually a bunch of bull. But unfortunately, others are too flattered or too naive to figure it out, and that mistake is many of their downfalls. I could provide you with statistics on the number of women having babies out of wedlock. And those smooth-talking, irresponsible men, who refuse to claim their role as fathers, have moved on to hit some other unsuspecting female with the same line."

"Syneda—"

"No, Madaris, you started this so let me wrap it up." She came to stand in front of him. "And age has nothing to do with it. Neither does occupation or status in life. So what if I'm a single, twenty-eight-year-old attorney living on my own. That doesn't necessarily mean I have loose morals. What law says I have to sleep with any man I date? People shouldn't get intimately involved with each other until they're ready, both physically and mentally."

Clayton grabbed Syneda's hand. "I apologize if I offended you, I didn't mean to. It's just hard to believe."

When her frown darkened he added, "However, I do believe you. But what about that guy you recently broke up with? The one you had been dating for the past six or seven months."

Syneda yanked away from his grasp. "What about him?"

"Wasn't he special to you? Didn't the two of you ever want to . . . you know?"

"My relationship with Marcus is not open for discussion. All you need to know is that there has never been a special man in my life. And as far as me sleeping with him, I didn't want to and he respected my decision."

"The man was a fool. There's no way in hell you would have been my woman and not shared my bed."

"Then it's a good thing I'm not your woman, Madaris. So you can take your sexist way of thinking right back to Texas."

When she made a move to walk away, Clayton reached out and gently brought her against him. "Let me go, Clayton."

"Not on your life." He calmed her struggling and pulled her against him, holding her tight.

When he bent down and kissed her, she reluctantly returned it. "I want you to leave, Clayton," she said unconvincingly between their kisses.

"I'm staying, Syneda."

He picked her up into his arms and carried her back to the sofa. Sitting down, he again placed her in his lap and continued kissing her.

"Stay then," she muttered against his moist lips. "Just as long as you know I'm mad."

"Stay mad," he responded, against the angry quiver he felt while tasting her bottom lip. He lifted his head and looked down at her. "Nothing brings out passion quicker than anger."

"Then this weekend should be rather interesting since we argue most of the time, Madaris."

He traced the line of her lips with his finger. "Not this weekend," he replied easily. "For the next two days, we're going to spend time doing something else. We'll argue the next weekend we spend together."

Syneda gazed up at him, wanting to remind him that this would be their only weekend together. Instead, she pulled his face down and kissed him long and deeply.

Clayton stood with her in his arms and carried her to the bedroom. Once there he gently placed her on the bed. The colorful bedcover was pulled back invitingly. He stood back to look down at her.

"I'm not a very good hostess. I didn't even offer you a drink," Syneda said silkily.

"You offered me something a whole lot better and definitely more precious."

"What?"

"Yourself."

His words made what little control Syneda had slip even further. It was evident that he wanted her. His body was growing hard with desire. He reached down and drew her up slowly toward him. His lips touched hers lightly at first, nibbling at her mouth softly.

Syneda moaned as she opened her mouth fully to him and tightened her arms around his neck. Her tongue slipped into his mouth and met his, returning his kiss with an intensity and hunger that he absorbed.

Syneda, Clayton discovered, had an intensely passionate nature and it set him on fire. A tremor inside him heated his thighs and groin. Pulling her into his arms, he ran his hands over the slender curves of her body through her clothes, bestowing kisses to her that were more hot and demanding than any of his others had been.

Still holding her, he swept back the bedcovers with a one-handed motion, and placed her on the mauve-colored sheet, gently coming down on top of her. They kissed again. No words needed to be spoken.

Syneda clung to Clayton, kissing him with as much hunger as he was kissing her. Everything was swept from her mind except him and how he was making her feel.

Clayton was driven by a need to become a part of her. He undressed her quickly, removing every stitch of her clothing. When she lay unclothed before him, he let his hands glide over her body to the slender curves of it.

Syneda's breath caught. She closed her eyes. A flash of blazing heat roared within her. "Clayton." She whispered his name in a yearning urgency.

"I'm here baby. The only place I'm going is inside of you."

His words made her sizzle. She reached up and pulled his head down to her, capturing his mouth with hers. She conveyed to him in her kiss just how much she wanted him.

Clayton's breath grew ragged. He felt possessive, protective, and vulnerable. Those feelings were strange to him, but for some reason, quickly acceptable. With their mouths still joined, he somehow managed to unbutton his shirt. However, he had to break their kiss to completely remove it.

"Clayton, please," Syneda pleaded. She wanted him. She wanted his hands on her, she wanted his kisses.

"Just a second sweetheart," he breathed against her neck as he tugged on the belt to his pants with shaking hands. He removed the foil packet from his pocket. He intended to take every precaution to keep her safe.

Moments later Syneda gazed at the magnificent nude male body before her. "You're beautiful, Clayton."

He grinned broadly, rejoining her in bed. "Thank you. You're beautiful, too."

Syneda smiled. She felt neither shy nor ashamed with Clayton, just a sense of wanting and readiness. What she was about to share with him somehow felt right. It felt like this was how it was supposed to be.

She caught her breath when she felt his lips open against her skin as he placed kisses over her body.

"Sweet. You taste very sweet," he whispered. His hand began moving slowly up her hips, tenderly stroking her bare skin. She thought she would go up in flames when his hands moved upward, his touch lingering just below her breasts.

Syneda arched her back, welcoming the feel of his hands on her, feeling her body's response to him. She searched for words to describe how she felt but couldn't come up with any. Nothing had ever felt like this before. When he began stroking her breasts, a moan of pleasure escaped her followed by the words, "I want you, Clayton."

Her words inflamed him. Instinctively he ground his hips against her, feeling himself grow harder, heavier, less in control. He willed himself to hang on. He wanted their first time together to be special.

Desire, deeper than he'd ever known before tore through him. He couldn't last much longer. He lowered his head and let his lips take hers with an all-consuming hunger. Her taste filled him completely. He wanted this woman and it wasn't just due to a physical need. He felt an even stronger need, one he had never felt before in his life. It was the need a man had to bind a woman to him forever.

He raised his head slightly and looked deeply into her eyes, wondering why he felt this way, and why with this woman. Some emotion he had never felt before coursed through his entire body. Shivers passed through him when he leaned down and kissed her again. It was a surprisingly gentle kiss as his lips brushed lightly over hers. Then he lifted his head and their eyes met once more.

"Syneda, are you sure?"

Syneda looked up at him in a passion-filled state. She heard his words. His voice was a mere whisper but his features were as serious as the question he was asking her again.

"Are you sure about this, Syneda?"

She met his gaze, fully understanding what he was asking her. If she had any apprehensions about what they were about to do, he was giving her the opportunity to stop things from going any further. For them to go beyond the bounds of friends to become lovers would be a mutual decision.

She had no apprehensions. Maybe it was because of the tenderness she saw in the dark brown eyes looking down at her, or the feel of the light strokes his fingers were tracing from her throat to her breast, and the feel of the heat of him pressed against her. And when she felt his hand dip low to touch her stomach, she thought her breathing had stopped.

She was lost.

A part of her, a part she had never shared with any man was taking over. It was that part she seldom allowed to surface. It was a part of her that up until now, had kept her from losing all concept of reason and logic. But now she felt vulnerable to the man who held her in his arms. She was steadily losing control of her senses and was rapidly spiraling beyond what she had the ability to contain.

She couldn't stop herself from cupping his face in her hands and saying. "I'm sure, Clayton. Very sure."

As if he'd been waiting to hear her say those words, Clayton crushed her to him in a torrid kiss at the same time he joined their bodies as one, making Syneda totally aware of the heat of him deep within her. He stopped moving, giving her body time to adjust to his.

Moments later, Clayton moved again and Syneda gave a sharp intake of breath. She reveled in the fullness of him inside her, filling an emptiness she'd just discovered existed. She couldn't help giving herself up to the enthralling sensuality flowing between them.

The ultimate pleasure of their lovemaking exploded, wrapping them in a delicious convulsion of ecstasy. The long, shattering release carried them to the heights of sensuous splendor where they were somehow united in body, soul, and spirit.

It was a long time before either of them could move. They lay together completely depleted of strength.

"Clayton," Syneda whispered drowsily. Her body was totally satiated. She wanted to do nothing but sleep. However, it appeared Clayton had other ideas. She felt his strong hands pull her closer to him. She felt his fingers as they began to trace lightly over her body. She felt the hardness of him pressing against her.

He was ready again.

She wondered how on earth such a degree of sensuality and passion could exist between two people. He had already taken her to the peak of sexual pleasure. Surely, something that strong, potent, and powerful could not be repeated. At least not this soon.

Syneda tuned out her thoughts when she felt his hand touch her intimately. She automatically began responding, giving herself up to the luscious waves of pleasure rippling through her all over again.

Clayton only paused briefly in his ministrations to protect her again before sheathing himself deep inside her.

Syneda sighed heavily as her body matched the primitive sensual rhythm of his. Soon after, once again together, they flowed together in a sensuous haze of passioned fulfillment.

Hours later, Syneda's last thought before sleep overtook her was that it could be repeated. Several times.

Clayton's chest expanded as he drew in a deep breath. Never before had he experienced anything liked he'd done tonight with Syneda. He tilted his head back to watch her sleep. Her hair fell like a silky curtain on either side of her face, and she wore such a peaceful and serene look.

He gathered her closer to him. From the time he had begun high school, women had always been readily available to him. And like most men, he appreciated them, desired them and enjoyed them. But never until tonight had he actually loved one.

Oh, God he loved her!

That sudden realization settled on him with the weight of a ton of bricks, and it scared the hell out of him. He probably would have bolted out of bed right then and there if Syneda had not been sound asleep in his arms. Instead he looked down at Syneda, really looked at her before pressing his head back against the pillow and closing his eyes. *What in the world had he gotten himself into?*

Clayton released a deep sigh as he held Syneda even closer, lightly caressing her back and shoulders. He suddenly understood as he had never understood before. There could be no other explanation for what he had been feeling since he had seen her that morning walking on the beach, and the jealousy, possessiveness, wanting, and need he'd been experiencing ever since. And it had nothing to do with lust. He'd been there, he'd done that. What he was feeling now was totally different. What he felt for Syneda went a lot deeper than just the physical relationship they had just shared. He loved her. There could be no other explanation for what he was feeling at this very minute. He slowly opened his eyes.

A part of him still wanted to run for cover and deny the strong emotions he felt. That was the part of him that had been a bachelor all of his life and had been quite proud of that status. But another part of him, the part that recently had had him subconsciously longing for something more, acknowledged easy acceptance of the fact that for the first time in his life he had actually made love with a woman. There was an astounding difference in having sex with a woman and making love to one.

Tonight he had made love to Syneda. Every movement of his body, every touch he had bestowed upon her, and every kiss he had given her had conveyed the words his lips had not spoken. There was no way he could deny that he loved her.

He didn't fully understand how it had happened and why it had happened. All he knew was that it had happened. Somehow, once they had gotten to Florida, he had begun to stop thinking of her as just a good friend and an antagonist. He'd begun regarding her as a very desirable woman. He had appreciated her fun-loving nature, her intelligence and sensitivity.

He shook his head and grinned ruefully, wondering how on earth would he survive a relationship with Syneda. She was definitely a handful. She could be outright stubborn at times, temperamental and too outspoken. He would even conclude that she was somewhat of a female chauvinist. But one thing was for certain, a life with her would never, ever be boring.

A smile touched Clayton's lips at the thought that Syneda was now his. He knew he would have to give her plenty of time to adjust to the notion that she belonged to anyone but herself. But he was willing to give her all the time she needed because he had no intentions of ever letting her go.

CHAPTER 8

A slow, lazy smile spread across Syneda's face when she felt the warmth of Clayton's lips near her ear. "It's morning," he whispered.

She opened one eye and peered up at him. He was standing next to the bed leaning over her. And from the casual way he was dressed, she could only assume he'd been up for some time. "I hate morning people Clayton. Don't you believe in sleeping late?"

"I'm usually up before the crack of dawn every day, including Saturdays," he said, sitting on the bed beside her. "But I would not have had any problems staying in bed late this morning," he added, his meaning clear. "None-what-so-ever." He leaned down and kissed her. "Are you ready to get up now?"

Syneda closed her eyes and snuggled deeper under the covers. "No! And I forgot to mention rule number three."

"Which is?"

"Don't ever wake me up on Saturdays before nine o'clock."

"It's nine-fifteen."

"Then don't ever wake me on Saturdays before ten."

Clayton laughed. "I admire a woman who's flexible only when it suits her."

Syneda began to turn away from him but Clayton touched his lips to her shoulder. "I'm serving breakfast at ten."

She opened her eyes. A frown lowered her dark eyebrows. "Breakfast? There's nothing here to eat for breakfast."

Clayton stood. "So I noticed. I walked down to that deli on the corner and grabbed us something. See you at ten." He turned and walked out of the bedroom.

Clayton had no trouble finding his way around Syneda's kitchen. There wasn't much to it; at least in the way of supplies. It was one his father would refer to as an unstocked kitchen. During his search, he'd been unable to find any dishes, glasses or silverware. He wondered if that meant she dined out every day.

"What are you looking for?"

Clayton looked up. Syneda was leaning against the door frame wearing nothing but his dress shirt. The shirt hit her midthigh and she looked very sexy in it.

They stared at each other for a long, silent moment, and he knew her thoughts were probably similar to his. He couldn't help but remember them together, wrapped in each other's arms last night.

"You're late. It's almost ten-thirty," Clayton finally said, breaking the silence. Didn't she know what seeing her dressed in his shirt was doing to him? The only reason he had gotten up and left her alone in bed was to give her and her body a break. They had made love through most of the night. The more he was around her, the more he wanted her. He couldn't seem to keep his hands off her.

Syneda laughed softly. "Better late than never. Now what were you looking for?"

"Place settings."

"Oh. Everything's in the dishwasher."

Clayton moved to the dishwasher and opened it. He then turned and raised a brow at her. "Saving space?"

"What do you mean?" Syneda came into the kitchen and sat down at the table.

Clayton couldn't help noticing how the shirt had ridden higher when she'd sat down, exposing one luscious looking bare thigh. He tore his gaze away from her thigh and back up to her face. "A month's supply of place settings are in your dishwasher."

Syneda shrugged. "They're clean, aren't they?"

Clayton nodded. "Yes, they're clean. But don't you put your dishes away in the cabinets after they're washed?"

"No. But I suppose you do."

"Yes."

Syneda's lips tightened and she glared at him. "Well, I don't. I see no sense in going to all that trouble when I'll be using them again. So don't start in on me, Madaris."

Clayton grinned. "Are we about to get into an argument?"

"If you start it, I'll sure enough finish it for you," she said, giving him a look that said she meant business.

"Does that goes for anything else I start?" he asked in a challenging voice, walking toward her.

Syneda stood and met his gaze. "Just try me."

Clayton looked at her, his dark eyes thoughtful. He had one hell of a woman on his hands. She was full of fire, and he was determined to make sure her fire burned just for him. He swept her into his arms. "You're on."

She glowered up at him. "You have a one-track mind, Madaris. I wasn't talking about this and you know it. And what about breakfast?"

He smiled down at her. "We'll have it in bed."

So much for wanting to do the right thing and leave her alone for a while, Clayton thought, snuggling closer to the woman in his arms. He and Syneda were two strong, stubborn, argumentative people who were accustomed to having their own way. It seemed it was only while in the throes of heated passion, they were totally and completely of one accord.

He gathered her closer to him. Even while she slept, his hands continued to caress her. He would never get tired of touching her.

He glanced at the clock. It was past noon. They hadn't eaten breakfast yet, but during the past couple of hours neither of them had cared. They'd been too busy satisfying another type of hunger.

A frown lit his brow. Syneda was turning into a sort of a mystery. She was definitely full of surprises. There were some things about her that he didn't understand; things that didn't make sense. Like the spiel she'd given him about why she'd remained a virgin. Had she been talking for Syneda or was she the spokesperson for someone else? Had some man once fed her or someone she'd cared for a line they had believed? And then there was the question that he had pondered since their trip to Florida. Who was the man responsible for her never wanting to love again?

He wrapped his arms around Syneda. She belonged to him now. She was his. And he would always see to her happiness.

His thoughts quieted and, like the woman he held in his arms, he drifted off to sleep.

Syneda's eyes slowly opened and they flickered over the sleeping man holding her in his arms. He was as solid as a rock. His muscular thighs were entwined with hers in an unnervingly sexual way, almost holding her to him in bondage. If she'd wanted to get out of bed, she'd have to wake him to do so.

She snuggled closer to him, satisfied for the moment to remain just where she was as memories washed over her. Last night when he had stood before her completely undressed, she couldn't help appreciating his powerful masculine frame. No wonder women were drawn to him. His physique absolutely radiated virility. She shivered when she remembered the sheer male size of him and the arousing effect seeing him had had on her. At first she had felt wary wondering how on earth she would handle it all.

A satisfying smile touched her lips. Somehow she had handled all of him, and had enjoyed every tantalizing moment doing so. He had entered her easily, filling her with all his masculine power and strength. She had felt very little pain.

"I hope that smile is for me."

Clayton's words startled her. She thought he was still asleep.

"No, sorry. It's for someone else." She could tell by the gleam in his eyes that he didn't believe her.

"Then maybe I better try this all over again," he said, leaning over her on one elbow.

"If we try this any more today, I won't be able to walk for a week."

"Did the bath help any?"

Syneda noticed the concern in his voice. Last night after they'd made love a number of times, he had gotten up and gone into the bathroom. A few minutes later, she had heard the sound of running water. He'd come back and gathered her up in his arms. Carrying her into the bathroom, he had eased her body into the warm sudsy water. Dropping to his knees beside the tub, he had taken her bath sponge and gently lathered the soreness from her aching muscles. It had felt heavenly.

She gazed up into his eyes. "Yes, the bath last night helped tremendously. Thanks for taking such good care of me. But then somehow I knew that you would. Under that rough and tough exterior is a very caring man. You're a gentleman in every sense of the word."

"A gentleman?" At her nod, he shrugged. "I don't know about that. A part of me feels a real gentleman would have walked out the door last night and left you alone after discovering you were a virgin."

"But I wanted you as much as you wanted me. It was just that simple."

"There's nothing simple about being the first with a woman, Syneda. Some men may take it lightly, I don't."

Their gazes held and Syneda felt the seriousness in his words. "No, you wouldn't. Even with your womanizing ways, I knew deep down that you wouldn't. And that was one of the reasons for my decision to let it be you, Clayton."

"And the other reason?"

When moments passed and she said nothing, Clayton reached out and caressed her cheek with his finger. "Talk to me, Syneda. We're friends, remember. And after last night, I'd say we're very close friends." A smile touched his lips. "As close as any two friends could possibly be."

Syneda nodded. "The other reason is because you play by the rules."

"A man playing by the rules is very important to you, isn't it?"

"Yes."

"Why? Why are you so against falling in love?"

She frowned. "I've told you all this before, when we were in Florida. You and I are a lot alike. Love isn't for everybody. Take you for instance—"

"We're not talking about me, we're talking about you. You never told me what happened to make you so against falling in love."

Syneda quickly turned away from him. "I'm hungry. I think I'll go find something to eat," she said, attempting to get up from the bed and clearly sidestepping his question. But Clayton's huge muscular thigh across hers wouldn't budge.

She turned back to him. "Clayton," she said warningly. "Kindly move your leg off me."

"Not until you answer my question. Who was he, Syneda? Who was the man that hurt you so?"

She held her head down for a moment and when she lifted it again, Clayton couldn't help noticing the tears misting her eyes. "Please don't ask me about him, Clayton," she said softly.

"Syneda." He gathered her close in his arms. The last thing he wanted to do was to make her cry. In the two and a half years that he had known her, he had never seen her cry, except for the tears she'd shed at Justin's and Lorren's rushed wedding. But those had been tears of joy. What he saw in her eyes now were clearly tears of pain. His entire body shook. He was used to seeing fire and anger in her eyes, not hurt and pain.

"Talk to me baby. Please talk to me. Who was he?"

Twisting agony in her midsection made Syneda not want to talk about it. But another part of her, the part Clayton could so effortlessly bring out, wanted to share that period of her life with him.

"My father."

"Your father?" He frowned. "I don't understand."

Syneda drew a shuddering breath. The subject of the man who had fathered her was a subject she didn't like to discuss with anyone. But for some reason, she wanted to talk about it with Clayton.

"I never knew my father. From the information I was able to gather while growing up, my mother got pregnant while attending college. It must have been in her senior year because she did manage to graduate with a degree in nursing. She was an only child, and she too had been born out of wedlock."

Syneda's expression saddened. "There were two generations of Walters women who allowed men to feed them lines. I was determined not to follow in their footsteps and become a third."

She took a deep breath before continuing. "When I was ten, my mother caught a rare form of pneumonia and had to be hospitalized."

"Did you stay with your grandmother while your mother was in the hospital?" Clayton asked, pulling her closer into his arms.

"No, by that time, my grandmother had died. There was a lady my mother knew, another nurse name Clara Boyd who kept me. They weren't exactly close friends but she was a coworker who agreed to take me in while my mom got better. The only thing was my mom never got better. She died in the hospital."

A tender, pained smile came into Syneda's features. "The really sad thing is that she died still very much in love with my father. And for some reason, she died believing that he still loved her too and that he was deserving of both her love and trust. I don't understand how and why she could believe such a thing because he never came to see us."

Syneda quivered slightly. "For as long as I live, I'll never forget the day Clara took me to see Mom in the hospital. She had lost a lot of weight and I kept thinking how different she looked. She could barely talk but I remember her telling me that my father would be coming for me. She said Clara had already called him and he had agreed to come for me. She said he would love me and take good care of me."

Clayton stroked her shoulder gently. "What happened?"

Syneda lifted her head slightly to look at Clayton. The hurt, pain and tears in her eyes made his insides ache. "He never came. After my mom's funeral, I waited and waited but he never came. Even after the authorities turned me over to Mama Nora because I didn't have any other family, and Clara didn't want the responsibility of taking care of me, I still believed he would come. I believed it because my mom believed. She died believing it so I figured she couldn't be wrong. I remember waking up each day at Mama Nora's thinking that this would be the day. Sometimes for hours, I would stand by my bedroom window watching and waiting. But he never came."

Clayton's hands tightened around her and he pulled her closer into his arms, silently cursing the man who had caused her so much pain. "Why did he tell Clara he would come if he had no intentions of doing so?"

"I found out the truth later. Mama Nora and Poppa Paul told me the entire story years later when they thought I was old enough to handle it. Evidently the authorities questioned Clara, and she admitted to lying to my mom. She had called the man as my mother had asked her to do, but according to Clara, he had denied being my father. Clara said she didn't have the heart to tell my mother what he'd said, so she let her die believing I would be taken care of."

"What about the authorities? Couldn't they pursue it before making you a ward of the state? Evidently, Clara had this man's name and phone number, surely there was something they could do."

"Possibly, but they didn't get the chance to question Clara any further. I understand not long after my mom died, she quit her job at the hospital and moved to another city without leaving a forwarding address."

"So you still don't know who your father is?"

"No, and as far as I'm concerned Clayton, I never had a father."

Her eyes closed momentarily, and when her lashes lifted again, her eyes revealed deep inner pain. "That period in my life was very difficult. It was during that time that Lorren and I became the very best of friends. She would stand by the window and wait with me every day, and then later when I found out the truth, that my father wasn't coming, her being there made a very painful time easy for me. And then I had Mama Nora and her husband Papa Paul. They were also there for me. One day Papa Paul explained to me that part of growing up was accepting the fact that on this earth, you would always face disappointments and letdowns from mortal men, even fathers. But he used to assure me that although my biological father had let me down, I had another father, a heavenly father, who would never let me down, and that he would always be there for me, no matter what."

She sighed. "So I shifted my faith to my other father. He became my rock, my strength, and like Poppa Paul said, he has never let me down."

Clayton clenched his teeth, angry at the disappointments she'd had to endure as a child. He couldn't help but admire her spirit. She'd been a fighter, a believer, a survivor.

Syneda continued. "And I made up my mind that I would never give my love and trust blindly to any man like my mother did. Over the years, I've learned that only a few people are blessed with sharing that special love and the unwavering trust that goes with it. Mama Nora shared it with Papa Paul before he died, your parents, your sisters and their husbands, Lorren and Justin, and Dex and Caitlin, have all shown me that it's possible, for some people."

"But not for you?"

"No, not for me. I'll never fall in love. It's not for me. I don't need it."

Clayton's hands closed over Syneda's shoulders and the feel of his strong fingers soothed her. He leaned down and brushed his lips to her neck. "No, baby, I think love *is* for you," he said huskily. "You just don't know it yet."

"Clayton, you don't understand."

He met her eyes, his expression suddenly serious. "Yes, I do, Syneda. I really do." He understood more than she realized, he thought. He understood what her lifelong insecurities about love were, which had been so much a part of her childhood and evidently remained a part of her adult life. And because of how she felt, he knew he couldn't tell her that he loved her. Love would be the last thing she would want from him.

Knowing that he could never rid her of all the sadness and loneliness she had endured over the years, Clayton inwardly vowed to bring some happiness and pleasure into her life. Love was about more than being wanted. It was also about understanding, time and patience. He would do battle to have all those things with Syneda. First, he would be understanding whenever she would try keeping him, like she'd done other men, at arm's length. Second, he realized she needed time. Although she thought she had fully healed from the pain caused by her father, he sensed that deep down she really hadn't. And last, but above all, he would have to have patience. No matter what, he would not give up on her or his love. He was in it for the long haul.

He slowly got out of bed. "It's lunch time."

Syneda smiled up at him. "Will we really get to eat this time?"

He laughed. "Yes, this time we will."

After lunch Clayton had gotten dressed and gone to a video store and rented a number of movies. They had ordered pizza for dinner and after watching the movies had decided to go to bed early.

In bed Clayton had held her in his arms. He refused to make love to her any more that day, knowing her body was still tender.

"Thanks for protecting me last night . . . and this morning, Clayton. You must carry packs of condoms around with you," Syneda said with a teasing glint in her eyes.

Clayton chuckled. "Shut up, Walters, and go to sleep," he said, pulling her closer to him.

Syneda laughed as she snuggled closer. Her last thought before closing her eyes was that if she weren't too careful, she could get used to Clayton sleeping in her bed.

"This weekend was wonderful, Clayton."

Clayton stood by the door. His traveling bag was packed, and he was ready to leave. That morning she was the one who had awakened him to make love. Again they had skipped breakfast and ended up eating left over pizza for lunch.

"Was this weekend wonderful enough to get me an invitation for another visit?"

Syneda hesitated before answering. "Do you think that's a good idea?"

"Yes."

She frowned up at him. "This weekend was to be a lust-purging experience to get you out of my system, and me out of yours."

He pulled her closer to him. He felt the soft warmth of her skin, and inhaled her arousing feminine scent. He wanted nothing more than to take her back to bed and make love to her for the rest of the day. "Then we failed miserably, because you're definitely still in my system."

Syneda stared up at him, becoming increasingly uneasy because he was still definitely in hers, too. "Another weekend will be a mistake."

"No, it won't."

A warning voice whispered in her head. She had let her guard down more with Clayton this weekend than with any other man. She needed time to think, to revamp. "I'll be busy next weekend."

Clayton nodded, recognizing her attempt to put distance between them. His gaze lowered to her body. She was wearing his dress shirt. It was the only stitch of clothing she had worn all weekend.

He reached into the pants pocket of his jeans and pulled out a key and placed it in the palm of her hand. "This is a spare key to my apartment." He didn't add that he had never given the spare key to any woman other than members of his family on occasion. "That shirt you're wearing is one of my favorites. How about personally returning it to me. Soon."

Syneda nervously bit her bottom lip as she gazed at the key she held in her hand. She then raised her eyes to meet his. "If you'll wait a minute, I'll change and you can take it with you."

"No. I want you to return it to me. In Houston. This coming weekend."

"Clayton, I can't do that. Don't you realize what you're asking of me?" He was suggesting that they continue their affair beyond this weekend. There was no way she could do that. Tossing aside common sense for a wild, reckless, and passionate weekend with him once was enough. Considering doing it again would be asking for trouble.

"What do you think I'm asking of you, Syneda?"

Syneda closed her eyes momentarily. Clayton's voice, sexy and warm, wrapped about her like silken honey. Suddenly, sanity returned with full force and she opened her eyes. "To continue what we started this weekend."

Clayton reached up and tipped her chin up so their eyes could meet. "You're right, sweetheart. I'm not ready to end things. I still want you."

He lowered his head and kissed her tenderly. His lips slanted over hers, moving softly, yet boldly, making circular motions. His tongue, smooth as velvet, teased her own tongue in a taunting yet provocative play. When he lifted his head, he gazed deeply into her eyes. The heat of them scorched her, and took her breath away.

Gathering his baggage in his hand, Clayton opened the door and walked out. Syneda stared at him, her mouth still feeling the pressure of his gentle but heated kiss as she remembered his parting words.

CHAPTER 9

Monday morning over breakfast, Syneda was still fighting the state of rhapsody she had found herself in. Clayton's departure yesterday had done little to bring her senses and mind back to reality. She had refused to take off his shirt until her bath late Sunday night.

His masculine scent had been drenched in the material and an acute yearning for him had welled up inside her so strongly that at times, she couldn't breathe. She had gone to bed wearing her nightgown and missing the aroma of his deep, masculine skin the shirt had provided.

Not even the sore muscles she had encountered upon waking that morning or the marks of passion that Clayton's beard had left on various places over her body had dampened her spirits. That weekend they had soared to passionate, exhilarating heights, and her body was still tingling from the memories of it.

Taking a sip of her coffee, she realized that in order to make it through the coming weeks and months, she would have to get Clayton off her mind. The last thing she needed was to become involved with a man who had the ability to make her hot all over with just one look, and whose lovemaking surpassed anything she'd ever imagined.

On her way to work, she dropped Clayton's shirt off at the cleaners. She had made up her mind that the shirt would be returned to him but not personally as he'd requested. It would arrive at his place via Federal Express overnight delivery.

Joanna looked up at Syneda when she stepped off the elevator. "Whoever is trying to impress you, Ms. Walters, is doing a darn good job. I'm definitely impressed with him."

Syneda raised a brow at her secretary's comment. "What are you talking about, Joanna?"

"There was a delivery for you first thing this morning."

Upon opening the door to her office, Syneda halted, shocked. Vases of flowers were everywhere.

"These are for me?" Syneda asked. She stood there, blank and amazed. Joanna giggled. "Yes, they're all for you."

Joanna's response hit Syneda full force. "You're kidding."

"No, I'm not kidding. It took four guys to deliver them all. All these flowers make your office look like a flower shop. The guy definitely has great taste."

Syneda walked farther into the room. "They are beautiful, aren't they?"

"That's an understatement. Whoever sent these is definitely my kind of guy."

Syneda turned and faced her secretary with a smile on her lips that she couldn't contain. "Do me a favor and have another table brought in. Also, Joanna, I have a meeting with John Drayton. Please set up conference room B for our use. It will be a little too crowded for us to meet in here."

Joanna glanced around the room. "You think one table will do it? I think we need a couple of tables in here," she said teasingly, as she headed for the door. "The card that came with the flowers is in the middle of your desk." She left, closing the door behind her.

Syneda's hand shook nervously as she picked up the envelope and pulled out the card.

This weekend was more special to me than you'll ever know.

Clayton

Smiling, Syneda slipped the card back in the envelope and placed it in her desk.

"Ms. Walters?" Joanna's voice came through the intercom on her desk.

"Yes."

"Mr. Drayton has arrived. I have him settled in conference room B."

"Thanks, Joanna. I'm on my way."

Syneda looked at the distinguished-looking man sitting across the desk from her. His daughter, a young woman of twenty, had made a mistake and being from a well-respected and wealthy family, they were not eager to share her mistake with the world. Nor did they want to make her pay for it for the rest of her life.

"Why didn't your daughter come with you? Are you sure she wants to give her child up for adoption, Mr. Drayton?"

"She'll do what's best for the family."

Syneda sighed. The man had said earlier that his daughter would not consider an abortion, and Syneda couldn't help wondering if perhaps Cassie Drayton was giving up her child under duress. "What about the child's father?"

"What about him?" John Drayton did not try to disguise his annoyance with her question.

"Even if your daughter is willing to give her child up for adoption, we'll need the consent of the father, Mr. Drayton."

"Consider it done. He won't oppose it," he replied with easy smug confidence.

"I take it marriage has been ruled out as an option?" Syneda asked pointedly.

"Of course it has." His curt response held a note of impatience. "All I want is for your firm to arrange a private adoption. I'm sure there's some childless couple somewhere who would love to—"

"Adopt your grandchild?"

Mr. Drayton did not flinch at her words, nor did he seem remorseful when he answered. "Yes."

"We'll have to meet with your daughter, of course."

"That can be arranged."

"And the father?"

"Prepare the required papers. I'll see that he signs them."

Syneda angled her head and noted how John Drayton basked in the knowledge of his power. "Yes. I'm sure you will."

Restlessly, Syneda paced through her apartment that evening. Every room she went through reminded her of Clayton. Memories of their weekend together assailed her at every turn. He had spent less than seventy-two hours in her apartment and already his presence was missed.

It's not the quantity of time but the quality of time, her mind screamed. *And Clayton gave you top quality time.*

She stood in the doorway of her bedroom, remembering Clayton in it. A part of her wished he was there in it now. Another part of her knew that it was best that he wasn't, and that the best thing for her to do was to forget a weekend that she knew deep down she never would.

She had not even called to thank him for the flowers. She couldn't risk the sound of his sexy voice unnerving her. So she had chosen the coward's way out. During lunch, she had gone into a card shop and picked out a cute thank-you card, which she had signed and included in the box with his shirt that she'd sent back to him.

Taking a deep breath, she entered her bedroom. For the first time, it felt lonely to her. The bed was neatly made and looked nothing like the untidy and much used bed it had been during Clayton's visit.

Syneda felt her resolve wavering as she sat on her bed. For a smart woman, she was completely stupid about sex. She had felt so savvy when she had entered the drugstore during lunch on Friday for her condom purchase. Determined to be on the safe side, she had purchased three packs of condoms, one for each day of Clayton's visit.

It was a good thing he was an expert at practicing safe sex because not only had she not purchased enough of the darn things, she had not given thought to using them until Clayton had discreetly pulled out his own foil packet before they'd made love; not only that first time, but every single time.

She couldn't help but appreciate his care and concern for her welfare. He never made a big production out of using them, nor had he tried to analyze her reaction. It did, however, make her feel comfortable to know he was a man who believed in a simple, direct approach to being careful, and who took the thought of AIDS or an unwanted pregnancy seriously. The last thing she needed was to have a child out of wedlock from a man who didn't love her like her mother had done. She and Clayton had made love enough times for that to happen, had it not been for him taking the necessary precautions.

Thoughts of him and their lovemaking suddenly made her feel as if her skin was on fire. Never would she have thought she would have spent the better part of a weekend making love to a man she considered a friend, at times an adversary, and at others a mentor. A man who was also a freewheeling bachelor, a sexual predator, a man who never made promises or hinted at the possibility of never-ending devotion and fidelity.

She didn't want to kid herself, Clayton was smooth and experienced. He was a man she could lose her heart to and get hurt if she was not careful. More than anything, she must not get love confused with great sex. She must not forget her own rules.

With that thought firmly embedded in her mind, Syneda's resolve became a little stronger than before.

"Ms. Walters, you have a call from a Mr. Clayton Madaris."

Syneda bit her lower lip. She had been expecting Clayton's call. Evidently he had received the package she had sent to him. "Thanks, Joanna, I'll take it."

A few minutes later the connection was made. "Clayton?"

"Yes, Syneda. Thanks for the card, but no thanks for returning the shirt. I wanted you to return it in person," he said disappointedly.

Syneda smiled as she put her paperwork aside. Evidently he wasn't used to women not following his requests. "You can't always have what you want, Clayton. Thanks again for the flowers. You really shouldn't have."

"I couldn't help myself." What he had just said was the truth, Clayton thought. Upon arriving at the airport he had gone into a florist shop and ordered that the flowers be delivered to her first thing Monday morning. There had not been one particular arrangement that had suited him, so he had ended up ordering several. Although he was disappointed that she had not personally returned the shirt, at least she had not returned the spare key to his apartment with the shirt.

Clayton couldn't help being plagued with vivid memories of her wearing nothing but his shirt. Never could he remember wanting a woman so much. The incredible hunger he had for her suddenly made his body go taut. He had to make love to her again and soon.

"I want to see you, Syneda. This weekend," he said huskily.

Syneda took a deep breath. "I've told you, I'll be busy."

"What about next weekend?"

"I'll still be busy."

"We need to talk, Syneda."

"No."

"Yes. Just what are you afraid of?"

"I'm not afraid of anything, Madaris."

"Then we'll talk. We either talk tonight on the phone, or I'll fly up this weekend and we'll talk in person."

"Don't do that, Clayton," she said shakily. She wasn't ready to see him again. He had a way of making her come utterly unglued.

There was a pause. "Okay then, I'll call you tonight at eight. Goodbye, Syneda."

Syneda hung up the phone without saying goodbye.

Clayton called at exactly eight o'clock. He didn't waste time on pleasantries. He had preplanned his strategy and went straight to the heart of the problem.

"Okay, Syneda, you talk and I'll listen since there seems to be something bothering you about the idea of us continuing to see each other."

Syneda sighed. Something bothering her was an understatement. "All right, Clayton, since you insist upon forcing the issue, I think you've forgotten there was to be only one weekend for us. All we shared was satisfying a case of lust and a little bit of curiosity. We've gotten both out of our system."

"Can you honestly say we did?"

"Yes, you're out of my system," she lied.

"Well, you're not out of mine."

"Too bad, Madaris. You don't get a second try."

A grin appeared on Clayton's face. She was following just where he had wanted to lead her. "Does that mean we go back to being just friends?"

"Yes."

"Then there's no reason for me not to come visit you in two weeks, as nothing more than a friend. I'll even check into a hotel if you want me to."

Syneda heard the challenge in his voice. It was something she could not ignore. Her first instinct was to tell him in unladylike words just where he could go, but she thought better of it. In this situation, the age-old saying "actions speak louder than words" would have to be proven. It was obvious he did not believe they could go back to being just friends without anything sexual between them.

Syneda balled her hands into fists. She would jump to the challenge to contradict his beliefs and show him that he was out of her system. She only hoped that in two weeks he really and truly was.

"Okay, Clayton, I'll see you in two weeks. And it won't be necessary for you to check into a hotel. My sofa converts into a bed, and I have plenty of room here at my place."

"Are you sure?"

"Yes, I'm positive. Just as long as you remember my position."

Unfortunately he *was* remembering her position, and the one that stuck out uppermost in his mind was the one of her Sunday morning lying flat on her back, pinned beneath the heated weight of his aroused body.

"Yes, Syneda, I'll remember your position," he said in a deep husky voice. *At the present time, I can't seem to think of anything else.*

"I wasn't aware you'd be working late tonight, Braxter."

Braxter Montgomery looked up from the papers he'd been reading. "I really hadn't planned to stay this late, senator, but I'm picking up my date from work. I decided to stick around here and go over the guest list Jacob Madaris faxed today."

Senator Lansing smiled. "Ahh, yes. It's almost that time isn't it? I thought it was pretty nice of Jake to give me a kickoff party for my reelection campaign."

"Yes, it was." Braxter knew that Jacob Madaris was a personal friend of the senator, and a loyal, longtime supporter. He owned a large cattle ranch called Whispering Pines.

Whispering Pines was located several hundred miles from Houston. In addition to the cattle business, Madaris also owned stock in many business investments, including being a major investor in his nephew's oil exploration company. Last year, Madaris Oil Exploration, made national headlines when they had located a rich oil basin near Eagle Pass, Texas for Remington Oil Company.

"How's the list coming?"

Braxter smiled. "It's growing by leaps and bounds. There's quite a number of impressive names on it. People are coming from as far away as Hollywood, California, and Miami, Florida."

The senator laughed. "That doesn't surprise me. Everybody knows Jake Madaris seldom throws parties. But when he does, it's a good one, and most people don't want to be left out."

Braxter glanced down at the list. "Yes, I can believe that. How did you meet Mr. Madaris?"

"I met Jake through his brother Robert who was six years older than Jake. Robert Madaris and I served in Nam together and became good friends. Unfortunately, Robert never made it back home."

"How awful."

"Yes, it was for the Madaris family. They're good people. Well, good night, Braxter."

"Good night, sir."

After the senator left, Braxter checked his watch. It was almost time for Celeste to be closing her shop. She'd told him this was her busiest time of the year, the first weeks of June. During this time most people began making summer travel plans.

He smiled remembering how they had begun seeing each other. It was right after he had repaired her car that day in the parking lot. That had been almost two weeks ago, and they had dated steadily since then. She was witty and fun to be around. He thoroughly enjoyed her company.

Braxter pushed his papers aside. He stood and began putting on his jacket. He was looking forward to seeing Celeste again.

CHAPTER 10

"If there's some doubt in your mind about giving up your child for adoption, Miss Drayton, then why are you doing so without first exploring other options?"

Although Syneda tried remaining emotionally detached, she couldn't stop her heart from going out to the young woman sitting across the desk from her. She didn't fit the image of a wealthy and spoiled woman who had gotten herself in trouble and had run home to Daddy for help.

Syneda was assaulted with a terrible sense of wariness. Her earlier thoughts when she'd first met with John Drayton appeared to have been correct. Cassie Drayton, the only child of the wealthy New York clothing magnate, was giving up her child not because she wanted to but because she felt she was being forced to.

Glossy blond hair fell like a shimmering curtain over both sides of the young woman's face as she began sobbing into an embroidered handkerchief. "I have no other choice and neither does Larry."

"Larry?"

"Yes. Larry Morgan, my baby's father."

"Have you spoken to Mr. Morgan about any of this?"

"No. It's best I don't. He wants to marry me but that's impossible."

"Why?"

"Because I love him too much," she replied brokenly. "And my love may end up destroying him."

Syneda raised her brows in surprise. She had assumed the relationship between Cassie Drayton and the father of her child had not been a long-standing one, but one where sex and not love had been a factor. Evidently she'd been mistaken.

Syneda rose and rounded her desk. She laid her hand on Cassie Drayton's shoulder. "You're not a child, Miss Drayton. You're a twenty-year-old woman who has the right to make her own decisions. If you really don't want to give up your child for—"

"You don't understand, and why should you care, Ms. Walters? My father is obviously paying you a big fat retainer to quickly find a solution to my problem, especially since I refused to have an abortion. Your job is to place my baby with a couple who love each other and who'd love my child. But what really hurts is knowing that couple could just as well be me and Larry. We love each other deeply, and no one would love our baby more than the two of us."

The crack in Syneda's heart widened another degree. The young woman was totally distraught, and Syneda was at a loss for what to do. She wanted to help without stepping beyond the boundaries of her role as an attorney. But right now Cassie Drayton didn't need an attorney, she needed someone she could talk to, and most importantly, someone who would listen.

"Cassie, I owe the couple who may be adopting your child complete peace of mind that one day you won't show up demanding the child back. I'm presently working on a case such as that, and all it's done is caused pain for both sides. So, if you're having doubts about going through with this, I suggest we discuss them now. You mentioned you and the baby's father love each other, yet you said marriage is out of the question. Could you please explain why you feel that way?"

"Why should it matter to you?" the young woman asked sniffing.

"Because besides being an attorney, I'm also human. I have an ethical obligation to do more than just represent you. I want to hear you and listen to what you have to say."

"Are you in love, Ms. Walters?"

The question caught Syneda by surprise. "No," she replied gently.

"Have you ever been in love?"

Syneda met the young woman's curious tear-stained stare. "No, but that doesn't exempt me from understanding or trying to understand. And how about calling me Syneda."

Cassie Drayton hesitated only briefly before replying. "And I'm Cassie." She paused then spoke slowly. "I met Larry at college. He's a few years older and was obtaining a master's degree in accounting. He's brilliant," she said proudly.

"I fell in love with him the moment I saw him. We dated three months before I took him home to meet my family. As soon as my father discovered Larry's parents weren't a part of New York's society's best, he forbid me to see him again."

"I gather you continued seeing him anyway."

"Yes. By that time Larry had completed his studies and had gotten a really good job with a prestigious accounting firm here in the city. He encouraged me to finish school and our plans were to marry after I graduated. Everything was going fine until we goofed and I got pregnant. Although a baby was not in our plans, we were happy about it anyway."

"What happened?"

"My father found out. He paid us a visit and made a lot of threats. Within twenty-four hours, he had carried them out. When Larry reported to work the next morning, he was told he no longer had a job. We later discovered that my father has also made sure Larry doesn't find decent employment in this city or anywhere else as long as he continues to see me."

"What's Mr. Morgan's reaction to all of this?"

"He's furious. He tried telling my father that he loved me and would make me happy, but my father told him that he was not good enough for me and as long as he planned to include me in his future, he would make sure he didn't have one."

"So he gave in to your father's threats?"

"No, Larry would never do that. I'm the one who gave in. I know more than anyone what my father is capable of, Ms. Walters. He would destroy Larry's career completely without a moment's thought. I couldn't let him do that to Larry. I love him too much. I moved back home with my parents. I'm now back to being their puppet, letting them pull all the strings. But it doesn't matter as long as Larry isn't harmed."

"Where's Mr. Morgan now?"

"I don't know. He tried contacting me but I refuse to see him. It's for the best."

"Your father is so sure Larry will sign the forms to give up your child," Syneda said quietly.

"My father overestimates himself and underestimates Larry. He'll never sign those forms. Larry would never agree to give up our child."

A confused frown covered Syneda's features. John Drayton seemed so confident the man would do exactly the opposite. That was interesting, especially judging by Cassie's distress and opinion of her father's capabilities.

"Cassie, I suggest you give yourself a few weeks to think this over some more, then come back to see me."

"But what will I tell my father? He expects me to sign the papers today."

Syneda reached for a business card and pressed it into the young woman's hand. "You have time to make a decision, Cassie. This is something you should be absolutely sure about. If your father has any questions, just tell him to give me a call. If what you say is true, and Larry refuses to sign the papers, there's nothing your father can do."

Cassie nodded. "Thanks for listening, Syneda."

"You're welcome and Cassie, I have a feeling that somehow things will work out for you and Larry."

Cassie looked doubtful of that. She said goodbye and left Syneda's office.

Syneda returned to the chair behind her desk and propped her head in her hands, suddenly feeling extremely tired. It seemed all her cases this week had been either difficult or in some way mind draining. Or maybe she was in such a poor state of mind to deal with them. Knowing Clayton would be flying in this weekend was making her a basket case.

She had berated herself numerous times over the past two weeks for inviting him to stay at her place. She had been so sure she could handle it but now she seriously had her doubts. All it took was a few moments to think about their weekend together to know the man still was not out of her system.

She let out a deep sigh. This would be a rather interesting weekend.

It was Friday and not quite noon, Syneda noticed, glancing at her watch. Her right arm felt numb and she was positive that at any minute it was going to fall off. Also, her stomach was more than mildly protesting her lack of providing it with nourishment.

A donut and a cup of coffee were all she'd had for breakfast. She had too much work to take time to eat anything. Especially if she wanted to leave the office on time to be at home before Clayton arrived. He had phoned earlier in the week and indicated he would be arriving around six.

The smooth voice of Joanna on the intercom broke into Syneda's thoughts. "Ms. Walters?"

"Yes, Joanna, what is it?"

"I know you asked not to be disturbed but there's a gentleman here to see you. He doesn't have an appointment. He says he's a friend of yours by the name of Clayton Madaris."

The frown of annoyance on Syneda's lips was suddenly replaced by one of complete surprise. *Clayton was here in New York already!*

"Ms. Walters?"

Syneda could tell by the strain in Joanna's voice that she was getting frustrated with her lack of cooperation. "All right, Joanna, please show Mr. Madaris in."

Nervously gathering the scattered papers in a neat pile, Syneda placed them in a folder on the corner of her desk. Then she stood to face the man who had plagued her mind for the past couple of weeks; especially this morning before she had become totally absorbed in her work.

The door swung open and Syneda managed to place a friendly though strained smile on her lips.

Clayton entered her office escorted by Joanna. It was obvious Joanna was completely enthralled by the tall, dark, handsome man dressed impeccably in a dark suit.

"Thanks for showing Mr. Madaris in, Joanna. That will be all for now."

"All right," Joanna replied, not taking her eyes off of Clayton. "If you're absolutely sure there won't be anything else."

A slight frown of annoyance covered Syneda's face. Joanna appeared to be in a daze. She hadn't moved an inch. It bothered Syneda that Clayton had this effect on women. "I'm positive, Joanna. You may leave us alone now. And make sure I'm not disturbed."

Clayton raised a dark brow at the harsh tone of Syneda's voice.

"All right, Ms. Walters," Joanna replied, not ignoring the curtness of Syneda's words. She gave Clayton a warm smile before leaving.

"I wasn't expecting you until late this afternoon, Clayton. You're early."

"My case this morning was canceled, so I caught an earlier flight out. I had my secretary phone you a few times, but she couldn't get through to speak with you. She did leave a message though. I hope you don't mind me showing up like this, but I need the key."

A confused frown covered Syneda's features. "The key?"

"Yes, the key to your apartment."

"Oh," Syneda said, as understanding dawned. She went into her desk for her purse. "You need the key to get inside my apartment." She handed it to him. "Just make yourself at home. I should leave here by five. What would you like to do tonight? How about dinner someplace?" She had already decided it would be best if the two of them spent as little time as possible at her apartment.

"What do you usually do on Friday nights?" Clayton asked, taking the key she offered.

"Usually, I just grab something on the way home, then watch my favorite television program." As an afterthought she added. "That's if I don't have a date for the evening."

"Do you have a date for tonight?" Clayton asked quietly.

"No."

"Then you shouldn't change things just for me. However, since I'll have nothing to do until you get there, how about letting me prepare us something to eat."

"Clayton, that isn't necessary."

"I'd enjoy doing it. I'm not a bad cook you know."

Syneda knew that was an understatement. Thanks to their mother, who was superb in the kitchen, all three Madaris brothers were great cooks. "I just hate for you to go to all that trouble. You'll be showing up my insufficiencies as a hostess again."

As soon as the words had left her mouth, Syneda regretted them. They could dredge up memories of their last weekend together, and by the sudden silence in the room it appeared they had.

Clayton captured her eyes with his. "Trust me. You were a good hostess. You took very good care of me that weekend," he replied huskily. "I'll have dinner prepared by the time you get there. Don't work too hard."

Before Syneda could utter a response, Clayton had turned and walked out of the door.

"Clayton, I'm home."

Around five hours later, Syneda entered her apartment using the spare key. Her plans to leave work early had been aborted when she'd received another unexpected visitor. This time Larry Morgan.

He had told her in no uncertain terms that he would not agree to give his child up for adoption no matter what John Drayton did to him.

Syneda's thoughts came to a sudden halt when her nose picked up the aroma of food. She was starving. She'd skipped lunch to finish an important report only to have the completion delayed because of Larry Morgan's visit. Then not long after he had left, she'd gotten a call from John Drayton. He had not been pleased with her decision to give his daughter more time to make a final decision. As far as he was concerned the decision had been made. Therefore, he'd stated, he wanted to be represented by another attorney in the firm. That suited Syneda just fine.

"I was wondering when you'd get here," Clayton said, coming into the living room. He had changed into a pair of jeans and a white chambray shirt.

Syneda's mind began reeling as she eyed him from head to toe. He was an incredibly sexy man whether he was dressed in a suit, jeans . . . or nothing at all, she thought. She noticed he was holding two filled wine glasses. He handed her one of them.

"I thought you could probably use this. I take it you've had a bad day."

Syneda graciously took the drink he offered. "That's putting it mildly." She took a sip. "Thanks. Something smells wonderful. What is it?"

Clayton smiled. "It's a surprise. I just hope you're hungry."

Syneda laughed. "Clayton, I could eat a horse about now."

"Well, dinner is ready when you are. Would you like to take a warm bath to unwind first?"

"That's not a bad idea. I'll be back in a few minutes."

Clayton watched as Syneda rounded the sofa and went into her bedroom, closing the door behind her. He had found incredible hunger raging through him upon the sight of her. He only hoped his plan would work. He didn't want to push her into anything, but with Syneda, some things had to be forced on her, and accepting a relationship between the two of them was going to be one of them. She was so certain she didn't want or need the love of a man in her life that she was overlooking the obvious. A man who loved her was already in her life.

Over the past few days, he had done a lot of thinking about what she had told him the last night they had spent together; specifically, the information she had shared about her father. Whether she was willing to admit it to herself or not, the pain of her father's rejection and abandonment was clouding the way she thought about love.

He knew she had some deep-rooted fears. The first being her fear of ever becoming dependent upon anyone, especially a man. And for that reason he understood her need for more space than normal. She would never agree to a relationship that would be confining.

She was also a private person, and she thought she couldn't become seriously involved with a person for that reason. She didn't know that the key to that problem would be for her to become involved with someone with whom her privacy wouldn't be threatened.

And then there were her biggest fears, rejection and abandonment. It was plain she had decided the best way to avoid the heartache of both was by not getting close to anyone.

He could only imagine the pain, anguish, and disappointment she'd endured when her father had not shown up for her. In his mind, Clayton could envision her at the age of ten standing at the window peering out, waiting day after day after day.

Having been involved with Big Brothers of America, he'd always taken pleasure in watching a fatherless boy who'd been patiently waiting for a Big Brother finally get one. The joy, excitement, and happiness on the kid's face was priceless. But because Syneda's father had never shown up for her, she had been cheated out of experiencing any of those emotions.

Clayton expelled a deep breath and walked back into the kitchen. He had a big job on his hands. He was deeply in love with Syneda and was determined that in time, she would put the past behind her and return his love. What she needed was time to heal, and he had found a way to give her the time she needed while still sharing a relationship with him.

He hoped she would go along with what he would be proposing to her. She was a strong-willed woman, but he'd have to be even stronger to get her to do something she would be totally against doing. But he was determined that before he left on Sunday, she would have accepted the fact that there could never be a platonic relationship between them again.

* * *

The warm bath was a wonderful idea, Syneda thought. Turning on the faucet she added a generous amount of her favorite bubble-bath gel to the flowing water. Closing her eyes, she inhaled deeply as the fragrance of a flower garden began filling the steamy room.

Removing her clothes, Syneda sank to her neck in the bubbles a few minutes later. She felt somewhat guilty about how much Clayton had done since his arrival. From the smell of things in the kitchen, undoubtedly he had prepared quite a feast. There was no way he could have found the ingredients he had needed to cook with in her kitchen, which meant he had gone grocery shopping. That thought made her feel even more guilty. He was her guest, she was not his. It seemed Clayton was always going out of his way to take care of her.

Getting out of the bath some time later, she toweled herself dry before lotioning her body. She liked the way the fragrance of the lotion lingered on her skin. After changing into a pair of slacks and a top, she entered the living room.

Syneda found Clayton sitting on her sofa, finishing the rest of his wine. He looked up when she entered and smiled.

"How do you feel now?"

"A lot better, but my problem will still be there to haunt me on Monday."

"Is it a case you're working on?" Clayton asked, handing her another glass of wine.

"Yes and it's a bummer. My client is . . . or I should say was, since it seems I'm no longer representing her . . . the daughter of one of the wealthiest men in New York. She's unmarried and pregnant, and her father wants her to give the child up for adoption."

"What does she want?"

Syneda sat down on the sofa. "She wants to keep her baby and marry the father of her child. He wants to marry her, too."

"Then what's the problem?"

"John Drayton doesn't think Larry Morgan is good enough for his daughter. And he's determined to ruin the young man's career unless he agrees to give in and sign papers giving the child up for adoption."

"Unless the woman is a minor, Syneda, there's really nothing the father can do, however, it's understandable why he would want to."

Syneda raised arched brows. "And just what does that mean?"

"It means that although the man is playing his role of father a little too thick, I can understand him wanting the best for his daughter."

Clayton's response rankled her. "Wanting the best for his daughter? That has nothing to do with it, Madaris," Syneda snapped. "He just wants to control her life."

"A life she undoubtedly couldn't control on her own. If she could, then she wouldn't be pregnant now, would she?"

Syneda gave him a hostile glare. "Accidents *do* happen, Clayton. Everyone isn't as overly cautious as you are. I can't believe you've taken the father's side in this."

Clayton heaved an exasperated sigh. "I'm not taking anyone's side. For pete's sake, I don't even know these people. All I'm saying is that sometimes parents think they know what's best for their children. You can't hang the man because he think he's doing the right thing."

"But that's just it. He isn't doing the right thing. Cassie Drayton and Larry Morgan love each other. Their baby is a part of that love. But you wouldn't understand something like love, would you?"

"I guess not. But I suppose *you* do." Clayton could tell by her expression that his comment had nearly infuriated the life out of her. No doubt she felt like slapping him silly.

"I only know what I saw today, Madaris," she said after having stared at him for a long moment with angry eyes. "And today I met a man who desperately wants to be with the woman he loves."

"Ah, well now. It's good to know some men who say 'I love you' aren't just feeding women 'lines,' " he said sarcastically with a sweetness that he knew probably pushed Syneda beyond the boiling point. He hoped she was beginning to realize she couldn't judge every relationship in life based by what had happened between her parents.

Syneda's eyes narrowed. "Yes, but what you've failed to—"

"Let's just drop the subject. I don't want to argue with you."

"We aren't arguing. I just don't like—"

Before Syneda could finish what she was saying, she found herself lifted from the sofa and into Clayton's arms. "This is the only way I know to shut you up."

Before she could react, his mouth was opening over hers. Her struggles to free herself were useless. Clayton had her pinned into his arms while his mouth took over hers.

Syneda could not identify at what point she stopped resisting him as streaks of pleasure exploded deep within her. It seemed every desire she had tried suppressing since Clayton's last visit came pouring out. She couldn't help responding to the powerful sensual chemistry sizzling between them, and was unprepared for the sudden rush of hot passion that swept over her. She was a fool to have thought she had gotten this man out of her system.

She pressed herself against him, needing to feel his hard body and the strength of his arms holding her. She locked her arms around his neck and returned his kiss, wanting his taste to fill her mouth. Their kiss grew hotter, wilder, longer.

The sound of Syneda's stomach growling echoed in the room. Clayton slowly lifted his head to first stare down at the sea-green eyes glazed with passion before moving lower to her full, inviting lips.

"You're hungry," he said huskily

Syneda gazed into dark eyes that were starkly sexual. "Yes, I am," she replied, her words coming out soft as whipped cream.

Clayton wanted nothing more than to carry her into the bedroom. But he knew he couldn't. When they made love again, it would be on his terms. Terms he hoped she would agree to.

"Come on," he said, taking her hand. He led her to the kitchen and sat her down at the table. After placing various casserole dishes before her, he sat down across from her. "First, we eat."

Syneda's throat suddenly felt dry. She should not have let him kiss her. The last thing she wanted was for him to think her position had shifted and they could be more than just friends. "After we eat, then what?" she asked in a curious whisper, looking into his eyes.

Clayton's gaze held hers. The look in his eyes was intent, clear, and challenging. "Then I'll make you an offer I hope you can't refuse."

CHAPTER 11

At first Syneda pretended not to have heard Clayton's statement. She went about spooning the baked chicken, macaroni and cheese, okra and tomatoes and rice pilaf onto her plate. She put down her first mouthful, savoring the taste of the well-prepared meal. Finally, the strain of curiosity was too much for her.

"What kind of offer are you talking about?"

Clayton smiled. He'd known her nonchalant attitude wouldn't last long. She was an inquisitive person by nature. Most attorneys were. "I prefer we discuss it after dinner."

"Why can't we discuss it now?"

"I want to do it later."

Syneda sighed. Experience had taught her Clayton did things when it suited him. Evidently this would be one of those times. "All right, suit yourself but I may not want to hear anything you have to say after dinner."

"I'll take that chance."

She frowned. She also knew from experience he enjoyed getting in the last word.

"How does everything taste?"

"Good. You're an excellent cook."

"Thanks."

They ate in silence for several minutes, and then Clayton spoke. "Mom should be giving you a call in a few days."

Syneda lifted her brow. "Why?"

"Uncle Jake is giving Senator Lansing a kickoff party for his reelection campaign at Whispering Pines sometime next month. More than likely Mom will be contacting you to make sure you come."

Syneda smiled. "I'd love to come. You know how much I admire Senator Lansing. I've never met him, but I'm a big supporter of his."

Clayton nodded. "The day after Senator Lansing's party is Gramma Madaris's eightieth birthday. We'll be having another party to celebrate that, too. Knowing Mom she'll want all of us to spend the night at Whispering Pines so we'll all be accounted for on Sunday."

"Okay." Syneda knew that sleep-over also included her. Ever since Lorren had married into the Madaris family, they had not held any family gatherings that had not included her. She knew Clayton's mother, Marilyn Madaris, considered her more than just Lorren's best friend. The entire Madaris family thought of her as part of the family and she really appreciated that. Now that Mama Nora spent a lot of her time traveling with a group of other widows from church, Syneda enjoyed the rather close relationship she had developed with the Madaris family.

After dinner together she and Clayton cleared the dishes off the table and cleaned up the kitchen. Syneda couldn't help noticing Clayton had taken all the dishes out of the dishwasher and had stacked them neatly in the cabinets.

"Now we'll talk." Taking her hand, Clayton led her into the living room where he motioned for her to sit down on the sofa. He sat next to her.

"All right, Clayton, what is it?"

He took her hand in his, and gave her an engaging smile. "I propose that we become lovers," he came right out and said in a very controlled voice.

Syneda looked at him. He was serious! "That's out of the question."

"Why? Have you changed your mind about love and commitment?"

His question startled Syneda. "Of course not!"

"You still don't want anything to do with either?"

"That's right," she answered quickly, wondering where Clayton's line of questioning was leading to.

"Then we're perfectly suited for each other, and becoming involved will have a lot of advantages for the both of us," he said.

"Advantages like what?"

"Neither of us wants to get involved in any sort of permanent relationship. I live in Houston, you live here, so there won't be any crowding. We'll both get the space we need. Then there's the stability of a steady relationship, which means there won't be any risks since we won't be dating other people."

Clayton quickly searched her face to see if any of what he was saying was sinking in. When all he saw was an unreadable expression, he continued. "We're both private people but a relationship won't threaten our privacy because we trust each other. We enjoy each other's company, we're friends, we respect each other's profession, and we enjoy being together in every way a man and woman can be together. But most importantly," he murmured softly, "becoming lovers is the perfect solution to our problem."

"What problem?" Syneda looked into Clayton's dark eyes and felt the heat displayed in them with every nerve in her body.

"The fact that you want me as much as I want you. And no matter how much we try to convince ourselves otherwise, last weekend was not enough for either of us. What we shared was very special, but it only made me want you that much more. I want you more than I've ever wanted a woman in my life."

Syneda frowned. "That's impossible. You've had lots of women. Most of them a whole lot more experienced than I am. Why me, Clayton? And why are you even considering limiting yourself to dating just me? You've always enjoyed having lots of women."

Clayton didn't think she was quite ready to hear how much he loved her. So instead he answered. "I'm getting older, wiser and more cautious. There's no longer such things as 'safety in numbers' and 'no risk, no pleasure.' Now the present climate is more like 'unsafety in numbers,' and 'no risk, live longer.' And although I'm a careful man, I don't like the chances I take sleeping around. It's time for me to make some lifestyle changes. Therefore, you and I getting together is the perfect solution. Like I said, we're perfectly suited for each other. Besides, you're all the woman I need."

He lowered his head and touched his lips to hers. He deepened the kiss when he felt her immediate response. He heard himself release a groan of pleasure when her mouth began opening beneath his.

Syneda's hands slowly slid up his chest, wrapping themselves around his neck. He reveled in her fire, her heat, her scent, and her trembling warmth in his arms.

Clayton slowly broke off the kiss and looked deeply into her eyes. The passion he saw glittering in them was a mirror of his own. He then rested his forehead against hers. His breathing unsteady.

"You don't have to give me your answer tonight, or even this weekend if you need time to think about it," he said huskily, stroking her shoulder. He lifted his head to again look in her eyes. "I don't want to rush you into anything. Just promise me that you'll at least consider the idea."

Syneda nodded, unable to say anything. It wasn't too often she was at a loss for words. If anything, she usually had too many of them. But as usual, Clayton's kiss had zapped her of all logical thought.

Clayton heaved a deep sigh as he stood. "I think I'll go out for a while."

"Go out? Where?"

"No place in particular. I'll just take a walk."

"Take a walk? In New York? This late?"

Clayton grinned. "Yeah, I'll be all right. I might stop by that video store and pick up a movie or something." He reached up a hand and rubbed the back of his neck. "I just need to get out of here or I won't be responsible for my actions. I told you I would visit as a friend this weekend, and until you say otherwise that's all I'll be."

Syneda drew in a shuddering breath. He had left the decision in her hands. What did or did not happen between them this weekend and any weekend that followed would be her choice.

"I'll be back later."

She watched as he turned and walked out the door.

Alone, Syneda walked across the room, her arms cradling her middle. It was an instinctive protective action, and she needed all the protection she could get from Clayton Jerome Madaris.

How dare he suggest they become lovers! She didn't want to be *that* involved with any man. Men had a tendency to get too possessive, too domineering, too crazy. Her life was just fine without a man in it. She liked being in control of her life and not having to answer to anyone. And most of all she hated feeling vulnerable.

And with Clayton she felt vulnerable.

Even with the confrontational tension that usually surrounded them, lately there had been an increase in physical tension between them.

Syneda sighed, acknowledging the effect Clayton had on her. She was intelligent enough to know it wasn't based on love but on something for which she really didn't have a clue. Neither Thomas, Marcus, nor any of the other men she'd dated had made her feel the way Clayton did. None of them had even come close.

Her palms felt strangely damp. The neat, tidy case Clayton had presented to her was in no way a weak one. Like the brilliant attorney that he was, he had presented all the advantages of them becoming lovers. He had stated them so eloquently that there was no way she could even poke holes in his opening argument.

A cross-examination of the facts he'd presented would have been useless. He had, beyond a reasonable doubt, cited all the reasons she had avoided an intimate involvement. He had then used those very reasons not in favor of the defense, but to further the prosecution.

There was no way she could deny there would be some real benefits in becoming his lover. She would have the space she liked, the stability she wanted, and the privacy she craved. But most importantly, she would have relief from the intense combination of passion and desire Clayton had stirred up within her. She had become trapped in the depths of her own sensuality. It was a state that only Clayton could rectify. At least with him, she didn't have to worry about being fed a line, There would be no "I love you" and no promises of "forever after." With him she could enjoy the present without the pain of the past or the worry of a loveless future.

"It's all about mutual satisfaction," she said softly to herself. "Mutual satisfaction and nothing more."

Syneda nodded, her decision made. She would agree to become Clayton's lover only if he was willing to accept her conditions.

Nearly an hour had passed before Syneda heard the key rattle in the lock. Tossing aside her legal pad, she stood. She didn't care that the expression on her face clearly showed she'd been worried. When Clayton hadn't returned in what she had considered a reasonable amount of time, she had begun pacing the floor, peeking through drapes and gnawing nervously at her bottom lip.

The nerve of him to make her worry!

"Where have you been?" she demanded the moment he walked in.

Clayton gave her an inquiring glance before calmly saying "Out."

Syneda felt a surge of renewed anger. Here she had been driving herself crazy wondering if he had gotten mugged or run over by a speeding yellow cab. And all he had to say regarding his whereabouts was "out."

"I know you've been out, Clayton. But you've been gone for over an hour. Did it ever occur to you that I was worried?"

Clayton shook his head. "No. That thought never occurred to me."

Infuriated, Syneda walked up to him. Heaven help her, but she wanted to grab him and shake him one time. "Well, I was."

A hint of a smile played around Clayton's mouth. His hand slipped to her waist and pulled her closer. "I'm sorry that I made you worry about me. I stopped by that arcade shop around the corner and played a couple of games."

Syneda frowned at him. "Look, Madaris. If we're going to be lovers, we need to have an understanding about a few things. I don't believe in disappearing acts."

Clayton's heart almost stopped beating with Syneda's words: He cupped her face in his hands, smiling brightly. "Are we going to be lovers?"

With a gentle smile she said, "Yes."

Clayton pulled her closer to him. "Does this mean you've decided to accept my proposal?"

"Yes, counselor. You presented a pretty good argument, but I do have two conditions."

Clayton studied her eyes, noting the determined set in them. He knew that whatever her conditions were, there would be no negotiations. "What are they?"

"First, I want you to agree that at any time if either of us wants to end this relationship we can do so without any questions asked. Other than dating each other exclusively, we are not bound to each other."

Clayton didn't like that condition at all. More than ever he was determined to make sure she never wanted to end the relationship. "All right," he finally said.

"The next one involves your family."

Clayton raised a brow. "My family? What about my family?"

Syneda stepped out of the circle of his arms. "I don't want them knowing about us, Clayton. I don't want them to know we're involved."

He frowned. "Why?"

"I don't want to become one of those women they constantly tease you about; the kind they think you only date. I don't want to lose their love and respect."

"Syneda, that would never happen."

"I can't take that chance. I won't take it."

Clayton pulled her back into his arms. Although he didn't like what she was asking of him, he understood why she was doing it. Because of her deep-rooted doubts and fears, she needed an attachment to people she could count on and trust. His family had become that to her. They were her surrogate family, and she would never take the chance to be rejected and abandoned again. But what she failed to realize was that his family would always be there for her, no matter what. They would always love her. Nothing could or would ever change that. If anything, they would love her even more for finally opening his heart to love. But he knew nothing he said would convince her of that. Only time would prove it.

"Okay, Syneda, if that's the way you want it, I won't mention it. Justin and Lorren are the only ones that will know. But I want you to know upfront that I don't care who knows. We're adults and don't have to answer to anyone. I won't ever be ashamed of what we'll be sharing, and I don't want you to be either. You're very special to me."

The manly scent of Clayton filled Syneda's nostrils as he embraced her. She liked being held in the comfort of his arms. "And you're very special to me, Clayton."

Clayton's tongue traced the outline of Syneda's lips. He then moved his mouth from her lips to her neck and began kissing her there.

His caress on a sensitive part of her neck aroused her, setting her body on fire with desire. He lifted his head.

"Where do we go from here?"

Syneda smiled up at him. "How about the bedroom."

Smiling, he gathered her into his arms and took her to the very place she'd requested.

Late Sunday evening, Syneda walked Clayton to the door wearing his white dress shirt. She looked down at herself. "This is becoming a habit."

He smiled as he pulled her into his arms. "But it's one I like. You look good in my shirt. I want you to return it to me in New Orleans."

Syneda's eyes widen. "New Orleans?"

"Yes. Let's meet in New Orleans two weeks from now. Will you do it?"

She looked at him for a few minutes before saying. "Yes."

Clayton smiled. "I can't come back to New York this coming weekend. I promised Dex and Caitlin I'd babysit Jordan while they attend Caitlin's high school reunion in San Antonio. I would invite you to keep me company, but Jordan would love telling her parents when they returned that Aunt Neda spent the weekend with her too."

Syneda grinned. "Yes, I can just imagine Jordan doing that."

They looked into each other's eyes, momentarily becoming lost in the memories of the weekend. Clayton had been right, somehow this weekend had far surpassed the last. The last time they had spent together was due to a mixture of curiosity and hormones. This time they had become closer friends as well as lovers.

On Saturday morning over breakfast they had again discussed the Drayton case. And this time although they still didn't agree completely, they had respected the other's opinion.

"Waiting two weeks to see you again will seem like forever," Clayton said huskily. He pulled Syneda into his arms giving her a goodbye kiss that was destined to be the longest on record.

CHAPTER 12

Clayton Madaris's paced walk and relaxed smile reflected an extremely happy man. As far as he was concerned he was on top of the world. What man wouldn't be when he had found the woman of his dreams?

He could barely contain himself as he walked through the doors of the Remington Oil Building. The only thing that would make him any happier, he thought as he scribbled his name on the clipboard the security guard had handed to him, was for him and Syneda to have a Christmas wedding. But first he would have to make sure the future bride had fallen in love with him by then.

He shook his head grinning. Very few people would believe that he, a man who'd always avoided any serious involvements, would be contemplating something like marriage. At times it was hard for him to believe himself, and he would find himself spending a very long time in the shower doing some serious thinking.

Then all it would take was for him to remember some of the reasons why he had fallen in love with Syneda to bring him back to reality. From the start, although they'd been at odds with each other, there had always been very good open communication between them. He liked the fact she was a very up-front person. She didn't believe in sugar coating anything. And the truth of the matter was that he'd found her combustible nature absolutely irresistible. He still did.

Before, when he'd dated a lot of women, he'd had to date quite a number of them to obtain all the qualities he had found in the one he considered as the ideal woman, Syneda.

His thoughts drifted to the weekend they had spent in New Orleans a few weeks ago. He had been to New Orleans several times before, but never had he enjoyed the city the way he had done with her. They had wined and dined in the French Quarter, had been entertained at a number of hot spots, and had made love in the heat of the night in their hotel room. He had fallen even more hopelessly, madly, and passionately in love with her.

As Clayton stepped on the elevator, his thoughts turned to his brothers. Although they were now happily married to the women they loved, he could remember them going through some really tough times in the name of love. In fact he, of all people, had had to intervene to keep them from making a complete mess of things. If it hadn't been for him, Justin would not have had the good sense to accept Lorren as his fate, and poor, pitiful Dex would still be on the "pain and suffering list," working himself to death at Madaris Explorations trying to forget Caitlin.

Clayton was glad he wasn't going through any changes over a woman like his two brothers had. Things were progressing smoothly between him and Syneda. For most people, love didn't grow in a short time like it had done with him. That was the reason why he would give Syneda a little bit more time before springing his true feelings on her. By then, hopefully, she would be in love with him so much that she would agree to marry him right away. Nothing would please him more than coming home to her each and every night.

When the elevator stopped on the executive floor, he got off, checking his watch. He was right on time for his meeting with the president and CEO of Remington Oil, S. T. Remington.

He had gotten the opportunity to work closely with Mr. Remington last year when Dex's wife, Caitlin, owned a piece of land that Remington Oil had been interested in buying. Caitlin hadn't wanted to sell the property and instead she had leased it to Remington Oil. He had represented Caitlin as her attorney in the contract negotiations.

S. T. Remington, Clayton had soon discovered, was a sharp but fair businessman. He had taken an immediate liking to the man whose family's blue-blooded lineage could be traced all the way back to Texas's beginning when his great-great-great-grandfather rode alongside Sam Houston. Although Remington had been born to wealth and was considered to be a private person, he was caring and concerned for all aspects of human life. That was evident in his generous contributions to numerous charities.

"Good morning, Mr. Madaris," the secretary greeted. "Mr. Remington is expecting you. You can go right in."

"Thanks." Clayton entered the plush office and watched as the tall, distinguished-looking gentleman in his late forties stood to greet him.

"Madaris, how are you?" S. T. Remington said heartily, extending his hand to Clayton.

"Fine," Clayton responded, accepting the man's warm handshake. "And thanks for seeing me on such short notice. I hope it wasn't a problem."

"None whatsoever," the elder man said, gesturing toward the chair next to his large oak desk. "You mentioned something about a job referral."

"Yes," Clayton said, taking the seat.

"You didn't have to have a special meeting with me to refer someone for employment with Remington Oil. Stephen James is the manager over my Human Resources Department. He's always looking for energetic, career-minded individuals to bring on as part of our management team."

"Yes, but I thought it best to talk with you first. It's only fair that you know that if your company determines the person I want to refer is suitable for employment, and decides to hire him, there may be possible repercussions."

Remington lifted a brow. "I don't understand."

"Do you know John Drayton?"

"The John Drayton of Drayton Industries?" At Clayton's nod he said. "Yes, but not personally. Why?"

Clayton told Mr. Remington about the problems Larry Morgan was having finding employment because of John Drayton. He was careful to leave out confidential information or to reveal his source for the information he was sharing. "So, as you can see, no one will hire him."

"Is Morgan a friend of yours?"

"No, in fact I've never met him and he knows nothing of me, and I prefer to keep it that way. I know of him and the problems he's having through an acquaintance whose identify I prefer not disclosing. It's a rather complicated story."

Remington nodded. "You don't know him, yet you want to recommend that we hire him?"

"I've checked into his employment history. It's apparent he's an excellent employee. The only reason he was released from his former job, and the reason he can't find employment now is because of John Drayton."

Remington smiled. "If Larry Morgan is as good as you say he is, then there's no reason we can't call him in for an interview. And if he meets all of our qualifications, we will consider him for employment with us."

"Thanks."

"You're welcome, and I think it's commendable that you're taking such an interest in someone you really don't know."

Clayton smiled. "I have my reasons."

"I'm sure you do. And don't worry about John Drayton. If he wants to start something with Remington Oil let him. I'm just the person to finish it for him."

Clayton laughed as he stood. He liked Remington's grit. It reminded him of someone else he knew. The beautiful, feisty woman he was in love with. "Thanks. I appreciate it."

Go ahead and be daring, a devilish little voice droned in Syneda's ear.

Don't even think it, the voice of reason shot back, *Clayton may not like it. . . .*

Syneda closed the book with a thump. Why was she beginning to care what Clayton might or might not like? Why was she remembering that he'd once said he liked the way she wore her hair?

"Sorry about running off like that," Deborah, her hairdresser said, coming back to her. "But Ms. Jones claimed the relaxer was stinging, and God knows she can't afford to lose another strand of hair."

Syneda smiled. She liked Deborah and had been coming to this hair salon for over five years. The hairstylist was good at what she did.

"Did you see a style in that book you liked? You're long overdue for a new look," Deborah said, working quickly and efficiently as she applied the conditioner to Syneda's hair.

Syneda thought for a moment, then said, "Yeah, I saw a couple that I liked."

"Well?"

"Well, what?"

"You haven't done anything drastic to your hair since you went from curly to straight over a year ago. How about a short cut? I think it'll look good on you."

Syneda frowned. "Why do you want to cut my hair? Is this one of your scissor-happy days? I saw what you did to Carla Frazier's head."

Deborah shrugged as she continued to work the conditioner into Syneda's hair. "Carla got just what she asked for. She wanted her hair cut off like that. And you have to admit, she looks good with short hair. Some people wear short hair well, some do not. That's why I'm thankful for such a thing as weaved hair."

Syneda grinned. She could always count on Deborah to lighten her mood. Although the woman could be a chatterbox at times, she enjoyed coming to the full-service salon.

"Well, are you gonna get a cut?"

"Not this time. Let me think about it some more."

After getting home and settling in for the night, Syneda thought back to her conversation with Deborah and her decision not to make any drastic changes to her hair. For the first time in her life, she had taken into account what a man might or might not like about her. Specifically, she had not gotten her hair cut because she had cared how Clayton would feel about it. When she'd changed from the curly look to the straight look last year, he had complimented her several times about her hair and had told her how much he'd liked it.

She frowned, not liking the way her thoughts were going. In fact, she hadn't liked the way her thoughts had been going for quite some time. All she had to do, at any time and at any place, was to close her eyes to pick out one of several memorable moments she and Clayton had shared over the past couple of months. Even now, she could clearly remember their weekend together in New Orleans, especially that first night.

Vivid memories of their room, a romantic suite, filled her thoughts. It had been large and spacious with a king-sized bed. The room had been cool, supported by the air conditioning that had provided relief from the already hot "Nawlins" afternoon. But even the air conditioner had not withstood the powerful heat that began surging to unbearable degrees once Clayton had closed the room door, locking them inside.

He had ordered room service and the food had been delicious. But it was the things that had happened after the meal that still had her nearly groaning aloud at the memory. It was when he had scooped her up into his arms and had taken her into the bedroom, making beautiful, passionate love to her.

The ringing of the phone startled Syneda so much that she jumped. A part of her became angry at the intrusion. She picked up the phone.

"Yes?"

"Hmm, I like a woman who says yes, right off the bat," a husky masculine voice said.

Syneda smiled as she stretched across her bed. "I was just thinking about you."

Clayton smiled. "Were you? Good thoughts I hope."

"The best."

"Enlighten me. And be specific," he said mildly.

Syneda closed her eyes and blushed as her mind did a sort of instant mental replay. However, this time it zeroed in on more things in detail. She could see herself, how she had been that night in New Orleans, naked, languorous, in his arms. She could feel the silk bed sheet against her bare back and the weight of his body, hard as a rock, upon hers. She could conjure up the taste of him in her mouth as he kissed her senseless.

"Syneda?"

"Hmm?" She refused to open her eyes just yet. She could visualize more that way.

"You're moaning into the phone, baby."

Syneda's eyes snapped open. "I'm not."

"Yes, you were. Did you enjoy our time together in New Orleans?"

"Oh, yes. Tremendously," she whispered.

"How would you like to meet me again next weekend?"

Syneda felt her mouth arrange itself into a smile. "Where?"

"Atlanta."

"Atlanta? What's happening in Atlanta?"

"We'll be what's happening. How about it?"

Syneda began to tremble at the thought of being with Clayton again. It had already been two weeks since they had last been together. A part of her wanted to say yes, just name the place and the time, and I'll be there. But then another part of her, the one that had always kept her level-headed where men were concerned, wanted her to call time-out and take time to examine the feelings and changes slowly taking place within her.

She heaved a sigh, rolled onto her stomach and buried her face into the pillow.

"Hello? Syneda? Are you still there?"

"Yeah, I'm still here."

"Well then, what about it?"

Syneda sighed. The "I don't need a man" part of her was tempted to tell him no, but the "I enjoy being with Clayton Madaris" part of her overruled.

"Yes, Clayton. I'll meet you in Atlanta."

"Celeste?" Braxter whispered.

"Hmmm?" she answered, her voice sleepy.

"Do you want to spend the night?"

She opened her eyes and smiled up at him. "Since it's past midnight and I'm still in your bed, I think that's not a bad idea."

Braxter grinned. They had just finished making love. She was everything he wanted in a woman and more. "I'm going to have to leave town for a while."

She came awake and sat up in bed. "Why?"

He got out of the bed and stretched. "Reelection time. It's time for the senator to take his campaign on the road, back to his home state of Texas, and I'll be going with him."

Celeste frowned. She was clearly not happy with this news. She had spent one month with Braxter already, and had not been able to find out anything of particular interest about his employer. As far as Braxter Montgomery was concerned, Senator Lansing walked on water. The only thing she had stumbled on was the fact that around the same time of month in May of each year, Senator Lansing cleared his calendar for a few days and went back to Texas. She took a deep breath. There could be a number of reasons for him doing that. She would be the first to admit that everyone needed to get away by themselves once in awhile.

"Does that mean you're breaking things off between us?" she asked poutily, not really caring one way or another. The person who had hired her had paid her in full up-front. And although she didn't have anything against Braxter personally, in fact she thought under different circumstances, she could have found herself very much attracted to him. He was indeed handsome, and was definitely a terrific lover. But she had learned a long time ago not to mix business with pleasure.

"Breaking things off?" Braxter asked, laughing. "Of course not. I'll be coming home most weekends."

He got back in the bed and pulled her into his arms. "I got an idea. How would you like to be my guest at the senator's kickoff campaign party three weeks from now? A friend of his, this wealthy cattleman named Jacob Madaris, is giving this huge party for the senator at his ranch. The guest list is pretty impressive."

Celeste arched a brow, feigning disinterest by yawning. "Really? How impressive?"

He smiled. "Not that I think you'll really be interested," he teased "But I know for a fact that Sterling Hamilton is coming."

She bolted out of his arm. "Sterling Hamilton! The actor Sterling Hamilton?"

Braxter laughed, pulling her back to him. "Yes, but before you get overly excited, you may as well know that Diamond Swain is coming, too."

"Oh," Celeste said disappointedly. Anyone who kept up with the lifestyles of the rich and famous knew that Sterling Hamilton and the leading lady in most of his movies, Diamond Swain, were an item.

"Disappointed?"

"Crushed is more like it."

Braxter smiled. "Does that mean you don't want to be my guest at the party?"

She smiled up at him. "I said I was crushed, not crazy. Of course I'll attend the party with you."

She snuggled closer to him, smiling, pleased with the recent turn of events.

CHAPTER 13

Clayton glanced around the room, taking in the well-dressed, affluent people in their expensive suits and gowns. Around him the crowd swirled happily amid the soft, jazzy sound of Kenny G as he entertained a group on the other side of the huge room. As usual, Clayton thought, his uncle had spared no expense for his good friend, Senator Lansing.

He stopped at a table laden with food and helped himself to a little cracker covered with rich, dark caviar. Being at a party was the last thing he wanted. Especially a party where Syneda would be in attendance, and the two of them would pretend to be only friends. The thought of seeing her again inflamed him with desire.

He hadn't seen her since their romantic rendezvous in Atlanta three weeks ago. Because of the important court appeal she'd been working on, and a couple of business trips he'd taken to California, they had not been able to hook up. Although they had talked frequently on the phone, their conversations had been short and as far as he was concerned, unfulfilling.

Clayton searched the crowded room with a steady, sweeping glance, recognizing various members of his family, business associates, friends, as well as a number of unfamiliar faces. He continued to scan the room for the one person he wanted to see. Syneda.

A group of people shifted from the crowd surrounding Kenny G, and for a moment he had a clear view across the room. And then he saw her.

She was dancing with Lloyd Jones. Clayton frowned. Although he didn't know Jones personally, he knew of him. He knew that the man was in his early thirties, single, and considered by some to be a brilliant neurosurgeon.

"Don't look now, man, but you're glaring. And for some reason jealousy doesn't become you," a familiar voice said in a deep Texan drawl at his shoulder.

Clayton turned to face his brother Justin. "Am I that obvious?" he asked dryly.

Justin took a sip of his wine. "Right now, only to me because I know a little more than most. But if you keep it up, everyone in this room will know, especially Lloyd Jones. Do me a favor and behave yourself. I don't want to repair any broken bones tonight."

Clayton shrugged. "You won't have to," he said smoothly. "I promised Syneda that I would not give anything away."

"That should be interesting."

"If it was left up to me, everyone would know."

Justin chuckled when he saw Clayton's annoyed features. "I gather as much." He took another sip of wine. "Give her time, Clayton. Things will work out."

"That's what I keep telling myself."

Justin stared long and hard at his brother. An amused grin touched his features. "You really have it bad, don't you?"

"No worse than you had it for Lorren," Clayton shot back, his eyes narrowing.

"I think there's a major difference here though," Justin said smiling, thinking of his wife and the love affair they'd shared before they had married.

"What?" Clayton asked, reaching for another cracker from the table.

"I was in love with Lorren. My intentions were honorable."

Clayton put a hand on the sleeve of his brother's jacket, claiming his full attention. "So are mine. I'm in love with Syneda."

Justin stared at him, open mouthed. "Impossible. You would never allow yourself to fall in love," he finally managed to say.

"Then that should say a lot for Syneda's abilities, shouldn't it?"

Recovering from the initial shock, Justin eyed his brother thoughtfully, not knowing what else to say. A grin spread across his face. "Care to hang with me for a while?"

"Where's Lorren?"

"She's upstairs. She wanted to get the kids tucked in bed before coming down. Well, well, well, take a look at who just walked in."

It took all Clayton's strength to tear his gaze from Syneda and Lloyd Jones and to the person who had apparently caught Justin's attention.

"It's cousin Felicia Laverne. And take a look at her outfit."

Clayton's lips lifted in an amused smile. His attractive cousin was dressed in a silk leopard jumpsuit with matching short leopard boots and carrying a leopard clutch bag. Her face lit up in a warm smile when she saw them. She began walking their way.

"Justin, Clayton. It's good seeing you guys," she said giving them both a quick peck on the cheek. She glanced around the room. "Where's Dex?"

"He's around here someplace," Justin answered, scanning her from head to toe. "What's with this outfit?"

Her eyes darkened. "My man's been acting like a dog so I've decided to begin acting like a cat. I'm on the prowl tonight and would love to purr to any man for attention. So you better warn your rich friends to stay away from me. You know how much I like men with money."

Justin chuckled. "None of my friends can afford you. After husband number two, maybe you should consider marrying a poor man."

"Not on your life. I'm sure there's some man out there with both honey and money."

Clayton shook his head. He and Felicia were first cousins and had been born in the same year. Their grandmother said the moon must have been out of orbit that year, given his womanizing ways and Felicia's inability to keep a husband.

"Well, I'll see you guys later. I understand there's a lot of men here tonight, and I want to check them out."

"Yeah, see ya," Clayton said, turning his attention back to Syneda. Sometime during his conversation with Felicia, the dance had come to an end, and Syneda now stood across the room talking to his Aunt Delores. He sighed. At least Jones wasn't hanging around.

Clayton knew there was no way Syneda hadn't seen him, so why hadn't she come over and at least said hello? There would have been nothing conspicuous with her doing that. So why was she avoiding him?

Delores Brooks's happy chattering seemed to recede into the distance as Syneda's eyes drifted to Clayton. She had known the exact moment he had entered the room. Although the room was crowded. She had known.

Like a soft caress, his mere presence had touched her even while she had danced in the arms of another man. She frowned, getting annoyed with herself. Long ago she had made up her mind that getting deeply involved with a man was a personal complication she didn't want or need in her life.

But now, in a way she could not define, she was getting deeply involved with Clayton. And he was becoming a complication. She had picked up on that fact weeks ago, right after their trip to New Orleans. But she had convinced herself that he was the one man she could handle. She had believed an intimate relationship with him would not mean losing control over her emotions. After all, all she'd wanted to share with him was passion, and the man certainly was full of that.

But somewhere, somehow, for a little while, she had allowed herself to forget the promises she had made to herself, her goals, and her own personal established agenda. If she wasn't careful, she would forget the reasons she could never trust love. She had known firsthand the pain of believing that someone loved you and then being disappointed.

She met Clayton's glance across the room. The look in his eyes was heated, seductive, arousing. Memories of their weekend in Atlanta flowed between them and she read the message in his eyes. He had said nothing, he hadn't even bothered to move his lips. But then, he didn't really need to say anything. The message he was sending to her was plain and clear. He wanted her and sometime later tonight, family or no family, he intended to have her.

Shakily, Syneda took a deep breath. Even when she wanted to struggle against the sensuous pull he had on her mind and senses, she couldn't. And she knew that deep down, tonight of all nights, she wouldn't. She wanted him, too.

Only when Clayton's aunt touched her arm to regain her attention did she drop her eyes from his. When she looked back in his direction moments later, he was gone.

I need to start mingling more, Clayton thought, when Justin disappeared after being beeped by one of his patients.

Clayton moved in the direction of the bar that had been set up. Frustrations were beginning to overwhelm him. He wanted to take Syneda and go some place private, where the two of them could be alone. As usual, she looked good. His eyes had completely surveyed her sleek teal-colored gown. He had long ago accepted the fact that anything Syneda wore, she wore well, including his dress shirt.

Tonight her gown was totally alluring. The silky material fitted fluidly over her body, emphasizing her shapely figure. He not only wanted to hold her in his arms, but wanted to touch those familiar places that only a lover would be allowed to touch.

Glancing around, he noticed his sister and brother-in-law had just arrived. He walked over to them. "Good evening, folks."

"What's so good about it?" Traci answered with a pout on her lips.

Clayton met his brother-in-law's gaze and detected his well-hidden grin. He couldn't help but like Daniel Green, the man who had taken his sister off his parents' hands nearly ten years ago. Any man who could handle Letracia Madaris Green's raving-mad buying sprees definitely lifted a notch in his eyes.

Everyone in the family knew that Traci lived to spend money and that the shopping malls were her second home. "Shop till you drop" was her motto in life. Clayton smiled. No doubt Traci's state of unhappiness had nothing to do with PMS. Daniel must have pulled the plug on her buying power.

"Have Mom and Dad arrived yet?" Traci asked, interrupting Clayton's thoughts.

Clayton's smile widened. He wondered why she'd be looking for their parents. She definitely wouldn't get any pity from them. They were probably still paying for the things she had charged while in college. "Yeah, they're here someplace."

Traci walked off. And without having the decency to excuse herself, Clayton thought. "I take it she's not a happy camper tonight," he said to Daniel.

Daniel chuckled as he nodded. "That's putting it mildly. But she'll get over it."

"Yeah, but I'd hate to be at your house while she's in the process of doing so. Should I guess why she's ticked off?" Clayton asked, leaning against a column post. His arms were folded across his chest as he eyed Daniel with amusement.

"You think it's funny don't you, Clayton?"

"Hell, yeah, I think it's funny because Justin, Dex, and I tried to warn you, but you wouldn't listen to us."

Daniel laughed, remembering. "Being in love makes you do foolish things. But you'll be spared ever finding that out."

Clayton lifted a brow. "Why do you say that?"

"Because you're one of those men who'll never fall in love."

If only you knew. Clayton thought.

"You like hit-and-run relationships."

Not any more. Clayton wanted to say.

"And speaking of relationships, Clayton, I may as well warn you that, thanks to Traci, the buzz word is that there may be a special woman in your life."

That got Clayton's immediate attention. He began wondering if somehow he had given something away for Traci to pick up on. That couldn't have been possible since he hadn't seen her a lot lately. "What gave her that idea?"

"I don't know, but it sounds crazy doesn't it? Everyone knows you don't believe in getting serious about a woman."

"What makes Traci think otherwise?"

"I overheard a conversation she was having with Kattie. They're trying to figure out what's going on with you, and why you're going out of town so much. They're curious about all of your weekend trips; especially since you're being so secretive. No one knows where you go or who you're seeing. It's driving them nuts."

"Serves them right for trying to get into my business." He looked thoughtfully at Daniel. "And I guess they have their own ideas of just who the woman is."

Daniel laughed. "Yep. They figure it's someone you met while attending that attorneys' conference some months back."

"Is that a fact?" Clayton said, slightly annoyed but relieved. He grabbed a glass of wine off a passing waiter's tray and took a sip. At least his two nosey sisters hadn't put two and two together and come up with him and Syneda.

"Do me a favor, Daniel."

"What?"

"Put a muzzle on your wife's mouth, and I'll have a talk with Raymond about putting one on Kattie's."

Clayton strolled off, hearing his brother-in-law's laughter follow him. He headed back to the main area of the house, intent on at least saying a few words to the honoree. While making his way to the other side, he noticed a deep silence spread across the room. He glanced toward the door and understood. The actor, Sterling Hamilton, had arrived and just like the rumor mill had predicted, the very beautiful woman who appeared as his leading lady in a number of his films, Diamond Swain, was with him.

Clayton chuckled. Once again Hamilton and Swain's appearance together would start tongues wagging. There were already reports circulating around the country that the two of them were secretly married. He knew if that was true, it would cause the heartbreak of quite a few women.

Clayton shook his head. He had enough to deal with regarding the woman in his life. He didn't have time to speculate about the woman who was supposed to be in Sterling Hamilton's.

Senator Lansing was pleased with the turnout. As usual, Jake Madaris had outdone himself. He glanced around the room and caught Braxter Montgomery's eye and smiled at him and the lovely young lady he was with. He had been introduced to her earlier. He was glad Braxter had finally gotten interested in someone. He thought the young man worked a tad too hard at times.

The senator's smile faded when, for the second time that night, he noticed the attractive young woman in a teal-colored gown making her way around the crowded room. He couldn't put his finger on it but there was something oddly familiar about her. There was something about her that captured his attention, not in a sexual way, but in a way he couldn't explain. It had something to do with her smile, her mannerisms, and the way she tilted her head when talking to someone.

He continued to regard her with interest. She reminded him of some-one. But who?

Only a man as close to the senator as Braxter could have picked up on the senator's troubled expression, even from across a crowded room. "Celeste, please excuse me for a second."

He walked over to the senator. "Sir? Is something wrong?"

"I don't know," Senator Lansing said, his words barely a thread of a sound. He continued looking at the young woman across the room. "That woman, the one in the teal-colored gown. Do you know her?"

Braxter followed the senator's gaze. "Not personally, but I know who she is. She's Lorren Madaris's best friend."

"Lorren Madaris? Justin Madaris's wife?"

"Yes."

"What's her name?"

"Syneda. Syneda Walters."

Shakily the senator reached out to steady himself with a hand on the edge of an oak table. "Did you say Wal . . . Walters?"

Braxton frowned, clearly worried by the shocked expression on the senator's face. "Yes, Walters. Sir? Are you all right?"

"I need to get out of here for a moment, Braxter. I'm going up to my room for a while. Please make the necessary excuses."

Before Braxter could respond, Senator Lansing turned and went up the stairs.

Celeste stood on the other side of the room, grateful she had taken a lip reading class as an elective in college. She took a quick glance at the woman who had made the senator lose some of his color.

The attractive woman appeared to be around her age. Was she some-one with whom the senator had once had an affair? Well, whoever she was, the sight of her had shaken up the old man. She smiled. She would have to find out the woman's name, and more about her. There might be something about the senator's reaction to the woman that was worth checking into.

CHAPTER 14

Clayton glanced around the crowded room, his gaze seeking out Syneda. He saw her dancing again, this time it was with his uncle Jake.

He relaxed, not concerned about competition from his uncle, who was the youngest of the seven Madaris brothers. Although at the age of forty-four Jacob Madaris was still a strikingly handsome man, everyone knew Jake was married to the Whispering Pines ranch. He'd been married while in his early twenties, and the woman had left him after less than a year. She had been a city girl who had hated the rural life Jake loved.

"Where have you been?"

Clayton turned toward the sound of the familiar voice, and came face to face with his brother Dex. A smile formed on his lips. "I've been around."

Dex Madaris shook his head. "No, I don't mean tonight. I mean where have you been for the past couple of weeks? Caitlin and I haven't seen you since that weekend you kept Jordan for us. And you've been missing Sunday dinners at Mom's. It's not like you to pass up a free meal." Dex flashed him a grin. "Although with you not being there, there's more food to go around."

"Funny, Dex. Real funny. You're turning into a regular comedian," Clayton said, grabbing a handful of mixed nuts from the table.

"So, where have you been?"

Clayton frowned slightly. "Why is it that everyone wants to get in my business?"

Dex smiled. "Because you're usually in everyone else's."

"You can't deny that, Clayton," Justin said, coming to join them.

Clayton stopped munching for a moment and looked at the two brothers he loved and respected. But at the moment they were annoying. "Your opinions of me are touching," he said dryly.

Before the brothers could respond, an old acquaintance of Justin's walked up. Introductions were made and conversations began. But Clayton tuned out all the talk around him, although he forced a smile and nodded his head occasionally. His real interest was in the woman across the room. The dance had ended and she stood talking to Caitlin, Lorren, and Corinthians Avery, a woman who was the head geologist for Remington Oil.

"I see she has caught your interest as well."

"Who?" Clayton asked the man standing beside him who had been engaged in a conversation with Justin and Dex moments earlier.

"The woman in the teal gown. She's gorgeous. I've had my eyes on her all night."

Clayton tried to keep his features expressionless. "Really?" He searched his memory for the name of the man Justin had introduced him to just minutes ago. Ahh, yes, his name was Bernard Wilson, and according to Justin he owned a large pharmaceutical company in Waco.

Clayton balled his fists at his side. A part of him wanted to smash the man's face for even noticing Syneda.

"So what do you think of her?" Bernard Wilson asked.

On a long breath, Clayton fought back the anger consuming him. As nonchalantly as he could, he simply said, "She looks all right."

Bernard Wilson raised a brow. "I think she looks better than all right. I love the color of her hair, and the color of her eyes is so sexy. And look at the size of her waistline. I just love slender, well-built women." He then turned to Justin. "I understand she's a good friend of your wife, Justin. You'll have to introduce us."

Justin flicked a quick glance at Clayton, then back to Bernard and said. "Sure."

Clayton looked at his brother in disbelief, ignoring Justin's "what else could I say" expression. He then decided to take matters into his owns hands. If Wilson thought he was interested in Syneda, he may as well get disinterested.

"You like slender, well-built women, huh? Then you may want to think twice about asking Justin for an introduction."

Bernard Wilson frowned in confusion. "Why?"

"Because less than six months ago, Syneda was almost a hundred pounds heavier."

Dex, who had been quietly listening, and who had just taken a sip of wine, nearly choked when he heard Clayton's blatant lie. He coughed a few times to clear his throat.

Clayton gave Dex a few whacks on the back. "You shouldn't drink your wine so fast, Dex," he said calmly, as Dex tried to regain his composure.

"She used to weigh over a hundred pounds more?" Bernard asked incredulously.

So as not to get caught in the middle of Clayton's lie, Justin simply shrugged, and said nothing.

When Dex started to deny it, the look Clayton gave him clearly said he'd better keep his mouth shut.

"Yes, it's hard to believe, isn't it," Clayton answered smoothly. "I understand she went on one of those quick weight loss programs. She was determined to get in that particular dress tonight. And you're right, she does look good in it. But you know what they say."

"What?" Bernard, Justin and Dex all asked simultaneously. Bernard asked out of curiosity. Justin asked because he was eager to see just how far Clayton would go with this farce. And Dex asked because he was clearly in the dark and didn't have a clue as to what was going on. He cast Justin a curious glance, and all he got was a shrug for an answer.

"They say it never stays off when you get rid of it that fast. In a few months she'll be looking like her old self again. Plump."

Justin thought Clayton had gone a little bit too far and decided to step in. "There's more to a person than looks, Clayton."

"Yeah," Dex agreed, still clearly lost.

"I agree. And I'm sure Syneda feels her colored eye contacts will—"

"Colored eye contacts?" Dex asked, not believing what he was hearing. Clayton knew green was Syneda's real eye color.

"But I thought they were hers," Bernard said, his frown deepening.

"They are," Clayton answered him. "She bought them didn't she?"

Dex took a huge gulp of Jack Daniels from the glass he held in his hand. Justin suddenly became preoccupied with brushing off a nonexistent speck of lint from his suit.

"And her hair color?" Bernard asked dryly. His interest in Syneda clearly fading.

"From a bottle." Seeing Bernard's sullen expression Clayton added, "With all the enhancements available to women these days, you never know what's real and what's not."

Bernard nodded. "Thanks for leveling with me, man."

Clayton smiled. "Hey, don't mention it. We players have to stick together." He put his arm around Bernard's shoulder. "Don't look so down. I think there's a woman here tonight that's probably just what you're looking for. And I do believe you're just her type."

Bernard's mood brightened some. "Really? Where?"

"She's around here someplace. Her name is Felicia Laverne Evans. You'll know her when you see her. She's dressed in a leopard outfit."

Bernard smiled. "Hey, thanks, you're an all right guy." He turned to Justin. "Forget about that introduction, Justin. I'll see you guys later." Then he walked off.

"I don't know why you did what you just did," Dex said, glaring at his brother. "And maybe it's best that I don't know. All I have to say is that when Syneda finds out about those lies you just told Wilson, she's gonna give you hell."

Clayton smiled and calmly resumed eating his nuts. "Won't be the first time she's given me hell about something."

"No man should look that good," Kattie Madaris Barnes said to the other women standing with her. They were all staring at the man across the room, Sterling Hamilton. He and Diamond Swain were talking to Oprah.

"Don't forget you're a married woman," Lorren Madaris teased.

"I'm married, but I'm not blind," Kattie replied grinning.

"I heard he and Diamond Swain are secretly married," Caitlin Madaris said.

"She's not wearing a ring. I've already checked that out," Traci replied.

Syneda hid her smile as she reached for a cracker covered with cheese. She had to admit Sterling Hamilton was indeed a very handsome man. But then, so was Clayton, she thought to herself. She could have pointed that out to Traci and Kattie, but they might get curious as to why she even thought so. As Clayton's sisters, they wouldn't see their brother through the eyes as another woman.

She glanced across the room where Clayton, Dex, and Justin were involved in what appeared to be a deep conversation. In her opinion, and she knew Lorren and Caitlin would agree with her, the three Madaris brothers were three *fine* men. They gave true meaning to the words tall, dark, and handsome. And although they were different in personality and temperament, she didn't know any men more loving, considerate, and loyal to their families.

She glanced at her watch. It was getting late. She had hoped to have gotten the opportunity to meet Senator Lansing by now. During most of the evening, he'd been constantly surrounded by people, and now she didn't see him anywhere.

"Syneda, are you all right? You haven't had much to say all night," Kattie said with concern in her voice.

Syneda smiled. "I'm fine, just kind of tired. I've been keeping late nights working on a case I'm appealing. I think I'll turn in early tonight."

"All of us should turn in early. Especially you two," Traci said to Lorren and Caitlin. "Although it's been a long time since I was pregnant, the one thing I do remember is needing plenty of rest." She grinned. "And don't forget Gramma Madaris expects all of us in church tomorrow, bright and early, beginning with Sunday School."

"Sunday School starts at nine o'clock," Kattie said. "Boy is she asking for a lot."

Traci smiled. "I know, but with tomorrow being her birthday, I guess she feels she can ask her children, grandchildren, and great-grands for anything."

"Where will her birthday party be held?" Syneda asked.

"It will be right after the services tomorrow in the church dining room. Gramma Madaris has been a member of that church for over sixty years. In fact, she and Grampa got married there when she was seventeen."

"Good evening, ladies," Justin said coming over to join the group with Dex and Clayton with him. "I think you ladies are the most gorgeous ones here tonight. Don't you agree, Dex?" he asked, placing a soft kiss on Lorren's lips.

"Absolutely," Dex said smiling. His arms went around Caitlin protectively, gently pulling her against him. "All Madaris women are beautiful, and they're all Madaris women."

Syneda smiled. It was on the tip of her tongue to remind Dex she wasn't a Madaris but thought better of it. Like everyone else, Dex considered her as part of the family.

She liked Justin and Dex. Justin had been there for Lorren when she had needed someone to help her through a difficult time in her life. And for that reason he was very special to her. With Dex, there was such tenderness in him, as well as stubbornness and pride. He was the type of man who protected his own. Last year Caitlin's life had been threatened, and Dex had made it clear that no one messed with his wife unless they were willing to face his wrath.

Her gaze went to Clayton. He took another sip of his wine, watching her with dark eyes. A part of her came to life under his steady gaze. It was silently reaching out to her, touching her, making her want him and bringing forth memories she could never forget. Not being able to handle his gaze any longer, she looked down.

"Clayton, you've been scarce lately. I've heard you've been taking quite a few trips out of town. Any reason why?" Kattie asked, her dark eyes twinkling.

Clayton's eyes narrowed. His gaze went first to Kattie and then to Traci. "What I do does not concern the two of you. Remember that."

Syneda's stomach was in knots. *Had Kattie and Traci figured out what was going on between her and Clayton? Did they suspect anything?*

Clayton glanced at Syneda and couldn't help but see the worried look in her eyes. He wanted to go to her and take her in his arms and wipe

away that look. He decided to do the next best thing when he heard
Luther Vandross step to the microphone to sing. "Syneda, could I speak
to you for a minute?"

"I hope the two of you aren't going to start arguing about anything,"
Caitlin said smiling.

"Not tonight. I just want to dance." He knew that dancing provided a
socially acceptable way to be close to her. And he desperately needed to
hold Syneda in his arms.

Not giving Syneda a chance to refuse, he reached out and took her
hand in his and led her to the area where people were dancing. He took
her in his arms as Luther began singing, "You Are My Lady."

Clayton's arm tightened around Syneda and he whispered. "I missed
you."

Syneda relaxed in Clayton's arm. She knew the members of his family
wouldn't think anything of them dancing together. They usually danced
together often at all the family functions. His family had commented several times on how well they danced together. "And I missed you, too,"
she said truthfully.

"I'm coming to your room tonight, Syneda."

She looked into his eyes. "No. Don't. Someone might see you."

"I'll make sure I'm not seen, but I'm coming, so don't ask me not to. I
have to come. I want you so much I can barely stand it."

She lifted her face upward seemingly to invite the kiss he wanted to
give her, but both knew he couldn't. "Don't tempt me, Syneda."

Syneda smiled and placed her head against his chest. Clayton pulled
her closer to him. He wondered if she was listening to the words Luther
was singing. Syneda was indeed "his lady" and he would never let her go.
She is my lady, he whispered in his heart. *She is everything I need and more.*

Dex was walking across the room to get another glass of punch for
Caitlin when he glanced at his brother dancing with Syneda. He stopped
walking. He had seen them dance together several times before, but
never like this. It seemed they were so in tune to each other. There was
such a look of possession in Clayton's eyes as he held Syneda while they
danced. And there was another emotion on his face, the same emotion
he and Justin wore whenever they looked at their wives.

He had never seen that look on Clayton before. He glanced around
the room to see if anyone else had noticed and found that no one else
seemed to be paying any attention to them. Then he remembered the
scene earlier with Clayton and the lies he had told Bernard Wilson. Now
it all made sense.

A smile tilted Dex's lips. He hadn't thought he would ever live to see
the day Clayton fell for a woman. And of all people. Syneda. He won-

dered how the two of them had stopped arguing long enough to connect. His smile widened. Apparently they had enjoyed more than the beaches in Florida.

Clayton saw Dex across the room watching him and Syneda dance. He had seen the exact moment when the truth had hit Dex, and he'd put two and two together. Their eyes met and the shock he'd noticed in Dex's features gradually disappeared. He nodded to his brother and pulled the woman he loved closer into his arms.

Senator Lansing heard the knock on the door. "Yes?"

"It's me, senator, Braxter."

Senator Lansing opened the door. "Come in, Braxter. I was about to go back downstairs."

Braxter entered then closed the door behind him. He studied the senator curiously. "Are you all right, Senator?"

"I don't know. I may have overreacted just a little. It's just that that young lady reminded me of someone. And then her last name is Walters. It may all be a coincidence." He sighed. "Do me a favor, Braxter, find out everything there is to know about her."

"I'll talk to Jacob Madaris and—"

"No, I don't want to involve Jake in this. I want this handled discreetly. I don't want anyone to know I want information on her. Use an investigative agency, and make sure it's one we can trust. I want the report on my desk as soon as it's received."

Braxter frowned. "This sounds serious, sir."

"It may not be. I may be getting myself worked up for nothing. But until I see the report, I won't know for sure."

Braxter nodded, wondering who the young lady could possibly be and what part she played in the senator's life. Unfortunately, Senator Lansing wasn't saying. He hoped there was nothing he really needed to worry about. There had never been any sort of scandal linked to the senator before, and now was not the time for one to happen.

"I have this friend from college who has an investigative company. I'll talk to him on Monday."

Senator Lansing nodded. "Do you know whether the young lady is still here tonight?"

"I saw her leave just before coming upstairs. She left with some other members of the Madaris family. It's my understanding that Jake's putting them up for the night in the various guest cottages around the ranch. Tomorrow is their grandmother's birthday and they're all staying overnight, including Ms. Walters. She's considered a member of the family."

Senator Lansing nodded, remembering that tomorrow was Jake's mother's birthday. His friend had mentioned that to him months ago. "Then there's a possibility that I'll see her at breakfast before I leave. I'm going to make it my business to meet her."

CHAPTER 15

Clayton followed the path that led to the guest cottages. The party for Senator Lansing had ended over an hour ago, and after engaging in polite conversation with the senator, he had quickly cut across the wide swathe of yard and headed in the direction where the cottages were.

"Where are you going in such a hurry?"

Clayton turned quickly at the sound of the familiar voice. "Mom? What are you doing out here so late?"

Marilyn Madaris's face split in a smile. "I wanted to check on your grandmother. She was determined to sleep in the old house tonight, and Christy is staying with her."

Clayton nodded. The old house had been the original ranch house. It was the one his grandfather had built for his grandmother and where they had raised their seven sons.

"I was wondering why Christy left the party early," Clayton said.

Marilyn Madaris studied her son. "You never answered my question about where you're going in such a hurry."

"I'm not in a hurry. I thought I'd walk around a bit."

"Oh, I see."

Clayton couldn't help but notice his mother was giving him a strange look. It was one of those looks he recalled all too well from when he was a kid. It was a look that made you think you couldn't fool her about anything, no matter how hard you tried.

"Well, I'll see you in the morning, Mom."

"All right, Clayton, and don't forget your grandmother expects every-one to be in Sunday School in the morning, nine o'clock sharp."

"I won't forget. See ya."

Clayton waited until his mother was no longer in sight before climbing the porch to the row of cottages that sat off in a distance.

Syneda had just closed the book she'd been reading when she heard the faint knock on the door. The rapid beating of her heart, and the heat settling in the pit of her stomach, told her just who her late-night visitor was.

Pulling her robe together, she crossed the room. She paused within a few feet of the door knowing she should send Clayton away. She shouldn't take the risk of his family finding out about them. His sisters had already begun questioning his frequent weekend trips.

She sighed. As much as she knew she should send him away, she couldn't. She'd been under a lot of work-related stress the past couple of weeks, and she needed to lose herself in the kind of passion only Clayton could stir within her. "Yes?" she finally answered.

"It's me and turn off the lights before opening the door."

Syneda darkened the room then opened the door. She looked past Clayton into the velvety darkness that was lighted by only a few stars and a quarter moon.

"No one saw me come here," he said before she had a chance to ask. He stepped inside, closing the door behind him. He turned on a lamp near the door and the room became bathed in soft light.

Syneda studied him. Tonight he appeared as suave as always, but more unyielding and with less control. He reached out and tilted her chin up with his finger, and looked deep into her eyes.

Syneda's senses were piqued by his closeness and the desire she saw in his eyes. She could feel his heat and literally tasted his passion. An essence of electric tension was sharp and vibrated in the air between them. He reached out and took her hand in his, rubbing his thumb over the softness of her palm. The erotic touch sent her over the edge. He had first done that to the palm of her hand in Saint Augustine. And later when they began seeing each other, that had always been his silent code to her that he wanted her in the most intimate way.

Clayton leaned down and his lips brushed lightly over hers. He lifted his head and their eyes met for a brief moment before he was kissing her again, molding her mouth to his, covering it fully.

Syneda shivered and his arm tightened around her. "Are you cold?" he asked, breaking their kiss.

She shook her head. "No, actually I'm hot. I'm burning up . . . for you."

That was all Clayton needed to hear. He pushed the robe from her shoulders and soon her short gown followed, falling to the floor by her feet. His eyes roamed slowly over her and even in the dim light, Syneda could see the appreciation shining in their dark depths. Then he lifted her in his arms and carried her into the bedroom and positioned her on the bed.

He stood back and without his eyes leaving hers, he began removing his own clothes. Then he took the time to protect her. When he rejoined her on the bed, he began kissing her again, bestowing feathery kisses to her ear, her temple, the tip of her nose, and the corner of her mouth. His kisses then moved down her neck, and from there to her shoulder. "I love tasting you," he whispered huskily.

Syneda held on to him, the force of the passion she felt was overwhelming. It nearly took her breath away. His mouth claimed hers again. Her lips parted under the onslaught of his kiss. Her breath came in short gasps as his fingers touched her intimately, driving her to the point of total madness.

She softly moaned his name when she felt him ease into her, fusing their bodies together as one. They made love in a rhythm as old as time, but still as new as the early morning dew. With infinite tenderness and passion, he loved her. She bit her lip and tried to control her groans of pleasure, but she didn't have to. Clayton kissed the sounds from her lips. She arched her hips, bringing him deeper inside her. What they were sharing felt so good, and so right, she thought her body would surely shatter from the force of it.

Moments later, she did shatter when she reached the peak of total fulfillment and felt Clayton's body trembling with his own release, the sensations were extremely satisfying. Their pleasure built higher and higher, taking them both over the edge. Clayton's muffled groans combined with her own, as they both tumbled into pure ecstasy.

In a guest cottage not too far away, someone else was receiving a late-night visitor. The actress, Diamond Swain, quickly crossed the room after hearing the knock. She flung open the door and a smile spread across her face.

"Jacob. Oh, Jacob, I missed you so much." She reached for him. Her arms slid around his neck as their mouths met in a fierce, demanding kiss.

With their mouths still intimately joined, Jake Madaris's firm hands wrapped securely around her waist, lifting her higher in his arms and closed the door with his foot.

"I missed you, too." And then he was kissing her again, more fiercely and more passionately than before.

"Jacob," Diamond murmured against his moist lips moments later. "I hate to tell you this, but we have company."

"Yeah, remember me, cowboy?" a masculine voice asked from across the room.

Jake spared the man a brief glance before gathering Diamond closer into his arms. "Get lost, Sterling. Go find a woman of your own."

Sterling Hamilton threw back his head and laughed. "Good suggestion, and I would do that in a heartbeat if I hadn't promised a particular stubborn rancher that I would go around pretending his woman was really mine."

Slowly, Jake's eyes narrowed at his friend. "And from what I read in the papers, you're doing a pretty good job. Maybe too good a job. The last rumor I heard said the two of you were secretly married."

Sterling Hamilton smiled. "Jealous?"

"No, just cautious. Just don't forget who she belongs to."

"All right, stop it you two." With a half laugh Diamond pressed her head against Jake's chest. "And, Jacob, leave Sterling alone. He and I are doing a real good job fooling everyone. Besides, how can I be married to Sterling when I'm already married to you?"

Sterling chuckled. "Your wife has a valid point there, Jake. And with that bit of logic, I'm out of here," he said walking to the door.

"I put you up next door," Jake said to Sterling.

"Thanks," he said, turning back to the man who still held Diamond in his arms. He smiled. "Oh yeah, Jake, your faith in me is touching."

"I wouldn't trust my wife with just anyone, Sterling. Remember that."

Sterling chuckled. "Believe me, I will. And by the way, Garwood sends his best regards. He couldn't make it tonight because he, Kimara and the kids are spending a few weeks at Special K."

"How is Kyle?"

"He's doing fine. Kimara is pregnant."

"Again?"

With a throaty laugh Sterling opened the door. "Yes, again. Some people enjoy making babies." He gave Jake and Diamond a wide smile. "And others just like to practice. I'll see you guys later." He left, closing the door behind him.

CHAPTER 16

The sun was shining brightly through the bedroom window when Syneda awoke the next morning. She stretched lazily and rolled over only to discover she was alone in the bed. Clayton had left sometime before daybreak.

She sucked in her breath sharply as memories of their night together descended upon her. Each time they came together was better than the last. Their passion for each other had driven them to new heights, making their hunger more demanding, and making their wanting of each other more urgent.

She took a quick glance at the clock on the nightstand near the bed. It was after eight already. There was no way she could make breakfast and still get to Sunday School on time. She would just have to skip breakfast, she thought, quickly getting out of the bed. She just hoped that she and Clayton would not be the only two people missing at breakfast.

The first thing Clayton noticed when he entered the sanctuary of the Proverbs Baptist Church, was the fact he was late. Not only had he missed Sunday School, but the morning service had already begun. The second thing he noticed was that the church was packed with Madarises. They sat shoulder to shoulder, hip to hip, crowded in a church whose air conditioning, as usual, wasn't working very well.

"Don't worry about the heat in church," his grandmother had told him once as a kid when he had complained about it.

"Why not?" he'd ask her.

She had turned to him and calmly said. "The heat in here isn't so bad. Just remember it's even hotter in hell. Just make sure, Clayton Jerome Madaris, that you never have to find that out."

After hearing that bit of news, he had never complained about the heat in the church again. His grandmother's words that day, as far as he'd been concerned, had been the gospel.

Clayton sat on the last pew, hoping no one would notice his late arrival. No such luck. His grandmother's eyes met his, all the way from the front row corner pew where she sat as the oldest member and official mother of the church. He didn't mistake the frown she gave him.

He shrugged. He had had all intentions of making it to Sunday School, but a night spent making love to Syneda had practically drained him. It had taken all his strength to get out of her bed and make it back to his own before he'd been discovered missing. He didn't like this sneaking around stuff and was determined more than ever to bring it to an end very soon.

He glanced around the church, looking for Syneda. He spotted her a few pews up sitting with Justin, Lorren, and their kids. Jordan, Dex's and Caitlin's daughter, was sitting in her daddy's lap and waved when she saw him. He smiled at his niece and waved back.

He also noticed his uncle Nolan. Clayton smiled. Nolan Madaris was determined to bring the leisure suit back in style. Clayton shook his head. At the last family reunion, he, Justin, and Dex had purchased an expensive suit for their uncle as a birthday gift. Evidently he hadn't taken the hint.

The choir members were singing out of their souls, and Clayton appreciated the songs that had the entire church electrified. As far as he was concerned, nothing uplifted a church service more than good singing.

"Today I want to welcome the Madaris family to our services," Clayton heard the minister saying as he began his morning sermon. His loud booming voice filled the sanctuary. "And since we have an unusual number of men in the congregation today," the minister continued, "I've selected as my subject, 'When a Man Loves a Woman.'"

This shouldn't put anyone to sleep, Clayton thought, shifting in his seat to get comfortable. Reverend Moss was a person who believed in seizing every opportunity to preach to anyone he felt needed it. Evidently after glancing over some of the Madaris men in the audience and seeing their bored, half-asleep expressions, he had felt there was a need.

"There has been a lot of talk lately about spousal abuse, and I've come to the conclusion that some men have forgotten just how to treat a woman, and that saddens me. I think it's fitting for us to go back and talk about the relationship between a man and a woman as dictated by the Word."

Clayton couldn't help but glance over at his uncle Lee who was notorious for going to sleep in church. He smiled when he saw his uncle's eyes drift closed. Evidently today wouldn't be any different from any other Sunday.

"First and foremost," Reverend Moss went on, "I want to point out that woman was created as a helpmate for man. I suggest all of you go home and *reread* the book of Genesis. Woman came from man. She was not taken from his feet for the man to walk upon her, like some men enjoy doing; nor was she taken from his hand for a man to knock her around."

Clayton grinned when he heard a hearty amen from his aunt Dora. Evidently his uncle Milton got heavy handed at times. He shook his head not seeing how that was possible. Uncle Milton was such a little man, and aunt Dora was a huge woman.

"And women," Reverend Moss continued, glancing around at the females in the congregation, "you were not taken from the man's head to place yourself above him." Several loud amens from the men in the congregation filled the air.

"The woman was taken from the man's side, from his rib, to walk beside him, and to be equal to him. She should be cherished by him, loved, honored, and respected. The same thing applies, ladies, for the man."

The minister went further and spoke of several men in the Bible who cherished the women they loved. He told the congregation about Jacob and Rachel, Hosea and Goma, Boaz and Ruth, and a number of others. He wrapped up his sermon by saying, "When a man loves a woman, he places her above all else, and she becomes the most important person in his life. She becomes his queen."

By the time the sermon was over and the choir began singing again, Clayton was sure a good majority of the women in the audience were expecting overnight miracles from their husbands.

After the services were over, everyone was invited to the dining area for some of Mama Madaris's birthday cake and ice cream. The usher who had seated Clayton began leading members and visitors out of the church and toward the back where the dining area was located. When he passed the pew where Syneda sat, he thought about what the minister had said. Syneda was a woman to be loved, cherished, honored, and respected. She had become the most important person in his life. And whether she accepted it or not, their destinies were entwined.

Senator Lansing took his seat on the plane and fastened his seatbelt. If it wasn't for a meeting with the president back in Washington this afternoon, he would have extended this trip.

He'd been disappointed at breakfast that morning. Syneda Walters, like most of the younger members of the Madaris family, had slept late, skipping breakfast.

He had been tempted to ask Jake about her but hadn't. The possibility that she was Jan's child was a long shot, but he knew he wouldn't be satisfied until he knew for sure.

He would have to be patient and wait for the report Braxter was getting for him.

Celeste waited until Braxter had gone to claim their luggage before taking the cellular phone from her purse. She glanced around the airport terminal and when she no longer saw him she punched in a few numbers.

"Listen, I can't talk long. I want you to check out a woman by the name of Syneda Walters. She's an attorney in New York. There may have been something between her and Senator Lansing at one time."

Celeste frowned. "What do you mean he's a single man and has the right to date women? Well, how would the voters feel if they found out he'd been involved with a woman young enough to be his daughter?" She smiled. "Let me know if you find anything."

CHAPTER 17

Syneda had taken a break from work and stood at the office window staring down at the busy New York streets. It was hard to believe it was the end of September already. That meant she and Clayton had been seeing each other for almost five months.

Their relationship had fallen into a comfortable pattern for the both of them, proving that a long-distance affair could work in certain situations.

Not to overcrowd the other, they'd set a pattern of seeing each other every other weekend. Clayton either came to New York or they met somewhere in between. The weeks they were apart, he would send flowers, candy, balloons, cute stuffed animals, or some other sort of "I'm thinking of you" gift.

Not once had she visited him in Houston for fear of running into members of his family. And although she talked with Lorren regularly, they never discussed her relationship with Clayton. However, Lorren had mentioned some family members were getting more and more curious about his frequent out of town weekend trips that he was not discussing with anyone.

Usually whenever Clayton came to town, they spent a quiet evening with dinner at her place or at a restaurant. Once in a while they would order out. Sometimes they rented videos to watch, and at other times they went to a movie or took in a Broadway play or concert. A lot of times they just stayed inside the apartment simply listening to music and talking. Although they still disagreed on a number of things, they were attuned to each other in their perceptions and attitudes of what they considered important.

Syneda drew in a sigh. Their time together seemed so natural and so right. She refused to question the changes that were taking place in her life; positive changes Clayton was responsible for. And she tried not to think about how much he was beginning to mean to her. Things were good between them and she wanted them to stay that way.

She smiled. Clayton was flying in this weekend and she couldn't wait to see him. She hadn't seen him in a couple of weeks and she missed him.

After his shower, Clayton returned to the living room and found Syneda where he'd left her over twenty minutes ago. She was still sitting Indian style on the sofa with a law book in one hand and a legal pad in the other.

Busy writing, she hadn't noticed his presence so he took the opportunity to study her. He always enjoyed watching her this way, intense and absorbed with what she was doing. She had no guards up around him and was totally relaxed with him being there, invading her space, or rather, as he preferred thinking, being a part of it.

When Syneda stopped writing a few minutes later, she arched her back, working out the kinks that had settled there. Then she looked up and saw Clayton watching her.

She released a deep sigh that was from the satisfaction of him being there with her as much as from finally piecing together a new argument for the Jamison appeal. Putting down the book and legal pad, she stood and slowly walked over to him, placing her arms around his neck. She knew the desire in her eyes revealed what she needed and what she wanted. No words had to be spoken. He gathered her up in his arms and carried her to the bedroom.

Sometime later, they lay together in the dark silence of the room, their bodies still joined in the torrid, sweet aftermath of their lovemaking.

"I can't seem to get enough of you," Clayton said, his voice thick and dazed. His heart was beating rapidly in his chest. The emotional force of their lovemaking was beyond anything he had ever experienced.

"I feel the same way," Syneda said drowsily. "You're special, Clayton. You're my friend as well as my lover."

Clayton kissed her tenderly. "I know it might be a little early to ask, but are you planning to come to the big Madaris Thanksgiving bash?" he asked a few minutes later.

Syneda smiled up at him. "I wouldn't miss it for the world. In fact your mom called last week just to make sure I was coming. She invited me to stay with them again this year."

"You turned her down, of course."

A bemused frown covered Syneda's features. "Why would I do that?"

Clayton reached down and gently pinched her nose. "Because, sweetheart, when you come to Houston, I want you sleeping in my bed, and not some bed at my mom's house."

Syneda's eyes widen in surprise. "Clayton, you know I can't do that."

"Why not?"

"Because your family doesn't know about us."

"Then it's time they found out."

"No."

"Yes," Clayton countered, rolling to his side, disengaging their bodies but still cradling Syneda in his arms. Over the past few weeks, he had given serious thought to finally telling his family about them. He felt he and Syneda were ready to take that next step. However, by the look on her face, it was obvious she felt otherwise.

"I don't want to treat what we're doing like some cheap backroom affair when it's not. It really makes no sense for us to continue sneaking around like being together is wrong."

"Don't do this to us, Clayton," Syneda said softly, caressing his arm. "You know how I feel about your family finding out about us. You said you understood."

Clayton tilted Syneda's chin up so that their eyes could meet. "Somehow you have this notion that me understanding certain things is the same thing as me endorsing them. You were wrong in believing that about Cassie Drayton and Larry Morgan, and you're wrong in believing that about us. I do understand your fears, but after spending the past months together, I would have hoped I'd helped put some of them to rest. Especially your misconceived notions about my family. They love you. Don't you know that nothing could tarnish that?"

Syneda's chin trembled. "I can't take any chances. Other than Lorren and Mama Nora, your family is the closest thing to a real family that I've ever had." She gazed into the depths of his dark eyes. "I can't risk losing that. Not even for you."

Clayton frowned. "I still don't understand why you think you would. My parents weren't born in the Stone Age, Syneda. They stopped being shocked about anything when they thought they would surprise Kattie at college in New Orleans, and showed up unexpectedly to find her and Raymond were living together. They would understand us wanting to be together at my place."

"In other words, you want to openly flaunt our affair in front of them," Syneda said coolly.

"No, but I want them to know there's something special between us."

"Don't you understand what that will do? What happens next Thanksgiving when things have ended between us and you're dating someone else, perhaps seriously? How will they feel having both your old girlfriend and your present one there? It wouldn't be fair to place your family in a position of feeling obligated to continue to include me in the family gatherings, and it wouldn't be fair to your new girlfriend, who could possibly become your wife, to know you and I were once lovers. How do you think she would feel?"

"You don't have to worry about anything like that happening," Clayton snapped. "There won't be another woman."

"How can you be so sure of that?"

"Because I love you."

Syneda gasped and stared at him. It seemed her voice left her. "You can't mean that?"

This was not the way he had intended on revealing his feelings to her. "I do mean it," Clayton said curtly. "I love you and want to marry you."

Clayton's words hit Syneda with the force of a ton of bricks. Unable to lie passively in his arms any longer, she jumped out of bed. Glancing around the room, she noticed their clothing tossed carelessly about the room. Spying Clayton's dress shirt thrown on the floor, she automatically reached down and put it on.

Clayton watched Syneda through hooded eyes. She was not handling this the way he had hoped. "I really don't understand why you're trippin'. We've been seeing each other constantly for nearly five months, during which time I haven't seen any other woman. Why can't you believe that I love you?"

Syneda turned to face him. "I believe you may think you do."

"What's that supposed to mean?"

"It means that you see how happy and content Justin and Dex are, and think now is the time to try it for yourself."

"Don't try rationalizing my feelings for you, Syneda. I love you, plain and simple."

Syneda's eyes filled with tears. "No, Madaris. Nothing about love is plain and simple. Have you forgotten I can write a book on the word, or rather the lack of it? Sex is plain and simple, not love. My mom died not knowing the difference. But unfortunately, I had to find out the hard way that a night she spent in passion with some man, which may have been plain and simple love for her, was nothing but plain and simple sex for him."

"I'm not your father, Syneda. I love you and you're wrong. What we've shared these past months has nothing to do with sex. I fell in love with you in Florida. The reason I never told you was because I wanted to give our relationship a chance to grow gradually. You may deny it now, but I believe deep down you love me, too."

"No! I don't love you. I don't love any man. All I wanted to share with you was an affair. You broke the rules, Clayton, and I can't believe you've done that. I thought you'd be different from the others. You were supposed to understand." She turned and ran into the bathroom, slamming the door behind her.

When Syneda came out of the bathroom some time later, Clayton was dressed in a pair of jeans and a cashmere cardigan. His bags were packed.

They faced each other for a moment without speaking, then Clayton was the first to break the unnerving tension of silence. He walked over to stand before her.

"I felt it best that I leave, under the circumstances."

Syneda took a deep breath and lifted her tear-stained face to him. "I agree, you should leave. You're asking too much of me, Clayton. There can't ever be anything beyond what we've been sharing these past months."

"I want more, Syneda. I want an entire lifetime. I want you to be eternally mine."

"I can't give you that. When I accepted your proposal it was with the understanding that either of us could end it at any time. Well, I'm ending it."

"Don't do this to us, Syneda."

"I didn't do anything, you did."

"You think falling in love with you was wrong?"

"I don't want your love, Clayton. I didn't ask for it, and I don't want it."

Clayton flinched. Her rejection of his love hurt, and he felt his heart breaking into a million pieces.

Without saying a word, he picked up his baggage, turned and walked out of the bedroom. It was only after Syneda heard the sound of the door closing behind him that she gave in to her tears.

Celeste slipped out of bed when she heard Braxter singing in the shower. Moving quickly, she picked up the phone and began dialing.

"It's me," she whispered to the person who had picked up the phone. "What have you found out?"

She frowned. "What do you mean you haven't found out anything? It's been almost three weeks," she said angrily, her voice raising a little. "There has to be a connection. I saw the look on the senator's face every time he looked at her. Trust me, he knows Syneda Walters from somewhere, and I want you to find out where. I need to have—"

Celeste stopped talking when she heard noise behind her. She turned around. Braxter was standing in the bathroom doorway, his eyes a fuming dark as they locked with hers. There was no doubt in her mind that he had overheard her conversation. She quickly hung up the phone.

"Braxter, sweetheart, don't look at me that way."

"Who were you talking to on the phone?" he demanded in a loud voice. "And why is Syneda Walters of interest to you?"

Celeste backed up a little when he came toward her. His hand tightened on her arm when she didn't answer him. "I asked you a question, Celeste."

Celeste could feel his anger. "Turn me loose, Braxter. I don't have to tell you anything that I don't want to."

Braxter's eyes blazed. "Who the hell are you and just what is your game, lady?"

"I don't have any idea what you're talking about, and I said let me go, or so help me, I'll scream so loud all of the occupants of this apartment building will hear me. I can just see tomorrow's headlines—'Senator Lansing's top aide arrested for manhandling a woman in his apartment.' "

When Braxter released her arm, she turned her face up to him and smiled. "I thought you'd see it my way. You're always mindful of shielding the senator from any negative publicity."

She walked around him and began getting dressed. "It was fun while it lasted, Braxter."

"Who are you working for?"

Celeste heard the pain in his voice and ignored it. "I work for no one."

Braxter walked over to the dresser and grabbed her purse, emptying the contents in the middle of his bed.

"What do you think you're doing!"

Braxter said nothing as he picked up her small appointment book and thumbed through it. He didn't see anything unusual, just little notations about what he assumed to be job-related appointments.

Then he flipped through her driver's license and charge cards, which indicated the name she had given him was her real name. He threw them aside and picked up her checkbook and began flipping through it. His eyes widened at the large amount she had deposited in her personal account a few months ago. It was exactly two days before they had met. He turned around and his eyes met hers.

Celeste trembled. He didn't say anything, but if looks could kill she would be on her way to the morgue. She hesitantly walked over to him and snatched her purse from his hands, placing the contents back inside. She knew she had pushed him to his limit and the best thing to do was to get out of there.

She walked to the door then stopped before opening it. She slowly turned around and they stared at each other. She saw the pained and angered look on his face and a part of her almost shattered. For the first time, she felt her conscience pricking her. She actually regretted hurting him.

"It was nothing personal, Braxter. You're an all right guy," she said softly.

She turned and quickly hurried out of the apartment.

A physically and emotionally exhausted Clayton Madaris entered his office where he had come straight from the airport. He wasn't ready to go home just yet.

Sitting behind the big oak desk he leaned his head against the back of the chair and stared into private space. His mind was in deep thought as he replayed the scene with Syneda over and over again in his mind.

Moments later he checked his watch for the time. He needed to call Alexander Maxwell. Alex was the brother of his best friend, Trask Maxwell. His and Trask's friendship went all the way back to touch football when they were kids growing up in the same neighborhood. Trask had gone on to become the greatest running back in the history of the NFL. Having retired from playing football a few years ago, he was now living in Pennsylvania and was a recruiter for the Pittsburgh Steelers.

Clayton picked up the phone and dialed Alex's number. At the age of twenty-six, Alexander was a top notch private investigator. It was almost two in the morning, but he knew Alex was used to receiving calls at all times of night.

"Hello, Alex? I need your help. There's someone I want you to find for me."

Syneda awoke slowly, and the first thing she did was listen for the sounds she had grown accustomed to hearing whenever Clayton visited. Things like the sound of him in the shower, or the sound of him moving around her kitchen while he prepared breakfast.

But there was no noise. All she heard was silence.

She rolled her head on the pillow so she could look at the gift Clayton had given her this visit, a huge stuffed teddy bear. He'd said it had reminded him of her, all warm and cuddly.

She slowly sat up, and swung her legs over the side of the bed. She stood and the first thing she noticed was that she had slept in Clayton's shirt. She had been so upset after he'd left that she'd cried herself to sleep and didn't undress. His scent was all over her and lingered in the bed where they had made love last night.

"I'll get over him," she said to herself as she went into the bathroom. She stopped and looked around. Clayton's presence was everywhere, even in her bathroom. A bottle of his favorite cologne was sitting next to her perfume, as well as a number of other toiletries he kept at her apartment.

She walked back into her bedroom and went to her closet and pulled out an empty shoe box. Returning to the bathroom she began placing Clayton's items in the box to mail to him.

I can do this, she kept thinking over and over. *No man, other than my father, has made me cry after him. I have to keep my mind focused on what I'm doing and why I'm doing it.*

After packing the items, she squared her shoulders and returned to the bedroom where she placed the box on her dresser. She opened the drawer and took out the key he'd given her; the one to his apartment that she had never used. She placed it inside the box with the other items. With that completed, she turned her attention to another task. She wanted to strip her bed and replace the linens. There was no way she could sleep in that bed again tonight where Clayton's scent lingered on everything.

A few minutes later, after taking her shower, she walked into the kitchen. The day was just beginning and already she was feeling tired. She was sure the cause was more emotional than physical.

She opened the dishwasher to get a bowl for her cereal and found it empty. As usual Clayton had placed her dishes nice and neat in the cabinets instead of leaving them in the dishwasher.

He's done nothing but disrupt my life, she thought. *Before taking up with Clayton, I kept things just the way I wanted them. I used to sleep late on Saturdays and I used to spend a quiet weekend alone doing the things I enjoyed doing.*

She slammed the dishwasher shut, suddenly no longer hungry. She walked into the living room and sat down on the sofa. Clenching her hands together in her lap she tried pulling herself together. No man had ever made her lose her appetite.

Syneda looked down at her entwined fingers. There was no way she could deny the fact that during the past five months she and Clayton had bonded in a way she had never bonded with a man before. And deep down she knew she would never bond that way with another man.

She smoothed a hand back and forth across her forehead, feeling a headache coming on. Her apartment held too many memories of the times she and Clayton had spent together. She needed to get away. She didn't want to stay in the apartment all weekend alone.

Syneda stood and went into the bedroom to pack.

Braxter rose from the chair he had slept in all night. How could he have been so stupid? It had been nothing more than a setup. He had meant nothing to Celeste but a tool to gather the information she needed. But for whom?

He walked over to the window and looked out. He would have to contact the senator and tell him what was going on immediately. Someone was determined to ruin his credibility with the voters.

He thought about the portion of Celeste's telephone conversation he had overheard. Evidently she was trying to figure out what part, if any, Syneda Walters played in the senator's life.

For some reason, Braxter had a feeling when the answer came to light, all hell would break lose.

"I hope my unexpected visit won't throw the Madaris family schedule off balance," Syneda said jokingly as she entered the spacious and elegant ranch style home of Justin and Lorren Madaris.

"Of course not," Lorren replied, giving her best friend a hug. "Your visits never throw anything off balance. Justin and the kids will be glad to see you. Just leave your bags here. Justin went to Dallas and should be returning any minute. He'll take care of them when he gets back."

"Where are the kids?"

"They went with him so you came just in time. I was dying of boredom. Besides, it's about time you paid us a visit."

Syneda smiled. "I know and just look at you." She placed her hand on Lorren's stomach. "You're showing more now than you did at Whispering Pines last month. I'm so happy for you."

"Thanks." Lorren led them into the huge family room that was off the foyer. Syneda sat down on the sofa and Lorren sat across from her in a wingback chair. "So, how have things been going with you, Syneda?"

"Fine," Syneda said flatly. "Work is lightening up somewhat, and I take the Jamison case back to court in a couple of weeks."

Lorren studied her friend who had been a pillar of strength for her during her divorce from her first husband, and later when her relationship with Justin was at a delicate point. She had known Syneda long enough to know when something was bothering her. "I wasn't asking about work, I was referring to your personal life."

"My personal life? Why, everything's great!" Syneda replied enthusiastically, and at the same time she tried to stop the quick rush of emotional tears she felt filling her eyes. She swallowed hard and tried blinking them away, but the gesture was too late. Lorren had seen them and had immediately come over and sat next to her.

"What is it, Syneda?" she asked softly. "You know you can talk to me about anything. I may not have any answers but I promise to be a good listener. We haven't had a chance to really talk in a long time. Does what's bothering you have something to do with Clayton?"

Syneda nodded, not trusting herself to speak.

"Do you want to talk about it now?"

"No, not now," Syneda replied brokenly. "But I will later."

"All right, we'll talk later."

* * *

Hours later after taking a shower and changing into a pair of slacks and white blouse, Syneda walked down the stairs to where everyone was. Justin and the kids were in the pool playing a game of volleyball, and Lorren was sitting in a chair nearby.

"I thought you were going to take a nap," Lorren called out to her.

"I was but decided not to. I'm ready to talk now."

Lorren nodded and stood. "Let's take a walk. You haven't been here since Justin had the airstrip installed for the Cessna that he, Dex, and Clayton purchased together."

She then turned toward the pool. "I'll be right back. I need to let Justin know where we're going."

A few minutes later the two women were walking side by side along a narrow path that led to a clearing. Syneda spoke up. "It's over between Clayton and me."

Lorren sighed. Although she had never asked, she had been fairly certain Syneda was the mystery woman in Clayton's life. Apparently things had stretched beyond that one lone weekend Syneda had only planned for them to have. Lorren loved both her brother-in-law and her best friend dearly, but she had felt their involvement with each other had been headed for trouble from the very beginning. Evidently, Syneda had taken the affair more seriously than Clayton had. She could feel her friend's pain.

"It lasted longer than I thought it would. I tried to warn you about him."

Syneda stopped walking and turned to Lorren. "You don't understand, Lorren. It's not Clayton's fault. It's mine."

A bemused expression covered Lorren's face. "Yours? You're right, I don't understand."

Syneda took a deep breath. "Clayton thinks he's in love with me and wants me to marry him."

Whatever Lorren had expected Syneda to say, those words were not it. Shock and disbelief covered her face. "Clayton loves you and wants to marry you?"

"Yes."

"Are we talking about the same Clayton Madaris?"

"Yes, Lorren, we are. He thinks he loves me and wants to marry me."

Lorren shook her head. "From the way you're talking, I take it that you don't believe him," she said. It was a little hard for her to believe herself.

"In a way I believe him, and in a way I don't know what to believe."

"If you're concerned about his past involving other women, Syneda, the one thing I've discovered about Madaris men is that when they do fall in love, they're hard core lovers who are loyal, dedicated, and sincere."

"That's not it, Lorren."

"Then what's the problem?"

"I can't give back to him the love he wants."

Lorren knew about Syneda's feelings about falling in love. "You have to let go of the past some time."

"I've tried but I can't."

"Maybe you haven't tried hard enough because you've felt no man was worth the extra effort. Now you have to decide if Clayton is."

Syneda nodded. At the moment, she wasn't sure if perhaps Lorren's comment wasn't true. "I'm thinking about not attending the Madaris Thanksgiving dinner."

"Why? Because Clayton will be there? Unfortunately, there's going to be a lot of times when your two paths will cross. Have you forgotten you happen to be my best friend, Clayton is Justin's brother, and the two of you are godparents to Justina, Vincent, and our baby yet to be born? Avoiding Clayton will be impossible."

Syneda knew what Lorren said was true, however, she wasn't ready to accept that fact. "How about going shopping with me in Dallas?"

Lorren sighed as she accepted Syneda's hint that their discussion of her and Clayton was over for the time being. "I'd like that. We can look at baby gifts for Caitlin. But I want you to promise me something."

"What?"

"Try forgetting the past and follow your heart."

CHAPTER 18

"Ms. Walters, there's a couple here to see you. A Mr. and Mrs. Larry Morgan," Joanna announced over the intercom.

Syneda was sitting at her desk going over some notes she'd made on a case she was handling. She lifted her head in surprise. "Mr. and Mrs. Larry Morgan?"

"Yes."

She pushed the papers aside. "Please send them in."

Syneda stood when Joanna escorted the couple into her office. All it took was the smiles on their faces to let her know somehow things had worked out for them. "Congratulations," she said, returning their smiles and shaking both their hands.

"Thanks. We stopped by to do two things," Cassie said as they took the seats Syneda offered them. "First, we want to thank you."

Syneda raised a brow. "Thank me for what?"

"For taking the time to listen to me that day and for not trying to force me into giving up my baby for adoption," Cassie said.

"And I want to thank you for not throwing me out that day I showed up here unexpectedly," Larry added. "You took the time to listen to what I had to say." He grinned. "And I had quite a lot to get off my chest."

Syneda nodded, clearly remembering that day. She and Clayton had almost gotten into an argument over the issue of Cassie's father's interference.

"I take it your father has finally come around."

Cassie shook her head. "Unfortunately he hasn't. And that's our second reason for coming here today. We want to say goodbye. We're moving to Texas."

"Texas?"

"Yes, Austin, Texas. Larry has received a job offer there. He'll be working for Remington Oil."

Syneda raised an arched brow. "Remington Oil?"

Larry grinned. "Yes, I'm sure you've heard of them. Who hasn't? They're a very good company to work for. They offered me a very good salary and the benefits are excellent."

Syneda nodded. Remington Oil Company was one of the largest oil companies in America. They had made history last year when they became the first oil company in over fifty years to locate a major oil field. Dex's company, Madaris Explorations, had been used for the job. Also, a piece of land owned by Caitlin had been instrumental in making that discovery possible. Clayton had handled the negotiations in both situations. Syneda couldn't help but wonder if it was just a coincidence that Larry Morgan had gotten a job with a company in which Clayton had close ties.

She cleared her throat. "Did you seek out employment with Remington Oil?"

Larry smiled. "No, and that's the funny thing about all of this. According to the personnel manager at Remington Oil, I came highly recommended, but he wouldn't say who recommended me. As far as I'm concerned whoever recommended me is truly my guardian angel."

Syneda returned his smile. She had a funny feeling his guardian angel was none other than Clayton. The words he had spoken that last night in her apartment suddenly came back to her, *". . . Somehow you have this notion that me understanding certain things is the same thing as me endorsing them. You were wrong in believing that about Cassie Drayton and Larry Morgan, and you're wrong in believing that about us. . . ."*

"Ms. Walters? Are you all right?"

Cassie's soft voice cut through Syneda's thoughts. "Yes, I'm fine. How did your father handle the fact that Larry has found a job? Especially when he'd gone to a lot of trouble to make sure he wasn't hired anywhere."

"Not too well. In fact Larry and I found out that he called Mr. Remington personally and made threats. But believe it or not, he met his match."

"Really? What happened?"

Larry chuckled. "I heard Mr. Remington advised Cassie's father that he would be faced with a law suit if he tried anything. He further advised my father-in-law that he was considering diversifying Remington Oil and that the clothing industry would be the first avenue he looked at for a possible merger."

Cassie laughed. "I guess the thought of anyone attempting a corporate takeover of Drayton Industries was enough to make Dad think twice about carrying out his threats."

Syneda nodded in agreement. "Well, I'm glad things have worked out for you two."

"We're glad, too," Cassie said. "People in love deserve to be together. It's no fun being alone. Everyone needs someone to love and someone to love them."

"It's been a while, Clayton. Welcome to Sisters. You were missed."

"Thanks," Clayton said to the hostess. He leveled a long, hard look around the restaurant. Sisters was a place he used to frequent quite a bit. It was known for its good food, lively entertainment, and most importantly, its abundance of women. It was a place women came to hang out; some to cultivate sisterhood—so he'd been told, some to be noticed, and others to do the noticing because where there were women, you were sure to find men.

"Trevor's here and he's dining alone. Do you want to join him?"

"Yeah, that will be fine."

Clayton followed as she led the way to the table where his good friend, Trevor Grant, was sitting. Trevor was the head foreman for Dex's company.

As he was being led to the table, Clayton couldn't help noticing the number of women who called out a greeting to him or who were smiling openly at him. At any other time he would have made a clean sweep around the room, flirting with the women that he knew and getting ready to hit on those that he didn't know. But not now. He was only interested in one particular woman; a woman who had told him in no uncertain terms that she didn't want him.

"Well, well, well, aren't you a sight for sore eyes," Trevor Grant said, shaking hands with Clayton before he sat down. "This place hasn't seen the likes of you for months. Where on earth have you been?"

"Busy." He turned to their hostess. "Just give me the usual."

The woman nodded. "All right." A grin then curved her lips. "And by the way, Clayton. Kayla's been asking about you, but Evelyn hasn't. In fact she's now taken up with Al."

Clayton gave her a dry look. "I'm happy for her."

The hostess shook her head and walked off.

Trevor laughed. "Losing your touch, Clayton?"

He gave his friend a grim smile. "Just my interest."

Trevor lifted a brow. "You not being interested in a woman will be the day they prepare you for burial."

Clayton smiled and didn't say anything. Instead he stood and pulled several quarters out of his pocket. Since this was Monday night, there was no live entertainment. Music was being provided by a huge jukebox that sat in the corner of the room. It contained a number of the latest hits as well as quite a few of the oldies.

"Excuse me for a minute." He walked over to the jukebox and after depositing his quarters, punched a couple of songs, "The Track of My Tears" by Smokey Robinson and "What Becomes of a Broken Heart" by Jimmy Ruffin. He walked back over to the table and sat down. The songs he had selected were all indicative of how he felt.

Trevor folded his arms and pinned Clayton to his seat with a curious stare. "What's wrong with you? You're acting like a lovesick puppy." Trevor chuckled. "But since I know that can't be the case, at least not with you anyway, what's your problem?"

"Don't have one. And what's so bad about falling in love?"

Trevor looked up and frowned, not believing Clayton had asked such a question. "What's wrong with it? Everything's wrong with it. That's when a man's troubles begin, once he falls for a woman."

Clayton cocked his brow. "And I take it you've never fallen in love."

Trevor shrugged. "Not voluntarily, no."

"And involuntarily?"

Trevor squirmed slightly in his seat. "I may have had a short moment of madness." Trevor thought about the woman he had met over a year ago, Corinthians Avery. She was head geologist for Remington Oil. Their initial meeting was anything but normal. There was no doubt in his mind that she'd disliked him on sight and he'd disliked her equally as much . . . or so he had thought. But the few infrequent times he had seen her since their initial meeting, when they'd been thrown together due to work obligations, he had found himself wanting to seek her out and make hot, torrid, passionate love to her. He hadn't done that, of course. The woman hated his guts. But that hadn't stopped her from invading his dreams at night, or his thoughts during the day.

"What happened?" Clayton asked.

"Nothing happened. The woman doesn't like me. Besides, she's in love with someone else. She's in love with a married man."

Clayton arched one eyebrow. "You're kidding?"

Trevor shook his head. "Wish I was kidding. Can you believe that, especially after what happened with my old man. I almost fell for the same kind of woman who destroyed my parents' marriage."

After almost emptying a bottle of hot sauce over his fried chicken then topping it off with ketchup, Trevor tilted back in his chair and eyed his friend. The second song Clayton had selected was now playing. "Are you or are you not going to tell me what's going on with you?"

Clayton exhaled a deep, drawn-out sigh. "I've fallen in love."

Trevor didn't say anything for the longest moment. He just stared at Clayton in disbelief. Finally he spoke. "Must be one hell of a woman."

A smile tilted Clayton's lips. "She is."

"Who is she?"

"Don't ask."

Trevor rubbed his hand over his jaw thinking. "Man, she isn't married is she?"

Clayton glared at Trevor. "Of course not! You know I don't do married women."

Trevor smiled. "I thought you didn't do falling in love either, but you did."

Clayton couldn't help but return Trevor's smile. His friend had him there, unfortunately.

"So, what's the problem? Whoever the woman is I'm sure she's elated, since you're the biggest catch in Houston."

"She doesn't want me."

Trevor almost choked on his chicken. He grabbed his water to wash down the piece of meat caught in his throat. "A woman doesn't want you! Are you serious?"

"Yes, as serious as a heart attack."

Trevor pursed his lips. "She actually rejected you, man?"

"Yep."

Trevor shook his head. He then pushed his plate aside and tapped his thumbs together for a few seconds. "Do you have any more quarters?" he suddenly asked Clayton.

"Yeah. Why?"

"I want to play something on the jukebox."

Clayton stood and pulled out a couple of quarters and handed them to Trevor. He watched him cross the room to the jukebox, deposit the money and select a song. He then came back and sat down.

"I played this song for the both of us."

Clayton lifted a brow when the jukebox roared to life with Trevor's selection. He had chosen Toni Braxton's 'Unbreak My Heart.' "

Senator Lansing looked up in surprise. "Braxter, you're early. I wasn't expecting you to come in until around nine."

"There's an important matter I need to discuss, sir."

The senator nodded, noting the seriousness in Braxter's voice. "Have a seat over there. Is something wrong?"

"That will be for you to decide."

At the lift of the senator's brow, Braxter continued. "The woman, the one I've been seeing, the one I took to Texas with me and introduced you to . . ."

"Yes, what about her?"

"She was using me to get information about you."

The senator sat straight up. "What? How do you know that?"

"Last night I overheard a conversation she was having with someone, a private investigator. Somehow she must have found out about our interest in Syneda Walters and is doing her own investigating into it."

"Who is she working for?" the senator asked calmly.

"I don't know. But whoever it is, that person wants to make sure you're not reelected."

The senator frowned. He was running against Noel Frazier. He couldn't believe the man would stoop to something so low. In fact the two of them had vowed to run a clean campaign. "I want you to find out who's behind it."

"Yes, sir, and if you want me to, I'll turn in my resignation."

"Why?"

"Because I may have done more harm than good to you now. Because of me, the media may get a hold of something that you prefer kept private."

The senator smiled weakly. "When you're an elected official, Braxter, you don't have any privacy. I would have preferred getting the information on Ms. Walters before anyone else. However, if there's anything in the report that I need to be concerned with, I'll deal with it."

"But I let Celeste Rogers make a fool out of me. I can't believe I was so stupid, so inexcusably stupid."

"You weren't stupid, Braxter. You're a man who fell in love, and with love automatically comes trust. And the person you trusted betrayed you."

"So what will you do, sir?"

"Nothing. We'll just let the person who appears to be in control of things finish whatever game he or she is playing."

Syneda entered her apartment. She had gotten through the day . . . now if she could only get through the night. Then she would concentrate on the rest of the week.

The day hadn't been so bad with the visit from Cassie and Larry Morgan. An hour or so later, she had received notification of a date for the appeal's court to hear her oral argument.

She had immediately called the Jamisons to give them the news. They had cried over the phone. Barbara and Walter Jamison had been without their little girl for almost six months. They were hoping and praying to win the appeal so little Kasey would be returned to them.

Later that night when Syneda turned off the lamp and made herself comfortable in bed, she couldn't help but think of the Morgans and how

Clayton had helped to change their lives. The more she thought about it, the more convinced she became that somehow he had been instrumental in Larry Morgan finding employment with Remington Oil.

Then there was the Jamison case. Although she had come up with the new argument to use with the appeal, it had been Clayton's expertise and experience as an attorney that had given her food for thought and ideas for different avenues to pursue. Numerous times during his weekend visits, he had brought a law book or two from his own personal law library. She had enjoyed spending time with him researching cases and digging for precedents she could use. A part of her knew if she won the appeal, it would be because of Clayton's help.

As Syneda shifted in bed, she thought about something else she missed in not being with Clayton, the intimacy they shared. Although she wanted to believe it had only been about sex for them, she knew they had shared a whole lot more. There had been the sharing of emotions and feelings, and that's what she missed most of all. He had opened emotions in her she hadn't wanted opened. He had made her feel, he had made her need—regardless of whether she had wanted those things or not. Clayton had made her experience them. And she had experienced them with him. Perhaps in the end that was the main reason why she had fought against it, and why even now, she was still fighting against it. She was fighting the love she felt for him.

Syneda knew she had avoided the truth long enough and it was time to be honest with herself. She did love Clayton. She probably had always loved him. But even with that admission, she knew she would continue to fight her love for him. Her survival depended on it. As a child, her heart had not just gotten broken, it had gotten crushed. And it couldn't survive being crushed again. She couldn't take the chance.

No matter how much she loved him, she couldn't risk getting her heart destroyed. She just couldn't.

CHAPTER 19

Justin Madaris pounded on the door a good five minutes before it finally opened.

Clayton scowled at Justin and then at Dex before rubbing a hand across his eyes that were clouded with sleep. "What are the two of you doing here? And what are you doing in Houston, Justin?"

Justin studied his youngest brother with an intensity that came from being the oldest and always having to look out for his younger siblings. He knew immediately that something was wrong. A quick glance at Dex indicated that he had picked up on it as well. Clayton's robe looked rumpled and his ungroomed appearance made him look a little rough around the edges. His face had the look of a man who'd had a bad night. In fact, he looked like he'd had quite a few bad nights. "What are you still doing in bed, Clayton? It's almost two in the afternoon."

Swearing, Clayton rubbed the top of his head and stepped aside to let his brothers in. "Maybe I wanted to sleep late."

"Clayton, you don't know how to sleep late," Dex said with a half smile on his lips.

Clayton glared at Dex. "Just what is this? Gang up on Clayton day?"

Dex shrugged as he sat down on the sofa. He glanced around the room. "This place is a mess. I never knew you could be so sloppy."

"So now you know," Clayton said, moving through the untidy living room and sitting in a chair. Dex was right. His place was a mess and it wasn't like him to be sloppy. If anything, he was known to be extremely neat. He hated disorder of any kind. But now he didn't care. Lately he hadn't cared much about anything.

Clayton gave Dex a hard glare. "For a man who makes a living playing in dirt, I hardly think you have room to talk. The biggest mistake Mom has ever made was buying you that sand box for your fourth birthday."

"Kids, behave," Justin said, chuckling.

Clayton's response was a grunt. "You never did answer me, Justin. What are you doing in Houston?"

Justin dropped in the chair across from Clayton. "And you never answered me. Why are you still in bed?"

"You go first since you're the oldest."

Justin grinned and then conceded. "I drove Lorren down for Caitlin's baby shower. Did you forget it was this weekend?"

"Yeah, I forgot," Clayton said, and felt annoyed that he had forgotten. During the past few weeks, his mind had been preoccupied with other things.

"So why are you still in bed?"

Clayton rose and went into the kitchen. Dex and Justin followed him. Ignoring them he switched on the coffeemaker.

"We're not going away, Clayton."

Clayton turned to his brothers. "I can see that," he said, glaring at them, frowning. "The reason I was still in bed is because I had no reason to rush getting up this morning," he finally said, simply.

"I'm surprised to hear you say that considering the fact that Syneda flew in for the baby shower today."

Clayton's eyes became hard like volcanic rocks. "That's all the more reason," he said coolly. "She's the last person I want to see."

Dex looked at his brother, surprised. The last time he had seen Clayton and Syneda together was when the family had been at Whispering Pines. At the time, Syneda had been the only person Clayton had acted like he wanted to see. He hadn't been able to keep his eyes off of her. "I take it there's trouble in paradise."

Clayton turned toward him. "There is no paradise. There never was and there never will be. The only paradise was the one that I concocted in my mind. But the lady has set me straight. The only thing she's interested in is a surrogate family she can claim, and not a man who wants to love her."

Justin took a good look at his brother, hearing the deep pain in his voice. And there was also a coldness, a hardness within Clayton that had never existed before, and he immediately knew the cause—rejection. Syneda had done something to Clayton no other woman had done. She had rejected him. She had taken the love he had never confessed to another woman and had thrown it back in his face. And from the looks of things, he wasn't handling it too well.

"And the really funny thing about it," Clayton continued, "is that I watched the two of you go through your bouts of pain, and I used to think to myself that it could never happen to me. I used to tell myself I was above all that; that there wasn't a woman anywhere who could infiltrate my mind and my heart like that, and cause me that much pain, that much grief, that much anguish." With studied calmness, he sat down in the chair at the round oak table. He dropped his forehead to his joined hands, "Boy, was I wrong. I was so very wrong."

He then held up his head and looked at his brothers. The hurt and pain were evident in his eyes, plain for them to see. "How do you handle telling a woman for the first time in your life that you love her, only to have her tell you that she doesn't want you nor does she want your love. And that all she wants from you is a good time. And what's really hilarious is that that's the same thing I've been telling women for years."

He squeezed his eyes shut for a moment, then reopened them. "I guess it's payback time. And for me, payback came all nicely packaged in the form and shape of a woman by the name of Syneda Tremain Walters. And she got me just where it hurts the most—straight in the heart. How am I supposed to handle something like that? How am I supposed to handle the hurt and the pain?"

Justin and Dex watched their brother in silence, neither knew what to say but both were familiar with what he was going through. They had been there. Giving advice had always been Clayton's thing, even when the advice hadn't been wanted.

Justin shook his head. Clayton had done more than just given advice to him and Dex. He had deliberately undermined and manipulated their love life. He had done what he felt had been necessary to straighten out their problems with the women they loved. Now Clayton's own love life needed straightening out and Justin knew that his baby brother didn't have a clue of how to help himself.

Justin finally spoke. "Give her time, Clayton."

Clayton's response was a quiet laugh. "I've given her time, Justin. Maybe that's the problem. I've given her too much time."

"Then try being more patient with her," Dex put in. "How you and Syneda even got this far without killing each other beats the hell out of me," he said, shaking his head in amazement. "Both of your analytical and strongly opinionated minds are enough to rattle any relationship. Just chill and be patient. You know how I almost screwed things up with Caitlin by not being patient."

Clayton took a long, deep breath. "I have been patient, Dex. I've been patient for over five months. But now I'm tired of fighting for what I want against what Syneda evidently doesn't want. You can't make someone love you, and I'm sick and tired of even trying."

He stood. "The hurt and the pain aren't worth it anymore." He took another deep breath. "The two of you can let yourself out. I'm going back to bed."

He then walked out of the kitchen.

Clayton had lain across the bed for nearly an hour and knew from the sounds coming from the living room, Justin and Dex had not left. In fact, with the television blasting and the sound of his refrigerator opening and closing periodically, he could tell they had made themselves at home and were watching a football game and eating up his food.

Why on earth were they still hanging around? Did they think he was going to hang himself or something? He took a quick glance at the box that sat on his dresser. The package had been sent from Syneda and had arrived a couple of days ago. In it were items he'd made a habit of leaving at her place. She had returned all of his things along with the spare key he had given to her with a note that simply said, . . . *"It's better this way."* The thought of it increased his anger. It might be better for her but it certainly wasn't better for him.

Clayton got out of bed and went into the bathroom to take a shower. Since it appeared Justin and Dex weren't going anyplace, he might as well watch the game with them.

Syneda looked out the window as the cab drove through Houston on its way to the airport. She had flown in that morning and a little over seven hours later, she was flying back to New York. With her day in court for the appeal on Wednesday, she needed to be fully prepared.

Caitlin's baby shower had really been nice and she had received many nice things. Syneda smiled at the games they had played at the shower. She had really enjoyed herself, as she always did with the Madaris family.

She was glad that Clayton had not stopped by. She didn't think she could handle seeing him just yet. She knew that Justin and Dex had gone over to his place. Neither had returned before she'd left for the airport.

A part of her couldn't help wondering how Clayton was doing. Had he dismissed her from his mind already? Was he back to dating other women again?

She took a deep breath, irritated with herself for even caring. But she did care. She loved him and the thought of him with someone else . . .

But, she reminded herself, she had been the one to end things between them. She had sent him away. She'd had no choice. She could not start depending on anyone for her happiness. The only person she could always count on was herself.

As the cab continued to make its way through the city, Syneda couldn't help but think of Houston. This was Clayton's territory, his city. The city of his birth. In Houston, Clayton Madaris was a very well known and successful attorney. But when he had come to her in New York, he had been her friend, her mentor and her lover. And deep down she knew she had lost all three. No matter what she wanted to think, there was no way they could ever go back and reclaim that special friendship they once shared. She was only fooling herself if she thought they could.

Later that night Clayton received a call from Alexander Maxwell.

"You don't believe in giving me easy jobs do you?" his friend chuckled.

Clayton smiled. "What can I say, you're the best. Do you have any information for me yet?"

"No, not yet, but I've stumbled onto something pretty interesting. I thought I'd better bring it to your attention."

"What?"

"There are two other investigators checking out Syneda's past. Seems like you're not the only one interested."

Clayton sat up straight, frowning. "Who are they?"

"Don't know yet. I picked up on them in my database. I know about them but they don't know about me. We have an advantage."

"Let's keep it that way, Alex. I want to know who they are and what their interest is."

When he hung up the phone a few minutes later, Clayton couldn't help wondering who else besides him would be interested in Syneda's past.

CHAPTER 20

Syneda won the appeal and Kasey Jamison would be returned to her adoptive parents by the end of the week.

She knew she should celebrate, but her win had also been the result of someone else losing. Kasey's biological mother.

Syneda left the courtroom after getting the ruling when it was released. She had spoken immediately with the Jamisons and shared their happiness.

Entering her apartment, the first thought that came to her mind was that she needed Clayton. She wanted to share her victory with him. She looked around her apartment. Although she had returned all of Clayton's things, his presence was still there. It was there in the living room where they had made love occasionally. It was in her kitchen where he had whipped her up a number of tasty meals. His presence was in her bathroom where they had showered together frequently, and it dominated her bedroom where he had made her his.

He had made her his. He'd been the first man to capture her heart, making her irrevocably his. Syneda tilted her head back and drew in cold air, feeling the tears sting her cheeks. Her apartment was cold from the freezing weather outside, not unusual for New York the week before Thanksgiving. She quickly wiped away her tears.

Her tears were for all she had lost, at her own hands, because she hadn't been strong enough to take a chance on love—the kind of love Justin had for Lorren, the kind of love Dex had for Caitlin. Clayton had offered her that and she had refused it.

Cassie Drayton Morgan had been right when she'd said . . . "It's no fun being alone. Everyone needs someone to love and someone to love them . . ."

Syneda had never believed that until now.

And Clayton had been right when he'd said, that what happened with her father did not concern them. It was time she got beyond that and moved on. And she was ready to do so. But first, there was something she had to do before she could finally put the past behind her. There was someone she had to visit.

Syneda had won the appeal.

Clayton leaned back in his office chair. He had just gotten word from a fellow attorney who was working on a similar case. He wanted to call Syneda and tell her how happy he was for her, and how proud he was of her. But he didn't.

She had made it very clear things were over between them, yet he still wanted to talk to her. He still wanted to hear her voice. He picked up the phone and after hesitating a few seconds slammed it back down. The words she had said to him the last night they were together tore into him . . . *"I don't want your love, Clayton. I didn't ask for it and I don't want it."*

Clayton rose from his chair, balling his hands into his pockets. He was hurting in a way no person was supposed to hurt. He was hurting everywhere, both inside and out, and all at once.

He knew that although Justin and Dex had tried being supportive, they just didn't understand. The problems plaguing his and Syneda's relationship would not evaporate with time and patience. It would take love and trust, and she wasn't willing to take a chance on either.

Clayton tugged at his tie, wishing he could rip it off and then do the same thing to his heart—rip it out. But something in him made him bite back both his anger and his frustration. He refused to let any woman make him lose his mind, his self-respect, or his pride. In time, he would get over her, he would make sure of that.

And no woman would ever get close to his heart again.

Syneda took a deep breath as she leaned against the huge wrought-iron gate. Her plane had landed less than an hour ago and she had immediately taken a cab from the Dallas airport.

For the past eighteen years of her life she had avoided coming here. She used to tell herself that if she never came, her mother would never know the truth. Her mother would never know that the man she had died loving, trusting, and believing in had let them down.

Syneda straightened and began walking across the stretch of velvet green lawn. As she neared the area where the groundkeeper had instructed her to go, poignant memories of her childhood with her mother resurfaced.

The two of them had been close, almost inseparable, except for the time her mother was at work and she was at school. They had done a lot of things together. Although there hadn't been plenty of money, her mother had worked hard and had taken care of their needs.

The short walk was finally over and as Syneda stood before the headstone, she felt renewed pain followed by a deep sense of cleansing. She knew by the time she left to return to New York, a part of her past would be left here. It was the part she should have buried a long time ago.

She knelt down and placed the bouquet of flowers across the headstone. She squeezed her eyes shut from the mistiness that began clouding them. "Mama, I know it's been a long time, and your little girl is all grown up now. And I know in my heart you understand why I haven't come until now."

Syneda felt a momentary stab of pain when she thought of the man who had fathered her. "I never wanted you to know he didn't come for me, Mama, because more than anything I truly wanted you to rest in peace. And I knew you couldn't do that if you knew the truth. I didn't want you to worry about me."

Syneda's hands trembled as she wiped the tears from her eyes. "I'm okay now. I admit I wasn't in the beginning, the disappointment of him not coming hurt for a while, but I'm okay now. My heavenly father took very good care of me. He sent me to live with Mama Nora and Papa Paul. I know you would have liked them. They took me to church every Sunday just like you would have done. And I had Lorren. She's the sister I've always wanted."

Syneda took a deep breath as her fingers traced lazy patterns in the cold earth. "I made something of myself, Mama. I went to college and got a law degree. And I've met someone special by the name of Clayton Madaris. I know you would like him, too. He's kind, gentle, strong, and caring. And he loves me. I didn't want to believe it at first, but now I do. And I love him. I love him very much and one day soon I'm going to tell him just how I feel. I want to marry him and if we ever have children, I'll tell them all about you. I'll tell them how you took care of me all by yourself. I know it must have been hard being a single parent and all, but you did it. I'll tell my kids how you used to read me stories before tucking me in at night and how you would wake me up by singing a beautiful song in the morning. I'll tell them all about our good times."

Syneda hesitated briefly before continuing. "But most of all, Mama, I'll tell them how much you loved me and how much I loved you." Tears that she had held for so long were released and she wept.

Syneda wept for the mother who had been taken away from her at the age of ten, and for the father who hadn't cared enough to come and claim her as his daughter.

A few minutes later she wiped her eyes and slowly stood. "Goodbye, Mama," she whispered. "Continue to rest in peace. I love you."

She turned and walked out of the cemetery in the direction she had come in.

CHAPTER 21

How could he have let his mother talk him into coming here? Seeing Syneda was the very last thing he wanted, Clayton thought, walking toward the airport terminal. Passing through the entrance he moved in paced steps, ignoring the noisy sounds from the crowds. The airport was packed with people traveling to and fro to spend time with family over the Thanksgiving holiday. With a brief glance at the monitor, he checked the gate for the flight arriving from New York. Noting he was a few minutes early, he took a seat to wait.

He disregarded the attractive young woman sitting across from him who'd sent an inviting smile his way. Her eyes ran over him, and Clayton couldn't help but give her a half-amused smile before tipping his head back against the wall and resting his eyes.

When Syneda's flight was announced he stood and forced himself to relax. That brief moment of calmness came to an abrupt end the moment he saw her walk through the gate. She was dressed in a pair of white jeans that gracefully hugged her firm hips with total allurement and a peach-colored pullover sweater. She looked absolutely stunning.

Syneda's face registered surprise when she saw Clayton. His towering height made him quite visible over the crowd of people that were waiting for other passengers. She shivered slightly when she felt his hooded eyes on her.

He was dressed in a pair of faded snug-fitting jeans and a burgandy pullover sweater that outlined every detail of his muscled body. A body she had come to know rather well during the past few months.

How could I have thought I didn't love him? How could I have thought I didn't want him? Taking a deep breath, she walked over to where he was standing. "Clayton, I'm glad to see you."

"Yeah, I bet you are," he replied coolly, his lips forming in a taut line. "Mom sent me." He took the flight bag from her shoulder. "She would've come herself, but didn't trust me or Dad to watch her sweet potato pies that were in the oven."

"Oh," Syneda replied. Her gaze met Clayton's and the eyes staring back at her were like chipped ice. There were so many things she wanted to say to him, but she couldn't say them in a crowded airport. They needed privacy.

"Are you ready, Syneda?"

"Yes."

"Let's go then," he said gruffly.

Together they walked down the wide, crowded corridor. Syneda was having a little bit of trouble keeping up with Clayton's long strides.

"It will only take a minute to claim your bags," Clayton said curtly upon reaching the area where the rest of her bags were.

"Am I the first to arrive?" Syneda asked, pointing out her bags to Clayton. Then she felt foolish for doing so. They had taken enough trips together over the past few months that he would have recognized her luggage easily.

"No. Traci and Kattie were over earlier today to help peel the potatoes for the pies, but they left before noon. They'll be back later today. Dex and Caitlin will probably be there by the time we arrive. They had to wait for Jordan to get out of pre-school before coming over. And Justin, Lorren, and the kids are flying in this afternoon."

"What about Christy?"

"She's been home from college since Monday."

For the first time since seeing him, Syneda couldn't help but notice the fleeting smile that somewhat softened Clayton's features. "Let me rephrase that," he said. "Christy's been in Houston since Monday, however, she's seldom at home. She's making her rounds visiting friends. She only pops in to eat and sleep."

"What about Jake?"

Clayton frowned. "I don't know what's going on with Uncle Jake. For some reason he's not coming this year. He called Mom earlier this week and said he had other plans. It's not like him to miss Thanksgiving dinner with us."

As they stepped out of the building, Clayton led her over to a car parked nearby. He set down the bags and pulled the key out of his pocket. "Mom suggested I drive her car," he said, as he loaded Syneda's things into the trunk of the sleek champagne colored Seville. "I guess she figured all your things wouldn't fit in my two-seater."

Syneda nodded and again their eyes met. His eyes appeared colder than they had earlier. Suddenly, all the words she had wanted to say to him stuck in her throat. What could she say to undo what she'd done? What words could she use to make him understand she was ready to love him and she trusted him? She was the first to break the eye contact.

"Will my being here bother you, Clayton?" she asked, feeling a little unsure of herself and suddenly filled with self-doubt. His cold attitude toward her wasn't helping the situation.

"Not particularly," he said dispassionately, opening the car door.

"Maybe I should not have come."

The look Clayton gave her was as sharp as a broken piece of glass and as cold as the weather she had left in New York. It was definitely not filled with the warmth she was accustomed to. "Too late to think about that now. You're here, aren't you?" he said harshly, shutting the door. Then he walked around to get into the car.

His words had hurt, and when Clayton started the car, Syneda turned her attention to the scenery outside the car window. She couldn't help wondering if she had made a mistake by coming. What if he no longer had a place in his heart for her? What if he no longer wanted her? It had been over a month since they had been together, and she hadn't heard from him. The thought that he no longer cared for her sent her mind reeling in sheer panic.

When they arrived at Clayton's parents' home, Dex was in the driveway washing his father's pickup truck. Clayton brought the car to a stop and Syneda opened the door and got out of the car.

"Syneda's bags are in the trunk," Clayton told his brother gruffly, tossing him the keys. "Tell the folks that I'll be back later." He then got into his Mercedes and left.

Dex shook his head resignedly, then turned his handsome smile on Syneda. He came around the car and gave her a huge hug. His charcoal gray eyes were filled with concern. "Are you all right?"

Syneda gave Dex a forced smile. She wondered if he knew about her relationship with his brother, but at the moment she didn't care who knew. "Yes," she replied softly. "I'm fine."

"What in the world has Clayton in such a bad mood?"

"I don't know. I'm glad I'm not the only one who's picked up on it."

Syneda went about her job of grating the cheese for the casserole trying not to listen to the conversation going on between Clayton's sisters, Traci and Kattie.

Soon after she had arrived, the two women had returned to help with all the cooking that had to be done. It was an annual Madaris ritual that the women in the family prepared the entire Thanksgiving meal the night before, and the men were responsible for getting up on Thanksgiving Day morning to fix the special dessert. Rumor had it that this year it would be a delectable peach cobbler.

Working by Syneda's side in the kitchen was a very pregnant Caitlin, whose due date was less than two weeks away. She was busy chopping onions, celery, and bell peppers for the potato salad.

"I thought the two of you were convinced Clayton had a love interest," Caitlin said to Traci and Kattie without looking up from her task.

"All evidence seemed to lead that way," Traci replied as a smile touched her lips. "Especially all those weekend trips that he refuses to discuss."

"All right, girls," Marilyn Madaris spoke up. "Your brother has a right to his privacy. What he does and who he sees are none of your business."

"We know that, Mom. We're just trying to figure out what's bothering him."

Syneda was tempted to provide them with the answer they sought. She was what was bothering Clayton. He had been in a bad mood since picking her up from the airport.

"Has he mentioned bringing a surprise guest to dinner tomorrow?" Traci inquired.

Marilyn Madaris shook her head and smiled. "No, he hasn't."

"Where's Lorren?" Caitlin asked as she began peeling the shells off the boiled eggs.

"She's in the den with the kids, reading them a story. Bless her heart. How she can put up with all of them in her condition is beyond me," Kattie answered. "She has so much patience."

The conversation in the kitchen shifted from Clayton to other topics as the women continued working diligently on tomorrow's dinner.

"Are you all right, Syneda?" Caitlin asked a little while later when the two of them were left alone in the kitchen. "You've been rather quiet today."

Syneda liked Caitlin. She was a very likable person who was just as beautiful on the inside as she was on the outside. She and Dex had married within two weeks of their meeting. What followed not too long after that was a long and bitter separation that had lasted for nearly four years. Love had reunited them, and when you saw them together, you would never have guessed the problems their marriage had endured. Problems that Caitlin was quick to admit had made their love and marriage stronger.

"I'm fine," Syneda replied, giving Caitlin an assuring smile.

At that moment the kitchen door swung open and Clayton walked in. A frown covered his features. "Where's Mom?"

"She's upstairs trying to find a place for all the kids to sleep. Your dad wants all his grands under his roof tonight," Caitlin replied, eyeing her brother-in-law warily. His handsome face had become brooding and a scowl clouded his features. Her sisters-in-law had been right. He was in a rather bad mood.

"I think I'll go upstairs and offer my assistance. Do you want to come with me, Syneda?" Caitlin asked.

Syneda shook her head as her gaze met Clayton's. "I'll be up later. I would like to talk to Clayton for a while."

In his present mood, Caitlin wasn't sure that was such a good idea but kept her thoughts to herself. "Okay. I'll see you guys later."

When the door closed behind her, Clayton walked forward, stopping in front of Syneda. He looked down at her intensely. "What do you want to talk to me about?"

Taking a deep, unsteady breath, Syneda stepped back. His towering height seemed intimidating. "Let's step outside."

"No."

"No?"

"That's what I said. Why can't you say what you have to say right here? Are you afraid we'll make a scene and the family will find out about us?"

She frowned. "That's not it at all. I thought—"

"And what did you think, Syneda?"

"I thought that maybe we could go someplace where we could be alone."

Clayton stared at her. She had a lot of nerve trying to offer him a chance to put things back the way they used to be between them. She was still only interested in an affair with no commitment or complications. Didn't she understand that he could have what she was offering with a number of other women? Didn't she know that with her, he wanted more? Had she not gotten it through her head that he loved her with such a passion that even now, his hands were trembling from just being near her, wanting to touch her, to love her, and to keep her with him always? Just looking at her brought back memories he could very well do without.

"You're the last woman I want to be alone with, Syneda." He turned to leave.

His words hurt Syneda, but she was determined that he would hear her out. Moving quickly she blocked his exit. "You're going to listen to what I have to say, Madaris."

"Don't count on it. Now move your butt out of my way."

"No."

The stark coldness in his eyes made her shiver from the chill cast in the room, but Syneda didn't care. As far as she was concerned she was just as mad as he was. He could be so stubborn at times.

"You make me so mad, Madaris, I could just smack you."

"I wouldn't advise you to act crazy and do it," he said, threateningly, glaring down at her.

"Act crazy? You mean like this?" she asked angrily before smacking him.

The swiftness of Syneda's action caught Clayton completely off guard. Enraged, he grabbed her hand and yanked her to him and glared down at her. Then all of a sudden he was kissing her, his mouth hard on hers, his tongue thrusting into her warm moistness, probing and caressing.

He had wanted to be brutal in his kiss, to punish her for hurting him. But he found he couldn't. Especially when he felt her response. So he continued to kiss her, letting all his needs and frustrations take over.

Soon an inner part of him told him this was not the way. He loved her too much to take less than a full commitment, less than her total love. Feeling disgusted with himself for his lack of control where she was concerned, he shoved her away from him and spun around and walked in the opposite direction.

"Clayton, please wait and listen to me."

He stopped walking and turned back around. The look in his eyes told her he had been pushed beyond his limit "No, Syneda, *you* listen to me. You're here but that doesn't mean I have to like it. Just do me a favor and stay the hell away from me. You wanted my family so bad, well you can have them, but that doesn't include me. All I want is for you to leave me alone." He turned and walked out of the kitchen.

Shaken by his angry words, Syneda sat down in the nearest chair. Clayton no longer wanted her. She had been so sure that once she saw him again and they had a chance to talk, and she told him how much she loved him, things would be all right between them. She hadn't expected his anger, and she never expected him to not want to have anything to do with her. He actually acted like he hated her. She must have hurt him deeply for him to feel the way he now felt toward her.

Her shoulders drooped. There was no way she could stay here with his family knowing how he felt. Making a decision to find an excuse to leave first thing in the morning, she walked through the same door Clayton had walked through just moments earlier, almost colliding with Mrs. Madaris.

"We didn't mean to desert you, dear."

"You didn't. In fact I was just about to find you. Something has come up and I'm going to have to return to New York first thing in the morning."

Syneda found herself under the warm charcoal-gray gaze of the woman, who gave her an endearing smile. "I'm sorry to hear that. I really enjoy you being here with us."

Marilyn Madaris's eyes were lit from some inner glow. "I've been in this kitchen since six this morning, and I think I'm more than due a break. I've started taking afternoon walks around the neighborhood. Would you like to join me?"

Syneda nodded. She always enjoyed Clayton's mother's company. Besides, her conversation with Clayton had taken a toll on her.

The two women walked outside the house. The treetops stirred with the whisper of a cool breeze. They were ten minutes into their walk before either woman spoke. Then it was Clayton's mom who broke their silence. "Have I ever told you how Jonathan and I met?"

The question surprised Syneda. "No, I don't think you have."

The older woman smiled. "I was fresh out of college and had landed my first teaching job. It seemed good fortune was on my side because the elementary school I was assigned to was within a block of my apartment. I was grateful for that because money was tight, and I couldn't really afford a car payment."

They continued walking. "My first day on the job I came face-to-face with the principal. He was a stern but very tall, dark, handsome man by the name of Jonathan Madaris. I think we were attracted to each other immediately, although I tried my best to fight it. I had my own set of plans for my future, and they didn't include getting serious about anyone for a long while."

Her laughter mixed with the sustained whine of an ambulance siren in the distance. "Lucky for me, the school board had a policy that stated school administrators could not date their teaching personnel. However, Jonathan Madaris had made up his mind that he wanted me, and would not let some school administration policy stop him."

Syneda's interest was piqued. "What did he do?"

"Without me knowing what he was about, and after I had worked only a few weeks at his school, he had me transferred elsewhere. I was assigned to another school that was out of his district and over fifty miles from my home. I was furious. Not once did he consider the fact that such a move would be an inconvenience as well as a hardship for me. He was only thinking of himself. He had only one goal in mind and that was to have me, one way or another."

"And what did you do?"

"I rebelled and fought him every step of the way. But he didn't give up on me until I did something that's almost unforgivable to a Madaris man."

"What?"

"I injured his pride."

Syneda raised a brow. "How?"

"I filed a complaint against him with the district school superintendent. It was somewhat similar to a modern-day sexual harassment complaint. Fortunately, although I didn't know it at the time, the school superintendent was a good friend of Jonathan's. He called him in and told him what I'd done. By that time, I had cooled off and had regretted my actions and withdrew the complaint. But Jonathan was very upset with me. It took him a while to come around."

Marilyn Madaris stopped walking and Syneda also ceased her steps. She found herself caught under the older woman's soft gaze that seemed to probe deep within her soul. "My sons, especially Dex and Clayton, with Dex being the worse, are no different from their father when it comes to the issue of the Madaris pride. They can be stubborn men, but when they fall in love, it's forever and nothing, not even Madaris pride, can destroy that. It just takes a very strong woman to work around it."

Syneda's eyes widened suspiciously. "Why are you telling me this, Mrs. Madaris?"

"Because I thought you should know."

Syneda nodded. "All right," she replied with sudden calm. "And I only think it's fair that you know that I'm in love with Clayton, and that we've been seeing each other secretly for almost six months. But you knew that didn't you?"

Marilyn Madaris wore an open, friendly smile. "I had my suspicions, but I wasn't absolutely sure until that night at Whispering Pines when I saw the two of you dancing together. I knew then."

Syneda was operating on pure amazement as she took a much needed deep breath. "You picked up on it just by seeing us dance together? But we've danced together a lot of other times."

Marilyn Madaris's eyes lifted. A smile touched her lips. "But never like that. It was somehow different the way he was holding you, the way you were holding him, the way the two of you kept looking at each other. It was like the two of you were the only two people at that party."

She laughed. "I may be getting old but these eyes of mine don't miss too much, especially when it concerns my children." She smiled again. "However, I don't understand why you and Clayton wanted to keep it a secret."

A lump formed in Syneda's throat and she moved her shoulders under Mrs. Madaris's concentrated gaze. "I asked him to. I didn't want the family to know that we had been seeing each other."

"Why?"

Syneda took a deep breath. She silently admitted she was relieved to bring everything out in the open. "I was concerned about what you and the rest of the family would think of me getting involved with him."

"We would think what we've always known; you're a level-headed young lady and a special person. Clayton's falling in love with you makes you that much more special. For so long, his father and I were concerned that he would never find someone special to settle down with. I see that he has, and I'm glad it's you."

Syneda stared at the older woman. "We're having problems."

"Somehow I picked up on that, but I'm sure the two of you will work things out."

"And you don't mind that Clayton and I are having an affair?"

"An affair?" Marilyn Madaris's face broke into a wide grin. "Since Clayton is his father's son, I have every reason to believe something permanent is forthcoming. That's another thing about Madaris men," she continued, "once they find the woman they love, they need commitment. They believe when people just live together, it's too easy to walk away and call it quits. Forever to them means just that, forever."

She eyed the young woman standing before her. "What I don't understand is why Clayton is upset?"

Syneda blushed although the thought of confiding in Mrs. Madaris didn't bother her. She had long ago learned that the woman was very understanding. As they strolled back toward the house, Syneda told her everything, including the fact that Clayton was upset with her because she was staying with them instead of at his apartment.

Marilyn Madaris said very little as she listened to Syneda tell her about her mother's death, and about the father who had rejected her and the resulting childhood insecurities that had followed her through adulthood, and how she had let it come between her and Clayton.

Talking about it with the older woman made Syneda realize what Clayton had said all along was true. You can't let the past dictate the future. Before long the two women were back at the Madaris family home.

Before entering the door Syneda turned to the older woman. "Thanks, Mrs. Madaris, for listening."

"You don't have to thank me. I enjoyed our talk, and I know you're just the woman for my son. I've known that since the first time I saw you and Clayton together, and you were giving him hell about something the two of you had disagreed on."

An approving smile touched her lips. "I think Clayton is a very lucky man."

Syneda's entire face spread into a smile with her comment. "I think so, too, but only because he has you for a mother."

The two women embraced before entering the kitchen where they found Dex sitting at the table reading the paper.

"Where is everyone?" his mother asked. The house was unusually quiet.

"Caitlin is upstairs taking a nap, and Jordan talked her uncle Justin and her granpa into pizza. They thought it would be nice if they took everyone out for pizza instead of having it delivered here. I think they were trying to give you a break from all the noise."

Marilyn Madaris laughed. "Pizza on Thanksgiving eve? They better have room for turkey tomorrow. Did Clayton go with them?"

"No, he's left and said he won't be back until tomorrow. Why?"

"I hate to inconvenience him, but Syneda is staying over at his place tonight."

Ignoring the shocked and surprised look on Syneda's face, as well as that of her second-born son, Marilyn Madaris continued. "That way we can have plenty of room for the kids to sleep comfortably since your father insists they all spend the night."

She then turned to Syneda. "Go gather your things, dear. You may use my car," she said, placing her car keys in Syneda's hand. "I expect both you and Clayton here in the morning no later than eleven. Understood?"

Syneda nodded before rushing from the kitchen and up the stairs to grab her things.

Dex stood. His expression wary. He didn't know how much he could or should tell his mother about Clayton and Syneda's relationship. "I don't think that was such a good idea, Mom, to send Syneda over to Clayton's for the night. Caitlin and I have plenty of room at our place. She could have stayed with us."

He hesitated briefly before continuing. "You've probably been too busy to notice Clayton's mood today. It's been the pits. And I really don't think you want to subject Syneda to that. You know how disagreeable they are most of the time anyway. And with Clayton's present mood, one little spark could cause a big explosion. Being together is the last thing they need tonight."

A smile touched his mother's lips. "Perhaps. And perhaps not."

Less than an hour later Syneda stood in front of the door to Clayton's apartment. She had come prepared for anything but his rejection. She would not settle for that. Taking a deep breath, she rang the doorbell.

A somewhat tired and angry-looking Clayton opened the door. He lifted his brow in surprise. "What are you doing here? I thought I made it clear that I wanted to be left alone." There was a sharp edge to his voice.

Syneda swallowed nervously, but she refused to back down. "I need to talk to you, Clayton. Please."

Clayton hesitated a moment before moving aside. Syneda stepped inside his living room and turned to face him. The look on his face was inscrutable, and he was so distant that a knot of uncertainty coiled within her. However, she refused to give in to her anxiety. She was determined to accomplish what she came to do.

"I came to return something to you, Clayton."

Clayton shut the door and leaned back against it. His hand remained on the knob as if he needed support. "What? I thought you sent back everything."

"Everything but this," Syneda said. She opened the coat she was wearing.

Clayton's full attention was drawn to Syneda's outfit when she completely removed her coat and dropped it to the floor. His white dress shirt was the only thing she was wearing. His breath caught in his throat when she began unbuttoning the shirt.

"What do you think you're doing?" His voice was harsh with no vestige of softness.

Syneda stopped and met his gaze. The eyes staring back at her were cold, remote, and distant. "I had a long talk with your mom this evening, Clayton, after you left," she admitted quietly.

He stepped from the door and came to stand before her. She could tell he was seething with mounting rage. "So?"

"And she knows about us. I told her everything."

Clayton's mouth hardened. "And just what do you expect from me for doing that? Some sort of medal for bravery?"

His words infuriated her, and anger flared in Syneda's eyes. She lifted her chin. "I thought you would be pleased about it. Evidently, you're not. Coming here was a mistake." She snatched her coat from the floor and walked past him. She had just opened the door when Clayton's arm shot in front of her and slammed it back shut.

Grabbing her by the shoulders, he turned her around to face him. "What do you want from me, Syneda? The only woman I've ever loved throws my love back in my face, and you think all you have to do is strut your behind in here and I'm supposed to fall at your feet. Sorry, babe, it doesn't work that way. At least not for me. I'm a man with feelings. I can bleed just like the next person."

Syneda glanced up at him when she heard the pain in his voice and saw the hurt in his glare. Her heart squeezed in anguish when she realized what he'd been going through over the past month. And she understood what Marilyn Madaris had meant about the Madaris pride. She had trampled his pride by rejecting the love he had offered her.

She lowered her eyes, her long lashes fanning her cheeks. She stood nervously before him trying to find the right words to express just how she felt. She decided on the simple approach, to speak from her heart. She lifted her eyes slowly to meet his.

"I was wrong, Clayton. And I know that now. I do love you, and more than anything, I want your love in return. I know you offered it to me once, but at the time I was too scared and too unsure of myself to even consider accepting it. But now I know what I want, and if you'll offer your love to me again, I promise to take it in my heart and cherish it. And from this day forward, I will always and forever be, eternally yours."

Clayton stared down at her. They stood transfixed, mesmerized by a sensuous power that for the moment bonded them together in heart and mind.

Syneda saw his hands ball into fists at his side and knew he was fighting hard to resist her. But then, little by little, she saw the coldness leave him and watched as warmth crept back into his body, beginning with his eyes.

He slowly bent his head to kiss her, his mouth moist and gentle against hers, and she knew that love had won. When he lifted his head, a flood of warmth and love shone in his eyes.

Tears of happiness slowly found their way down Syneda's cheeks, and he tenderly kissed them away. With a raw ache in his voice he said, "I want more from you than my shirt, Syneda. I agree with what you said about there having to be more between us than sex. And I want more, a lot more."

He covered her hand with his and pressed her palm against his mouth. "I want everything you have to give and still more. I want you to marry me, to have my children, to be my partner in life and love. I want you to walk beside me, and to believe in me, and believe that I love you more than anything or anyone in this world. I need you."

Syneda's heart swelled with love for him. "And I love and need you, Clayton. I need a man in my life whom I can trust; a man whom I can believe in and depend on." Her lips quirked in a smile. "And I want a man who wants more than the shirt off my back."

Clayton laughed, pulling her gently into his arms. "You'll get everything you want and more."

Syneda pressed her face into his shoulder. "You'll never know how hard it was for me to get out of your parents' home unnoticed wearing my coat with only your shirt underneath."

Clayton grinned. "You're something else." He pulled her tighter. "How soon can we get married?"

Syneda laughed affectionately as she pulled back out of his arms. "I'm open to suggestions."

Clayton smiled. "How about tomorrow?"

"Tomorrow?" Syneda laughed. "That's kind of rushing things a bit isn't it?"

"I don't know if I'll be able to let you return to New York. Besides, I don't want to run the risk of you changing your mind on me."

"I won't change my mind. I want all the things you're offering; marriage, children, trust, and most of all love, your love."

"I guess I won't cheat my parents out of witnessing their last remaining son's marriage. Especially since they weren't present at Justin's and Dex's weddings. Do you have anything against a big wedding?"

Syneda shook her head. "No. In fact I think I'd like that. We may as well do it right. How about a June wedding?"

"How about December?"

"June."

"I'd like a Christmas wedding."

"Next Christmas?"

"No, this Christmas."

Syneda grinned, shaking her head. "That's too soon. I say June."

Clayton frowned. "June? I don't know if I can wait that long."

Syneda chuckled. "June's only seven months away, and believe me, time will go by quickly. That will give us time to really plan things. Caitlin and Lorren will have had their babies and Christy will be home from college for the summer. Then there are the cases I need to finalize or transfer to other attorneys, not to mention the fact that I need to look for another job here in Houston."

Clayton's hand moved slowly down her back as he stared down at her. "You'll have another job. I have plenty of room in my office to take on a partner. I like the sound of Madaris and Madaris, Attorneys at Law. Don't you?"

Syneda smiled up at him, her heart bursting with happiness. "Yes, it sounds wonderful, but I'm a little worried we might disagree on every case we take on."

Clayton smiled and folded her to him. "I'll take that chance." He silently pledged to love and protect her for the rest of her life. "I think," he rasped close to her ear as his hands came to rest on her smooth thighs, "that you can return my shirt now."

Syneda pulled away from him. "My things are in the car."

Clayton nodded. "I'll bring them in later. Right now I can think of other things I prefer doing. I've always thought that my shirts look better on you than they do on me," he said huskily as he continued the task of unbuttoning the shirt. He paused briefly to bend his head. His mouth claimed hers in a kiss of both violent tenderness and turbulent longing.

Syneda kissed him back with all her heart and with all of the love that she had accumulated through the years but had been afraid to give.

"Your mom expects us by eleven in the morning," she whispered shakily when Clayton lifted his mouth from hers and began removing his shirt from her body.

"Eleven?" He smiled down at her. "In that case, we shouldn't waste any time," he said moments before gathering her up into his arms.

"My sentiments exactly," Syneda said, returning his smile and pulling his mouth down to hers.

CHAPTER 22

"What do you mean the two of you are getting married? Is this some kind of joke?"

The living room of the Madaris family home was in a complete uproar as everyone began shouting questions at Clayton and Syneda all at once. "When? Where? How? Why?"

Clayton laughed at the look of surprise and shock on most of the faces staring at them. He and Syneda had made the announcement to the family after arriving a few minutes before eleven and finding them gathered around the breakfast table.

He pulled Syneda to his side. "When? . . . sometime in June. Where? . . . that's for Syneda to decide. How? . . . the usual way two people get married. And why? . . . because we love each other very much," he said, pulling her to him and placing a gentle kiss on her lips.

Kattie shook her head, still not convinced. "Okay you two, the joke is over. April Fool's Day is months away."

Syneda chuckled. "Believe us, Kattie. This isn't a joke. Clayton and I are really getting married."

Traci rolled her eyes heavenward. "Be for real. The two of you don't even get along most of the time. Besides, you haven't been romantically involved, and . . ."

Traci stopped talking in mid-sentence when a thought suddenly hit her. She gave Syneda a long, penetrating stare.

"You're her!" she exclaimed. "You're the one responsible for Clayton's out-of-town trips." She shook her head. "I don't believe it. Why didn't someone tell me?"

Dex chuckled. "Evidently they wanted to keep it a secret, and everyone knows you can't hold water, Traci."

Traci turned and glared at her next-to-the-oldest brother. "And I suppose you knew?"

Dex smiled at his sister. "Yes, but they didn't tell me either. I figured it out at Uncle Jake's party for Senator Lansing. All anyone had to do was to take a good look at them dancing together and figure it out."

"I saw them dancing together and didn't notice anything unusual," Kattie piped in.

"Probably because like most of the women there that night, you were more into noticing Sterling Hamilton," her husband Raymond suggested, grinning.

The majority of the women in the room nodded. That was a good possibility. A very good possibility.

"But why the secrecy? Why did the two of you hide the fact you were seeing each other?" Caitlin asked. She frowned at her husband. The nerve of him knowing and not sharing the information with her.

Syneda glanced up at Clayton. He took her hand in his. "When Syneda and I went to Florida together, it was as two good friends. However, we discovered something special while we were there. The reason we didn't tell any of you about it was because we wanted to go slow. We needed time to see where the attraction was going and what it meant. And we needed time to sort out our feelings."

He pulled her into his arms. "We have them sorted out now. We love each other very much and want to commit our lives to each other. I've asked her to make me the happiest man on earth by becoming my wife and she has agreed."

Syneda's gaze held Clayton's. He had made it all sound so romantic. He had eloquently and smoothly presented his family with an understandable, convincing, and acceptable reason why they'd kept their relationship a secret over the past months. Only the two of them knew things hadn't really been quite that way.

"We're happy for the both of you." Jonathan Madaris' words to his youngest son and future daughter-in-law were followed by similar ones from the others as they crowded around the happy couple offering words of congratulations once the surprise had officially worn off.

A poll was taken to see who else had known about the couple's involvement beforehand. Marilyn Madaris admitted knowing and confessed to passing the information to her husband that weekend at Whispering Pines.

Justin and Lorren admitted to finding out about the couple when they paid them a surprise visit to Florida.

And surprising his wife, Kattie, Raymond admitted to knowing. He recalled seeing them together in Atlanta during one of his business trips, although they hadn't seen him.

"The reason I didn't tell you, Kattie," Raymond said when she glared at him, "is because you don't hold water any better than Traci."

This was truly a day of Thanksgiving, Syneda thought hours later as she sat around the dinner table with Clayton at her side and his family around her. News of their engagement had quickly spread and the telephone calls from other members of Clayton's family—uncles, aunts, and cousins, began rolling in.

Everyone was more than happy to hear that the man who had loved his freedom, who often boasted of having to answer to no woman, and whose credo in life for the longest time had been . . . "all men are fools, except for bachelors" . . . was finally tying the knot. They were very pleased with his choice for a wife. And there was no need to welcome her to the family because as far as they were concerned, she was a member of the family already.

"Tomorrow is the biggest shopping day of the year, Syneda," Traci said from across the huge table in the Madaris family dining room. "If you like, we can go shopping for—"

"No!" It seemed the entire Madaris family echoed the single word at the same time. Traci turned and glared at them. "And what's wrong with Syneda going shopping tomorrow?"

Daniel gave his wife a serious look. "There's nothing wrong with Syneda going shopping. You just aren't going with her. You've been suspended from shopping, remember?"

Justin chuckled. "Suspended from shopping? That's a new one."

Daniel smiled. "When you're married to Traci, you have to do what you have to do." He held up his hand when Clayton opened his mouth to say something. "And don't you dare remind me that the three of you warned me, Clayton."

Traci gave her husband an imploring look. "But, Dan, I have to go shopping with Syneda. How else will I know what she wants me to wear in her wedding?"

"The wedding isn't until June. You have seven months to pay off your charge cards, Traci," he replied.

Syneda smiled. It had been decided that Lorren and Caitlin would be her matrons of honor, and Clayton's three sisters, and their cousin, Felicia Laverne, would be her bridemaids. She thought of asking two good friends from college to be her bridesmaids, too.

The wedding would be held at Gramma Madaris's church near Whispering Pines, and the way the plans were shaping up, the guest list would be enormous.

"Syneda won't be going shopping with anyone but me tomorrow," Clayton said. He captured her hand in his and held it tenderly. "The first thing I'm going to do in the morning is to take her to the jeweler."

"Make sure you pick out the most expensive ring," Clayton's youngest sister Christy suggested. "By the way, Syneda, who's giving you away at the wedding?"

Syneda met Clayton's eyes and smiled. "No one is giving me away, Christy. I'm giving myself away."

Dex laughed. "That should be interesting. But knowing you and Clayton, I guess we shouldn't expect the norm, should we?"

Syneda smiled at him. "No. As you can see, we're full of surprises."

Clayton watched as the morning light shone through his bedroom window. Its rays silhouetted Syneda, who still slept soundly in his arms.

He moved, shifting her closer to him, wanting to be a part of her again, but knowing that she needed to rest. They had spent the entire Thanksgiving Day at his parents' home. It had been after midnight before they had returned to his apartment.

His lovemaking last night, just like it had been the night before when she'd shown up at his place wearing only his dress shirt, had been aggressive, demanding. It was as though he couldn't get enough of her. And she had only added fuel to his fire by meeting him kiss for kiss, stroke for stroke, matching his demands with equal fever.

He leaned over and whispered in her ear. "I love you."

A smile touched Syneda's lips as she struggled to open her eyes. "And I love you, too, Madaris. Now kiss me awake."

"My pleasure." His mouth found hers in a passionate kiss that she returned.

Moments later, after he had broken off the kiss, she rested against him, feeling like the luckiest woman in the world. All the past fears, doubts, disappointments, and pain seemed to have left her under the onslaught of Clayton's love. And she knew that as long as he was a part of her life, she could deal with just about anything.

She sat up, ignoring the morning chill that was in the room. "I went to the cemetery to visit my mother last week, Clayton."

Clayton gently pulled her back down beside him. He understood that must have been an important undertaking for her. She had once told him that she had never visited her mother's grave, and had shared with him the reason why.

He raised himself up and looked down at her, concern on his face. "How did it go?"

"It went okay. I had to go there in order to close a chapter in my life forever. I knew I loved you and didn't want that deal with my father in my life any longer. I wanted to get rid of it once and for all."

"And did you?"

"Yes."

"I'm glad." He kissed her again, this kiss longer than before. Afterward when she lay in his arms snuggled close to him, he wondered if he should tell her about hiring Alex to find her father. It had been his original plan, right after she had broken things off with him, to find the man and beat the hell out of him for what he had done to her, and for being the cause of all their problems. But then, after rationality had set in, he had kept Alex looking for the man just out of pure curiosity. He wanted a name. He couldn't help but wonder what kind of man would do what her father had done to a child.

But now, there was a whole new element to everything with Alex's revelation that two other investigative agencies were looking into Syneda's past.

"Syneda?"

"Hmm?"

"Have you ever tried finding your father?"

He felt her tense. She looked up at him, frowning. "Of course not. Why would I?"

"And you know nothing about him?"

"Nothing other than the little bit I told you."

"So you have no idea how he looks? Your mother never kept a picture of him around the house?"

Syneda sat up again. "Why all the questions, Clayton?"

"Just curious. We don't have to talk about it if discussing him upsets you."

She shook her head. "No, discussing him doesn't bother me now." She lay back down in his arms. "I don't know how he looks, and I don't recall Mama ever having a picture of him. I assume he's some light-skin brother with light-colored eyes since my mother's coloring was darker than mine, and her eyes were dark brown."

Syneda frowned. "Now to think about it, I remember her telling me all the time when I was a lot younger how much I looked liked him. She stopped telling me that after I began asking questions about him."

Syneda shifted in his arms. "Now I want to ask you a question."

Clayton nodded, smiling. "What do you want to ask?"

"Do you know anything about Larry Morgan being hired at Remington Oil?"

He chuckled. "Why would I know anything about it, sweetheart?"

Syneda gave him a pointed look. "Because you do. I know it and you know it whether you admit it or not."

Clayton shrugged. "End of discussion."

She frowned at him knowing he wouldn't confess up. But she had a way to make him talk and confess all. She smiled sweetly up at him. "Can I see that case of condoms you have in your closet?"

Syneda held her left hand out in front her. Tears misted her eyes as she looked at the three carat diamond ring on her third finger that Clayton had just placed there. It was absolutely stunning.

It had been past noon before they had left Clayton's apartment. After showing her the case of condoms in his closet, he had proceeded to put a few of them to good use. The first place they had stopped on their shopping expedition was the jeweler.

"Oh, Clayton, this ring is absolutely gorgeous." She looked up at him. "Are you sure?"

Clayton glanced down at Syneda's face and saw the uncertainty lingering there. It was there in her eyes. Dear heaven! How could she still doubt anything about him? But then he remembered she had had eighteen years of doubt and pain from another man she had wanted to believe in. Placing her complete trust in someone didn't come easy for her.

"Am I sure about what, Syneda? That I want to marry you or that I love you?" he asked her quietly.

"Both." She bowed her head, unable to meet the intensity in his eyes any longer.

"Syneda?" He waited for her to look up at him. Waited for the abundance of golden bronze hair that fanned across her shoulders to fall back in place and frame her face.

When she lifted her eyes to him, her gaze was searching his for answers. "Yes?"

"I'm sure," he said, his voice low and soft. "I'm sure that I love you very much, and that you're the woman I've been waiting for all my life, even without knowing I was waiting. And I'm sure I want to marry you, to make you my wife. I want to give you my name and one day I want to give you my babies. I promise to be a good husband to you and a good father to our children."

She smiled through the tears that misted her eyes. "Babies? Meaning more than one?"

Clayton grinned. "Yes, babies, meaning more than one."

He tilted her chin up with a knuckle. His expression was serious. "Trust me, Syneda, and know that I would never deliberately hurt you." His tone suddenly became fierce. "Believe that I love you with all my heart and soul, and that I will love you for all eternity. And that I will always be here for you."

Brenda Jackson

He stepped back, and ignoring the fact there were other shoppers in the store, some more curious than others, he opened his arms to her.

Syneda stepped into his embrace, and he drew her to him. Reveling in his touch, she clung to him. "Thanks for loving me, Clayton."

He tightened his arms around her. "Thank you for letting me love you." After some moments had passed, he checked his watch. "We have a few more stores to hit before dinner."

Taking her hand in his, he asked "Ready?"

She nodded.

"Then let's go, baby."

"Are you certain you don't mind having dinner here?"

Syneda smiled. "I'm positive. I know about your past reputation and that it included other women, lots of them. And since this was your hangout, it wouldn't surprise me to run into a few here tonight. That really doesn't bother me. I'm woman enough to get beyond that. Besides, we are here for a worthy cause."

"True," Clayton said as they entered Sisters. They were meeting Justin and Lorren and Dex and Caitlin for dinner. Each year on the day after Thanksgiving, the local chapter of the Delta Sigma Theta Sorority sponsored a tree-decorating event at Sisters. Each ornament was individually purchased and placed on the tree and came with the name and address of an underpriviledged child they would sponsor for Christmas. The place was packed and Clayton was glad for the turnout.

"Welcome to Sisters, and I understand congratulations are in order, Clayton."

Clayton smiled down at Netherland Brooms, the attractive owner of Sisters. "Thanks and yes they are. I would like you to meet Syneda Walters, my fiancée. Syneda, this is Netherland Brooms, but we all call her Nettie. She's the owner of Sisters."

Nettie took Syneda's hand in hers. "I'm glad someone finally hooked this guy on in," Nettie said to Syneda grinning.

Syneda smiled at the woman's comment. "Yeah, and I'm glad I was fortunate enough to be the one to do it."

"The two of you make a lovely couple, and I wish you much happiness."

"Thanks."

Nettie turned to Clayton. "Your brothers and their wives are here. They have been quite busy this year haven't they?"

Clayton laughed knowing she was referring to the pregnant state of his two sisters-in-law. "Yes, it appears they have been pretty busy."

Clayton and Syneda followed Nettie over to the table where the Madaris party were sitting.

"We were wondering when the two of you were going to get here," Dex said smiling. "Justin and I can't starve our ladies too long, don't forget they're each eating for two."

"Sorry," Clayton said grinning. "We lost track of the time shopping."

"The ring!" Lorren suddenly exclaimed. "You got your ring!"

Syneda nodded, beaming happily and holding her hand out for the others to see. "Isn't it gorgeous?"

Lorren and Caitlin released ohs and aahs. Justin and Dex gave their brother nods of approvals.

The hostess came and took their order and within a reasonable time, their dinner was served. Afterward, Justin ordered champagne to toast the engaged couple.

"Well, well, well, look who just walked in," Dex said, slanting a grin in Clayton's direction. "And look who's with her."

Clayton turned and rolled his eyes to the ceiling, while muttering a silent curse. Why did his cousin Felicia have to show up now, and of all people, Bernard Wilson was with her.

"I'm sure she appreciates you sending Bernard her way," Justin grinned.

Syneda lifted a brow after seeing an uncomfortable look on Clayton's face. "Is something wrong?"

He shrugged. "No."

Clayton heard the sounds of Justin and Dex chuckling and glared across the table at them.

Syneda looked around her. Her attention focused on Clayton's cousin and the handsome man who was with her. They had seen them and were headed over to their table.

"Hi, everyone," Felicia said when she reached the table. "Glad to see everyone out for a good cause. Let me introduce Bernard. But I think he knows everyone already."

Bernard smiled as they sat down to join them. "I met everyone at that party for Senator Lansing, except for you," he said to Syneda. "We were never officially introduced," he said extending his hand to her. "Bernard Wilson."

Syneda took the hand he offered. "Syneda Walters."

"Soon to be Syneda Madaris," Felicia said smiling. "And thanks for asking me to be in the wedding."

"The two of you are getting married?" Bernard asked Syneda in surprise, letting his gaze move from her to Clayton.

"That's right," Clayton said, sipping some of his champagne. "Why?"

"But I thought . . ."

He didn't finish his statement when the hostess came to take the newcomers' order.

They got into talking about other things. Dex and Justin began enlightening everyone about the small airplane the brothers had purchased together.

Bernard couldn't help noticing Syneda and the amount of candy and nuts she was nibbling on. And that was after she had finished eating a slice of coconut pie with vanilla ice cream.

Syneda felt Bernard's gaze on her and stopped munching. She lifted a brow. "Is anything wrong, Bernard?"

He smiled at her. "No, I was just noticing how much you're enjoying those nuts. You do know they're fattening don't you?"

Syneda heard Dex and Justin clear their throats. She raised a brow to Bernard. "They're fattening?"

"Extremely fattening since they're filled with oil. I know how hard it is to lose weight and how it's even harder to keep it off. You've done an excellent job, and I admire you for it."

Syneda smiled at him. "Thanks but you must have me confused with someone else. I've never had a weight problem. I can eat like a horse and never gain a pound."

He raised a brow at her before turning to frown at Clayton. The sly smile Clayton gave him let him know he'd been had. "And I guess you are not wearing eye contacts," Bernard said drily.

Syneda grinned, wondering why he would think she was. "No, I'm not. Why would you think I was?"

"Because I was deliberately led to believe you were. In fact I was led to believe a number of things about you that evidently aren't true."

"Really? And who would tell you untrue things about me?"

Bernard laughed, shaking his head. "Someone who evidently felt a need to protect his interest."

Syneda raised an arched brow, then dawning surfaced. She turned to Clayton and glared at him. "Would you like to tell me what's going on?"

As on cue, Justin and Dex stood and turning to their wives, suddenly suggested they use that time to select their ornament for the Christmas tree. Felicia and Bernard quickly decided to do the same.

When the table had cleared, Syneda asked Clayton again. "Would you like to explain what's going on? What did you tell Bernard about me?"

Dark eyes looked at her. "He had plans to hit on you that night, so I decided to take action."

"By telling him I had a weight problem and wore contacts? And just what else did you tell him?"

Clayton shrugged. "I told him that wasn't your natural hair color."

"You did what! I don't believe you did such a thing." Syneda glared at him. "Why all the lies? I could have handled the likes of Bernard Wilson that night."

"I'm sure you could have. I just didn't want him near you, that's all."

Syneda shook her head at Clayton's admission. It was hard to believe he had been jealous. She then remembered his behavior in Florida. At the time it hadn't made sense. Now considering everything, it did.

After a few minutes, she couldn't help the smile that stole across her lips. She should be furious with him but wasn't. He was at times her nemesis, but mostly her friend. He was her lover and soon, in seven months, he would be her husband.

"What am I going to do with you, Clayton Madaris?"

"Love me."

She leaned over and kissed his cheek. "Heaven help me but I do that already." She took his hand in hers. "Come on, let's go purchase our ornaments and help decorate the tree."

Clayton's alarm went off at six o'clock Monday morning. He missed Syneda already. It had been hard putting her back on the plane for New York yesterday afternoon.

He got out of bed and went into the bathroom. He returned to the bedroom moments later when the sound of the phone interrupted his shower.

"Hello."

"I hear congratulations are in order."

Clayton chuckled. "Good morning, Alex. I see news travel fast."

"Yes, especially when a fellow bachelor defects. Trask called last night and I told him the news. He asked me had you gone crazy or something."

Clayton laughed. "The next time you talk to Trask tell him I said I'm not crazy. I just happen to be a man very much in love. His time will come one day, so will yours."

"I hope not. Besides, speaking for myself, I promised your kid sister on her thirteenth birthday I'd wait for her to grow up," he teased. "Congratulations anyway. The only saving grace for you is I happen to think the woman you're marrying is first class. It's about time you noticed it."

Clayton couldn't help but agree.

"The reason I'm calling so bright and early is because I have that information you wanted. I have the names of the other two investigating agencies as well as the identity of Syneda's father."

For some reason, Clayton felt uneasy. "And?"

"I've located him, Clayton, and you won't believe in a million years just who he is. And I prefer not having this conversation over the phone. Are you free for breakfast?"

"No. I have to be in court by eight thirty. How about lunch?"

"Lunch is fine, and I prefer somewhere private."

Clayton frowned. "Sounds serious."

After a moment of hesitation, Alex said. "Depends on how you look at it. I'll let you decide."

"All right. We'll have lunch in my office. I'll order sandwiches."

"Okay, and remember I don't do mayo, and I do just a tad of mustard."

"Okay."

"And Clayton."

"Yeah?"

"I'm tired of turkey."

Clayton shook his head, laughing. "Got it."

CHAPTER 23

"I understand congratulations are in order."
Syneda lifted her gaze from the paper she was reading and saw
Thomas Rackley standing in the doorway of her office.

An easy smile played at the corners of her mouth. "Thanks. I guess I
don't have to ask how you found out do I?"

He grinned, shaking his head. "Office gossip is at its best today."

She leaned back in her chair. "I assumed that it would be."

Thomas stepped inside her office and saw the radiance of her smile.
He cocked his head to the side and studied her for a moment. "You're
happy aren't you?"

The smile on Syneda's face widened. "I think I'm happier than anyone
has a right to be."

He weighed her answer with a critical squint before his eyes grew
openly sincere. "I'm glad. You deserve to be happy. I'm glad you met
someone and fell in love."

"It wasn't easy."

Thomas chuckled. "And no doubt you gave the poor guy pure hell."

Syneda tried suppressing the grin that crossed her face. "No doubt."

His smile deepened into laughter. "I'm glad he hung on in there."

The amused look left Syneda's eyes when she thought about what
Thomas had just said. Clayton had hung on in there when most men
would not have. "I'm glad he did, too."

* * *

Clayton gave Alexander Maxwell a long, penetrating stare. He was absolutely speechless and had been since Alex had provided him with the information he'd wanted, especially the identity of Syneda's father.

He stood and walked over to the window and looked out. His mind felt bruised by the bitter truths Alex had just hit him with. Of all the men who could have fathered Syneda, it was hard to believe the one man he would never have suspected in a million years was the one.

"So what are you planning to do with this information?"

Alex's question abruptly invaded his thoughts. Clayton shrugged heavy shoulders. He felt like the weight of the world was sitting on them. He turned to Alex. "I don't know."

"You're surprised, aren't you?"

Keeping Alex's gaze, he nodded, his breath feeling heavy in his chest. "Weren't you?"

"Sure, I was. When I decided to do a little further investigating, surprise isn't quite the word I would use with what I found out. Hell-shocked is more like it. This was one of the most challenging puzzles I've pieced together in a long time."

"I believe you," Clayton said returning to his seat behind the desk. "Is there any way you could be mistaken about any of this?"

"No. That's why I went the extra mile on this one and located Syneda's mother's friend, that nurse, Clara Boyd, who conveniently disappeared after Jan Walters died. I knew there had to be a missing link someplace. And now when you really think about it, you'll agree that Syneda is the spittin' image of her father."

Clayton nodded as he absently traced the pattern of the wood grain across his desk. "Just for sanity purposes, let's go over all of this again."

Alex nodded, understanding completely. "All right," he said, stretching his legs out in front of him, trying to get comfortable in the chair. That wasn't too easy for his six-foot-four frame. "Those other two private investigators are based in Washington, D.C. That immediately told me something. Whatever was going on was somehow linked to the political scene. I just didn't make Syneda's connection until Senator Lansing's name popped up. Then I figured out that one of the investigators was trying to get the lowdown on the senator."

He stood when the chair became too uncomfortable. "Since it seems Senator Lansing was dating Syneda's mother during her senior year of college, the year Syneda was conceived, it appears he's her father. A father who didn't claim his child. It's my guess they plan to release their scoop to the media. When they do, all hell is going to break loose, and Syneda will be caught right smack in the middle. I can see the headlines now, and they definitely won't be positive for Senator Lansing. He'll have a lot of explaining to do."

"What about the other investigator?"

"I believe he's working for the senator. I think Senator Lansing somehow got wind of what was going on and decided to check things out for himself. Both investigators are turning in what they think are accurate reports."

Clayton rubbed his chin. "Accurate reports? That's a laugh."

"Yeah, and the only person who knows the truth, besides you and me, is Senator Lansing."

"Let's not forget Clara Boyd."

Alex's face hardened as he remembered his interview with the woman. She had broken down and told him the truth under his intense questioning. "Yeah, some friend she turned out to be." He sat back down after stretching his legs some. "So going back to my earlier question, what are you going to do with the information?"

Clayton stood. "I'm going to do everything I can to protect Syneda. She's been hurt enough. The first thing I'm going to do is to see Senator Lansing." He leaned over his desk and punched the intercom button. "Serena, book me a flight to D.C. as soon as possible."

Senator Lansing looked up upon hearing the knock on the door. "Come in."

Braxter walked in. "The investigator's report is here, sir," he said, handing the senator the huge envelope he carried. "It was delivered a few moments ago."

The senator nodded, taking the packet Braxter handed him. "Have you read it?"

"No. I considered it a private matter."

"Thanks, I appreciate it."

"Just keep in mind, senator, someone intends to ruin your reputation if they can with that same report."

The senator rubbed a hand across his face. "I haven't forgotten. And Braxter, please hold my calls for a while. I want to go through this report immediately." He checked his watch. "It's almost closing time, you can go on home if you'd like."

Braxter shook his head. "There's some things I need to work on. I'll be out front if you need me."

"Thanks."

"Oh yeah. On Sundays I always buy newspapers from major cities in Texas to see how well you're doing in the polls. This article appeared in the society column of a Houston paper and caught my attention." He handed the newspaper clipping to the senator. "I thought you might be interested."

The senator scanned the article that announced Texas attorney, Clayton Madaris's engagement to fellow New York attorney, Syneda Walters. The wedding was planned for June of next year.

"It seems Syneda Walters will be marrying Jacob Madaris's nephew," Braxter said, breaking the silence in the room.

Senator Lansing took a deep breath. "Yes, it appears that way doesn't it. I've known Clayton Madaris a long time. He's a fine young man, and an outstanding attorney."

Once Braxton left, closing the door behind him, the senator pulled the papers out of the packet and began reading.

Laying aside the packet that had just been delivered to her, Celeste stood and walked to her bedroom and sprawled out in a chair next to her bed. She raked a hand through her shoulder-length hair, wondering why she felt so awful.

The job was completed. She was sure the packet in her living room contained information Senator Harris would be eager to get his hands on. Although Emery Fulton, her friend from college who had done the investigative work for her hadn't told her exactly what was in the report, he had said it contained some information on Senator Lansing that if released to the media, could be damaging.

Standing, she walked back into the living room and picked up the packet. She should call Senator Harris and let him know that she had the information he'd paid her to get. But for some reason she couldn't make herself pick up the phone and do that.

For the past two years she had cultivated a pretty good life for herself. It was a life she enjoyed with the material things she had always wanted as a child but never had. Thanks to a mother who ran off and left her with an alcoholic father at the age of twelve, she had learned to survive without help from anyone. And she had never wanted or needed anyone.

She had met Senator Harris a couple of years ago when he had come into her travel agency to arrange a cruise for him and his wife. It didn't take long for him to figure out that in her profession, since she came in contact with a lot of people, especially those in the political circle by planning trips for them, she could be an asset to him.

At first he had only been interested in inside information on some of his supposedly close friends. She had passed information to him about Senator Mat Williams's affair with a woman young enough to be his daughter, Senator Paul Dunlap's daughter's abortion, and Senator Carl Booker's son's drug addiction.

He had paid her well for the information she had obtained with Emery's help. But this assignment involving Braxter had been the first that she had gotten personally involved with to the point of going so far as to sleep with someone to get information. And since the day Braxter had discovered the truth, her life had not been the same. Somehow his pain had become hers, especially knowing she'd been the cause of it.

She picked up the phone to make the call to Senator Harris and then slammed it back down. She just couldn't do it. The amount of money he had paid her no longer mattered. She would pay back every penny of it to him.

She went into the bedroom and slipped into her coat. Going back into the living room she picked up the packet, grabbed her purse, then walked out of the door.

Nedwyn Lansing felt his back hit against the desk chair as he released a long-drawn breath. Suddenly all the anger he had ever felt in his entire lifetime hit him with the force of a tidal wave.

How could this have happened? How could such a mistake be made? How could Jan's child be turned over to the authorities when her father was very much alive and would have wanted her had he known about her?

He shook his head to calm his temper. There was no doubt in his mind that Syneda Walters was Jan's child. The report clearly named Jan as Syneda's biological mother and gave the reason she'd been placed in a foster home after Jan's death. Her father had not come to claim his child.

He picked up the phone knowing the one person he had to call immediately. He paused when there was a knock on his door. He then remembered that Braxter had not yet left.

"What is it Braxter?"

Braxter opened the door and came in. He immediately noticed the intense expression the senator wore. "I just got a call from security downstairs. Clayton Madaris is here to see you."

"Clayton Madaris?" The senator shook his head slowly, glancing down at the report before him. He sat silently for a moment before saying. "Have security send him up."

Clayton frowned when he stepped into the senator's office and saw the other man standing there. "I was hoping to get a chance to speak with you privately, Senator."

The senator nodded. He then proceeded to introduce the two men. "Braxter is my top aide, Clayton, and we can talk openly in front of him. Besides, it's about time I let him in on what's going on since I have a pretty good idea as to why you're here. Let's sit down."

Once everyone was seated, Clayton began. "I'm sure by now you're aware someone is trying to ruin your political career, Senator."

The senator's gaze didn't flicker from Clayton's. "Yes, I'm aware of it. What I would like to know is what's your connection, and how do you know so much about it?"

Clayton breathed an annoyed sigh but calmly contained himself. Although he had known the senator a number of years due to the senator's close relationship with his late Uncle Robert and his Uncle Jake, Clayton understood his need to be cautious in certain situations. This was one of those situations.

"My connection is the woman I plan to marry. Someone is planning to use her as a weapon in an attempt to destroy your credibility with the people. The reason I know so much about it is because I hired a private investigator to find her father for me."

"And you think you've found him." It was a statement rather than a question.

"I know I have."

The senator took a deep breath and stood. He paced the room several times before coming to a stop in front of Clayton. "And you believe I'm your man, don't you?"

Clayton's gaze never left the senator. "No. I know for a fact that you're not."

The senator raised a surprised brow. "Do you?"

"Yes. My investigator is a very thorough man who loves putting together puzzles. The only reason I came here before going to see her father is to get some answers about a few things."

"If you're going to ask me if he knew about her, the answer is a definite no. There's no way he would have known and not claimed his child. He was too deeply in love with Jan. In fact he still loves her. Her dying changed nothing. The second week of May of each year, on the date they met, he tortures himself by first visiting her grave, then later he tries to erase the pain by drinking himself to death for two days. And he's not a drinker. I'm the only one he'll let see him that way. And I make it a point to go visit him every year in May to help him through that painful period."

Braxter had been sitting quietly listening to Clayton and the senator, trying to follow along and piece together what they were talking about. The only thing he understood was the explanation for the senator's mysterious trips each May.

"Excuse me," he interrupted the two men. "I'm trying to follow the two of you here." He turned to the senator. "Are you saying that report I gave you from the investigator indicates you're Syneda Walters's father?"

"After reading it one would assume that, yes."

"But you're not?"

"No, I'm not."

Braxter shook his head. "I don't understand. Why would anyone assume you're her father if you aren't?"

The senator went over to the window and looked out. He could see the Lincoln Monument in the distance even in the dusk of night. He turned back to Braxter. "Most people thought Syneda's mother, Jan Walters, and I dated exclusively during our senior year of college."

"But that wasn't the case?"

"No. We just wanted people to think that we did."

A look of ungoverned confusion shone in Braxter's eyes. "Why?"

Sadness shone in the senator's gaze. "Because society wasn't ready to accept what they considered as forbidden love."

When Braxter looked even more confused, Clayton decided to intercede by asking him. "Have you ever heard the term 'jungle fever'?"

"Yes, of course." Braxter stared first at Clayton then back at the senator when understanding dawned. He paused for a moment before finally asking. "And just who is Syneda Walters's father?"

The senator hesitated briefly before saying quietly. "Syntel Tremain Remington."

Braxter was shocked into silence. "S. T. Remington of Remington Oil?" His voice was filled with disbelief.

"Yes, and I need to talk to Syntel as soon as possible. He knows nothing about any of this. The shock may be too much for him. Arrange a flight that will take me to Austin tonight."

"I'm going with you," Clayton spoke up.

"I think this is something he needs to hear from me personally."

"I agree, but I intend to be there when he hears it. Like I said earlier, there are a number of questions that I want answered. My main concern is Syneda and how she's going to handle all of this. For years she assumed her father abandoned her. Now from what I understand that's not the case. I want to know if he knew his father had intercepted a phone call meant for him and paid the caller good money not to give Syntel's name to the authorities as Syneda's father."

"Is that what happened?"

"Yes. We were able to find the woman, and she told us everything. She even admitted taking the money."

The senator shook his head. "He will never forgive his father for that. He loved Jan deeply."

At that moment there was a soft knock on the door.

"Yes, come in," the senator called out.

The door to the senator's office swung open and Celeste walked in.

"What are you doing here?" Braxter snapped. He was both surprised and upset to see her. His chest heaved with outrage at the sight of her. "Who gave security the approval to let you in here?"

Celeste nodded to the other two men in the room before answering Braxter. "I deliver travel packages to occupants of this building all the time. Security is used to seeing me."

"What do you want?"

She placed the packet on the desk. "I came to give you this and to say I'm sorry. I hope one day you'll forgive me for what I did." She turned to leave.

"Excuse me, Miss," Clayton said, putting together what was transpiring between the two individuals. "Who hired you to get information on Senator Lansing?"

Celeste turned back around. She remembered Clayton from the party at Whispering Pines. She bit her lower lip. It had taken every scrap of courage for her to come here tonight to make amends. But she had to come. She had to do the right thing.

Her gaze left Clayton, then went to the senator, before finally coming to rest on Braxter. She knew he hated her and would never forgive her. The piercing dark eyes staring back at her did not show any signs of forgiveness.

She knew at that moment why she hadn't been able to go through with passing the report on to Senator Harris. She had fallen in love with Braxter. Her eyes closed momentarily, shielding his angry glare from her. When she reopened them, she shifted her gaze back to Clayton. "The person who hired me is Senator John Harris."

She then turned and quickly walked out of Senator Lansing's office.

CHAPTER 24

"**A**re you sure he's going to be here?" Clayton asked as he and Senator Lansing stepped into the elevator of an elegant apartment building near downtown Austin.

"I'm pretty positive," Senator Lansing replied, keying a special code into the elevator door panel box. "During the week Syntel stays here instead of commuting back and forth to the ranch. And he seldom goes out in the evenings."

Clayton nodded. Since discovering Syntel Remington was Syneda's father, he had begun searching his mind for whatever personal information he knew about him. It was a known fact that he had never married. He also remembered reading somewhere that he had taken over the running of Remington Oil fifteen years ago, upon his father's death.

Clayton's thoughts came to an end when the elevator door opened and they stepped into a plushly carpeted hallway and walked toward the only door on the floor.

The door was opened on the second knock. A surprised expression lit Syntel Remington's face. He moved aside to let the two men enter. "Ned, I didn't know you were in Austin." He then turned questioning eyes to Clayton. "Madaris, this is a pleasant surprise."

For the first time since meeting him over a year ago, Clayton looked deeply into Syntel Remington's eyes. They were eyes so much like Syneda's in color and shape that he couldn't believe he hadn't noticed them before. But then he hadn't been aware that the man standing before him was her father. He also noticed that Syntel and Syneda shared similar smiles and the same well-defined features.

"I just arrived in Austin less than an hour ago," Senator Lansing said. "I flew in from Washington. We both did. There's an important matter we need to discuss with you, Syntel."

Syntel Remington's brow lifted. "This sounds serious, Ned."

"Trust me, it is."

"Let's go into the study. I was just about to settle down and get some reading done."

He led them to a brightly lit room where bookcases lined both sides. He gestured them to take a seat. He then took a seat behind a large oak desk.

"All right, Ned, what is it? What's so important to send you racing to my door from Washington with one of Texas's most dynamic attorneys in tow?" he asked, managing a wobbly smile. He was confused and concerned with the expression his best friend wore.

The room fell silent, and a few moments later Senator Lansing spoke. "It's about Jan."

Syntel Remington's eyes suddenly became distant and pained. "What about Janeda?"

The senator's lips lifted in a faint smile. Janeda had disliked her birth name and in college she had shortened it to Jan. No one got away with calling her Janeda. No one except Syntel.

Syntel Remington stood, crossing his arms like a protective shield. Clayton couldn't help but note it was something Syneda did occasionally.

"Ned, I asked you what about Janeda?"

The room fell silent once more and before Senator Lansing could respond Syntel spoke again. "All right, I think I get it now. If the two of you are here to warn me that you've gotten wind that one of those slick and sleazy tabloids have somehow dug up information about my relationship with Janeda and plan to print it, don't concern yourselves with it. I will never deny ever loving her. You should know that, Ned."

Nedwyn Lansing nodded. "Yes, I know, Syntel, but that's not it. That's not why we're here. There's something else, something you should know. And I think you should sit back down before hearing it."

Syntel looked for a moment like he wasn't going to take the senator's suggestion, but then he took his seat again. "What is it, Ned?"

"Jan had a child. Your child."

Clayton watched the color drain from the man's face with Senator Lansing's words.

"What did you say?" Syntel's lips barely moved when he asked the question.

Senator Lansing forced himself to respond calmly. "I said Jan had a child. Your child. A girl."

Syntel jumped up out of his seat, nearly knocking a plant off his desk in the process. His face was filled with rage. "Who told you that lie, Ned? How could you believe such a thing?"

"It's true, Syntel. I checked it out myself. If you remember, Jan disappeared right after you'd left for the Air Force Academy. I think she did it because she knew she was pregnant."

"If what you say is true, why wouldn't she have told me? She knew I loved her. There was nothing I would not have done for her."

"I think she knew that, and that's the reason she left without telling you. She didn't see a place for her in your life. You and I know that society would never have accepted a marriage between the two of you. At least not back then. She knew it too, and left."

Syntel slumped back down in his chair. He buried his face in his hands, shaking his head. "No, I don't believe it. I refuse to believe Janeda would give our child away."

"She didn't give the child away. She raised your child alone as a single parent until her death."

Syntel's head snapped up. "Are you saying I have a child somewhere? A daughter?"

"Yes. She was ten years old when Jan died."

Syntel shook his head as if dazed with disbelief. "What happened to her?"

"Because the authorities assumed she didn't have any living relatives after Jan died, she became a ward of this state and was placed in a foster home."

"No!"

Clayton watched as Syntel Remington's entire body jerked as if it had been struck. His face filled with rage. "Are you saying my child was raised by strangers?"

Clayton spoke for the first time. "That was the only recourse under the circumstances. But I can tell you that the Phillips were good people and she was treated very well."

Syntel looked at Clayton as if he had forgotten he was there. His shoulders slumped. "So no one knew I was her father?"

With a sigh of resignation, Senator Lansing stood, knowing he had to tell his friend the rest of the story. During the flight from D.C. to Austin, Clayton had told him everything, including his investigator's personal interview with Clara Boyd. It had been a case of downright deceit and betrayal by Syntel's father.

"That's not true, Syntel. There were two others who knew you were the child's father. When Jan knew she was dying, she told someone she thought she could trust to contact you. In fact she died believing you were contacted and were coming for your child. She even told your daughter you would be coming for her."

He wiped a film of perspiration from his forehead before continuing.

"However, instead of getting you, the person who'd made the call for Jan spoke to your father instead. And . . ."

"And what?"

"Your father made the decision not to pass the information on to you and to make sure your name was never connected to Jan's child. Clayton hired an investigator who has located the woman. She admits receiving money from your father in payment for not revealing your identity to the Children's Services Department."

Syntel raked his fingers through his tousled hair. The expression on his face was pained, disbelieving, enraged. "That can't be true," he said in a strained voice choked with deep emotion. "My father would not have been that cruel, that heartless, that hateful. He would not have turned his back on his own grandchild, my child, my own flesh and blood," he said, as if trying to convince himself. But looking at the sympathy in his best friend's eyes, and Clayton's, he knew deep down his father had done just that.

"Where is she? Oh, God, please tell me you know where she is now."

Clayton stood and faced the man. He had to swallow in an attempt to remove the lump in his throat. "She lives in New York."

"New York?"

"Yes." Pulling his wallet from his pant pocket Clayton took out a picture he'd had taken of Syneda when they had visited Atlanta. As she smiled for the camera, her sea-green eyes shone brightly, her golden bronze hair flowed about her shoulders and highlighted her light brown complexion.

"This is your daughter, Syntel, the woman I love and plan to marry in June."

A wry smile touched Clayton's lips as he realized something. "I often wondered about the origin of her name since it's unusual. Now I know where it came from. Janeda was thinking of you when she named your daughter. It's a combination of both your names. However, her middle name is all yours. The woman in this picture is Syneda Tremain Walters." He handed the picture to Syntel.

Syntel nervously accepted the photograph Clayton handed to him. There was complete silence in the room as he looked at it. His eyes began filling with tears. Suddenly, the only sounds in the room were the sounds of Syntel Remington's heartwrenching sobs.

After Nedwyn and Clayton had left, Syntel Remington sat slumped down in a chair. A spasm of pain flitted across his face when he thought of what his father had done.

Janeda had given him a daughter, and in the end she had believed in their love enough to want him to know about their child, to want him to take care of her, even when they had not seen each other in ten years.

But she had known that his love for her would have survived the test of time and that he would want their child, and that he would take care of her. Janeda had died believing in him.

He couldn't help but remember the last night he and Janeda had spent together. He was to report to the Air Force Academy the day after graduation. The Viet Nam War was on everyone's mind, and it had been the main thing on his that night. Maybe if it hadn't been, he would have paid more attention to her mood and the words she had spoken to him. And maybe he would have sensed some sort of a change in her, and noted that something was bothering her.

She had been the joy of his life, his true love. To him the color of their skin had never made a difference. But to her it had. She'd always been afraid of what others would think about it. Interracial relationships had not been accepted during that time, and that was the reason Ned had been used as their go-between and their cover.

Syntel hadn't cared what others thought, and he had told her that countless times. His love for her was the only thing that mattered to him. But because she had cared, he had respected her wishes.

He closed his eyes remembering that night, their last one together, the night before graduation. They had just made love and he'd been holding her in his arms, never wanting to let her go . . .

Janeda snuggled closer to him. "We're so different," she said, looking deep into his eyes.

He smiled down at her. "No we aren't. You just got a better tan than I do," he said jokingly.

She smiled back at him, then suddenly her expression became serious. "I'm afraid."

He pulled her closer. "Don't be. Everything's going to work out all right. I'll have six weeks at the academy and then I'll come back for you. It's not certain that I'll be sent overseas, but if I do, we'll get married before I go. You're the most important person in my life. I want to tell my parents about us so that if you need anything while I'm gone you can contact them."

"No. Please don't tell them anything, at least not yet. I'll be all right. Just be careful, and always know that I love you. No matter where you go or what you do, just believe that I love you, and will love you forever."

He pulled her closer into his arms. "And I love you. I always will. I will make you my wife one day, and I don't care who may not like it as long as I have you . . ."

*   *   *

Syntel opened his eyes. He had been at the academy only a couple of days when Ned had contacted him that Janeda had moved out of her apartment and hadn't told anyone where she had gone. He had almost gone out of his mind with worry, and when days passed with no word from her, he'd almost gone crazy. The only thing that had gotten him through his days at the academy was the belief that sooner or later she would contact him.

She never did.

He was sent to Viet Nam directly from the academy. His father had tried to stop the order but had soon discovered that the Remington name hadn't meant a thing to Uncle Sam.

Janeda never contacted him and when he returned to the States nearly twenty-four months later, he had tried finding her but couldn't. He'd tried forgetting her but had been unsuccessful in that attempt, too. Years later, he'd hired an investigator who within weeks had concluded his report. Janeda had died of a bad case of acute pneumonia at the age of thirty while living in Dallas, Texas. The report had not mentioned anything about the fact that she had been survived by a child. His child.

The lump in his throat seemed to grow larger. He stood and walked to the window and looked out into the darkness. He had a daughter. A twenty-eight-year-old daughter that he hadn't known about until tonight.

His child . . . Janeda's child . . . Their child.

Syneda Tremain Walters.

Syneda recognized the smell of spaghetti the moment she entered her apartment. A broad smile covered her face.

Clayton was here!

She called out to him and moments later he walked out of the kitchen and swept her into his arms, kissing her with a need that she returned. Finally she lifted her head after he had placed her back on her feet. "What are you doing here?"

He leaned down and kissed her moist lips. "Aren't you glad to see me?"

"Yes, but it's Wednesday. I wasn't expecting you until the weekend."

"I missed you," he responded huskily, cupping her chin and leaning down and kissing her once more. It was a deep kiss, long and warm. His lips left hers then moved to her ear, her temple, and her nose before retracing the path back to her mouth. The sensual force about to explode between them was acute. He pulled her closer to him. "Do we eat first or make love?"

Syneda looked up and studied the face of the man she loved, the man she was going to marry. Desire-filled eyes stared down at her. She had missed him, too, and wanted nothing more than to lose herself in his arms, to lose her body in his.

Her hands slowly slid up his chest and around his neck. "Make love to me, Clayton. Now."

He kissed her again as he swept her into his arms and carried her into the bedroom.

"I'm hungry."

Clayton smiled at Syneda's words. He lowered his head and placed a kiss on her lips. "You could have eaten first. I did give you a choice."

"I know but I preferred doing this first," she said smiling against his lips. She eased up on her elbow and looked down at him. "At this moment I'm happier than anyone deserves to be."

He reached up and captured her face in the palm of his hand. "If there's anyone who deserves to be happy, you're that person."

Clayton kissed her knowing he had to discuss the reason he had come to see her during the middle of the week. He would never forget how Syntel had taken the news of Syneda's existence. He had been filled with joy, sorrow, and anger. Joy that Janeda had given him a daughter, sorrow that he had been cheated out of twenty-eight years of her life, and anger in knowing his father had been the cause of it.

A deep sigh escaped Clayton's lips. He had had to explain to Syntel why it was so important how they handled revealing his identity to Syneda. As best he could, he had told him about Syneda's rejection and abandonment complex, and how at first she would not accept a serious relationship between them because she had associated loving a man with abandonment and rejection. He had seen fresh tears cloud the older man's eyes when he had told him how confident Janeda Walters had been when she'd been told upon her death bed that he would be coming for his daughter; and how Syneda had waited patiently for him to come for her.

"Clayton, I'm hungry."

Syneda's words cut into Clayton's thoughts. He smiled at her. "Then I guess I'd better feed you. But first I need to tell you something."

She looked up at him curiously. "What?"

"We've been invited somewhere this weekend."

"Oh? Where?"

Clayton reached up and traced his knuckle across her smooth skin. "To S. T. Remington's ranch."

Syneda's eyes widened. "Really? Why?"

"He wants to meet you."

She laughed. "Why would S. T. Remington want to meet me?"

He smiled, a slow, lazy smile. "He's eaten up with curiosity about the woman who nabbed me from the throes of bachelorhood. Trust me, he's dying to meet you." Dying to meet her was an understatement, Clayton thought. Syntel had been ready to fly to New York and claim his daughter.

"Well, what about it, baby?"

Syneda leaned up and kissed him. "I had relished the idea of spending this weekend here alone with you. But if you want us to go, I will. Is anyone else going to be there?"

"Yes. Senator Lansing will be there, too. They've been best friends since college."

Syneda nodded. "Then I'll finally get the opportunity to meet the senator. I never did meet him at Whispering Pines."

"Now you'll have your chance."

Syneda snuggled closer to Clayton. "Hmmm, sounds like it will be a rather interesting weekend."

Clayton pulled her to him. "Yeah, I have a feeling that it will be."

"How did things go with S. T. Remington?" Braxter asked as he entered the senator's office.

Senator Lansing sighed raggedly, pushing his chair back from his desk. "No different than I expected. Syntel loved Jan very much and to discover he had a child he didn't know anything about because of the deceit of his father was a lot for him to take in."

Braxter nodded. "I'm sure it was. Has Ms. Walters been told anything yet?"

"No. Clayton strongly suggested we wait until the weekend. He's bringing her to Syntel's ranch then."

"I hope things turn out all right. In their own way, both of them have suffered enough."

"I fully agree."

"Have you decided what you're going to do about Senator Harris?"

"Yes. I'm not going to do anything. He didn't get the report and nothing has happened."

"But he tried to ruin you."

"And no doubt he'll probably try again. I can't go around worrying about people like him, Braxter. All I can do is continue to do the job I was sent here to do. I don't have time to play games like Senator Harris is inclined to do."

"So you're going to let him get away with it?"

"Thanks to Celeste Rogers, he didn't get away with anything."

"Yes, thanks to Celeste Rogers," Braxter said bitterly.

"Have you seen her since that night she brought the report here?"

"No, and I don't intend to either."

"She apologized for what she'd done."

"How can you forgive someone who has betrayed you? Someone who deliberately used you?"

A few seconds followed before the senator answered. "It can be done, Braxter, but you have to want to do it. None of us are perfect. All of us have flaws, and we all make mistakes. We don't know why she did what she did initially. The only thing we do know is that in the end, because of you, she couldn't go through with it. Forgiving someone never is easy. It takes a big person to say I'm sorry, but it takes an even bigger person to say I accept your apology and you're forgiven."

Braxter didn't respond for the longest moment, then nodding his head he turned and walked out of the office.

The snow was coming down in light flakes, the first for D.C. this winter. It took all of Braxter's concentration to operate the car and not think about Celeste. He had not gotten a lot of work done today from thinking about her.

Suddenly his mind became filled with what the senator had said to him earlier that day. . . . "It takes a big person to say I'm sorry, but it takes an even bigger person to say I accept your apology and you're forgiven."

He took a long deep breath. For so long he had not allowed himself the time to get interested in anyone. He had been too busy to include a woman in his life, at least not seriously.

Not until he'd met Celeste.

When the car came to a stop at a traffic light, he shifted his weight in the seat and massaged the tightness at the base of his neck. No matter how much he tried, he couldn't stop thinking of her. And no matter how much he tried he couldn't stop loving her.

When the light signaled it was time to go, he found himself heading in the direction of Celeste's apartment.

Celeste answered the knock at her door and was surprised to find Braxter's tall figure filling the doorway.

"May I come in?"

Numb, she simply nodded and stepped aside.

For the longest time Braxter didn't say anything to her, he just stood looking at her.

"Braxter, why are you here?"

He shook his head as if to clear it. "I asked myself a similar question while driving over here. I wasn't completely sure until you opened the door. Now I know."

He took her hand in his and led her over to the sofa where they sat down. "There's a lot of things I don't understand, but I want you to talk to me, let's get things out in the open. I want you to help me to understand your connection with Senator Harris, and why you did what you did."

Celeste met his gaze not believing he had actually come and was giving her an opportunity to explain things to him. She really couldn't ask for any more than that.

At least it was a start.

CHAPTER 25

"You're pretty good at flying this thing," Syneda said, watching Clayton at the controls of the Cessna 310. She glanced around the cockpit of the small plane before returning her eyes to him. Although she disliked small planes, she couldn't help admiring his abilities as a pilot. He handled the controls with both ease and competency. They had been in the air fifteen minutes, and she had not experienced even the tiniest bit of queasiness.

"Thanks," Clayton replied casting her a smile. "And thanks again for taking this trip with me."

"I didn't mind. In fact I'm looking forward to it." Her lips twitched in amusement. "You evidently made a darn good impression on S. T. Remington when representing Caitlin in that land deal for the two of you to have gotten so chummy. I'm sure not too many people get invited to his ranch for the weekend. Anyone who keeps up with the lives of the rich and famous knows S. T. Remington is a very private person. I understand he's very selective when choosing his friends and associates."

Clayton grinned. "Remington and I aren't chummy. I told you, you're the reason for the invitation. He wanted to meet you."

Syneda rolled her eyes upward. "Yeah, right."

He smiled. He knew Syneda didn't believe him. She thought he was getting together with Syntel Remington on business and had merely invited her along.

Syntel had contacted him yesterday to make sure they were still coming. He had also advised Clayton that after making a few phone calls, he'd been able to track down the investigator who had handled his search for Janeda years ago. Now retired, the man had remembered the assignment well, and what he'd told Syntel was no longer hard for him to believe. He had been paid a hefty sum by Syntel's father to omit certain information in his report. Specifically, any information regarding Janeda's child.

"Tighten up. It's time to take this baby down," Clayton said to Syneda moments later.

Clayton smoothly landed the small aircraft. "Syntel has sent someone to get us," he told Syneda as he motioned to the Pathfinder parked near the runway. "We'll be on our way to the ranch as soon as I check in."

Not long afterward, they were on their way to the home of one of Texas's richest oilmen. Syneda was not disappointed when the vehicle came to a stop in front of the big sprawling Spanish-style ranch house moments later. She had always thought the ranch house at Whispering Pines was huge but this one took the icing off the cake. It was surrounded by numerous flowering trees, plants, and shrubs. "It's beautiful," she whispered to Clayton. "I can't believe he lives here alone."

Clayton took her hand in his. "He doesn't live alone. He has an entire house staff and this is an operating ranch. In addition to being in the oil business, Syntel raises Arabian horses. There's a slew of ranch hands living around here."

"What I meant is that I can't believe he isn't married. He's one of Texas's wealthiest bachelors, and from the pictures I've seen of him, he's extremely good looking. I'm surprised no one has snatched him up by now."

"I understand he fell in love rather young . . . in his twenties. The woman died and he never wanted anyone else after that," Clayton replied as the door to the vehicle was opened for them. "He loved her very much."

"How sad."

"Yes it was, but they did have a daughter together."

Syneda accepted Clayton's words without any further comments or questions. Her attention was immediately drawn to the tall, broad-shouldered, handsome, older man who had come out of the house to greet them. Clayton introduced Syneda to Syntel.

"Welcome to Viscaya." Syntel captured Syneda's hand in his. A lump formed in his throat as he tried suppressing any outward emotions he felt in knowing this young woman was *his* child, his and Janeda's. She had been created in their love.

Syneda smiled up into eyes that she failed to notice were the exact color of her own. "Thanks for the invitation."

Syntel beamed down at her. "Clayton told me how beautiful you were, but I didn't believe him. Now I see he really didn't exaggerate."

"Thank you. You're very kind, Mr. Remington," Syneda replied. For some reason, she had taken an immediate liking to the man. He seemed full of warmth and friendliness and was nothing like the private, closed person the media had painted him to be. "You have a beautiful home."

"I'm glad you like it. And please call me Syntel. Come on inside," he said, leading them through the huge front door made of dark wood. "Emilie is my housekeeper, and she'll show you to your rooms. Later today after the two of you have unpacked and relaxed a bit, I'll show you around."

Once inside, Syneda couldn't help but view with approval the decor of the house. A few minutes later she and Clayton were led down a long hall where the guest rooms were. The rooms they were given were next to each other. Her room was beautifully decorated and contained a fireplace. A huge window overlooked an interior courtyard filled with lush plants and a small man-made pond. There was also a swimming pool within her sight.

Syneda smiled as she began unpacking her belongings, anticipating what she deemed to be a weekend of fun spent on a ranch deep in the heart of Texas.

True to his word, Syntel took Syneda and Clayton on a personal tour of his ranch. More than once Syneda looked up to find his intense gaze upon her. It wasn't the look of male interest, but a look of something she couldn't quite figure out.

That night she retired to bed early to give Clayton and Syntel a chance to talk privately. After taking a bath in the huge bathtub she walked out of the bathroom dressed in a silky mauve-colored slip-style nightgown to find Clayton stretched out on her bed.

Her heart began beating rapidly from the sight of him on the bed. He looked so big, powerful, and strong. The jeans he wore hugged his muscular thighs and the shirt he wore greatly emphasized his broad shoulders.

Before she had a chance to realize what he was up to, he reached out and grabbed her wrist, pulling her down to him on the huge bed.

"Clayton, what do you think you're doing?" she asked laughing.

"I think it's obvious," he said huskily, closing his arms around her like steel bands.

"What will Syntel think if he finds out you're in my room?" Syneda asked moments before her breath caught in her throat. Clayton's hands had begun roaming underneath her gown.

Clayton had thought of that. Syntel had given them separate rooms. Evidently he didn't think it was too late to be a protective father to his daughter. However as far as Clayton was concerned, it would take more than separate rooms to keep him away from the woman he loved.

"Don't worry about Syntel. He knows we're engaged to be married. Besides, his bedroom is on the other side of the house. There's no one in this wing but the two of us."

"Are you sure?"

Clayton swiftly and expertly removed the gown from Syneda's body. "I'm positive," he answered moments before savoring the taste of her mouth. And at the same time he let his hands move leisurely over her, finding pleasure in her soft nakedness.

"I want you, baby." He whispered the words against her lips before claiming them again, pressing her back against the pillow.

Syneda was completely aware of Clayton's tenderness as he went about pleasing her. She automatically surrendered to the passion he was stirring inside of her. He teased her by keeping his mouth on hers lightly, toying with her tongue and nipping at the corners of her mouth.

He lifted his mouth from hers and met her gaze. Deep desire flared in his eyes. "I want to love you tonight in the full sense of the word, Syneda. I don't want anything separating us. Not anything. I want to give you all of me. But doing so will put you at risk of getting pregnant, and I don't want to do that. I want you to have my baby but only after we've gotten married and feel the time is right."

Clayton's words echoed in Syneda's head. A rush of emotions surged through her. Clayton Madaris, a man who thrived on being careful and in control, wanted to be careless and out of control with her. What he had held back from numerous other women, he now wanted to give to her. He wanted to be a part of her in the most elemental way, in the most special way. But he thought doing so would put her at risk of getting pregnant.

She looked up at him. Love swelled in her heart. "And I don't want anything separating us either. I want all of you." Syneda's voice was a mere notch above a whisper when she spoke.

"And don't worry about placing me in any kind of risk. I'm on birth control."

Clayton's surprised gaze held hers for a moment before asking. "You're on the pill?"

Syneda shook her head. "No. I didn't think I'd remember to take one of those things everyday. They're only as reliable as the person who takes them. I had an injection."

His look was thoughtful when he asked. "When?"

"Right after our trip to New Orleans."

"Why didn't you tell me?" he asked, threading his fingers through the softness of her hair.

"I started to tell you a number of times then changed my mind. Using a condom always seemed to be the most comfortable and safest method to you." She smiled slightly. "Not too many men can boast of having a case of them in their closet. The reason I didn't tell you was because I didn't want you to feel you had to change your way of doing things just for me." She lowered her eyes from his.

"Look at me, Syneda."

When she raised her eyes to his, he brushed his lips across her lips before saying. "I've always believed in safe sex. More men should take responsibility for their actions in the bedroom. But there was never a time when I made love to you that I didn't think about how it would feel to be skin to skin with you, without having some type of covering, not matter how thin, separating us."

He pulled her closer into his embrace. "You don't know how often I wondered how it would feel to make love to you knowing the very essence of me would become a part of you. I've never made love to a woman without using a condom but that's all I've ever thought of not doing with you."

Anticipation combined with heated desire flowed through Syneda's body with his words. "Then do it, Clayton. I'm not at risk. I want the full Clayton Madaris experience."

Clayton's heart raced. There was no mistaking the love and trust he read in her eyes. Excitement and desire tore through him. She was a very special woman. His woman. Then he kissed her in a way that left her shivering and murmuring his name. He touched her in a way that made her tremble, taking his time to build their passion until Syneda almost shattered in his arms.

Reveling in his touch, Syneda clung to him. His scent exuded a virility that was a combination of man and heat. His body was warm and hard. She loved the feel of him on her and was ready for the feel of him inside her. She kissed the tender skin underneath his ear and whispered. "Love me, Clayton. Now!"

He did, both mentally and physically.

As he slipped into her body, he gazed down into the depths of her sea-green eyes that were dark with passion. He felt himself losing control. He was powerless in her arms.

They began moving together in rapturous rhythm, the heat of his passion inciting her to move under him and cling to him tighter as he filled her completely.

"I love you." Clayton whispered the words in Syneda's ear just moments before their passion soared to greater heights. All sense of time and place escaped them as their bodies convulsed and their passion crested.

Syneda flexed her inner muscles to hold him tighter within her. She heard herself make a low sexy sound as her senses began slipping. She soon heard Clayton's groan mingle with that sound and felt his body trembling as they simultaneously reached the peak of total fulfillment together. She strained against him when she felt him emptying himself into her.

"Clayton!"

The force of what was taking place made Syneda's entire body grow still as a tidal wave of sensuous pleasure flooded over her. It was a violent culmination for the both of them as together they reached the pinnacle of sexual pleasure.

A long time afterward, Clayton lay holding Syneda as she slept in his arms. Her head rested on his shoulder, her soft body was tucked into the curve of his.

He leaned down and brushed his lips across hers. Sometime tomorrow her eighteen-year wait for her father would end. He hoped and prayed she would not resent him for interfering in her past, but she needed to deal with her past before the two of them could have a future.

"Did you get a good night's sleep, Syneda?"

A blush crept in Syneda's cheek. She quickly took a huge swallow of orange juice before answering Syntel's question. "Yes, thanks for asking."

Out of the corner of her eye she saw Clayton's thin smile. Of all the things she had gotten last night, a good night's sleep wasn't one of them. The memories of her lovemaking with Clayton made her body ache with both desire and soreness. She cast a quick glance at him and the delicious tension within her intensified when she watched his lips form a silent message, *I love you.*

"I have a little celebration planned for tonight," Syntel said, unknowingly interrupting the soundless byplay between Clayton and Syneda.

Syneda shifted in her chair. "Oh? What's the occasion?"

"My daughter," he replied smoothly. "She's coming for a visit."

Syneda smiled up at him. "That's really nice."

Syntel took a sip of his coffee. Then he tilted his head and a proud smile touched his lips. "Yes, and I'm looking forward to it."

Syneda sat next to Clayton on the sofa. She glanced at her watch before turning toward him. "What if Syntel's daughter doesn't show up? It's almost seven o'clock," she whispered softly. "He's been acting rather anxious since he mentioned she was coming."

Clayton pulled Syneda closer to his side and pressed a kiss at her temple. "She'll be here."

Syneda lifted a brow wondering how Clayton was so sure of that and was about to ask him, when she noticed Syntel and Senator Lansing returning to the room. The senator had arrived over an hour ago, and Syneda had finally gotten to meet him.

"I hope you're right. I'd hate for him to be disappointed. He's such a kind person," she said softly before the two men approached.

Clayton smiled. His dark eyes slid lazily over the woman at his side. "So are you. And a rather beautiful one I might add. You look sensational tonight."

Syneda basked in Clayton's compliment. She was wearing an elegant egg-shell-colored silk dress that was cut in modest, classic lines. "I wanted to wear something nice for the special occasion."

Syntel and Nedwyn joined them and sat in chairs across from them.

"Tell me about your daughter, Syntel," Syneda asked politely in an attempt to keep conversation flowing.

Unnoticed by Syneda, the three men looked at each other fleetingly before Syntel cleared his throat. "There isn't much I can tell you about her, Syneda. The two of us will be meeting as father and daughter for the first time tonight. I only discovered I have a daughter a few days ago," he replied quietly.

Syneda's eyes widen in surprise. "I don't understand. How could you not know you had a daughter?"

Sadness shone in Syntel's eyes. "It's a rather long and sad story."

Clayton intertwined his fingers with Syneda's. "We would love hearing it anyway, Syntel. That is, if it's not too personal."

Taking a deep breath the older man began. "Almost thirty years ago while attending college, I met and fell in love with the most beautiful woman to walk the face of this earth. I've never met or seen a more exquisite individual. But she wasn't just beautiful on the outside, she was beautiful on the inside as well. I lost my heart the first time I saw her."

Syntel took a deep breath before continuing. "She'd been in one of Ned's classes and thanks to him, we were introduced."

He paused thoughtfully before going on to say. "I asked her out and she turned me down." He smiled at the memory. "In fact she turned me down several times, but I refused to give up. Finally, she gave in on the condition that no one was to know we were seeing each other."

"Why didn't she want anyone to know the two of you were dating?" Syneda asked.

"Because I'm white and she was black. During that time interracial dating was not acceptable."

Syneda nodded. She knew that even in this day and time, some people were pretty close-minded when it came to interracial relationships. She couldn't even imagine how such a relationship would have survived over thirty years ago. Some people refused to accept the fact that true love was color-blind.

Syntel stood, continuing. "She found out she was pregnant before we graduated but didn't tell me. I had to report to the Air Force Academy the day after graduation. She used that time to disappear, telling no one where she was going. I nearly went out of my mind worrying, but in my heart I believed she would get in touch with me. But she didn't. I never saw her again."

"If you never saw her again, how did you find out about your daughter?" Syneda asked, totally intrigued with the story being told.

"A few days ago her fiancé showed up at my office and told me. He had hired a private investigator to find me with the sole intention of ripping me to shreds for hurting the woman he loved."

A lump formed in his throat. "You see, Syneda, eighteen years ago, the woman I loved died leaving my daughter all alone. All alone but with a promise that I would come for her."

Syneda startled and her fingers turned to ice as they clutched Clayton's. She gazed deeply into Syntel's eyes as he continued speaking. "I'm told her mother had a telephone call placed to me. It was a phone call I never received. That's the only reason I didn't come. There's no way that had I gotten that phone call, I would not have come for my daughter."

He held back an emotional choke. "I loved *your* mother deeply and I believe she loved me. You're living proof of just how much she loved me, and the sacrifices she made. It was her choice not to continue our relationship because of the problems she felt we would have endured as an interracial couple, but it wasn't my choice not to know about you."

He took a deep breath. "There's no way I can turn back the hands of time and undo everything you've endured because of your mother and me. All I can ask is that you find it in your heart to give me a chance, and to allow me to become a part of your life. A life I've already missed twenty-eight years of sharing."

Syneda was transfixed in place, unable to move as her shocked mind absorbed Syntel's words. Tears clouded her eyes.

Clayton's gaze intercepted Senator Lansing's nod. Neither he nor the senator was noticed as they slipped from the room, leaving father and daughter alone.

"I still can't believe S. T. Remington is actually my father." Syneda lay in bed with her head cradled on Clayton's shoulder, staring at the roaring fire in the fireplace. She had returned from talking with Syntel for over two and a half hours to find Clayton pacing the floor waiting for her. She had walked across the room and gone into his arms without hesitation. Then she had cried while he had comforted her.

Clayton leaned on one elbow, smiling down at her. "You may as well get used to the idea. As soon as the media finds out everyone and their mama will know it."

Syneda nodded. "Syntel and I talked about that, too, and wondered what would be the best way to handle it." She smiled. "One thing is for sure, he doesn't want to keep me a secret."

She snuggled closer to Clayton. "For so long I wanted to hate the man who fathered me, the man I thought let me and my mother down. And now I find it was all lies. Just listening to him talk let me know he loved my mother very much."

Clayton wound his hand in Syneda's silky hair. "Yes, he did. It's just sad your mother allowed what society thought dictate her happiness. Who knows, they could have married and lived happily ever after."

Syneda's smile faded. "Somehow I doubt it. Just look at what Syntel's father did. I don't believe his family would have accepted a marriage between him and my mother."

Clayton raised a brow. "Why are you calling him Syntel's father? He was your grandfather."

"But I can't think of him that way. He didn't think of me as his grandchild, did he?"

"No, he didn't." Clayton had to agree with her on that. "But he's dead now so what he thinks really doesn't matter anymore does it?"

"No, but it hurts to know he didn't want me as his grandchild."

"And how do you feel about having Syntel for a father?"

Syneda looked up at him. "Scared, overwhelmed. I've had eighteen years of bitterness to fester inside of me. It will take time for all of it to completely go away. It won't dissolve overnight and he understands that. We've decided to take things one day at a time and get to know each other. There's so much we have to catch up on, so much I want to share with him and so little time. I have to begin making plans for our wedding soon. With Christmas right around the corner, June will be here before you know it."

Clayton slipped out of bed to put another log on the fire. When he returned to bed, Syneda couldn't help noticing the serious expression he wore. He pulled her back into his arms.

"Do you want to postpone our wedding for a while?" he asked.

Syneda raised a confused brow and looked at him. "No, why do you ask? Do you want to postpone our wedding?"

"No. I just didn't want you to feel rushed about anything."

She threw her arms around him. "Oh, Clayton, the day I marry you will be the happiest day of my life. Syntel and I will have plenty of time to get to know each other, both before and after our wedding."

Clayton smiled, feeling relieved. "So the wedding is still on?"

"Absolutely."

They kissed with all the deep longing and all the love they had for each other in their hearts. Both of them had waited years to find true, everlasting, and eternal love.

"Clayton?"

"Umm?" he asked, brushing small kisses against the base of her throat.

"Have you thought about where we can go on our honeymoon?"

He paused thoughtfully before placing another heated kiss on her lips. He was beginning to ache for her all over again. "No, sweetheart, I haven't thought about it. Any suggestions?"

"Yes." The palm of her hand gently caressed his chin. "I heard St. Thomas is a beautiful place that time of the year, and I've always wanted to go there."

Clayton was grinning. "St. Thomas? Will I get the chance to preapprove the clothes you bring along?"

Syneda smiled. "Do you think you need to?"

"Yes."

Suddenly they were laughing together.

"If you think for one minute, Clayton Madaris, that you're going to start dictating what I can or cannot wear once we're married, you're out of your mind. We need to get a few things straight. No man is going to—"

Clayton kissed her to shut her up. When he lifted his head, his eyes gleamed with amusement. "One thing is for sure, sweetheart, with you I'll never be bored. I can't wait for June to get here."

"Neither can I," Syneda said, pulling his head down for another kiss. "Neither can I."

CHAPTER 26

A beautiful day in June

Clayton Madaris glared at the seven men standing on the other side of the room. Three of them, Alexander Maxwell, Trevor Grant and Trask Maxwell, were his closest friends. Two others were his brothers-in-law, Daniel Green and Raymond Barnes. But his full glare, the darkest it had been in months, was directed at his two brothers, Justin and Dex, who stood nonchalantly by the window.

"What do you mean Uncle Jake's not coming?" he finally shouted after taking in the announcement Justin had just made. "He has to come! He's in the wedding!"

Jonathan Madaris, dressed elegantly in a white tuxedo, stood leaning against the mantel as he watched his youngest son begin pacing the length of the room in angry strides. He could feel the tension growing in the room. Clayton was a nervous wreck as it was, and at the moment the last thing he needed was his brothers playing devil's advocates. He made a quick decision to intervene before he had a murder on his hands instead of a wedding.

"All right, settle down, Clayton. Jake will be here. He called and said he's running a little late but he'll make it in time for the wedding. Justin and Dex were just teasing you."

Jonathan then turned his serious attention to his other two sons. "Justin Stuart and Dexter Jordan, behave yourselves. Your brother is nervous enough as it is. Don't make matters worse. And I might add that at least he thought enough of me and his mother to let us share in his wedding day. Something neither of you did."

Justin grinned at his father's observation. "I would have loved having you and Mom at my wedding, but if you'll recall, I didn't know about the wedding myself until an hour before the ceremony was scheduled to take place. You have Clayton to thank for that. He schemed with Lorren to pull that one off. So he won't be getting much pity from me today."

Dex Madaris, whose charcoal gray eyes were warm with amusement, chuckled throatily before coming to his own defense. "I would have loved inviting you and Mom to my wedding, but unfortunately I had to move fast and marry Caitlin. From all appearances, Clayton was trying to make a move on her. I didn't know at the time that he was doing it just to make me jealous."

Clayton had stopped his pacing to listen to what his brothers were saying. He couldn't stop the slow smile that spread across his lips. "The way I see it, both of you owe me a lot of gratitude for Lorren and Caitlin. Without my intervention neither of you would be happily married men."

Dex and Justin looked at each other before smiles of agreement covered their faces. It was a known fact that they loved their wives dearly. "You do have a point there, `Lil' Bro," Justin said grinning.

"However, your situation hasn't changed. Although we were teasing you about Uncle Jake, you still have to deal with your other problem. There's no way Gramma Madaris is going to let you see Syneda before the wedding," Justin continued. "It's a tradition that the groom sees the bride for the first time on their wedding day when she walks down the aisle. So the way I figure it, you have a couple of hours to go."

Clayton began his pacing again. "This entire thing is totally ridiculous. Gramma has deliberately kept Syneda from me all day."

Jonathan Madaris shook his head. "You know how your grandmother is, Clayton. She's not doing this to torture you. At your sisters' weddings, Raymond and Dan couldn't see them either. And if I remember correctly, at the time you thought the entire thing was downright funny."

"Well, today is my wedding day, and I don't find anything funny about not being able to see Syneda. And I'm not going to stand for it a minute longer."

Justin chuckled. "What are you going to do? Force your way inside that room where Syneda and all the ladies are being held hostage by Gramma?"

A devilish gleam appeared in Clayton's eyes. "That's not a bad idea."

Jonathan Madaris straightened his stance, recognizing immediately the look of defiance in his youngest son's eyes. He could just see Clayton going head to head with his mother. "All right, Clayton, don't do anything foolish. Your grandmother—"

"Means well, Dad, but this time I can't abide by her wishes."

Before anyone could say anything further, Clayton stalked out of the room and headed down the church's long hall which was adjacent to the corridor where Syneda was. Without knocking, he walked right into the room.

Ignoring the gasps and surprised expressions of the numerous women in the room, his gaze collided with Lorren's. "Where is she?"

"Clayton! You know you can't come in here. Your grandmother will have a fit if she finds you here."

"Where is Syneda, Lorren?" His patience was beginning to wear thin.

Lorren glared at him. "Clayton Madaris, you just march right back out that door—"

"Where is she, Lorren?" he asked again.

Seeing the determined expression etched on his face, Lorren pointed to another room. "She's in there with your mother getting dressed."

Clayton turned to the other women in the room who were staring at him like he'd gone crazy. "Please make yourselves scarce for a few minutes."

Felicia was the only one brave enough to speak up. "You can't run us out of here, Clayton. This is where we belong. You're the one out of place."

"Out!" Clayton shouted like a madman to the women staring at him. "Out! Now!"

The room quickly emptied.

"What on earth is going on out here?"

Clayton turned when his mother came into the room. A frown covered her face when she saw him. Leave it to her youngest son to be difficult on his wedding day. "Clayton, what are you doing here?"

"I want to see Syneda, Mom."

"That's impossible, Clayton. You know how your grandmother likes traditions. She will have your hide when she returns, and she'll be back any minute. She and Mama Nora left to give last minute instructions to the florist."

Clayton looked deeply into his mother's eyes pleading understanding. "I don't mean to cause problems, Mom. Really I don't. But I need to see her. These past few months have been hell. I've barely spent any time with her at all. First it was Syntel demanding most of her time, and then it was you, Mama Nora, and Gramma spending all that time with her planning this wedding. And let's not forget all those bridal showers she had to attend. I feel like an outcast."

Marilyn Madaris was startled by her son's admission. Insecurity was something he rarely had to deal with. Even as a child growing up, he'd always been totally sure of himself. Too sure of himself at times.

She took a deep breath. "All right, Clayton. I'll give you five minutes. Syneda is in there."

Clayton gazed at the closed door. "Does she know I'm out here?"

Marilyn Madaris grinned. "With all that racket you were making, how could she not know." A firm expression covered her face. "Five minutes, Clayton, that's all you got. Besides," she said chuckling. "I have a feeling someone has alerted your grandmother to your behavior and she's on her way to toss you out on your rear end." She turned and left the room closing the door behind her.

Clayton walked over to the other door and opened it. His breath caught in his throat.

Standing in the middle of the room wearing her bath robe was his soon to be wife. The essence of her radiant beauty almost brought tears to his eyes. Her hair was arranged on top of her head in a bevy of soft curls. It was a very exquisite looking style.

Clayton thought his heart had stopped beating when she smiled at him. "Causing problems, Madaris?"

He returned her smile. "Don't I always where you're concerned?" He locked the door before walking over to her. "I had to see you, Syneda."

"You weren't supposed to see me until the wedding."

Clayton raised his hands to cup her face. "I know and I'm sorry if I've ruined this day for you by not sticking to tradition, but I had to see you. It doesn't matter when I see you, Syneda. Your beauty will always have me spellbound."

Syneda's heart burst with happiness. She thought he looked so handsome dressed in his white tuxedo with tails, and didn't hesitate to tell him so. "You look so good in a tux."

"Thanks. I have something to tell you," he said quietly, taking her hand in his.

"What?" Syneda asked. A nervous tremor touched her.

"I just wanted to tell you how much I love you. So much has happened since you agreed to marry me. We really haven't had a chance to spend a lot of time together lately." He placed her hand over his heart. "Every beat you feel under your palm is for your heart only. I love you very much and will spend the rest of my life showing you just how much. From this day forward, I am eternally yours."

Tears glistened in Syneda's eyes. "And from this day forward, I am eternally yours." She repeated the words he had just spoken. "I love you so very much, Clayton."

Slowly, Clayton pulled her into his arms. He couldn't help looking at her lips, full and sensuous. A shock of overwhelming heat spread through him. He suddenly felt hot and hungry for the woman he was about to marry.

"Clayton Jerome Madaris! Open this door!"

The sound of his grandmother's demand from the other side of the locked door echoed loudly in the room.

"I think I'm in trouble," he said to Syneda as his mouth hovered closely over hers. "I may as well make it worth my while, don't you think?"

Syneda nodded, smiling. "Definitely. There's no trouble like big trouble," she replied seconds before placing her arms around his neck to bring her body more fully against his.

Clayton's mouth moved hungrily over hers as Syneda's lips parted for him. She made a small, soft sound when his tongue entered her mouth and rubbed sensuously against hers. The byplay was deliciously erotic, and promised things to come later.

The heady taste of Clayton made a glowing heat blossom deep within Syneda's belly. The masculine scent of him was embedded in her nostrils, and the desire for him was an ache deep within the core of her.

"Clayton Madaris if you don't unlock this door, I'll have your father and brothers break it down!"

Abruptly, Clayton ended the kiss, and looked down into Syneda's passion-filled face. He enfolded her tightly into his arms. "I'd better do as she said, or she *will* have them break the door down." He leaned down and kissed her again. "Remember how much I love you when you walk down that aisle to me."

Syneda nodded. Love was shining in the depths of her sea-green eyes. "I'll remember."

Clayton smiled as he unlocked the door to discover not only his grandmother, but his parents, the minister, Mama Nora, Syntel and the entire wedding party crowded around the door. His grandmother had an annoyed and a disgusted expression on her face.

Before she could say anything he leaned over and kissed her on the cheek. "She's all yours now, Gramma, but in just a little while, she'll be all mine."

Whistling the tune of the bridal march, a much happier Clayton Madaris walked past the crowd of stunned onlookers.

Reverend Moss checked his watch. He then smiled at the faces of the men lined across the room all dressed in white tuxedos. Everyone was accounted for. He frowned when his gaze came to rest on Clayton. He shook his head. Even after the ruckus he'd caused a few hours earlier, Clayton Madaris didn't have the decency to look guilty or ashamed.

"Well then, gentlemen, it's about that time," he said adjusting his glasses and smoothing his white robe. "If you'll just follow me, we can get things started. We don't want to keep the bride waiting."

Before turning to leave, he gave Clayton a stern look. "And no more shenanigans out of you, young man. I've had enough excitement for one day."

* * *

Beautiful white lit candles lined the aisles and the altar of the church. The sultry sound of Whitney Houston floated through the building as she enchanted and dazzled the wedding guests by singing a song. Senator Lansing, who was a close friend of the Houston family, had made the arrangements for Whitney's special appearance.

When Whitney's song ended, Syneda watched her six bridesmaids drift down the aisle dressed in tea length peach gowns. Lorren and Caitlin were her matrons of honor. Lorren handed her her floral bouquet while Caitlin was busy straightening her train. Caitlin had given birth to another girl, Ashley Reneé, and Lorren had presented Justin with another son, Christopher Stuart.

Lorren gave her best friend's hand a little squeeze. "I'm so happy. I've always wanted this for you. You deserve to be happy."

Syneda smiled as tears misted her eyes. "Thanks for always being there for me."

Lorren returned her smile. "And thanks for always being there for me. I have something for you. It's something borrowed." She placed on Syneda's wrist a beautiful pearl bracelet.

"Oh, Lorren. It's your mom's bracelet." She hugged her friend. "Thanks."

When the wedding coordinator took the two flower girls off to the side to give them last-minute instructions, Syneda found herself alone with her father.

The last five months had been somewhat stressful for both of them. After her initial shock had worn off, Syneda went through a few weeks of resentment at Syntel Remington's appearance in her life. Like she had told him in the beginning, she had had eighteen years of hurt and anger to deal with. But through it all, he had been understanding and refused to let her put distance between them or deny him a place in her life as her father. He had braved, tolerated, and survived her overwrought and, at times, pushed-to-the-limit emotions. Now she was grateful he had not taken her behavior personally.

Once she had gotten beyond the frenzy of the media's headlines labeling her Syntel Remington's love child, and their constant encampment on her doorstep and place of employment in their search for the entire story, she had discovered something. She and Syntel shared more than just physical resemblance. They had quite a number of ways alike. They were both outspoken, neither believed in sugar-coating anything and they both didn't mind standing up for what they believed in.

Somehow they had gotten close over the past few months, regretting but accepting Syntel's father's and Clara Boyd's deceit. In the end, father and daughter had forged a strong bond between the two of them. Last month, as he'd done every year for the past fifteen years, Syntel had gone to visit her mother's grave. But this time she had gone with him. Somehow she believed her mother was now truly resting in peace knowing father and daughter were finally united as she had wanted. After the graveside visit, they had returned to the ranch and had been joined by Senator Lansing and Clayton. With the three of them there, Syntel had not indulged in his two-day drinking spree to drown out his pain. Instead, over ice tea, Syneda and Clayton had sat and listened to the two college friends share fond memories of the time they had spent with her mother, and how difficult it had been trying to keep Syntel's and Janeda's relationship a secret. Syntel even shared photographs with her that he and Janeda had taken together. Tears had formed in Syneda's eyes when she had looked at the photos and had seen her parents, young and very much in love. She was thankful to Syntel for sharing that part of his and her mother's past with her. She had had something to share with him too, a photo album her mother had kept during Syneda's growing years. The very first picture in the album had been her newborn baby picture that had been taken in the hospital nursery. Following that picture had been others that Syneda had taken each year for the first ten years. Some of them had been pictures she had taken alone. Others were those that she and her mother had taken together. The rest of the pictures in the album had been those she had taken during her junior and senior high school years while living with Mama Nora and Papa Paul. All the pictures had provided Syntel with a pictorial journal of her life; a life he'd been unable to share with her. Their sharing of the photographs had been a special time for them, and had some how strengthened the bond between them.

"Nervous?"

Syntel's question brought Syneda's thoughts back to the present. She looked up at him, nodding her head. "A little. What about you?"

He smiled. "I'm nervous a little, too." He released a deep sigh before saying. "It seems so unfair."

Syneda raised an arched brow. "What does?"

Syntel took her hand in his, to take his place at her side. "I just found my daughter. It's a pity that already I have to give her away," he said in an oddly hoarse voice.

Syneda looked at him and saw the sadness openly displayed in his eyes. "Be happy for me, Daddy," she said, surprising him by calling him that for the very first time. Up to now she had always referred to him as Syntel.

"I'm marrying a good man. I think he's the best. And don't ever worry about you and me. Now that you're in my life, you're here to stay. Count on it."

She leaned up and kissed his cheek. "Thanks for loving my mother. I know she was only able to make it through all those years without you because she knew she had found true love once in her life. And I know each and every time she looked at me, she must have seen you. That's why she often called me her most precious gift. I was a gift of life she'd received from the man she loved."

Syntel's eyes were misty when he hugged his daughter. "Thank you for telling me that and for believing it. I loved your mother deeply, and I love you. I'm honored to be your father."

"I love you too, and I'm honored to be your daughter."

Clayton stood next to his father, who was his best man, and watched Jordan, who looked so beautiful dressed in a peach floor-length gown, walk carefully down the aisle, tossing rose petals on the red carpet.

Next came two-year-old Justina. She began tossing rose petals from her basket just like the nice lady had told her to do. She was doing a pretty good job at it until she saw her daddy standing at the altar.

"Daddy!" She tossed the basket down as if saying, "later for this," and skipped happily down the aisle to her father.

Justin scooped his daughter up in his arms, shaking his head. He looked over at Lorren who was grinning from ear to ear.

Next came the ring bearer, the four-year-old son of their cousin Felicia. He was followed by Vincent, Justin's and Lorren's eight-year-old son, who entered and gave a loud blast from a golden horn. He then proclaimed in a loud voice. "The bride is coming! The bride is coming!"

The sanctuary got quiet. And then the organ began playing the bridal march. In awe, the wedding guests stood on their feet and watched Syneda and her father begin their walk down the long aisle.

A knot got caught in Clayton's throat. He had never seen a more beautiful bride. She looked absolutely radiant. Her bridal gown was a soft white satin with a crystal pleated portrait neckline. That neckline gently curved around her shoulders to a cluster of dropped authentic pearls and sequin trim. A lace-trimmed train with embroidered appliques added the finishing touch to the gown. A romantic floral hat that was lavished with fabric flowers, authentic pearls, net pouf and a fingertip-length veil adorned her head.

Both pride and love burst within Clayton. The woman coming to him was everything he could possibly ever want in a woman. They were still both strongly opinionated and at times argumentative, but now they would have a different way of settling their disputes. He smiled. Namely in the bedroom.

As he continued to watch her, the sermon Reverend Moss had preached on his grandmother's birthday suddenly came back to him. "... *when a man loves a woman he places her above all else, and she becomes the most important person in his life. She becomes his queen . . .*"

"She's my queen," Clayton whispered in his heart.

The crowd watched as Syntel walked Syneda three-fourths of the way down the aisle. As planned, Clayton was coming the rest of the way for her.

The guests looked on, most of them with misty eyes and breathless anticipation, when Syneda turned and hugged her father. Then they watched as Clayton strode down the aisle toward them.

Upon reaching them he shook hands with Syntel and said, "I promise to take care of her, sir."

Nodding, Syntel then relinquished his place at his daughter's side.

Clayton stood before the woman who had consented to become his wife. She was the woman he loved. He took her hands in his, smiling. Unable to help himself, he leaned down and placed a tender kiss on her lips.

"Lordy, the boy wasn't supposed to do that until after the ceremony."

Clayton smiled when his grandmother's words reached his ears. He then led Syneda to the altar, winking at his grandmother when he passed her sitting on the front pew. He could tell by her deep frown that she was not too happy with what he had done.

Upon reaching the others, he drew Syneda forward as they knelt in front of the altar. After Reverend Moss's brief prayer, they once again stood on their feet. The minister began.

Syneda's hand was held securely in Clayton's. When Reverend Moss asked her to repeat her vows, she looked into Clayton's eyes. "I, Syneda Tremain Walters, take this man, Clayton Jerome Madaris, to be my lawfully wedded husband."

She felt the heat of Clayton's gaze on her as she continued, ". . . to love and to cherish, from this day forward, for better or for worse . . ."

Clayton was stunned by the intensity of the emotions he felt, hearing Syneda's words. With iron-clad control he forced himself not to take her into his arms.

"Clayton," Reverend Moss was saying to him. "Please repeat after me. I, Clayton Jerome Madaris, take this woman, Syneda Tremain Walters, to be my lawfully wedded wife."

Finally, after all the vows were said, and wedding rings exchanged, Clayton and Syneda turned to face each other and held hands while Whitney Houston came forward to sing the song Syneda had requested, "I Believe In You and Me."

Syneda looked deeply into Clayton's eyes while the words to the song floated around them, encompassing them in a mist of their love. Tears misted her eyes as she looked at him remembering how his love had brought her through a difficult time, how he had refused to give up on her until she had sent him away, and how in the end she'd come to her senses and reclaimed his love. She knew the love she felt for him was unhidden and clearly visible for him to see.

Clayton held Syneda's hand in his as the words of Whitney's song touched him. For so long he had not believed in love. He had thought love was not for him. But the woman whose hands he now held in his had changed that. Now he believed in miracles.

After Whitney's song ended, Reverend Moss said, "By the powers invested in me by this great state of Texas, I now pronounce you man and wife." He smiled broadly. "You may kiss your bride, Clayton."

Clayton was more than ready for this part. Lifting Syneda's veil, he whispered. "I love you, Mrs. Madaris." He then took Syneda in his arms and kissed her.

When the kiss seemed endless, Reverend Moss tapped Clayton on the back. "That's enough, son."

Clayton kept right on kissing Syneda.

Reverend Moss frowned. He again tapped Clayton on the back, a little more forceful this time. "You can finish that later, young man."

Clayton released Syneda's mouth. He smiled at the minister. "I kind of got carried away."

Minister Moss frowned at him. "Apparently you did."

Clayton grinned and then to everyone's surprise and unfortunately to his grandmother's horror, he swung Syneda up in his arms and after tossing her long, winding train across his shoulder, he carried her out the church leaving a stunned wedding party behind to follow.

The grand ballroom of the Hilton Hotel was a spectacular sight. Syntel had gone beyond himself in hosting his daughter's wedding reception.

After the traditional first dance of the bride and groom, Syneda danced first with her father, then with Senator Lansing, who had declared himself her godfather.

Clayton had approached his mother but she strongly suggested that he dance with his grandmother first. "She's pretty upset with you, Clayton. If you ever want to taste her bread pudding again, I suggest you do something to rectify that situation."

Being the smart man that he was, Clayton had immediately taken his mother's suggestion. By the end of their dance his grandmother was all smiles again. But that was only after she had sweetly raked him over the coals.

Trevor Grant stood leaning a shoulder against the wall, holding a half-filled champagne glass in his hand. He smiled, happy for his friend.

His gaze swept over the ballroom. When it rested upon a particular young woman, it stopped. Corinthians Avery, who was head geologist for Remington Oil, was a beautiful woman. She was everything male fantasies were made of. He of all people should know. There wasn't a single night he went to sleep without her invading his dreams.

As if sensing his gaze upon her, Corinthians' head lifted, her gaze met his. She frowned and narrowed her eyes at him.

Trevor gave her his most charming smile then lifted the champagne glass in a silent toast to her. He knew she could tell that his gaze was moving down the full length of her, remembering a night when he'd seen her, wearing nearly nothing at all. It was a night he would never forget.

He smiled when she continued to meet his gaze head on. He had to hand it to her, the woman was something else. He took a sip of champagne, and still her leveled gaze never flickered from his. He knew she was trying to look straight through him, and deny his existence. But he was not about to let her do that. He blamed her for many of his sleepless nights, and one day soon, very soon, she would pay for it.

"How soon can we leave and go upstairs?" Clayton asked his wife as they moved slowly around on the dance floor.

Syneda lifted her head from his shoulder. "It won't be too much longer. You wouldn't leave before most of your guests would you?"

"Watch me. Besides, they've been well fed, plied with good wine and champagne, entertained with good music and thanks to your father, most of them have been given plush rooms to spend the night. What more could they ask for?"

Syneda smiled. "I'm so glad all of your friends made it. It was nice getting the chance to meet Alex's brother, Trask Maxwell. He's really nice."

Clayton grinned. "But all of my friends are single. I hope each of them finds a woman to love and who'll make them happy. Like you've done for me." He leaned down and brushed a light kiss across her mouth.

"All right, you two," the wedding coordinator said from behind Clayton. "It's time for more pictures. Then, Syneda, you need to toss your bouquet and Clayton, you need to take your wife's garter off and toss it to one of those single, unattached, handsome friends of yours."

He smiled. "It will be my pleasure."

Moments later, Syneda was ready to toss her bouquet. All the single women were asked to go to one side of the room. Everyone laughed when Gramma Madaris marched over and pulled Felicia out of the group. Evidently she thought with two failed marriages to her credit, her wild and reckless granddaughter did not need a third.

Syneda had all intentions of aiming her bouquet straight toward Christy in hopes of shaking the three over-protective Madaris brothers up a bit over the thought of their nineteen-year old baby sister being next in line for marriage. Unfortunately, Syneda's aim was off and instead her bouquet landed right smack in Corinthians Avery's hands.

* * *

Jonathan Madaris came over to join his youngest brother, who was standing against a wall. Both of their tall forms looked elegant in their white tuxedoes.

"I thought I'd better warn you that Clayton is about ready to do the garter toss, and Mama is herding together all the single men to participate," Jonathan said, his eyes twinkling with humor.

Jake raised a dark brow. "Why would you want to warn me about something like that?"

Jonathan smiled. "Because I know for a fact she wants you included in on that. With Clayton out of the way, she wants you to be next. She thinks it's time for you to remarry."

Jake took a sip of his champagne. He then met his brother's gaze. "I have remarried."

Jonathan smiled. "But she doesn't know that and unless you're ready to share your secret with the family, I suggest you make yourself scarce for a few minutes."

Jake took another sip of his champagne. Only a few people knew about his marriage to Diamond Swain, and Jonathan was one of them. He loved all of his brothers, but Jonathan was the one he was closest to.

"By the way," Jonathan said a few moments later. "How's Diamond? I guess it was hard coming here and leaving her at Whispering Pines."

Jake lifted an inquiring eyebrow. "How did you know she was at the ranch, Jon?"

Jonathan chuckled. "That was pretty easy to figure out. You couldn't leave the rehearsal dinner quick enough last night; you seemed somewhat relieved when Syntel offered to put up the wedding guests at this hotel, which eliminated you from having to put them up at Whispering Pines; and you barely made it to the church on time today. You almost gave Clayton heart failure." He shook his head, smiling. "Even now you're biting at the bit to get out of here."

Jake laughed a rich throaty laugh. "Am I that obvious?"

"Only to me and Marilyn. And she picked up on it right away. She says you always have a better disposition whenever Diamond is around. She thinks your wife is good for you."

"Oh? And does she still think Diamond and I are making a mistake by keeping our marriage a secret for now?"

"I think she's decided differently after seeing how the media hounded Syneda when word got out that Syntel Remington was her father. Marilyn knows they'll do the same thing to you and Diamond."

Jake nodded. "I want Whispering Pines to always be a place Diamond can come to when she wants to escape the lights and glamour and stress of California for a while."

"And how long will her infrequent visits be enough for you? I can't help but remember why your marriage to Jessie didn't work out."

Jake rubbed the top of his head, struggling to ignore the resentment and old feelings of anger whenever his first wife was mentioned. "I swore after Jessie I would never get involved with another city woman. But when Diamond came along, I couldn't help myself. For as long as Diamond is comfortable with our arrangements, this is the way we'll do things."

Jonathan studied his brother. "And what about you? Are you comfortable with the arrangements?"

Jake's dark eyes met Jonathan's. There was no way he could lie to him. "Not really, but I really don't have a choice. I knew what the deal was when I fell in love with her." His gaze sharpened when he saw his mother headed in their direction.

"Look Jon, here comes Mama so I'm out of here. Tell the newlyweds that I'll see them after they get back from their honeymoon."

He turned and quickly made his exit.

Clayton looked at the fifteen or so single men gathered around him. None of them looked overly anxious to participate in this part of the wedding ceremony. At least three of them he knew for a fact did not relish the thought of possibly being next in line for marriage.

His gaze sought out those three, Alex Maxwell, Trevor Grant, and Trask Maxwell. They were deliberately standing as far away in the back as they could. He smiled when he noticed Trask walking toward him.

"Why do we have to do this?" Trask Maxwell asked when he had reached Clayton.

"Because Gramma Madaris said so. She's all wrapped up in traditions today." Then he used the same tactic on Trask that his mother had used on him earlier. "And if you want to risk making her mad and never eating any of her bread pudding again, then go right ahead and not participate."

Trask shook his head smiling. "Do I look like a fool? Now toss the darn thing. Let's get this over with. Just make sure you throw it to one of those guys in the front." He turned and walked off, returning to his spot in the back.

A few minutes later, Clayton sent Syneda's blue garter sailing through the air and over the heads of most of the men in the front before it finally landed right in Trevor Grant's hands.

"I thought I was never going to get you alone," Clayton said to his wife a hour or so later. Pulling that garter from around her thigh while hundreds of people looked on had been difficult. The feel of his hand on her skin had almost made him lose control. He had wanted to begin making love to her right then and there.

They would spend the night here in the hotel and bright and early tomorrow morning, they would catch a flight to St. Thomas. He was more than ready for his honeymoon to begin.

He pulled Syneda closer into his arms. "And how do you like my present?"

Syneda laughed softly and tipped her head up to meet Clayton's gaze. "I like it."

When she had entered their hotel room, the honeymoon suite on the twenty-eighth floor, a beautiful gift-wrapped box was in the center of the bed. The card attached to it had indicated it was from Clayton. Like a child on Christmas morning, she had eagerly opened it up to find five brand new men's dress shirts with designer labels.

"Although you always look sexy as hell in those things, I prefer you not start wearing them until we get back from our honeymoon."

She lifted a brow. "Why can't I take them with me?"

"Because I prefer you not wear anything at all in St. Thomas. I plan to keep you under lock and key those two weeks."

Syneda smiled and placed her arms around his neck. "I think I'm going to like that."

"I'm going to make sure you do," Clayton said, cradling her body even closer to his. "I love you, Syneda."

"And I love you. We aren't going to argue about anything in St. Thomas are we?"

Clayton smiled down at her. "We'll make love not war." Clayton kissed the side of her neck. "Besides, I have a new way of dealing with you whenever you get too opinionated and sassy, Mrs. Madaris."

"Oh? And what way is that?"

Clayton grinned as he picked her up in his arms. He began walking toward the bedroom. "You're about to find out."

Hours later, in their darkened hotel room, Clayton and Syneda lay wrapped in each other's arms. Both were very satisfied with how their special day had turned out.

It had been a day filled with love, joy, and tears. They had been blessed with the presence of a multitude of family and friends. But most importantly, it had been a day filled with anticipation, confidence, and trust. It was a day they had committed themselves to each other.

"Happy?"

Syneda smiled up at Clayton, mesmerized by the handsome face staring down at her. His features held all the love, tenderness, and passion she had come to adore. "Tremendously happy. What about you?"

"Extremely happy." Clayton slipped an arm around her shoulder and leaned down to take her lips in a long kiss.

Syneda wrapped her arms around him, lost in the cravings and desires he could stir within her so easily again. Then in a surprised move, she shifted around until her body was on top of his. She looked down into his dark eyes.

"Now, Mr. Madaris, it's my time to show you how I plan to deal with you when you get too opinionated and arrogant for your own good."

Clayton smiled. "Is that a fact?"

"No, Madaris, that's a promise."

Syneda's scent drifted all around him, and Clayton's passion began flaring anew under the onslaught of her warm lips when she began placing kisses all over his face, neck and shoulders.

His hand came up and cupped her face. He looked up into her eyes, at the love, peace, and contentment he saw there. He silently thanked God for bringing this special woman into his life, and for opening his eyes to her beauty, both inside and out. She was the half that made him whole. She was his sunshine after a storm. She would never bore him. With her his life would be filled with never-ending excitement.

She was eternally his and he was eternally hers. Forever.